THE

White

DRAGON

In Fire Forged, PART ONE

Tor books by Laura Resnick

In Legend Born

The White Dragon: In Fire Forged, Part One

The Destroyer Goddess: In Fire Forged, Part Two (forthcoming)

THE
White
DRAGON

In Fire Forged, PART ONE

LAURA RESNICK

TOR®

A Tom Doherty Associates Book New York

THE WHITE DRAGON: IN FIRE FORGED, PART ONE

Copyright © 2003 by Laura Resnick

Edited by James Frenkel

Map by Ellisa Mitchell

A Tor Book
Published by Tom Doherty Associates, LLC
175 Fifth Avenue
New York, NY 10010

www.tor.com

Tor® is a registered trademark of Tom Doherty Associates, LLC.

Library of Congress Cataloging-in-Publication Data

Resnick, Laura, 1962–
    The white dragon / Laura Resnick.—1st ed.
        p.   cm.—(In fire forged ; bk. 1)
    "A Tom Doherty Associates book."
    ISBN 0-312-89056-7(alk. paper)
    I. Title.
 PS3568.E689W47   2003
 813'.54—dc21

                                    2003041017

First Edition: June 2003

Printed in the United States of America

0 9 8 7 6 5 4 3 2 1

To the memory of Aunt Sima—to know her was to adore her

To my cousin Robert, his wife, Glenda, and their son, Brian

And to my cousin Julie, who loaned me Kiloran's name

THE
White
DRAGON
In Fire Forged, PART ONE

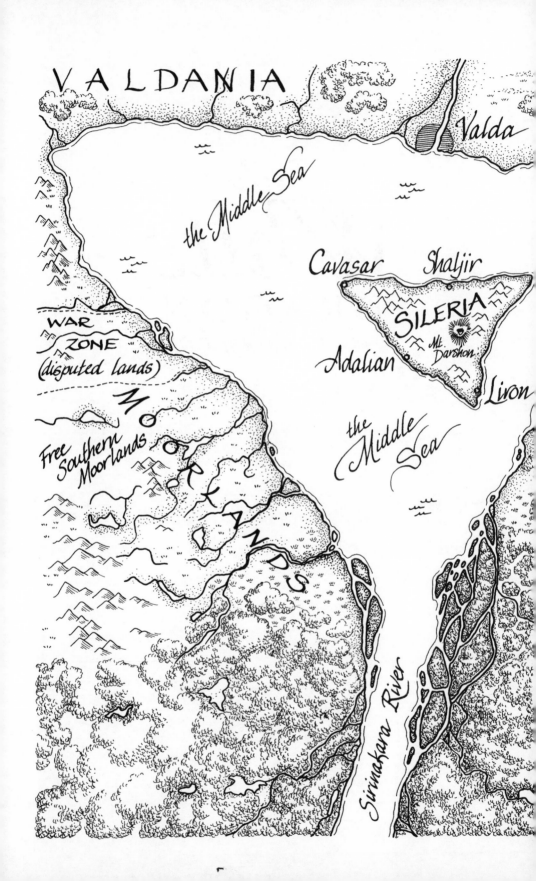

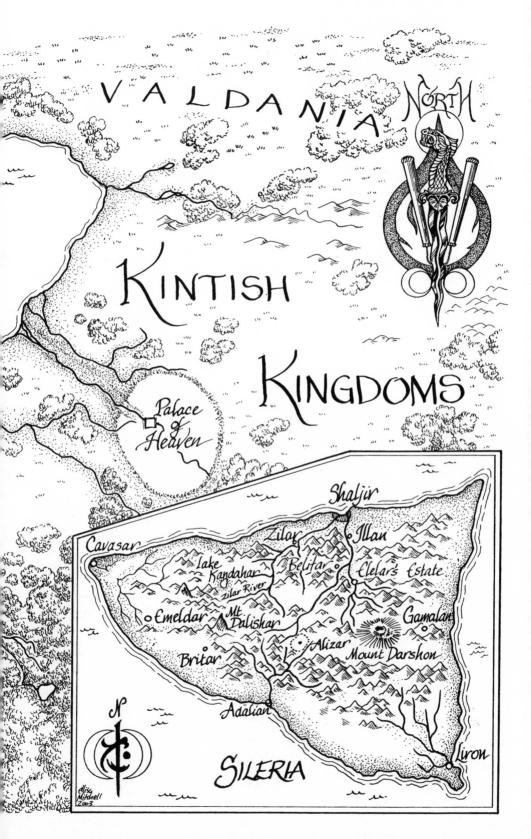

Prologue

DAR, THE DESTROYER GODDESS, CHOSE SILERIA AS
HER HOME; FORTUNATELY, WE ARE NOT SO EASY TO
DESTROY.

—Silerian Proverb

THE VAST ISLAND nation of Sileria rose majestically out of the
azure waters of the Middle Sea. Surrounded by mainland empires which
arose and fell as the eons passed, Sileria had suffered invasion and conquest
many times. She was a great prize, since possession of Sileria was necessary
for domination of the Middle Sea, once named Sirkara—heart of the
world—by an ancient people whose forgotten empire had been the first of
many to rise in glory and descend in flames. This inland ocean was bordered by the vast Moorlands, the sprawling Empire of Valdania, the ancient
Kintish Kingdoms, and the delta created by the north-flowing Sirinakara
River.

For a thousand years, the island nation of fertile fields, rich mines, harsh
mountains, and bustling ports had endured foreign domination as one conquering power after another claimed Sileria, the sun-drenched jewel of the
Middle Sea, for itself. For a thousand years, her disparate peoples had suffered humiliation, servitude, and contempt. For a thousand years, Silerians
had looked to Dar, the most powerful goddess in a nation of many sects and
cults, to liberate them from the 'yoke of slavery.

The goddess's home was the sacred volcano of Mount Darshon, whose
snow-capped, cloud-piercing peak dwarfed the rest of this rugged, moun-
tainous land. In the center of Darshon's caldera was the seething, bubbling,
red-hot lake of molten lava wherein dwelled Dar, goddess of fire and of the
Otherworld. Forged from a union of earth and sky, Dar had traveled the
three corners of the world in search of a home before finally coming to rest
at Darshon, the mightiest of mountains in the most beautiful of nations.

She was the destroyer goddess, wiping out whole villages on a whim,
exploding in showers of lava and molten rock which set the surrounding
mountains on fire and blackened the sky with ash. Her fiery nature had
shaped Her people, making them ruthless, unforgiving, and violent. Yet it

was also Dar who had made them the strongest, fiercest, and bravest people in the world.

She was a creator, too, renewing the tired earth again and again, enriching the lowlands, leaving fertile fields in the wake of Her tempestuous fury. Without Dar, the harvests would be perpetually poor, the mines would be barren, and Sileria's people would be bereft of the Otherworld. Without Dar, Silerians would still be hopeless slaves of the Valdani; it was Dar who had given Her people Josarian the Firebringer, the prophesied warrior who united all Silerians for the first time in a thousand years and led the Silerian rebellion against Valdania.

Silerians were a profoundly devout people, and so, even in the face of foreign laws prohibiting their native religious practices, they had never neglected Dar or failed to thank Her for these blessings. The *zanareen,* fanatics once considered insane by most Silerians, had worshipped at the rim of Darshon's fierce volcano for centuries, and many had died flinging themselves into the Fires of Dar in hopes of becoming the Firebringer. After Dar chose Josarian as the Firebringer, the *zanareen* served Her by serving him.

The city-dwellers, the lowlanders, and the earth magic cult of the Sisterhood made offerings to Dar of flowers, fruit, wine, and grain. The *toreni,* Sileria's landed aristocrats, made Her rich offerings of livestock, even of gold and jewels. The *shallaheen*—the mountain peasants who were Sileria's poorest and most numerous people—worshipped Her even more devoutly than the others and offered their very blood to Her, slicing open their palms to swear bloodpacts and bloodfeuds as they chanted their prayers to Dar. They made pilgrimages from all over Sileria, coming to Darshon to offer the bones of their dead to the goddess.

The Guardians of the Otherworld were closest of all to Dar, for She had blessed them with fire magic and with the ability to commune with shades of the dead sojourning in the Otherworld. For centuries the Guardians had devoted every day of their lives to Dar even though their kind had been outlawed by the Valdani for two hundred years—and sought by the deadly waterlords and assassins of the Honored Society for far longer than that.

Yes, despite the bloodfeuds which destroyed whole clans and the fanaticism for which various sects killed and died, despite the terrible poverty of the *shallaheen* and the mixed blood of so many *toreni* and city-dwellers, despite centuries of foreign domination and exposure to foreign gods . . . Despite all this, most of Sileria's people still remembered to pay their respects to the fierce goddess who dwelled in the fiery heart of Mount Darshon.

It was not enough.

Deep in the heart of Darshon's raging, fire-spewing sea of lava, Dar rumbled with discontent and claimed the right of a goddess to demand more from a people who, She knew, would now need more from Her.

1

WHEN THE LAST DRAGONFISH IS DEAD, THEN WILL I
SET MY FOOT UPON LAND.
—Motto of the Lascari Clan

THE DECK OF the fishing boat rolled beneath Zarien's feet,
rocking and soothing him as it had every day of his life, since the moment
he'd been hauled out of the sea where he had been born. For as long as Sileria's sea-born folk had existed, their women had given birth to their generations in sacred coves, then midwives blessed the infants with ritual
immersions before passing them to waiting paternal arms aboard nearby
boats. It had now been some fourteen years since the midwife had held
Zarien underwater to introduce his spirit to the spirit of the dragonfish,
whom his people feared, fought, and must someday vanquish.

And for fourteen years Zarien had lived by the creed which bound his
clan, the Lascari—and many other sea-born clans—to life upon the waves:
He had not set foot upon land, not once in his life.

True, many sea-born folk did walk among the landfolk of Sileria. They
traded on shore and supplied the floating markets upon which sea-bound
clans like the Lascari relied for those things which the sea did not provide.
They met with smugglers, rebels, and outlaws on land. They personally
delivered cargoes, carried from the nations surrounding the Middle Sea, to
wealthy merchants, aristocrats, and waterlords. Some had even marched
inland to meet the Firebringer himself, Josarian, to pledge the many clans
of Sileria's sea-born folk to his cause.

But the Lascari did not walk the dryland, nor would they until the last
dragonfish in the Middle Sea was finally dead. Since before memory began,
since before there had been waterlords in Sileria or the Palace of Heaven in
Kinto, since before the empire of the Moorlanders had risen from the mists
or disappeared centuries later into ashes, since before the Valdani had built
the great city of Valda and struck out to conquer so much of the world,
including Sileria . . . Since before all this, the sea-bound Lascari had thrived
without going ashore; indeed, to do so ensured banishment from the clan,
without exception. Theirs was a proud and ancient tradition, one to which
they clung fiercely. Zarien had been taught not to rudely ridicule clans who
mingled with the untattooed landfolk or who profaned their sea-born her-

itage by treading on solid ground while yet a dragonfish lived, but he was proud to be coming to manhood in a clan which did not do such unworthy things.

During the Festival of the New Year this year, he had finally received the tattoos of adulthood, as had all other sea-born children born fourteen years earlier, in the Year of Dark Skies. The intricate indigo markings he now bore on his hands, face, and forearms forever marked him as sea-born, as Lascari, and as a man. But only now might he become a man in truth; if he presented his mother with the heart of his very first dragonfish kill, then he would earn the right to say to her, as generations of sea-born males before him had said to their mothers, "Today I am a man."

They called it *Bharata Ma-al* in sea-born dialect: the Time of Slaughter. Now, as spring ripened into its full promise in Sileria, the dragonfish swam close to shore to lay their eggs in warm coastal waters. Now they were vulnerable. Now the sea-born showed them no mercy.

The rest of the year, these ferocious creatures might strike the sea-born folk anytime, anywhere in the Middle Sea. Many a boat had never returned from the open sea, many a man had died in those voracious jaws. No one—not marauding Moorlanders, not Kintish pirates, not the Valdani themselves with their sleek warships—had ever killed as many sea-born folk as the dragonfish had. Zarien's people had faced and fought this enemy since they first took to the sea, and until they had spilled the dark purple blood of the very last one left alive, there could be no peace. Only then would their destiny be complete. Only then might the children of their children's children set their feet upon land.

Zarien shrugged and lifted his face to the wind, indifferent to the knowledge that he would never walk the dryland. Why would anyone want to? The sea was the only life for real men, the dragonfish the only enemy worth facing. Let the *shallaheen,* Sileria's mountain peasants, slaughter each other in their endless bloodfeuds. Let the assassins of the Honored Society kill and be killed in bloodvows which were sworn to serve the power struggles of their masters, the waterlords. Let the vast armies of the world's rising and falling empires grapple for supremacy on the mainland all around the Middle Sea. What concern was any of this to the Lascari and their kind, whose enemy had been chosen for them by their gods at the dawn of time?

The sturdy two-masted boat upon which Zarien's family lived drew near the ancient killing grounds of the Lascari, the stretch of coastal waters which they had claimed as their own centuries ago. Zarien's heart began thudding with mingled pride, fear, and excitement. Tonight, for the first time, he would join the men of his clan in the bloody ritual through which they honored their gods and proved their manhood by voluntarily facing the dragonfish. It was during the Time of Slaughter that, for once, the sea-born folk rather than the dragonfish staged the ambush, chose the time and place of the confrontation, and challenged the enemy rather than simply awaiting their unpredictable attacks.

By the time the *bharata* was over, the shores of Sileria would be stained with blood and the sea would be dark with it. Not all of it would be purple either; *Bharata Ma-al* claimed many sea-born lives, too, every year.

The season of slaughter was a short one, lasting only while the first new moon glowed alone, before the second one appeared to join it in the night sky, during the fourth month of the year. It was a sacred span of three days and nights, an opportunity which came only once a year. If Zarien did not slay a dragonfish during the *bharata,* the traditional time for a first kill, then he would have to rely on chance until next year, on the mingled hope and fear that a dragonfish would attack him somewhere in the open sea. And until he finally killed one, he would be excluded from the rights and privileges granted only to those who had done so. He would also, he reflected sourly, be obliged to meekly listen to the other men's endless boasts wherever boats met and mingled at sea or in Sileria's harbors.

"Stop scowling," his mother advised him, brushing past him as she busily prepared the deck to receive the first dragonfish corpse of the *bharata*.

"I wasn't scowling," he corrected. "I was thinking."

"You were thinking?" Her dark brows rose. "Ah, for that alone, we should hold a special festival."

He scowled at her but didn't retort. A sea-born man who was not respectful to women—especially to his mother—would be dragonfish bait before long.

He didn't help her with her work, nor did she ask him to. Work was strictly divided among the sea-born, and each person stayed out of the other's way when it came to chores and duties; boats were small and unsteady, after all, and the sea-born couldn't afford to trip over and bump into each other all the time like clumsy landfolk. So Zarien stayed out of his mother's way and attended to his own work—which currently meant trimming the foresail as the boat drew near the killing waters.

Some of the boats of the Lascari clan were already there, and others were arriving even as Zarien's family brailed their sails up to the yard and prepared to drop anchor, positioning their boat for the setting of the nets. The women of each family had folded the huge nets aboard their own boats with care so that they would feed out smoothly and quickly when they were being set.

Only let this slaughter make me a man, he prayed to the spirits which ruled the sea. Without his manhood, he would not be allowed to carry the *stahra* he knew his parents had already acquired for him and tried to hide belowdecks without his knowledge. Among the sea-born, the *stahra* was a deadly weapon with which a sea-born man protected himself and his family from enemies, pirates, landfolk, and dragonfish. To ignorant eyes, though, it simply looked like an oar, something which even the Valdani didn't object to Silerians possessing.

Of course, the need to conceal weaponry from the Valdani was changing with the coming of Josarian the Firebringer. A simple *shallah* turned
rebel leader, Josarian had proven himself to be the long-prophesied chosen
one of Dar, the destroyer goddess who dwelled in the volcano of Mount
Darshon. With few exceptions, all of Sileria's disparate population worshipped Dar. The Honored Society, of course, was one of the exceptions.
They had turned their backs on Dar a thousand years ago, during the time
of Marjan, the very first waterlord, who had founded the Society. But even
the Society—like the sea-born folk—was not openly disrespectful of Dar.
After all, Zarien knew, to worship a land goddess like some mountain peasant was one thing, but to openly insult Her and risk Her vengeance was
quite another.

Sileria and all her peoples had toiled under the rule of various foreign
nations for a thousand years, since the days of the Conquest when the Moorlanders had sailed out of their misty western homeland in search of slaves
and gold. After them came the Kints, founders of the ancient union of
exotic kingdoms east of the Middle Sea; they had ruled here for six hundred
years. Two centuries ago, they had lost Sileria to the Valdani, builders of the
most powerful empire the Middle Sea had ever known.

Through it all, prophecy, prayer, song, and story had spoken of a great
warrior who would drive out the conquering powers which enslaved Sileria
so that it could be, once again, a free and proud nation. He would prove
himself by leaping into the volcano atop Mount Darshon and surviving. For
centuries, of course, the mad *zanareen* kept flinging themselves into the
Fires of Dar in an attempt to achieve that ecstatic union with the goddess—
and failing. Then Josarian had come along.

Everyone knew the story. Hundreds of witnesses, including many skep-
tics, had been there to see the event. The rebel leader, the *shallah* who sacked
Valdani supply posts and killed their uniformed Outlookers, had flung himself into the heart of the volcano and survived. Spewing fire and ecstasy,
Dar had safely returned him to the volcano rim after having Her fill of
him. And so Josarian's legend, born on the twin-moon night he had killed
his first Valdani Outlooker, had ripened into fulfillment.

Some of the other famous rebel leaders had been with him at Darshon,
too, it was said. Tansen, Josarian's bloodbrother, was also a *shallah,* but he
was rumored to be different from the other mountain peasants. He bore a
strange foreign symbol on his chest, branded into his flesh by the gods of
Kinto, which made him invincible. He carried two magically engraved
Kintish swords which he used with the skill of a sorcerer; they could leap
out of their sheathes and slaughter men by themselves. It was said that he
had actually gone to Darshon to stop Josarian from jumping, afraid his
bloodbrother would die in the Fires of Dar, but had arrived too late. And it
was Mirabar, the stories said, who had led Josarian to Darshon. She was the

flame-eyed, fire-haired Guardian whose visions had foretold Josarian and Tansen's joint destiny to lead Sileria to freedom.

The *shallaheen,* Zarien knew, feared beings like Mirabar—some silly mountain superstition about such people being demons. Yes, *shallaheen* were ignorant; but Zarien's father said that one must nonetheless honor the way they had flocked to Josarian's banner even before the events at Darshon. One must respect the many lives they had sacrificed to free Sileria from the Valdani.

The sea-born folk had joined Josarian's cause after his transformation at Darshon, and now many of them were also dying. The Valdani were losing the war, and Josarian's destiny would soon be fulfilled. But the Valdani had not abandoned Sileria entirely. That day was yet to come.

When we take Shaljir, Zarien thought, *then the war will end, then the Valdani will finally surrender and leave forever.*

All of Sileria waited for Josarian to commence the attack on Shaljir. For the sea-born folk, it would be the deadliest and most important battle of the entire rebellion; Shaljir, the ancient capital city, was the largest and most active port in Sileria. Zarien knew his father thought that Josarian should have laid siege to the walled city before now, that he was waiting too long. The delay was due to dissension among different factions of the fragile rebel alliance. The landfolk liked nothing better than quarreling among themselves, and even war against the Valdani had not changed that. Josarian the Firebringer had become enemies with Kiloran, the most powerful waterlord in Sileria, and their feud weakened them both when it came to fighting the Valdani. And so the expected attack on Shaljir had yet to be launched.

Zarien, however, was glad for the delay. If he killed a dragonfish now, then he could join in the final great sea battle of the rebellion and fight alongside his father and elder brother for the port of Shaljir. Although they sailed primarily off the Adalian coast, the Lascari had no intention of being left out of the siege of Shaljir. Only *Bharata Ma-al* had prevented the entire clan from sailing towards Shaljir before now; no one ever skipped the *bharata.* But when the new crescent of Ejara, the second moon, appeared in the night sky and the slaughter ended, then the Lascari would sail east, via the sacred rainbow-chalk cliffs of Liron, and then turn north towards Shaljir.

Oh, let me kill a dragonfish, that I may share the honor of driving the Valdani from the waters of Shaljir, Zarien prayed fervently to the eight gods who ruled the wind and to the nine goddesses who ruled the sea.

After he placed the bloody purple heart of a dragonfish at his mother's feet, he would also be eligible to acquire a boat which he would someday offer as a wedding gift to the woman of his choice. Like his elder brother, Orman, he would continue living on his mother's boat until he finally married, and he would use the years between now and his marriage to make his own boat one that any woman would be proud to accept.

Still praying for success during the *bharata,* Zarien watched the other arriving boats of his clan drop anchor and await his grandfather's signal to begin setting the nets. When he'd exhausted his promises to the gods about all he would do for them in exchange for the heart of a dragonfish, he thought again about the extraordinary events sweeping across Sileria now that the age of the Firebringer was at hand. Freedom from the Valdani. Freedom from crippling tribute and taxes, from sudden seizures and searches, from arrest, execution, and death by slow torture for violating the smallest of their endless laws. Freedom from the threat of transportation to the mines of Alizar, somewhere in the mountains of Sileria; no one sea-born had ever returned alive from Alizar. Zarien grinned, recalling the day they'd received word that Josarian had attacked and seized the mines. His father had opened a smuggled cargo of Kintish spirits and urged his family to drink freely.

Zarien knew the number of his clan's square-sailed boats as well as he knew the number of his own fingers, so he knew when they had all arrived and were in position. The sun blazed gloriously down upon the yellow sails and the azure waters as his grandfather blew into the ritual dragonfish horn, giving the first signal of the slaughter.

"Zarien!" his father, Sorin, called from the bow. "Prepare to drop the nets!"

Zarien glowed with pride. The order meant that he would be the one to lead his own family in the setting of the nets. It was a great honor, one his father had hinted he would bestow upon him even though it was only his first *bharata*. Orman had led the setting of the nets before, so he wouldn't challenge Zarien's right to do so today—though Zarien knew he wouldn't get to do it two years in a row. His brother wasn't *that* generous.

Now his younger brother, Morven, weighed anchor, allowing the boat to creep forward again with their mother at the helm as Sorin and Orman unfurled the foresail. Zarien lifted the first iron weight, his muscles straining as he prepared to heave it over the side. Orman, Morven, and their father took their places near him on the starboard side. The boat bobbed gently in the coastal current, and Zarien only noticed his slight adjustments to its motion because of the awkward weight he held in his arms.

Taut silence replaced the typically gregarious boat-to-boat greetings of the sea-born people. Even the wind died down, awaiting the moment. Only the ever-present dull roar of the sea remained, the never-ending song of Sirkara. Then Zarien heard his grandmother's piercing wail, invoking the women of the clan to commence the chant of *Bharata Ma-al*. Zarien heaved the iron weight overboard, then heard his mother's voice strike the first note of the ritual chant at the very moment the weight struck the water.

Now there was no time to think, no time to worry about disgracing himself or his family if he failed to live up to his father's expectations. He fell into the rhythm of the chant, ordering his father and brothers to guide the massive net overboard as he hoisted the next weight into his arms. This second weight was at the end of the first net, and it must be dropped into the water exactly as the first chant ended, carrying with it the women's entreaty to the nine goddesses that the net be filled with a good catch.

One by one, they dropped the nets into the water, working in tandem with the rest of the clan to form a vast maze in the sea. The nets hung from huge cords which were floated by corks, stretched taut through the water and weighted at the bottom by the precisely spaced iron weights. The open ends of the maze all faced the open sea, from which the dragonfish would come. Any dragonfish which entered the nets would get caught in the maze and eventually swim into one of the dead ends, or death chambers, to which the underwater corridors led.

Stringing the *bharata* maze across the killing grounds was a long, hard task. The Lascari men worked efficiently under the fierce Silerian sky, sweat pouring down their beardless faces and naked backs as they dropped weights and lowered nets in time to the rhythmic chanting which filled the salty air. The singing women guided the boats skillfully, weaving a pattern on the sea's surface which defined the shape of the maze in its depths.

The ritual chant entered Zarien's blood, became part of his heartbeat, matched its pace to his breath. He no longer had to concentrate to ensure that he set the nets in time to the singing which blessed them. He moved and the movement was right, he breathed and the breath was song and prayer, he sweat and the sweat became the sea.

This was what it was to be sea-born, to marry these glimmering azure waters at the moment of your birth, to carry the sea's mystery within your veins for the rest of your life. To work in pure harmony with the rest of your kind, afloat on a bit of bobbing wood amidst the endless wave and roar of the Middle Sea. To know your course based on the slightest touch of the wind against your skin, to smell the silent approach of land even in a fog, to shift your weight with currents and waves even in your sleep . . . There was simply no other life worth living.

Arms trembling with exhaustion, Zarien helped his father lower the final iron weight into the water. The women's chanting ceased at the exact moment the weight slipped below the shimmering surface. Zarien's ears rang in the sudden silence. The weight sank to the bottom, carrying their hopes and prayers with it.

"*Aiola!*" Zarien cried, and everyone on the boat followed his lead, shouting the guttural cheer in sea-born dialect that marked the end of setting the nets. *Aiola, aiola, aiola!* May they die!

Above their own shouts and the gleeful cries from the other boats, they

heard the clan leader blow the dragonfish horn again. This was their signal
to salute the eight winds, turning on deck to honor each god as the horn
wailed eight times in succession.

Each of the eight gods was consort to one of the nine goddesses of the
sea. The ninth goddess, however—Sharifar—had no consort. According to
legend, she had been betrayed by the god who had originally been her consort, the ninth wind, and had cast him off. In his bitterness, he became the
whirlwind—whom the sea-born folk loved no better than they loved the
dragonfish. Ever since then, Sharifar had sought a new consort, but she had
yet to find a man who satisfied her. If she ever chose one (which Zarien
thought seemed unlikely after all this time), he would become the king of
all the sea-born folk—their first acknowledged leader since before the
Moorlanders had conquered Sileria a thousand years ago.

Concluding his salute to the eighth wind, Zarien looked over his shoulder to meet his father's gaze. Sorin's dark face was creased with smiles now.
His green eyes—a souvenir of the Moorlanders' long-ago Conquest not
only of Sileria, but of many of its women—glowed with pride as he clapped
Zarien on the back.

"The nets are set well, son," he said, his grin broadening in response to
Zarien's. "Perhaps I shouldn't have waited, perhaps I should have gone
ahead and got you a *stahra*."

Zarien smiled to himself, having already spotted the *stahra* in the exact
same hiding place Sorin had used for Orman's coming-of-age gift two years
ago. Neither Sorin's habits nor his teasing were original, but they were as
much a rite of passage aboard this boat as was the *bharata* itself.

"You didn't get me a *stahra*?" Zarien feigned outrage. "Don't you have
faith in me?"

His father shrugged. "Well, the dragonfish are not even here yet. We
shall see, we shall see . . ." His eyes met those of his wife, Palomar, sharing
the joke.

"Yes," Zarien said, letting them enjoy what they fondly imagined was
their secret. "You shall see. And then you'll be sorry you didn't get me a
stahra before we left port."

Now the Lascari floated their boats away from the *bharata* maze they
had constructed with such care. When the first dragonfish was sighted tonight, the men would row into the maze in small oarboats, armed for the
slaughter. Until nightfall, though, clan members rowed from boat to boat,
visiting relatives and enjoying conversation. New wounds and scars were
exclaimed over, new babies admired, new wives inspected. Cousins and in-
laws shared gossip about friends and enemies in other sea-born clans. Everyone talked about the Firebringer and his bloodfeud with Kiloran the
waterlord. Would it destroy the rebellion, or would Kiloran and Josarian
concentrate on driving out the remaining Valdani in Sileria before one of
them finally eliminated the other? Which of those two giants was most

likely to survive their enmity? True, Josarian had entered the Fires of Darshon and survived. But Kiloran . . . even the sea-born folk, who had little to do with the Honored Society, whispered his name with awe, almost afraid to say it aloud. He was the most powerful waterlord in Sileria, perhaps even the most powerful who had ever lived.

"If anyone can defeat the Firebringer," said Linyan, Zarien's grandfather, "surely it would be Kiloran."

"Then we must remember Josarian in our prayers," said one of Zarien's uncles. The others resoundingly agreed with this, since the sea-born had sworn loyalty to Josarian, not to Kiloran.

"Two days ago," said Sorin, "we met with three boats of the Kurvari clan. They say that Kiloran has seized control of Cavasar." The Valdani had fiercely held onto Sileria's westernmost port city, even though its citizens had been among the first whom Josarian had inspired to riot and rebel.

"So the Valdani have finally surrendered Cavasar?" one of Sorin's brothers asked.

"But to Kiloran," Sorin pointed out, "not to Josarian."

"To Sileria," his brother corrected. "All that really matters is that now Cavasar is free."

"Ah, but is it?" Linyan asked.

"Of course!" Zarien ventured, emboldened by his new tattoos to participate in the conversation as a man. "If the Valdani have abandoned Cavasar as they abandoned Liron and Adalian, then the city is free."

"Or have the Cavasari merely traded one master for another?" Sorin suggested. He and Linyan exchanged troubled looks.

Another of Zarien's uncles shrugged. "At least now they have a Silerian master."

"And the landfolk," Zarien said, "will always be mastered by someone." Not like the sea-born, who were meant to be free, beholden to no one except their own clans.

"But the rule of a waterlord is harsh," Linyan said heavily. "You'll understand this soon enough, Zarien. Such men bring terrible suffering to the lives that they touch."

Zarien's father agreed with this. Then, after a moment of contemplative silence, the men all began discussing other matters.

As the sun set, painting a fantastic canvas of amber and amethyst across the endless sky, the Lascari sang songs and told stories. But when the lone new moon, Abayara, rose in the night sky, they fell silent. Soon the dragonfish would come, and nothing must warn them of the trap which awaited them. The Lascari lit no lanterns aboard their vessels tonight, and they ate cold meals this evening rather than risk lighting their braziers to cook. In silence and darkness, they awaited the enemy.

Zarien was sitting between his father and brother in their long, low, wooden oarboat when the signal came. One of his cousins, keeping watch over the dark sea under a crescent-moon sky, had spotted the telltale horn of a dragonfish breaking the surface. His warning signal was soft, careful not to alarm the enemy swimming towards the maze. Sorin nodded to Zarien who, pleasantly aware of his younger brother's envious gaze, pushed the oarboat away from his mother's vessel and dipped his oars into the water to glide closer to the maze.

Sorin silently directed Zarien with his right hand. In his left he held an oil-soaked torch which he would light when the attack began, and it was too late for the enemy to escape to the open sea. Their harpoons and tackle, along with Orman's and Sorin's *stahra,* were ready, neatly ordered at their feet or fastened to the sides of the boat. Now Zarien heard more signals from the lookouts as the number of sightings increased.

"It will be a great slaughter this year," Sorin murmured, his low voice rich with anticipation.

Please let me kill one, Zarien prayed to the wind and the sea. What could be worse than failing to make his first kill during a *bharata* which would long be remembered as a particularly good one?

As the sightings continued, he heard his brother say softly behind him, "So many this year, papa!"

Yes, Zarien decided firmly, he would rather die than endure the shame of failing to make his first kill now. Only some bumbling drylander would fail to take a dragonfish when so many were entering the maze!

The boat heaved beneath him suddenly. A geyser of water drenched him as he caught his balance. "There's one underneath us!" Zarien released one oar and reached for a harpoon.

Sorin laughed with exultation. "Let it go, Zarien. There will be enough in the maze for us."

Heart pounding, Zarien watched the sleek, deadly creature disappear back into the dark water. It was huge! Bigger than the oarboat. What a fine first kill it would make! But he supposed his father was right. They'd waste time chasing it down, and probably wind up losing it in the dark, anyhow, unless it turned and attacked. Better to keep rowing towards the maze.

More than twenty oarboats took their places around the bobbing corks which defined the vast and elaborate maze the Lascari had laid out under the brilliant sun. Now the men watched the water's opaque surface as they awaited the moment which would commence the slaughter. Zarien was so excited he could scarcely breathe. He stared unblinking at the water until his eyes burned.

Then it came! The sudden, thrashing rise to the surface of the first dragonfish to reach a death chamber and realize it was trapped.

"*Aiola!*" Zarien shouted. May they die!

The exultant cry was repeated by all the Lascari as torches now flamed into life in every boat on the water.

More trapped dragonfish began rising to the surface, their massive curling horns reflecting the torchlight as they surged out of the water. Boats rocked wildly as the enormous bodies fell back down, noisily hitting the sea's surface and sending up showers of cool, salty water to drench the Lascari.

"*Bharata Ma-al!*" cried Linyan, setting his clan free of all restraint. And the slaughter began!

Zarien moved quickly, but not quickly enough. His brother's blood was high, and his generosity in letting Zarien lead the setting of the nets without argument did not extend to letting Zarien make the family's first kill of the *bharata*. Orman whooped wildly beside Zarien as his harpoon sailed through the night and sank into the silver-gray and shiny-green scales of the nearest dragonfish. A terrible roar rose up from the water and echoed through the night. The dragonfish's agonized thrashing brought it crashing against the oarboat. Zarien braced himself as the boat rocked wildly and nearly flung him into his father's flaming torch. A dark stain spread through the water, absorbing the glow of the torches. It was the glorious cloud of the dragonfish's dark purple blood.

"That one was mine!" Zarien said fiercely.

"You can have the next one!" Orman shot back.

"You do that again, and I'll—"

"Easy, son," Sorin interrupted, "you'll get your chance. Let's finish this one!"

"*Aiola!*" Orman howled. He raised his *stahra* and then brought its sharp edge down on the dragonfish's writhing back, again and again, until the spine was finally broken. The creature's sticky purple blood covered Orman, Zarien, and Sorin by the time the great body lay still in the water.

Another silvery horn broke through the water's surface as yet another dragonfish tried to escape the deadly maze. It flailed its powerful spiked tail in a desperate attempt to clear a space for itself, hitting Orman's fresh kill hard enough to send geysers of bloody water high into the air. Its wild thrashing started pushing the just-slaughtered corpse away from the oarboat. Orman leaned perilously far over the side, reaching for the *stahra*, which stuck out of the dead monster's back, in an effort to retrieve his kill.

This one, Zarien thought as the living one hurled itself frantically towards the surface again. *This one will be mine!* He fixed his aim on the massive heaving body which twisted and flailed in fear and anger.

"Damn it!" Orman leaned out a little farther, ignoring his father's warning not to, trying to haul in his kill. The thrashing of the second dragonfish was driving the corpse beneath the surface. "It's sinking! Zarien—"

"Let go of me!"

"Help me—"

Poised to make his first kill, Zarien tried to shake off his brother's grasping hand. He scarcely heard Linyan's nearby shout or his father's cry of alarm. It was only when the impact of their colliding boats nearly knocked him into the water that he realized the danger. He braced himself against the sudden pitch of the boat. His balance would have held—had not Orman's nagging grasp turned into a reflexive yank which tumbled him headlong into the sea.

"*Zarien!*"

Cool water engulfed him. Fear filled him, drowned all thoughts but one: *Get out!*

His legs were propelling him back towards the surface almost before he realized what had happened. He crashed into the underbelly of a writhing dragonfish, a beast so huge it blotted out the flickering torches he had briefly glimpsed through the blood-clouded water.

No, no, no!

Another dragonfish rose beneath him. Its mouth brushed his legs.

No! Not my legs!

Horrible memories of legless men hauled out of the sea clouded his mind with panic. He'd rather drown than bleed to death on deck in terrible agony.

Help!

He *would* drown if he didn't get to the surface. He'd had no time to fill his lungs with air before—

A flailing spiked tail broadsided him, snapping his head around, tearing open his flesh and nearly knocking him unconscious. Only the trained instincts of the sea-born kept him from involuntarily inhaling—and drowning.

Get out, get out, get out!

He boldly pushed between two enormous, heaving bodies which struggled in the maze. He prayed they were too panicked to notice a puny thing like him right now. He prayed that the scent of his blood, now clouding around him, would be concealed by the scent of their own.

Through the wine-dark water, he saw lights flickering above him again. Hope blossomed in him. If he could break the surface. If his family could pull him out before—

A huge body sank down upon him from overhead, pushing him back down.

No!

He kicked wildly. Swam out from under it. Got tangled in the net of the maze.

The heavy weight of another dragonfish careened into him, trapping him against the net. The tough fiber of the net cut into his skin as he was pushed harder and harder against it.

His lungs burned like the Fires of Dar. He was dizzy, growing weak. The weight of the dragonfish would crush him in another moment, leaving his mangled carcass dangling from the net.

Sanity came to him a moment before death did. What a fool he was! Instead of pushing uselessly against the net, he now reached through it, then let his right arm grasp the small knife sheathed at his waist. All sea-born folk carried one to cut tangled lines, nets, and seaweed.

Fighting the fatal instinct to inhale, Zarien cut through the net's tough fibers and freed himself, slipping out of the deadly maze. He had sunk far below the surface, but hope renewed his strength as he rose through the blood-darkened water.

It was the blood, of course, that prevented him from seeing the dragon-fish until it was upon him.

As its great jaws closed around his torso and its gleaming ivory teeth sank into his flesh, Zarien screamed. Water filled his mouth, his throat, his lungs, but the agony of the dragonfish's attack was the only sensation he knew as it dragged him down to the age-old destiny of the sea-born folk.

2

FROM ONE THING, ANOTHER IS BORN.

—Tansen

THE ARMS WHICH held Zarien were cool and soft, pulling him ever deeper into the dark water.

His thoughts returned slowly, coming to him one by one, like lazy waves lapping at the side of a boat. He was underwater. He felt peaceful and serene. He wasn't holding his breath, nor was he drowning. Someone soft and voluptuous and cool-skinned embraced him. He felt no pain. No pain. . . .

The dragonfish!

He gave a panicked start as terror quickened his heart. The lush arms tightened their hold around him. He struggled against the embrace, confused and scared.

There is nothing to fear.

The rich and unfamiliar feminine voice filled his head. It seemed to come from within him as much as from all around him. Increasingly alarmed, he struggled harder.

You're safe now.

They were going deeper and deeper, strong strokes propelling them ever further from the surface and survival.

What happened to the dragonfish? Zarien wondered.

I took you from her.

He went rigidly still. A cold certainty flooded him. He tried to speak, but water filled his mouth. So he asked the question in silence: *Are you Death?*

The gentle laughter which greeted this question seemed so incongruous that his eyes snapped open—which was when he finally realized they'd been closed.

The darkness surrounding him at this depth was made all the more apparent by the brilliant incandescence of the female creature which held him in her arms. Zarien drew in a sharp breath of astonishment. The fact that this action didn't make him gag or cough, even as he felt the cool water flood his lungs, was startling enough to distract him for a moment. He stared at his companion in bewilderment, now also realizing how inexplicably clear his vision was.

You're safe now, she repeated.

She was as beautiful as she was strange, with veil-like fins flaring around her translucent body, revealing and concealing her voluptuous form as they flowed back and forth. Zarien, who had never before seen a naked woman who wasn't a blood relative, couldn't help staring. Her diaphanous skin glowed silvery-pale, like the moons on a misty night. Her full hips flowed down to a sleek tail whose undulations kept propelling both of them away from all that Zarien knew. Heat crept through his cold limbs as he became aware of the soft globes of her breasts pressed against him. Instead of hair, something like spun pearls grew from her scalp, flowing around her in pellucid strands. She must be a dream. Or perhaps . . .

A goddess?

No, he *must* be dreaming.

You're not dreaming. You fell overboard and were killed by a dragonfish.

Then I am dead? he asked in sorrow.

Not for long.

You will return me to my family?

In a way.

Bewildered, he risked another question. *What has happened?*

Ah.

She slowly released him from her grasp, then slid her cool palms along his arms until she was holding his hands. She felt like both flesh and water, both real and unreal, firm and fluid all at once.

The moment he was free of her protective embrace, he could feel the tremendous power of the underwater current. It pulled at his body, dragging fiercely at his weight. Only the grip on his hands kept him from being swept into the current's eddy.

Face-to-face with the sea goddess now, his gaze was inexorably drawn to hers. He looked into the depthless pools of her eyes and saw his fate revealed there, the events of the *bharata* reenacted within her glimmering gaze. He saw himself, foolish in his eagerness, fall overboard when Linyan's oarboat collided with his own. He watched his own struggles beneath the sea's surface, and he wanted to weep when he saw how ferociously the dragonfish had attacked, mauled, and killed him. He saw the goddess tangle fiercely with the dragonfish, then carry his lifeless body away in victory. Embarrassment flooded him as he saw her press her translucent lips against his to breathe life back into him, and he nearly had to look away when he saw her nurse him from those lush breasts to restore his lifeblood.

He watched his father return to his mother's boat and tell her and Morven of his death. His mother wept violently as she took a knife and repeatedly cut herself in mourning—an ancient sea-born custom which the Valdani had tried to outlaw. His father, his brother, and his grandfather all blamed themselves for Zarien's death. His mother hoisted dark purple banners from both masts to announce that one of her family had been taken by a dragonfish.

I must go back, Zarien said.

His mother's suffering made his heart raw. The guilt and self-condemnation of his male relatives were like the blows of a *stahra*. But he would end their sorrow, would bring rejoicing and celebration to his clan, if he returned.

When the goddess didn't respond, he added more insistently, *Let me go—please!*

I didn't save you for them. Now the voice in his head, so seductive earlier, was as cold as the sea.

He pulled himself out of the visions in her depthless eyes and tried to think. He knew enough about the gods to realize that this one would probably want something in return for giving him life after what the dragonfish had done to him. She hadn't saved him just to send him back to his family.

Of course, he said, aware of the current tugging at his body, aware that the price for life would probably be very high—and death a certainty if he refused. *I thank you for my life. What must I do to earn it?*

He could have drowned in the beauty of her smile. *You must bring me my consort.*

If Zarien were alive in the normal sense, he would have choked on his surprise. *Your consort?*

The time has come. I must have him, and the sea-born folk need him.
Then you are Sharifar? he guessed.
Yes.

His body bobbed in the current as he considered her demand.
I will be honored to bring him to you, Sharifar. Where will I find him?
On land.

He recoiled so sharply that the goddess's own body jerked in response to the tug of his hands, rippling as water rippled in response to sudden movement. *I can't set foot on land,* he protested. It was unthinkable. She might as well ask the sun to rise in the west.

Yes, you can.

I am sea-bound! We do not—

No, you're not, she said.

Yes, I am. I'm Lascari!

Not really.

My father is—

Your father was a drylander.

Take that back! he snapped, heedless of her divinity. *My mother has never*—

Your real mother died long ago.

My moth— He stopped abruptly, realizing what she had just said. *My real mother?*

Yes.

He stared at the goddess in bewildered astonishment for a moment. *No, you're wrong.*

You are not Sorin and Palomar's son.

Of course I am!

No.

Sorin and Palomar are—

They lied to you, she told him gently. *Your whole life.*

No! His father a drylander? Absolutely not! No. *You're wrong.*

I am Sharifar. I know.

I don't believe you!

You—

You're lying!

—must—

No, I won't listen! I am Lascari!

Zarien.... She warned him against such disrespect by releasing one of his hands. The current tossed him around violently. Sharifar's cool grip on his other hand was his only anchor, his only link to survival. The gods only knew where this current would take him if she let go.

Darkness surrounded him. Cold filled him. He needed air. He needed to breathe. He would die any moment if he couldn't get air! Panic seized him. Pain consumed him. The deep wounds of the dragonfish's teeth began bleeding again. He'd be dead in moments, whether he drowned, bled to death, or was scented and attacked by another dragonfish.

He had always believed he would die at sea, perhaps just this way— wounded and drowning . . . but now he would die not knowing the truth about himself, consumed by this terrible doubt, poisoned by Sharifar's humiliating claim.

I am Lascari! And he would prove it.

He would die soon enough. Perhaps even from another dragonfish attack. But he would die knowing who he was, knowing the pride of the Lascari was his by birth. He didn't want to die now, like this, in doubt and shame.

I will listen, he conceded at last.

A strong, cool hand grasped his flailing one and brought him face-to-face with the goddess again. His pain faded, his blood stopped flowing, his lungs stopped burning. Angry and resentful, Zarien regarded Sharifar stonily and resisted the lure of her exquisite beauty. She smiled sympathetically.

It's time for you to seek your true father, she told him, *just as it is time for me to embrace my consort.*

My true father, he repeated without belief or enthusiasm.

You will bring my consort to me.

As you wish, he replied obediently, burning with outrage.

You will make your own choices about your father.

He couldn't stop himself, for thoughts flowed with far less control than words: *Sorin is my father.*

Sorin raised you, but he is not your father.

Then why didn't he tell me that himself?

Because you were only a child.

Suddenly, despite the goddess's protection, he felt the full weight and chill of the sea's depths again. Could Sharifar's claims possibly be true? Was this appalling discovery something Sorin would have revealed to him once he truly became a man?

The affectionate name by which he had always known Sorin came unbidden to his thoughts: *Papa* . . .

Sorin cannot be your father any longer.

But when he knows I'm alive—

You're going to walk the dryland, she said. *You can never be Lascari again. Your sea-bound life is over.*

But I . . . His mind went blank as her words ripened in his heart. She was right. No matter who was really his father, and no matter how glad the Lascari would be to learn he was alive, setting foot upon land would ensure banishment from the clan for the rest of his life.

This was the price of his life. He could never be Lascari again.

He would have preferred death, except that he could not let Sharifar send him incomplete to that shore which had no other shore. He had to know the truth about his birth, about his blood, before he sailed into death.

I . . . *I will be an outcast.* If he weren't hovering beyond life, somewhere in the domain of the gods, he would have had to fight tears.

You will find your own life ashore, she promised.

The sea is my life.

The world is changing, Zarien. You must change with it.

I want to see my—I want to see Sorin, he said suddenly. *I want him to tell me. To my face.*

In time, perhaps. Now you must go in search of my consort.

On land?

Yes.

Your consort is . . . No, surely not. *Your consort is a drylander?*

Yes.

You can't take a drylander as your consort! How can the sea-born accept him as their king?

He is chosen by Dar.

Dar is . . . She is not . . .

The volcano rules even the sea-born.

But the sea-born do not worship—

The sea-born will accept my consort, as I will accept Dar's choice for my mate.

Then I . . . I will bring him, Zarien said with far more resignation than hope. *To earn my life, I will bring him to you.*

Perhaps sensing all the doubts he tried to hide from her, Sharifar added, *It will be no small thing, Zarien, to bring back the first king of the sea-born in a thousand years.*

That, at least, was true. *How will I know him?*

She smiled again. *It's enough that I will know him.*

But I— He gasped when she suddenly released both his hands, abandoning him to the fierce current. *Sharifar!*

She spread her graceful fins through the water and moved forward, following him. The shimmering veils grew larger and larger, covering Zarien, spreading around him like the open sky on a clear day. From this veiled covering emerged a long slender object, slowly floating towards him. He recognized what it was only moments before colliding with it—a *stahra,* the weapon of a man. Sharifar's gift to him, he supposed.

He seized the metal-tipped oar in bitter resignation and let it take him where it would. The shimmering veils of the goddess drifted away, leaving him alone in the endless sea. The current shifted and pulled him in a new direction. Free of pain or the need to breathe, he let it carry him according to Sharifar's will, away from her and away from his own death.

He couldn't believe the sea-born would accept a drylander as their first king in centuries. He couldn't understand why a sea goddess was bowing to Dar's will. How much could the world possibly be changing? How much more would it need to change for Sharifar to be satisfied and for Dar's will to be done?

And he . . . he would never sail as a Lascari again. If Sharifar was to be believed, he had never been one in the first place . . .

He must return to Sorin and Palomar, must make them tell him the truth!

The sea soothed his desperate thoughts, carrying him safely through this strange realm between life and death. He supposed Sharifar would protect him until he reached the shore, so he had no fear of reefs, rocks, nets, or dragonfish.

Once he reached shore, though . . . The fear of *that* threatened to consume him. He knew nothing about life on land. He would be as helpless as a baby among the landfolk. How would he survive?

His musings ended when, contrary to his previous expectations, the current hurled him against a rock. He gasped—and immediately began coughing as he inhaled saltwater. The goddess's protection was evidently withdrawn, he reflected sourly, now that he had reached land. He was on his own from now on.

Zarien braced himself as the waves broke against the rocks again, then he grappled for purchase with one hand while holding on to the *stahra* with the other. His seeking hand slipped on slime at first, but then he finally got firm hold of a rough surface and hauled himself out of the water. Breathing hard, he sat down on a rock and looked around. It was still nighttime, and now thick clouds obscured even the faint light of the first new moon. He couldn't see far or make out any details beyond observing some rocky shoreline. He wouldn't know much more until morning.

However, assuming he was on the Adalian coast—since he'd fallen overboard in Adalian's coastal waters—he tried to come up with a plan. He wanted most of all to return to the open sea, to find his parents . . . to find Sorin and Palomar, that was, and confront them with the goddess's tale of his dead mother and drylander father. But he looked longingly out at the dark sea, listening to its familiar roar, and knew it was hopeless. He had no boat. No sea-born folk would be in port right now, even if he could find a port in the morning; all sea-born clans were at sea for *Bharata Ma-al*. There were usually foreign ships in any sizeable port, but he had no money and so couldn't pay them to take him back to his family. And certainly no *toren's* yacht would escort him to the Lascari; the aristocratic *toreni* did not make a habit of exerting themselves for commoners.

By the time any sea-born folk returned to port, the *bharata* would be over and the Lascari would be sailing for Shaljir. Zarien's presumed death wouldn't change those plans.

So perhaps he should go overland to Shaljir, searching for Sharifar's consort along the way. And whether or not he found him by the time he reached Shaljir, he could try to contact the Lascari once he reached Sileria's greatest port.

As for finding Sharifar's consort . . . It occurred to Zarien that there was already a likely candidate. Who better to embrace Sharifar than the man who had already survived the embrace of Dar? Who better to become the sea king than the Firebringer himself? Who better to unite the volcano and the sea than Josarian, who had already united the landfolk and the sea-born against the Valdani?

He must find Josarian. He must take the Firebringer to Sharifar. Who else could Dar have chosen for her consort?

Of course, finding Josarian would be no easy task. Even Zarien knew that Josarian's movements were a closely guarded secret. Not only did the

Valdani keep increasing the reward offered for his death, but now Kiloran, the great waterlord, was his enemy and sought to slay him, too—which meant many assassins, as well as many other waterlords of the Honored Society, were now after the Firebringer.

Although the sea-born folk remained Josarian's loyal allies, Zarien knew enough about landfolk to realize that asking them to tell him where Josarian was would be useless. The *shallaheen* wouldn't trust a sea-born boy any more than the lowlanders would trust a city-dweller or a *toren* would trust an assassin. Josarian's unique gift was that he had somehow made Sileria's feuding and disparate peoples work together towards a common goal: freedom from the Valdani. For a time, at least. Now that Kiloran was his enemy, who knew how much longer the Firebringer's day of glory would last? The rebel alliance was crumbling even with victory against the Valdani in sight. Life in Sileria never really changed.

I must find Josarian before Kiloran or the Society do, before the Valdani do.

He shivered a bit as the coastal breeze swept over his wet skin and clothing. He shivered a little with loneliness and fear, too. He had not yet become a man according to the customs of the sea-born, and now he faced a task that he believed would make most men tremble. But, he reminded himself, he bore the tattoos of a man and his *stahra* had been given to him by a sea goddess. Manhood was upon him, whether or not this was the way he had expected to earn it. Surrounded by darkness and comforted only by the never-silent sea, he wondered where to start his search for the Firebringer.

"Dalishar," he suddenly realized.

Mount Dalishar, a sacred site of the mysterious Guardians of the Otherworld, had been Josarian's base since the beginning of the rebellion. For months now, the country around it had been rebel-held territory, a vast section of Sileria finally free of Valdani laws and Outlooker patrols. And Dalishar was said to be so heavily imbued with Guardian magic that even the Honored Society and its powerful waterlords couldn't attack Josarian there.

If there was one place to find Josarian—or at least to find someone Josarian trusted, someone who could somehow be convinced to take Zarien to him—Dalishar would be the place.

All Zarien really knew about Dalishar's location was that it was high up, somewhere in Sileria's merciless mountains, deep in the heart of the clannish, violent world of Josarian's own kind, the *shallaheen*.

For a moment, Zarien almost wished he were back in the water with the dragonfish.

Sileria's mountain peasants might be good fighters, but everyone knew they were dirty, ignorant, superstitious, dishonest, violent, and unforgiving of the slightest misunderstanding or offense. Few sea-born folk had ever ventured into the mountains; even fewer had come back out.

Many *shallaheen* didn't even speak common Silerian, the language by which Sileria's diverse ethnic groups communicated with each other. Zarien had heard the guttural mountain dialect of *shallah* smugglers a few times and could only understand about one word in three. So even if they didn't kill him or steal what little he possessed, they might just not understand what he was saying to them.

Josarian speaks common Silerian. He even speaks Valdan. Everyone says so, he reminded himself, trying to summon up hope. *Some of the others will, too.*

Contemplating the difficulties of undertaking his enormous task without friends, family, money, or food, Zarien summoned all his will and rose to his feet. Tonight he would go the rest of the way ashore and get some sleep. Tomorrow, he would set out for Dalishar. Somehow, he would survive and do what he had to do. He had died and been reborn tonight, so he could certainly do this.

Sharply aware of how motionless the surface beneath his feet was, he began picking his way through the rocks. They were wet and slippery, but they were no challenge to a boy used to the heaving decks of storm-tossed boats.

Beyond the rocks was a narrow beach. Zarien had touched sand before, of course, diving in coastal seabeds. This was particularly coarse stuff, though, strewn with seaweed that tangled in his toes and rocks that poked the arches of his bare feet. He ambled along for a while, hoping to find a more comfortable surface for sleep. He wasn't ready to go farther inland in search of a good spot, though. Tomorrow would be soon enough to leave behind the familiar scent and sound of the sea, the familiar tickle of salty air in his nostrils and on his tongue. Tonight he needed to sleep near the soothing murmur and roar of her waves.

Finally abandoning hope of encountering a stretch of smoother sand, Zarien chose a spot, cleared away the seaweed and rocks as best he could in the dark, and lay down on the sand. The cloudy night sky overhead was soothing and familiar, since he usually slept on deck. But there was no gentle rolling, no comforting bob and sway beneath him.

The clouds drifted apart and the glimmering light of the moonlit sky slowly spread across land and sea. Restless and edgy, Zarien sat up and glanced around. The rocky beach looked no better now that he could see more of it. Depressed, he lowered his gaze.

His breath caught when he saw, for the first time, the great scars left on his torso by the teeth of the dragonfish. Its terrible fang marks made a half-circle which went from his right shoulder, across his chest and belly, to his right hip. He reached awkwardly behind him as horrifying memories of the attack returned to him. Yes, he could feel corresponding scar tissue on the parts of his back which he could reach.

Contemplating the mystery of his survival, Zarien lay back in the coarse sand again, folding his arms beneath his head. He gazed up at the endless night sky . . . and that was when he noticed that Ejara, the second moon, was now a glowing crescent beside Abayara, which was waxing.

That meant *Bharata Ma-al* was already over.

He had been underwater for more than three days.

3

ONLY ONE THING IS BETTER THAN LEARNING THAT
AN ENEMY IS DEAD: LEARNING THAT HE IS IN SILERIA.
—Valdani Proverb

JOSARIAN IS DEAD.

The words burned in Tansen's mind the way the seeping wound in his side burned his flesh. His heart hadn't known pain like this since that night, so long ago, when he had returned to his native village of Gamalan to find his entire family slain by the Valdani. Only a boy of fifteen then, he had turned to Armian, who eventually became his bloodfather, for courage. Now, more than ten years later, he was a man—a rebel leader, a warrior already embraced and embellished in Silerian legend—and, in the wake of this catastrophe, others would look to *him* for courage.

But he had none left to give, and he found that the coming of day didn't change that. Sorrow consumed him. Despair stole the last of his will. Pain and exhaustion clouded his mind.

The trek from the village of Chandar to the sacred caves of Dalishar wasn't far as *shallaheen* reckoned things, and Tansen had been born to Sileria's mountains; but he had used the last of his strength during the night and had nothing left now.

His wound had reopened—was it only two nights ago?—when he had abandoned Sanctuary to try to save Josarian's life. The deep wound burned with cold fire now, sucking his life away. It wasn't fresh; it had been made many days ago, but it was a *shir* wound, and the wavy-edged dagger of a Society assassin wounded as no other blade did. Created by the dark sorcery of a waterlord, a *shir* was fashioned out of water and imbued with a power so deadly that it ensured the assassins of the Honored Society were feared throughout Sileria.

Ironically, Tansen's wound hadn't been delivered by an assassin, but by a Valdan, the late and unlamented Commander Koroll; he had managed to slay an assassin at some point, during the long months of fighting between the Silerian rebels and the Valdani, and thereby acquired a *shir*.

Since a *shir* could be used even against a waterlord, the waterlords ensorcelled them so that only the trusted assassin for whom a *shir* was made could actually touch it. Only by killing an assassin could you make his *shir* your own. By now, Tansen had made more than a few *shir* his own, including the one which had belonged to Armian; but he didn't use or keep them. The two slender swords of a *shatai* were his weapons—earned with discipline and pain, wielded with honor and skill—and he had proved often that they were all he needed for killing Valdani Outlookers, Society assassins, or anyone else.

I'll have to kill more assassins now . . .

After all the broken vows, betrayals, and deadly plots, Kiloran had finally succeeded in his goal. Two nights ago, when his latest plan to destroy Josarian—by having Josarian's trusted cousin Zimran betray him to the Valdani—had failed, he had fallen back on an even darker scheme. He had summoned the White Dragon from the waters of the Zilar River. Tansen hadn't even believed the wild tales whispered about such creatures until he saw it with his own eyes, grotesquely forming itself out of the shallow river, gathering itself into a huge and hideous monster under the two full moons which illuminated the night sky. A billion glittering drops of water crystallized into slashing claws, dripping fangs, and voracious jaws. Born of a mystical union between water and wizard, Kiloran's terrible offspring had seized and killed Josarian.

And I couldn't stop it.

Tansen had tried, but his swords swept ineffectually through that monstrous creature made only of water. Mirabar had tried, too, but even her fire magic couldn't stop that thing. Now Josarian's dying screams of agony still rang in Tansen's head, and probably would for the rest of his life.

After completing the task for which it had been born, the White Dragon simply sank back into the Zilar River. Quiescent. Gone. As if it had never been. There wasn't anything left for Tansen to fight, to kill.

Except Kiloran.

Josarian was dead, but as a victim of the White Dragon, he would endure its vicious torment until its creator finally died.

All the more reason to kill Kiloran.

The old waterlord meant to rule Sileria. He meant to make the *shallaheen* and all the other peoples of this troubled land toil under the yoke of the Honored Society. Kiloran now intended to dominate the whole nation, rather than just his traditional territory, with violence and terror, with thirst and drought, with bloodshed and extortion. He would subject Sileria to worse misery than it had known during a thousand years of brutal foreign domination. And to ensure his success, he would use the Society to slaughter every last Guardian in Sileria. After centuries of enmity, the masters of water would eagerly employ their power to destroy the servants of fire once and for all.

Mirabar...

Mirabar, gifted with powers strong enough to frighten most waterlords, burdened with prophetic visions which even Kiloran respected. Young and hot-headed, sharp-tongued and quick-thinking, foolishly brave as a sorceress, unsure and inexperienced as a woman... Her death was now surely Kiloran's first priority.

Or my death, perhaps? For old times' sake.

Tansen's lungs burned from working so hard to make up for the loss of blood from his wound and the lack of food and sleep during the past two days and nights. His whole body ached from the blows of the White Dragon. His flesh burned in a thousand places from the drops of ensorcelled water which had dripped onto him from that grotesque beast. The cuts which its claws had left upon him burned coldly, like cuts made by a *shir.* He was covered in dried blood: his own, Josarian's, his enemies'...

You've wanted me dead for so long, old man, perhaps you will want me first, before her.

He paused to rest, something he almost never did in the long-distance trekking over brutal terrain that was a normal part of daily life in Sileria's harsh mountains. Unlike most *shallaheen,* he knew how to ride a horse, but horses were rare in Sileria, impractical deep in the mountains, and out of the question on the treacherous paths ascending to Dalishar.

He had been back in Sileria—back from exile in foreign lands, back in these loved and hated mountains—for more than a year now. He was normally conditioned to this life. But not today. Not wounded, exhausted, and weak from blood loss. Head pounding, he bent over, breathing hard, and braced his hands on his thighs, aware that he hadn't covered nearly the distance he had expected to since leaving Chandar before dawn.

Well past midday, he guessed, squinting up at the brassy Silerian sunshine. And he was still very far from the caves.

After Josarian's death in the Zilar River, Tansen had sent Mirabar to Dalishar, safe from Kiloran's reach, and told her to wait for him. He had gone to Chandar for one simple task. And he had failed at Chandar, as he had failed at the Zilar River. Now he must tell Mirabar he had failed. He must somehow make her understand why he couldn't do it.

I can't kill her, Mirabar, I can't.

His chest ached. His throat hurt. All of Sileria's sins were his, and he could think of no one whom he had never disappointed or betrayed.

Focus on the task at hand.

Later, he hoped, there would be time enough for mourning. Later, he knew, he would pay for his sins and his failings. Dar would see to that in the end. But for now, there was so much work to be done.

He must reach Dalishar. They must make plans and protect the crumbling rebel alliance. When word of Josarian's death spread, the *shallaheen* would be frightened and confused. Some of them had already reverted to old loyalties and sided with Kiloran; now many others might follow in fear and ignorance. The lowlanders, the *toreni*, the city-dwellers, the sea-born folk—everyone who had joined the cause because they believed in Josarian—might now drift away, splintering Sileria once again into disparate and warring factions incapable of resisting either the Society or yet another foreign conquest.

If he couldn't improve his pace, Tansen finally acknowledged, he wouldn't reach the caves of Dalishar by nightfall.

Another day lost.

Another day wherein Kiloran could gain ascendancy. Another day wherein the world which Josarian had tried to build would now tear itself apart. . . . Grief overwhelmed him again.

Josarian is dead. My brother is dead.

Tansen had thought so once before, when Josarian had flung himself into the Fires of Darshon. Tansen, busy battling the will of the destroyer goddess in flame and fury below the summit, had heard Mirabar's terrible scream, had heard Dar's triumphant roar, and he'd known it was too late to save the man who was his ally, his friend, and his bloodbrother. Who could have known that the goddess would embrace Josarian like a lover and then return him to his people, forever changed, but unharmed? Tansen had believed, right up until that moment, that Armian had been the Firebringer, as the stories of his childhood had always claimed.

Only Armian never had a chance to embrace Dar, because I killed him. . . .

Bile rose in his throat. His head swam. Tansen pressed a filthy hand to the bitterly painful wound at his side. His thoughts were wandering too much.

Focus on the task at hand.

That was his training, part of the discipline that made him who he was, the man he had become out of the wreckage of his boyhood. He was a *shatai*, a member of the finest warrior caste in the three corners of the world. Nine years of exile to escape the bloodvow he had earned from Kiloran the night he had murdered Armian . . . *Father, father* . . . Five of those years spent training under a *shatai-kaj* in Kinto, a great swordmaster who'd been just eccentric enough to take on an ignorant and unkempt Silerian peasant boy as his apprentice.

Kiloran had wanted him dead before, and wanted him dead now. The Valdani had placed a high price on Tansen's head, second only to that of Josarian. Society assassins had come for him, as had Valdani Outlookers. But the brand carved into his chest—the mark of a *shatai*—wasn't just for show. He had earned it with five years of training that many apprentices didn't survive. He had faced not only Kiloran, but Dar Herself, and he knew that some people now even believed that he couldn't be killed.

But every man can be killed. Every *man.*

Certainly he had killed enough men to know how true that was, but it was something he had learned upon his first killing, long before becoming a *shatai;* the night he had murdered Armian, the greatest warrior he had ever seen up until then . . .

The night I betrayed and slaughtered my bloodfather . . .

He straightened up and continued walking, pushing the memory of Armian deep into the recesses of his mind, where he knew it would lurk in wait for him. When he slept, yes, when he slept . . . that was when he inevitably remembered the father he had murdered.

Every man can be killed.

True, he had faced many enemies and always won. A *shatai* was very hard to kill, and he knew without boasting that he was harder to kill than most. But he had no illusions about being invincible. His *shatai-kaj* had seen to that. For five years, every single day of Tansen's training as a *shatai* had begun with the ritual phrase he was supposed to utter with every challenge and before every fight: *I am prepared to die today. Are you?*

The sudden leap of his senses warned him of danger before any conscious thought. The years of training, the endless repetitions and mind-numbing exercises had not gone to waste. He unsheathed his sword and spun to face his attacker before the first blow of the assassin's ambush could strike him.

"I'm not *that* prepared to die," he rasped, light-headed from the sudden movement.

He parried another stab of the assassin's glittering *shir* as he shifted in response to the movement of air on his left—a second attacker. Sensing the opening even before he saw it, Tansen killed that one with a quick slash across the throat. Messy, he acknowledged as the hot blood sprayed him, but effective.

Where you know there is one, fight as if there were many, his *kaj* had taught him, *for you'll find that there often are.*

He slashed the wrist of the first attacker and moved to fight the imagined others—who, as it turned out, did indeed exist.

"Kaja was right again," he muttered, fighting for air and balance. With the first attacker on his knees and the second attacker dead, Tansen confronted four more surrounding him.

Six assassins. An ambush. Kiloran had learned from his mistakes, and so had his men. Gone were the days when a sole assassin would openly challenge Tansen in the traditional manner of the Society.

He ignored the weakness claiming his body, the fierce pain of his wound, the vicious memories the White Dragon had left on his flesh. A *shatai* was contemptuous of pain, clear-headed in combat, and most focused at the moment when other men were most terrified. Tansen fought on eight sides and three levels, as he had been taught, taking control of the fight, of the footing, of the pace. He made a second kill, under the ribs and into the heart. The thrust took strength and a little too much time under the circumstances, but the opening was there and he took it rather than wait for another.

Out of the corner of his eye he saw the first attacker slide into unconsciousness, soon to bleed to death. Tansen knew, without the panic or fear which shackled lesser men to failure and death, that he must kill the remaining three quickly, before the last of his strength failed him and he made his first mistake. Kiloran had not sent inexperienced young braggarts after him. Tansen could tell that these men needed only one mistake, a single opening, to make their kill.

Of the three who still faced him, one carried two *shir,* as Tansen carried two swords. The other two assassins fought more traditionally, each swinging a *yahr* in one hand and wielding a *shir* in the other. That meant that, like Tansen, these two had probably been born to the mountains; the *yahr,* a deadly striking weapon, was typically used by the mountain-born *shallaheen.* It was made of two smooth, short, wooden sticks, sometimes metal-tipped, which were joined by a short rope or chain. To someone who didn't know what it was, it merely looked like a small bundle of sticks, or a distinctive *shallah* grain flail, the tool which had inspired the weapon. Developed two hundred years ago as a response to Valdani laws against Silerians carrying weapons, it had remained largely secret from the Valdani until the rebellion.

Tansen blocked a blow from one of the *yahr* and could tell, by the feel of it against his blade, that it was made of petrified Kintish wood—an expensive luxury, as typical of assassins as were the black-dyed gossamer tunics these men wore. Even one careless blow of such a *yahr* could crush bones in Tansen's hand. A solid hit would probably break his forearm or shatter his kneecap. And a good blow to the head . . . One would stun him, another blow or two would crush his skull. He knew, because he had killed Armian that way. . . .

Focus on the task at hand.

His lungs were burning. He stepped away from a thrust before it even came, knowing by the shift of the assassins' shoulders and the flicker of their eyes what they would do before they did it. A *shatai* trained to know his enemies in combat even better than they knew themselves. Killing was a passion among Silerians, but only work to a *shatai.* Clear, focused, skilled work.

Tansen spun to kill one of his opponents—and missed. His left blade tangled with a *yahr* while his right blocked the jab of a *shir.* He flipped the glittering water-born blade out of the assassin's hand and completed the arc of his move by slashing the man's face. His vision swam briefly from the effort, but luckily the assassin fell back, clutching his bloody face in pain. Tansen heard the labored rasp of his own breath, felt sluggishness creeping into his limbs, and knew how little time he had left to finish this.

A *yahr* swung at his head. He dropped to one knee and spun quickly, arms whirling. One assassin screamed horribly as his belly split open and his guts spilled out. Another leaped forward—and collapsed when his leg refused to support his weight. He looked down and saw blood spurting from the huge gash in his thigh. His confused gaze flashed back to Tansen a moment before the *shatai* slit his throat.

Tansen heard a footstep behind him and knew the assassin with the slashed face was making another attack. Still on one knee, Tansen blocked the overhead blow from behind with his left blade and simultaneously flipped his right-hand sword into a reverse grip and thrust behind him, sinking it deep into the assassin's vitals.

The assassin collapsed on top of him. The fall wrenched the sword out of Tansen's hand before he could withdraw the thrust. The man's *shir* touched his cheek, burning him with its icy fury. Tan tumbled to the ground under the assault of the assassin's full body weight. They rolled sideways, locked together, the assassin behind Tansen, and grappled on the rocky blood-soaked soil.

My swords . . .

Fighting to stay conscious, Tansen realized he had let go of *both* swords now.

Never let go of—

His mind went blank with hot white pain when the assassin's murderous struggles drove his burning *shir* wound against a rock poking out of the ground. His vision swam with cold fire, with the black burning agony of sharp stone digging into the open wound.

Come on, he's the last one, finish him and you can live, damn it.

Grinding his teeth together, Tansen groped behind him for the sword sticking out of the assassin's torso. He found it—and lost his grip as his hand slipped on the bloody hilt. He felt the *shir* at his throat—*Sweet Dar, he hasn't dropped it?*—and forgot about his sword hilt as he grabbed at the dagger a moment before it killed him. He grunted in pain as the wavy blade bit into his palm. Nothing hurt like a *shir,* not even the branding iron which his *kaj* had used on his chest to mark him as a *shatai.*

Ice and death, all of Kiloran's sharp-edged power, burned into his flesh and ignited his blood as he wrestled for the *shir,* so close to his throat that it stung the flesh there. The blade bit deeper into his palm, the blood making its water-smooth surface too slick to grasp firmly.

Think, think . . . use your head.

He rocked back and rolled harder onto his wound, fighting the blackout threatened by his pain-swamped senses. He shifted just enough to grope wildly with his other hand and found the hilt of his sword again. Just barely able to reach it . . . The assassin screamed as Tansen's groping hand finally bumped hard into the sword buried in his torso.

This is it—move!

Tansen knocked the *shir* away from his throat, got a better grip on his sword hilt, and yanked it up with the last of his strength. When he felt the hot flow of his enemy's vitals, the death-sag of the body clinging to him, he knew he had won.

He wasn't so sure he would live, though.

Six dead.

Was that all of them? Would more come now, a second wave? He hoped not. He wasn't sure he could even stand up, never mind fight a few more assassins. Darfire, hadn't Josarian told him only two days ago to get his strength back before going into combat again?

Josarian . . .

No, he couldn't think about Josarian. Not now.

Get up. You have work to do.

All they had dreamed together, all they had fought for side by side, Sileria united and free . . .

Six dead.

It had come to this. As it always did. Silerians fighting each other to the death, killing each other in murderous feuds over past insults, over the countless betrayals and injuries they committed against each other only because they couldn't seem to help themselves. Only because it had always been this way here. Only because they had always hated each other even more than they hated any of their conquerors.

He himself had come here straight from Elelar's bedchamber, where he had gone to kill her in vengeance for her betrayal of Josarian. Wouldn't Mirabar hate him forever now, only because he hadn't been able to do it, after all, and she would see that as betrayal, too? Hadn't he been driven there by the horror of Kiloran's vengeance against Josarian—Josarian who had killed the waterlord's only son in vengeance over Kiloran's betrayal of him? And Kiloran had always wanted Tansen dead, Tansen most of all, in vengeance for what he had done to Armian.

Must it always be this way here?

The wound in his side hurt so much that every breath was agony. His bleeding hand hurt like all the Fires of Dar. His palms were scarred, like those of all *shallaheen,* from slicing them open for bloodpacts and blood-vows; but no one was ever crazy enough to do that with a *shir.* He could hardly move the wounded hand, it was so painful.

Get up.

He couldn't lie here all day, just waiting for another assassin to come along and find him. And he'd never make it to Dalishar's caves now, not in this condition.

Sanctuary.

He must find a Sanctuary of the Sisterhood. He would be safe there. No Silerian ever violated Sanctuary; not feuding clans, not vengeful *toreni,* not even the Society.

There was a Sanctuary east of here, down another of Mount Dalishar's treacherous paths. It was inhabited by Sister Velikar, who was old, ugly, and notoriously mean, but a gifted healer.

I'll never make it.

He had to make it.

Focus on the task at hand—which, in this case, would be not dying in a pool of assassin's blood.

He lifted his head . . . and was promptly and humiliatingly sick.

Some legendary warrior.

He took steady, controlled, agonizing breaths, fighting to stay conscious. When he thought there was a reasonable chance that he wouldn't pass out, he slowly pushed the ground away and rose to one hand and both knees. Body trembling, head spinning, wounds throbbing, he stayed there awhile, concentrating on the heroic tasks of not fainting and not vomiting again.

My swords.

He looked around, found one lying close at hand. The motto of his *kaj*, carved into the blade in Kintish hieroglyphs—*Draw it with honor, sheathe it with courage*—was now obscured by filth. For the first time in his entire career as a *shatai,* Tansen didn't flip the blood off before resheathing it, didn't wipe it or clean it. Just slid the dusty, blood-encrusted blade into its sheath.

He knew damn well where the other sword was, the one with his own motto carved into its blade. *From one thing, another is born*—as the *shatai* was born of the orphaned *shallah* boy, so long ago.

He gripped the sword's hilt, now sticky with blood rather than slick with it, braced his knee against the assassin's corpse, and pulled. He thought he'd vomit again, or at least that his skull would split wide open. He tried to breathe without actually letting his wounded side move, but that only made him dizzier.

There was enough of the assassin still clinging to this blade that Tansen made the monumental effort of wiping it—on the leggings of another nearby corpse—before sheathing it in the soft leather harness which fit him like a second skin.

Then, somehow, he was on his feet, leaning over, one hand resting on his knee while he studied the bleeding palm of the other hand. He slowly closed the coldly burning hand into a fist. He should wrap it, try to stop the bleeding, but he lacked the energy.

He was filthy. And thirsty. *Water*. He should find water.

Dar have mercy, let it be safe water.

Kiloran's secret control of the Zilar River had shocked them all, and had enabled the old waterlord to ambush and kill Josarian. If Kiloran controlled any water supplies this close to the Dalishar caves, this deep in Josarian's territory, then they were in desperate trouble. Tansen could fight as many assassins as Kiloran could send, but no one could do without water. That was, of course, what made the waterlords so powerful.

Water. I need water.

Yes, he would find water . . . *Damn it, where is there water around here?* He couldn't remember. Had he ever needed to know before?

He took a good look around . . . and finally saw the extent of the carnage. Six brutally slain men lay in a sea of blood. Some of their eyes were open. One's head was barely attached to his body. Another's guts had spilled all around him.

Tansen didn't even have the energy to roll them into the brush or make them look more decent. He pitied whoever came upon this scene, but he had reached the end of his strength. There was nothing he could do about the sight of this bloodbath now.

Focus.

He would find water, then he would head towards Sanctuary. Once there, he would try to get a message to Mirabar.

Awaiting news of Elelar's death.

Yes, that was what Mirabar would want to know, even more than she'd want to know where in the Fires Tansen was.

Don't come back until it is done, she had said.

He had seen the look in her eyes when they had gone their separate ways after Josarian's death, when he had sent her to safety at Dalishar and had set out for Chandar to kill Elelar in the night. He had heard the steel in her voice.

Don't come back to me unless you can show me Elelar's blood on your sword.

She'd never forgive him for not doing it. And he'd have to be a much braver man not to dread a woman's wrath. He'd rather walk all the way to Lake Kandahar now, to face Kiloran in his underwater palace, than ascend the rest of Mount Dalishar and tell Mirabar, as he must, that he—

A terrible fear suddenly seized him, his dazed mind finally realizing what this ambush meant. If Kiloran had set a trap for him on the slopes of Dalishar, then he might have done the same for Mirabar. Perhaps with these very men.

Dar have mercy, could she already be dead? Did she make it to the sacred caves, or was she lying in a pool of her own blood somewhere farther up the mountain?

She was far from helpless even when alone, and he knew that Najdan had been with her—Najdan, the assassin who had betrayed Kiloran to protect Mirabar and save the Firebringer. So even if there was an attack, Mirabar might well have survived it.

But he had to be sure. He couldn't go to Sanctuary now, not until he was sure she was alive. She might hate him for all eternity for letting Elelar live, but he . . .

I need to know she's safe. I need to know that much.

He staggered forward, gritting his teeth, refusing to think about the punishing hike ahead, the great distance he would have to go in this condition—*if I don't find her body only a hundred paces ahead of me*—much of it in the dark.

He had taken perhaps a dozen steps when he fell to his knees.

He tried to get up. Fell down. Tried again. Collapsed facedown on the hard, dusty ground.

Mira . . .

He pressed a hand to his aching wound. The hand came away drenched in blood.

That's not good.

He put his hand back over the wound and pressed hard. The pain made his vision go black, but pressure was the only way he could think of to slow the blood flow.

Josarian, I will join you . . .

No, he wouldn't, after all. Even if he, so long a skeptic, went to the Otherworld, Josarian would not. A lifelong believer, Josarian had died in the dripping crystalline jaws of the White Dragon, from which the only escape was oblivion when Kiloran finally died. Josarian, who had never feared death because he believed it would unite him in the Otherworld with his beloved Calidar, the wife who had died in childbirth . . . Josarian was forever gone. He had believed in sacrifice, had served Dar to the exclusion of all else . . .

And You betrayed him, Dar. You let him die. Damn You forever.

Sacrilege seemed an irrelevant sin now.

I am prepared to die today . . .

He felt dust inside his mouth. He hadn't even been aware of speaking aloud. He should probably say his prayers—and his curses—silently, given that he was dying facedown in the dirt.

A warrior's death. Definitely less glorious than most people imagine.

What did the Moorlanders say? May you die on a day which is good for it. Moorlanders also said things like: May your death be a good one. And: I will give you a good death.

Not exactly a cheerful race.

Barbarians by any standards. But he had liked living among them briefly, even so. Their bloodlust made them like Silerians, in a way, and he had been homesick.

Focus . . .

All those years in exile . . . nine years, and not a day had passed without him longing for Sileria, for her harsh and merciless mountains, her lush and fertile lowlands, the scents of rosemary and wild fennel which filled the air after the long rains, the blossoming of the almond trees, the ripening of the lemon trees, the brassy Silerian sunshine glinting off the red-tiled roofs of crumbling Kintish temples and shrines, the towering cliffs overlooking sun-drenched beaches . . .

I am prepared . . .

Of course, he'd mostly visited the beaches on dark-moon nights, on those long-ago smuggling expeditions with his grandfather. . . . Until the night his grandfather was too old to come and had stayed behind in Gamalan . . . The night Tansen's life changed forever, when he found a great warrior lying close to death on the beach of a rocky cove . . .

Armian . . .

He felt his life seeping away. If the next person to find him was an enemy, he would certainly die.

Armian . . .

He'd probably die anyway. He wouldn't reach help if he couldn't walk, and he couldn't walk if he couldn't even get up. He didn't know if his eyes were closed or if his vision had simply gone black.

Now he saw nothing.

Nothing but memories. Nothing but the past.

Father . . . I am coming.

He should get up, should try once more.

I am coming at last.

4

ENTER NOT PRAYERLESS INTO THE DOMAIN OF DAR,
FOR SHE FORGIVES NO SLIGHT.
—Silerian Proverb

Eastern Sileria,
The Year of Late Rains

TANSEN MAR DUSTAN shah Gamalani—Tansen son of Dustan, clan of Gamalan—was fifteen years old the night his life changed forever.

He had ventured forth from his native mountain village and come down to the sea tonight, to a hidden rocky cove, to await Aljuna, the half-Kintish, half-Moorlander pirate with whom he and his grandfather regularly engaged in a modestly profitable smuggling trade.

It was a dark-moon night, as it always was for their smuggling runs; both moons, Ejara and Abayara, had turned their faces from Sirkara for a few nights. This was their way, Tan's grandfather said, of granting their blessing to smugglers.

In better times, his grandfather also said, the last of the Gamalani (there were very few left, thanks to a decades-long bloodfeud with the Sirdari clan) wouldn't stoop to dealing with a pirate. But better times were long ago and far away. The Valdani were draining Sileria with the demands wrought by their endless wars of conquest and by the ever-growing population of Valdania, the empire ruled from the great city of Valda. Everything good was either scarce in Sileria or forbidden to Silerians by Valdani law. So anyone in Sileria with a little money—*toreni,* merchants, waterlords, assassins, and even some Valdani—appreciated the goods discreetly made available by Sileria's hard-working smugglers. Even people without money (the *shallaheen,* namely, who accounted for more people and less money than any other group in Sileria) could always use the necessities, and even the occasional little luxuries, which had become so scarce during two centuries of Valdani rule in Sileria.

After sharing the profits of their smuggling trade with the Society, as was customary in exchange for protection (or at least for benevolent disinterest), Tansen and his grandfather usually had enough left over to keep the family fed and clothed. Their womenfolk—Tansen's mother and sister— relied entirely upon the two of them. Before Tansen had spoken his first word or learned to lie (which, among the *shallaheen,* was at roughly the same time), his father had been killed by Outlookers, the gray-clad occupation army of the Valdani; so the Gamalani had lit his funeral pyre and scattered his ashes long ago.

More than once since then, Tansen's mother had ventured higher into the mountains on the anniversary of his father's death, to ask the Guardians to Call him forth from the Otherworld. She seldom found the Guardians on these expeditions, though. They had once been the most honored sect in the nation, advisors to the Yahrdan himself, the traditional ruler of Sileria; but now they all lived in hiding and on the run, hunted not only by the Valdani, who had outlawed them, but also by their ancient blood enemies, the Honored Society. And even when Tansen's mother did find Guardians high up in the mountains, they had never been able to Call his father. If the Otherworld was anything more than a pretty tale, it seemed that his father had failed to reach it.

Tansen's mother did claim, however, to have once seen his dead brother in the flames of a sacred Guardian fire. Tansen himself had seen nothing during that Calling, at which he had been present, and so he remained skeptical. He scarcely remembered his brother, either. When Tansen was still very young, his brother had gone off, like so many men these days, to join the mad *zanareen,* those wild-eyed religious fanatics who lived atop the snowy peak of Mount Darshon and awaited the coming of the Firebringer. One day, suffering from the common delusion of a *zanar* that he himself was Dar's chosen one, he had flung himself into the fiery volcano—and died, as they all did.

As Tansen approached manhood, times got even harder. And so the Gamalani had entered the smuggling trade and offered the pirate Aljuna a bloodpact to ensure trust and loyalty in their mutual business. Aljuna had agreed to it without having any idea what a *shallah* bloodpact entailed; Tansen thought the pirate would faint when they made the diagonal cut across his palm to mingle their blood with his.

Foreigners, Tansen's grandfather said, were thin-skinned, weak-stomached, and pale-blooded.

His grandfather was not here tonight, though, as Tansen awaited the weak-stomached pirate with whom they did business. The rainy season had long since passed and the hot dry season was approaching, but his grand-father's knees now pained him terribly even so. So Tansen had insisted he could come alone. Was he not a man—or nearly so? His mother had added her exhortations to his own, and the old man had finally agreed to remain behind.

Now, as he approached the shore, Tansen heard someone else moving through the dark night. He didn't doubt for a moment that it must be Out-lookers. Who else would be so clumsy, so loud? He watched two of them, clad their in anonymous gray tunics, pass by without ever looking into the shadows where he crouched. He could have stolen the purse of the nearest one, they were so close, but he was no thief. Besides, he knew the penalty for stealing from a Valdan, and he had no wish to wind up in the mines of Alizar.

Not that he would be caught. His grandfather said that only a deaf one-eyed half-wit would let himself be caught by Outlookers. (Tansen always hoped this wasn't a description of his father, who *had* been caught and killed by Outlookers.)

Tansen paused behind a rock as more Outlookers passed him in the night. He could hear still more of them overhead, high up on the cliffs, call-ing to someone else farther down the coast. The beach was practically swarming with them tonight!

This could make things difficult, Tansen realized. Not that he had any intention of giving up and going home. The stubborn streak, which had kept his clan locked in a bloodfeud with the Sirdari long after anyone left alive even knew why it had started, now spurred him on to outwit the Out-lookers patrolling the coast. His family needed the income too much for him to scurry away like a coward just because the Valdani evidently had decided to start cracking down on smugglers.

He looked over his shoulder, up past the dark cliffs, up to where Mount Darshon rose to loom over Sileria. It was the home of Dar, the fiery goddess whose sighs had the power to sweep Gamalan clear off its own mountain perch. Even on a moonless night like this, Tan could see the snow atop

Darshon reflecting the starlight. On a twin-moon night, it always gleamed so brightly that it almost hurt the eye to look upon it.

Enter not prayerless into the domain of Dar, his grandfather always said. And so Tansen prayed now, because, as his grandfather also said, *If Dar is on our side, then who in the Fires could possibly be on theirs?* With Dar at his back, Tansen crept through the shadows and braved the wrath of the Out-lookers, and the all-powerful empire which stood behind them, to collect his shipment of contraband from the pirate Aljuna.

Unfortunately, all his daring proved to be pointless. He waited for hours at the usual place, twice slipping into the shadows as more Outlookers passed by, but Aljuna never came. Tansen strained his eyes, fruitlessly peer-ing out at the black infinity of the sea, but there was never any sign of the pirate's oarboat. At one point he saw a light out there, glowing erratically in the distance for a while, but then it disappeared without ever coming any closer. Just some ship, he supposed, sliding over the curve of the dark hori-zon as it made its way to some port in the Kintish Kingdoms.

Although he was annoyed, Tansen liked Aljuna, so he hoped the pirate wasn't dead or in chains. Aljuna reputedly led a dangerous life even apart from risking the wrath of Outlooker patrols; it was whispered that he had business with the Society itself. If that was the case, Tansen's grandfather said, then the less they knew—or even thought—about it, the better. But Tansen did think about it. Who did not think about the Society, after all?

He had not yet told anyone of his own ambitions to become an assassin, not even his grandfather. He knew his family would worry, might even object, considering what a dangerous life it was. But he was strong, quick, a good fighter compared to others his age. What else was there for him in Sileria, if not the Society and the life of an assassin?

His clan's bloodfeud with the Sirdari was finally over. The Sirdari had even given a bride to Gamalan in honor of the truce. So Tansen wouldn't be required to slice open his palm and pledge vengeance against that clan. Instead, he could choose his own destiny. He could go to a waterlord and offer his loyalty, his service, his life. Perhaps he would gain entry into the Society by fulfilling a bloodvow, by killing the enemy of a waterlord. Not only would it put his borning talents to better use than smuggling—or, he thought with disdain, than tending sheep—but it would also enable him to protect and care for his family.

Tansen yawned sleepily, then realized with disgust that the night was nearly gone. Sitting here dreaming about being inducted into the Honored Society wasn't accomplishing anything. And if he got so tired he fell asleep on the beach, even the Outlookers were bound to notice him once the sun rose. He got up and quietly started heading back towards the hidden trail he'd used to descend the cliffs hours ago.

Tansen froze when he heard one rock strike another softly in the dark, as if displaced by a foot moving over the uneven ground. He had kept to the shadows and felt sure he had made no sound to betray his presence—but not sure enough to bet his life on it. When more stones shifted, his hand moved to his *yahr,* preparing to use it if necessary. He had never killed a man and didn't want the first time to be tonight. There would, of course, be a first time—for a *shallah,* there inevitably was—but he didn't especially want it to be now, alone in the dark, on a failed smuggling run, with Outlookers crawling all over the beach.

Please, Dar, he prayed devoutly, *let that be another smuggler I hear.*

Being caught by an Outlooker would be too humiliating. And killing one . . . Well, that would cause a lot more trouble than it was worth. The Valdani rarely interfered with Silerians killing each other, but they were so ruthless in punishing even the slightest offense against a Valdan that no one dared actually murder one. Tansen didn't think anyone had killed an Outlooker since the days of Harlon the waterlord some thirty years ago.

He considered his options for escape, in case that was an Outlooker stalking him in the dark rather than another smuggler trying, as he was, to go unnoticed.

Now several rocks slid against each other at once.

If that's a smuggler, he's a very noisy one, Tansen thought critically.

He heard a stumble, a fall—and a stifled sound of pain.

Not an Outlooker. Surely an Outlooker would call for help?

This was someone who, like Tansen, wanted to keep his presence on the coast tonight a secret; someone who didn't want the Outlookers to catch him.

Another smuggler, then? Tansen thought it would be better not to get involved, better to escape quietly before more Outlookers happened along. But what if it was an assassin? Someone from the Society, who would remember the young *shallah* who had helped him tonight, and who would perhaps even bring Tansen to the attention of a waterlord?

Suddenly, it seemed worth the risk. Tansen decided to approach the unseen figure and, if it wasn't an Outlooker, offer assistance.

He crept closer to where the stranger had fallen. Now he could hear harsh breathing. Someone in pain, trying to make no sound. Moving silently, Tansen came closer still—and slipped on a wet stone. He recovered quickly, believed he made no sound . . . but the harsh breathing stopped that instant. Tansen peered into the syrupy darkness but could still see nothing, for the stranger had chosen to hide in the murkiest crevices of the rocks even in the moonless night. Now they listened to each other's deadly silence, each awaiting a sign from the other: friend or enemy?

Since Tansen was the one creeping up on a wounded person, he decided to speak first. "Who are you?" he asked in *shallah* dialect, giving away his location.

He heard a slight whisper of movement and guessed the stranger was rolling to face him.

"Who are *you?*" came the reply, issued in common Silerian. A grown man's voice, deep and probably powerful under normal circumstances, but laced with pain now and kept soft lest they be overheard.

Many *shallaheen* didn't speak common Silerian, but Tansen did. He and his grandfather had been coming down to the coast for several years, after all, and Silerian wasn't all that different from *shallah*—just enough to be confusing until you got used to it. Tansen hesitated, still unsure. Very few Outlookers spoke any native Silerian dialects, but those that did invariably spoke only common Silerian.

Friend or enemy?

"I am a *shallah*," Tansen said in Silerian. He figured it was a safely vague answer.

After a pause, the man said, "So am I, come to think of it."

Tansen switched to the mountain dialect again. "Then why don't you speak *shallah*?"

"I do, but not very . . . well." This time the reply was in *shallah*, though the stranger had hesitated over a word.

"Why not?"

There was a longer pause. Finally he answered, "I was born in the mountains, as was my father. But I was not raised there, I don't remember him, and my mother spoke only common Silerian with me. You are . . ." The man gave up and switched to Silerian again. "You are the first *shallah* I've spoken to in years."

"That's strange," Tansen said rudely. Strange for someone born to a *shallah* clan, certainly. Blood ties were everything among the *shallaheen*. A man was no one without his clan.

"Yes, I suppose it does seem strange." When Tansen didn't reply, the man added, "The Outlookers are after me."

"Why?"

"It's not for smuggling." The voice sounded dry, despite the pain. The stranger obviously knew why a lone *shallah* would be creeping around the coast in the middle of the night.

Tansen didn't bother to ask again why the Outlookers were hunting for him. Any reason—or no reason at all—could suffice. Tansen was starting to suspect this was just some stupid *toren* who'd gotten himself into trouble, because, after all, what assassin didn't know any *shallaheen*? However, a *toren* was bound to have wealth or influence of some kind. Anyhow, it would be bad manners to leave him dying here now that they had spoken.

So Tansen said politely, "I will help you."

"Good." The voice was even dryer as it said, "Because I didn't come all this way to die on the beach."

Tansen knelt down, close enough now to discover the stranger was soaking wet. "What's happened to you?"

"I was on a smuggling ship—"

"Whose ship?" Tansen interrupted, already dreading the answer.

"Ah. You were waiting for Aljuna?"

"What's happened to him?"

"You're the smugglers he had to deliver some cargo to?"

"Yes."

"Weren't there supposed to be two of you?"

"The other one couldn't come."

"I'm sorry," the stranger said, his breath still harsh and labored. "Aljuna's dead by now. I suppose everyone aboard died, unless someone else jumped overboard, too, and made it this far."

"Why would they be d—"

"The Valdani burned Aljuna's ship."

"They *burned* it?" That must have been the light he'd seen hovering on the dark horizon a while ago. "They burned a smuggling ship? Why didn't they just arrest Aljuna's crew and confisca—"

"They weren't after his cargo."

"What were they after?" Tansen asked, bewildered. *Poor Aljuna.*

The man gasped as a new wave of pain assaulted him. "We've got to get off this beach."

"The Outlookers. Of course. Will they be searching for survivors?"

"They'll be searching for *me.*"

"I have two donkeys hidden in a cave in the cliffs. The Outlookers won't find us there."

"How far?"

"Not far, but the way is very steep. It'll be a hard trek for you, if you're badly hurt." When there was no answer, he prodded, "How badly are you hurt?"

"I'm not sure."

"How'd you get hurt? When they attacked the ship?"

"No. After I jumped overboard. A dragonfish."

"Fires of Dar," Tansen whispered.

Like most *shallaheen,* he was secretly afraid of the sea and completely terrified of dragonfish. The sea-born folk might be strange, ignorant, and smelly, but no one could deny their courage. They risked death from the dragonfish every day of their lives, and once a year they openly confronted dragonfish in deadly combat during *Bharata Ma-al.* Tansen was thankful they didn't hold the *bharata* during the dark-moon, since the shore was awash with purple dragonfish blood throughout the Time of Slaughter, and he wouldn't relish sloshing around in it while he and Aljuna . . . *Dead,* he realized with sorrow. The colorful pirate was dead.

He asked the stranger, "Where did the dragonfish get you?"

"I'm not sure. I got banged against some rocks, too, and right now, I can't tell what parts of me have been mauled by the dragonfish and what parts have been smashed against the rocks."

"May I . . ." Tansen put his hand on the stranger. His back was soaking wet. It was too dark to tell if it was water or blood. And he was cold, terribly cold.

This isn't good.

"I don't think anything's broken," the man said. "I made it this far, after all."

Not just through the water and onto the beach, Tansen realized, but away from the exposed shoreline and into the rocky crevices below the cliffs. It must have taken tremendous will.

"But if I leave a trail of blood," the stranger added wearily, "the Outlookers will see it as soon as the sun rises."

If this was indeed a *toren,* then he was tough, Tansen thought, as tough as any assassin.

"I must find the wounds," Tan said decisively, "and bind them. But since I won't be able to see if we're leaving a trail of blood . . ." He took a breath and broke the news. "I'm sorry, we'll have to leave a false trail. That will mean a longer journey to reach the cave."

"But it's a good idea." The man tried to move, then gasped in pain. "It got my leg. *Now* I feel it."

Tansen felt for the stranger's leg. He heard the sharp intake of breath when his fingers found the wound. He stripped off his worn tunic, used his teeth to tear it, and bound the man's wounded leg. The wound he found on the stranger's shoulder was worse and took longer to bind. By then, his hands were coated with blood, and he realized the stranger might die before they reached the safety of the cave.

Outlookers passed their hiding place in the shadows once. Tansen and the stranger froze, scarcely daring to breathe.

If they catch me now, with him . . . Tansen decided not to finish the thought. Instead, he strained his ears to hear what they were saying.

Unlike many *shallaheen,* he understood Valdan, the official language of Sileria for two hundred years. His grandfather had insisted he learn it, saying that a shrewd man understood his enemies, and so Tansen had dutifully spent a year of his childhood at the Valdani school in the largest town of his native district. However, he couldn't make out the Outlookers' hushed words now. He heard the urgency in their voices, though. After they passed by, he asked the stranger again, "Who are you, *roshah?*"

"*Roshah* . . . That means . . . outsider in *shallah,* doesn't it?"

"Outsider, stranger, foreigner. All of these things." Tansen shrugged, then realized the *roshah* couldn't see the gesture in the dark. "I didn't mean it as an insult," he assured the man. It often *was* meant as an insult, since few things were worse to a *shallah* than being an outsider, unknown and distrusted. "But without knowing your name . . ." He paused and waited, then finally repeated, "Who are you?"

"Help me up," was the only reply.

He was a big man, and heavy with muscle. Whoever he was, Tan realized, he was in the prime of life and honed for combat and endurance. When Tansen slung the stranger's arm over his shoulder and supported his sagging weight as best he could, the man froze for a moment.

"By all the gods above and below," he said, his voice sharp with surprise as he uttered the strange phrase. "You're just a boy. I thought from your voice—"

"I am man enough," Tansen said flatly.

"Yes." There was both humor and apology in the man's voice as he added, "Yes, I've already noticed that."

"And Dar will shield us."

"Really? Why will She do that?"

Tansen heard the amusement and wondered at it. "Because they are Valdani," he said simply, "and we are *shallaheen*."

"She hasn't done such a good job of shielding you, so far."

"Me?"

"All of you. Everyone sweeps through Sileria: Moorlanders, Kints, Valdani. And Dar does nothing—"

"Shh . . ." Tansen pretended to hear more Outlookers coming, but really he was just trying to save the *roshah* from sacrilege. He didn't think it was wise to speak disrespectfully of Dar, especially not tonight when they so needed Her favor.

They proceeded in silence, moving carefully. The *roshah* tried not to be a burden, tried to carry his own weight, but he was growing steadily weaker. Tansen was strong and used to long treks over rough terrain, but he was drained by bearing more and more of his companion's weight as dawn chased them along the rocky cliffs and steep smuggling trails.

The sun was rising by the time they reached the cave, which was rich with the smell of Tansen's bored donkeys. Tansen left the man in the cave, barely pausing long enough to hand him the waterskin before he left to double back alone and cover their trail as best he could. Only when he was satisfied that no one could follow them did he return to the cave.

The *roshah* was lying where Tansen had left him, deep inside the cave, in a second chamber whose entrance was hard to find unless you knew it was there. Tansen spoke to him, received no reply, and realized he must be asleep or unconscious. So he fed and watered his two donkeys, ate and drank a little himself, and then took his lantern to the stranger's side to better examine his wounds in the dark cave.

It was his first real opportunity to study the man. His clothes were foreign, strange styles made of good materials. *Very* nice boots, Tansen noted with envy. Yet the stranger looked Silerian, albeit a little big for a Silerian—olive-skinned, dark-haired, strong-boned. He even wore a *jashar* around his waist, though it was now grubby with sand and red with his own blood.

At least it will tell me who he is.

Like most of his people, Tansen could neither read nor write. But the *shallaheen* communicated messages and information with *jashareen*—elaborately knotted and woven ropes, strands, and cords dotted with colored beads. The *jashar* a man wore around his waist—like the one a woman wore as a headdress on special occasions—identified him and his history. More elaborate ones covered doorways and walls, identifying merchants and craftsmen, codifying religious creeds, commemorating special events, and even relating *shallah* history and legends.

As Tansen started to untie the *jashar* from the unconscious man's waist so he could get a better look at it, he suddenly realized that it wasn't red from blood—it was just *red*, made that way to begin with.

Darfire, he is an assassin!

No one who wasn't would dare to wear the traditional red *jashar* of the Honored Society.

Thank You, Dar, thank You for placing him in my path.

Surely this was a sign that Tansen's destiny was at hand, that the time had come for his ambitions to bear fruit.

He tugged more insistently at the tangled fastening of the *jashar*, then pulled it away from the stranger's body and held it closer to the lantern light to study it.

Yes, he was right, some of the beads were yellow—the yellow beads which only an assassin or his family members wore on a *jashar*. He fingered the woven strands and knots, looking for the man's name, his clan, the identity of the waterlord he served . . .

He stopped breathing when he saw it. His blood ran hot and cold at once. Not all the beads were yellow, were they? He grabbed the waterskin and spilled water over the beads, wasting the precious substance in his haste. He washed away the dried blood and wiped the beads on his leggings, then held them up to the light again. Yes, now he was sure of it: some of the beads were clear, made of water crystallized by sorcery.

Clear beads on a red *jashar*.

A waterlord?

No, not quite a waterlord. Son of a waterlord, heir to one, according to the way the knots were tied around the beads.

And the name . . .

Armian . . .

Armian mar Harlon shah Idalari.

Armian, son of Harlon, clan of Idalar.

The Idalari, possibly the most powerful clan in the Society. Harlon, the great waterlord who had fought the Valdani for years, until they finally murdered him, throwing the Society into chaos for a time.

And Armian, the baby hidden from the Valdani who hunted him after Harlon's death, determined to kill him, too. Everyone knew the story. The infant had been spirited out of Sileria so that he might live, so that he would fulfill his destiny to return one day and free Sileria from the Valdani. *Armian . . .* whom everyone said was the awaited one, the chosen one . . .

The Firebringer.

Tansen heard the blood roaring in his ears. His hands shook as he fingered the *jashar* of Armian, the heroic warrior about whom he had heard his whole life. *The Firebringer.* He felt dizzy. He must be dreaming. He looked again at the strong face of the unconscious man he had brought to this cave.

That's the Firebringer lying there.

He had saved the life of the Firebringer! Dar had smiled upon him, had shown him Her favor, and had made his life count for something. The Firebringer had stumbled while coming home to fulfill his destiny, and a *shallah* boy from Gamalan had caught him before he fell from grace.

Tansen couldn't wait to tell his grandfather.

And we will be free. He's here, alive, and he will . . .

Actually . . . now that he took a hard look, Tansen realized that Armian didn't look like he was going to do much besides die in this cave.

Panic flooded him. He couldn't let the Firebringer die! Especially not after hauling him all this way like a sack of wet grain, he thought with a touch of annoyance.

A Sister. I've got to find a Sister.

He jumped to his feet, recalling that there was a Sanctuary not far from here. He could get there and be back with a Sister before midday. He started to sort through the spare supplies he and his grandfather kept stored here, looking for another tunic.

No wonder the Outlookers were searching for him. No wonder there were so many of them on the coast!

He found the spare tunic and pulled it over his head, then retied his *jashar*—plain hemp dotted with the rough clay beads of a *shallah*—around his waist.

No wonder the Valdani burned Aljuna's ship. He froze briefly as he realized that the rumors had been true. Aljuna did indeed have business with the Society. The most serious and secret business of all: *Bringing Armian out of hiding and back to Sileria to free us all.*

He returned to the assassin's side and tried to rouse him. "*Siran,*" he said, using the traditional term of respect. No response. "*Siran . . .*" Nothing. "Armian?" A flicker of the eyelids this time.

Tansen gritted his teeth and shook him. "Armian!"

Suddenly Tansen was lying on his back, dizzy from the hard thud his head made against the stone floor of the cave. He didn't gasp though. He couldn't. A big hand was wrapped around his throat, cutting off all air.

After a tense and confusing moment, Armian released his hold. His face screwed up in pain as his injuries punished him for his violent reflexes.

Tansen stayed where he was, too stunned to move.

Armian rolled away. "Sorry."

"I . . . I understand. You . . . I . . ." *I frightened you,* didn't really seem the right thing to say. Indeed, Tan couldn't think of anything to say. So he just sat up and silently rubbed his throat, gulping down some air now that he had the chance.

"Where are we?" Armian asked in a strained voice.

"The cave I told you about."

"Oh. Yes. And did you tell me your name?"

"Tansen mar Dustan shah Gamalani."

"Ah. Tansen." He lay still for a few moments, obviously trying to master the pain. Then he looked hard at Tan. "Why did you call me Armian?"

Tansen crossed his fists over his chest and bowed his head. A formal greeting, a gesture of respect. "Forgive my impertinence, *siran.*"

Armian sighed. "I didn't mean that. You don't have to call me 'master.'"

"It doesn't really mean mast . . ." Well, actually, yes, it did. "We say it to show respect for someone, *siran,*" he explained. "And who deserves respect more than you?"

"I see." Armian watched him closely. "When did I tell you who I am?"

"You didn't."

"Then who did?" He looked menacing now, despite the weakness and the wounds. He looked like an assassin.

Tansen met his gaze and spoke carefully. "The *jashar.*"

Armian's expression changed. "Ah. Of course. The *jashar.* I'm not used to . . ." He sighed again, then winced. "No one in the Moorlands knows what it means. It's just decoration to them."

"You were in the Moorlands? But everyone said you had been taken to Kinto."

"Well, of course." The humor was back in his voice, tinged with exhaustion. "You didn't think my clan wanted to draw the Valdani a map, do you? They convinced everyone I was clear on the other side of the Middle Sea from where they had really sent me."

"Your clothes are Moorlander?"

"Mmmm . . . But the *jashar* . . ."

"You wore it so *we* would know who you are, but the Valdani wouldn't, not even if they found you."

"And they nearly did find me. Someone betrayed us. The Valdani attacked Aljuna's ship knowing I was supposed to be on it." He closed his eyes, looking as if keeping them open was too much of an effort. "I jumped just before they boarded. I saw them set fire to it . . ."

"Did you *see* Aljuna die?" Tansen asked, reaching for hope.

"No, but he's dead." Seeing Tansen's doubt, he explained, "They weren't taking prisoners, Tansen. But perhaps Aljuna died quickly," Armian added with a touch of kindness. "I just hope they believe a dragonfish finished me before I reached shore."

"The dragonfish. Your wounds," Tansen said suddenly. "I'm going to find a Sister to tend you. I should be back here with her by midday."

"A Sister?"

"Yes. The Sisterhood. You know."

"I've never seen one, but I've been told about them." Armian's dark eyes opened again. Tansen marveled at the strength of will he saw in them, the courage. "Can she be trusted?"

"She doesn't need to know the truth. I'll hide your *jashar* before I go."

"I mean, can she be trusted not to tell the Outlookers there's a wounded stranger lying in this cave?"

The question surprised Tansen. "Of course. The Sisters would never—"

"There's no 'of course' about it," Armian said. "I'm in this condition because I've been betrayed once already. And Silerians are famous for betrayal, aren't they—we?" He paused, then added, "Nothing ever really changes here, does it?"

"How do you know about . . . about . . ."

"About you? Sileria? *Us?*" He closed his eyes again, drifting away. "My mother, her brother, and the two assassins that came with us to the Moorlands."

"Where are they now? Didn't they want to come home with you?"

"It was a long time ago. Almost thirty years have passed. Only my uncle is left alive now, and he's too old and sick for a journey like this." He sighed. "But he and the others all made sure I would be ready."

"Ready?" Tansen held his breath waiting for the answer.

"To come back. To, uh, come home." His breath was shallow, his eyes sunken as he added, "To fight the Valdani."

"It *is* you," Tansen breathed in awe.

"Of course it's me," was the weary response.

The Firebringer.

"I'll . . . I'll get help. You'll get well. I promise."

Armian didn't reply. Perhaps he was already asleep.

Tansen hid Armian's *jashar,* put the waterskin within his reach, blew out the lantern, and left the cave.

Outside, the brassy Silerian sunshine beat down upon the gold-and-amber mountains, so lovely in their harshness, so stark in their beauty. Darshon loomed overhead, its snowcapped peak piercing thin morning clouds, wisps of steam coiling up from the heart of the volcano. A faint scent of smoke rode the breeze, perhaps from some brush fire; the season was advancing, and soon such fires would be common. But for now, wild fennel and rosemary still lushly perfumed the air while Silerians enjoyed the blessings of the island's most seductive season.

And under a sky more fiercely blue than any other, Tansen knew that his destiny had finally found him. It promised to be a glorious one.

5

ANYONE CAN HOLD THE HELM WHEN THE SEA IS CALM; BUT A SAILOR IS NEEDED FOR THE STORM.
—Proverb of the Sea-Born Folk

ZARIEN'S FEET WERE killing him.

Walking the dryland was proving to be nearly as painful as being attacked by a dragonfish, and he knew better than anyone alive just how painful *that* was.

His feet had become blistered, bloody, and swollen soon after setting out on his quest. The calloused bare soles which were used to the wooden decks of small boats didn't adjust well to the harsh and unpredictable surface of the dryland—particularly not when required to walk farther each day now than Zarien had walked in the whole previous fourteen years of his life.

His second night on land, he had stolen a pair of boots. It was humiliating to resort to stealing—the Lascari despised thieves—but he didn't know how else to get the things he needed for his overland journey to Josarian's stronghold atop Mount Dalishar. So he stole food and clothing, hoping Sharifar's blessing would protect him here. However, his first crime was a failure. The boots fit so badly he discarded them halfway through the following morning and stole a pair of shoes that afternoon. The soles of his feet benefitted, but his toes and heels suffered terribly from the unaccustomed chafing.

He could swim for hours without tiring, diving the coastal shallows, untangling nets, setting traps, gathering catch, and spearing prey. He could work from dawn till dusk, repairing boats, mending sails, hauling nets, heaving weights. But now that he was on land, he could barely get through each day without collapsing in an exhausted and discouraged heap. Sometimes he thought his heart would burst if he had to trek uphill for one more moment.

However, at least struggling up and down Sileria's treacherous mountain paths distracted him somewhat from the pain of his feet. When he edged along crumbing cliffside trails, which seemed ready to tumble into the gorges below, at least he wasn't thinking about the aching blisters on his heels. When his lungs burned like the Fires of Dar and his legs shook with fatigue as he hauled himself up yet another punishingly steep path, at least he forgot about his bleeding toes. Whereas when he walked through the fertile lowlands or lush valleys, he thought so much about how badly his feet hurt that he scarcely appreciated breathing normally and not worrying about falling to his death.

When he sat down to rest, then he mostly just thought about how hungry he was. He had managed to steal some fish in the first few days, mostly from the backs of carts on their way to market. He'd eaten it raw the first time, since he had no coals or brazier; that was when he discovered that raw fish from a drylander market tasted a *lot* different than the succulent flesh sometimes eaten raw at sea only moments after taking catch from the water. His first attempt to build a fire like landfolk, using wood, was so discouraging that he'd resorted to spying on some *shallah* shepherd to see how it was done. His next attempt nearly set a whole valley on fire, and he hoped the *toren* who had run him off his land wasn't still trying to hunt him down.

He had no interest in eating animal flesh as the landfolk did. Even cooked, it looked disgusting, and the thought of eating it raw and bloody— just the sight and smell of those butchered carcasses—turned his stomach when he passed through market towns. And he soon gave up trying to catch wildfowl—traps seemed to be sadly unreliable on land, since birds here could perch anywhere, whereas at sea their choices were very limited.

So now, nine days after emerging reborn from the sea, he was subsisting solely on stolen bread and cheese, and whatever he could scavenge in the hills, valleys, and groves through which he passed: nuts, berries, fruit, baby potatoes, wild onions. Some of it he had discovered by himself, some he had learned about by watching the landfolk.

Water, at least, was no problem. Although sweetwater had to be carefully rationed at sea, it seemed easy enough to find on land. Despite all the drylanders' whining about the ruthless power of the waterlords, Zarien had yet to go thirsty.

The farther inland he ventured, the more drylanders he encountered who had never seen the sea-born. The landfolk stared openly at his indigo tattoos, making him feel self-conscious about something which was normally a source of considerable pride to him. People eyed his *stahra* and, not realizing it was his weapon, often asked why he was carrying an oar.

Zarien had walked in the wrong direction for an entire morning on one occasion before discovering that three *shallaheen* had lied to him about the location of Mount Dalishar. What did his father . . . what did Sorin always say? *Shallaheen* learned to lie before they learned to walk. He marveled that Sorin, who had never once set foot on land, knew them so well.

They called it *lirtahar*. It was a Society creed which had spread throughout Sileria until even the island nation's sea-born folk accepted its basic tenets; the *shallaheen,* however, had taken it to extremes. *Lirtahar* was the law of silence. In principle, it meant that no one ever told anything to the conquerors of Sileria. From the Moorlander Conquest, through the Kintish invasions, to the Valdani occupation, the people of Sileria offered their foreign rulers nothing but lies, half-truths, evasions, and silence. In practice, however, a thousand years of *lirtahar* meant that Sileria's disparate and quarreling people had evolved into a secretive and suspicious culture where information was hoarded and guarded like the diamonds of Alizar, particularly among the *shallaheen.* This made it a little challenging for a harmless sea-born stranger to find Mount Dalishar, despite its being one of the most famous landmarks in all of Sileria.

No one asked why he was going to Dalishar—perhaps they assumed he would lie or refuse to answer—but everyone stared at him with open curiosity. And, as he went deeper into the mountains, curiosity seemed close kin to hostility. *Shallaheen* were suspicious of strangers—*roshah,* they called him, "outsider"—and fiercely territorial.

The war had left many of their women unguarded by male relatives, and not everyone seemed to consider Zarien too young to be a threat in this respect. Some villages had been decimated by the Valdani, attacked and burned in retaliatory raids made by the Outlookers; some of these villagers resented the sea-born for waiting so long to join Josarian's cause. Other villages Zarien passed through now seemed to be deeply divided, as was much of Sileria, due to the rift between Josarian and the Society; those who were loyal to the Society seemed to know that the sea-born were not. And in one dreary village where he stopped, an assassin claimed a bloodvow and challenged a *shallah* to fight to the death.

Zarien had seen people die, for the sea-born life was a dangerous one, but he had never seen one man kill another before. It left him feeling hollow. He had no idea what that particular bloodvow was about, but he had learned by now that vengeance was always the motive. Josarian's world was every bit as strange and violent as Zarien had feared.

He wanted his family. He wanted his clan. Above all, he missed the sea. Every waking and sleeping moment, he longed for it. The scent of the ocean, the salty spray thrown up by the waves, the gentle lapping at the hull, the easy roll of the boat, the glimmering azure waters which mirrored the fiercely blue sky, the long reflection that the moons cast on the calms at night . . .

Don't think about it. Not now.

He would go home, in time. He would find Sharifar's mate—*Please let it be Josarian; where will I even look if it's not him?*—and he would return to the sea. And although the Lascari would never accept him as one of their own again, he would at least confront his parents and find out who he really was.

Besides, if I bring home the sea king, maybe the Lascari will overlook my sojourn on land.

There had never been an exception. He knew that. To walk the dryland was to be declared dead by the Lascari, to ensure that your name was never even mentioned again. But surely there had never before been a situation like this? He was in uncharted waters now, cutting new wind in the storm-tossed world of the Firebringer.

He came upon another village now and decided to again ask the way to Dalishar. He must be close by now.

The first two *shallaheen* he spoke to claimed, with every appearance of honesty, that they didn't even know the name of this village, never mind the location of Mount Dalishar.

"I'm not a Valdan," he said impatiently, having encountered this sort of behavior too often lately.

"Neither are you one of us, *roshah*." The two men turned and walked away.

Many men were gathered around a large fountain in the village's main square. They were speaking loudly, engaged in a passionate debate about something. Zarien only caught a few words of the volatile conversation, since it was all in *shallah* and everyone seemed to be talking at once. They said something about a *torena,* then about the *torena*'s servants . . . A journey to Shaljir . . . The *torena* had left this morning at first light . . . Something about Josarian . . . Now they were talking about Kiloran.

Suddenly there was a lot of shouting. Some of the men seemed furious, ready to fight. Others were trying to reason with them, or at least get between them to prevent a fight. Someone pulled out a *yahr.* Zarien had never even seen one before coming ashore nine days ago, but he recognized it easily by now and realized how menacing that simple weapon of two short sticks really was. This one gleamed darkly in the sunshine as its owner swung it in a circle over his head, making a soft *whooshing* sound while people stepped back and watched him warily.

Someone backing away from the scene stepped on Zarien's foot; given how sore it was, Zarien yelped. The man whirled around, his long black hair swinging like a loose sail. His apology faded in mid-sentence as his gaze traveled over Zarien. He stared for a moment, then said something in *shallah* about Dalishar.

Zarien nodded and replied in common Silerian, "Yes, I'm looking for Dalishar." He wondered how the *shallah* knew. "Where am I now?"

"This is Chandar."

It sounded like a real answer. Zarien plunged in and asked, "Are we near Dalishar?"

Instead of replying, the man said something which sounded like, *Do you know about Josarian?* Or maybe it was just, *Do you know Josarian?*

"No," he replied.

The *shallah* continued staring at him. He seemed more puzzled than unfriendly. At last he said, "They say Josarian . . . They say he is . . ."

"What?"

"Why are you going to Dalishar?"

I understood that. This is getting easier.

He tried the answer he thought would work best: "It is the will of Dar."

The man frowned at him, though Zarien wasn't sure what the expression indicated, then looked briefly over his shoulder at the crowd behind him. More talking seemed to have forestalled the threatened violence, but passions were still running high.

Finally the *shallah* pointed northwest.

Zarien gazed up at the mountain which loomed over this village. It looked steep and rocky, but he half-thought he could live through the climb. "That's Dalishar?"

"No, Dalishar is above it. Do you see?"

"Oh." Now he saw. Dalishar wasn't as high as Darshon, but it towered over the mountains around it—and over the nearer mountain—with imposing height and ferocity.

He wanted to curse Dar, as She deserved, but that seemed unwise under the circumstances, so he just prayed, "May the wind be at my back."

TANSEN RETURNED TO *the cave before midday, as promised, with a Sister to tend Armian. She asked no questions upon being shown the bloody, unconscious man hidden in the stone heart of the mountain. The Sisters tended everyone impartially, gave Sanctuary to all Silerians without discrimination, and so she asked Tansen nothing about the wounded man beyond what she needed to know to treat his injuries.*

If the Outlookers eventually found her and—like the barbarians they were—pressed her for answers about today, she would probably die under interrogation, as did so many people, rather than tell them anything. Lirtahar, the law of silence, ruled the mountains. To break silence, to tell the Outlookers anything, always brought terrible shame—and usually terrible vengeance, too. When a man or woman broke lirtahar and talked, revealed anything to the Valdani, he or she was shunned by everyone—village, clan, sect—and often severely punished, too. To betray the Society in any way meant certain death, of course, but ordinary people might be just as quick to kill for vengeance when lirtahar was violated, because silence protected them all from the roshaheen and must therefore never be broken. Burning down a house, killing someone's livestock, declaring a bloodvow, or commencing a bloodfeud—all of this might be done to punish someone who'd spoken instead of remaining silent.

So Tansen had no fear that the Sister would betray them to the Valdani.

IT WAS CLOSE to sundown when Zarien rounded a bend in the rocky path—and nearly tripped over an open-eyed corpse lying in a fly-swarming pool of blood.

"By the eight winds . . ."

He held his baggy sleeve to his nose as the stench of death and blood assailed his nostrils. His mouth sagged open in shock as he took in the horrifying scene.

Four . . . Six . . . No *seven* men lay dead. . . . Mangled bodies were twisted awkwardly, sprawled and broken, guts exposed, a head hacked off . . . or mostly off . . . *The blood* . . . It was thick and red and everywhere. . . . All over them, the ground, the rocks, their clothes, their weapons . . .

Zarien whirled away from the sight. He dropped his *stahra* and fell to his knees, retching violently again and again. The world faded away as nausea seized his body, his breath, his reflexes.

When he finally stopped, he rested on his hands and knees. His head felt heavy. The air was sticky and foul. Spots swam before his eyes. The partly digested meal that his stomach had just surrendered now assumed the horror of his surroundings.

I'll never eat onions again, he thought in a daze, his mind shying away from the bloodbath he was afraid to look at again.

He tried to blink away the blurriness in his vision. Something wet dropped onto his cheeks. That's when he realized his eyes were watering.

He drew in a steadying breath—and smelled it all again.

No, no, no . . .

"May the gods have mercy, may the winds guide me, may the waters be calm and my sails be strong," he prayed mindlessly, the familiar words pouring out of his mouth in a terrified rush. "May the current carry me far . . . May I . . . I . . ." His mind clouded. Flies swarmed around the dead. A river of drying blood stained the harsh rocks of the dryland.

"*Sharifar!*" he cried, alone and afraid.

Someone groaned. A low, weak, pained sound.

Zarien leapt to his feet, poised to run.

Another groan. A slight movement from a body lying facedown, just the faintest turn of the head.

They're not all dead.

His heart pounded so hard it hurt. His teeth were chattering. He clenched his jaw. His hands were shaking. Should he help or should he run?

Think. Who are they?

He forced himself to study the slain bodies. He finally noticed the wavy-edged daggers lying among them, along with the *yahr.* He knew what a *shir* was. Everyone knew, even those who'd never seen one before. Now he saw the black leggings and tunics, too. Presumably their tangled *jashareen* had originally been red, though they were so blood-soaked now that he couldn't be sure.

Assassins.

He didn't want to get involved in anything to do with assassins. Or their remains.

His breath was rasping through his clenched teeth. He brushed at his eyes and swallowed hard.

He flinched when the figure that had groaned now moved again. An arm fumbled briefly in the dirt, as if its owner were seeking purchase to rise or roll over. The body bore a leather harness and a sword sheathed at its back. That was unusual.

Zarien realized that this man's clothes weren't black. They were the rough homespun of an ordinary *shallah*. The left sleeve had escaped a complete drenching in blood. It still revealed its true pale color, albeit dirty and dusty.

Six assassins and an armed *shallah,* all dead or nearly dead after a terrible fight . . . So close to the stronghold of Kiloran's enemy . . . Hope suddenly filled Zarien's heart.

Josarian?

He leaped forward, heedless of the blood, making his way past the dead assassins. Without hesitation now, he bent over the *shallah*'s body, took his shoulders in a firm grip, and gently rolled him onto his side.

"Josari—"

"*Argh!*"

"Sorry!"

The man's lean face was screwed up in pain. His long black hair was filthy—sweat, dust, blood, mud. His eyes were squeezed shut as he muttered, "Darfire . . ." His deep voice was thin, his breath harsh. He rolled a little further onto his back and pressed a hand against his side. Zarien looked down and saw that he was bleeding from a wound beneath his ruined tunic. The rest of him looked terrible, too. Cuts, burns, bruises, blood, scars . . .

Scars . . . What in the Fires is that?

There was a huge, elaborate scar on the man's chest. Zarien could see it through the shreds of the tunic. Why did someone do that to him? And surely it wasn't a battle wound? It was too regular, too patterned. It almost looked like the marks the Kints made on their loads of cargo. . . .

The dryland seemed to tilt as Zarien realized who this was.

Tansen.

Except for Josarian, no one in Sileria was more famous than Tansen, the Firebringer's bloodbrother, the great warrior who carried two Kintish swords . . . *And a brand carved onto his chest by the gods of Kinto.* Trying to be gentle, Zarien rolled Tansen just a little further, all the way onto his back . . . until the movement revealed the evidence that confirmed the warrior's identity: He had been lying on his second sword, sheathed at his left side.

Two swords. The brand on his chest. Six attacking assassins dead around him.

Oh, yes. You're Tansen.

But he was near death now, already sailing towards that shore which had no other shore.

"I will tow you back," Zarien promised him.

At the sound of his voice, the dark eyes flickered open. Tansen looked dazed. "Wh . . . Who . . . Who—"

"I'm Zarien. I will help you."

"Where . . ." He tried to lick cracked lips. His tongue had the whitened look of someone who'd gone too long without water.

"I'll get you some water." Zarien spotted a satchel lying nearby and realized, from the Kintish symbols on it, that it must be Tansen's. "Is there a waterskin in there?"

"Where . . ."

Zarien looked around again, his mind racing. When these six assassins failed to return to wherever they came from, someone else might be sent to find out what had happened to them.

"I'll get you some water," he repeated, "but first we must find a place to hide. Can you walk?"

"Mmmm . . . Help . . . me . . ."

Tansen was only average in size, but he seemed to be made of iron as Zarien hauled him off the blood-drenched ground, all hard muscle and wiry sinew, lean but heavy with the steely strength people spoke about when they mentioned his name with such awe.

"I can't carry you," Zarien said as his throbbing feet protested the extra weight.

"Help . . . walk . . . ," Tansen mumbled as he leaned heavily on him. "You're . . . boy . . . small . . ."

"I'm not that small," Zarien snapped. Yes, landfolk were a little bigger than the sea-born, but he was hardly a runt.

He heard a snort and glanced up quickly. A slight smile touched Tansen's lips, though his face contorted in pain again. "Didn't mean to . . . offend," he said, clearly speaking common Silerian now. Zarien hadn't been sure, before.

"Where can we go?" he asked.

"Not up. Down."

"Oh. Good."

"If more assassins come . . . they'll search past here . . . above . . . not below . . . to try to catch me. . . ." But as Zarien turned slowly and started down the path, with Tansen's arm slung over his shoulder, Tansen said, "No. Not the path."

"Through the scrub?" Zarien asked without enthusiasm.

"And . . . we mustn't leave . . . a trail of blood."

"This is my only shirt," Zarien said, already resigned.

"Sorry," Tansen muttered as Zarien struggled out of the garment while trying to keep his hold on the warrior. "Get you another. Promise."

Zarien used his small stolen knife to tear up his stolen homespun tunic and fashion an adequate dressing for the wound. Tansen was silent throughout the bandaging process, his sunken eyes closed, his breathing fast and shallow. Zarien let him rest for a few moments while he went to retrieve Tansen's satchel and his own *stahra,* which was still lying where he had dropped it earlier. When he returned with the metal-tipped oar, he thought for a terrible moment that the unmoving warrior was dead, so still was he as he leaned against a boulder.

"*Siran?*" Zarien used the *shallah* term of respect which had become common throughout Silerian culture.

"Not dead yet," was the weary reply.

But soon, perhaps. I'd better ask before he dies, Zarien decided. "Where's Josarian?"

Tansen's eyes snapped open. "Why?"

"I must find him."

"Why?"

"I'll explain later."

"Then I'll answer you later."

Zarien stared at him with a touch of exasperation. "You really are a *shallah*. Not Kint or a *toren*, as some say—"

"And you're sea-born, aren't you?" Tansen still looked exhausted, but more alert now. "Those tattoos, that *stahra* . . ."

"Yes." Zarien supposed he shouldn't be surprised that Tansen knew what the weapon was called. A great warrior like him probably even knew how to use one. "I am Lascari." He hesitated, then added more honestly, "Or I used to be."

"Why are you looking for Josarian?"

Be patient. He guards Josarian's back. Of course he won't simply come out and tell you where he is.

"The sea-born need him," Zarien began.

"Everyone needs him."

"It's complicated."

"I believe you."

"I have to find him," Zarien said. "My life depends on it."

Tansen lowered his head. "You're in trouble, then."

"What do you mean?"

Tansen didn't answer for a moment. When he lifted his head again, his face looked terrible. Haunted. Grief-stricken. "Josarian is dead."

Zarien felt it like a blow. "*What?*"

"Two nights ago. At the Zilar River."

"*Dead?*"

"Dead."

"You're sure?"

"I was there."

"What happened? How could you let him die?"

Pale from blood loss, Tansen seemed to go even whiter.

Zarien faltered. "I'm sorry. I didn't . . . didn't mean—"

"Go back to the sea, boy."

"I can't."

"He's dead."

"Then there must be another—"

"There's nothing for you here."

"There must be!"

"Shhh . . ." Tansen lifted his head. He seemed to be listening for something. Zarien froze. More assassins? After a moment, Tansen shook his head. "We can't stay here and argue about it now." He winced, pressed a hand over the bandaged wound, and said, "You've helped me. That will be enough for them, if they come."

"Yes, we must hurry." Zarien dreaded the prospect of facing more assassins when Tansen couldn't even stand up by himself. "And night is coming."

"Night is always coming," the legendary warrior replied.

"SIRAN?" TANSEN SAID *softly.*

Armian awoke with a start. His gaze flashed around the cave, glowing dimly in the lantern light, until he saw Tansen. "Tan? I . . . I thought there was a woman here . . ."

"There is." Tansen gestured to the Sister who lay sleeping in a far corner of the cave. "I brought her yesterday. She will stay until she's sure you will recover."

Armian inhaled, tensing and flexing his muscles. "I will," he said with certainty. "I feel much better."

"She says you are very strong."

"You're very strong, too." Armian studied him in the flickering light for a moment. "Not many boys could do all you've done for me."

Tansen felt his face glow with pleasure at the compliment, but he shrugged it off like a man. "You have been away from the mountains too long. Here, I am not special."

Armian smiled. "Then Sileria's mountains must be a remarkable place."

"Yes, siran. The only place. No other place matters." Armian's smile emboldened Tansen to add, "It's good that you have come home, siran. We have waited so long."

"For what?"

"For you."

"Because I'm Harlon's son?"

How could he not know? "Because you're the Firebringer."

Armian grinned. "You seem like a bright lad, Tansen. You don't really believe that, do you?"

Tansen stared at him in shock. "Of course I do." An incredible thought occurred to him. "Don't you?"

"No."

"Then you . . . you aren't going to Mount Darshon—"

"No."

"—to embrace Dar?"

"Throw myself into the volcano?"

"Yes."

Armian laughed. "No! Why would I do such a crazy thing?"

"Because you're the—"

"No, I'm not." Armian shook his head, still grinning. "I know the story— and that's all it is, Tan. A story. Probably made up by some hungry peasants who'd smoked a little too much Kintish dreamweed one night, hundreds of years ago."

Tansen stared at the Firebringer, so strong, so powerful, so brave. The Firebringer . . . who evidently had no intention of proving his identity in Dar's embrace.

Armian's expression was almost kind as he continued, "Men must solve their own problems, Tansen, rather than dreaming of someone who will do it for them."

"Yes, a man like you, siran, but . . ."

"And the man you will be, too, son," Armian said.

SOMETIME AFTER SUNDOWN, they found a shallow cave where they could spend the night. Zarien explored it with shrinking horror, since he had learned by now that such places often harbored all manner of land creatures, from the disgusting to the genuinely dangerous: bats, worms, mice, rats, snakes, mountain lions . . . and, he supposed, bandits, rebels, Guardians, and assassins.

I miss the sea, he thought for the thousandth time as he limped back to Tansen on aching feet and said, "It will do."

Tansen was leaning heavily on the *stahra.* Zarien didn't really mind this undignified use of the honored weapon, since he himself had taken to using it as a staff ever since coming ashore. Besides, this was *Tansen,* so Zarien wouldn't protest about the *stahra* even if he did mind.

He led Tansen into the cave and tried to help him lower himself to the ground. The warrior's skin was hot and dry, his limbs weak and limp as he tumbled to the cave floor in a sudden collapse, nearly taking Zarien with him.

This is bad.

"I'll get water," Zarien said. There was no reply. "*Siran?*" Still no reply. Tansen was unconscious again.

Zarien found a waterskin in Tansen's satchel, as he had hoped. He left the cave and stumbled through the dark, tripping over rocks, vines, plants, and tree roots. On a bright twin-moon night like this, he'd be fine at sea. On land, though, with its constant obstacles and strange surprises, he stumbled and strayed, no more capable than a drunken *toren* letting a pleasure yacht run straight into a reef.

He tried not to dwell on the fears which threatened to consume him. Josarian was dead, and Tansen seemed barely alive. Zarien's own life hung on a fragile bargain struck with Sharifar. His search for the goddess's mate, the truth about his birth, the destiny of the sea-born . . . the weight of it all pressed down upon him in the mysterious night world of the dryland.

Water, he thought, focusing on the first task he must accomplish before he could confront the overwhelming problems which lay beyond it. He was thirsty, too, now. *I want water.*

He heard it then, trickling softly down the mountainside. *Water.* A comforting musical sound amidst all the unfamiliar ones which crowded the night on land. He approached it, tripping several more times and once nearly walking into a sapling. He smelled it now, too, the soft scent of sweetwater, so different from the salty tang of the Middle Sea. Different, too, from the loamy smell of the north-flowing Sirinakara River, the great southern waterway which splintered into a thousand swamps, brackish lagoons, and dying streams on its way to the Middle Sea.

He found the water trickling from overhead, through a crack in an overhanging ledge. Consumed by his own thirst, he stood beneath it and opened his mouth, letting it run down his parched throat. Clear, cold, sweet.

When he had drunk enough to quench the worst of his thirst, he let the water run over his head, his shoulders, his back. He washed the dried blood off his hands, then drank some more. Finally, he filled the waterskin and brought it back to the cave.

Tansen was still unconscious. He didn't respond when Zarien tried to wake him. Zarien removed Tansen's ruined tunic, tore up a sleeve, soaked part of it in water, and forced it into the unconscious warrior's mouth. His mother . . . Palomar had once done this when Morven was very sick and too weak, at first, to drink.

Zarien wondered briefly if Morven was Palomar and Sorin's real son. He hoped so. He didn't want his little brother to feel the shame and betrayal he'd felt ever since coming alive in Sharifar's embrace. For the rest of his life, Zarien would bear the tattoos identifying him as a sea-bound Lascari born to Palomar and Sorin—and it would never be true.

Immersed in the cave's darkness, he placed his hand on Tansen's throat and waited. It seemed a long time before he finally felt it move reflexively, swallowing the bit of liquid trickling from the cloth to the back of Tansen's throat.

Encouraged, Zarien poured more water onto the cloth. It soaked through into Tansen's mouth and, eventually, his throat moved again.

It took a long time to empty the waterskin this way. Zarien's back was stiff by the time he stopped bending over Tansen's prone body and, after taking the rag out of the warrior's mouth, left the cave to get more water. He wouldn't try to clean Tansen's wounds before morning, since he couldn't see them in the dark cave and didn't dare risk building a fire. Even if he managed to do it right, it could be spotted by any assassins searching for them.

He returned to the cave again. "*Siran?*" No reply. He crouched and felt for the bandage he had bound to Tansen's side. It was wet. Blood must still be flowing from the wound.

"The winds carry me," Zarien murmured in despair. Maybe the stories were wrong. It seemed this man could indeed be killed, after all, and might even be dead by morning.

He turned away, wondering what else to do for the warrior right now, when a strange rumbling sound made him pause.

"What is . . ." The ground started trembling. "What *is* that?"

The rumbling turned into a grating roar. The ground started shaking in earnest. The whole cave seemed to be moving, like a small oarboat on the back of a dragonfish.

Rocks started falling from overhead. Zarien flung himself across Tansen. He heard a pained groan as his weight assailed the wounded body, but the warrior remained limp beneath him.

Zarien shouted in fear as the cave floor heaved wildly and its walls shook around him. The rumbling roar was pierced by a great thundering crash in the distance which seemed to echo through his own veins.

Terror consumed him. The ground roiled like rough seas. Rocks tumbled down on him as he tried to shield Tansen. The furious roar of the angry earth deafened him to the painful thundering of his own heart.

And Dar moved the mountains in Her fury.

6

MAKE NO VOWS OR PROMISES IN THE DARK.
ALWAYS WAIT UNTIL DAWN.

—Najdan the Assassin

MIRABAR HAD NOT been asleep when the earthquake began, so she was slightly—but only slightly—less disoriented by it than everyone else atop Mount Dalishar.

She had been through a few tremors in her lifetime—a span of barely twenty years, she guessed, though she didn't know for certain. Tonight's quake was far worse, though. It felt as if the ground was being pulled out from under her. The walls of Dalishar's six multichambered caves shook. The simple belongings of the forty or fifty rebels living up here tumbled around as if thrown by unseen hands. A terrible roaring filled the air, like the world screaming in its death throes.

And in the distance, Mount Darshon gave a terrible, thundering crack of rage.

Mirabar fled from the cave where she was spending the night, dragging Sister Rahilar with her as she escaped the shelter which had now become a potential deathtrap. When they reached the open ground outside their cave, she saw that everyone else at Dalishar was doing the same. The sentries were shouting wildly to alert everyone—*As if anyone could sleep through this!*—as people poured out of the caves, confused, armed, and frightened.

No, it's not Kiloran, not yet. Just an earthquake.

That was bad enough, she realized, as another violent tremor threw her to the hard ground. Kiloran wouldn't have to kill them all if Dar did it for him. And Dar was furious with them, for Sileria had killed the Firebringer.

Kiloran. Elelar. The Valdani. They killed him, Dar, not me. And You let it happen. So stop this!

Mirabar tried to rise, furious at her goddess, even as the ground continued shaking.

"*Sirana!* Stay down, *sirana!*"

She didn't know whose voice she heard shouting in the chaos, but she knew it was directed at her. *Sirana,* they called her now, a term of the highest respect. Her, an illiterate *shallah,* a clanless orphan who'd grown up wild in the mountains. She had survived like an animal and barely been able to speak like a human child when first found by Tashinar, the Guardian who caught and tamed her all those years ago. The sick old woman was her mentor and the closest thing she'd ever had to a mother.

She prayed fervently that the earthquake wasn't this bad at Mount Niran, where Tashinar was tonight. Mirabar and Sister Rahilar clutched each other in fear, huddled on the ground, and tried to protect their heads from falling rocks.

Please Dar, shield Tashinar, shield her.

She only realized that the terrible rumbling which filled her senses was finally fading away when she heard the rasping sound of Rahilar's breath. Mirabar cautiously lifted her head.

"It is over, *sirana?*" Rahilar asked, her voice high and thready with terror.

Mirabar waited another moment. "Yes, it's over."

"*Sirana! Sirana!*"

She knew *that* voice. "I'm here!" she called. "I'm fine!"

Hard, calloused hands hauled her off the ground a moment later. She saw the black clothes of an assassin, the yellow beads woven into the red *jashar,* the harshly lined face and long black hair—now showing some gray—of her protector. His *shir* trembled slightly, as it always did in response to her presence. She supposed Najdan had grown used to that by now.

He released her quickly, showing a *shallah*'s respect for a woman's sanctity, a servant's respect for the *sirana*'s dignity.

"You are not hurt?" he asked, his gaze traveling over her with proprietary concern. She knew he regarded her safety as his destined duty; if she came to harm, it stained his honor. The habits and values absorbed during his twenty years as Kiloran's trusted assassin remained with him, and now he applied them to the young Guardian to whom he had pledged his loyalty, the prophetess for whom he had betrayed his master.

"I'm fine." She was shaking, but unhurt.

Najdan's breath was coming fast, and his face gleamed with the sweat of fear. He was a brave man, but no one liked earthquakes. Least of all *shallaheen,* whose villages were perched so precariously on Sileria's steep mountain slopes and high cliffs. Now Najdan would be worried, she knew, about his mistress, Haydar, whom he had left in the mountain Sanctuary of Sister Basimar. Haydar would be safe from Kiloran's vengeance there, but earthquakes didn't respect Sanctuary the way the Society did.

Mirabar was even more worried about Tansen. "He should have been here by now," she said, scarcely aware that she spoke aloud.

"He was wounded, *sirana*. He must be making the journey slowly," Najdan answered without needing to ask whom she meant. "He will surely be here tomorrow." He paused. "Today?" He shrugged and settled on, "After sunrise." He bent over and politely helped Sister Rahilar to her feet. She was shaking, too, but not, Dar be thanked, weeping or complaining.

"Sister!" A *shallah* rebel named Galian, known for always fighting with two *yahr,* came running over to where the three of them stood. "Sis—" He stopped when he saw Mirabar, crossed his fists over his chest and bowed his head respectfully. "You are unhurt, *sirana?*"

"Yes, yes," she replied, still unused to how much her life had changed. Her fiery red hair and flame-bright eyes had once, not long ago, made the *shallaheen* shun her, fear her, even violently drive her from their villages. Now most of them treated her with the deference usually paid only to a *torena*. Or a waterlord. "You need the Sister for something?"

"Lann slept through the earthquake and—"

"He *what?*"

Galian grinned. "And he was hit by some falling rocks inside the cave. I don't think it's serious, but that thick skull of his is bleeding a little."

"I will see to him," Rahilar said. "Bring any other wounded there, too, and I will tend to them."

"Yes, Sister."

"We should remember not to leave Lann on sentry duty," Mirabar said to Najdan as the other two hurried away.

"It would perhaps be unwise," he agreed dryly.

Mirabar walked to the edge of the clearing and stood atop a sharp cliff left on Dalishar's craggy face long ago, presumably by a night even more violent than this one. She looked out across the dark expanse of Sileria and could see many mountains outlined by the rich light of the two full moons.

In the distance was Mount Darshon, so high and vast, its snow-capped peak so bold and bright, she could see it even from here on a twin-moon night like this. Now lightning flashed around the snowy summit at uneven intervals. Mirabar fell back a step as flame shot into the night, piercing the clouds which shone palely in the harsh flashes of light flickering above Darshon.

"Dar is angry," Najdan guessed.

"Then Dar should have protected him," Mirabar replied bitterly.

"Josarian chose his way, *sirana*. As I have chosen mine. As you have chosen yours."

"Now we must wait only to see what Tansen's choice will be."

"He said he would execute the *torena*."

"So die all who betray Josarian," she quoted softly, remembering. It was the death sentence of anyone who betrayed the Firebringer, the Silerian peasant who had struck out from his humble mountain village to change the world.

"Yes, and *Torena* Elelar did betray him." He paused and added, "As I betrayed Kiloran."

"Revenge is Kiloran's strength," Mirabar said, "whereas Elelar is Tansen's weakness." She hated the knowledge of that more than she should.

Najdan smiled. An assassin's smile. "Mercy is his weakness."

She turned away, chilled by him, as she sometimes was, despite trusting him with her life. "Then may he be ruthless where that . . . woman is concerned."

"If he isn't, *sirana,* it would be a simple matter for me to assassinate her myself."

"No."

"I have never killed a woman," he said, tactfully avoiding mention of the time he had once tried to kill Mirabar, "and I would rather not, as it is not honorable. But if you wish—"

"No," she repeated, in a tone which prohibited argument.

"Ah. Must it be done," Najdan asked, "or must *he* do it?"

"It must be done," she replied, "and he must do it."

"Then let us hope that he already has, *sirana,* as he vowed."

"Let us hope that he is still alive." She shivered, though the night was only pleasantly cool, and returned to the thought which had kept her wide awake before the start of the earthquake. "He should have been here by now."

"Give him another day, *sirana,*" Najdan advised. "He is very hard to kill, you know."

"Yes," she agreed. "That much is true."

She rubbed her forehead. Now that the thundering chaos of the earthquake was fading into memory, the ever-present song of Dalishar was returning to haunt her. The six caves up here were sacred to the Guardians of the Otherworld, claimed by the sect centuries ago. Guardian power here remained so strong that the waterlords had never challenged their supremacy at Dalishar and, Mirabar sincerely hoped, never would. Sacred fires, blown into life long ago and left burning ever since—woodless, enchanted, mystically linked to the Otherworld—kept the caves perpetually bright, day and night.

Fresh springs kept Dalishar well supplied with water year round, even at the height of the dry season. The caves were decorated with strange paintings, older than memory, left by a race of peaceful water wizards called the Beyah-Olvari, the first inhabitants of Sileria. Most people thought they were extinct, but Mirabar knew otherwise. She had never seen one, but she knew the well-guarded secret, as did Tansen: Though few in number, the Beyah-Olvari still existed; small blue-skinned beings, a dying race living in ancient tunnels below Shaljir. This mountaintop, like all of Sileria, had once belonged to them.

The Otherworld was very close up here, separated from this world only by a thin veil eternally pierced by the sacred fires of Dalishar. Shades of the dead called through the night to Mirabar now, their silent voices echoing around her, making her head ache. After a few days at Dalishar, she became so exhausted from the twin realities of this world and the Other one that it was hard to function, difficult to concentrate.

But she was safe from Kiloran at Dalishar, and so Tansen had insisted she come and await him here. It was not far from Chandar and the ruined villa where Elelar had been living in recent months, ever since Tansen and Zimran risked their lives to break her out of prison in Shaljir. *Torena* Elelar had been caught spying on her Valdani lover, Imperial Advisor Borell, and giving information to the Silerian rebels; she had been beaten, raped, imprisoned, and condemned to death by that same man.

Mirabar hated Elelar, but even she had to admit that the woman was no coward. The *torena* was part of the Alliance, a rebel group which had existed since long before Josarian's birth, and she had devoted her whole life to ridding Sileria of the Valdani. Unfortunately, she was also willing to betray anyone—Josarian, Tansen, *anyone*—to achieve this goal. Long ago, she had betrayed Tansen to Kiloran. Now that Josarian was dead, Mirabar was the only other person left alive who knew why: Tansen killed Armian, and Elelar told Kiloran to ensure that he would not blame the Alliance for his comrade's death.

When the Valdani finally realized they were losing the war against Josarian in Sileria, they met in secret with the aristocratic leaders of the Alliance—which had been largely ineffectual before Josarian commenced the rebellion and united Sileria against its conquerors—and demanded Josarian's death in exchange for Valdani withdrawal from Sileria. For reasons which Mirabar would never, ever understand, Elelar had not only agreed, she had personally plotted Josarian's murder. She seduced his cousin Zimran—who typically thought with an organ very distant from his brain—and convinced Zim to lead Josarian into an Outlooker ambush.

As much as Mirabar loathed Elelar, she also knew the *torena* wasn't stupid, so it bewildered her that she hadn't suspected what any fool should—that Kiloran was behind the plan all along. He had alerted the Valdani that the Alliance could be convinced to betray Josarian, and he had convinced the Alliance that his own enmity ensured that Josarian ought to be sacrificed to save Sileria. The shrewd old waterlord had undoubtedly counted on Elelar's mingled arrogance and fanaticism to lead her straight to the well of betrayal he had secretly chosen for her.

But Kiloran, who valued and richly rewarded loyalty, hadn't suspected that, during the course of the costly war with Valdania, Najdan's loyalty had switched from him to Mirabar. Najdan abandoned his master and betrayed Kiloran's plans to Tansen and Mirabar, who were Josarian's sword and shield, thus condemning himself to a bloodvow from the waterlord.

Thanks to Najdan's warning, they had found Josarian in time to save him from the Outlooker ambush. Although letting Josarian be murdered by the Valdani would have been the tidiest solution for Kiloran, the waterlord had foreseen the possibility of failure, and so he had another plan, a far more horrible scheme, in reserve: the White Dragon.

So Elelar hadn't really killed Josarian. But she had tried. She had betrayed him. Had she not done so . . .

Would he be alive now?

Probably not, for Kiloran had set his final trap well. But that changed nothing. Vengeance must now be swift and merciless. This was Sileria, where mercy was indeed a weakness, compassion was dangerous, and forgiveness was a fool's delusion. Elelar must pay for what she had done.

If Tansen hasn't killed her, as he promised that night, then I will do it, she vowed. *And I will never forgive him.*

As for Kiloran . . . Mirabar shuddered as she remembered the White Dragon rising out of the Zilar River. Unstoppable. Unkillable. Kiloran's hideous, evil offspring, its water-born form dripping death in icy droplets that burned the flesh. Josarian's dying screams now filled her head, competing with the clamoring music of the Otherworld. How Tansen had wept afterwards. Covered in blood—including that of Zimran, whom he had killed that night—covered in bruises, in burns, in cuts and abrasions, swaying from the reopened *shir* wound in his side, panting from his fruitless battle against the White Dragon . . . He had wept like a child for the bloodbrother he couldn't save.

"Are you cold, *sirana*?"

Mirabar flinched, having forgotten Najdan was there. "What?"

"You're shivering."

"Oh. I . . ."

"I believe it is safe to return to your cave now."

"No, I don't . . ."

"I will move any fallen rocks, and then you will lie down."

She knew that tone. He could bicker like an overprotective mother if she resisted once he had decided what was best for her. "As you wish."

She was following him into the mouth of the cave when she heard the Beckoning.

Come to me . . .

She was tired. She was grieving. But she well knew the penalty of resisting the Beckoner. If the Otherworld sometimes clamored inside her head, the Beckoner could thunder until her knees gave way from the force of his will.

Come . . .

Najdan sensed her hesitation. "*Sirana?*"

"Go," she said, staring into the dark wilderness which bordered this cave. "I'll lie down later."

"But—"

"It's the Beckoner."

Najdan froze, then crossed his fists, bowed his head, and quietly retreated. This, after all, was what made her the *sirana* for whom he had betrayed Kiloran: the gift of prophecy.

The strange visitant whom Mirabar called the Beckoner—for lack of a more accurate notion of what he was—had opened the gates of destiny to a young Guardian initiate one night on the slopes of Mount Niran, and she had helped Josarian change the world. She saw the Beckoner again now, as she had many times since that first night: the ghostly shape of a strong man with flame-red hair and fire-gold eyes, his skin glowing with the light of the Otherworld, his feet never touching the ground. Not a shade of the dead. A god, perhaps? She didn't know. She only knew that whether or not she liked it—and she often didn't—she served Dar and Sileria through the prophecies given to her by the Beckoner.

His lava-rich coloring was rare, as rare as her own. In all her life, she'd never seen another person with hair like hers, and only one other with eyes like hers: Cheylan, a *toren* turned Guardian, whose kisses she well remembered and whose stunning secret she couldn't forget . . .

Come to me . . . the Beckoner urged in the seductive silence of her vision, driving all thoughts of Cheylan from her head. He glowed like the clouds above Darshon tonight as he floated into the forest beyond the sacred caves.

You must come . . .

That much, she knew, was true. She had been chosen, and she had no choice. She had tried to resist before, and it was not permitted. Was it only last night she had refused the Beckoner while she grieved over Josarian's death, betrayed by all she had wrought? But he had not allowed it; he had forced her to bend to his will. Again.

"Our work is not yet done," she said, following him, repeating what she had learned from him in the previous vision. "The new Yahrdan is coming . . ."

"*Sirana?*"

She heard a puzzled voice behind her, someone who wasn't familiar with her strange fits and visions, someone who had never seen her wander into the dark wilderness muttering like a madwoman, had never seen her suddenly fall to the ground when tormented by unseen forces.

Then she heard Najdan's voice: "Leave her."

"But . . ."

Their voices faded from Mirabar's senses as she followed the Beckoner into the fragile borderlands between this world and the Other one.

"The Yahrdan," she said, using the title of the traditional ruler of Sileria.

There hadn't been a Yahrdan here since the death of Daurion, a thousand years ago, the Guardian and great warrior who had ruled this island nation with a fist of iron in a velvet glove before being betrayed by Marjan, the very first waterlord. Marjan was the Guardian who had unraveled the secrets of water magic encoded in the cave paintings which the Beyah-Olvari had left all over Sileria. He had betrayed Daurion and thereby weakened Sileria for the Moorlander Conquest. Marjan invented the *shir,* turned men into assassins, demanded tribute in exchange for water from the rivers and lakes he controlled . . . As much as the Valdani, Marjan had created the world into which Mirabar had been born.

"The new Yahrdan," she repeated into the darkness which now danced around her, blotting out the gossamer trees, the caves, the ground, the moon-bright sky. "How will I know him?"

The ground disappeared beneath her feet, and she fell into the swimming emptiness of the Beckoner's domain. A hollow world beyond life and death, a region where the past and the future collided, where will was power and flesh was nothing.

Hot sparks ignited in the murky void and something liquid trickled musically past Mirabar's senses. Fire and water: the two elements which ruled Sileria. Incompatible, forever apart, forever at odds.

The sparks fell into the liquid, and the two substances united, becoming one, becoming something new, something which grew. Now fire whirled around her, strange blue flames of incandescent water, a burning liquid that scorched and froze her at once.

Fire and water, water and fire . . .

"No," she protested, "we are enemies. Now and forever."

He comes, he comes . . . Welcome him.

"Who? The Yahrdan?"

Fire and water, water and fire . . .

"Are you saying he's a waterlord?" she asked in horror.

Her whirling nest of blue fire became a cradle. The birthing screams of the world surrounded her, roared across space and time, filled her head. The agony of childbirth, strange and yet strangely familiar, seized her body, the pain causing her to double over as her screams blended with those which echoed around her. A river of fire poured out of her womb, turning into a flow of icy water that chilled and burned all at once.

Only when the pain finally faded did she understand.

"Am I looking for a child?"

A child of fire . . .

"Yes?"

A child of water . . .

"No!"

Blue fire pierced her like a spear. She screamed in agony.

"*Siran!*" she cried, her eyes streaming lava as she pleaded for mercy. "Please, don't!"

A child of sorrow . . .

Mirabar gasped for breath, choking on a sudden, terrible sadness. Her heart wailed inside her chest, broken and empty. "Whose . . . sorrow is this?" she asked weakly. But grief was her only answer, longing her only comfort.

She fell through the stars, inhaling the watery blue fire all around her, drowning in it as it burned her throat and flooded her lungs. Tears of lava continued to flow down her cheeks. She caught them with her fingers and saw them turn into diamonds, glittering stones like those mined at Alizar. They gleamed beautifully for a moment, then turned into water so cold she gasped and dropped them. They coalesced around her and turned into a circle of fire, glorious flames rising through the dark.

He is coming!

"How will I know him?" she begged.

Prepare the way.

"What must I do?"

Shield him . . .

"How?" she asked bitterly. "I couldn't shield Josarian."

The night exploded like an eruption of Mount Darshon, showers of lava consuming her flesh. The ground pushed upward against her falling body, surging towards the tumbling sky, birth and death twining together in the heaving soil beneath her, in the liquid fire flowing through her veins, in the deadly water glittering on her skin.

"How will I know him?" she cried again.

Before she lost consciousness, she felt the answer sliding along her skin, filling her hands, whispering in her ears. She felt it and knew it was there, but she couldn't understand it.

A frustrated sob escaped her before her vision went black and she returned to her world, empty and helpless in the night.

NAJDAN WAITED UNTIL dawn to search for the *sirana*.

He didn't fear the darkness. An enemy who awaited him in the dark could see no better than he could, after all. He didn't fear the assassins undoubtedly plotting his death right now, perhaps even haunting the slopes of Dalishar at this very moment. He had survived too long as an assassin to fear another of his kind.

He feared very few things, in fact, for there wasn't much that he, who had served Kiloran for twenty years, hadn't already faced and survived. But he feared whatever it was the *sirana* so often confronted in her strange visions. And because she did not shrink from it—from something powerful beyond his experience, strange beyond his understanding—he served her, as she served this thing which ruled her destiny.

She was a prophetess, cursed and gifted with visions which had helped change the world. Najdan had little interest in the toils and struggles of the *shallaheen,* sheep whom his former master had always herded with ease, and he himself had not seen Josarian's transformation at Mount Darshon. He had, however, seen this small, impoverished girl, without family or clan or influence, face Kiloran and win his respect. Najdan had seen her win the respect, even earn the fear, of many of the Society's waterlords and assassins. She had initially faced Najdan himself as an enemy and, after a few misunderstandings during which he had tried to kill her, won his respect, too—and, eventually, his devotion.

Najdan knew a hundred ways to kill a man, and at least as many ways to force him to submit and obey. He had pledged his life and skills to the Society long ago, so he knew little of the Guardians or their religion. Until Mirabar, in fact, he had only known them as enemies to be killed whenever possible. He hadn't prayed to Dar in many years; the Society discouraged any devotion to Her. He had consecrated his life to serving Kiloran, who had rewarded him richly, ensuring that he would never go hungry again.

Loyalty was basic to his nature, and he hadn't wanted to betray Kiloran. But his master had eventually forced him to choose—by ordering him to kill Mirabar. Najdan would have accepted Kiloran's plan to kill Josarian, because Josarian had murdered the waterlord's only son, Srijan; and spilled blood called for vengeance. But Najdan couldn't kill Mirabar. That was the push which shoved him into the strange and unstable land of betrayal.

He was not an educated man like Searlon, Kiloran's most favored assassin. He wasn't worldly, like Tansen, who had traveled far and wide during the nine years he'd spent in exile for some crime against Kiloran which neither man had ever revealed. And he didn't possess the gifts of leadership and imagination which had made people follow Josarian even before he'd become the Firebringer. Apart from being very good at killing, Najdan supposed he wasn't special at all. However, he could certainly recognize those who were, and he had built a worthy life by using his skills to serve them. In the course of many years spent among Sileria's most powerful wizards, Najdan had never known anyone as special as Mirabar. So when Kiloran had forced him to choose between them, he had known what the choice must be.

Kiloran's power was extraordinary, still the greatest in Sileria, perhaps in the world. But Najdan could not kill this lone girl who faced the torment of gods in the darkness without flinching and consecrated her life to the service of something Najdan didn't understand but knew could change the world.

On the other hand, he also wouldn't stumble blindly into the midst of one of these strange visitations which consumed her without mercy. The gods which tormented Mirabar didn't like interruptions, and *he* didn't like the chill of Otherworldly magic which permeated these scenes. He had felt it the other night—they had all felt it, here at Dalishar—when Mirabar's visions had spilled over into this world for once, filling the night sky with sound and fury, with images which she, at least, seemed to understand.

"He is coming," she had said. "The next Yahrdan. Our work is not yet done."

Najdan still felt queasy when he recalled those moments of wonder and terror. He didn't know how Mirabar regularly faced these things with such resolve, and he himself didn't want to come so close to them again. However, he also didn't like the thought of her lying somewhere out there, sprawled on the damp ground, easy prey to anyone or anything that might happen along.

When dawn came, when he felt sure the visions must have passed and the thing she called the Beckoner must have retreated, Najdan went in search of Mirabar. He brought Sister Rahilar with him, because he didn't know what Mirabar would need, and it wasn't fitting that he, a man, should handle her.

The Sister was rather pretty, in the almost-harsh way of *shallah* women, but she chattered far too much. He missed Haydar, his mistress of many years. He hoped she was safe, that the earthquake had not hit hard at Sister Basimar's Sanctuary.

He was scanning the hillside and ignoring Rahilar's vapid babbling when he spotted Mirabar lying in a heap, her fire-bright hair glistening with morning dew. Her long homespun tunic was hiked up, exposing her bare stomach. The modest pantaloons of a *shallah* female were now torn, leaving one golden knee naked.

He turned his back on Mirabar and said to Rahilar, "Tend her." At least the woman was good at that.

Rahilar arranged Mirabar's clothing and woke her with some smelling salts. Najdan knew Mirabar was well when she snapped, "Ugh! What in the Fires are you doing?"

"You had fainted," Rahilar murmured.

"I did not faint. I was . . . hit on the head with a volcano."

Rahilar looked at Najdan. He ignored her. "Would you care to return to camp now, *sirana*?" he suggested.

"No, I'd like to sit on the damp ground in the middle of nowhere all day." Her eyes glowed almost yellow with bad temper.

Yes, she would be fine. He had learned by now to expect a little crankiness after these encounters, as if she'd drunk too much wine or indulged in Moorlander cloud syrup.

"Oh, my *head*," she said, cradling it.

"I have something that will help that," Rahilar said. "Back at camp."

"Camp . . ." Mirabar met Najdan's gaze. "Has he come?"

Najdan knew whom she meant. "No, *sirana*. Tansen hasn't arrived yet."

"Dar shield him," she murmured.

"Yes, *sirana*." He had not prayed since his youth, but now he tried the words with an unaccustomed tongue: "Dar shield him."

From Kiloran. From himself. From the earthquake. From his destiny.

Yes, Dar had much to shield the *shatai* from.

7

To KNOW IS NOTHING AT ALL.
To BELIEVE — THAT IS EVERYTHING.

         —Kintish Proverb

TANSEN FELT THE reopened *shir* wound throbbing, draining his life away with the cold magic of a waterlord.

It seemed like such a long time since he'd gotten this wound. Tansen remembered killing High Commander Koroll before collapsing. He'd never even seen the *shir* with which Koroll had done this to him. But he did remember one of his men later saying that it evinced Baran's distinctive workmanship, with its silver and jade inlays on a hilt of Kintish petrified wood.

And Baran isn't even my enemy.

Well, not back then. Perhaps he was now. Who knew? An immensely powerful waterlord, Baran was nothing if not unpredictable. And who could say which was more dangerous in Sileria, anyhow: a friend or an enemy? As Josarian had said: *I can take care of my enemies, but Dar shield me from my friends.*

Tansen grunted in pain. Not from the *shir* wound, but from the memory of Josarian's death, which now returned to him with the pain of a sharp stab to his vitals.

"Are you awake, *siran?*"

He tensed with surprise, coming into his senses as he realized he wasn't alone. With tremendous effort, he opened his eyes. The world whirled dizzyingly for a moment, a cacophony of sight and sound as sunlit shadows flickered over rough stone and the unfamiliar voice spoke to him again.

"*Siran?*"

His eyes came to rest on the figure addressing him. Dark-haired, dark-skinned, dark-eyed. Short hair. Intricate indigo tattoos on the face, forearms, and hands. None on the torso, as a fair-skinned Moorlander might have.

Sea-born.

And young. Caught in that bewildering web between childhood and adulthood, but still clearly more boy than man.

Memories started to drift back into Tansen's conscious mind. The ambush on the path to Dalishar, his collapse afterwards, the voice which had roused him, the sea-born boy who had helped him.

What's he doing so far inland? And all alone?

They were in a cave, hiding because Tansen was too weak to defend himself—let alone the boy who had helped him—and incapable of making the journey to Dalishar or to Sanctuary.

What's your name?

His lips moved, but no sound came out. The boy seemed to understand the problem and, lifting Tansen's head, held the waterskin to his lips.

He choked briefly on the water, and his side felt like all the Fires of Dar were consuming him. His left hand burned coldly, too, and he now remembered the wound inflicted upon it during his struggle with the last of the six assassins who'd ambushed him. He drank more, letting the water soothe his parched throat.

"What's your name?" he croaked at last.

"Zarien." The boy hesitated, then awkwardly crossed his fists over his chest and bowed his head. "I know who you are, *siran.*"

No surprise there. His swords and the brand on his chest made him easy to identify in Sileria, even without the *jashar* he wore around his waist.

The boy's tattoos, Tansen knew, were like a *jashar*; but Tan was, after all, what the sea-born rather contemptuously referred to as "landfolk," and so he couldn't interpret them. "Family? Clan?" he asked, wondering whence this boy had come.

"I . . . was raised by the sea-bound Lascari."

"You're sea-bound?" Astonishment lent strength to his voice.

"I was."

"Ah . . ." He only knew a little about the sea-born folk. Even those sea-born who spent much of their lives ashore seldom came inland and rarely mingled with landfolk. He was aware, though, that the sea-bound clans were regarded as anything from slightly exotic to rigidly fanatical even by their sea-born cousins who willingly traversed the land. "This means . . . banishment from your clan, doesn't it?"

"Yes, *siran*. I am dead to my people." The stern, youthful pride in the boy's expression dared Tansen to pity him.

He finally noticed the bruises on the boy's face, and a fresh cut along his cheek. "What happened to you?"

Zarien reached up to touch a bruise on his forehead. "The land shook."

"Earthquake?"

"Is that what it was?"

"When the land shakes, yes."

"The ground heaved. The cave walls moved. There were falling rocks." He frowned. "I'm not used to caves. I didn't know it was unsafe until it was too late. Anyhow, you were here, and unconscious . . ." He shrugged.

He didn't remember any of this. "You shielded me?"

"I didn't know what else to do."

"I owe you my life," Tansen said. However, it felt like there would soon be nothing left to collect of the debt. His body was immobile, his mind weak and sluggish with fever and blood loss.

"It is my honor, *siran*," Zarien said.

"All the same . . . I am . . . very grate . . ."

Zarien lifted his head and gave him more water. It revived him, but less than it had before. He was weary, so weary. . . .

His gazed drifted downwards as he fought to stay awake. He caught his breath when he studied the terrible scars on the boy's naked torso and finally realized what they were.

"Dragonfish," Tansen murmured, remembering Armian's wounds. Only these scars were from a much, much worse attack. The beast's jaws had closed over the child's entire torso. Its broad teeth had sunk far into his flesh, Tansen judged, based on the width of the marks left behind. How in the Fires had the boy survived *that*?

"Yes." Zarien took a deep breath and then blurted, "A dragonfish killed me during *Bharata Ma-al*."

Tansen digested this, wondering if he was hallucinating. "And then?"

"And then I was rescued by Sharifar—"

"One of the nine goddesses of the sea."

"Yes."

A *detailed* hallucination.

The boy added, "I thought that most drylanders didn't know the names of the sea goddesses." He sounded pleased with Tansen.

So my hallucinations are blessed with accuracy.

"I have a broad education," Tansen told him.

"Of course, *siran*." Zarien continued, "And then Sharifar made a bargain for my life."

The tale which followed was as compelling as it was extraordinary. The boy seemed sane enough, though Tansen didn't place a great deal of faith in his own judgment while he lay bleeding to death, feverish, weak, and confused. However, having seen Josarian emerge alive from the Fires of Dar to drive the Valdani out of Sileria, and having seen Kiloran's White Dragon emerge from the icy waters of the Zilar River to destroy the Firebringer, he supposed anything was possible.

"I'm sorry," he said, aware of the boy awaiting his reaction. "But Josarian isn't your sea king. Not now, anyhow. He's dead."

"Yes, I know that now. You told me yesterday."

He vaguely remembered. "Was it only yesterday?"

"I'm disappointed, of course," Zarien said, "but that is the way of the landfolk, isn't it?"

"Hmm?"

"To betray, to kill in vengeance, to fight among themselves."

He felt both depressed and irritated. "And the way of the sea-born is what?" he challenged.

"To fight the dragonfish."

He grunted and felt himself drifting away again. He felt compassion for this boy, so far from home, bent on a seemingly impossible task in a world which did not welcome him. "But you're . . . a strong boy." Zarien had come this far. He had faced the bloody mess Tansen had left on the path to Dalishar. He had helped Tan to this cave and shielded him during an earthquake which must have scared him half to death. Tansen figured Zarien's chances of surviving were better than average. "Strong," he repeated, too weak to say the rest.

"I am Lascari," the boy said, with a creditable attempt to sound casual.

. . . Tansen felt his face glow with pleasure at the compliment, but he shrugged it off like a man. "You have been away from the mountains too long. Here, I am not special. . . ."

"There are ghosts here," Tansen whispered.

"Where?" He heard apprehension in the boy's voice.

"Don't worry," he murmured. "They are only *my* ghosts."

"I don't understand."

"No, I don't imagine you do."

"I've been thinking, *siran* . . ."

He closed his eyes, trying to decide what to do. Send the boy to Dalishar? Would he make it? To Sanctuary? Would he find it? If Zarien remained here, Tansen would probably die, whereas there was a slight chance that a Sister could arrive in time to save him . . . if, that is, a sea-born boy could find one *and* also remember where this cave was. Meanwhile, if assassins found them here together, the boy would certainly be killed.

And Mirabar, he wondered with sudden, confused urgency. Was she safe? Was she even alive?

His mind reeled as all his fears now assailed him. How long before news of Josarian's death spread through the mountains and into the lowlands? How soon would panic seize people? Would the Valdani honor their secret treaty with the Alliance and withdraw from Sileria now that Josarian was dead? Could Elelar convince them to abandon Shaljir before they discovered that Sileria was about to descend into the inferno of civil war?

Before they realize all they have to do is hold on to Shaljir long enough for us to destroy ourselves, and then—

"*Siran?* This wound . . ." Zarien lifted a saturated bandage away from Tansen's side. Tan vaguely realized that it was the remains of the boy's tunic. "If my mother were here, I think she would cauterize it. So perhaps I should try to build a fire, and—"

"You can't cauterize it," Tansen interrupted, his vision swimming blackly. "It's a *shir* wound."

"An assassin did this to you?"

"No, a Valdan."

"I thought only assa—"

"It doesn't matter now."

"No."

With monumental effort, Tansen spoke again. "I want y—"

"But if we cauterized it—"

"*Shir* wound," Tan repeated. He explained to the sea-born boy what any *shallah* knew. "Water magic. Put a hot poker to the wound, all you get is steam. Doesn't close or heal or stop bleeding."

"The winds take me." Zarien's voice came from very far away. "What do we do?"

"You've got to go—"

"Go? No!"

"Go to—"

"I can't leave you."

"Yes, you must. Go to—"

"No!"

He was too weak to argue. "Zarien . . ."

"No, I won't." The stubbornness Tansen heard in the boy's voice made his heart sink.

If assassins find you with me . . .

"I've come all this way to find you," Zarien said. "I won't let you out of my sight now."

This startled him enough to open his eyes. "Me?"

"I thought it was Josarian, but now I know it must be you."

"Me?" he repeated stupidly, falling through the dark night of death, barely able to hear the tattooed boy's desperate voice.

"Yes. Don't you see? You're the sea king!"

AFTER THREE DAYS *of the Sister's care, Armian climbed out of the depths of his weakness and recovered with great speed.*

However, he remained adamant about not going to Mount Darshon to embrace Dar.

"I've got to get to Shaljir," he told Tansen, in a voice which allowed no further debate.

Tansen had never been west of Darshon in his life, let alone as far away as the capital city. "I will take you back to Gamalan," he offered. "My grandfather will know what to do."

Armian decided not to wear his jashar *while they traveled through Sileria. Both his mission and Tansen, he said, would be safer if no one recognized him. "So don't tell anyone. Understood?"*

"No, sira . . . No, Armian," Tansen corrected himself, for the Firebringer had insisted he accept the privilege of using his name. "I will die to protect your secret!"

"You don't need to go that far," Armian said dryly. "Just use that blank-faced discretion the shallaheen *are known for. Lirtahar?"*

"Yes." Tansen smiled, pleased that Armian was becoming more Silerian with every day he spent here. "Lirtahar."

Armian let him look at the shir *which had been concealed in one of his well-made boots the night he had washed ashore; but, of course, Tansen couldn't touch it. A* shir *could never harm its owner, which was why neither Armian nor any other assassin needed a sheath for his water-born dagger. If a* shir *belonged to you, you could even sleep with it tucked inside your clothes, its deadly blade as harmless as a kiss against your skin. However, just the whisper of its touch was terribly painful to anyone else. Even the waterlord who made a* shir *was vulnerable if the weapon was wielded against him. When Tansen tried to touch Armian's* shir, *it burned cruelly with the cold fire instilled in it by Kiloran, the great waterlord who had made it as a gift—a sign of trust, a mark of good faith—when Armian had been born to Harlon's woman.*

"*I've come to find him,*" *Armian said.*

"*To find Kiloran?*" *Tansen breathed in awe.*

"*Yes.*"

"*He lives in hiding, like all the waterlords, ever since the Valdani Emperor swore he would destroy the Honored Society in his lifetime.*" *He bit his lip when he realized Armian would already know this, since his own father, Harlon, had died after battling the Outlookers for years.*

"*There are people who can help me find Kiloran,*" *Armian said,* "*who can make arrangements.*"

"*In Shaljir?*"

"*It's called the Alliance. Have you ever heard of it?*"

"*No.*"

"*Maybe your grandfather has.*"

"*I don't think so, Armian.*"

"*We'll ask him when we reach Gamalan.*"

"*Yes, of course. He will know the best way to reach Shaljir.*"

"*Good.*"

And after Armian found Kiloran, Tansen thought, perhaps then he would go to Darshon.

IT WAS LATE morning when Mirabar awoke, still groggy from the violent and restless night, but feeling considerably better than she had when Najdan and Rahilar had found her lying unconscious in the morning dew.

Just once, couldn't I have visions in my own bedroll?

With wakefulness came the weight of worry again. Where was Tansen? She knew he still hadn't arrived, because someone would have awakened her—

She sat bolt upright when she heard the shrill whistle of a sentry. Someone was coming up the southern path, identity still unknown. The southern path—the way Tansen would come, journeying here from Chandar.

She leaped out of her worn bedroll, pulled on her shoes, and went outside. Lann was there, larger than life, his long Moorlander sword unsheathed as he waited in readiness for whatever would happen now. He was bearded, an unusual trait in Sileria, and now his head was wrapped in the bandage Rahilar had used on the injury he'd gotten while sleeping—of all things!—through the earthquake. He was from Emeldar, Josarian's native village, and had known Josarian his whole life. A boisterous, openly emotional man, he had wept piteously upon seeing the Firebringer die at the Zilar River. Lann always wept when his friends died.

"Someone is coming," Najdan said, trying to force Mirabar back into her cave.

She resisted, "Yes, I heard. It might be—"

"It might be anyone," he interrupted.

She was about to argue when another signal from the sentry riveted her attention. "A friend," she said, praying to Dar that it was Tansen.

She rushed across the clearing and to the edge of the plateau, then ran surefootedly down the path watched over by the sentries. She felt the sharp edge of something cutting across her inner senses and mistook it for excitement. Only when she rounded a bend in the steep trail and saw him did she realize it was sorcery, the echo of power she always sensed in his presence.

"Cheylan," she said in disappointment.

His handsome, aristocratic features were made all the more arresting by the fiery glow of his golden eyes. His long hair was braided in the intricate style of a *toren*. Like her, he wore the broach of a Guardian pinned to his tunic, a single flame in a circle of fire. But Cheylan had been born to a wealthy family, and so his was made of silver, whereas Mirabar's was only copper.

"Mirabar! I didn't know you'd be here."

He smiled and held out his hands, no doubt expecting a warm welcome. Though his hair was black rather than the fiery red of her own, he had the Dar-blessed—or Dar-cursed, depending on your point of view—fire-golden eyes which had once been common among the Guardians of Sileria long ago, before the Society had begun slaughtering them and encouraging others to do the same. A sign of the great power which was feared and persecuted by the Society, those eyes had made Cheylan, too, an outcast, despite his aristocratic birth and wealthy upbringing.

This similarity had created a common bond between the two of them when they met during the rebellion. It was even a source of attraction between them. Cheylan was the first man who had ever looked at Mirabar as a woman, rather than as a demon girl or a sorceress, and certainly the first who had ever touched her as a man touched a woman. She had tumbled willingly into the fiery warmth of the few stolen embraces they had shared.

So he seemed understandably perturbed when she brushed past him now without even a nod and gazed down the path behind him. "You came alone?" she asked, turning back to him.

He lifted a dark brow at her tone. "Yes."

"You saw no one else?"

"Such as?"

"Tansen."

"Ah." He studied her for a moment before saying, "Then he's not here? I thought he might be."

"Why?"

"I thought that mess lower down the mountain might have been his doing. But evidently—"

"What mess?" she pounced.

"You don't know?"

"Know what?"

"There are half a dozen assassins lying dead down there. All in one place. All killed with a sword. Or two swords, perhaps."

Her heart leaped with panic. "Fresh?"

"A day old, I'd say."

"Yesterday. He would have . . ." Her voice gave out for a moment. "He would have been there yesterday." She whirled and raced back up the path, heedless of Cheylan's puzzled voice behind her. "Najdan!" she called urgently. "*Najdan!*"

He appeared, *shir* in hand, before she had finished crying his name a second time. His face darkened when he saw Cheylan, whom he didn't like, and he moved towards him with open menace. "What has he done t—"

"No, no," she said impatiently. "It's about Tansen."

The rebels crowded around her, full of questions. She made Cheylan repeat what he had just told her.

"You think he walked into a trap?" Lann asked her.

"And survived," she said, "since Cheylan didn't see his body."

"Six," Najdan mused. "Yes, even wounded, perhaps he could defeat six."

"But if he survived, then where in the Fires is he?" Lann wondered.

TANSEN KNEW SOMETHING *was terribly wrong even as he and Armian approached the village. There was no activity, no call of greeting. No old men sat outside the public house, or* tirshah, *at the edge of the village to exchange stories, share news, and play obscure Kintish games of strategy with intricately carved pieces worn smooth by years of handling. No children on the mountain path, no women at the water well, no shepherds on the hillside . . .*

And then they entered the main square of Gamalan and saw the site of the massacre. Dozens of bodies. Everyone who had lived in the tiny, forgotten, impoverished village, a community badly depleted by its long bloodfeud with the Sirdari clan.

The stench of death was unbelievable. The bodies lay under the merciless Silerian sun while flies swarmed around them, the ceaseless buzzing creating a thrumming drone which further disoriented Tan's stunned senses.

"No!" he cried. "No! No!" Over and over. No other word penetrated his thoughts, no other sound could emerge from his lips.

"Outlookers!" Armian warned suddenly.

"No!"

He felt Armian's grip and struggled against it. He felt Armian grasp something in his jashar *and heard him mutter, "I need your* yahr." *He stumbled as Armian shoved him and said, "Stay behind me." He didn't understand, didn't care, knew nothing but the horror roaring through his veins.*

"No! No!" He broke away from Armian, ran to the mute corpses, and

started handling the stinking, heavy, blood-soaked bodies, looking for his own family. "No!"

"Tan, get back! Tansen!"

He saw the Outlookers then, their gray tunics, their clipped hair, their short Valdani swords. He didn't care. "No!"

Armian's shir *glittered in the sunlight, its water-born blade slitting the throat of the first Outlooker to venture close to him. He swung Tansen's* yahr *at one who hung back slightly. The wood lashed through the air and connected with the Valdan's nose. Blood sprayed across Armian's face just before he whirled to confront another attacker.*

Tansen turned his back on them and continued looking for the proud flow of his grandfather's white mane, the tapered elegance of his peasant mother's work-roughened hands, the womanly curves of his once-skinny elder sister. He found friends, cousins, and aunts among the dead, but not his family.

"Are they here?" *Armian asked. His voice was breathless.*

Tansen looked up, barely able to see him through the flow of his tears.

"Your family," *Armian clarified.* "Are they here?"

He shook his head, staring. Three Outlookers lay motionless around Armian. The fourth was on his knees. Armian held him by the hair and pressed the shir *against his throat.*

"Are they dead?" *Tansen asked blankly, looking at the three Outlookers lying on the ground.*

"Two are dead," *Armian said tersely.* "The other will be dead soon, and why should I make it quicker for him?"

Hatred seared Tansen's blood as he looked at the Outlooker kneeling before Armian. A boiling rage flooded him, a thirst for vengeance so fierce it choked him. "Let me kill this one."

"Later, when we're done with him," *Armian promised. He yanked the Outlooker's hair and prompted in Valdan,* "The boy's family?"

"I don't—"

Armian drew blood with the shir. *The Outlooker screamed in pain, then babbled,* "I didn't participate in the interrogation. I swear I didn't! I was just left behind to take you in case you came here, after all. We waited for two whole days, and then our commanding officer decided you weren't coming, you'd either died at sea or were already on your way to your destination. So he took the rest of his men with him and left us behind to—"

"How did he know about me?" *Armian snapped.*

"The pirate."

"Aljuna?" *Tansen blurted.*

"We had information, and when we caught the pirate at sea and you weren't on board anymore, we took him into custody before burning his ship. He broke under torture."

Tansen suddenly remembered the way Aljuna had squealed like a pig when they'd cut his palm for the bloodpact. It had seemed funny at the time. "He couldn't take pain," he said in a daze.

"And the pirate told you what?" Armian demanded.

"A boy and an old man from a mountain village called Gamalan. He was coming ashore to meet them that night. Smugglers. They might have helped you if you made it to shore." The Outlooker's voice was shaking. He was panting with fear. "Please! I'll tell you anything you want to know."

"You certainly will," Armian said grimly.

"Only don't kill me!"

Tansen felt sick. "They're dead, aren't they?" When the Outlooker didn't reply, Tansen said, "Dead?" in Valdan, unable to choke out more.

"Who?" the man bleated. "The pirate? Yes."

Armian threw him to the ground and kicked him in the stomach. "The boy's family, you dung-eater!"

"Three have mercy, don't kill me!" The Outlooker started weeping with fear. "Please! I swear I had nothing to do with the interrogation! Don't kill me!"

Tansen felt even sicker. He had never seen a man beg for his life.

"This wasn't interrogation, you festering worm," Armian snarled, "this was a massacre!" He yanked the Outlooker's head up by the hair again and forced him to look at the dead of Gamalan. "There are children there, you maggot! Women and old men, girls and unarmed boys!"

"What..." Tansen swallowed and tried again, already knowing, in his churning gut, what the answer would be. "What interrogation?"

"The old s— sm— smuggler and h— his women," the Outlooker stammered, his eyes rolling with terror.

Tansen met Armian's gaze. "My grandfather. My mo— My..." He couldn't say it. Bile rose in his throat. His heart pounded with horror.

"My commander wanted to know wh— where the b— boy was," the Outlooker said, still weeping. "But they w— woul— would..."

"Wouldn't talk." Armian's voice was flat and hard.

"N— No."

Armian pulled on the Outlooker's hair until he was standing up, then said, "Show me." When Tansen followed, Armian turned and said to him, "Stay here."

"No."

"Tan—"

"They are my family."

Armian hesitated a moment longer, then nodded. "Show us," he ordered the Outlooker.

"Please..." the man whispered. "P— please, soron..."

"It's siran, you pig. And don't pollute our language with your filthy tongue."

"I'm sorr—"

"Shut up," Armian snapped.

The Outlooker led them into the best house in the village, a three-room dwelling in good repair. Tansen saw the village headman, who had lived here, dead inside.

Along with Tan's grandfather, his mother, and his sister.

It was worse than anything he could have imagined. He would see it in his nightmares as long as he lived. He would never forget, never forgive, and never recover from what the Valdani had done to his family while he tended Armian in a coastal cave, blissfully ignorant of the slaughter of the innocents in Gamalan.

His beautiful, work-worn mother, with her small hands and her soft brown eyes, now lay gutted, her entrails streaming away from her corpse. They had raped his sister and stained her bruised thighs with her own blood. He tried to arrange her clothes, lest any man see what only her husband should . . .

"Tansen," Armian said.

. . . but she would never marry now. He looked away from her lifeless body and turned to his grandfather. They had broken all the old man's fingers and gouged out his eyes.

"But you did not . . . tell them . . . wh— where I w—" Tansen couldn't stop crying, couldn't draw enough breath, couldn't look away from the old man's ruined face, from the empty, blood-drenched eye sockets.

"I didn't do this, I didn't do this, I swear to you, I didn't do this," the Outlooker kept repeating, his strained voice the only sound besides Tansen's choked sobs in this dead village.

"We must burn them," Tansen finally said.

"No," Armian replied. "We will let others do that."

"No, I must burn them. My grandfather says a person cannot journey to the Otherworld if the body is not purified through fire, and we can't just—"

"People should see the Outlookers' work," Armian said. "The murder of women and children. The torture of an unarmed old man . . ." He put a hand on Tansen's shoulder and tried to make him understand. "If you burn them all, no one will know. The Valdani can claim it was disease or sorcery or a bloodfeud."

"I don't care what they cl—"

"We want people to know," Armian said. "When they see this, when the mountains talk of it, then people will hate them as much as you and I do."

"People hate them already," Tansen said dully.

"Not enough," Armian said. "Not yet."

Tansen looked around, his mind blank with shock. "Then . . . we will just leave them like this?"

"Yes," Armian said. "I'm sorry."

"Do you think . . ." He met Armian's eyes. "If I had been here . . ."

"You'd be dead, too."

"Perhaps I c—"

"You'd be dead, too," Armian repeated. "Even if we hadn't met, even if you had come straight home from the coast . . ." Armian shook his head. "The Val-

dani came here on a hunch. They did all this—" He gestured to the devastation around them. "*—on a chance, a guess.*"

Tansen's eyes clouded with tears again.

"*You couldn't have stopped them,*" Armian told him. "*I couldn't have stopped them.*"

"*Then . . .*" He took his last look at his murdered loved ones. "*Then I am left alive to avenge them.*"

"*Yes. We will avenge them,*" Armian promised.

When they emerged from the headman's house, dragging the quivering Out-looker with them, Armian asked Tansen, "*Is there anything you want to get from your own house before we go?*"

He couldn't think. He could only hear the buzzing of the flies and smell the acrid odor of death under the brassy Silerian sun. "*I just want to leave,*" he said at last.

Armian thrust the Outlooker in front of him. "*You wanted to kill this one yourself?*"

Though Armian spoke to Tansen in Silerian, the Outlooker seemed to under-stand the gesture, the moment. "*No!*" he wailed. "*Please, don't! I beg you!*"

Armian held the yahr out to Tansen.

Tan met the Firebringer's eyes, the cold eyes of an assassin.

He looked at the trembling Outlooker, drenched in sweat, weeping with fear. Begging, pleading, wailing for mercy.

He felt the hard wood of the yahr in his hand. He felt the thick cord which held the two sticks together, which turned a couple of pieces of polished wood into such a deadly weapon.

I'll have to beat him to death.

The yahr *was a striking weapon. How many blows would it take, Tansen wondered? When would the Outlooker stop screaming? After the second? The third? Or maybe not until the seventh or eighth?*

How will I know when he's dead?

Should he completely crush the skull to be sure, only stopping when he saw the splatter of brains? Or would Armian, who had killed before, tell him when he could stop? What would it feel like, the death of a man at his hands?

He turned away and was abruptly sick, retching as humiliating waves of nausea overwhelmed him.

"*Dar have mercy,*" he croaked.

"*May the Three have mercy on me,*" the Outlooker whispered, waiting for his uncertain fate.

Tansen handed the yahr back to Armian, ashamed. "*I can't.*"

"*It's all right,*" Armian told him. "*The first time is always the hardest. Today was not the day, that's all.*" He looked down at the Outlooker. "*We're leaving now.*"

The Outlooker nodded, too afraid to speak, watching the hypnotic sway of the yahr as Armian toyed with it.

"You will return to your commanding officer," Armian instructed, "and tell him nothing."

"Nothing," the Outlooker repeated in a choked voice.

Armian put the end of the yahr under the Outlooker's chin and tilted his face up, so that their eyes met. "If anyone follows me to Liron, I will know that you have given me away, and I will return to kill you."

"Yes." The Outlooker licked his lips. "I understand. I will say nothing."

"Tansen." Armian met his eyes. "Let us leave this place."

Only when they were far outside the village did Tansen finally ask, "Why did you let him live?"

"Never destroy a useful tool, son. He will send the Outlookers haring off to Liron in the south while we go north to Shaljir."

"But he said he wouldn't tell them."

"You didn't believe him, did you?" Armian grinned. "By the time his commanding officer demands a complete account of what happened in Gamalan, he will have convinced himself that he acted shrewdly after his three companions died. He will assure himself—and especially others—that he wasn't truly afraid of a couple of barbarians like us, and he will be eager to think he tricked me into revealing our destination—which he will gladly report to his commander. That," he added, "is the way of men everywhere."

"I have never seen a man beg for his life," Tansen said slowly. "It made me—"

"Don't dwell on it now." Armian slapped him on the back. "You'll learn not to let it bother you."

"I will?" He didn't think so. He wasn't sure he wanted to. But perhaps an assassin must. And he . . . "I want to be an assassin," he said suddenly. "There's nothing else left for me now."

"What about the rest of your clan? W—"

"There is no rest." He explained about the bloodfeud with the Sirdari. "There were only a few Gamalani left, and they were all in my village."

"Then I'm even sorrier," Armian said after a long pause. "They died because of me, because I am here."

"So you must understand now," Tansen said, "you must see."

"See what?"

"Why the Valdani fear you so. Why the Outlookers will do anything to stop you."

"You think they know about the Alliance?" Armian asked, frowning. "About the plan the Moorlanders have sent me to discuss with Kiloran?"

"No." Tansen impatiently waved aside things he didn't understand or care about. "They know you're the Firebringer!"

THE SUN BEAT down on Zarien's head as he returned to the water he had found in the night, still trickling fluidly down the rockface, and refilled

Tansen's waterskin. His bruises ached where rocks had struck him during the earthquake. His feet hurt; as the drylanders said, like all the Fires. He was so hungry he felt lightheaded, but he didn't want to leave Tansen alone long enough to find food.

The warrior was even worse off now, stirring fitfully in his fever dreams, lost in the shoreless world of near-death. Whatever he saw there troubled him greatly, for his muttered exhortations were harsh and angry, or else full of sorrow and grief. His skin was hot, and the bleeding wouldn't stop.

Zarien knew he must clean the wound so he could see it more clearly. If it couldn't be cauterized, perhaps it could be stitched. If the thought of pressing a red-hot poker to human flesh had made him queasy, the idea of darning Tansen's skin like cloth positively appalled him. He was no healer. But that was Sharifar's mate lying in that cave, and Zarien was not about to let him die. He would do whatever he had to . . . On the other hand, how could he stitch the wound with no thread or needle?

He returned to the cave with the water. Tansen was murmuring unintelligible words. When he tried to rise, Zarien pushed him back down, surprised by how hard that was when he was obviously so weak and disoriented. Then again, here was no ordinary man.

The sea king.

Dar had helped Zarien, after all. She had thrown Sharifar's mate right into his path. Why, he had practically tripped over Tansen! What else could their meeting mean? With Josarian dead, who but the Firebringer's blood-brother could be a fitting mate for the sea goddess? What drylander but the greatest warrior in Sileria could be accepted by the sea-born as their king?

Zarien poured water over the wound and wiped away fresh blood, as well as a lot of older residue. Tansen recoiled in unconscious protest at first, then fell into a motionless stupor. As daylight flickered through the shallow cave, Zarien studied the wound and felt despair creep through him. He finished washing it, then took the cleanest cloth he could find and pressed it hard against the ravaged, blood-seeping flesh. If pressure couldn't stop the crimson flow, he wondered fearfully, what would he do?

"Please Dar," he prayed to the goddess who held sway here on land, "please help him. He must be the sea king. I cannot go back without him. *Please.*"

He pressed down on the wound, willing the blood to stop flowing. He begged Dar to make it stop bleeding. He prayed to all the gods of the wind and sea to save Tansen. He admonished the warrior to heal.

"Dar," Tansen rasped in his fever dreams.

Zarien glanced at the warrior's lean face, but he still seemed unconscious even as more whispered words poured from his cracked lips: "Dar . . . shield . . . sword . . . fire . . . firebr . . . mercy . . . Father, father . . ."

Heal him, heal him, Zarien begged in silence.

A chilling heat passed through him, a cold fire that made him shiver even as it burned him. He gasped and snatched his hand away from

Tansen's body, startled, a little afraid. An icy mist rose from the wound, a crystalline glow that shimmered in the dappled sunlight creeping into the cave.

Zarien watched unblinking as it slowly faded away, leaving only Tansen's flesh in its wake. With his own breath rasping in his ears, Zarien leaned closer and peered at it in amazement.

The angry, bleeding, life-stealing wound was gone. Only a silvery scar was left in its place.

"Dar be praised," he murmured in awe. "I have found him."

The sea king.

8

THERE IS NO REAL SWORD OUTSIDE THE HEART.
—Kintish Proverb

ARMIAN TOOK CARE *of everything—food, money, clothing, supplies, shelter at night, water by day, finding the way to Shaljir while avoiding the Outlookers, inventing a plausible background for himself and the boy at his side. Everything.*

Tansen thought of little besides his loss, his grief, and the howling guilt which haunted him day and night. If he had returned home sooner, if he had not left home at all . . . His mind knew that Armian was right: He'd had no hand in what the Outlookers had done to his people. Yet he couldn't deny the conviction swamping his heart that it was he, not his entire village, who should have died at Valdani hands.

Armian showed him compassion for his loss, but he himself seemed untroubled by guilt. But Armian was the Firebringer, and his destiny was great. He would free all of Sileria, Tansen realized, so he knew that his life, in the end, counted for more than those of a few villagers.

If Tansen's grandfather or anyone else had given in and led the Outlookers to that cave in the cliffs . . . But they had died rather than tell. That was lirtahar. *That was the honor of the* shallaheen. *That was the terrible, destructive courage of Sileria.*

He and Armian traveled fast, crossing the mountains on foot. They usually only asked the way to Shaljir if Tansen judged someone apt to give them a true answer. The rest of the time, Armian, who was an educated man, relied on the position of the sun and his knowledge of Sileria's geography.

Armian adjusted quickly to life in Sileria's harsh mountains. His shallah *dialect improved daily. His strong physique adapted to the punishing climbs, deadly descents, and long treks over uneven terrain which a* shallah *boy scarcely even noticed. He kept Tansen's mind busy by distracting him with many questions about Sileria's ways and her peoples. He knew much already, but now, he said, he needed to see Sileria through the eyes of someone who lived here.*

However, he was not much interested in discussing Dar, the zanar *prophecies, or the Firebringer, and Tansen's grief made him too apathetic to press the point. Armian was curious, though, about why a man would abandon everything to go live at the airless, wind-swept, snow-capped peak of the volcano—and perhaps one day even throw himself in.*

"The zanareen *come from all walks of life," Tansen explained as they passed through a lush valley of blossoming almond trees. "My brother was one. He felt a calling one day, they say. That can happen even to a man who seems to have everything—a* toren, *a* merchant, *a* wealthy city-dweller. *Most often, though, they are men who've lost too much. Their livestock has all died, or their wives are lost in childbirth, or their fields have dried up and no waterlord will help them, or an assassin seeks them for a bloodvow . . . or their entire clan is killed in a bloodfeud." Tansen paused, then added, "A man without a clan is no one in the mountains. A* shallah *is nothing without his kin."*

Armian gazed at him thoughtfully. "What about bloodpact relations?"

Tansen shrugged. "I have none."

Armian grasped the back of his neck and shook it, a gesture of affection, an attempt to lighten Tan's dark mood. "Don't tell me you're going to run off and become a zanar?*"*

Tansen smiled. "No, that I will not do."

"Good."

"There is no need. The Firebringer has come."

Armian grunted in exasperation, then drenched him with spray from the waterskin. It was the first time Tansen laughed since meeting him.

TANSEN DRIFTED SLOWLY into consciousness, feeling his way out of death's dark domain and back towards the world of the living. He remembered that he was in a cave, and he could smell daylight in the breeze which drifted in through its mouth.

Only in Sileria, the most beautiful of nations, was the scent of day so ripely, pungently different from that of night. The burgeoning blossoms, the ripening fruits, the tender leaves, even the peach-and-amber rocks themselves seemed to soak up the sun and then, by midday, start sweating it back into the air, drenching a man's senses. Afternoon was traditionally a time of rest in Sileria, though the war had changed that for many people. Even at the height of the fighting, though, it was hard to think about killing, hard to seek blood, when Sileria wrapped Tansen in her perfumed embrace and coaxed him to sleep in her scented shadows.

He inhaled deeply, surrendering to the seduction of his native land . . . and realized that his wound didn't hurt.

His eyes snapped open in surprise. Something else occurred to him, too: "I feel better."

The words came out as a croaking whisper. He turned his head. The movement made him a little dizzy, but without the sickening, whirling weakness he'd felt before. He didn't see the waterskin, though. Had the boy gone, after all? He should have left the water, but perhaps he expected to return soon. Tansen tried to remember what had happened after Zarien's startling declaration that, since Josarian was dead, he must be the sea king.

Dar spare me.

The boy had refused to leave his side. Had Tansen stayed awake long enough to tell him how to find the nearest Sanctuary? Or where an alternate path up to the caves of Dalishar was? Had he instructed him what to do and how to remember where this cave was? He didn't think so, but he couldn't remember for sure.

However, Zarien seemed very capable, even if out of his element, so perhaps he could make it to help and back even so. If not, then . . .

I'll have to make it alone.

Perhaps he should start right away, while he was feeling a cautious return of his strength. He rolled to his side and slowly rose to a sitting position. His head swam for a moment, but his vision didn't go black. Was the wound healing on its own? He looked down—and caught his breath in astonishment.

His seeping, open, pain-ridden wound was gone. Only a thick, silver scar was left in its place. A scar! As if it had healed long ago.

One thing he *was* sure of was that he hadn't been lying here for the months it would take for that to happen naturally.

Sorcery?

No one had been here but the boy. How had he done it?

Tansen remembered Zarien wanting to treat the wound and not knowing that it couldn't be cauterized. Perhaps he had more suggestions which Tansen had not stayed conscious long enough to hear. Certainly the sea-born—their women, usually—were reputed to be gifted healers. They had to be, since their boats were often far from help when disaster struck. And hadn't Josarian once told him that his own wife, believing she was barren, had sought help from the sea-born women in the port of Cavasar who were supposed to possess the secrets of fertility?

If the sea-born could do this for a *shir* wound, Tansen thought as he fingered his new scar, he sincerely wished more of them would come inland.

Then again, he acknowledged, Zarien was no ordinary boy. Regardless of what one thought about his tale of being reborn in the depths of the sea at a goddess's will—Tansen merely reserved judgment for the time being—

he bore the most death-defying scars Tansen had ever seen. No one should have lived through the attack evinced by those terrible teethmarks. If Zarien had somehow healed himself after that attack, then he could probably heal a *shir* wound even in his sleep.

Tansen hoped they'd never have cause to find out, but the events now unfolding in Sileria suggested there'd be many, many *shir* wounds before the year was out.

His hand throbbed painfully, and he wondered why Zarien—who had cleaned and wrapped the fresh *shir* wound—hadn't healed it, too. Fortunately, though, it wasn't life-threatening, just damned inconvenient. A Sister's balms would at least make it hurt less so he could wield a sword with that hand while it healed over the course of time.

Knowing he couldn't afford to waste more time, he rose slowly to his feet. When he was sure he could stay on them, he looked around for his tunic. He saw a pile of blood-soaked rags in the corner and realized that was probably what was left of it, as well as of Zarien's. The boy should have burned those, rather than leave them here to attract animals, but he probably wasn't used to thinking about that; the carnivores of the sea only smelled blood in the water, after all, not aboard a boat. It didn't matter now, anyhow, since Tansen was leaving.

He knelt by his satchel, moving carefully, and opened it in search of his spare tunic. It wasn't there.

Damn him, he thought, momentarily forgetting that the boy had saved his life.

He heard footsteps outside the cave. Now ingrained habits ruled his healing body. He reached for the harness lying nearby, scooped it up with his injured hand, and unsheathed a sword with the other hand as he turned to face the cave entrance.

The sudden action left him a little dizzy, so it was just as well that the intruder was only Zarien.

"*Siran?*"

"That's my tunic," was Tansen's irritable reply to the boy's questioning expression. The thin homespun shirt was a little baggy even on Tansen; Zarien was practically swimming in it.

"Mine is ruined." Zarien gave a pointed glance to the bloody rags in the corner. Tansen sheathed his sword.

"Where have you been?" The moment he spoke the words he realized what a stupid question that was. The boy was carrying not only the waterskin, but an unappetizing assortment of wild onions, baby potatoes, and underripe figs.

"I went to get more water, and some food." He paused, then added, "You may have all the onions."

"Thanks, I'm not hungry."

"You should eat," Zarien insisted.

"I'll wait until we reach Dalishar." Whatever food they had up there when he arrived, it would be better than this.

"I thought this *was* Mount Dalishar."

"I meant the sacred caves."

Zarien looked dismayed. "Must we?"

"*I* must. What you do is your own decision, of course, but we can feed and protect you at Dalishar until—"

"I go where you go."

"Good. Let's—"

"But we should rest another night here, and then make for the sea."

"I can't," Tansen replied, "I have to—"

"Sharifar awaits you. The sea-born await you."

"No," he snapped.

He saw the distress in the young face and immediately felt guilty. He sighed and tried to explain. "You've saved my life, and I am very grateful. I'll do whatever I can for you, help you in any way—"

"Then come with me!"

"—that I can, provide you with whatever you need to return to your people—"

"They won't take me back. I can't go back without you!"

"—or to find this . . . this man you seek, but—"

"It's you, I *know* it is."

"—I can't—"

"They have saved you for your destiny." Zarien gestured to the healed *shir* wound.

"—go haring off—" Tansen stopped abruptly and stared at the boy. "Didn't *you* heal me?"

"No." Zarien shook his head. "I only prayed to them. They healed you."

"They?" He didn't like this. "Who?"

Zarien brushed a hand across his own torso, indicating the scars now hidden by the tunic. "Whoever did this for me. Sharifar, or—"

"This is land, not s—"

"—or Dar, or perhaps they worked together." Zarien's tattooed hand moved back and forth, gesturing to them both. "To heal us both. To save us both. So that I would come here and find you, as I did, and bring you back to sea with me, as I must."

He could be a very convincing young man. Nonetheless, Tansen shook his head. "If Dar healed me . . ." That thought alone was incredible, but Dar had spared his life before that he might fulfill his destiny, whatever it was, and perhaps She had done so again. He hoped not. He was angry at Dar and didn't want to owe Her anything now. But: "If Dar healed me, it's so that I can finish Josarian's work."

"What if it was his work to unite the sea-born, as their king?"

Darfire, he was a persistent little brat.

"Then, in the fullness of time, perhaps I will," Tansen offered, trying to end the argument, "but for now, I must make sure the Valdani withdraw from Sileria and that the Society doesn't rule it in their wake. And," he added, when Zarien drew breath to speak again, "I must begin by going to Dalishar to—"

He stopped speaking abruptly and lifted his head, listening, his mountain-born senses tuned to an intrusion.

"Wh—"

Gently but quickly, Tansen put a hand over Zarien's mouth, then whispered, "Someone's out there."

The boy went still and wide-eyed, looking to him for direction.

Since Tansen had heard whoever was out there, they'd probably heard enough to know someone was in here.

"Let them see you," he whispered to Zarien. "Convince them you're alone." He couldn't risk more detailed instructions now. He only hoped Zarien could lie as well as any *shallah* boy. "I'll be right here, in case they don't believe you."

Breathing a little fast, Zarien nodded and moved to the mouth of the cave. Tansen crept along its wall, staying in the shadows near the entrance, both swords drawn as he waited. He felt sweat trickle down his face. His left hand throbbed fiercely, with the kind of pain only a *shir* could inflict. He felt stiff, his mouth was dry, and he was still weak from blood loss.

He could pray to Dar to make the intruders go away, he supposed, but he had a vivid memory of cursing Her as he lay bleeding on the path to Dalishar. No, he and the volcano goddess were not on good terms. So he merely cleared his thoughts and focused on the task at hand.

"Is someone there?" Zarien called out.

Tansen heard nothing, and that paradoxically convinced him that someone was indeed there—someone moving with stealth now that Zarien had evinced awareness of the intrusion.

"Hello?" the boy tried again.

Something distracted Tansen. A soft rattling sound, a strange vibration. He looked down and saw the boy's oar, the *stahra,* lying on the floor of the cave. It was shaking—*shaking?*—with increasing intensity even as Tansen stared at it in astonishment.

He flashed a puzzled look at Zarien, but the boy's back was to him. He glanced at the quivering *stahra* again.

What's going on?

He started to reach for Zarien, worried, but for once he wasn't fast enough. Zarien stuck his head out of the cave. A dark hand snaked around from the side, grabbed the boy's hair, and roughly yanked him the rest of the way out of the cave.

"Assassins!" Zarien's startled exclamation was followed by a harsh grunt of pain. The *stahra* shuddered wildly, nearly tripping Tansen as he stepped past it. Instinct convinced him the thing's agitation meant Zarien was in danger.

Tansen dived out of the cave, a move designed to avoid the kind of trap which had caught Zarien, and rolled to his feet, swords flashing as he—

He stopped abruptly and stared in surprise.

"Well, only one assassin," Zarien admitted. The boy gulped as the assassin's wavy blade kissed his throat, the grip on his hair keeping him on his toes.

"Najdan." Tansen sagged with relief.

"Yes, and you are very lucky," Najdan said, "since a blind beggar could have followed the trail you left."

"I wasn't quite myself at the time."

Najdan regarded the youth in his grasp with interest and added, "However, until I found this boy, I thought there might be assassins here, so I am lucky, too."

Tansen sheathed his swords and said, "Let go of him."

"As you wish."

Najdan released Zarien, who rubbed the painful *shir* burn on his throat as he warily backed away from the assassin. Older than most assassins, since it was not a profession which usually counted longevity among its benefits, Najdan nonetheless looked very impressive. He bore more than a dozen scars, all gotten in combat—except for a couple of burn marks acquired during his first encounter with Mirabar, when he had been her mortal enemy rather than her devoted servant. Najdan's eyes were hard, even when he smiled, and his ways were both violent and unyielding. However, he had condemned himself to a bloodvow from Kiloran in order to save Mirabar's life and to try to save Josarian's, and that ensured he had Tansen's loyalty.

Najdan's eyes narrowed as he studied the boy. "You are sea-born."

"This is Zarien," Tansen said. "He saved my life."

"Don't tell me *he* fought the assassins lying dead o—"

"No, I did, but . . . It's a long story. I'll tell you later. Where is Mir—"

"Tansen!"

He knew that voice as well as he knew the face which now appeared as Mirabar emerged from the scrub, accompanied by Lann.

Najdan scowled with disapproval. "*Sirana,* you were to wait—"

"Dar be praised," she said, "you're alive!"

"I told you he would be." Lann's voice boomed with its usual vigor. He grinned, big and bearded and robust, fully recovered from the severe wounds he had incurred several months ago during Kiloran's first ambush of Josarian. Tansen wondered briefly why he bore a fresh bandage on his head.

Mirabar ran to where Tansen stood, hesitated for a moment, then embraced him. He put his arms around her and closed his eyes. He had held her once or twice before, but only in fear or sorrow. Never like this, relieved, glad to see each other. Her smooth cheek against his bare chest, her hair spilling over his shoulder, tickling his skin . . . That fire-bright hair, almost supernatural in its intensity, was a lava-rich color uniquely her own, like her flame-gold eyes, stirring him. Yet her Dar-blessed beauty had actually repulsed him the first time he ever saw her. And, if he were honest, for a while thereafter.

He had traveled the world, seen many things, learned even more, but he was still prey to the superstitions of his youth. The waterlords so feared the power of people born with Mirabar's unusual coloring—and thereby blessed with great gifts of fire and communion with the Otherworld—that they had, centuries ago, convinced Silerians, particularly the *shallaheen,* that such people were demons, cursed in the womb by Dar, who must be killed on sight. As an adult, he knew better, but the fears and prejudices of a child could lurk deep in even the most worldly of men.

Now Mirabar pulled away, her eyes almost glowing in their fiery intensity as she met his gaze. "I looked into the circle of fire at Dalishar, but you were not there."

"Not dead yet," he said wryly, knowing that she meant she had searched in a Guardian fire for his shade, the shadow of a person which sometimes sojourned in the Otherworld after the body's death.

"All the same, I was afraid . . ."

"I'm all right now," he assured her.

Her hand slid down his side, touching the bare skin which had been an open wound when last they had seen each other, only days ago. She gasped at the sight of the scar. "What happened?"

"We'll discuss it later," he replied.

"Your wound is healed," Najdan said slowly, staring.

"But," Mirabar said, "how could—"

"I'm not sure," Tansen admitted.

"You don't remember?" Najdan asked.

"No."

Tansen glanced at Zarien, who was looking at Mirabar with open-mouthed fascination. Being sea-born, he didn't share the dark superstitions of Tansen's childhood about orange-eyed demons with fiery hair, but it was safe to assume he'd never seen anyone like Mirabar. Once she was willing to take her gaze off Tansen, Mirabar studied the tattooed sea-born boy with interest, too. This deep in the mountains, he was as unique as she was.

"A child is coming," she murmured suddenly, taking a step towards Zarien.

The boy lifted his chin, evidently understanding the words she had spoken in *shallah*. "I am a man among my people." He paused and added reluctantly, "Well, almost."

"Are you?" She scarcely seemed to have heard his words.

"He has certainly shown all the courage of one." Tansen introduced

Zarien to Mira and Lann, speaking in common Silerian for the boy's benefit. He told them briefly about the ambush and explained how Zarien had
found him and brought him here.

Mirabar returned her attention to the healed *shir* wound. "But what
about—"

"Perhaps we shouldn't stay here," Najdan said suddenly.

Tansen was too accustomed to his brusqueness to be surprised. "Are the
bodies where I left them?" he asked.

"The assassins?" Mirabar grimaced. "Yes."

"When I found your trail," Najdan said, "I left the *sirana* behind to burn
the corpses."

"But Lann and I followed Najdan, instead," Mirabar concluded.

"Let's go back there," Tansen said. "I want to get their *shir*."

Mirabar was surprised. "But you never take the *sh*—"

"We'll need them for an idea I have," he said. "And we should burn
those bodies." He didn't want to send Kiloran's assassins to the Otherworld,
if assassins even went there, but custom was custom: Silerians burned their
dead, whether friend or foe. The island nation's native people were revolted
by the Valdani custom of burying the dead, and they avoided the Valdani
graveyards in Sileria, viewing them with profound distaste.

"We should certainly do *something* with those bodies," Zarien agreed
with a grimace.

Tansen could imagine what stumbling across six violently slain men had
been like for the boy.

Mirabar asked Tansen, "What's your idea f—"

"*Sirana*." Uncharacteristically, Najdan interrupted her yet again. "Let us
leave this place."

"Najdan's right," Tansen agreed. "My pace is slow right now. We
should move if we're going to reach the caves by sundown."

He waited as Zarien slipped back into the cave to fetch his *stahra* and
Tansen's satchel. The oar was quiescent now, revealing no signs of its earlier
spine-chilling animation. Tansen knew he had not imagined that bizarre
occurrence, though. The weapon was yet another aspect of this unusual boy
about which he intended to get answers.

Meanwhile, Lann looked at Zarien and laughed. "An oar? You won't
need an oar in the mountains!"

Zarien sighed. "It's a *stahra*."

"A what?"

"His weapon," Tansen said.

"Let's go," Najdan prompted, forestalling further discussion.

"An easy pace," Mirabar warned the others, looking at Tansen with
concern.

"I'll manage," he assured her, concealing that he was tired already.

As they trekked back towards the scene of the ambush, though, Tansen realized that it was Zarien, not he, who would determine their pace. "What's wrong with your feet?" he asked the boy after a while, realizing that they pained him.

Zarien shrugged, embarrassed. "I am not used to the dryland." Then he quickly changed the subject. "*Siran*, we should be thinking about returning to sea where—"

"Zarien," Tansen warned, "not now." He wasn't up to walking *and* arguing. After studying the boy's shoes for a moment, he ventured, "Those aren't yours, are they?"

"I . . . I, uh—" Zarien's sun-bronzed complexion darkened.

"Stole them?" Tansen guessed.

"My bare feet were not used to all these . . . these rocks and pebbles and thorns and—"

"No, I suppose not."

"And I am not used to walking so much."

"Why not?" asked Mirabar. She was directly ahead of Tansen, and turned often to look at both him and the boy with a thoughtful expression. Najdan led the way and Lann brought up the rear.

"He's from a sea-bound clan," Tansen answered so that Zarien, who looked self-conscious, wouldn't have to.

"I've heard about them. People—whole clans—never going ashore," Mirabar said. "That seems so strange."

Zarien bristled. "Have you ever been to sea?"

"No," she admitted.

"Not once in your whole life?"

"No."

"That seems very strange to *me*."

"Generation after generation?" she persisted. "Your parents, their parents, your ancestors . . . No one ever comes ashore?"

Zarien looked uncomfortable and shrugged. "Have your *shallah* parents ever been to sea?"

"I don't know who they were," Mirabar replied.

Zarien's face darkened again. "I'm sorry. I only meant—"

"I know what you meant," Mirabar said without rancor. "I'm used to not knowing."

"Can you . . ." Zarien frowned and asked her, "Can you really get used to that?"

"You can get used to anything," she replied, and Tansen knew she spoke from experience.

Her response seemed to send Zarien into deep thought. Tansen wondered if he was considering all he would now have to get used to if his clan really wouldn't take him back. Tan himself had gone alone into exile at a young age, so he understood some of what the boy must be going through, though he had only a very vague idea of the life Zarien had led until now.

Now that Tansen was somewhat rested and his wound healed, he discovered that the distance he had previously covered with Zarien was not nearly as far as he had thought. They reached the scene of the ambush sooner than he expected, even at this slow pace. The corpses had ripened under Sileria's strong sun and truly stank. Zarien made a sound of disgust and moved upwind.

"Six," Najdan said, gazing at the bodies. "And you were already wounded." He eyed Tansen and paid him a rare compliment. "Speaking as an assassin, I'm glad you're the only *shatai* in Sileria."

"I'm lucky Searlon is in Shaljir," Tansen admitted. "They were good, but had he been among them . . ." He shook his head, knowing he might well have died had Searlon been among them. Searlon was even better at killing than Najdan, and Najdan was among the very best. He shook off the thought and asked, "Do you know any of them?"

"Yes. All but this one. He must have been new." He touched the nearest corpse with the toe of his well-made boot. "That one . . ." He pointed briefly with his chin to the one who had been so hard to kill, the one who had nearly finished Tansen. "He and I were friends." Najdan's voice didn't change and his expression remained hard. After a moment he added, "We are better off with him dead."

"He was a brave man," Tansen said politely. "A strong fighter."

"Yes," Najdan agreed. He turned his back on his former friend and met Tansen's gaze. "He was. You did well."

Tansen knew there was nothing else to say, so he turned to see where Zarien had gone. The boy was sitting on a rock, resting his sore feet and keeping his face turned away from the carnage.

Lann and Najdan began piling up the bodies while Tansen, now feeling the sting of his many smaller wounds and burns, collected the six *shir* which, by virtue of victorious combat with the assassins, were now his and his alone. Although two of the assassins' *jashareen* were too fouled to be of use even after washing, he took the other four from the bodies. Like the *shir,* they would be useful in the plan he was forming.

He put all these things in his satchel and joined Zarien upwind as Mirabar began chanting over the bodies. Najdan's *shir,* never entirely still in her presence, began shuddering wildly in his *jashar.* A moment later, the six *shir* in Tansen's satchel started doing the same, making noise as they rattled against each other.

Zarien jumped to his feet, snatched up his *stahra* as if ready for a fight, and demanded, "What's happening?"

"It's nothing," Tansen told him. "*Shir* do that in response to Guardian magic." The *stahra* was doing nothing, he noticed, in response to Mirabar's gathering power. It must only respond when Zarien was threatened. "Are all *stahra* enchanted?" he asked.

Zarien's expression suggested this was a stupid question. "None of them are."

Could the boy not know? Tansen decided this was a discussion which could wait until later.

Mirabar, having recited the traditional blessings over the bodies of their enemies, spread her hands wide and blew gently onto the bodies of the dead. Her breath turned into a fiery mist which grew into a glowing flame.

Tansen heard Zarien make a stifled sound of astonishment as the flame suddenly expanded to ignite the entire pile of six men into a blazing bonfire which took only seconds to tower well above its creator. Mirabar kept chanting, her voice melodious and slightly husky, spinning through Tansen's senses as she sent his enemies to . . . whatever the ultimate fate of assassins was.

"So . . ." Zarien swallowed, watching the scene with wide-eyed fascination. "So that's Guardian fire magic?"

Tansen replied, "That's only some of it. She has many gifts."

"Do they all?"

"The Guardians all have gifts, some more than others. But she," he said with a touch of pride which he supposed was not really his to feel, "is unique."

"In the way she looks?"

"In her gifts." He paused and added, "And in her looks, as far as I know."

"She would be . . . well, *startling* to come upon unexpectedly in the night," Zarien admitted.

The boy obviously meant it without any of the superstition which had so often characterized people's attitudes in the mountains, including Tansen's own, so he merely said, "Yes."

"And an assassin."

"Yes."

"Your friends are . . . dangerous people," Zarien ventured.

And these are the ones I trust, Tansen reflected wryly, but he only repeated, "Yes."

When she was done with her ritual, Mirabar joined them upwind of the fire. "You have no tunic?" she asked, glancing at Tansen's bare chest.

"No."

"Perhaps Najdan would loan you his."

"I'll be all right until we reach the caves." What few spare personal possessions he owned were kept there.

She looked uncertain. "We agreed to meet Cheylan back here after—"

"Cheylan is here?" He was surprised—and not pleased.

"Yes. He returned this morning from the east. He told us about this." She gestured to the bonfire, indicating the six bodies Tansen had left lying in bloody disarray on the path to Dalishar. "So we came in search of you."

"Where is he?"

"There's a Sanctuary not far from here."

"Sister Velikar's Sanctuary. I know."

"We thought you might have tried to reach it if you were too badly hurt to make it to Dalishar, so Cheylan and three of the men have gone there."

"But Najdan saw my trail—"

"Only after Cheylan had gone," she replied.

"Ah." He said nothing else, but he doubted, after what Najdan had said earlier about the trail he and Zarien had left, that Najdan had failed to notice it immediately. Tansen thought it far more likely that Najdan had simply been eager to get rid of Cheylan, whom he didn't like, for a while. Since Tansen didn't like him, either, he was in sympathy with the ploy. Cheylan was an ally, but no friend. "Why is Cheylan back?"

"I didn't ask. When we realized you had been attacked and were missing, I just . . ." She sighed and looked off into the distance. "I didn't even tell him about Josarian's death."

"But word must be spreading," he said, aware of the flush of pleasure inside him. She had cared so much she'd forgotten about everything else. Unlike Elelar, the woman who had held him in thrall for so long, this one cared. "Every moment that we lose—"

"Did you do it?" she asked suddenly, without looking at him, her voice low.

The warm pleasure inside him died in the chill of reality.

He didn't have to ask what she meant. He had known, ever since leaving Elelar alive that night, that he would have to face this moment. Had Mirabar not feared him dead and been so relieved to see him alive, it would have been the first thing she said to him: *Did you do it?*

"No," he replied. Evasion would only make it worse. "I didn't kill her."

Out of the corner of his eye, he saw Zarien's head swivel suddenly in his direction, the discussion now drawing his attention away from the magical fire which continued to burn so brightly, so silently compared to an earthly fire.

Mirabar didn't move, didn't look at him, but he could sense her tension building, could practically feel the heat of her anger. There was so much to tell her, so many reasons why he couldn't kill Elelar for what she had done. And this particular moment wasn't the right time or place to talk about it. He tried to think of what to say—and waited too long.

"That's it?" she said at last, her voice barely more than a whisper. "That's all you have to say about it?"

"No." Since the time and place would probably never be right, he realized, he ignored Zarien's fascinated stare and said, "I didn't kill her because—"

"I don't care why you didn't do it!"

Zarien jumped as Mirabar leaped to her feet in fury. Even Tansen flinched a little. Lann and Najdan, standing too far away to distinguish Mirabar's words but close enough to hear her tone, whirled to face them.

Lann took a step forward but Najdan stopped him from coming any closer.

Tansen rose to his feet, too. "Mira—"

"She betrayed Josarian, and you let her live!" The hot rage in her voice was matched by the yellow fury flashing from her eyes. "She betrayed us all, and you swore you would kill her. And you didn't!"

"I realized—"

"I know why you didn't do it," she snapped bitterly.

Tears filled her eyes. She clenched her teeth angrily and raised her arm. He saw the blow coming. He watched her arm swing, and he didn't move. He felt her palm connect with his cheek, and he welcomed the flash of pain, the loud crack of flesh against flesh. He welcomed the way his head whipped around with the force of her blow, the way his ears rang. He wanted the hot sting to be worse, to last longer than it would.

He could make no other decision than the one he had made that night in Elelar's shadowed bedchamber, but he wanted Mirabar to punish him for it as he deserved. He had not avenged the betrayal of his bloodbrother. He had not avenged the *torena*'s betrayal of them all. And he had neglected this woman in the throes of his obsession with another.

Now Najdan came closer, though Lann held back.

Hit me again, Tansen thought, because Mirabar was too small and too unaccustomed to violence for the first blow to hurt as he deserved. *Hit me again.*

But she didn't. She merely said, her voice low and trembling with the effort to hold back more tears, "I will never forgive you."

It hurt more than being hit.

"Mirabar . . ." He laid a hand upon her arm.

She jerked away. "Don't *touch* me."

Much more than being hit.

"If you ever touch me again," she ground out, "I will tell Najdan to kill you."

"*Sirana?*" Najdan was at her side now, frowning as he glanced from her to Tansen.

"We're going to Sanctuary," Mirabar told Najdan.

"Wait," Tansen said, trying to fend off this blow, "we have to make plans f—"

"No," she said. "You've chosen your way. Now I choose mine."

"We're in this together," he told her.

"We *were*."

"Mira, let's—"

"I hope they kill you next time."

"*Sirana* . . . ," Najdan said uneasily.

"I never want to see you again," she told Tansen.

She turned and walked away.

That was the blow which nearly drove him to his knees.

9

SPILLED BLOOD CALLS FOR VENGEANCE.

—Silerian Proverb

TORENA ELELAR MAR Odilan yesh Ronall shah Hasnari was exhausted by the time she reached the great city of Shaljir.

Elelar had roused her household in the ruined villa outside Chandar with her screams of rage and fury the night Tansen had slipped inside to awaken her, tell her of Josarian's death, and avenge her betrayal of the Fire-bringer. After Tansen had decided to spare her life—though she had not asked him to and was now almost sorry that he had—she immediately ordered her servants to begin packing while she wrote letters, issued instructions, and set her household on its ears with her sudden decision to travel halfway across Sileria. She had followed Tansen's orders and left at first light that very day. She had pushed herself, the servants who traveled with her, and their mounts to the limits of endurance in order to reach Shaljir as soon as possible. She hadn't even let that terrifying earthquake slow her down, though one of the servants had been injured. She'd left him in Sanctuary the following morning and continued her journey, anxious to reach Shaljir and carry out her duty.

Now that she was here, arriving at sunset, exhausted, depressed, guilt-ridden, and afraid, all she had to do was move mountains.

Oh, Dar, as I have been faithful and true—in my way—I humbly beseech You to help me now, she prayed as she waited at the Lion's Gate for entry into the city.

But the prayers were probably useless, as was the remorse, for she had betrayed Dar's Chosen One. The destroyer goddess forgave no slight, after all, and what Elelar had done was considerably worse than neglecting her devotions or denying offerings to Dar. Her punishment for betraying the Firebringer would surely be swift and terrible.

It was bewildering to remember how pragmatic, how necessary, the decision had seemed at the time. The Valdani demanded Josarian's death in exchange for their final withdrawal from Sileria, for the surrender of Shaljir. Elelar's cohort *Toren* Varian reminded her that the *zanar* prophecies never said *how* the Firebringer would finally drive the foreign invaders out of Sileria; so, Varian suggested, perhaps he was destined to do so as a sacrificial offering rather than as a warrior. Josarian himself knew that the prophecies said nothing of his destiny beyond ridding Sileria of the Valdani; his ultimate future was as uncertain as any man's. And he was locked in a deadly bloodfeud with Kiloran, a wizard so invincible that few doubted he could destroy even the Firebringer. Kiloran wanted Josarian dead, and the Valdani wanted Josarian dead . . . and Elelar had believed that his death was the way to free Sileria.

A hot wave of shame washed over her every time she thought of it. Kiloran had used her. Even worse, she had let him. She had been so obsessed with her lifelong goal, so focused on her hatred of the Valdani, that she had let Kiloran make her his tool in Josarian's destruction, every bit as much as Zimran had been Elelar's tool.

The *shallaheen* had a word for someone like her: *sriliah*. It was the worst thing one Silerian could call another. Worse than liar, thief, cuckold, coward, murderer, or whore: *traitor*. Among Silerians, betrayal was the very worst crime a person could commit. The irony of their culture, the tragedy of their history, was that it was also perhaps their most common crime against one another. And it was always punished with blood vengeance.

Who will punish me?

She knew now that it would never be Tansen. Not because he loved her. She was almost certain he didn't. And even if he ever had, even if he still could, she knew he would never want the woman who had betrayed his blood-brother.

He had still wanted her when he had returned to Sileria after his nine years in exile. She had seen it in his eyes, had felt it in the sharp tension which ran through him like pain when she touched him. She had smelled desire on his skin more than once and had believed he could be hers if she chose. But she always chose duty, and Tansen always chose loyalty to Josarian.

Elelar had betrayed Tansen to Kiloran years ago for murdering Armian; she had sacrificed Tansen's young life to protect the Alliance, and yet he had continued to want her. Nine years in exile, nine years of wandering foreign lands and knowing other women, and yet he was not indifferent to her upon his eventual return to Sileria. If Tansen had not precisely forgiven her, he had at least never forgotten her.

However, while a man of honor might overlook a woman's sins against him, if he desired her enough, he could never ignore what she had done to his brother or his nation. Elelar's betrayal of Josarian had damaged more than Tansen's dreams; it had stained his honor and bloodied his heart. Tansen had introduced his bloodbrother to Elelar, had brought the mountain rebel into association with the Alliance. If not for Tansen, Josarian and Zimran would never even have known Elelar, let alone been vulnerable to her.

This was Sileria, where spilled blood called for vengeance. Josarian had killed Kiloran's only son, Srijan, in vengeance for betrayal. That act had incited Josarian's bloodfeud with Kiloran, had splintered the rebellion, and had made most of the Society into his enemies overnight. Yet even Elelar, who had tried to stop Josarian from killing Srijan, understood why he had done it: Kiloran's offense against him must be avenged, swiftly and ruthlessly, or the *shallaheen* would never again respect and follow Josarian, even though he was the Firebringer.

No matter how worldly Tansen had become, he had been born and raised a *shallah,* so Elelar knew that his honor now depended on avenging his brother. He had killed Zimran and he certainly intended to kill Kiloran, but he hadn't taken his vengeance against her. She knew the *shallah* in him would hereafter see his dishonor every time he looked at her. And no matter how strong he was, he had loved Josarian and was devastated by his death. He would be reminded of this pain every time he looked at her.

Nor could he ever forgive her betrayal of Sileria, even knowing she did it in ignorance. He had loved Armian and had killed him even so, committing an unforgivable sin by murdering a bloodpact relative and offending Dar by slaying the man he thought was the Firebringer, all to save their nation from the Society. Now, by betraying Josarian, Elelar had paved the way for Kiloran to seize power and, a thousand years after Marjan first envisioned it, finally condemn Sileria to the absolute rule of the Society.

Tansen should have killed me.

It was she, after all, who had convinced Zimran, Josarian's beloved cousin, to betray him. Zimran had possessed many of the virtues most prized among the *shallaheen*—reckless courage, wily shrewdness, and blood loyalty—but none of the virtues needed by a rebel in a war-torn land, none of the virtues Josarian needed in his followers. Zimran had lacked vision, imagination, or dreams. He was too selfish to be a leader, too cynical to believe in freedom, too jealous to share Josarian with others, and too shortsighted to understand that his boyhood playmate was no longer the simple mountain peasant he had always known. In the midst of world-changing events and fire-born prophecy, Zimran had stubbornly continued to long for nothing more glorious than a return to the simple life of a *shallah* smuggler in Valdani-occupied Sileria.

Elelar had seduced Zimran, letting him believe he had seduced her. Though Tansen hid his pain and his jealousy behind the schooled mask of a *shatai,* Elelar sensed how he hated her relationship with Zimran. It was his own fault, she'd told herself more than once. Had Tansen been willing, as Zimran ultimately was, to switch his loyalty from Josarian to Elelar, then he could have been her lover; but Tansen always chose loyalty to Josarian.

She used Zimran as a conduit to Josarian when the Firebringer quarreled with the Society and turned his back on the Alliance. And she used him as her weapon against Josarian in the end, convincing Zimran to betray Josarian to the Valdani—Zimran, who had once daily risked his life to protect Josarian from them, back in the days when Josarian had merely been an outlaw on the run, rather than a rebel leader or the Firebringer.

It was happenstance that Elelar's plan failed, that Tansen discovered the plot, executed Zimran, and stopped the Valdani. Nonetheless, the Firebringer was dead, and she doubted Kiloran would have known enough about Josarian's movements to kill him that fateful night had Elelar not betrayed him to Advisor Kaynall.

Tansen was right. She was such a fool. How could she never have guessed, never suspected, that Kiloran was behind the secret treaty all along? Searlon himself, Kiloran's most favored assassin, had escorted Elelar to the meeting between the Alliance and Advisor Kaynall! Yet she had never guessed. Her hatred for the Valdani and all they had done to Sileria had made her blind to the terrible danger of her own allies. What had Josarian himself often said? *I can take care of my enemies, but Dar shield me from my friends.* She should have listened. He was much wiser than she had ever realized.

But she had been so certain that she knew better than an illiterate mountain peasant, even one chosen by Dar. She saw the arrogance that overcame Josarian after his transformation at Darshon and was afraid. She was so accustomed to fearing the power of the Society that she had wanted the Firebringer himself to placate them rather than challenge them. She was so terrified that the Valdani, the only enemies she knew how to hate, would take advantage of the division among the Silerian rebels that she had agreed to eliminate . . .

Dar, how could I have done it? What madness was in my mind?

Her own actions may have destroyed the only dream she had ever lived for: freedom in Sileria.

Whatever Dar did to her now, it couldn't be punishment enough. Elelar, who did not believe in forgiveness, would never seek salvation for helping Kiloran destroy Josarian. But she knew that Tansen had let her live because he counted on her to accomplish something that mattered much more than her life or death: She must ensure that the Valdani honored their treaty and withdrew from Sileria. Then she must help ensure that the Society did not dominate Sileria in their wake. Once that was done, she could at least die with honor. Regardless of her terrible sin against Dar, her life's work would be fulfilled, her dream realized. Her people—Dar's people—would finally be free.

Tansen, who had been the one to teach Josarian to think like a leader, knew this. He had held a sword to Elelar's throat, burning with vengeance, craving her blood, yet he had let her live. With the strength of will that had driven him to kill the bloodfather he loved, he spared the woman who had betrayed his brother—and sent her to Shaljir to do her duty.

Unfortunately, he was right about something else, too: She had to seek Searlon's help. The thought of facing him again galled her. Searlon had used her, duped her, made her not only a traitor, but also a fool; all on behalf of his master, of course. Elelar had made the fatal mistake of underestimating Kiloran and the inexcusable blunder of taking Searlon at face value. Now she trembled with shame and rage when she thought of seeking Searlon's help, but she knew she must.

Freedom from the Valdani was her life's work. Freedom from the Society was Tansen's. She must earn the life he had granted her at swordpoint by helping him defeat them both.

The secret treaty with the Valdani called for the Alliance to bring Josarian's body, or at least indisputable proof of the Firebringer's death, to Advisor Kaynall. Some sort of trophy, Elelar supposed, for the Outlookers to parade through the streets of Valda, the great city which was noisy with horrified gossip about the mountain rebel's crimes against the Valdani in Sileria. However, Josarian's death in the magical jaws of the White Dragon left no evidence whatsoever. Fortunately, an Outlooker prisoner had witnessed the event. Tansen had released him and sent him back to Shaljir to report Josarian's death to Kaynall. Nonetheless, Sileria couldn't rely solely on one scared Outlooker to convince the Imperial Advisor that Josarian was truly dead and the Valdani should honor their treaty.

Tansen had learned from the Outlooker prisoner that Searlon was in Shaljir with Advisor Kaynall. The assassin was supposed to identify Josarian's body when the Outlookers brought it back from the ambush Zimran led his cousin into. Since there was no body now, Tansen had ordered Elelar to get Searlon to help her convince Kaynall that Josarian was indeed dead and the secret treaty must now be honored. The rebels had one thing left in common with the Society, after all: They all still wanted the Valdani to surrender and withdraw from Sileria.

Elelar would do whatever she had to. Once again, she chose duty—and did not shrink from its dictates.

"*Torena.*"

Derlen, a member of her household, interrupted her thoughts.

"Yes?" she replied.

"We are next at the gate, *torena.*"

She looked around in the golden glow of early evening and realized this was his polite way of suggesting she urge her mount forward. She did so, then ensured that the woven cords of her headdress modestly concealed her face from the Outlookers at the gate. They would not be able to interpret the way its knotted, braided strands and shiny aquamarine beads identified her name, family, and rank, but even Outlookers knew that such an elaborate headdress signified she was a *torena*. The headdress she wore today was relatively new, having been recently made by her personal maid, Faradar, to replace the one Elelar had lost here, at the Lion's Gate, when she'd been arrested months ago for spying.

Inside the gatehouse, Imperial Advisor Borell had raped her while the guards outside listened to her painful humiliation. It was here that her servants had died, except for Faradar, who had managed to escape and go into the mountains to alert the rebels. It was here that Elelar had been placed in chains and hauled off to prison to await execution.

It was not a memory she cared to dwell on. Her stomach churned now as she dismounted and identified herself to the Outlookers manning the Lion's Gate. She saw by their expressions that they had heard her name before. Well, her arrest hadn't exactly been secret. And after Tansen and Zimran had succeeded in their insanely dangerous rescue of her and she had escaped the city, the Valdani had hunted her far and wide.

Now, as two Outlookers unsheathed their swords and ordered her to surrender, she realized that news of her pardon had not been nearly as widespread as news of her arrest and her escape. However, since her pardon was a minor addition she had made to the Alliance's entirely secret treaty with Kaynall, this was hardly surprising. Maintaining her dignity at the point of the Outlookers' short Valdani swords, Elelar ordered Derlen to present her pardon, an official document written in Valdan and signed by Imperial Advisor Kaynall himself.

After one of the guards read it aloud, Derlen said in his punctilious way, "You will now sheathe your swords and treat the *torena* with the respect which is her due."

It was a fairly impetuous comment for a Silerian to make. Although some fighting continued throughout Sileria, the Valdani had essentially withdrawn all the way back to Shaljir. Most of the country was already under rebel control. Outlookers were busily surrendering their remaining outposts throughout rural Sileria and fleeing to the dubious safety of Shaljir. This was their final stronghold, the site of their last stand in the island nation they had conquered two hundred years ago. They were awaiting Josarian's siege of the city, mentally braced for the ultimate battle in this bloody war, and they were clearly not in a humor to tolerate *anything* from their enemies.

The city walls were gruesomely decorated with the heads of slain rebels. Dispossessed Silerians were leaving Shaljir in a steady stream. Most Silerians trying to enter the city had been turned away from this gate while Elelar had been awaiting her turn. Anyone who made it past the initial examination, as Elelar now did, was required to submit to a lengthy search. Elelar had anticipated that her baggage and her male servants would be searched, but she was appalled to discover that she and her maid, Faradar, must now submit to the pawing hands of two Outlookers if they wanted to reach their destination inside the city walls.

"I am a *torena* of the Hasnari clan," she snapped with regal anger, "wife of a Valdan, and I have already shown you my imperial pardon. How dare—"

"Body search or back to the mountains," a tall Outlooker interrupted with open rudeness. "The choice is yours, *torena*." He made her title sound like an insult.

Some more Silerians were being turned away from the gate. Elelar suspected it was only her status as a Valdan's wife—a situation made clear in her written pardon—that had let her get this far.

"My husband, *Toren* Ronall, will hear about this," she bluffed, still hoping to avoid the indignity of a search. Silerian women, even a Silerian woman with morals as flexible as Elelar's, had always been in service of the Alliance, and did not submit to the touch of strangers.

"He will doubtless understand that we're doing this for his safety," the Outlooker replied, moving towards her with purpose. "No weapons enter Shaljir except those which will be used in defense of the Empire."

"Oh, for the love of Dar." She had to get into the city, and there was no other way. She ordered Derlen and her other two male servants to cooperate, and she kept Faradar close to her as they submitted to the disgusting intrusion of the Outlookers' search. It was humiliating, particularly when the tall one felt between her legs without any warning or apology. She had to grind her teeth together to control her fury. However, she knew that Faradar had smuggled Tansen's swords into Shaljir by strapping them to her inner thighs, when he had come here to rescue her, so she realized the Outlookers weren't doing this for pleasure. They had simply stopped being careless. Besides, this man gave the impression of being bored beyond measure as his hands roamed freely over the two well-dressed women before him. Elelar supposed it was a small blessing that he had evidently done this so often that any prurience had by now faded into indifference.

As for telling Ronall . . . Actually, Elelar sincerely hoped her half-caste husband had already fled Shaljir for the mainland. She had married that whoring drunkard, born of a Valdani father and a Silerian mother, strictly out of duty. She had taken advantage of his wealth and his Valdani connections to serve the Alliance. It was through Ronall, in fact, that she had met Borell, the former Imperial Advisor in Sileria. No matter how distasteful Elelar found Borell's bed, becoming his mistress had given her access to information which helped Josarian drive the Valdani out of the mountains. Soon after Elelar's arrest, Borell committed suicide when he realized he couldn't avoid the public disgrace earned by his careless passion for a Silerian woman who had repeatedly betrayed his trust to help Josarian's rebellion.

Ronall had, in his ineffectual way, tried to get Elelar out of prison by convincing his Valdani father to petition the Imperial Council on her behalf. When Ronall visited her once in prison, Elelar discovered, with mingled confusion and exasperation, that he even loved her in his strange and self-pitying way. The Valdani took Ronall hostage after Elelar's escape, but they eventually released him. Elelar didn't care, either way. What happened to Ronall was no longer any concern of hers. With her true loyalties exposed and with freedom so close she could smell it, the reasons for which she had married Ronall no longer applied. He was a Valdan and should go back to Valda. She hoped he already had. If not, if he was still in Shaljir, she would make sure he left immediately. It shouldn't be hard, after all, to convince a coward like Ronall to flee Shaljir before it came under Silerian control.

Which it must. No matter what I have to do.

When the Outlookers were finally done with their lengthy search, Elelar was allowed to mount her horse and proceed through the Lion's Gate into the exotic city of Shaljir.

Here, in Sileria's ancient capital, the island nation wore her long and tumultuous history like the jewels of an aging courtesan. Thirty-seven sky-reaching marble spires still rose gracefully above the city, though there had reputedly been three hundred of them during the reign of Daurion, the last Yahrdan of Sileria. The tall, round towers of the Moorlanders, who built thick walls around the city they had conquered after Daurion's death, still guarded Shaljir from enemies; and the enormous stone dragons and horned creatures which decorated these towers still protected Shaljir from the demons whom those hairy barbarians had feared more than they feared any mortal.

The complex and sophisticated culture of the Kints, who had taken Sileria from the Moorlanders, had gifted Shaljir with hundreds of red-domed stone buildings which had lasted even longer than Kintish rule in Sileria. The Kints had made Shaljir a city of fountains and flowing water, of bathhouses and floating gardens.

The Society, of course, had changed much of that, gaining strength and power as the centuries passed, and making all of Sileria pay heavy tribute for the blessings of water. Even the Valdani, whose Emperor had waged relentless war against the Society for the past forty years, gave the waterlords what they wanted in order to ensure the flow of water into the conquered cities of Sileria.

And even the Valdani, Elelar admitted grudgingly, had contributed to the beauty of Shaljir. Their elaborate public palaces, ornate villas, and fine homes were impressive, if sometimes vulgarly ostentatious. Their broad boulevards and massive city-squares gave Shaljir an aura of grandeur which belied its humble status as a conquered city.

Some of Elelar's tension faded in her pleasure at returning home. She loved this city and had been away for too long, exiled in the mountains while her enemies continued to strategize an increasingly desperate war from Shaljir's Santorell Palace, the seat of imperial power in Sileria.

People from all the nations of Sirkara, the watery heart of the world, usually filled the crowded streets of the city. Men and women from all walks of life normally bustled and jostled for their place in the throng. But all that had changed since Elelar was last in Shaljir. If Advisor Kaynall had received news of Josarian's death, he had evidently not yet announced it to the city. Shaljir was still awaiting the rebels' planned siege—the long, costly, bloody battle which the Alliance's betrayal of the Firebringer was supposed to make unnecessary. Josarian's death was meant to secure surrender and peace, to spare the Silerian rebels what promised to be the worst fight of the war. Shaljir had been conquered too many times to be thought impregnable, but it would be very costly for the rebels to take the city by force.

Houses, palaces, and shops were now boarded up and abandoned. Foreigners were conspicuously absent, though Elelar supposed that might be due to Valdania's two-front war on the mainland as much as to the battle expected in Shaljir. The colorful Kintish merchants and free Moorlander traders who were usually so abundant in Shaljir might have deemed it prudent to depart the Valdani-ruled city while their own nations were locked in an increasingly deadly struggle with the Empire. It was the two-front war on the mainland, of course, which had created the opportunity Sileria had needed to make its bid for freedom. The Valdani had never expected it, and they couldn't rally the men, money, and supplies needed to suppress the Silerian rebellion before Josarian had driven them all the way back to Shaljir. But if they could hold onto the capital for a year, perhaps even just half a year, who knew which way the wars on the mainland would go? If the Kintish Kingdoms or the last free tribes of the Moorlands surrendered, the rebels in Sileria could never withstand the might which the Valdani could then bring down upon them with the mainland armies they would then be able to spare.

Whether through the secret treaty or—Dar forbid—the expected siege, Sileria must take Shaljir *now*. Delay could well mean disaster, an end to the rebellion, the death of all their dreams, and a brutal Valdani reconquest of Elelar's homeland.

"I feel almost as if we are strangers here," Elelar heard Faradar murmur to Derlen. "Everything has changed so much since we were last in the city."

Now there were no *shallaheen*, no sea-born, no Society assassins, no *zanareen*, and even very few lowlanders to be seen in Shaljir. Any faction known to support Josarian couldn't safely enter the last Valdani-ruled domain in Sileria.

There were Valdani everywhere, however, and many, many Outlookers. Even as darkness descended, Elelar saw long lines outside the few shops which were still doing business; people were evidently trying to hoard what food they could still find. So much water had been stored that Elelar even saw barrels on roofs and in courtyards. They thought Josarian would convince Kiloran to turn the Idalar River back on itself and starve the city of water. Or that, failing that, he could convince his ally and Kiloran's notorious enemy, Baran, to find a way to do it.

Thinking of this brought a sick lump of dread back into Elelar's belly. What would Kiloran do now? Whose side would Baran take in the coming struggle? How would the *shallaheen* respond to the news of Josarian's death? And what would Advisor Kaynall do?

It was with relief that she found her own house looking relatively normal under the encroaching night sky. Although Ronall was Valdani, they lived in a Silerian section of the city—because they lived in Elelar's house, the palatial residence she had inherited from her grandfather, Gaborian, who had founded the Alliance. Along with Elelar's parents, who had died when she was young, Gaborian had taught her to devote her life to the Alliance. She loved this house, as she had loved her grandfather. She had guarded its many secrets, as he had. Since her arrest, however, only one of its secrets remained: the mystical Beyah-Olvari who lived in the ancient tunnels running beneath the cellars.

"*Torena,*" Derlen said, gaining her attention again. "I will go in first and ensure that you are properly received."

She thought that was a little absurd, given the circumstances. She been in prison since last inhabiting this house, had spent most of the rainy season in a cave on Mount Niran, and lately had been living in a drafty, ruined villa outside of Chandar—and openly sharing her bed with Zimran, a *shallah* rebel. She knew that her house here had been sacked by the Outlookers when she was arrested, and she didn't even know if any servants had been inside since then. It seemed doubtful, since no torches blazed outside the massive doors to herald the night. So Derlen's concern for her being received with the dignity due a *torena* almost made her laugh.

However, she nodded her head graciously and allowed him to do as he thought best, watching him as he entered the house.

Derlen was a Guardian, though he did not, of course, wear his insignia here in Shaljir. Guardians had been outlawed by the Valdani centuries before the rebellion, and they were now known to have been among Josarian's earliest supporters. Derlen was a fussy, slightly pompous widower whose rather irritating young son (left safely behind in Chandar for now) probably accounted for the early graying of his short hair. Born to a family of wealthy city-dwelling merchants from Shaljir, he had left the mountains to become part of Elelar's household during the rebellion, pleased to return to the city and act as a link between the Alliance and the Guardians. After escaping Shaljir when Elelar was arrested, he had, like most of her other servants, eventually rejoined her when she settled temporarily near Chandar. They had never actually discussed it, but now he seemed to be a permanent part of her household. He still carried messages between the Alliance and the Guardians, but he was increasingly devoted to ministering to her household's spiritual needs. Although more than a little lapsed in her religious observances, Elelar accepted his presence as fitting. It had once been the custom for any *toren*'s household to have at least one Guardian in residence. It should, she decided, become the custom again.

Whatever she was expecting next, it certainly wasn't that Derlen would come flying backwards out of the imposing front door of her house and roll painfully down the broad stone steps to land in a heap before her startled mount.

"Derlen!"

Elelar slid off her nervously prancing horse and bent over the Guardian's prone, panting body. The woven cords of her headdress swung across her eyes, obscuring her view of his face. She impatiently ripped off the headdress and tossed it aside.

"Derlen," she repeated, but got no answer. He lay stunned, possibly unconscious.

"*Torena?*" Faradar dismounted and knelt beside her.

"Someone's hit him," Elelar noted. His gushing nose had already dirtied her silk tunic with blood.

"Come away, *torena,*" one of her male servants urged. "We have no weapons to defend you."

It was a good point. But when she glanced up, she saw no attack issuing from the vast, dark doorway of her house. "Derlen?" She shook him. "What happened?"

He mumbled incoherently. Then his eyes opened. He put a hand to his face, then snatched it away and scowled when he saw the blood on his fingers. "Dar *curse* that stinking drunk, that whoring, half-witted . . ." His voice trailed off awkwardly as his rolling eyes met Elelar's.

"Yes?" she prodded.

"I beg your pardon, *torena.*"

"Oh, no," she sighed, already guessing the truth.

"*Toren* Ronall," the Guardian informed her with strained courtesy, "is in residence."

10

HONOR MY HOME, EAT AT MY TABLE, SLEEP BENEATH MY ROOF.
—Traditional Silerian Welcome

THE CLIMB TO Dalishar might have made Zarien weep with the pain it caused his feet had he not been so preoccupied with curiosity about the strange scene between Tansen and Mirabar.

The flame-haired Guardian had abandoned them in a blaze of rage, followed by the assassin—whose company Zarien couldn't honestly say he missed. Then the big, bearded *shallah,* Lann, had talked a great deal, though he'd only said one thing that mattered: They could leave immediately for the sacred caves, since the funeral pyre burned with Mirabar's disciplined magic and wouldn't set the hillside on fire even if a stray breeze came along.

It was quickly obvious to Zarien that although Lann was discomfited by the fight between Tansen and Mirabar, he had been too far away to hear their angry exchange of words and had no idea what it was about. Tansen, after a few absentminded attempts to distract Zarien's obvious train of thought, had simply ordered him to stop asking questions and to concentrate on keeping up. Though Zarien would never say so aloud, it was good advice; even a weakened *shallah* could make that punishing climb with more speed than a footsore sea-born lad. By the time they finally reached the caves after dark, Zarien scarcely even noticed the woodless fires, the strange paintings (made by the Beyah-something-or-other), the staring *shallaheen,* or anything else. He collapsed in a breathless, pained heap while Tansen was welcomed with obvious relief by a lot of heavily armed rebels.

Zarien was sitting at the edge of the clearing, resting his unhappy feet, when Tansen finally came to his side. "Are you all right?"

"I think I was in more pain when the dragonfish killed me," Zarien said, "but I'm not sure."

"I've spoken to Rahilar—"

"Who?"

"The Sister staying up here right now," Tansen clarified. "She's going to tend your feet."

"What's she going to do?" Zarien asked suspiciously.

He saw that slight tightening at the corner of Tansen's mouth, which he was starting to recognize as a smile chased away before it could offend. "You can trust her. She's a Sister." Tansen sat beside him and added, "But first, we'll eat. You must be hungry."

"I have been hungry since the last time I ate my mother's cooking," he grumbled irritably.

"And tired," Tansen observed.

"Not *that* tired," he said significantly.

"We'll talk tomorrow."

"I would rather talk now."

"I'm sure you would. But I've decided we'll talk tomorrow," was the inflexible reply, "so that's the way it will be."

Zarien was annoyed enough to blurt, "No wonder she hates you."

Tansen glanced at him. "Mirabar doesn't hate me. She's just very angry."

"On that woman," Zarien observed, "anger looks a lot like hate." When Tansen's only response was a sigh, he probed, "Who were you supposed to kill?"

"Didn't I just say we'll talk tomorrow?"

"Whoever it is—did she really betray Josarian? Is that why he's dead?"

"If I could say 'we'll talk tomorrow' in sea-born dialect, *then* would you—"

"It seems very strange that a *shallah,* of all things, wouldn't avenge a—"

"Zarien."

He heard the warning note this time, something else he was learning to recognize in Tansen, and decided it might be prudent to wait until tomorrow, after all.

A scarred, one-eyed *shallah* wearing a Valdani swordbelt and sword brought them a basket filled with food. Zarien's stomach rumbled, but then he smelled something repulsive, and he recoiled with an exclamation of disgust.

"What's wrong?" Tansen asked.

"Ugh. *That.*" He pointed to the offending item.

"The venison?"

"The cooked flesh."

"Cooked flesh?" Tansen regarded the grease-gleaming blood-dark pieces of animal flesh for a moment and admitted, "I suppose I wouldn't be very enthused, either, if I thought of it that way."

"How do you think of it?" Zarien asked without real interest.

"It's meat."

"Whatever."

"It's good."

"It's revolting."

"Have you tried any?"

"No, and I don't intend to."

"A boy your age should—"

"Should stick to food that won't make him gag."

Tansen sighed again. "Have it your way. But you won't get much fish up here."

"Surely there are fish in the sweetwater?" He hadn't had time to investigate, but it seemed an obvious conclusion.

"You mean in lakes and rivers?"

Zarien nodded.

"Yes, but . . ." Tansen shrugged.

"You don't fish?"

"Poaching from waterlords has never seemed wise."

"They even own the water here?"

"Not here at Dalishar," Tansen said, "but there are no fish in the water up here."

"But do the waterlords control the water further down the mountain?"

"I don't think so—Darfire, I hope not—but it's all gotten very confusing since the rebellion started. Everyone's territory has changed, and some waterlords have been killed by the Valdani. Some of the water the Society controlled may even be free now. But," he added, "I don't want you fishing anywhere without asking me first."

"Yes, *siran*."

"My name is Tansen."

"I know your name," he replied, surprised.

"I mean, you can use my name."

"Call you Tansen?" he asked doubtfully.

"My friends do."

"But they don't know—"

"And let's not tell them."

"But I must take—"

"We'll talk about it tomorrow," Tansen repeated wearily. "Now eat something."

Zarien peered suspiciously into the basket. "What is that?"

"Those are roasted vegetables."

"I've never seen them before."

"They're wild mountain beets. I don't suppose they'd be sold in the floating markets."

"And that?"

"Goat cheese."

"And that?"

"Just taste it."

"The flesh is touching it."

"If I take the flesh out of the basket, will you stop complaining and just eat?"

"I am not complaining. I'm just asking. Would you put strange things into your mouth?"

"If I'd been living on wild onions, raw potatoes, and underripe figs since leaving home, I'd eat anything a hospitable person put in front of me."

Zarien realized he'd been rude and felt chastened. "I'm sorry, *sira*—Tansen." While he might not be a Lascari by birth anymore, he still bore the tattoos of one and would not shame them before the landfolk by behaving badly. "Everything has been so strange ever since I fell overboard and died and then came ashore that I—"

"Yes, I can only imagine. I'm . . ." Tansen made a funny, stifled sound and said, "I'm sorry, too. I was impatient. I, uh, I haven't been at my best since we met."

"Perhaps . . ." Zarien stared at the legendary warrior and now saw the immense sorrow and fatigue in that lean face. The dancing light of the woodless fire lent a haunted look to Tansen's dark eyes. His filthy long hair made him look savage, and his many minor injuries showed starkly against his blood-drained skin. Even the sea king could not spring back quickly from near-death, Zarien acknowledged, and Mirabar's angry words had wounded him, too. "Perhaps you are right," he said at last, "perhaps tomorrow will be better for talking."

After all, Zarien was not at his best right now, either. He was even, he privately admitted, a bit cranky tonight. It had been a long, hard day preceded by too many days of fear and confusion.

"You're a good lad." The compliment was casual, but Zarien heard its sincerity and felt his stature grow. Tansen returned his attention to the food. "I'll take the, uh, cooked flesh out of the basket." He took one of the leaves lining the basket and starting putting the chunks of meat on it.

A woman approached them with a bowl of some steaming liquid and said to Tansen, "You shouldn't eat that. Not tonight. I've made this for you." She wore a long, plain gown of the Sisterhood rather than the draped tunic and pantaloons typical of a *shallah* woman. This was, Zarien realized, the Sister whom Tansen had mentioned.

"What is this, Rahilar?" Tansen asked as she handed him the bowl.

"Blood broth."

Zarien rose quickly. "I'll think I'll sit upwind, if you don't mind."

Sister Rahilar frowned. "It doesn't smell bad."

"Humor him," Tansen advised. He regarded the bowl's contents with something less than favor. "Must I?"

"You must," she replied. "And often for the next few days."

"I won't be here for a few days."

"But you—"

"I'll drink it tonight and tomorrow." He gazed down into the bowl again and amended, "Well, tonight, anyhow."

"You've lost too much bl—"

"Time is what I've lost," Tansen said.

"You can't—"

"Rahilar."

Zarien noted with satisfaction that Tansen's warning tone worked on the Sister, too.

She pursed her lips for a moment, then said, "When you're both done eating, I will tend to your wounds. Then you may both feel free to go get yourselves killed." She turned and stalked away, her posture rigid with indignation.

Zarien watched Tansen pick up a piece bread to dunk in the blood broth, then asked, "Do *any* women like you?"

Tansen threw the chunk of bread at him. It was the first time Zarien laughed since meeting him.

"I CAN'T EAT," Mirabar said and pushed herself away from the crude wooden table inside Sister Velikar's humble Sanctuary.

The Sister, who was as old as the mountains and notoriously ill-tempered, ignored her and kept on devouring the lamb-and-fig stew she was sharing, as befitted the hospitality of the Sisterhood, with her unexpected guests: Cheylan, Najdan, Mirabar, and the three *shallaheen* who had come here with Cheylan earlier today in search of Tansen. That was a lot of people to feed unexpectedly, but the rebels at Dalishar often hunted fresh meat for the Sister and gave her supplies seized from the Valdani, so her larder was usually well stocked.

Cheylan and the *shallaheen* had met up with Mirabar and Najdan, who advised them the *shatai* had been found, and they had decided not to return to the sacred caves until morning. No one liked Velikar, but they all knew she was a reasonably good cook, in addition to being a gifted healer.

Mirabar felt Najdan's brooding eyes upon her and was aware of his disapproval. It made the raging fury inside her even harder to bear, but at least snapping at him gave her some relief: "What are *you* staring at?"

He ignored her and said courteously to the Sister, "I, however, have an excellent appetite. May I trouble you for some more?"

"Trouble yourself," Velikar said, jerking her head in the direction of the fat, black pot hanging above the glowing embers on the stone hearth in the corner.

Cheylan remained silent, but his glowing golden gaze rested often on Mirabar as he toyed with his food. Since the stone abode was so small, the three *shallah* rebels had chosen to eat outside.

Had their hostess been anyone other than Sister Velikar, Mirabar would have apologized for her rudeness. Even she, less schooled than most in matters of etiquette, knew what an insult it was to push away a full plate after taking scarcely a bite. However, if Velikar was less than charming, one of the distinct advantages of her company was that she didn't care how anyone behaved as long as they didn't pester her.

If anyone *was* so foolish as to pester her, she—in defiance of all teachings of the Sisterhood—usually drove them away with a *yahr,* which she could swing as well as half the men in Sileria.

Predictably, Josarian was the only person she had ever seemed to be fond of; it was a rare person who hadn't liked Josarian. Mirabar had not been pleased to announce his death to Velikar upon arriving here. The old Sister had asked no questions. She merely burned an offering to Dar, in mourning, and grumbled nastily at anyone who tried to speak to her thereafter. Filling her belly at dinner didn't noticeably improve her mood, either.

Cheylan, however, undoubtedly had plenty of questions, and Mirabar could sense his tension as he waited for this awkward meal to end so he could speak privately with her.

Angered by Najdan's coldly composed expression and exasperated with Velikar's presence, Mirabar suddenly blurted, "I need air." She whirled around and left the Sister's hut without a backward glance, escaping outside, past the three *shallaheen* finishing their meal, and into the head-clearing mountain air of the twin-moon night. Mindful of the dangers beyond Sanctuary, though, she was careful to stay on Velikar's grounds.

He didn't kill her, he couldn't kill her, he let her get away with it.

Her head pounded in time with her heart, in time with the bitter refrain which filled her thoughts: *He let her live, he let her live, he let her live.*

Tansen had killed everyone who had ever threatened Josarian, who had stood in his way or gone against him. He had been Josarian's sword, as Mirabar had been his shield. Tansen could be ruthless when he needed to be; no one knew that better than Mirabar, who had communed with Armian, who now sojourned in the Otherworld.

But Tansen had spared Elelar, the lying, traitorous whore who had helped destroy the Firebringer.

And I will hate him forever for this.

It was impossible to understand, to accept, to tolerate his obsession with Elelar. The *torena* had betrayed him to Kiloran for killing Armian. She had taken many other men to her bed, ignoring his passion for her. After her arrest and near-death in Shaljir, she had chosen Zimran, not Tansen, as her lover; she had even flaunted this liaison before Tansen's brooding eyes. She had negotiated a secret treaty with the Valdani and used Tansen's weakness—as he lay helpless for many days after Commander Koroll stabbed him with a *shir*—to have Josarian ambushed while he was unprotected by his bloodbrother.

Tansen's honor demanded vengeance for what Elelar had done to him, to Josarian, and to Sileria.

Yet he spared her.

Mirabar knew why. She had seen the veiled desire in his dark eyes whenever the *torena* was in their presence. She had seen how he secretly watched Elelar even when his attention seemed wholly fixed on something else. She'd noticed the tension in his body when Elelar came close, the carefully neutral way he spoke of her, the hot urgency which escaped his control when he learned she'd been arrested in Shaljir, the reckless obsession which drove him to risk everything to rescue her from prison, the sudden shift of his attention whenever she arrived, his loss of focus after her departures . . .

Mirabar had seen all of this in the *shatai* and knew there was no other woman in the three corners of the world whom he would forgive the things he forgave Elelar for, no other woman who could paralyze and befuddle him as did the *torena*.

There was also no other woman who could make him forget Elelar.

It doesn't matter now.

There was also no other woman as skilled as Elelar at taking advantage of Tansen's weakness, his private hunger, his ungovernable thirst for what she would not give.

How had Elelar talked Tansen out of killing her? Had she even needed to? Or had he simply seen her and lost all sense of purpose, all desire to spill her blood?

Pain pierced Mirabar's heart. She sank to her knees.

Why? Why? Why her?

She knew what she really meant, and she was ashamed of herself: *Why not me?*

She remembered how Tansen had recoiled upon first seeing her, when she tumbled in a ball of fire through the icy waters of Kandahar into Kiloran's strange water-walled palace of air. Driven by visions and prophecy, she had gone there in search of the *shatai,* to save him from the waterlord, to help him find his destiny, to bring enemies together in the visionary flame of the Beckoner.

Tansen had seen her lava-bright hair and her flame-rich eyes, and he had recoiled like a *shallah* boy hunted by demons in his darkest nightmares. She had come to save him, and he had shielded Elelar from her—Elelar, who had betrayed him before and who would do so again.

Why her?

Mirabar still protected his secret, the murder of Armian, whereas Elelar had cost him his youth by going straight to Kiloran with the story.

When he lay near death after being wounded by a *shir,* Mirabar had protected and tended him. Elelar had seen his weakness and used it to prey upon Josarian.

Why? Why her?

Mirabar thought of the vow she had made in the dark last night. Could she really kill Elelar? She had committed acts of violence since becoming the Beckoner's conduit and Josarian's shield, but she had never killed anyone. Of course, she didn't necessarily need to. When Najdan got over his glowering disapproval, he would kill Elelar for her if she asked him; but she didn't think she would.

Must it be done, Najdan had asked, *or must he do it?*

The assassin, once an enemy who had tried to kill her, now knew her so terribly well. Elelar had to die, but Mirabar wanted Tansen to be her executioner. It was Tansen's place, his duty, to avenge Josarian and to protect Sileria. It was also the only thing which would heal this raging wound inside Mirabar.

The night stirred with a sense of hot and cold, something which touched Mirabar's instincts more than her senses. She knew it meant Cheylan was coming, for she could always feel his presence even before she heard his footsteps. He was the only Guardian whose approach affected her this way.

"Do you feel it, too?" she whispered, knowing without looking that he was now close enough to hear her.

"Yes." He came closer.

"That . . . power."

"Mmmm." The heat of his body reached out to her as he hovered just behind her and lowered his head to scent her hair. "Yes."

"Have you ever felt it with any other Guardian?" She had never seen another person like him, but she knew he had seen one like her, a child in eastern Sileria, so she wondered.

"No," he whispered, taking her hand and raising it to his lips. "Have you?"

"I've felt this way near very powerful waterlords," she admitted. "Kiloran, Baran . . . but never with another Guardian. Only you."

"Then perhaps it's really this," he murmured a moment before turning her in his arms to kiss her.

She initially welcomed the hot promise of that embrace, longing for Cheylan to banish her sorrow and anger, her hurt and bitter yearning. But the more she sought oblivion in his kiss, the more she found it eluded her.

"Mirabar?" He sounded puzzled.

She pushed him gently away. "I'm sorry."

His eyes glowed in the moonlit night as he studied her. "There's more to Josarian's death than you've told me, isn't there? More than just a sudden attack by Kiloran's White Dragon?"

"Much more," she admitted.

"Tell me."

She saw him open his palm and start to blow glowing flame into it. "No, don't start a fire," she cautioned. "Not out here." Even being outside under the twin moons wasn't smart, she knew, but she couldn't face returning to the stone hut. "There may be assassins just beyond Sanctuary grounds who'll see us if we—"

"Yes, of course. After that ambush on Tansen, I should know better." He paused and added, "Why is Najdan with you? Didn't he return to Kiloran after Josarian killed Kiloran's son?"

"Yes, but . . ." Mirabar realized there was a great need to tell him. So she began relating the bare facts of recent events, speaking until she concluded wearily, "So Tansen and I argued, and I came here." She wondered what Cheylan's steady silence signified.

The answer came when he said succinctly, "He has betrayed you."

Perversely, though she herself thought so, it sounded unreasonable when she heard it from someone else. "She's his weakness." The knowledge was bitter.

"We cannot afford a leader with weakness."

She shrugged stiffly. "Surely every leader has *some* weakness." Agreeing with Cheylan right now seemed like it might lead her down a path she wasn't prepared to tread yet.

After an uncomfortable pause, Cheylan said, "Tell me more about this child you're supposed to shield."

"A child of fire, a child of water," she murmured, "a child of sorrow."

"What does that mean?"

"I don't know."

"A child of fire, a child of water, a child of sorrow," he repeated. "Interesting."

"Vague," she mumbled dispiritedly.

"But a *child*?"

"I think so, but . . ." She shrugged. The unfolding of her visions had repeatedly confounded all her expectations, so she knew better than to deny or insist upon any possibility.

"How could a child lead us?" Cheylan persisted. "Become the new Yahrdan amidst rebellion and bloodfeuds and—"

"Dar only knows," she said on a sigh.

"How will you know him?"

"Good question."

"Perhaps . . ."

"What?"

"Nothing," he answered at last.

When the silence lengthened, she ventured, "Tansen wanted to know why you've returned from the east."

"Verlon sent me with a message for Josarian."

His hot eyes shone coldly now. Verlon, the most powerful waterlord in the east, had once sworn a bloodvow against Cheylan. He had rescinded it for the sake of the rebellion, so that they—like so many other enemies in Sileria—could work together to help Josarian fight the Valdani. At the start of the rebellion, Kiloran had rescinded his own bloodvow against Tansen for the same reason. But now hatred and the lust for power had fanned the embers of old feuds into raging flames again.

However, Cheylan's situation was unique with regard to the Society, and this was the dark secret with which he had chosen to trust Mirabar: Verlon was his grandfather.

When he confessed this to her, Cheylan didn't tell her why his own grandfather had sworn a bloodvow against him and tried hard to see it fulfilled. And she had been too stunned to ask. She hadn't known that a Guardian, least of all one with Cheylan's Dar-blessed eyes, could be so closely linked by blood to a waterlord.

"What is Verlon's message?" Mirabar asked.

"He knows Kiloran has control of Cavasar and the mines of Alizar. He knows that either Kiloran or Baran will ultimately gain full control of the Idalar River and, through it, control of Shaljir once the Valdani surrender."

"So he wants Liron," Mirabar guessed. The great city of the east, so close to the sacred rainbow chalk cliffs where Dar's fiery consort had dwelled eons ago before falling into the unforgiving sea, had been the first of Sileria's cities to fall to the rebels.

"He claims it is his due, after all he contributed to the rebellion in the east."

"Why does he need Josarian's permission? Kiloran didn't—"

"The Lironi," Cheylan said, naming one of the largest and most powerful clans in all of Sileria, "have decided, in the wake of the Valdani evacuation of eastern Sileria, that they like not having any masters."

"They're fighting Verlon for control of the city?" she breathed, scarcely daring to believe it could be so.

"Yes. For control of the whole district, in fact."

"What are the eastern *toreni* doing?"

"Mostly trying to protect their lands."

"Have any of them sided with the Lironi?"

"Some." He added, "Not my family, but a few."

She stepped forward and gripped Cheylan's arm, which was firm beneath the fine fabric of his tunic. "The Lironi are really fighting the Society in the east?"

"Yes." She could tell Cheylan was puzzled by her growing excitement. "Verlon supposes that Josarian doesn't want . . . didn't want civil war. He sent me to ask Josarian to, er, make them see reason."

"In other words, on the eve of the siege of Shaljir, when Josarian would need the entire nation behind him, Verlon meant to make the city of Liron the price he would demand in exchange for supporting Josarian."

"The question now, I gather," Cheylan said, "is whether or not there will even be a siege of Shaljir. And if there is, who will lead it?"

"Tansen, of course," she said in surprise.

The silence was long and awkward.

"So . . . this thing you've told me about *Torena* Elelar," he said at last. "None of it is common knowledge?"

"Even Josarian's death isn't common knowledge yet."

"Word will spread quickly."

"Yes. But the part about Elelar . . ." She paused, lost in thought. "The Lironi are fighting Verlon."

"What does that have to do with the *torena*'s betray—"

"It has to do with Kiloran," she said suddenly.

"I don't understand."

"Damn Elelar," she said with bitter vehemence. "*Damn* her. She wins again."

"She does?"

"Don't you see? We can't expose her. We can kill her, but we can't expose her." She looked up at the glowing moons. "If we're to convince people to fight Kiloran—to fight the Society—then we've got to make sure they know he killed the Firebringer. We can't . . . complicate things by telling people about the Alliance's secrets and the *torena*'s betrayal. This is Sileria. Revealing the whole truth would just incite bloodfeuds, chaos, and a perfect opportunity for the Society to seize power the moment the Valdani leave."

"Do you really think people can be convinced to fight the Society?"

"Don't you? You just told me that the Lironi already *are* fighting them."

"Yes, I did, didn't I?" Cheylan paused for a moment, then said, "So perhaps we . . ." He took her hand again and raised it to his lips. "We can be full of hope."

She felt the damp warmth of his mouth against her skin. She felt the tingle along her senses that his presence created.

No, not you, she realized sadly.

In her inexperience, in her ignorance of men, she had previously thought the tumult of her senses whenever she was with Cheylan might be the sparks of love. Tonight, though, she finally knew better. The power of his sorcery was what made the air quiver around her and created the hot-and-cold confusion inside her. And the touch of his lips, the touch of his skin . . . Well, it was certainly pleasing, but it was not the touch of the man who had, without realizing it, taught her the pain of love rather than the pleasure of mere desire.

Damn Tansen.

"Are you all right?" Cheylan asked.

"I'm . . . just tired," she lied.

Damn Elelar.

"You've been through a lot."

"Yes. And now there's so much more to come."

May they both burn like the Fires of Dar for all eternity.

NAJDAN WAS NOT usually credulous of common gossip, but he tended to believe the rumor that Sister Velikar had been *born* old and mean. Not even among the assassins of the Honored Society had he ever known such a foul temper. And learning of the Firebringer's death this evening had only made her nastier. She had, as improbable as such a gentle emotion seemed in Velikar, been fond of Josarian.

When Mirabar and Cheylan abandoned Najdan to this dreadful woman's sour company, he was tempted to assassinate her just so he could enjoy the rest of his meal in peace. However, he didn't kill women, and violence on Sanctuary grounds was forbidden to all Silerians. If Kiloran himself walked through that door right now, they'd have to tolerate each other's company in peace.

One of Velikar's few virtues was that she was a rather good cook, and he was glad of that. Learning that Tansen had not killed *Torena* Elelar shah Hasnari, as vowed, may have ruined the *sirana's* appetite, but not his.

Young women were hard to understand, and Mirabar was more complicated than most. Najdan wished his mistress Haydar were here to advise him, perhaps even to deal with Mirabar in his stead, for once. He wondered briefly how he could find the time and safe means to bring Haydar here from Sister Basimar's Sanctuary, but then dismissed the idea; it was doubtful they'd be here for long, anyhow. Tansen knew he had to move quickly against the Society and, unless she'd lost all her wits since sunrise, the *sirana* knew it, too.

But young women could, Najdan was starting to realize, make bewildering decisions based on incomprehensible notions.

He had vaguely suspected before, and now finally felt convinced, that Mirabar's interest in Tansen was not based solely on the visions which had led her to him and kept her linked to him. He now even believed that the *shatai* returned this more personal interest, if in a confused and sadly blundering way.

The old ways were the best ways, Najdan reflected. He pushed aside the heavily beaded *jashar* which covered Velikar's doorway, and paused there to enjoy the night air and escape the Sister's unpleasant grumbling. He had first seen Haydar in a marketplace more than fifteen years ago. He wanted her, he gave her father fifteen sheep and several bolts of imported Kintish silk as a bride-price for her, and so she became his. And—after some initial difficulties, during which she kept threatening to run away and join the Sisterhood—they had been content together ever since. He had never legally married her, since he was unwilling to mouth the pledges to Dar which were required before cutting open a palm with the marriage knife, but he was devoted to Haydar and had no doubts of her devotion to him.

However, while Najdan's life might be easier if Sileria's rebel leaders could sort out their affairs of the heart as simply as he had his own, he didn't really envision Tansen collecting sheep for a bride-price—or Mirabar feeling honored by such an effort. And if the *shatai* simply tried to take her home with him, as men sometimes did upon choosing a woman whom they couldn't afford, then Najdan would be obliged to kill him.

Or die trying anyhow.

The carnage Najdan had seen on the path to Dalishar today only confirmed what he'd realized long ago. He was glad he had never had the opportunity to claim Kiloran's bloodvow against Tansen. Anything was always possible in combat, of course, but he knew that it would be the wildest stroke of luck for him to survive attacking the *shatai*.

In any event, Tansen had no home to carry Mirabar off to, and after their argument today about his failure to execute the *torena,* Mirabar would probably incinerate him if he tried, anyhow. No one knew better than Najdan that the *sirana* was far from helpless. She had captured, imprisoned, and terrorized him upon their first meeting, and survived his two attempts to kill her. She was unlikely ever to need him to defend her honor, though it was, of course, his duty to do so.

That was why he now hovered in Velikar's doorway and kept an eye on

Mirabar and Cheylan, who were speaking together at the edge of Sanctuary grounds. Respectable young women did not visit alone with men in the dark, and Najdan realized he had too often been negligent in this respect. It was sometimes easy to forget that, for all her sorcery, courage, and prophecy, the *sirana* was, after all, a marriageable young woman—albeit a very unusual one—and therefore as vulnerable to her own inexperienced judgment as she was to the presumptuous attentions of disrespectful young men.

Young men such as Cheylan. Whom Najdan had never liked.

Just because Tansen, for all his worldly experience, evidently had no idea how to present his honorable intentions—and they had *better* be honorable—to a woman, that was no reason for Mirabar to compromise herself with another man. True, the *shatai* was somewhat enthralled by *Torena* Elelar, and that may even be why he had spared her; but sparing a woman was hardly dishonorable. Moreover, the *torena* was married, which certainly settled the question of which woman Tansen would choose; Najdan felt fairly certain that the *shatai* would not murder another man just to have his wife.

However, the *sirana* had become enraged beyond reason today. Threatening to set Najdan against Tansen. Embarrassing the *shatai* in front of Lann and the sea-born boy. Wishing aloud that Kiloran's assassins would succeed in killing him next time. Najdan particularly didn't like that; such wishes could well be powerful curses, he suspected, when uttered by such a capable sorceress.

Mirabar's hot-tempered inexperience and Tansen's ill-advised neglect of her feelings could cost them both—and everyone around them—a lot more than a broken heart. It was a woman's right, of course, to spurn a man, even after her parents had agreed to the bride-price. But Mirabar didn't have the luxury of abandoning her duty to Sileria because a man had hurt and angered her. Regardless of her personal feelings, she belonged at the caves of Dalishar tonight, conferring with the man who must lead Sileria's rebels now that Josarian was dead—not dallying in Sanctuary with Cheylan.

She knew it, too. If she didn't come to her senses by morning, Najdan would explain it clearly to her, but he didn't anticipate this would be necessary. He had never known her to shirk her duty, no matter how unpleasant. He disapproved of her behavior today, but young women were difficult to understand and so he was trying to be tolerant. Until sunrise, anyhow.

It was unfortunate that Cheylan happened to be here now. Najdan knew little about him beyond what everyone knew. A powerful sorcerer, a *toren* by birth, and a former enemy of Verlon, Cheylan had followed his orders loyally throughout the rebellion, acting as a liaison between the Guardians and the Society, and between eastern and western Sileria. Despite this respectable history, though, Najdan found Cheylan's arrogant manners unpleasant and his reticence more suspect than modest.

So now, under the glowing light of the twin moons, Najdan scowled when he thought he saw Mirabar permit Cheylan to kiss her hand. Fortunately, she seemed disinclined to permit additional liberties, particularly of the kind she had allowed Cheylan in the past. Najdan had once come upon the two of them locked in a passionate embrace. He had been too stunned at the time to warn Cheylan about the consequences of such behavior.

Now Mirabar made a brief gesture, evidently bidding Cheylan good-night. Najdan decided he had rudely shunned Velikar's company for long enough, and he retired to the stone hut before Mirabar turned in this direction.

"It's late," Velikar growled at him. "Go sleep outside."

"Of course," he said, seating himself at the table again.

"I said—"

"Ah, here comes the *sirana*." He rose courteously as Mirabar pushed aside the door *jashar* and entered the hut.

Mirabar seemed unusually hesitant as she met his gaze, her fire-bright eyes now dull with fatigue. "We, uh . . . Tomorrow we need to . . ." She shifted restlessly and tried again. "I should . . ."

Ah. This, at least, Najdan felt he understood. And since Mirabar was very proud, he knew what to do. "I'm uneasy about the *shir* wound," he said.

She blinked. "What?"

"Tansen's wound."

She frowned thoughtfully. "The one that healed so suddenly. As if . . ."

"By magic."

She nodded. "It bothered you. You wanted to leave that place."

"Yes. But now I think it may not be the place."

"The boy, then?" She murmured distractedly, "A child of water . . . I need to speak with that boy. I need to know why he's here."

"The boy, perhaps." He shrugged. "Or Tansen himself." He held her gaze and said, "Who knows what might occur when Dar wants Her will done?"

"You're not afraid of Dar," she challenged. "That's not what you're worried about."

"No . . ."

"What do you think it was, then?"

"Water magic."

She drew in a quick breath. "What should we do?"

Najdan made it easy for her. "I think we should return to Tansen's side."

"You do, do you?"

"Especially if you want to speak with the boy," he added helpfully.

Mirabar brushed her hair way from her face. "All right. If you insist."

"It's best."

"We'll go in the morning," she agreed.

"I'm glad you understand, *sirana*." He headed for the door. "I will sleep outside. Goodnight."

"It's about time," Velikar grumbled. "Leave, already."

"Goodnight, Najdan." Mirabar paused, then added, "Cheylan—"

"Will sleep outside, too," Najdan said loudly as the *jashar* flapped into place behind him.

ALTHOUGH RAISED IN wealth and physical comfort by the aristocratic family he now seldom even spoke to and had never regarded with any warmth, Cheylan's Dar-given talents ensured that he had spent most of his adult life among the Guardians. So he was accustomed to sleeping outside, living in caves, appreciating whatever food and shelter he could find, and doing without it when he had to. He was not poor, for the Guardians did not require one to renounce one's personal wealth or worldly goods the way the Sisterhood did, but his family's money couldn't protect him from Valdani laws—and no one could protect him from the Society.

He had first met Josarian when the *shallah* was nothing more than a notorious local outlaw, a peasant who had rebelliously killed a couple of Outlookers who tried to beat him to death one night after they caught him helping his cousin Zimran with a little smuggling.

Like all the Guardians at that time, Cheylan had appreciated Josarian's bold defiance of the Valdani. And he had been willing to help. Outlawed by the Valdani and hunted by the Society, Cheylan—like all Guardians—had too little to lose to worry about possible punishment for assisting the outlaw. But Cheylan had had no more expectation than anyone else that the local mountain bandit would literally change the world.

Unlike so many people, however, he hadn't needed Josarian's transformation at Darshon to convince him that a great destiny was at hand. Cheylan had realized it the moment he had first heard about Mirabar, an immensely gifted prophetess blessed with the fiery coloring that was a portent of great and terrible power.

Tansen, who knew her well, was always reticent about her, and so Cheylan had learned little of value from the *shatai* during the time they had spent working together—as allies, but never as friends—in the east. Most others Cheylan spoke to were in awe of the demon-girl who talked to gods, Called shades of the dead from the Otherworld, and whom even Kiloran respected. Little of value could be learned from the superstitious admiration of the *shallaheen,* but Cheylan heard enough to recognize that Mirabar's visions were as important as Josarian's deeds.

It was only upon meeting her at last that Cheylan discovered, with mingled surprise and frustration, how little she herself understood the visions, how incapable she was of seeing where they would lead. She was cautious, too, about what she would relate. He had taken pains to win her affection and her trust, even sharing a deadly secret or two of his own to gain her confidence. He had cultivated patience his whole life, and now he recognized how wise he had been to do so.

Tonight was the first time Mirabar had ever spoken to him freely, without any reserve whatsoever, about this thing she called the Beckoner, the Otherworldly demigod who had led a parentless peasant girl out of obscurity and straight into legend. Tonight was the first time Cheylan began to realize the full weight of the Beckoner's power, the inexorable nature of its will. Tonight was the first time he'd been certain his own destiny—at last—was beginning to unfold.

A child of fire, a child of water, a child of sorrow.

Yes.

Now, as Cheylan bedded down at some distance from where Najdan the assassin ostentatiously stretched out in front of the threshold of the stone hut, he considered the things Mirabar had also told him tonight about the splintering rebel factions. He lay on his back and gazed up at the moon-bright sky, wondering what he should do now. The time for patience was nearly over. The day for action was almost at hand.

Torena Elelar's betrayal might be irrelevant. Kiloran's brutal actions might be ill-advised. The Alliance might have been right or wrong. Cheylan would let Tansen, Mirabar, and Sileria's quarreling factions worry about all that. There would undoubtedly be bloodshed and chaos; this was Sileria, after all. The future remained uncertain, and Mirabar's visions were still too vague to act upon for the time being.

However, one shining beacon of light, one promising turn of events assured Cheylan that his patience had not been wasted.

The Firebringer is dead, he thought. *Dar be praised.*

11

FIRST THE MAN TAKES A DRINK; THEN THE DRINK
TAKES THE MAN.

—Kintish Proverb

HIS OWN WIFE refused to see him.

Ronall sat in the luxuriously furnished library of his aristocratic wife's palatial house in Shaljir and fumed in bitter hurt as he poured himself another generous glass of jasmine wine. It wasn't strong enough, but there was nothing stronger left in the house—he had drunk it all, and now he was too tired to go out in search of more. He could send the servants—he was *toren,* damn it; he was supposed to be waited upon!—but they were all *her* servants, and they were bustling around to make the *torena* comfortable now that she was back. To make the house suitable for the wandering traitoress who had finally come home.

Ronall had been living here with just one servant on loan from his father's house, since being released from prison. He'd been held for several months in the old Kintish fortress not far from Santorell Square, as hostage for his wife, who had staged a violent escape from prison after being accused of high treason against the Empire.

He swallowed more wine.

Just one servant. Yes, all right, he supposed the house had become a bit dirty and shabby during his wife's long absence. She was right about that.

"Who gives a damn?" he muttered and drank some more.

What could one servant do, after all?

And why get more? The Silerian rebels were going to descend on Shaljir at any moment and probably use their fire sorcerers to burn the whole city to the ground. Or maybe they would just get their waterlords to flood it, or to wrap the Idalar River around it like a noose until no one was left alive.

When Ronall was a child, many people had died of thirst in Shaljir before the Outlookers relented and met Kiloran's demands. In later years, the legendary waterlord's struggles with Baran, some crazy upstart from who-knew-where, had caused even worse problems. When those two giants battled for control of the Idalar River, Shaljir starved for water; even sending generous tribute to Kiloran didn't solve the problem, since Baran didn't relent.

"Who owns it now?" Ronall asked the engraved silver chalice in his hands, noting absently that Elelar owned such fine, fine things.

If anyone knew, in all this chaos, which waterlord currently controlled the Idalar River, Ronall supposed it would be his dear wife. She kept company with such people, after all.

"Keeps company with everyone but her husband," he mumbled.

Their marriage had been a living inferno since the day it began. His desire, her disgust. His desperate love, her cold rejection. His cowardly sniping, her unyielding contempt. His wild violence, her bitter tears. His self-disgust, her vicious sarcasm.

His drinking, his dreamweed, his cloud syrup.

Their marriage bed had been a place of conflict, never comfort. And he'd hurt her there more than once. Hurt her badly more than once.

Afterwards, he was always ashamed, always wondered how he could have done it. But sooner or later, he always did it again.

So maybe he deserved everything that had happened to him in the past year.

"At any rate, *she* certainly thinks I deserve it," he told the priceless Kintish sculpture on the mantel of the vast fireplace. A woodless fire burned in the hearth, the enchanted flames blown into life months ago by Elelar's pet

Guardian. Ronall didn't know how to put out the damn thing. Maybe now that Derlen was back, he'd finally douse it. Ronall hoped so. Forbidden fire sorcery right here in his own house . . . it made him queasy.

Just another of those unexpected little consequences of his marriage.

Upon his wife's arrest, Ronall had finally discovered who she really was and why she had married him. She had poured an enormous amount of his money into her rebel cause and used his family's Valdani connections to help Josarian the Firebringer. And she had spread her legs for every man who could help her—or so Advisor Borell told Ronall, in his rage.

Remembering it now, Ronall quipped, "He was so furious that my wife had cheated on him."

Ronall thought this over and started laughing. The more he thought about Borell's red-faced rage over the promiscuity of the married woman he'd been bedding, the funnier it seemed. Tears misted his eyes as his shoulders shook with bitter amusement. In his slack-limbed mirth, he spilled his wine. Dazed, his vision not quite in focus, he watched the chalice roll across the floor.

"Enjoying yourself, I see." Elelar's chill voice pierced his muddled reflections.

He whirled to face her, staggering a little as he did so.

"Elelar," he whispered.

He had barely seen her upon her arrival. A few angry words about the intruder he'd hit—Three Into One, how was he supposed to know it was Derlen, suddenly appearing out of nowhere after months with no word from Elelar or any of her escaped servants?—and then she'd gone up to her bedchamber, barring the door and telling him she would see him when she damn well felt up to it and not before.

Now he saw that she was as lovely as he remembered her, even lovelier than the day they'd first met nearly seven years ago. Her softly waving black hair was pulled away from her face, braided and coiled in the elaborate style of a *torena*. She had never taken to wearing Valdani fashions, as did so many Silerian *toreni* in the city, not even after marrying into Ronall's family; and how her shapely body flattered the flowing lines of her silk pantaloons and the long tunic which hugged her lush breasts and her slim waist. Her dark, long-lashed eyes still transfixed him after all these years. Her soft, wide mouth still made him hungry for her. Yes, he had seen more beautiful women, but he had never known one with his wife's allure.

"What are you doing here?" she asked with all the warmth and charm of an executioner.

He had also never known a woman who could so easily make him feel like something to be scraped off the bottom of a boot.

He replied, "I thought you would come in here after you—"

"I don't mean in the library," she said impatiently, "I mean *here*."

He was a little confused. "I live here."

"This is my house," she snapped.

"I'm your husband." He peered at her. "I've been living here for six years."

"What could y—"

"*You* haven't, though," he continued. "You've been gone since before the long rains. Since before Josarian supposedly leaped into the volcano of Darshon and survived."

"He did leap and s—"

"Where in the Fires have you been?" Ronall demanded.

"In the mountains, obviously."

"What do you mean, 'obviously'?" Suddenly he was angry. Hotly, head-spinningly angry. "You escape from prison—with a body count that made the Fifth Moorlander War look like a minor squabble, I might add—and disappear for *months*. You send no word, make no effort to let me know you're alive, let alone where you are."

"As if you wouldn't be watched," she spat.

"Watched? I was *imprisoned,* damn you!"

She paused. "I know," she said in a more moderate voice. "I'm sor—"

"You *know*? How do you know? Who told you?"

"Advisor Kaynall."

"Kaynall? When did *you* have time to talk to the Imperial Advisor appointed after Borell killed himself because of you?"

"During peace negotiations," she said shortly. "But what are you still doing in Sh—"

"Peace negotiations?" he repeated. "Ah. For your rebels. They want peace, do they?"

"They want the Valdani out of Sileria."

"Negotiations," he mused. "Josarian's giving Kaynall a chance to withdraw before Shaljir goes up in flames?"

She went terribly still and stared at him, looking uneasy.

"Before thousands of Outlookers die here?" he continued. "Empire's last stand in Sileria, and all that." When she didn't reply, he asked, "Josarian thinks he can talk them out of fighting for it?" He snorted and bent down to pick up the chalice. "He doesn't know the Valdani very well, does he?"

"He . . . He's . . ." She suddenly turned away from him and moved towards the fire.

"What?" When she didn't reply, he prodded, "Are you sleeping with him, too?"

To his surprise, she merely said, "No."

He struck out again. "Lost your touch?"

She shook her head, staring into the flames. "He always belonged to the memory of his late wife. To her and to Dar."

He thought he'd heard her wrong. "Belonged?"

Now she looked at him, her eyes churning with something so terrible that he wasn't surprised when she finally said, "Josarian is dead."

He digested that for a moment. "Valdani?"

"No."

"Silerians?" he asked incredulously.

"The Society."

"Ah."

"Kiloran."

Ronall nodded. "Well, that figures. If what they say about Josarian was true . . ." He shrugged. "Who but Kiloran could eliminate the Firebringer? And one Silerian killing another . . ." He sighed. "Nothing ever really changes here, does it?"

Suddenly her temper broke. "What are you *doing* here?"

He flinched a little at the tone. "You and I are not the only couple in Shaljir who share a house without sharing a bed," he pointed out.

"I mean, why haven't you gone home?"

"I will not let even you shame me into scurrying back to my father's house like a child." He swayed a little and muttered, "I'm sobering up. This is no good." He found the decanter and poured more jasmine wine.

"I didn't mean your father's house," she said, "though that would be an acceptable start."

He swallowed a life-giving, hurt-soothing gulp and said, "Huh?"

Her mouth tightened with bad temper. "I mean, why haven't you already left for Valda?"

"Valda?" he repeated blankly.

"Yes!"

He stared at her in confusion. "I'm not planning . . ." He wondered if he was drunker than he'd realized. "Valda?"

"I didn't think you'd be here."

Or maybe he just wasn't drunk enough. "Where did you think I'd be? In prison still?"

"Valdani are fleeing Sileria by the thousands," she said wearily, sinking into a chair without her usual grace.

"May the Three have mercy upon them," he said politely, finishing his wine and reaching for more.

"Why haven't you left, too?"

"Leave Sileria?" He finally understood. "For Valda?"

"Yes." She sounded exasperated. "How many cups of that wine have you already had?"

"Far fewer than you've had men," he said nastily.

"When it came to fidelity," she struck back, "I followed your example."

"How I've missed you," he said dryly. "I only hope we have enough wine for me to get through this reunion." He sat down in a chair opposite hers and tried to focus for a moment. "Elelar, I've never even been to Valda."

She made an impatient gesture. "Somewhere in Valdania then, wherever your—"

"I've never been to the mainland."

"Wherever your people come from."

"They come from here."

"Your father's people," she clarified.

"They come from here, too."

"They are Valdani," she said between clenched teeth.

"And like many Valdani in Sileria," he said, "I've never been off the
island, not once in my life."

"Nonetheless, it's time to go," she said inflexibly. "You don't belong
here."

Her words hurt him, but for once he didn't think they were personal. In
this matter he wasn't her despised husband, he was his bloodline. He was
the Valdani stain on Silerian honor, the Valdani seed in a Silerian woman's
belly, a Valdani name with a Silerian face. And given the woman that he
had only recently learned Elelar was, he now realized that he was an anomaly she couldn't accept.

"Go?" he repeated. "Go where, Elelar? To a city I've never even seen,
to a mainland empire nearly as foreign to me as the Kintish Kingdoms
would be?"

"You will not be a foreigner there, you—"

"I look like a Silerian." He was a little fairer than most full-blooded
Silerians, true, but no one would take him for a Valdan, not with his coloring and features. "And I speak better Silerian than Valdan."

"Not really," she muttered sullenly.

"When I speak Valdan, I have Silerian accent." He knew she couldn't
deny that. "Just like you."

"Even so—"

"I don't know the mainland, or their ways, or their culture."

"You are not a Silerian," she hissed.

"I'm not a Valdan, either." He took more wine and then concluded, "If
I'm not going to belong anywhere, I'd rather not belong in the country that
I know than in the foreign lands that I don't."

She sneered. "You think the rebels will spare you when they take the
city?"

"So you're positive they'll take it?" His wife seemed more likely to
know the rebels' true strength than anyone else he'd talked to lately.

"Kaynall will give it up or they will take it," she said. "Either way, we
will have native rule in Sileria, Ronall."

He saw the passion in her eyes and knew she wouldn't understand when
he said, "I've never cared who ruled Sileria."

Her contempt was as familiar as it was painful. "No, as long as you're
protected by your rank and your wealth—"

"That's right," he admitted. Why deny the truth?

"As long as you've got liquor in your cellar, dreamweed in your pipe, and women in your bed—"

"Though seldom my wife."

"Never again." Her voice was low and rough. "You will never touch me as a husband again."

He knew she meant it, had even been expecting it, but he still couldn't accept it. "We are still married, we still need an heir, and—"

"Divorce me."

The room seemed to tilt. "What?"

"You heard me. Divorce me. It's an easy enough matter for a Valdan. Claim that I'm barren. It's probably true."

"We were also married as Silerians," he reminded her. A mixed-blood couple, they had married twice in one day: once before a priest of the Three, and once before a Sister who witnessed them reciting vows to Dar.

Seeing how deflated she looked, he said, "You shouldn't have married me under Silerian law if you were planning—"

"*I* didn't know what would happen, what the future held! I had my position to think of. I couldn't share a man's bed without—"

"*How* many beds have you shared?"

"I mean," she said with obvious irritation, "I couldn't live respectably as your wife without a Silerian wedding."

"So now, even if I divorced you as a Val—"

"If you leave Sileria," she said, "I can claim abandonment and dissolve the marriage when you don't return within three years."

It was, he knew, one of the very few ways to end a marriage under Silerian law. The Valdani didn't care whether or not Silerians stayed married to each other, but Silerians themselves were extremely inflexible about such things. This was a land where blood-ties and family alliances mattered even more than wealth, rank, or property.

"I see you've thought this over," he said.

"We've never had children," Elelar continued, warming to her theme. "There's no reason—"

"No!" He didn't want to hear this. "I'm not leaving Sileria, Elelar, and I'm *especially* not leaving Sileria just so *you*—"

"—for us to continue this—"

"*No!*" he shouted. He rose to his feet, swaying, and flung his half-full chalice across the room. It flew into a delicate sculpture and broke it in a smashing shower of noise.

Elelar gasped and jumped up. "You drunken—"

"That's right," he snarled, smarting under her openly disgusted glare. "That's *right*. I'm the drunken, whoring pig you married, the fool you robbed, the cuckold you betrayed again and again."

"I won't st—"

"I'm the only one who shares your bed by right of law—"

"You will *never*—"

"You're my wife!" he shouted, seizing her by the shoulders.

"*Torena!*" It was a man's voice.

Ronall glanced over his shoulder and saw Derlen in the doorway. Then Faradar, bless her insolent little heart, tried to drag the Guardian away, saying, "No, Derlen, no, let the *torena* deal with this."

"I went to prison for you," Ronall growled at Elelar, shaking her as he spoke.

"And sobered up there, according to Kaynall," she said breathlessly. "Why couldn't you have stayed that way?"

He didn't know. Dar help him, Three have mercy . . . He didn't know why. He had actually tried. The effort had lasted for only moments after his release from prison.

"*Torena?*" That idiot Derlen still hadn't gone away, and Faradar's soft chatter urging him to do so was getting on Ronall's nerves.

Elelar's shoulders were firm under the fine silk of her tunic. Her black hair gleamed in the firelight. A flush of anger showed on her soft skin, which was darker than that of a Valdani woman but exquisitely fair by Silerian standards. She smelled sweetly of whatever scent she'd used in her bathing water upstairs. She was his *wife* . . . and he felt his body quickening in response to the knowledge, to the hunger that had assaulted him a thousand times in her presence and which would rule him until the day he died.

Her breasts swelled luxuriantly against the thin silk of her tunic with every panting breath she took as she stared up at him with those wine-dark eyes. He thought of their marriage bed, now cold and empty for so long. He remembered the warmth of her breath on his naked skin, the feel of their bare bellies pressed together, the damp friction of her thighs . . . His head swam with urgent passion.

"This . . ." Her voice failed her and she tried again. "This is usually the part of the evening where you rape me, isn't it?" Her tone was rich with loathing.

It had the intended effect. His desire shriveled like parchment going up in flames until nothing was left but ashes.

He released her and turned away, swallowing the familiar potion of shame, hurt, and humiliation, which Elelar knew so well how to brew for him.

He saw Derlen gaping at him from the doorway, his jaw hanging open. Faradar, who had been with Elelar since before their marriage, was more accustomed to such scenes, of course; she merely looked steadily at the floor.

Ronall was pretty sure he felt embarrassed, but a little more wine would wash that away, so he didn't dwell on it. However, he was done amusing the servants.

"Go away," he ordered.

Derlen didn't move. Ronall decided it was a good enough reason to hit him again, and so he did.

Derlen cried out and fell back against Faradar, who recommenced trying to drag him away. Ronall noted with pleasure that the Guardian's nose started bleeding again. On the other hand, now Ronall's hand hurt.

More wine, he decided.

Ronall slammed the door as he turned away to seek the decanter. It was only after he had drained an entire cup that he realized Elelar was still in the room with him.

"Why are you still here?" he asked.

"I believe that's what *I've* been saying."

"You shouldn't have married me." He said it to blame her for their predicament. But he reflected on the statement and realized what a profound truth he had just uttered. "You shouldn't have married me."

"Probably not, but as long as I'm stuck with you . . ."

The room was reeling. The wine was working. He felt better—which was to say, he felt less. And feeling less had been his primary interest for as long as he could remember.

"Are you listening?" Elelar asked.

He realized she had been talking. He'd heard none of it. "Hmmm?"

"I want you to do something for me."

That struck him as wildly amusing. He burst out laughing. The long-suffering patience on his wife's face was so uncharacteristic that it made him laugh even harder. He tumbled sloppily into another chair, spilling wine all over himself, clutching his side when it started to ache.

Ache. That was bad. It meant he could still feel something.

"Wine," he muttered.

"You've had enough."

"Wine," he insisted.

"In a moment. In fact . . ." She picked up the decanter and waved it slowly, enticingly, just beyond his reach. When he made a clumsy grab for it, she backed away. "I'll give you all you want, and even get the servants to go find more at this Darforsaken hour, if . . ."

More, he thought, *more.*

"If?" he prompted.

"If you'll go to Santorell Palace tomorrow," she said. "There's an assassin there named Searlon whom I must speak with in private, without Kaynall knowing about it."

He didn't understand, but it didn't matter. "All right."

"I know you don't care who rules Sileria," she said, "but you probably don't want to see Shaljir destroyed."

"No," he agreed, "I don't."

"All the taverns—"

"*Tirshaheen,*" he said, showing her he knew—and used—the traditional Silerian word for a public house.

"All the brothels, all the gambling halls, all—"

"How can an assassin save all that?" he asked, bewildered and longing for the decanter.

"He's going to help me convince Kaynall to give it all up," she said. "No matter what I have to do."

He heard those words and discovered he could still get angry. He wanted the decanter. "Not in my house, Elelar."

"This is my house," she reminded him.

"Don't bed him here." He feared he would beg, and he didn't want to. "Don't bed him in my . . . in this house."

She looked surprised. "Searlon?"

"Or Kaynall."

He saw her lush lips curve in a slight smile. "I promise I won't." She shook her head and added, "That is not the bait which will lure either of them. Not these men."

"Then what?"

"That's my problem, not yours."

"My problem is to find this assassin in Santorell Palace?" When she nodded, he asked, "How?"

"Ask to speak to Kaynall. Tell him I've returned home and, based on something your overheard me say, you have reason to believe that there's an assassin lurking in Santorell Palace."

"Searlon."

"No, say only what I've just told you. You don't know his name, you only know that it's your duty as a Valdan—"

"But I—"

"—to warn the Imperial Advisor that his life may be in danger."

"That's all?"

"That's all."

"How will that secure a meeting with this . . . Searlon?"

"He's there, somewhere in the Palace, close to Kaynall. He'll hear about it."

"So?"

"He'll want to know how I knew, what I'm planning. Searlon is very clever. He may even suspect it's a message from me." She shrugged. "But I doubt Kaynall will."

"And?"

"And Searlon will come. He'll find me."

"Why?"

"Because he, like his master, lives according to the old proverb."

"Which is?"

"Keep your friends close, but keep your enemies closer."

"I was right," Ronall said with bitter satisfaction. "Nothing ever really changes here."

She sighed. "Will you remember any of this in the morning?"

"Probably not."

"We'll go over it again tomorrow, then."

"Fine. Can I have the decanter now?"

"You promise you'll do it? You'll go to Kaynall?"

"I promise," he said wearily. "You married me for my Valdani blood, so I suppose you can't help trying to use it yet again."

"Yes," she said quietly. "That's why I married you."

"And because you thought I'd always be too drunk to notice your activities." He remembered their conversation when he visited her in prison—the first honest conversation of their marriage.

"And you were."

"So let me be once again the man you married," he said. "Give me the damned decanter, Elelar."

She came closer and handed it to him. He didn't even bother fumbling for his cup, just raised the bottle to his lips and drank deeply.

Soon his senses spun away from his sorrows, and his blood felt that longed-for flow of comfort. Soon the world reeled around him, enchanted instead of bleak, gentle instead of harsh, forgiving instead of condemning. His thoughts flowed more calmly as the jasmine-tinged liquid warmed his belly, and his heart stopped aching as the wine cooled his grievances.

He didn't know when Elelar had left the room, he only knew she was gone now. But he had the wine and so he didn't miss her.

So Elelar thought she and some assassin could convince Kaynall to surrender Shaljir without a fight? So Josarian was dead, slaughtered by his own kind? So Elelar would never let Ronall touch her again? So he wouldn't belong to native-ruled Sileria any more than he had belonged to Valdani-occupied Sileria . . .

So what?

More wine, he thought.

Dar had raged wildly the other night and shaken the ground from Liron to Cavasar, but Shaljir's walls were still standing, awaiting violent assault and massive bloodshed. The Valdani fled this land by the thousands, and Ronall couldn't go with them. Silerians celebrated every new victory for the rebels, every Valdan they killed, and he couldn't celebrate with them.

More.

His wife despised him. The Outlookers who'd guarded his cell had despised him. His father was disappointed in him and his mother made excuses for him.

He felt tears of futile shame slide down his cheeks, and he poured wine down his throat, wishing for something stronger, longing for oblivion.

He was wrong. So wrong. Sileria *was* changing. Everything was changing. Unprecedented days of glory and of horror washed across the only land he could ever call home, yet he hid here in his wife's house, confused, afraid, and useless.

How would his life end?

Had it ever even begun?

More . . .

12

IN THE EMBRACE OF MEMORY, THE HEART ALWAYS
BLEEDS ANEW.

—Kintish Proverb

"FATHER!"

Armian didn't respond. The wind was high, carrying away Tansen's voice, and the assassin's attention was fixed on the coast below them.

They were on the cliffs east of Adalian, walking rather than riding, since it was a dark-moon night and the landscape was too treacherous for horses. The long rains had finally come, the season of heavy storms when the sun-baked land renewed itself. A fierce coastal wind swept the downpour sideways, drenching Tansen and his companions. Elelar was lagging behind. The young torena *was tired, unused to such hardship and exertion.*

Tansen knew he should do it now.

"Father," he said again.

Armian still didn't hear him, and now he knew it was just as well. He couldn't look into his father's eyes and do this terrible thing. And he certainly couldn't succeed if Armian saw it coming.

He must do it now, before Elelar caught up to them, to where Armian stood boldly at the cliff's edge searching the cove below for some sign of the Moorlanders he awaited. Tansen must do it before Elelar came closer, for a young woman shouldn't see such a thing.

His heart sick with anguish, his stomach churning with mingled guilt and terror, Tansen fingered the new yahr *his bloodfather had recently given him. Armian had gotten it from Kiloran while they were the waterlord's guests. Something special for his son, he had said, something to honor such a fine young man. Made of petrified Kintish wood, it would do the job.*

Fast, please Dar, let it be fast. Let him not suffer. I can't bear to make him suffer . . .

It was Tansen's weakness, Armian said, this distaste for suffering. Armian had no such weakness. By now, Tansen had seen him make too many men suffer to doubt this. Now he knew that an assassin wasn't indifferent to killing. An assassin relished it.

Tansen withdrew his yahr *from his* jashar, *the belt which would now never be knotted to identify him as Armian's bloodson, which would never bear the yellow beads of an assassin.*

He must be quick.

Father!

He must be stealthy, must take him by surprise. The moment Armian knew what he intended, it would be too late. Armian was bigger than Tansen. Armian was so fast, so strong, so skilled.

My father is a great warrior.

He saw the black-clad silhouette faintly outlined against the tormented coastal sky and crept forward, squinting against the rain, ignoring the howling wind and the keening cry of protest in his own heart.

My father is a cold-blooded killer who will rule this land in darkness and drought, in terror and bloodshed, with Kiloran, if I don't do this now.

Armian's back was still to him, but now he sensed his son's presence; he said something over his shoulder to Tansen. It sounded like he was cursing the weather, the darkness which made it impossible to see if a ship was down there in the cove.

Now, Tansen knew, it must be now.

He swung his yahr.

Good-bye, father.

He struck out. The blow connected, reverberating through Tansen's soul. Armian fell to his knees.

Father!

Armian was stunned but not unconscious. The yahr *continued its arc as Tansen swung it back around over his head, without pausing, to strike again. Armian had been instructing him, had taught him not to hesitate over the death blow lest his still-living opponent seize the opportunity to fight back.*

A great fighter, Armian now instinctively rolled away from the next blow, moving so fast he escaped it entirely, while simultaneously reaching for his shir. *Even in the dark, the wavy-edged dagger gleamed boldly with Kiloran's sorcery.*

I'm dead, Tansen thought.

But Armian froze, like a statue, when he saw his son standing above him on that windswept cliff, swinging his yahr *with deadly intent.*

If Tansen lived for all eternity, he would never forget the sound of Armian's voice as he said, "Tansen?"

Tansen had learned well from Armian. He took advantage of the moment of surprise, of his opponent's brief hesitation. He struck Armian in the face with another blow of that fatally hard yahr.

Now Armian knew, now he realized, now he moved to fight. But he was injured, and it was too late for him. That shocked pause, that stunned moment of inaction when he couldn't believe his attacker was Tansen, had ensured his defeat. On the next blow, he dropped his shir. *By the fifth blow, he was dead.*

Tansen stood in the rain, staring down at Armian's corpse. After a moment, he sank to his knees.

"Forgive me, father," he whispered.

The night rained down upon him in dark condemnation for what he had done. Dar would punish him terribly for this, he knew. How could She not? The prayer he had uttered before murdering the Firebringer, his plea that Armian should not suffer, was the last time he would ever ask Dar for anything, the last time he would ever pray to Her.

Enter not prayerless into the domain of Dar . . .

Dark, the night was dark. His grief was forever stained with shame, his sorrow forever marred by guilt.

. . . for She forgives no slight . . .

. . . forgives no slight . . .

. . . forgive . . .

"I imagine he was not altogether bad," Josarian said.

"No," Tansen agreed, "he was not."

Josarian? Where had Josarian come from?

"Dar gives and Dar takes away," Josarian said.

"Dar didn't do this," Tansen said. "But She let you *die." He looked up at his brother. "You were the Firebringer, not Armian. Why did She let you die?"*

"That's right," Josarian said, looking surprised, "I'm dead. Like him."

Now Armian opened his dead eyes and repeated, "Tansen?" in that voice Tan would never forget, that shocked, disbelieving voice, that voice so rich with betrayal, so wounded by treachery . . .

"No!"

Tansen came hurling out of the dark world of his nightmares, scrambling wildly away from the memories which had chased him across the years and through many foreign lands ever since the night he had killed Armian.

His chest heaved with panting breaths as the world reeled around him, reality slowly taking shape out of dreams, the windswept cliffs of the Adalian coast gradually fading into the glowing interior of one of Dalishar's safe, sacred, silent caves.

He was sticky with sweat, shaking with fear, dizzy with nausea.

"*Siran?*"

He recognized the boy's voice.

"I'm all right." He heard how breathless and thin his own voice sounded, and he focused on making it more reassuring. "I'm fine."

"What is it?" Zarien mumbled, still half asleep.

"Nothing," he said. "Go back to sleep. It's nothing."

Just my ghosts. Just the demons of my dreams. They won't hurt you, son. It's not you they've come for.

The boy squinted briefly, then lowered his head. Watching him, Tansen thought he fell asleep again the moment his cheek touched the borrowed bedroll. Tan gazed down at the sea-born youth for a moment, sad and envious all at once. He hadn't slept like that, in such deep innocence, for ten years. His nights were riddled with guilt, his dreams laced with his sins.

He needed air. He stalked past Lann, whom, the others had delighted in telling him upon his arrival, even an earthquake couldn't wake, and escaped from the cave. A sentry outside glanced at him questioningly. He shook his head and went to the edge of the clearing, gazing across the moonlit night to where Darshon rose majestically in the distance.

The night breeze wafted through his hair, clean at last. He had bathed after eating, washing off the filth of violence and illness. The *shir* cut on his left palm was freshly dressed by Rahilar's expert hands, and her practiced healing magic had made it hurt less. He hoped the sea-born boy's feet hurt less, too, now; they had looked terrible when Sister Rahilar removed Zarien's stolen shoes to examine them.

He hoped the boy's dreams would not be troubled by the memory of those six ravaged corpses he'd stumbled across yesterday. No one that young should see something like that.

Don't dwell on it, Armian would have said, shrugging off violent death with the ease of a born assassin.

Armian . . .

Tansen's bloodfather had been right—the first time was indeed the hardest. Tansen, who had killed so many men by now, couldn't remember another death which had been so hard to inflict.

Except Elelar's, of course. And so he hadn't done it.

If he had never cared about her, never been enthralled by her, never once believed himself in love with her, perhaps he could have done it.

But perhaps not, even so.

His sins were too close to hers. She had tried to kill the Firebringer and, in slaying Armian, so had Tansen. She had betrayed Josarian, an ally, believing she did so to save Sileria from the Valdani; Tansen had betrayed his own bloodfather, believing he did it to save Sileria from the Society.

He knew with all his heart that Elelar was wrong. Josarian's death put them in desperate peril. And he knew that she had believed that night on the cliffs, and believed to this very day, that Tansen had been wrong when he killed Armian, thus destroying Armian's plan to use Moorlander forces to drive the Valdani out of Sileria and then rule the island nation with Kiloran.

Yes, Elelar was still his weakness, but Mirabar—*What in the Fires am I going to do about her?*—was wrong about the reason.

Elelar's sins were his sins. She was the mirror of his life, the banner of their culture, the sorrow of their times. She was Sileria, in all its shameful glory, in all its self-destructive courage, in all its bitter sacrifice and traitorous ferocity. And in the end, so was he.

If they couldn't change, then how could Sileria? If they couldn't reap something worthy from their bloodstained past, then how could their country?

Josarian had been all that was good in Sileria, the purity of intent and strength of heart which had somehow survived the centuries of servitude, poverty, and humiliation. Who else could have united Sileria's feuding, disparate factions and been embraced by Dar Herself? Who else could have resurrected Sileria's pride in itself and sown belief in place of resignation?

But even Josarian had been caught in the web of Sileria's worst flaws, and he always knew it: *I can take care of my enemies, but Dar shield me from my friends.*

If they were to triumph and survive as a nation, then betrayal and vengeance must cease to be their whole way of life. Tansen had started by not killing Elelar. He would finish by destroying the Society and killing Kiloran, not as a *shallah* seeking vengeance, but as a *shatai* eliminating the worst threat to freedom in Sileria.

Unfortunately, he also knew the *shallaheen* were far more likely to understand vengeance as a motive for fighting the Society than anything else. They were far more likely to oppose Kiloran if fired by revenge than if coaxed by abstract philosophy.

Leadership called for compromise, and war called for expedience. In the morning, he would motivate his people according to their past. In the end, though, he must somehow help them find a new future.

Tansen sighed wearily and stretched his stiff muscles. He knew he should try to get more sleep. Dawn was far away, and he was still weak. He had too much to do, too many responsibilities, to indulge in a slow physical recovery.

So, after another deep breath of cool night air, he reluctantly returned to the cave and his bedroll. Lann was snoring. As Tansen lay down, Zarien started murmuring in his sleep.

Tansen closed his eyes and tried to ignore them both.

. . . Armian froze, like a statue, when he saw his son standing above him on that windswept cliff, swinging his yahr *with deadly intent.*

"Tansen?" he said in a voice torn by shock and disbelief. . . .

Tansen's eyes snapped open.

"Sea king . . . ," Zarien muttered.

Lann's snoring was louder than an eruption of Darshon.

Tansen sighed. Dawn would be a long time coming.

13

HE WHO HAS WARNED YOU HAS NOT KILLED YOU—AS
YET.

—Harlon the Waterlord

Northern Sileria,
The Year of Late Rains

TRAVELING TOWARDS SHALJIR, where they would seek out this
thing called the Alliance, Tansen and Armian avoided the Outlookers by
sticking to the high mountain paths and old smuggling trails of northern
Sileria. Sometimes they found them without help. Sometimes a local *shallah*
recognized something special enough in the man or sorrowful enough in
the boy that he'd simply tell them which way to go. And sometimes Armian
forced people to give him the information he sought.

The first time Armian struck a stranger without provocation, Tansen was
shocked. He would see it again, would even grow used to it by the time they
reached Shaljir, but the first time befuddled him with stunned confusion.

It was the act of an assassin, he knew. It was exactly the sort of penalty
some of them had inflicted upon Tansen's own people from time to time,
leaving tears, blood, and humility in their wake. It was Armian's birthright,
Tansen knew, the merciless strength of his kind.

Somehow, though, knowing this didn't actually prepare Tansen for it,
nor did the knowledge govern his reaction.

"*Siran!*" Tansen protested, watching Armian beat a spicemonger who'd
just refused to answer Tansen's question about a safe pass through the next
mountain range. Some women screamed. Children scattered. Men backed
away. Tansen never used Armian's name in front of others, since the Outlookers were undoubtedly still searching for the Firebringer. "*Siran,*" he repeated.

Armian ignored him, grabbed the hair of the man he had just knocked
down, and smashed his face into a table in the marketplace of the village
they were in.

"Now," Armian said pleasantly to the man who lay dazed and bleeding, "perhaps we can count on a more courteous answer to the boy's question?"

"Ah . . . Uh . . ." The man panted with incoherent fear.

"Please, *siran,*" Tansen whispered. People were staring, murmuring, waiting to see what would happen next. "We can find the pass without—"

"This man will be happy to guide us to the pass." Armian shook his victim. "Won't you?"

"Yes!" the man wailed. "Yes, *siran!*"

"Then show us now." Armian released him and kicked him into the middle of the street.

While the tense crowd stared, the spicemonger picked himself and up and said, "Yes, *siran,* this way, *siran.*"

No one interfered.

No one ever interfered with the Society in Sileria. And while Armian wasn't wearing his *jashar* and had not withdrawn his *shir*—which was hidden in his boot—everyone here could see that this was an assassin. A powerful one. A ruthless one.

Throughout Tansen's whole life, he had been part of the humble crowds who watched assassins take what they wanted and do as they pleased. He had admired their courage, respected their position, and envied their power. He had secretly wanted to be one of them, and he had even stated this ambition aloud to Armian, who took him seriously.

Now he discovered that being among the ones the crowd stared at with fear wasn't as thrilling as he had supposed. Seeing Armian attack Outlookers in Gamalan had felt very different from watching him beat an unarmed merchant. Armian hadn't needed to do this, not really. They could have found their way without help, or they could have asked someone else for directions. The assassin's sudden burst of violence against a recalcitrant spicemonger . . . well, it was far from glorious. And now the man's obsequious fear and babbled pleas gave Tansen no pleasure, no sense of power.

In fact, he felt . . . ashamed. He was eager to leave this village and hopeful that he'd never have to come back.

So he responded with alacrity to Armian's clipped command that he keep up. He maintained an uneasy silence as the sun rose higher, following Armian and the man who led them, having no idea what to say or how to behave. When they reached the hidden trail leading to a pass which would get them safely past a town swarming with Valdani, the spicemonger gladly accepted Armian's dismissal. Tansen avoided the man's eyes as he departed.

Armian's dark gaze followed the man, but his words were for Tansen. "Pardon one offense, and you encourage the commission of many."

"I . . ." Tansen didn't know what to say.

"I'm telling you this for your own good," Armian continued. "Permit rudeness, and you're offered insolence next. Permit insolence, and opposition follows. And opposition . . ." Armian looked at him now. "That we cannot allow."

"No, *siran.*"

Armian was right. Of course Armian was right.

"If you want to be one of us," Armian told him, "you cannot be one of them. It is the first rule."

"Who . . ." Tansen nodded his understanding, then asked, "Who taught it to you?"

"My father's assassins. The ones who went into exile with me, my mother, and my uncle."

"Oh. Yes. Of course."

"They taught me what they had learned from my father."

"Harlon was . . ." A wise man? A shrewd man? ". . . a great waterlord," Tansen concluded at last. "I've heard many stories about him."

"Our destiny," Armian taught him, "is to be obeyed. Demanding obedience is the source of the Society's power."

"I thought water—"

"And what do the waterlords seek when they withhold water?"

He hesitated only a moment. "They seek obedience."

"Now do you understand?"

"Yes, Armian, now I understand."

THEY WERE ENJOYING the hospitality of Sanctuary the night Armian asked Tansen to become his son. The three Sisters who lived here were old and timid. One of them was deaf, and another had been maimed by Valdani torture. Armian was polite to them, but when they began their evening prayers to Dar, he vacated their spacious stone dwelling.

Tansen, who knew better than to offend the destroyer goddess, prayed with the Sisters before following Armian outside. The night air was cool and slightly damp.

"I've been thinking about what you said," Armian announced when Tansen joined him around a small fire he had built at the edge of Sanctuary grounds. "A man without a clan is no one in the mountains, a *shallah* is nothing without his kin."

"Yes." It hurt to dwell on it.

"Now you're alone," Armian continued, his voice kind despite the bleak words, "as I am alone."

"You? But there are many Idalari. You clan is very—"

Armian made a dismissive gesture. "My parents are dead. I've never met any of the Idalari, and they will be strangers to me when I finally do. At least, at first. I have no brothers. No wife." He paused and added with emphasis, "No son."

Tansen stared at him in the firelight as Armian held up his right palm, showing Tansen its scarred flesh.

"My father sliced my palm when I was named. Years later, his assassins cut my palm when they made me one of them." Then he held up his left hand. It was smooth, unmarked by bloodpact relations or bloodfeuds. "I know that here in the mountains you can choose a new father to replace the one you've lost."

"I . . ." Tansen didn't want to presume, though his heart pounded as he realized what Armian must be leading up to. "I lost him so long ago that I don't remember him."

"A boy needs a father. Even," Armian added quickly, "a very brave, capable boy who is nearly a man."

Tansen's eyes misted, embarrassing him. Pride filled his throat, making it impossible for words to escape. The greatest moment of his life was taking place in the dark, far from anyone else who might have cared, and only after his family was dead. Were a man's great moments always like this, he wondered?

"Will you honor me, Tansen," Armian asked formally, "and become my son?"

The Firebringer wants to be my bloodfather.

Tansen's chest rose and fell, breath gusting in and out as his feelings welled up, threatening to propel him across the sky like a shooting star.

A man whose name lived in Silerian legend wanted Tansen as his blood-son. He was a man whom no one dared to insult, a man whose great destiny shone plainly in his proud face and ready courage.

Tansen crossed his fists and bowed his head. "The honor would be mine, *siran.*"

Armian smiled. Then he took the small knife which they carried among their few possessions and stuck it into the fire, heating the blade for the bloodpact ceremony.

"And perhaps," Armian suggested, "you could stop calling me that."

"Yes, Armian."

"Actually, I was thinking . . ."

"Yes?"

"Well . . . you could call me 'father.'" Armian shrugged casually, staring into the fire. "If you wanted to."

The wind stirred the vast leaves of the gossamer trees. In the darkened forest, something stalked and caught its prey, which squealed in panic a moment before dying. Overhead, the twin moons gleamed on the snow-capped peak of Darshon, which had never looked more beautiful.

"Yes, father," Tansen replied.

"THAT MUST BE Illan," Armian said, gazing down at a large town from the mountaintop where they stood together, surveying the countryside below.

The diagonal cut of the bloodpact ceremony still made Tansen's palm throb, but then, it was supposed to. The privileges and responsibilities of a bloodpact relation were as binding as those which a *shallah* owed to the family he'd been born into. The pain was meant to remind him of the commitment he had made, and the scar it would leave was meant to remind him of its permanence.

The Sisters had cleaned and dressed the cut on his hand, as well as the one on Armian's. Then the two of them left Sanctuary and continued the journey to Shaljir.

Now Tansen pointed to the broad ribbon of silver-blue descending from the mountains to weave through the lowlands below them. "Then that would be the Idalar River."

"The Idalar," Armian breathed, his interest sharpening as he gazed upon it.

It was, after all, the foundation of his clan's power, the water source which Harlon had used to bring the Valdani to their knees. The reprisals for Harlon's sorcery had been terrible, costing thousands of Silerian lives, but he was remembered as a hero in the mountains: a Silerian waterlord had opposed the Empire and made the Outlookers bleed.

Now Kiloran, who was himself reputed to have learned water magic from one of the Idalari waterlords, controlled the Idalar. It was the chief source of water for the great city of Shaljir, where Armian hoped to find the Alliance.

Armian finally pulled his gaze away from the river below them and looked back at the mountains they would now leave. "By all the gods above and below, this is a beautiful country."

"More beautiful than others?" Tansen asked.

"Oh, yes," Armian said, "more beautiful than anything I've ever seen."

"Is that why the Valdani want it?"

Armian grimaced. "They want it because it is their nature to want what is not rightfully theirs." He clapped Tansen on the back and said, "Let's go. If we move fast, we can make Illan by sunset. Doesn't a bed sound good for a change?"

"Yes, father."

"And after that, Shaljir."

THE EXOTIC MAZE of Shaljir's streets and the sparkling glory of its many fountains faded from Tansen's mind as he and Armian were shown into the home of *Toren* Gaborian shah Hasnari. Armian said that the *toren* was supposedly the leader of the Alliance in Sileria and could take him to Kiloran. Tansen had never heard of the Hasnari, but this palatial house with its luxuriant furnishings left him in no doubt of their wealth and status.

"I've never seen anything like this," he whispered to Armian, who had led him here through a long afternoon of asking throughout Shaljir where the *toren* lived. The city-dwellers of Shaljir were not as reticent as *shallaheen,* but the city was so enormous that, even so, finding this house had taken some time.

"It's impressive," Armian agreed. "But even here, you can see what it means to be ruled by the Valdani." He gestured to a large, discolored square on the floor. When Armian saw that Tansen didn't understand its significance, he explained, "They've been selling things—there was once a rug there—to pay their taxes."

"We had to." Startled, Tansen whirled around to face a young woman who spoke from the doorway. "The Outlookers beggared us with their demands for grain from our estates last year, and then the Society depleted our savings by abducting my grandfather." She arched her brows. "The ransom was very high."

The abduction would have occurred during the long rains, of course, when the Society had trouble exacting tribute from the populace. It was the one time of year when water was so plentiful in Sileria, the rivers so fast-flowing and abundant, that even the waterlords couldn't keep Sileria thirsty with their power. Abducting *toreni* and wealthy merchants was an old custom, a secondary source of income for the Society.

"And you did not apply to Kiloran for help?" Armian asked.

Tansen supposed that if these people could help Armian find Kiloran, they must be under his protection.

The young woman studied Armian with obvious interest as she replied, "We did. However, the captor was an enemy of his who would not listen to reason."

"Who?"

"It doesn't matter now. He's dead." She added significantly, "He was an enemy of Kiloran's, you see."

Tansen stood transfixed, scarcely hearing her words. She was the most beautiful woman he had ever seen. Long-lashed dark eyes commanded a face of intelligent beauty which was framed by elaborately styled black hair. Her silken clothes were so much finer than those of any *shallah* woman, and noticeably less modest; he could see the shape of her breasts and her waist under the clinging fabric, and her pantaloons tapered down to hug her trim ankles like a lover.

Heat flooded him, making his body alert and his wits dull. Her glance fluttered over him, and for the first time in his life, he wished he had better clothes, wished he were taller, broader, older. He could tell that several years separated them, and her gaze quickly dismissed him as a mere boy before she returned her attention to Armian. He saw Armian take her hand, a liberty which few respectable *shallah* girls would permit upon meeting a strange man. But the *toreni,* Tansen knew, were different. Without introducing himself, Armian asked to see Gaborian.

"Since the abduction, my grandfather is frequently too unwell to receive visitors," she said. "I am Elelar mar Odilan shah Hasnari, and I run this household now."

Armian let his surprise show on his face. Even Tansen knew that, though of marriageable age, she was very young to run such an obviously large household. He wondered what his father would do now, but the girl surprised them again.

"And you," she said, "must be Armian." She smiled at Armian's wary expression and added, "The Alliance has been awaiting you, though we feared you might be dead."

THEY SLEPT IN one of the vast house's bedchambers that night. The following morning, Gaborian was feeling strong enough to meet them briefly. It was the only time Tansen ever saw the dying old aristocrat. Later in the day, the young *torena* advised them that she had set in motion the slow procedure of contacting Kiloran to arrange a meeting.

She added, "So perhaps you should tell me why you're here."

"I've come home," Armian replied simply.

"Why?" She sounded a little impatient.

"To drive the Valdani out of Sileria, *torena,* why else?"

"I know what the *shallaheen* say about you, but I'm not a credulous peasant, and neither is Kiloran." She ignored Tansen, who gaped at her, shocked by such disrespect. "Do you actually have a plan?"

Armian merely grinned. "It is a plan, young *torena,* which should please even you."

"Go on," she urged.

"When I meet Kiloran, then I will go on." He shook his head when she started to protest. "I've already been betrayed once on this quest, *torena,* so I think it best to keep the details of my plans to myself for now. Until I meet Kiloran, all you need to know is that the Moorlanders propose . . . an alliance." He smiled beguilingly at her. Tansen would have been jealous had the *torena* responded in kind, but she only looked annoyed.

However, she was born to centuries of practiced courtesy, so she said, "And how may we amuse you in Shaljir until such time as we receive a message from Kiloran?"

"Ah, *torena.*" Armian smiled again. "You will find that I'm really very easy to amuse."

AN ASSASSIN AND a *shallah* boy staying as guests of a *toren* were bound to arouse interest if discovered, and that was the last thing they wanted. So, Elelar informed them, Gaborian advised her to move their guests to a safe *tirshah* in the oldest part of the city. The public house squatted deep in a maze of narrow, tangled streets which the wind never reached; it took days for Tansen to get used to the smell, the closeness, the ancient odors, and encroaching buildings.

However, although he'd have liked to see more of the beautiful young *torena,* he felt more at ease in the humble *tirshah* than he had in her grand home. And Elelar did meet with them several times. Meanwhile, Tansen became friendly with the chubby, good-natured man who owned the *tirshah* and who, he soon learned, was also part of this Alliance.

The Alliance was a secret organization composed of people from many walks of Silerian life: *toreni,* merchants, Sisters, city-dwellers, and even certain members of the Honored Society—most notably, Kiloran himself. There were no *shallaheen* in this Alliance ("they're wild, violent, and distrustful of everyone who isn't a *shallah,*" said the *torena*), and also no *zanareen* ("all mad") or Guardians ("not as long as the Society is in the Alliance"). However, there were many *roshaheen*; individuals from several tribes of the Moorlands and from more than a dozen of the Kintish Kingdoms were involved in the Alliance.

"Freedom from the Valdani," she explained to Tansen, "is our purpose, the goal we all work for."

Her grandfather, Gaborian, had founded this Alliance. Elelar had been raised to participate in the work of the Alliance, and, though still young, she'd taken over many heavy responsibilities since Gaborian had become ill.

It was a world Tansen had never imagined before, having known only the daily struggle of a humble mountain peasant's existence. Until finding Armian lying on the beach that first night, he had never even considered the possibility of freedom from the Valdani. Since then, he had believed Armian alone would somehow achieve it, with Dar's help. Now he realized that hundreds, perhaps thousands, of people believed in it, regardless of Armian. People had been working for it since before he was born.

"So why haven't you accomplished it in all these years?" he asked.

Elelar's indignation over this simple question seemed unreasonable; after all, she had just admitted that Gaborian had been trying to get rid of the Valdani for nearly forty years.

Armian's theory, related privately to Tansen over some particularly good ale at the *tirshah,* was that the members of the Alliance could scheme and plot and spy all they liked, but nothing could replace action—and they seemed sadly inadequate at that.

"But now you are here," Tansen said.

"Now I'm here," Armian agreed, "and we will have action. I guarantee it."

Armian told him what he wouldn't tell Elelar: the details of the Moorlanders' proposal. Tansen was his son, after all. Armian trusted him.

"Control of Sileria is essential for control of the Middle Sea," Armian told him, "and control of the Middle Sea is essential for control of a mainland empire the size of Valdania—especially if the Valdani want to keep extending their borders, which seems to be the case.

"The free Moorlanders know this. Valdania breaks treaty after treaty with them, and some of them have finally started to realize that the Valdani won't rest until they've swallowed the Moorlands whole, down to the very last tribe."

A keystone of the Moorlanders' plan to stop the Valdani advance, therefore, was to destroy their power in Sileria. They wanted to unite with the only organized force in the island nation, the only faction which had ever made the Valdani bleed: the Society. Even in the Moorlands, they had heard of Kiloran and knew that he was the waterlord best able to speak on behalf of the entire Honored Society.

The free tribes had an obvious envoy among them, the only person in all of the Moorlands whom Kiloran was likely to trust: the exiled Silerian assassin who lived among them even had the honor of being the son of Harlon, the waterlord whom the Moorlanders remembered for his fabled opposition to the Empire.

However, they didn't know how to contact Kiloran, nor did Armian, who had spent his whole life on the mainland. So finding the waterlord through Sileria's secretive network of strange bedfellows, the Alliance, was their solution.

"So you will . . ." Tansen shrugged, trying to work it out. "Abandon the Alliance once you find Kiloran?"

"No." Armian clapped him on the head, a playful blow of admonishment. "What did I tell you before?"

"Um . . ."

"Never destroy a useful tool."

"Oh! Yes, I remember." He frowned. "How is the Alliance useful?"

"I'm not sure yet, but they're bound to be. Money, contacts, networks, influence." Armian shrugged. "Kiloran will know. And he will keep them in their place."

An important matter continued to trouble Tansen, however. "After we find Kiloran . . ."

"Yes?"

"Will we go to Darshon?"

Armian sighed. "You're not still thinking about that, are you?"

"Father, surely your destiny—"

"Is too bright to throw away by jumping into the damned volcano."

"Then what will you do?"

"I'll fight a war."

"To get rid of the Valdani."

"Yes."

"But—"

"With the Society. And then I'll become Kiloran's heir."

I'm his son, Tansen thought, *it's my duty to say this.* "That doesn't seem fitting, father. You're the Fire—"

"Kiloran will teach me everything he knows," Armian said, looking a little exasperated by now. "Including water magic."

"You'll become a waterlord?"

"I'm Harlon's son."

"Waterlords' sons don't always . . . The gift doesn't always go from father to son."

"Let's just hope it has in my case."

"Are there any signs that you h—"

"No." He shrugged. "But I've never been in Sileria before, and I've never met a waterlord who might teach me. So there's never been any way of knowing."

"If you don't—"

"If I don't master water magic, then it will be very hard to rule Sileria." *A waterlord ruling Sileria.*

It was not the same thing as the Firebringer.

It was not the same.

TANSEN HAD NEVER seen a woman like Elelar, had never known the painful, tongue-tied yearning which overwhelmed him in her presence. He didn't know how to control the lust that swept through him when she brushed past him or stood so close he could feel the heat of her skin.

He had also never before experienced the acute embarrassment he felt over her amusement at his rustic habits or clumsy infatuation. For the first time in his life, he was embarrassed that he was poor, illiterate, and ignorant; her pity humiliated him and her impatience shamed him.

He was a *shallah* and she was a *torena.* Even worse, he was still just a boy, and she was already a woman.

"She's a lovely girl," Armian said one day, following Tansen's gaze as it followed the *torena,* who departed from a private meeting with them.

"I suppose so," Tansen said with a show of indifference.

"I believe that even in Sileria," Armian said dryly, "women are moved by compliments, gifts, and acts of gallantry."

Tansen glanced suspiciously at him. "Oh?"

"So if you want to win the girl's affection—"

"I didn't say that."

Armian sighed. "Never mind."

After a few moments, Tansen ventured, "Acts of gallantry?"

"Show her the courtesies a woman likes."

"The courtesies a woman likes," he repeated blankly.

"For example, perhaps if you let her precede you through a doorway, rather than always going ahead of her—"

"But a man must always go first through a door! To protect a woman from the danger which may lie on the other side."

Armian frowned. "Yes, there are certain differences between the *shalla-heen* and the *toreni* which . . ." He shook his head. "Perhaps compliments would be a better thing to focus on."

"Compliments," Tansen said without enthusiasm, morosely considering how tongue-tied Elelar's mere presence made him.

"A young woman like the *torena* . . ." Armian thought it over and continued, "She will be indifferent to comments about her beauty, but compliments about her mind will flatter her."

Tansen took his father's advice to heart and tried to compliment the *torena*'s intelligence when next they met. But he was a clumsy peasant, lacking the polished manners of Elelar's kind, and his awkward passion made his words sound foolish. She seemed more amused than flattered, and he quickly retreated into mortified silence. After that, he brusquely rejected Armian's encouragement in this matter.

"Well," Armian said philosophically, "she's a *torena,* after all, so I suppose things are best left as they are. And you're both still young enough that the age difference matters a great deal."

"Won't it always?" Tansen muttered.

Armian clapped him on the back. "No. In the ways that matter, she won't always be older. However, she will always be a *torena*."

"And I will always be a *shallah*."

"No. You will be more than that someday. Much more."

Smarting under the pain of hopeless love, what happened "someday" hardly seemed to matter, but he obediently replied, "Yes, father."

14

WHO WILL BE BRAVE AND STAND WITH ME?
—Daurion, the Last Yahrdan

SLEEP ELUDED TANSEN, so by the time dawn's amber glow finally kissed the sky above Mount Dalishar, he had been practicing forms and drills, with and without his swords, for nearly an hour. Sister Rahilar's dressing on his wounded palm ensured that it didn't disable him, though it was starting to throb again, and her disgusting blood broth seemed to have set him on the road to recovery. He was slower than usual and tired more easily, but with the life-threatening wound in his side completely healed, he was at least strong enough today for action and would, he knew, soon be fully recovered.

The mysteriously healed wound was just one of many concerns he must deal with today, and not the most pressing one. This morning, while a coil of dark smoke rose menacingly out of distant Darshon's caldera, he must take the first real steps in the necessary feat he had dreaded since Josarian's death: taking his bloodbrother's place.

After the rebels were all awake and the morning chores were done, Tansen called for everyone's attention. Only he, Najdan, and Mirabar knew the truth about Elelar; but eight of these men had been with Tansen when he saved Josarian from the ambush Zimran had led him into, so Tansen had no doubt that the news of Zimran's betrayal had already been discussed at Dalishar and might even soon spread across Sileria.

Looking at nearly fifty attentive faces now, he began with a judicious half-truth. "As most of you already know, I discovered that Zimran planned to betray Josarian to the Outlookers."

Galian, a *shallah* from Garabar who always fought with two *yahr,* asked, "Why did he do it?"

The disgusted reply came from Radyan, a young man from Illan whose intelligence Tansen had learned to appreciate: "Probably for the money the Valdani must have promised him."

"That," Lann said morosely, "seems likely." He had known Zimran well, having grown up with him and Josarian. "He always wanted more money, lots of money. I suppose his . . . his friendship with *Torena* Elelar beguiled him into believing she'd leave her Valdani husband permanently for him if he had wealth worthy of her position." Lann shook his head sadly. "As if a *torena* would favor a *shallah* for long."

"And presumably the Outlookers offered him a pardon," Tansen added. His blood simmered with guilt while his mind coolly noted that his lies would evidently satisfy these men. "However, as you know, Zimran failed."

"Because of you," Lann proclaimed.

"But Kiloran succeeded," Tansen continued.

Sister Rahilar started crying. Lann's eyes misted in his dark, bearded face. Even Yorin, a notoriously tough one-eyed *shallah,* looked as if he was fighting back tears.

Tansen had thought about his next move a great deal and had decided that the harshest words must come from him. If not, then he would wind up defending his plans against criticism; and Armian had taught Tansen that a defensive fight was almost always a doomed one.

Always attack, and never hesitate.

"Now," he told the rebels at Dalishar, "we are caught between Josarian's enemies, between the Valdani and the Society, between Advisor Kaynall in Shaljir and Kiloran in our very own mountains." The rebels' gazes were sharp and unblinking. "Now we face the worst odds, the hardest tasks, the heaviest fighting." The air was thick with tension. "Here, between the sword and the wall, between fire and water, between the past and the future," he said, praying for some of Josarian's charisma, "we must make our choice and, having made it, never waver from it."

He saw Zarien's young face, festive with sea-born tattoos, and suddenly felt the weight of the boy's expectations. "Now, here, today," Tansen said, "we must decide: Do we stand and fight, or do we surrender and submit?"

Lann's voice was hoarse with emotion: "Stand and fight!"

"At least *pretend* to think it over," Radyan suggested dryly.

"Josarian must be avenged!" Yorin cried.

"Do you know what that means?" Tansen challenged him.

"*I* know what it means," Radyan said. "I'm from Illan. I grew up on the banks of the Idalar River."

"If you want to surrender," Yorin snapped, "then there's no room for you at Dalishar."

Radyan sighed. "I didn't say I wanted to surrender. I'm saying you'd better be damned sure you know what you're getting into before you charge off in a blaze of vengeful glory."

"He's right," Tansen agreed. "To avenge Josarian is to challenge Kiloran. To challenge Kiloran is to oppose the Society. And that," he said, remembering so well how he had learned it, "they will not allow."

"War against the Society?" asked Pyron, who had lost both of his brothers in the mines of Alizar under Valdani rule.

"War against the Society," Tansen confirmed.

This stopped their debate and made their faces tight with fear. This, they knew, was an even madder dream than Josarian's rebellion against Valdania.

"War against the masters of water and the assassins who kill for them," Tansen said, relentless.

"But . . ." Radyan studied him with a puzzled frown. "What about the Valdani? What about the siege of Shaljir?"

He gambled everything on Elelar now. The future of Sileria, the rest of his life, the lives of Sileria's people. He counted on the *torena,* who had proven time and time again that she could talk men into doing the unthinkable and sacrificing the unimaginable.

"There will be no siege of Shaljir," he announced.

"What?" Lann blurted.

"We move against the Society now," Tansen said, "immediately, starting today."

"And Shaljir," Yorin demanded, his sole remaining eye glinting angrily. "We just leave it to the Valdani, to the *roshaheen* who've killed so many of us?"

"We can't afford to lose time and men taking Shaljir," Tansen said. "Not now. Not after what's happened. Kiloran's already killed Josarian, and he'll use every moment we waste to extend and consolidate his power. Do you want to die freeing Shaljir for *him*? Because if we expend our energy now on the siege of Shaljir, this nation *will* belong to him. We'll have given it to him."

"But if we leave the Valdani in Shaljir ..." Galian shrugged, his two *yahr* clicking lightly against each other in his *jashar* as he did so.

"The Alliance has been deep in negotiations with the Valdani." That much, at least, was true. "Kaynall is on the verge of surrendering Shaljir. And since the Alliance includes members of the Society, I've made arrangements for Searlon to help *Torena* Elelar convince Advisor Kaynall to abandon Sileria at last."

"Searlon?" Pyron asked incredulously.

"Yes," Tansen confirmed, "speaking on behalf of Kiloran. We are all still agreed that we want our mutual enemies out of our country."

But this was Sileria, so the enemies of their enemies weren't necessarily their friends. There was always enough hatred to go around in Sileria.

"Ahhh." Radyan thought it over. "In other words, you mean to let the Society free Shaljir for *us*?" When Tansen nodded, he grinned and said, "I *like* that plan."

It's got to work. Please, Dar, for their sakes, it's got to work.

"Will it work?" Galian asked.

"Yes," Tansen said.

"You seem very sure," Yorin noted.

"Which brings us back to the decision we must make today: Do we make war on the Society for our freedom, or do we give up now?"

There was a long, uneasy silence. He let them have it. He saw the look on Zarien's face and knew the lad thought he was losing. He wondered how much of the debate, all in *shallah,* Zarien was actually able to follow.

"When I was a boy," Tansen said at last, "people whispered Kiloran's name, afraid to say it aloud. My village paid tribute every year to an eastern waterlord, who was killed by Outlookers years later. Between what we gave him and what we gave the Valdani, there was nothing left for us. We lived in hunger and hardship." He paused and added, "And so did all of you.

"Sometimes the Outlookers came into our village, taking what they wanted, abusing our men, insulting our women, terrifying our children. Sometimes assassins came, and they did the same thing." His gaze swept the crowd. "And they did it in your villages, too.

"When Harlon the waterlord made his stand against the Valdani forty years ago, some Outlookers died and some assassins died. But mostly, thousands of *us* died.

"When the Firebringer came to free us from the Valdani, when he gave men a choice about their destinies and a nation to be proud of, who opposed him? Who thwarted him? Who betrayed and killed him?" Tansen's blood roared in his ears. His voice grew louder with each word of condemnation. "When it became Dar's will that we should be free, that we should fulfill prophecy and regain the lost glory of Sileria, who cared more about their own power than about the will of the goddess or the fate of this country?"

"Avenge Josarian!" Yorin shouted, leaping to his feet and waving his stolen Valdani sword in the air. "Avenge him!"

"You know what the Society can do to you if we oppose them," Tansen continued. "You know the lakes they can turn into crystal, the rivers they can stop from flowing, the wells they can make so cold your hands will fall off if you touch the water."

"Avenge Josarian!" Lann bellowed.

"You know they can pull a lake up over your heads to drown you, reach out to cover your faces with suffocating masks of water, strangle you with liquid tentacles stronger than a man's arms."

"Kiloran must die!"

"I've seen the White Dragon," Tansen warned them, "and now I know that it's not a legend. Kiloran killed the Firebringer—"

"Avenge the Firebringer!"

"—and will be harder to defeat than the Valdani, who are only men."

"We fought the Valdani!" Galian shouted. "We drove them all the way back to Shaljir!"

"I may not survive this war," Tan said. "You may not survive. We will suffer."

"And we will end the suffering!" Lann vowed.

"Dar demands vengeance!" Pyron cried. "My brothers didn't die at Alizar so that a waterlord could reap the wealth of the mines!"

This is it. Make it good.

"You will decide what you must," Tansen said, "but I made my choice the night Kiloran murdered the Firebringer. My choice was made the night he betrayed Dar, Sileria, and our destiny!"

"So was mine!" Lann declared.

"I am Josarian's bloodbrother!" Their love for Josarian made them cheer Tansen now. "And I will defeat Kiloran or die trying!"

The wild enthusiasm which met this pledge left him in no doubt of their decision. They would go to war against the waterlords. They would fight.

They were Silerians and they understood vengeance. Craved it. Lived for it.

No, it wasn't the future he wanted, the creed by which he believed Sileria could survive and thrive. But it was the first step along the way.

They seized him now and hoisted him up on their shoulders. Josarian had always let such outpourings of emotion flow over him naturally, easy with the crowd's enthusiasm, casually accepting the adulation which, privately, had made him wryly humble. Tansen hated it now, felt embarrassed and awkward; but he knew that his feelings were irrelevant and mustn't be allowed to destroy the wave of faith which had to carry these men through bloodshed, terror, and loss before finally taking them to a safe shore.

He was the Firebringer's brother and, as such, knew he was a symbol in which they needed to believe. Like Josarian himself, he couldn't be just a man in the eyes of the people he must lead.

Josarian, however, had at least had a bloodbrother with whom he could enjoy the ease of being just a man. Whereas Tansen . . .

He suddenly saw a flash of fiery hair gleaming under the sun and felt his heart quiver.

She had come back.

Mirabar.

Whereas Tansen . . . Ah, yes, Tansen always had women to remind him that he was just a man.

THE LIRONI WERE fighting Verlon the waterlord, opposing the power he'd always held in the east, rebelling against the stranglehold he wanted to clamp on the port city of Liron.

It was extraordinary news, and Mirabar couldn't have made the announcement to the rebels at a better moment. They were so fired with ambition, in fact, that Tansen now had his hands full trying to keep them here long enough to issue orders. The people loyal to Josarian's memory couldn't defy and defeat the Honored Society without strategy and tactics, after all.

Mirabar said nothing about Elelar, contradicted no one's belief at Dalishar that Zimran had acted alone. She said only, in response to curses the rebels pronounced on Zimran's memory, "But Kiloran is the one who killed Josarian, and that's all that matters now. Kiloran is the enemy we must fight."

That was when Tansen knew that however much she might hate him for not killing Elelar (and Zarien was right, it really did look like hatred), she wasn't going to confuse their cause with her private grievances. He supposed he should have expected that. Mirabar always put Sileria first. Strangely, it was the one thing she had in common with Elelar.

"Where are the *zanareen*?" he asked Mirabar now, holding council in the golden sunshine with her, Lann, Najdan, and Cheylan. Zarien was currently in one of the caves, where Rahilar again tended his bloody, blistered feet. When she was done with that, Rahilar would finish brewing up the pot of black dye Tansen had requested first thing that morning.

Still looking at Mirabar, Tansen said, "There were fifty *zanareen* with you when we parted company after Josarian's death, and I see none here now." Some of the *zanareen* had clung to Josarian like a shadow during the final months of his life.

"Some returned to the Zilar River after dawn," she replied, "to do who knows what. Mourn Josarian, I suppose. Some said they were returning to Darshon. Others scattered to spread the word."

"That Kiloran killed Josarian?"

"Yes."

"And Jalan?" Tan prompted, asking about the wild-eyed mystic who was something of a leader among the *zanareen*.

Mirabar's eyes widened. "Of course! I should have told you. He's gone east in search of Josarian's sister."

"Jalilar."

"He thought if Kiloran had gone to such effort to kill the Firebringer, then the Firebringer's sister might be in danger."

Dar be praised, this was now one less task Tansen had to assign. He had realized the necessity of it soon after leaving Elelar's villa near Chandar, but he'd had no opportunity yet to send someone after Jalilar—and now he wouldn't have to. Upon learning that Josarian was dead, Jalilar's husband, Emelen, a valuable rebel leader, would know what to do: get Jalilar safely to Sanctuary and then rally with Tansen.

Neither he nor Mirabar alluded to why she hadn't mentioned this before now, since yesterday's quarrel was not a subject for the many ears around them. He could tell by the rigid coolness of her manner, though, that nothing was forgotten or forgiven.

Focus on the task at hand.

"Cheylan," he said to the Guardian, "you'll need to go east again, first thing tomorrow." He sensed Cheylan's reluctance, caught the sudden flash of Mirabar's eyes, and he ignored it. "I want you to take messages to the Lironi as soon as possible, assuring them of our support against Verlon and getting theirs against Kiloran."

"As you wish," Cheylan replied.

"Lann, you need to send a runner to Zilar to tell them I'm coming."

"You're going to Zilar?" Lann asked.

"Yes. Hundreds—possibly thousands—of rebels have been massing near there, awaiting Josarian's arrival. We can't let them panic over his death."

"And you want a runner to precede you?"

"Yes. We've got to get word to everyone around the town of Zilar, as soon as possible, that I'm coming in Josarian's place and they should wait for me."

Lann nodded. "What else?"

"We've got to establish more sentries and better vantage points between here and Chandar. I don't want any more assassins ambushing us in our own stronghold. And send someone all the way down to Chandar to organize them there and send news through the mountains. Tell your runners—tell everyone—to see me for instructions before leaving."

"Is that all?" Lann asked.

"No. There'll be more before I leave today, but—"

"You're leaving today?" Mirabar blurted.

Cheylan glanced at her.

"—but for now, gather five of the best fighters we've currently got up here. I'll speak with them . . ." He looked at Mirabar. "After I'm done speaking with the *sirana*."

Lann nodded and rose to carry out his orders.

"You're leaving today?" Mirabar repeated.

"Before sundown," he replied. "You and I need to talk."

"We—"

"There's something I need to ask you about." He rose to his feet and, with a hand under her arm, forced her to do the same. Najdan, who could be very touchy about any disrespect to the *sirana,* didn't protest or even glare warningly at Tansen; his attention seemed fixed on Cheylan.

Cheylan's news from the east, of Verlon's demands and the Lironi opposition, was important enough to explain his unexpected arrival at Dalishar; but Tansen was glad it also ensured there was good reason to order him to return immediately to the district of Liron. Even without the aristocratic Guardian's interest in Mirabar, Tansen had never much cared for Cheylan's company.

And what's the point of being in charge, after all, if I can't indulge my petty dislikes?

"What do you need to ask me about?" Mirabar's voice was cold as Tansen led her towards the cave where Rahilar was tending Zarien.

"I promise you'll find it interesting."

The Sister was just finishing wrapping Zarien's feet in clean linen bandages when Tansen and Mirabar entered the chamber. Guardian fires burned magically in several places on the stone walls, their dancing flames glinting on the surface of the bubbling spring which formed a pool in the center of the cave.

"When that dye is ready," Tansen told Rahilar, "I'll need you to dye clothes for six men, including me. We're leaving before sundown, so they'll need to be ready by then."

"They'll still be damp," she warned.

"As long as they're not soaking wet. We won't actually wear them for a couple of days."

She nodded and left the cave to accomplish her task.

Alone now with Mirabar and Zarien, Tansen said to the boy, "Tell her what you told me."

"About . . ."

"About why you're here," Tansen clarified.

Now Mirabar's hostile gaze flashed with interest. "Yes," she said suddenly. "I need to know why you're here."

"Ah." Zarien looked from her to Tansen, then back again. "You understand this sort of thing. This is your realm, isn't it?"

"Go on," she urged, sitting down.

However, whatever she had been hoping or expecting the boy to say, it quickly became clear that she found his tale as astonishing as Tansen had. Her eyes widened when Zarien, at Tansen's request, showed her the scars left by the dragonfish attack, and her brow furrowed with thought as he described Sharifar's instructions. She looked particularly stunned when Zarien announced that Tansen was the sea king he sought.

Her reply to Zarien's urgent request that she agree with him was not quite what Tansen had hoped for: "It's possible."

"You see?" Zarien said triumphantly to Tansen. "*Now* will you come w—"

"However," Mirabar interrupted, to Tansen's relief, "it's certainly not what I've seen in my visions."

Zarien faltered. "It's not?"

"No. According to the Beckoner—"

"Who's that?"

"The one who brings my visions."

"Oh."

"According to the Beckoner, Tansen and I must prepare the way for the coming of the new Yahrdan."

"*What?*" Tansen said.

She looked a little sheepish. "I suppose I've neglected to mention that I've had more visions since . . . since Josarian died."

"Yes, you've left that out entirely," he said with a snap in his voice.

"But surely," Zarien said, "the sea kin—"

"The new Yahrdan?" Tansen repeated, almost enjoying his irritation with Mirabar; it felt good to attack rather than defend, for a change.

"Yes."

"You didn't think this was important enough to mention to me?"

"I just did," she replied stonily.

"No," he contradicted, pointing at Zarien, "it slipped out while you were talking to him."

"I had other things on my mind!"

"Like castigating me for not committing a murder."

"You can say that?" she cried. "After what she did?"

"She is in Shaljir right now," he replied, enjoying the sudden release of frustration in anger, "convincing Kaynall to honor their treaty—"

"How can you even use the word 'honor' in the same sentence with—"

"—and surrender Shaljir to us!"

"—that blood-soaked secret treaty?"

"Who else could do that, Mira? Who else could work with Searlon *now*? And Searlon is the key to convincing Kaynall—"

"You can make all the excuses you want!" she raged. "But I know the truth. No one else—"

"I'm tired of vengeance—"

"—could have betrayed Josarian with impunity!"

"—of killing in retribution for past killings!"

"You would have forgiven no one else!"

"I haven't forgiven her! I'll never forgive her! Fires of Dar, do you think it was *easy* to spare her?"

The sudden silence between them was thunderous.

Tansen was aware of Zarien's fascinated, open-mouthed stare. Mirabar's sun-kissed complexion was flushed with anger. His own breath was coming fast in his agitation.

"I think," Mirabar said at last, her voice low and harsh, "it was easier for you than killing her would have been."

"Maybe it was," he admitted at last, "but neither thing is easy." He added, "You've never killed. You condemn me without knowing what it means to take a life."

"True, but you've taken plenty."

"The feel of the blade cutting into flesh, the spray of blood. You don't know how that f—"

"How did she talk you out of it? Or did she even need to?"

Her tone bit into him. "By pointing out how similar our sins are," he admitted wearily. "She betrayed Josarian, and I . . ."

Darfire, he didn't want to think about it now.

Mirabar knew instantly. She had discovered his worst secret by Calling Armian from the Otherworld, after all. "She used *that* against you?" When he didn't deny it, she said, "How like her."

They fell silent.

Zarien finally ventured, "Used what?"

Tansen shook off the weight of warring emotions and said, "Never mind." He looked at the boy. "What we should be talking about is you."

"Yes," Mirabar agreed quietly, "that would be better."

"Can you help him find this sea king?" Tansen asked her.

"I don't know. It's certainly a brand-new—"

"I've found him," Zarien said stubbornly.

"I'm sorry, Zarien," Tansen said, "but I just don't think—"

"You didn't think Josarian was the Firebringer, either," Zarien interrupted. "So why sh—"

"How do you know that?" Tansen asked.

"Everyone knows that. You went to Darshon to stop him from jumping." Zarien nodded. "People talk."

"They certainly do," Tansen agreed tiredly. "However, I really don't believe I'm your—"

"And Josarian? Did *he* know he was the Firebringer?" Zarien challenged. "Before he jumped into the volcano, I mean."

Tansen searched his memories. "No, but he did have dreams. Portents.

And there were believers." Long before Josarian actually went to Darshon, Tansen had started fearing he eventually would.

"And there were signs in the circle of fire, too," Mirabar said, "in the Calling I did for him the night he decided to go to Darshon."

Tansen noticed that Mirabar didn't mention that she, too, had tried to stop Josarian, still terrified he would die at Darshon despite what she had seen in her Guardian fires. They had both failed, though, and Josarian had fulfilled prophecy.

By all the gods above and below, Tansen suddenly thought. *Could I possibly be this sea king?*

Nothing in him felt that it was true, but he had been wrong about such things before—convinced that Armian was the Firebringer, certain that Josarian wasn't.

"But surely you've had signs of your destiny, too," Zarien said to him. "The brand on your chest was carved by the gods of Kinto, showing you their fav—"

"No, it wasn't."

"It wasn't?"

Mirabar blinked. "Is that what people say?"

Zarien replied, "Yes."

"I'm afraid not, son," Tan said. "I got it the old-fashioned way. My *kaj* used—"

"Your what?"

"My teacher, the one who trained me to be a *shatai*—a Kintish sword-master—gave me this brand with a red-hot poker. All *shatai* have one. It's nothing magical."

Zarien looked deflated. "No?"

"No."

"And your swords?" Zarien asked. "They . . . they aren't enchanted?"

"No." He hadn't known people said so.

"They don't jump out of their sheaths by themselves?"

"I wouldn't have had to spend five years learning to use them if that were the case," Tansen pointed out.

Zarien looked extremely disappointed in him. Mention of magical weapons brought to mind the boy's quivering *stahra*. He was going to ask him about it when Zarien's face brightened as he said, "What about your healed wound?"

"Actually, that's among my questions," Tansen replied.

"Mine, too," Mirabar intervened. "Who healed it?"

"He did," Tan said.

Zarien shook his head.

"Did a waterlord find you?" Mirabar asked sharply.

Tansen's gaze snapped to hers. "A waterlord?"

She nodded. "Najdan says that healing a *shir* wound like that is water magic."

They both looked at the boy. He shook his head. "No one came." His expression was confused as he returned Tansen's equally puzzled regard.

"Tell me exactly what happened," Mirabar said.

"I prayed," Zarien said. "To Dar, to Sharifar, to all the gods of the wind and sea."

"That's all? You just prayed?"

"So did Tansen."

"I was unconscious," Tansen argued.

"You were feverish, but speaking," Zarien explained.

"I prayed?"

"Yes. To Dar. To the Firebringer. You asked for mercy. You called out to your father . . . Is he dead, too?"

"Yes." Both of his fathers were dead, but he remembered only one of them. He had called only one of them "father." Only one of them haunted his dreams.

"As you prayed to them," Zarien said, "as we prayed together . . ." He shrugged. "There was, I don't know, heat or something. Mist rose from the wound, silvery and glowing. And it healed."

Mirabar answered Tansen's questioning gaze with a frown. "It could be water magic," she admitted. "But that would mean one of you . . ."

When they both looked at Zarien, he immediately said, "Don't look at *me*."

"I thought it might be the place," Mirabar admitted, "but I investigated it on the way here today." She shook her head. "Nothing."

"What other possibilities can you think of?" Tansen asked.

"It could well be related to the magic which healed his dragonfish wounds. In which case . . ."

"We should go down to the sea right away," Zarien urged.

"And who do you think will lead us against the Society?" Mirabar asked Zarien.

The boy rose to his feet, stepping gingerly. "I don't care," he declared. "That is a dryland quarrel and doesn't concern me."

"Oh, yes, it does," Tansen insisted. "Sea-born clans have been in the Alliance since it was founded."

"Not the sea-bound Las—"

"All the sea-born swore loyalty to Josarian." He studied the boy's resentful expression and pressed, "Do you take your vows so lightly at sea?"

"We take nothing lightly," Zarien protested angrily. "But if you were sea king, then the sea-born would happily go wherever you led. Have you thought of *that*?" And he stormed—well, limped with offended dignity—out of the cave.

"He has a point," Mirabar said.

"He does at that," Tansen admitted. "But I can't abandon everything here to venture out to sea in search of a goddess's embrace based on the strange tale—"

"Josarian long resisted going to Darshon," she reminded him.

"So did Armian."

"And he . . ." She nodded, understanding. "He wasn't the Firebringer."

"Not even though one ignorant boy was utterly and completely convinced he was."

"More than one boy."

"More than one boy," he agreed. "Half the *shallaheen* in Sileria probably believed it. But Armian never did."

"What about your healed wound?"

"I think it's more about Zarien than about me. There's too much about that boy that's . . . unusual."

"Those scars," she said. "No one should have lived through that."

"And his *stahra*." He told her about what he'd seen in the cave where he'd been healed.

"You think it responds if Zarien is threatened?" she guessed.

"He says the sea goddess gave it to him." He shrugged. "It looks like any other *stahra* to me, but . . . I didn't imagine what I saw. I wasn't still feverish. He doesn't seem to know about its magic, but I'm sure it's not an ordinary weapon."

"He is no ordinary boy." She paused. "If Zarien remains convinced you're the man he seeks, the one this goddess wants, you may have to return to the sea with him. Sooner or later."

"I saw what being loved by a goddess did for Josarian." He could admit this to her. She would understand. "It's not what I want."

Her expression was sympathetic for the first time since coming here. The memories glowed in her fire-rich eyes. "There were many ways in which he would have preferred to remain an ordinary man. I know." She was quiet for a moment before adding, "But then, he had been a happy man."

Tansen looked away. "A wife he loved. A quiet life in his native village. A clan and a family . . . And no memories that haunted him."

"You may even find peace as the consort of a goddess," she suggested quietly.

"Do you want me to go to her?" he whispered.

"This isn't about what I want." Her voice was equally soft.

"Isn't it?" Now he met her gaze again, drowning in its exotic heat. "If I go to another's embrace . . ."

He put his hand on hers. He felt her startled reflex, but she neither withdrew nor protested. Her skin was warm from the sun outside, her bones as fine as an aristocrat's. He explored farther and found the remembered feel of her work-hardened palm.

He asked, "It will mean nothing to you?"

To be alone with her now, to see her look at him without anger, to smell her skin and feel its warmth . . .

Her fire-tipped lashes fluttered over lava-rich eyes. "You've already gone . . ."

"No." He leaned closer, his gaze drifting down to her mouth, to those soft, young lips.

". . . gone to . . ." Her breath was shallow, her voice vague, until it settled on a word full of hurt: "*Her*."

"No," he said. "Never."

"Only because she—"

"Don't bring her in here with us." He heard pleading in his voice and didn't care. "Not now."

She jerked away from him, startling him. "She is *always* here with us." Her voice was low and rough.

"Mira."

"And it's not my fault. You're the one who carries her image with you." She rose to her feet with the swift agility of a mountain girl. "You're the one who will have to eliminate it."

He watched her go, knowing no way to stop her, no way to reap what he wanted out of what he had sown with this woman.

15

WHY SHOULD WE HATE SILERIANS WHEN THEY'RE SO
GOOD AT HATING EACH OTHER?
—Imperial Advisor Kaynall

IF YOU EVER touch me again, I will tell Najdan to kill you.

So much for those fine, proud words, Mirabar thought as she left the cave and emerged into Sileria's brassy sunshine.

She couldn't ask Najdan to avenge a touch which she couldn't honestly claim to have found insulting, let alone unpleasant. On the other hand, if Tansen's touch was the one she wanted, it was also the one which hurt her.

He had looked at her that way once before, had touched her with longing one other time . . . and had promptly forgotten her the moment Elelar appeared. Mirabar would not tolerate such dismissal again.

When he kills Elelar, when he does as he promised . . .

Then she would welcome him. Not before.

But he would never kill Elelar. Mirabar had seen that in his eyes as they argued. She had heard it in his words. Had felt it in his shame.

"She betrayed Josarian, and I . . ."

Oh, the *torena* was clever. How many more ways would she find to punish and torment Tansen for that night, so long ago, when a lone boy had stopped the Society from taking over Sileria?

Mirabar's feelings were causing a storm in her which must show on her face, since Cheylan crossed the clearing and said quietly, "He's upset you."

The last thing she wanted was to go straight from facing one man to dealing with the other. How had her personal life become so complicated? She could almost feel a twinge of sympathy for Elelar, whose every waking moment seemed to involve juggling the men who claimed—or wanted to claim—a right to her company. Mirabar, by nature and experience, was far less prepared than Elelar to cope with such pressures. The greatest difference, of course, was that Mirabar cared about both of the men who troubled her peace, whereas she doubted Elelar had ever cared about anyone.

"If you're not needed right now," Cheylan said, "then perhaps we c—"

"I am," she blurted, wanting to avoid a tryst with Cheylan on the heels of her confrontation with Tansen. Seeing his questioning expression, she added, "It's something to do with Zarien."

"*Did* he heal the *shir* wound?" Cheylan asked, his gaze going to where the tattooed boy sat glumly at the edge of the clearing, ignoring the activity all around him as rebels prepared to depart Dalishar in pursuit of their newly assigned duties.

Mirabar had confided her interest in the boy to Cheylan while he and Najdan helped her investigate the cave where Tansen had lain dying.

"He says he didn't," she replied. "I'm inclined to believe him, but I want to know more." She called to Zarien. He rose to his feet and, bringing his *stahra,* came to join her and Cheylan. His expression was a little sulky.

"Come with us," Mirabar said.

She turned and led the way to the sixth sacred cave of Dalishar, which she entered. She passed through the successive chambers of the cave until they reached the fourth chamber. A huge Guardian fire, as old as the sect itself, burned in here, its flames rising up from the stone floor. A gateway to the Otherworld, perpetually open, its pull was so strong that Mirabar could hear souls streaming into its flames even now, their silent song reverberating through her head, disrupting her thoughts and making ordinary conversation difficult. She knew by the increased tension in Cheylan's face that it was the same for him.

Zarien's *stahra* remained immobile in his hand, with no sign of the life Tansen had described. If it was enchanted, at least it didn't hate fire magic the way all *shir* did, and that made Mirabar feel easier about it. There was no inherent enmity between her kind and whatever sorcery protected this boy.

Mirabar met Zarien's gaze and asked, "What have you brought to Dalishar from the sea, from your old life?" Seeing his puzzled expression, she clarified, "Personal possessions."

"Only my *stahra.*"

"It's probably all that matters, anyhow," Mirabar said.

"What do you m— Hey!" Zarien protested when Cheylan took the *stahra* from him.

"We're going to try to do a Calling with it," Mirabar explained.

The boy looked suspicious. "What exactly does that involve?"

She replied, "We communicate with the Otherworld. Usually, as in this case, to try to understand this world better."

Zarien looked even more suspicious. "Do I have to do anything? Or let you do anything to me?"

"No. We usually take a physical object, something which belonged to someone who's now dead—"

"I don't have anything—"

"In most cases, we can only Call shades from the Otherworld near the anniversary of their deaths."

"Why?" Interest was slowly replacing suspicion.

"The Otherworld revolves in relation to this one, time rolling over into time."

Zarien glanced at the *stahra,* now in Cheylan's hands, and reminded Mirabar, "That didn't belong to a dead person."

She pointed to the huge fire before them. "This is believed to be the oldest Guardian fire in Sileria. Ancient, sacred, very powerful." Mirabar gestured to the *stahra.* "Your weapon's origin is unusual, to say the least." She looked at Cheylan, whose eyes glowed hotly as he studied the oar. "Perhaps we can use it to learn more."

"I've told you everything I know," Zarien said.

Cheylan asked, "And don't you want to know more?"

Zarien looked at them both for a moment longer before saying, "All right, let's do this . . . this Calling."

He seemed to change his mind abruptly when Cheylan tossed the oar into the fire. "Wait! What are you doing?"

Cheylan held him back. "It won't burn."

"Won't burn?" the boy repeated in outrage, struggling out of Cheylan's grasp. "That's a fire, you— *Ow!*" He snatched his hand away from the flames.

"See?" Mirabar pointed out the way the *stahra* danced unharmed in the fire. "It doesn't burn."

Zarien stared open-mouthed. "How is that possible?"

The two Guardians ignored the question and started chanting, their voices blending together as if they'd done this often. In fact, Mirabar realized, this was the first time she and Cheylan had ever worked together. They did it well, as if they had been Calling the Otherworld in tandem for years.

It wasn't long before she felt a new presence among them, a powerful energy emanating from the fire. She could tell by the slight stiffening in Cheylan's posture that he felt it, too. Although their bodies remained immobile, the spirit was strong enough to pull their souls closer to the ensorcelled flames, dragging them towards the fragile boundary between this world and the Other one, towards that void where Guardians were sometimes lost forever.

"She is coming," Cheylan murmured.

He was right, it was a female presence. Mirabar added, "And her name is . . ."

Cheylan concluded, "Sharifar."

"Sharifar!" Zarien's excited voice barely penetrated Mirabar's senses, so absorbed was she in the fire, in the struggle not to go too far into the flames, and in the immensely powerful voice which she felt echoing through her blood now.

Shimmering veils rose through the fire, finer than gossamer leaves, translucent and glowing. They undulated as if underwater, swaying in a gentle, unseen current. The golden glow of the fire faded and was replaced by dancing flames of pale blue, like the azure waters of the Middle Sea, tipped with frothy white foam.

Even Mirabar, who had seen many strange things in Guardian fires, gasped when Sharifar's body took shape, some incandescent sea creature merged with a woman of inhumanly opalescent beauty.

"Sharifar!" Zarien came as close to the fire as its heat would permit. "Am I right? Have I found the sea king?"

Stay in the current you have found. Let it carry you.

Mirabar heard the reply in her head and was about to repeat it aloud; but when Zarien responded, she realized he'd heard it, too. A shade of the Otherworld normally needed to answer the living with a Guardian's tongue; but in this, too, a goddess was different. Or perhaps it was Zarien who was different?

"Stay with Tansen, you mean?" he asked.

He will lead you home.

"To the sea?"

Follow him until you cannot.

"When will that be?"

You will know.

Mirabar risked intruding. "How can we help Zarien?"

You cannot help him. You must not shield him.

"I must not shield him?"

You were born to shield another.

"Then you know?" Mirabar breathed.

Zarien interrupted, "When you say I will know . . ."

Yes, I know.

"How exactly will I know?" Zarien persisted.

"Can you tell us about Zarien's gifts?" Mirabar asked.

His gifts will lead him home.

Zarien said, "I thought *Tansen* would—"

Cheylan interrupted, "Do you know whom Mirabar must shield?"

Dar knows.

"Does Dar also know," Zarien asked, "how I'm supposed to convince Tansen to . . . to . . ." His eyes widened as a low, angry rumbling invaded the cave. "Is that . . . Is that another . . ."

Mirabar's senses, wholly immersed in the sacred fire, were slow to respond to the ferocious growling which began in the mountain's belly and slowly surrounded them.

Equally torn between this world and the Other one, Cheylan was sluggish, too.

When she felt the ground trembling beneath her, Mirabar tried to pull away from the fire, but her distraction weakened her, letting her soul tumble farther from her body and closer to the void. She felt a current tugging at her, drawing her deeper into the foaming blue flames, deeper into the Otherworldly embrace of the goddess she had brought forth to answer their questions.

Sharifar, let me go!

The goddess answered, *He is coming!*

And then Mirabar was tumbling backwards onto the heaving ground, her head hitting the floor of the cave as the roaring in her blood changed to a roaring in her ears. She opened her eyes, and the world spun wildly as Cheylan took her arms in a firm grip and dragged her to her feet.

Earthquake!

"Come on!" Cheylan shouted to Zarien.

"My *stahra*!"

Mirabar winced as the boy reached into the fire and grabbed the oar. Fear might shield him from the pain right now, but he'd suffer for days to come—if they escaped the cave alive. They could easily be trapped if a ceiling gave way in any of the chambers they must pass through.

Dizzy and disoriented, Mirabar just concentrated on moving her feet; she let Cheylan, who led her by the hand, determine their direction. Zarien's urgent hand on her back ensured that her pace didn't lag, and the two men yanked her to her feet whenever she stumbled.

She could see the light of day at the same moment she became aware of someone shouting her name. Tansen's voice. Tansen's face. He was there in the cave now, pushing her ahead of him, then dragging Zarien with him as rocks tumbled around them. One hit her on the shoulder, but she was in the sunlight before the pain became sharp. Then she was lying on the ground in a panting heap with Cheylan, Tansen, and Zarien.

A terrible thundering crash filled the air, different from the rumbling roar of the earthquake. She lifted her head and saw a thick cloud of smoke rising from the distant volcano of Darshon, billowing upward with the speed of water pouring downward.

Were there any *zanareen* living on the snowy, wind-swept volcano rim now? There had been hundreds in residence the day Josarian had jumped, but Mirabar knew that most had scattered afterwards, either to follow Josarian or to spread across Sileria and announce the long-awaited arrival of the Firebringer.

If there were any of them left at Darshon, she wondered if they had just died up there.

STILL SHAKEN FROM the earthquake which had assaulted Shaljir today, Elelar made sure the servants were all right, then assessed the damage to her household. Apart from some oil jars which had fallen, creating a slick mess of shattered shards, there was relatively little to concern her.

Next, she went deep into the cellars, through a concealed door, and down into the dank tunnels which ran underneath her house. Even further down into the belly of the world, behind a secret entrance, was a low-ceilinged maze of ancient tunnels carved eons ago by the now-extinct volcano of Mount Shaljir. It was here that the Beyah-Olvari lived.

The original inhabitants of Sileria, they were a fragile, peaceful, diminutive people driven to near-extinction by the New Race, Elelar's kind, who had invaded Sileria thousands of years ago. While some people thought that Elelar's race may have come from the Kintish Kingdoms before they *were* the Kintish Kingdoms, the Beyah-Olvari said the New Race had come from the south, pouring out of the mouth of the north-flowing Sirinakara River in search of an island nation promised to them in prophecy.

A land-hungry people of conquest, the New Race brought violence and warfare with them, as well as disease. Not even the Beyah-Olvari knew whether they had brought fire magic with them or discovered it for the first time here in Sileria, but they soon developed a powerful communion with the volcano goddess and had little interest in the gentle water magic of the Beyah-Olvari.

Time, disease, the hardships of competition with a stronger race . . . All this took its toll on the Beyah-Olvari. Most of them died. Some may have set sail for the mainland, though no one knew for sure. Others moved to higher and higher ground, fading into memory, into legend and song, and leaving behind only their mysterious cave paintings to show that they had ever existed. And a few hundred had come here, to underground tunnels ancient beyond memory, hiding for eons and assiduously avoiding the New Race as they built the great city of Shaljir overhead.

Elelar had learned about the Beyah-Olvari from her grandfather. Gaborian had envisioned a free Sileria for all Silerians, and so he had brought the

Beyah-Olvari into the Alliance. Their existence was still largely a secret, though, known only to a few inhabitants of Shaljir, several trusted members of Elelar's household, and certain members of the Alliance. As Gaborian had once warned Elelar, the more people who knew about the Beyah-Olvari, the more chance there was of the Society learning about them. And the Society was unlikely to tolerate the existence of another water magic cult in Sileria.

Elelar had not sent a message to warn the Beyah-Olvari—the Followers of the Olvar—of her imminent arrival. This was an unplanned visit, inspired by the earthquake. It had been a violent one, even worse than the other night's, and she wanted to know if there'd been any injuries among "our old friends," as they were discreetly referred to in the Alliance, from falling rocks or collapsing tunnels.

However, though unexpected, she was soon greeted by a small welcoming party sent in search of her. She didn't bother asking, since the Olvar was the only one among them who made a habit of speaking directly to members of the New Race, but she supposed that the aged Olvar had foreseen her arrival in the Sacred Pool—a small, deep spring imbued with all his considerable power. Among the Olvar's gifts was one which the waterlords had never developed: divination. Unfortunately, it was a gift of limited use, since the Olvar usually only foresaw things of interest to the Beyah-Olvari. Not only were they extremely different from the New Race in virtually every way, but they led a very circumscribed life down here in the tunnels. Consequently, Elelar seldom found much practical use for the Olvar's gifts of foresight.

The half dozen blue-skinned beings who now welcomed Elelar with much chanting and blessing were tiny, coming up only to her waist, with fragile bones and innocent faces. Whereas the New Race, even the *toreni,* were a modest people who covered most of their bodies, the Beyah-Olvari, male and female, covered only their loins. Although the Olvar could speak archaic High Silerian, which was how he and Elelar communicated, she seldom heard any of the others speak anything but their own language—a chattering, musical sound well suited to chants, blessings, banishing prayers, and mourning songs.

They guided her now to the Chamber of the Sacred Pool, where the Olvar could always be found. All around her, the tunnels glowed with phosphorescent plant and animal life; most of it comprised the diet of the Beyah-Olvari. When Elelar came face-to-face with the Olvar and his praise singer announced her arrival, there was a great deal more chanting and blessing, both before and after the lengthy greeting ceremony which was always required.

"I came to see if your people are well after the earthquake, *siran,*" Elelar finally said.

The dozens of Beyah-Olvari around her, only a portion of the hundreds which she estimated lived in the tunnels under the city, chanted a banishing prayer.

The Olvar's aged face was shadowed as he dipped and stirred his hands in the water of the Sacred Pool, which glowed with his sorcery. "We have not suffered from it, *torena*," he replied in his thick accent.

Shame and sorrow washed over Elelar as she said, "There have been many changes since last we met, *siran*."

"Yes, I know. The Firebringer is dead." The Beyah-Olvari began a mourning chant.

"Now there will be a struggle for ultimate rule of Sileria."

He looked up from the Sacred Pool, his watery eyes full of pity. "It is always so with your kind, isn't it?"

The mourning chant grew louder, making her head spin.

"Can you see who will win?" she asked suddenly.

He gave what might have been a sigh and returned his gaze to the Sacred Pool. "A child is coming."

"A child?"

"To rule us all."

"How can a child unite Sileria?"

"A woman of fire awaits him."

"Mirabar?"

"But her heart is so set on vengeance that she may not shield the child. She may fail her duty."

Of course it was Mirabar. Elelar could readily guess how much Mirabar wanted vengeance, wanted both her and Kiloran dead.

"What happens if she fails her duty?" Elelar asked.

"The waterlords will destroy her."

A banishing prayer replaced the mourning song. The Beyah-Olvari always uttered banishing prayers when the waterlords were mentioned.

"And," the Olvar added, "they will destroy us, too."

Some of the Beyah-Olvari now seemed to wail in panic. The noise rattled Elelar's nerves and made her eager to escape the tunnels. But she had to know, had to ask: "How can I help, *siran*?"

The Olvar's wrinkled blue face and sad eyes gazed deep into the Sacred Pool as his frail hands stirred the eerily glowing water. "Yes," he said at last, his head bobbing lightly on his thin neck, almost as if it floated. "What you do will change everything."

Elelar's heart pounded. "What must I do to save Sileria?"

"You must surrender."

Her stomach clenched with fear. "Surrender?"

"When the one with eyes of fire finally comes for you, you must not resist."

*   *   *

BY THE TIME Tansen finished giving everyone their orders, as well as preparing the men Lann had picked for the raid he was planning, he was exhausted. And he still had a long journey ahead of him. There had already been enough delays since Josarian's death, so he knew he must leave now; he couldn't afford to lose more time.

That sudden, terrifying earthquake earlier today had made everyone jumpy, and few things caused more dread among the *shallaheen* than seeing Dar throw a tantrum. Smoke had billowed wildly out of Darshon's caldera for hours, blackening the sky and creating an oppressive atmosphere.

The worst part of the day, though, had been those few dreadful moments at the start of the earthquake when someone told him Mirabar and Zarien were inside the sixth cave. Even now, his heart hadn't quite recovered from the plunge it had taken then. He still remembered the wild flood of relief he'd felt upon bumping into them at the rear of the first chamber as they made their frantic escape. His hands, steady against every opponent he'd ever faced, had been shaking.

Now, as the smoke-darkened sky over Dalishar threatened to bring on an early night, Tansen finished examining the clothes he'd ordered Sister Rahilar to dye black. Then he asked for Najdan and Mirabar. He didn't have any important orders for the assassin, who he already knew would protect Mirabar with his life, but he didn't think she'd want to be alone with him again so soon after what had happened earlier today. He wasn't sure he wanted to be alone with her, either.

When they sat down with him, Tansen said to Mirabar, "I want you to leave for Zilar in the morning. I want the people there to see you, to see how powerful you are, to hear from your own lips that you've had a vision about the coming of a new Yahrdan."

"Where will you be?"

"I'll meet you in Zilar," he promised. "I've got something I need to do first."

"Something that requires you to dress like an assassin?" Najdan asked with a glance at where Sister Rahilar was packing the black-dyed clothes.

"Yes."

"Something that involves those *shir* and *jashareen* you took from those bodies yesterday?"

"Yes."

"Ah," Najdan said. "A good idea."

"What's a good idea?" Mirabar asked impatiently.

"He's going to begin sowing distrust among the waterlords," Najdan said.

"They'll be hard enough to defeat individually," Tansen admitted, keeping his voice low. "Unless we can destroy their unity, we haven't got a chance."

Mirabar figured it out. "Who are you going to attack?"

"Wyldon. He still resides, as far as I know, in the Amalidar Mountains south of Lake Kandahar. With luck, he'll think Kiloran is trying to eliminate him so he can take over his territory."

"And Wyldon is loud," Najdan said.

"Precisely. If he believes it, he'll tell his troubles to others—and convince some of them that they may be next."

"What about Baran?" Mirabar asked. "He sided with Josarian against Kiloran. Among the waterlords, surely he's our best chance of an ally."

"He is," Tansen agreed. "Baran's half mad and wholly unpredictable, but there's a chance he might join us just to thwart Kiloran again. And he's strong enough for his defection to hurt the Society. That's why I'm sending a message to him, taken by Sister Velikar, offering our friendship and asking for his."

"Velikar?" Mirabar repeated incredulously.

"Yes, well, I needed a Sister who isn't afraid of waterlords. Even one as volatile as Baran."

"Ah, but will Velikar frighten Baran?" Najdan asked dryly.

"She's a strange ambassador," Tansen agreed, "but these are strange times."

"About Zilar . . . ," Mirabar said slowly. "There's more you should know."

"About your visions?"

"Yes. I think the new Yahrdan will be a child."

Tansen's heart took another plunge. "Could it be Zarien? Could that be why—"

"I don't think so." She told him about bringing the sea goddess forth in the Guardian flames.

"No wonder Zarien's been looking so stunned all afternoon," he said wryly. "I thought it was just the earthquake."

In the irritating manner Tansen had learned to expect of visions and Otherworldly matters, Sharifar hadn't come right out and said whether or not he was the sea king. However, she had advised Zarien to stay with Tansen and predicted that Tansen would lead the boy home.

"That's open to almost any interpretation," he protested.

"I can guess what interpretation the boy will place on it," Najdan said.

"So can I." He asked Mirabar, "But you don't think his coming here is related to your visions?"

She shrugged, her expression revealing some of her own frustration. "I don't know. I don't think so, but . . ." She sighed. "A child of fire, a child of water, a child of sorrow . . ."

"The child you're looking for will be all of those things?"

"Perhaps," she said vaguely.

"Fire and water?"

She heard his doubt. "I know, I know."

"And you have no idea who it could be?"

"Actually . . ."

"What?" he prompted.

"The first time I ever met Cheylan, he told me of a child who lives in the east. A Guardian boy named Semeon." She took a deep breath and added, "A child like me."

Tansen saw from Najdan's surprised expression that she had kept this a secret until now. "Can he find this boy?"

"Yes, though it may take time."

"He's going east again in the morning. I'll speak to him before I leave today and tell him to search for this boy—Semeon?—put him someplace safe where you can meet him."

She nodded, then changed the subject. "I think you may be right about Shaljir."

"About not attacking it?"

She nodded. "The Beckoner says the Valdani will leave Sileria."

Tansen said, "We've believed that for months. I just want to know how much more blood we'll have to shed to make them do it. How many more of us will have to die to get rid of them?"

"That question," she admitted, "the Beckoner did not address."

"No, of course not."

She looked perturbed. "I only repeat—"

"I know."

"If I knew more—"

"I know." He eyed her warily. "So perhaps I've done the best thing." After all, without Elelar, who in Shaljir could speak on their behalf to the Valdani?

Mirabar's expression was hot and cold at once as she replied, "I didn't say that."

He sighed. "Never mind. Is there anything else you should tell me?"

"Nothing I can think of now."

He looked at Najdan. "I've arranged for six men to accompany you. It's all I can spare right now. Travel only by day, stay in Sanctuaries every night, and don't let her out of your sight." When the assassin nodded in acknowledgment, he added, "Stay well away from the Zilar River until you get north of the delta, where it flows into the Shaljir River." It was unlikely that Kiloran's power extended that far. As far as Tansen knew, the Shaljir River was still under the control of two brothers, Abidan and Liadan, neither one of whom was strong enough to control it alone.

"We will," Najdan said.

Tansen rose to his feet when Mirabar did. Their gazes locked in the strange light of the smoke-clouded afternoon.

"Until Zilar," she said, and turned away.

"Until Zilar." He watched her go.

"Perhaps you should consider sheep, after all," Najdan mused.

"What?" He stared at the assassin.

Najdan sighed. "Never mind."

ZARIEN SPUTTERED WITH outrage as he protested to Tansen, "I'm not staying up here, on the roof of the world, with ensorcelled fires and earthquakes and attacking assassins—"

"There won't be any more assass—"

"You don't know that!"

"We're posting—"

"And that's not the point! The point is, I came all this way to find you, and I will not stay—"

"It isn't safe—"

"—alone here in this strange place!"

"You won't be alone. I'm leaving Sister Rahilar and a number of men here."

Not wishing to be rude, Zarien lowered his voice as he said, "These are landfolk."

"So am I."

"Sharifar said—"

"Please, let's not go over this again."

Zarien fell silent, burning with frustration the way his neck still burned where the assassin had pressed a *shir* to it yesterday. Tansen stubbornly refused to accept what the goddess had told Zarien when called forth in that strange fire.

By the winds, my hand hurts!

Sister Rahilar had dressed it for him, and her burnt offerings and strange chanting had actually made it feel better for a while, but now it was bothering him again. He should have made one of those Guardians retrieve the *stahra* from their damned fire, but everything was so confusing, so terrifying once that earthquake started, he had simply reached into the flames without thinking.

"I will not be left here," Zarien said.

"I'm not leaving you here permanently." Tansen's voice was getting edgy with irritation.

"You're not leaving me here at a—"

"Enough!" Tansen rose to his feet. "You will stay here. I will either send for you, or come back for you. That's the way it will be, Zarien."

Heart pounding, Zarien rose to his feet, too, and looked up into the warrior's dark eyes. "Or?" he challenged.

Tansen lifted one brow. "Or I will never, under any circumstances, no matter what, go to sea with you."

Zarien's jaw dropped. "But—but—"

"Be polite to the Sister while I'm gone and let her help your feet get better. Understood?"

Zarien studied his face, trying to determine if he really meant it, if Tansen could really be that stubborn, inflexible, and willful.

Stay in the current you have found.

"This is for the best," Tansen assured him. "Trust me."

Follow him until you cannot.

"Zarien?"

He realized Tansen was awaiting an answer. "Um . . ."

Tansen sighed. "I know this is a pointless—even foolish—thing to say to someone your age, but . . . Do as you're told, all right?"

"Where are you going?" Zarien asked.

"Oh, to make new enemies." Tansen smiled wryly. "It's what I do best. Winning friends . . . That was what Josarian did best."

"You miss him," Zarien said suddenly, surprised again that Tansen was so human, so like other men in some ways. It wasn't what he had expected of the legendary warrior, let alone the sea king.

Tansen nodded. "Yes, I miss him. The way you miss your brother, I am sure."

"Brothers," Zarien corrected absently. "I had two."

"Had?" Tansen asked, peering at him. "Is your family—"

"I mean," he said quickly, "Morven and Orman. Two. When I was at sea."

He wasn't going to tell Tansen the rest. It was his private shame, and not one he cared to expose to Tansen, second only to Josarian in glory and greatness.

Tansen slapped Zarien on the back. "Two brothers, that's good fortune. And your family will be happy to see you alive again."

"Yes." He added hesitantly, "But I'll be banished, even so."

Tansen frowned. "Maybe not, under the circumstances."

It was his own secret hope, but he said bravely, "There has never been an exception. The sea-bound never even speak the name of someone who has gone ashore."

"I'll talk to them."

"You're a drylander, they won't care what you—" He clapped a hand over his mouth as he realized what he had said.

"Ah, you see?" Tansen grinned. "Even you aren't as sure as you pretend to be."

Stay in the current you have found.

"I only meant—"

"I have to go," Tansen said. "But we'll meet again soon, Zarien. I promise."

"Yes, Tansen."

He came to his decision the moment Tansen turned away from him. He intended no disrespect, he truly didn't. But the dictates of a goddess must come before those of a man.

Follow him until you cannot.

16

IT TAKES ONLY THREE THINGS TO BECOME A WATER-LORD: A GREAT TALENT, A TERRIBLE THIRST, AND A HEART OF STONE.

—Kiloran

HE WAS THE greatest waterlord in all of Sileria.

He had dominated a vast territory of Sileria, the jewel of the Middle Sea, for more than thirty years, rising to preeminence in the Honored Society during the bloody feuding and chaos which followed Harlon's death nearly forty years ago. Now an old man, he continued to hone and increase his power over water at an age when most other waterlords had been dead for years. Some said he was not only the greatest waterlord in Sileria, but the greatest since Marjan himself, the very first waterlord; yes, perhaps even the greatest waterlord who had ever lived.

It was true, Kiloran knew. He was the best.

Not because he had more talent. If truth be known, he privately believed he had less talent than Harlon had had, and he secretly suspected that Baran was the most talented water wizard he'd ever seen. But they were ruled by their emotions. Harlon had invariably acted without thought, driven by his hot temper and bloodthirsty nature. And Baran, whose sanity was frequently questioned . . . Oh, yes, Kiloran knew what ruled Baran: heartsick longing, hatred, and the lust for vengeance.

He should thank me. Hating me gave him the will to develop his talent.

Nor was Kiloran the best because he was the cruelest or most ruthless. Cruelty was merely a weapon to Kiloran, ruthlessness merely an exercise in common sense. Whereas cruelty was a passion for some of them—Verlon, for example—and ruthlessness a pleasure in which they reveled. In fact, Verlon was even older than Kiloran, but did that fool have power and influence to match Kiloran's? No, of course not.

The lesser waterlords in Sileria, of which there were nearly one hundred, were perhaps younger, less experienced, less talented than Kiloran. This was irrelevant; young men eventually grew older and gained experience, after all, and Kiloran had already proven that talent was merely one factor in the struggle for ultimate power.

What mattered was that Kiloran had yet to see anyone among the lesser waterlords who possessed the one thing which could threaten him, the one quality which set him apart from the others: the cold intelligence which had ensured his ascendancy in the face of overwhelming odds and opposition, a shrewd cunning which had kept him at the head of the Honored Society longer than most assassins had even been alive.

It was fortunate, he reflected, that Searlon had never shown even the slightest hint of a gift for water magic. As an assassin, he was invaluable— and unfailingly loyal. If he had ever shown promise as a waterlord, though, then there would have been trouble.

Armian had been the sort of ally Kiloran knew he could control. A talented, bold, educated, quick-thinking man of courage and decisive action, Armian had nonetheless been wild and emotional, prone to reckless violence, sensual appetites, and unthinking sentimentality. His ill-considered devotion to that quiet, serious, willful peasant boy, for example . . . Then again, a father's love was a common weakness, even a noble one. Kiloran himself had loved his son Srijan, despite the lad's many faults.

Ah, mistakes. They are so easily made. Especially when we love . . .

Yes, he could have handled Armian as an ally, as he had handled so many others, some of them even—as in the case of *Torena* Elelar—unwitting to the alliance. But Searlon . . . No, Searlon would have been too dangerous an apprentice to water magic, too ungovernable a waterlord. Kiloran would have had to exercise a little sensible ruthlessness and eliminate him, had he been so gifted. Searlon's intelligence, like Kiloran's, ruled his passions, governed his appetites, and kept his judgment clear.

This was the quality that made a man superior to others, as well as more dangerous than the rest. It was the quality which made Searlon a servant who inspired envy among the other waterlords and respect—not to mention healthy competition—among Kiloran's other assassins. And it was the quality which made Kiloran the greatest waterlord in Sileria.

Could any other waterlord have beaten the Firebringer? He thought not. Did the others imagine he did it with sheer talent? Did the rest of them believe that his craving for vengeance, after Josarian had murdered Srijan, was so strong it superceded Dar's divine power? Well, let them think it. It was not Kiloran's duty to set them straight, to explain how the world worked, to teach them how power was exercised most effectively.

When Josarian assumed the mantle of the Firebringer, Kiloran understood the danger in a way that none of the others did. *Power is much easier to withhold than it is to take away,* he had told Elelar when the rift began to develop between him and Josarian.

Unlike so many others, Kiloran knew the difference between someone who must be watched carefully and someone who must simply be eliminated. A lava-eyed peasant like Mirabar, gifted with prophecy and blessed with extraordinary fire sorcery, was very dangerous, of course, but for a long time she had been more valuable alive than dead. Besides, the girl was no leader, and half the *shallaheen* in Sileria would probably still go screaming into the night if they came upon her suddenly in the dark. A father-slaying *sriliah* like Tansen could be allowed to live for a little while longer, Kiloran had initially decided, if it meant ridding Sileria of the Valdani; so he had rescinded his bloodvow.

Even Josarian, a charismatic rebel leader, hadn't been a threat in the beginning. After all, the one thing everyone in Sileria had in common— probably the only thing—was that they all hated the Valdani and wanted them to leave. Josarian's gift was that he had somehow been able to make everyone in Sileria willing to do virtually anything—even work together— to achieve this goal.

However, after Josarian's transformation into a Dar-blessed demigod issuing orders to the Society about how to manage its affairs, insisting on the waterlords' obedience to his rule, and increasingly supported in his intoler-able interference by an ever-bolder population . . . That was when he became someone who must be eliminated as quickly and cleanly as possible.

The *zanar* prophecies might say nothing about the Firebringer's ulti-mate destiny after driving the foreign invaders out of Sileria, but Kiloran could certainly see the future clearly enough after Josarian survived jump-ing into the volcano at Darshon. The Firebringer would rule Sileria unop-posed and grind the Society beneath the heels of his shoddy *shallah* boots.

Fire and water had competed for a thousand years in Sileria, eternal ene-mies. Kiloran had finally understood, when confronted with the Fire-bringer, that it was his destiny to end the struggle once and for all. Until Josarian, Dar had ignored the waterlords, leaving Her fire-blessed Guardians of the Otherworld to defend themselves as best they could against the Honored Society. But Josarian changed everything.

Had Armian been the Firebringer, as people once said, then the Society could have ruled Sileria in power and security for centuries. Of course, Armian himself had never believed it, having spent his whole life in foreign lands where Silerian beliefs were regarded with indifference. Kiloran, skep-tical but interested in the possibilities, had seen no reason to press the issue at the time—since he'd had no idea that that pestilent brat Armian had adopted would murder him and thus effectively sever negotiations with the Moorlanders. The silence from the Moorlands ever since then indicated that Armian's death was taken as Kiloran's answer to their proposal, just as Tansen had planned.

Tansen, when only a boy, had outwitted him. So now that Kiloran had slain Josarian, he knew better than to underestimate Tansen. Both the *shatai* and the fire-eyed prophetess must be eliminated. There would be no con-

tentment in Sileria while they lived, and Kiloran would ensure that the rest
of the Society understood and accepted this. He must lead them, as he
always had, as was his rightful place. And in the end, he would rule all of
Sileria, as was his destiny.

After all, he had already triumphed over the Firebringer and proved
himself greater than Dar's Chosen One.

Not that it had been easy. His first attempt to kill Josarian, by using Outlookers to ambush him in Sanctuary, had failed. The Valdani were such
incompetent blunderers, Kiloran would never understand how they'd managed to conquer more than half the nations of Sirkara.

Nonetheless, only the weak wavered from a goal in the face of discour-
agement, so Kiloran had persisted. After Josarian killed Srijan, vengeance
became as important as expedience. No one would respect a waterlord who
did not protect his own and avenge his son. Failure to punish Josarian for
Srijan's death would ensure Kiloran's own destruction. So he invested a
great deal of time and effort in his next attempt, knowing he must succeed.
It would have been best, of course, had the Valdani seized Josarian in the
ambush which *Torena* Elelar planned for him. But the Valdani failed
again—this time because Najdan betrayed Kiloran.

Ah, mistakes. They are so easily made.

After twenty years of Najdan's loyal service, it never once occurred to
Kiloran that the assassin would betray him. Najdan, of all men! Obedient,
servile, unimaginative—totally faithful even to his own woman, let alone to
the master who had always rewarded him richly for his service. Kiloran had
actually been fond of Najdan, had valued him and let him know it, had
trusted and relied on him. When he discovered that Haydar, Najdan's mistress, had disappeared, he was reluctant to accept the conclusion he would
have drawn immediately, without hesitation, had it been anyone else: Najdan hid her—in some Sanctuary, no doubt—to protect her from Kiloran,
because he was going to betray his master.

That was when Kiloran realized that his clean, clever plan to let the
Alliance and the Valdani together kill Josarian would probably fail. That
was when he knew he would have to do it himself—for he was half the
White Dragon, as the water from which it grew was its other half.

It was a terrible risk, in more ways than one. Until he had done it, even
he wasn't entirely sure that water magic could kill the Firebringer. The
Society did not pay homage to Dar, but attacking Her Chosen One was
undeniably dangerous. However, Kiloran couldn't delay any longer. Josarian
was preparing to lay siege to Shaljir. Whether it surrendered quickly or held
out for months, the fall of Shaljir would end the war in Sileria. And Josarian must not be alive on the day native rule was declared.

Power is much harder to take away than it is to withhold.

Nonetheless, despite everything, Kiloran hadn't wanted to kill Josarian;

he had desperately wanted the damned Valdani to kill Josarian, and he hated them bitterly for failing.

Being the murderer of the Firebringer could lessen his influence, he knew, if only temporarily. Most of Sileria had loved Josarian, would mourn his death, and would resent his executioner—even a father claiming vengeance; after all, Josarian had made sure that all of Sileria knew he'd killed Srijan in vengeance for Kiloran's betrayal.

However, Kiloran had done what he must and didn't regret it. Sileria's people might hate Josarian's executioner, but they would also fear the water-lord who had proven himself more powerful than the Firebringer.

Fear and love . . . Well, this was Sileria, where the two tended to be closely entwined. But it was not convenient, because he could well guess what that damned bloodson of Armian's planned now, knowing, as he undoubtedly already did, that Kiloran was responsible for Josarian's death.

Kiloran wondered what was happening in Shaljir, where Searlon waited to identify Josarian's body for the Valdani. Since there would be no body, of course, the Valdani might make excuses, might refuse to honor their secret treaty with the Alliance and surrender Shaljir. It was troubling to think about, particularly since Kiloran knew Searlon might not receive the message he had sent about Josarian's death; in anticipation of attack, Shaljir was locked up tighter than a *toren*'s wine cellar. However, Kiloran was a patient man, and he knew that Searlon was equal to whatever new challenges now arose in Santorell Palace.

Meanwhile, here in Cavasar, the city he had seized from the Valdani and now ruled, he had other concerns to occupy him. With Najdan gone forever and Searlon in Shaljir, Kiloran allocated additional authority to a green-eyed assassin named Dyshon, who had been in his service for almost six years. Dyshon was a little impetuous, but also smart, brave, quick, reli-able—and too eager to become a waterlord to get sentimental about the Firebringer, Mirabar, or the rebels, as Najdan evidently had.

"I want to send messengers across Sileria," Kiloran told Dyshon now, admiring the view of Cavasar at night from his tower window in the old fortress from which the Valdani had, until recently, ruled the city.

"*Siran?*"

"To call for cooperation among the waterlords. To ensure that no feuds or quarrels erupt to divide us. We cannot afford trouble now."

"But if Josarian is dead . . ."

"He is." It would take time for word to spread, but although he had not precisely been there in person when Josarian died, Kiloran, as sire of the White Dragon which had devoured him, had felt his death. Even now, if he tried very hard, he could hear Josarian's screams of agony, which would endure for the rest of his own life. However, it was an ugly sound and so he did not bother to try.

"*Siran,* are the Valdani not therefore obliged to—"

"That is a separate matter." Kiloran turned away from the window and regarded the assassin. The green eyes meant foreign blood somewhere in his family's history; Moorlander or Valdani. Nonetheless, now that Kiloran had finally agreed to let him study water magic, he showed some slight promise.

Dyshon nodded. "Ah. Then your concern is that those loyal to Josarian would have the impudence—"

"Tansen is still alive. So is the Guardian."

"Mirabar."

"Yes. So we can count on impudence."

"But surely the people would never dare oppose—"

"That," Kiloran said, "is undoubtedly what the Valdani said when Josarian started urging rebellion. But they were fools and I am not. I will expect anything."

"Yes, *siran*."

"And prepare for everything." He smiled coldly. "Which is why I want to arrange a meeting with Baran."

Dyshon's green eyes flashed with surprise. "But he was loyal to Josarian."

"Precisely."

"Baran is your enemy, *siran*. He always has been."

"Exactly."

"I'm sorry, *siran*, I don't understand. Why wo—"

"Because now everyone in Sileria must choose sides. Everyone. Even Baran. Will he join forces with a bunch of malcontents seeking vengeance for the death of a leader they can't resurrect and can't replace? Or will he come home, once again, to his own kind—the Honored Society, the water-lords, the destined rulers of Sileria?"

"Ah. He will see that you have won."

"He will see where his only real future lies."

"You think he will make peace with you?"

Dyshon didn't know why Baran hated Kiloran so much. No one left alive knew, not even Najdan or Searlon. "No. Baran will never make peace with me."

"Then why—"

"But I believe he can be persuaded to accept another truce."

"But why, *siran*?"

"Because he lives to destroy me."

"Then surely—"

"And he'll want to go on living until the day he finally *can* destroy me. He won't side with my enemies unless he's certain they can win. And now that Josarian's dead, he'll know they can't."

"So . . ." Dyshon frowned in puzzlement as he thought it over. Kiloran missed Searlon, who would have understood instantly. "So you're saying that he'll become your ally rather than your enemy now . . . because he'd rather wait for the chance to destroy you in the future instead of risk losing that chance now by . . ." Dyshon shrugged and concluded, "By dying futilely alongside your doomed enemies?"

"Precisely. He has done it before," Kiloran pointed out, "has become my temporary ally to preserve his chance of vengeance at a later time."

"Yes," Dyshon said slowly, "I suppose he has, hasn't he?"

"He's less than perfectly sane," Kiloran said dryly, "but he's not a fool."

Kiloran and Baran had not only joined forces when Josarian united Sileria against the Valdani, which was what Dyshon was undoubtedly thinking about, they had also called a brief truce some seven years ago when Valdani reprisals against the Society had been particularly harsh. Baran might be the single greatest nuisance of Kiloran's long life, but at least the man could usually see the larger tapestry and often adjusted his plans accordingly.

"The strength of the Society," Kiloran continued, "is that we know how to put aside our differences—if only temporarily—to unite against a common threat."

"Where shall we invite Baran to meet with you?" Dyshon asked. "He won't come here, and he certainly won't agree to go to Kandahar. And I assume you don't want to go to Belitar."

Dyshon assumed correctly. It was ironic that Baran—whose longtime feud with Kiloran made him an enemy of Kiloran's adoptive clan, the Idalari—inhabited Belitar, the abandoned stronghold of Harlon, the long-dead leader of the Idalari clan. Considering how many men—not all of them Valdani—had died in the ensorcelled lake surrounding the castle, it wasn't surprising that people said the place was haunted by demons, evil spirits, and wandering shades of the dead. Kiloran, content in his own unique underwater fortress at Kandahar, had never much cared what happened to Harlon's crumbling old ruin, a place he'd only entered once during his youth, anyhow. Legend claimed that Marjan himself, the first waterlord, had once lived there. Perhaps it was true; Kiloran found Belitar's damp, dreary ruins so decayed, he could well believe the foundations were at least a thousand years old.

By the time Kiloran learned, more than a dozen years ago, that Baran had moved into the long-abandoned ruins of Belitar, Baran had already secured the surrounding lake with sorcery. Then he went about establishing his territory by killing off several rivals and forging alliances with others. As the years passed, Baran became the second most powerful waterlord in Sileria, challenging Kiloran at every turn.

That, Kiloran acknowledged, was what came of not killing your friends before they became your enemies.

However, the damage was done, and he must deal with what Baran had become rather than reviewing his regrets.

"No, I certainly won't go to Belitar," Kiloran agreed with Dyshon. "Suggest to Baran that we meet in Emeldar."

"Josarian's native village?"

Kiloran nodded. "It's been deserted since the start of the rebellion."

One of Josarian's first acts had been to slaughter an army of Outlookers which rode into Emeldar with the intention of punishing Josarian by punishing his clan. After that, Josarian ordered his people to abandon Emeldar. Then High Commander Daroll and more than one hundred Outlookers occupied the deserted village . . . and all died slowly of the poison Josarian had ordered put in the main water supply.

Even now that the Valdani had abandoned the district, Josarian's people couldn't go home. No one but a waterlord could cure Emeldar's water supply.

"I will send a messenger," Dyshon said.

"Invite some of the other western waterlords to come witness our truce," Kiloran ordered. "Baran will be more apt to come if he knows half a dozen others will be there." Baran knew Kiloran wouldn't murder him at a truce meeting in front of witnesses. The appearance of honor was, after all, rather important in the Honored Society. "We will set a good example for the other waterlords, putting aside our private quarrel for the good of the Society."

"Is that all for now, *siran?*" Dyshon asked.

"No, one more thing."

"Yes?"

"Find Najdan's family. He came from some miserable little village east of Britar. As far as I know, his mother is still alive, and I believe he has sisters. Presumably married by now."

"Do you want them all assassinated?"

"On the contrary. I want you to send someone to them with wine, food, money, and gifts. Make sure they have everything they need. Promise them my protection, and establish a means for them to contact me if they ever have problems of any kind."

"*Siran?*"

"Assure them I don't blame them for Najdan's shameful betrayal. Tell them I will look after them, in his place, for the rest of their lives."

"That is very generous of you, *siran.*"

Kiloran gazed out the window again. Yes, Sileria could be ruled through terror, and often had to be. But why bother in cases where it was so much easier to cultivate devotion? If Kiloran slaughtered the womenfolk of a rogue assassin, he'd be feared—but also hated. Whereas if he tenderly cared for them . . . Ah, yes, who would be shamed now? Indeed, it probably wouldn't be long before Najdan's native village, and perhaps even his own family, were ready to kill him for betraying Kiloran.

"That will be all for now, Dyshon," Kiloran said.

"You . . ."

"Yes?" He glanced over his shoulder at the assassin.

"You seem tired, *siran*. Perhaps you should rest now."

"Yes. You're right. I will."

He turned away and, a moment later, heard the door close behind him.

Of course he was tired. As Marjan had once said, to rule water was to rule Sileria—but, as Marjan must have also known, it was far from easy.

Even in his sleep, Kiloran could feel Baran's grasping will struggling for full control of the Idalar River—something which was not so easy to rule even without fighting such a talented sorcerer day and night for it. The concentration required to keep Baran from seizing it was indeed tiring, especially at this distance.

Kiloran meanwhile maintained his grasp on the mines of Alizar. This was far less taxing, since they were dormant, completely flooded by water so cold a man could lose a finger just touching it. However, he couldn't safely access the mines—one of the greatest sources of wealth in the three corners of the world, a place so rich that even the Emperor of Valdania felt its loss—while his energy was absorbed by so many other demands. Most important, the power to drain the mines might distract him long enough for Baran to seize complete control of the Idalar, which was yet another reason Kiloran needed the proposed truce.

In addition, Kiloran now controlled the Zilar River—where Josarian had died—deep in the mountains, before it merged with the Shaljir River. He continued to rule water throughout his traditional territory, and he was slowly taking control of all of Cavasar. Not just the people and the government, as any conqueror would—as Josarian surely would have—but also the many deep-bored wells which were the city's primary source of water.

He had already, of course, quietly killed the two waterlords who had previously controlled the water in Cavasar. Neither of them had been powerful enough to be a threat, but together they were strong enough at least to cause trouble and be a distraction. Now that they were dead, some of the water in Cavasar was free—neither controlled nor requiring tribute—for the first time in centuries. That would change soon, of course.

Kiloran stretched his senses out towards the city now and could hear it, smell it, feel it—the water which lay deep, deep under Cavasar. Some of it was his already, though he had chosen to do nothing with it for the time being. Let Cavasar celebrate, let her people rejoice. The Valdani had fled, the Outlookers were gone, and no foreigner would ever again rule this city. Let the fountains flow, the wells bubble joyously, the people quench their thirst for freedom. In the end, he believed, it always paid to be a little generous, a little kind. You could beat a dog every day, but it remained loyal if you fed it, and mindlessly devoted if you let it sleep at your feet at night. People were much the same, and when the time came to be ruthless, the city of Cavasar would do as its new conqueror ordered. When tribute for water was required, they would remember how kindly Kiloran had let it flow in celebration of the Valdani surrender, and so they'd be that much more likely to pay it without resistance, to obey without resentment.

Obedience was essential. Opposition was intolerable.

Yes, there was water out there. Some of it answered his will, his ensorcelled reach, even now. He pushed slightly, and felt the course of a stream adjust to his desire. He grasped, and the level of a well lowered a bit. He willed it, and a fountain stopped flowing.

This was the power that made Silerians obey him. This was the mysterious glory of the waterlords, the only wizards of their kind in the three corners of the world.

You had to love water to command it. You had to understand it as more than just a substance. It had life, music, character, a will which must be coaxed, harnessed, bullied, beguiled. It had a scent which could fill you from far away, sound which could flood your whole being long before others heard it. It offered sensation, demanded focus, required discipline, and responded—to one who could access its deep, hidden, secret heart—with power beyond most men's understanding.

He knew now that his mother had suspected from his earliest childhood that he had the gift. She had brought him to an Idalari waterlord for apprenticeship, though, only after another waterlord's assassins killed her husband when she couldn't pay the ransom required after he'd been abducted during the long rains; like so many *toreni*, Kiloran's family had been beggared by the Valdani. Typically Silerian, his mother wanted vengeance. Before she died, a few years later, Kiloran ensured that she had it. By then, of course, the rest of his family had disowned him for joining the Society. Few people now knew where he came from, though the legends about his origins were many.

So many of the people who had influenced his life were gone now: His mother, who died soon after satisfied vengeance emptied her of the fury which was the source of her strength. The old Idalari waterlord who had taught him the mysteries of water magic. Harlon, so reckless in his opposition to the Empire, so exhilarated by the long and bloody conflict in which the Outlookers had destroyed him. *Toren* Gaborian, weak in body but with a heart full of visionary enthusiasm; they had never been friends—Kiloran didn't have friends—but they had broken centuries of tradition, a waterlord and a *toren*, by becoming allies. Armian, perhaps the most ambitious man Kiloran had ever known, defeated by the ordinary things in life—most notably, fatherhood . . .

Yes, how Armian had struggled with that role, loving the boy but ignorant of how to manage him.

"Siran, *what do you do when your son disobeys you?*" Armian had once asked him. Srijan had been only three years younger than Tansen.

"*I punish him.*"

"*What if he disobeys you because he thinks you are wrong?*"

"*I teach him.*"

"What if he doesn't accept what you teach him?"

"That has never happened."

On another occasion, Armian had mused, *"Sometimes the boy seems like a stranger."*

"He is a stranger. You've only known him a short time."

"His family is gone. He looks to me for guidance."

"Then give it to him."

"I try, but— I often feel he wants to see someone else when he looks at me."

"His real father?"

"No. A different man."

"Different?"

"Different from me. Perhaps . . . perhaps the man he expected me to be."

"Ah. Yes. Being a legend can be inconvenient."

"Very inconvenient for a father, anyhow," Armian had agreed.

Armian had shown some talent for water magic, if not for fatherhood, during the brief time he'd spent with Kiloran. Armian's father, Harlon, would have been proud. Kiloran himself believed he had found his successor, since his own son was devoid of the gift and none of the other prospects appealed to Kiloran. Yes, Armian had flaws, but there had been much promise there. . . . Not least of which was the possibility of Kiloran's complete and unopposed domination of Sileria if Armian's plan worked.

Kiloran cooled the rage which boiled inside him even now, ten years later, at the memory of all Tansen had taken from him by killing Armian. He forced himself to recall what Armian's shade, floating in Mirabar's strange Guardian fire, had said the night the girl had tumbled through the waters of Lake Kandahar in time to prevent Kiloran from killing Tansen upon his return to Sileria after nine years in exile.

"Now is the time. We were wrong. Now is the time."

Ah, destiny was a strange thing. Would their plan really have failed ten years ago even if Armian had lived? And without Tansen's guidance, would Josarian's enthusiastic but unfocused bloodfeud against the Outlookers ever have grown into a national rebellion? There was no way of knowing.

Unfortunately, the orphaned *shallah* boy had grown into a dangerous and powerful enemy. Kiloran thought it unlikely Tansen could convince Sileria to forever abandon the habits of centuries and to openly oppose the waterlords for long, but any opposition at all was intolerable.

If Tansen had even one hundred men at his back—and Kiloran was sure he must—those were one hundred men whom one thousand others would watch with interest. If not crushed immediately and ruthlessly, they would gain new recruits. Perhaps not as rapidly as Josarian's rebellion had, for hatred of the Valdani was universal, whereas loyalty to the Society was an ingrained tradition among many clans and villages throughout Sileria. But all opposition was dangerous, and none of it could ever be regarded with complacency.

When one Silerian saw another rise up and refuse to obey, and get away with it—even thrive—then he was likely to try it himself.

One hundred men could easily be defeated. But one thousand? Perhaps not. Ten thousand men? That was civil war. And all of Sileria? That might be the end of the Society. However, Kiloran knew it needn't come to that.

The waterlords and their assassins were not Valdani, not *roshaheen,* not hated conquerors from the mainland. They were as Silerian as the mountains themselves. They were the weft in the tapestry of their culture, the pillars which supported its bleeding sky, the discipline which held its inherent chaos in check. The Society traced its origins back a thousand years. There would always be water magic in Sileria; only a fool could think otherwise, and so there would always be waterlords.

Silerians knew this, accepted this. Those who had forgotten must be reminded. Those who opposed Kiloran must be destroyed.

They knew his power, his inexorable will, his relentless strength. They were his children and would obey.

What could Tansen offer them, in the end, to embolden them to challenge their masters? With Josarian gone, who was left for the nation to follow?

This was Kiloran's destiny. His time had come. He would triumph. Truly, what could Tansen promise Silerians beyond chaos, drought, bloodshed, and sorrow?

Nothing.

Who was left for Sileria to follow?

There is only me.

17

KEEP YOUR FRIENDS CLOSE, BUT KEEP YOUR ENEMIES CLOSER.

—Silerian Proverb

A CHILD OF *fire* . . .

Mirabar reeled in the eddy of stars swimming around her . . .

A child of water . . .

In the divine liquid fire of history and destiny, of past, present, and future . . .

A child of sorrow . . .

In the bitter longing of a broken heart, in the vengeful dreams of a wasted life . . .

"Where am I?" she asked the Beckoner.

It was a dark place full of light, a bright place shadowed by darkness. A vast cavern, heavy yet airy, immense yet encroaching.

"It seems like a big prison."

Fire and water were all around her. The churning lava of the restless volcano extended its reach to this forgotten place, dripping into the water which flowed through strange tunnels lit by unfamiliar glowing shapes. Each time lava touched water, angry hissing filled the air and steam rose to obscure her vision.

"Why do I feel imprisoned?" she asked.

A child of fire . . .

She thought the phosphorescent lumps on the walls and ceilings were plants, but now one moved.

She gave an aborted shriek, inspired by a purely worldly fear of strange crawling things.

Now she noticed other glowing shapes moving, too. Some with long spindly legs, some with no legs at all . . . And some with what appeared to be a thousand tiny legs.

"Blegh," she said with feeling.

However, they all scurried away, apparently as frightened as she was disgusted, so there was no threat from them.

A child of water . . .

"Are they one and the same?"

It was not a pleasing prospect, but she had learned to expect almost anything by now.

Protect what you most long to destroy.

"What?"

The strange surroundings evaporated in hissing steam, then a breath of wind blew the vision away. Or so she thought, until she looked up at the night sky overhead and saw two golden, glowing eyes gazing back at her.

"Daurion?" she whispered. She crossed her fists and lowered her head. "*Siran.*"

He is coming.

"How will I know him?"

The eyes faded, and only the night remained.

"All right," said Pyron, a *shallah* rebel who had lost two brothers in the mines of Alizar. His voice was startlingly loud behind her. "Did anyone else see that?"

Mirabar glanced over her shoulder. Since there'd been two earthquakes so recently, no one at Dalishar slept in the caves tonight. Everyone was outside, sleeping on open ground, and whatever noise she had made in the throes of her visions seemed to have awoken many of them in time to see what she had seen in the night sky.

"Because," Pyron continued, "I really don't want to be the only one who saw that."

"Welcome to my world," Mirabar said a touch sourly.

Yorin stood staring up at the sky with his sole eye, his stolen Outlooker sword drawn and ready for battle. "That was . . . That was . . . That was . . ."

"Very interesting." Lann's voice was unusually thin and high.

Sister Rahilar, who sat hugging her knees, glanced at Mirabar. "Did you do that?"

"I don't think so," she replied.

"He is coming?" Lann ventured.

Mirabar brightened. "You heard it, too?"

"Well, no, I didn't hear anything. I just . . ." He shrugged. "I don't know. Those words just came into my head."

"Yes," Pyron said, sitting down suddenly. "He is coming."

Mirabar looked hesitantly at her protector, who lay at a respectful distance from her and ensured that everyone but Rahilar—the only other woman here—did the same. "Najdan?"

"Yes, I saw." His voice was stony. He sat up slowly and repeated with concentrated calm, "I saw."

She knew he didn't like contact with anything Otherworldly, but she was pleased. "This could be good."

"Sure, that was my first reaction," Pyron said shakily. "This could be good."

"I mean," Mirabar said, "it'll be a lot easier to convince people of my visions if I'm not the only one who's seen them."

"That was a vision?" Rahilar started rocking back and forth.

"Well, just part of one."

"Pyron," Lann said suddenly, "where's that almond wine Josarian always liked so mu—" He stumbled over the memory, paused, then tried again. "Where's the almond wine?"

Pyron nodded and rose clumsily. "Um, there's a lot left, actually. I'll get some."

Rahilar followed him with her eyes and protested, "Are you sure you should go inside the—"

"Yes, I'm sure," he called over his shoulder as he disappeared into one of the caves.

Yorin caught Mirabar's eye with his own and winked, a surprisingly frivolous gesture in that tough, scarred face. "Sleep," he said with a shrug. "Who needs it anyhow?"

This was the second time Mirabar's visions had leaked through the night to ensnare others. The first was the night after Josarian died. Had it happened only here at Dalishar, in her presence? Or were others in Sileria now being alerted to the coming of the new Yahrdan?

She would, she supposed, find out starting tomorrow, when she quit Dalishar and set out for Zilar, as Tansen had ordered.

He was gone now, having departed at sunset with five other men. The bustle and excitement here should have made his absence scarcely noticeable, but Mirabar felt it sharply. He had not rested enough, and he was once again off courting death. There were things she might have said . . .

Then again, there were things he should have done.

Stop, she ordered herself. Her head reeled every time she reviewed their quarrel and the hopelessness of settling it to their mutual satisfaction.

Overhead, Abayara was starting to wane, but Ejara remained full. The moons' normally alabaster faces were a faint reddish color now and the stars were obscured, thanks to the smoky rages of the volcano, but the night was still a bright one for mountain-born eyes. Mirabar looked in the direction of Darshon—and rose to her feet even as Lann muttered, "Look!"

One by one, the rebels followed his gaze. Mirabar walked to the edge of the clearing, to the craggy cliff's edge, and stared into the distance, apprehensively studying the snow-capped peak of the volcano wherein dwelled Dar, the destroyer goddess.

Lightning flashed violently above Darshon, again and again, illuminating the mountaintop as columns of colored smoke rose from the caldera. Pink, red, orange, yellow, and ghostly white, the spirals of smoke and steam coiled upwards into the tumultuous storm, then swayed and shifted, as if shying away from the restless lightning which broke the sky open, time after time.

Mirabar didn't realize she was holding her breath until she heard Najdan, now standing close to her, release his.

"Have . . ." She felt her lower lip tremble and bit down on it for a moment. "Have you ever seen anything like that before?"

"No." His voice was scarcely recognizable. "Not even as a child in the Year of Red Moons."

Colored clouds rose and spread around Darshon's icy summit, swaying this way and that, sometimes snatching their heads back like snakes in response to the high winds and the angry bursts of lightning. Shifting and galloping light turned colors in the night and danced wildly all around the sacred home of Dar.

"My father . . . ," Lann said hoarsely. "He once said you could see the dead dance, in the right light . . ."

"That isn't the dead," Mirabar said with certainty.

"No," Cheylan agreed. Mirabar had forgotten about him. She had forgotten everything for a few moments. She tore her gaze away from Darshon now and met his eyes. Like her, he had seen shades of the dead. Often. Like her, he knew this was nothing like that.

"What is *that*?" Pyron demanded, carrying a large wineskin as he joined them and stared wide-eyed at Darshon.

"We don't know," Mirabar admitted.

"Well, you're supposed to know!" There was a shadow of panic in his voice. "This is your . . . your sort of . . . you know."

"Give me that wine," Mirabar said.

"Wine all around, I think," Lann added.

"Good idea," Pyron said. "There's plenty more where this came from, blessed be Josarian's memory."

"Josarian!" Yorin exclaimed. Everyone else looked at him. "Don't you see? Dar is angry that the Firebringer is dead."

Everyone immediately shifted their attention to Mirabar. All she could say was, "Possibly." She looked back at the swimming, colored mists and the lights whirling around Darshon with increasing urgency. "But since we didn't kill him, we have nothing to fear."

"I like that theory," Pyron said. "I respectfully accept the *sirana's* interpretation of—"

"And if Dar is angry," Mirabar continued, "then She shouldn't have let him die."

A crack of volcanic thunder roared in the distance as a column of flame, clearly visible even from here, shot straight up into the tumultuous sky over the caldera. Mirabar fell back a step, while many of the *shallaheen* ran halfway to the dubious safety of the caves before collecting their wits.

"Disrespectful comments—" Najdan began.

"I don't care," Mirabar snapped. "Whatever gods rule us, they have used me, tormented me, and led me around at their will." Her eyes were misty with frustrated rage. "If Dar wants my continued service, then She had damn well better be worthy of it."

"Mirabar . . . ," Najdan said, surprising her with his almost unprecedented use of her name.

She looked at him now. She saw his confusion, his uncertainty. She saw his age, his scars, the hard life he had led. She saw him wandering the unknown territory into which he had ventured, following her with such stern devotion.

And she realized she must be stronger than this; for him, and for the others.

With the Firebringer dead, they counted on her to understand Dar for them. To reassure them. To soothe their fears of the destroyer goddess and convince them of Her continuing love.

She didn't feel strong, she wasn't convinced there was nothing to fear from Darshon, and she had no idea if Dar still loved them. But she knew—because she had known Josarian, and knew Tansen—that her private fears were irrelevant and mustn't dictate her actions. Especially not in front of others.

"I'm sorry," she said quietly to Najdan. Then she turned and announced to everyone else, "We have nothing to fear. We were the Firebringer's friends. We tried to save him. We will avenge him. And Darshon . . . is very far away tonight."

These statements, and a few additional ones, had the desired effect—as did the almond wine which Josarian had favored so much that his men ensured there was always a good supply of it here at Dalishar. This, like almost everything else they had, they had stolen from the Valdani. Like everything the Valdani had taken from Silerians, it was rightfully theirs.

Only Cheylan did not join in the rather determined drinking and nervous conversation with which Josarian's friends now tried to comfort themselves. He remained at the edge of the clearing, his gaze fixed on Darshon's distant drama.

Mirabar eventually joined him. "What do you think?" she asked quietly.

"I'm not sure." His dark hair absorbed the light of the sacred fires of Dalishar and the torches the rebels had used to further illuminate this strange night. His golden eyes glowed as he gazed across Sileria. "But I find it . . . interesting."

"I'm afraid for you," she said. "Going east again tomorrow."

He smiled and finally looked at her. "I'll be fine. I'm from the east, after all." He shrugged. "This display is new, but we in the east are accustomed to living with Dar's moods and tantrums."

"Please be careful." Her voice almost broke. She had said good-bye to friends too often lately. Sometimes unwillingly. And, more than once, permanently. "Please don't . . ." She made a little sound and concluded lamely, "Don't fail to return."

He placed his palm against her cheek. The unscarred palm of a *toren*. "I will return to you. Nothing will stop me."

His wasn't the touch which made her blood run hot like lava and her heart swell like gossamer leaves soaking up the rain. But he understood what it was like to be her; more so, probably, than anyone else—even her mentor, Tashinar. Tonight, maybe because she felt lost and afraid and lonely, Mirabar felt a tremendous kinship with Cheylan. Even if another man had stolen her heart, this one would always have her trust.

"I saw it," Cheylan whispered to her.

She frowned.

He elaborated, "The vision."

"Ah."

"The eyes in the night sky. He is coming."

"Yes."

"The glowing eyes."

"Yes."

"Golden."

"Yes," she repeated.

He stroked her hair, his gaze bright with excitement. "Like yours and mine."

"Is that all you saw?" she asked, trying to casually move away from his caress without appearing to reject him.

"There was more?" he asked, his attention sharpening.

"Yes, much more!" She frowned. "You didn't see?"

He took hold of her shoulders, ignoring the way she tried to evade his grasp. "Tell me."

"A place . . . A watery place with lava dripping into it, making steam rise. I don't know, maybe a cave or cavern . . . Perhaps underground . . . Glowing things . . ."

"Glowing things," he repeated, his voice soft yet urgent.

"Glowing plants and, ugh, crawly things."

"Ah." Cheylan nodded, his expression intense. "And this is where . . . what? You'll find him?"

She shrugged. "I don't even know if it's a real place."

"But—"

"Fire and water. Water and fire. A child of fire, a child of water . . ."

"And a place." There was something insistent in his tone. "Caverns of fire and water."

Memory flashed through her mind. "Protect what you most long to destroy," she murmured.

"What?" His grip on her arms was starting to hurt.

"That's what the Beckoner told me." She glanced briefly around, looking at the core of rebels sworn to support Tansen against the Society. He hoped to bring thousands more to his cause at Zilar, she knew. "Could we be wrong?"

"About what?"

"The Society? Surely . . ." Her heart pounded as she tried to articulate a possibility she could never accept. "Did Dar let Josarian die so the Society would rule Sileria?"

"No. I don't believe that," Cheylan replied with certainty, finally slackening his hold on her.

Mirabar stepped back. "I can't believe it either, but . . ."

Why did You let him die, Dar?

"Protect what you most long to destroy," she repeated.

Fire and water, water and fire . . .

"Are we wrong," she asked Cheylan, "to go against Kiloran? To try to destroy the Society?"

"You think they could be part of the future?" he asked. "Part of this . . . this ruler you must shield?"

Hatred, vengeance, and panic all battled her attempts to consider this dispassionately. Finally she admitted, "If so, then it may already be too late."

He tried another approach. "What about Zarien. After what we saw in the fire today, surely he's not—"

"*Zarien*," she said suddenly. She turned away from Cheylan to inspect the crowd of wakeful rebels. In a loud voice, she asked, "Has anyone see Zarien?"

"Certainly," Rahilar said. "He was . . ." She looked around vaguely for a moment, then her expression went blank. "He . . ." She met Mirabar's gaze. "Now that you mention it . . ."

Pyron frowned. "I haven't seen him since . . . since, uh . . ."

"Where's Zarien?" Mirabar demanded.

Yorin looked at Lann. "Weren't you supposed to keep an eye on him?"

"In a general way," Lann admitted defensively, "but I didn't think that meant I was supposed to watch him like a virgin near Outlookers. And in case you haven't noticed, I've been very busy!"

"But where is he?" Rahilar asked.

"We can't have misplaced a whole boy," Pyron said.

Oh, no.

"We didn't misplace him," Mirabar said wearily. "He's run away."

"Should we send someone after him?"

"Who could we spare?"

"It's the middle of the night!"

"He could get hurt."

"Or lost."

"I suspect that boy can take care of himself," Cheylan mused.

"*I* suspect," Lann said, stroking his beard nervously, "that Tansen's going to be very annoyed with me."

"Where do you suppose Zarien's gone?"

"Back to sea, maybe?"

"Good riddance."

"He seemed like a nice enough boy."

"But he didn't belong here."

Mirabar recalled what she'd seen in the fire. "I'll bet he's following Tansen."

"Then he's in trouble. Even *I* can't follow Tansen when he's covering his trail," Yorin pointed out.

Pyron asked, "What should we do?"

"I'm not sure," Mirabar admitted.

"I wonder how long he's been missing?"

"He's probably been gone for hours." Rahilar glanced at Lann and added, "That's a little embarrassing."

Lann sighed. "Pass the wine."

ELELAR AWOKE TO the sensation of cold fire pressed against her throat. She opened her eyes and saw a man's shape hovering over her, faintly outlined in the shadowy moonlight streaming through the window.

Assassin!

Panic filled her chest and flooded her mind . . . until she realized who this must be.

"Searlon?" she whispered.

The tip of the *shir* blade left her throat and traveled insinuatingly down the length of the bedclothes. She held her breath and clenched her teeth, still afraid.

Then he suddenly reached down to slip his *shir* into his boot. "You wanted to see me, *torena*?" he asked politely.

She sagged with relief, glad he was as shrewd as she had believed. "Yes." Her voice was breathless. "But I had hoped you would call at a more conventional hour."

"I cannot escape Santorell Palace unnoticed at a more conventional hour," he replied. "My humble apologies, *torena*."

She had encountered Searlon's smooth courtesy many times. The more outrageous the circumstances, the more absurdly polite he was likely to be. It seemed to amuse him.

"You heard about my husband's visit to Advisor Kaynall?" she ventured, waiting for her heartbeat to resume a more normal pace.

"Yes. And I would not dream," he added, "of disturbing your conjugal chamber in the middle of the night, had I not already seen *Toren* Ronall downstairs in deep communion with some cloud syrup."

It had been years since she felt even the slightest interest in what Ronall did with his nights, let alone expected any husbandly protection from him, so she ignored the comment and proceeded to business. "Kaynall didn't realize it was a message from me to you?"

"No. The Advisor evinced little interest in your husband's comments, beyond briefly wondering if you did indeed know I was here. Other than that . . . he seemed to believe it was even possible that *Toren* Ronall had completely imagined your return to Shaljir." Searlon paused briefly before adding, "I gather the *toren* saw many imaginary things while he was in prison."

"Imaginary things?" she repeated blankly.

"To one who is used to a surfeit of pleasures, their sudden and complete absence can easily unbalance the mind."

She had no trouble believing that *anything* could unbalance Ronall's mind, and there was no question that he loved his liquor and dreamweed, so she dismissed this allusion with disinterest. Slipping out of the far side of the bed, she donned a dressing gown, then lit a few candles so they wouldn't have to continue this conversation in the dark.

She came directly to the point. "And what was Advisor Kaynall's opinion of the Outlooker's story about the White Dragon killing Josarian?"

"Ah. Then you do know. When I recognized your message to me, naturally I wondered."

He was a big, well-muscled man in the prime of life, who wore his coal-black hair short—which gave credence to the rumors that he originally came from a family of wealthy city-dwelling merchants. In the mountains, he usually wore the black clothing and red *jashar* of an assassin. Here in Shaljir, where no assassins were allowed, he was dressed in dark leggings which hugged his muscular thighs, and a neatly tailored tunic of wild gossamer dyed deepest blue. His face was notoriously handsome, despite the long scar running down one cheek; legend said he'd acquired that scar while making his first kill, the murder which had earned him a place in the Honored Society and brought him to Kiloran's attention.

"Yes, I know," she snapped. "So does Tansen. So does Mirabar. So do the *shallaheen* and the *zanareen* who were with Josarian when it happened. And soon—"

"Yes, I understand." He looked slightly disappointed. "Soon everyone will know."

"Surely Kiloran didn't think he could murder the Firebringer in secret?"

"Why not?" He smiled, his scar flowing into a long dimple which should have looked out of place on that menacing face, but somehow didn't. "After all, *you* did."

She gasped as if he'd hit her. Tears of rage and frustration threatened to cloud her eyes, but she willed them back. Yes, he was right. She had tried to lead Josarian to his death and keep her part in his murder a secret by letting Zimran commit the betrayal and the Outlookers wield the blade. She had acted according to Kiloran's will without even knowing it.

She was guilty. The Firebringer's blood was on her hands, though she had never touched a weapon. His screams of agony were in her ears, though she had never actually heard them. His fate was her burden, and she would carry it until she died—when Mirabar killed her, if the Olvar was right.

It wasn't a good idea to dwell on that now. But if her days were indeed numbered, then she must make each one count.

Shame flushed her skin as she realized what a mistake it would be to exchange further insults with Searlon. Their crimes were inextricably linked together; but he'd already realized that, unlike him, she was ashamed of her part in what they had done—and he would enjoy using that knowledge against her every time she gave him the chance.

"Dare I ask what went wrong?" Searlon asked.

"What?"

"With your plan. The Outlooker ambush," he clarified. "I thought it was all—"

"Tansen learned about the ambush."

"And spoiled your plans?"

"Yes." Shame flooded her again. She had been so sure, so certain . . .

Don't dwell on it. Not now.

"How did Tansen know?" Searlon asked.

"Ah. Of course. You haven't heard yet." She enjoyed herself as she said, "Najdan betrayed Kiloran."

She had the pleasure of seeing momentary surprise flash across his face, followed by consternation. He quickly collected himself, though, and said only, "Then it will be my pleasure to assassinate the *sriliah*."

"I've seen him," she said, still enjoying the moment. "He does not look so easy to kill."

"Fortunately," he replied, "I enjoy a challenge."

His expression chilled her. Then again, she'd found Najdan rather chilling, too, the few times she'd encountered him. Assassination was usually business among the assassins, but Elelar wondered if there might be a personal element this time; Najdan and Searlon had served the same waterlord together for years, after all. The fact that Searlon had betrayed any reaction at all indicated to her how shocked he was by the news. Maybe Najdan's defection hurt. Maybe it wounded.

She certainly hoped so.

"In any event," she said decisively, "you and I have a more immediate concern."

"Agreed, *torena*. There is no body to prove Josarian's death to the satisfaction of the Valdani."

"So I ask again: What was Kaynall's reaction to the Outlooker's tale?"

"Unfortunately, the Outlooker who witnessed Josarian's death was less than perfectly coherent when he arrived at Santorell Palace."

"Less than perfectly coherent," she repeated, sensing this was a remarkable understatement. It shouldn't surprise her. She'd never seen a White Dragon, but she remembered the haunted look on Tansen's face when he'd described it to her that night in Chandar. The sight must have left the Outlooker, who didn't even know what that water-born creature was, with a large hole in his powers of reason. "But if he told Kaynall that the White Dragon—"

"He didn't know what it was called. He only knew that some terrible monster of glowing ice and crystal had risen from the water to devour Josarian, and that the Silerians wanted Kaynall to know Josarian was dead, though there was no body to prove it."

"And?"

"Kaynall was, needless to say, extremely interested though noticeably skeptical. He ordered the man to eat and rest, then return for a more detailed report when he had calmed down."

"Well?"

"Unfortunately, the Outlooker seems to have gone straight to the docks and boarded the very first vessel leaving Sileria which he could find. No one has seen him since."

She sighed wearily. "Just our luck."

"Indeed."

"And you? Have you tried to convince Kaynall that the White Dragon k—"

"In the absence of any instructions from my master or any explanation other than one hand-fed to an Outlooker by Josarian's friends? No."

"That's all you have to say?" she asked sharply. " 'No'?"

"While it's true that the White Dragon leaves no corpse, there were other possible explanations," he pointed out. "I had to consider that Josarian might still be alive and the Outlooker fooled—or even convinced to lie."

"The story is true," she said bitterly.

"Yes, that much is clear to me now."

"And you made no attempt to—"

"I'm a patient man, *torena,* and it hasn't been long. You will soon learn, if you have not already, that it's hard to get messages in and out of Shaljir at the moment." He shrugged. "I knew that, one way or another, something would happen to show me what to do next." He smiled beguilingly. "And then today, *Toren* Ronall came to Santorell Palace."

"I see." She sighed. "The absence of a corpse . . . It's very inconvenient."

"Yes."

"But not irreparable."

"No?" His gaze sharpened momentarily, and then he smiled, already understanding. "Ah, *torena.* I'm so glad you've returned to Shaljir."

"I'm flattered," she said dryly.

"Perhaps we can prevail, now that you're here to speak for the Alliance with regard to the secret treaty."

He grinned openly at her icy stare, obviously realizing that she'd recently learned—due to his master's murder of Josarian—that he knew exactly what was in that treaty, including the final accord: Josarian's life in exchange for Shaljir. That damned treaty had been Kiloran's creature all along. And now that she knew it, Searlon clearly enjoyed the boiling, betrayed rage it created inside of her.

"I suggest, *torena,*" he continued, "that you and I meet with Advisor Kaynall and Commander Cyrill at the earliest opportunity."

"Cyrill," she repeated without enthusiasm. He was the nephew of her oft-betrayed Valdani lover, the late Advisor Borell. Cyrill had briefly been Commander of Cavasar, before the city fell to the rebels and came under Kiloran's control.

"Yes. He's preparing for the siege of Shaljir." Searlon lifted one brow. "But we are all eager to see these *roshaheen* finally gone from our land forever without further cost to us, are we not?"

"That is the objective," she agreed.

Yes, they all wanted the Valdani gone. There was nothing the Silerians wanted more than to be rid of their foreign conquerors . . . so that they could all set about slaughtering each other without further distractions.

Searlon's smile made Elelar's bones cold. "Only think, *torena*. If you and I succeed here in Shaljir ... then the Guardians and the Society, after a thousand years of enmity, will finally have the opportunity to prove, once and for all, who is the strongest."

She wanted to shake with the chill he caused, but she was a Hasnari and would not tremble before an assassin. So she lifted her chin and said, "But if we fail here, then all your posturing will have been rather pointless, won't it?"

She expected anger, but she should have known better. Searlon was not a man of heat, not a man of rash passions or tender spots.

His scar dimpled again and he replied, "How true, *torena*. How very true."

18

IF YOU LOOK FOR TROUBLE, YOU WILL SURELY FIND IT.
—Silerian Proverb

ZARIEN'S STAHRA QUIVERED slightly, letting him know which way to go when he came to a new intersection on the steep, rocky, narrow mountain path.

Every time it did that, he practically jumped out of his skin. Yes, the metal-tipped oar was given to him by Sharifar herself and had led him into the current which carried him to safety after she had ordered him to go ashore ... but he'd had no *idea*! It was enchanted—indeed, there were moments when it almost seemed alive.

Sneaking away from the throng of people at the caves of Dalishar hadn't been easy, and he'd had to wait until long after Tansen's departure to make his escape unnoticed. That meant that he'd soon realized he had no idea which way Tansen had gone. As the sky grew dark, Zarien recalled Sharifar's words—*follow him until you cannot*—and began to fear he'd been hasty in his decision and foolish in his actions. He certainly seemed to have reached the "cannot" moment of his quest, and so he decided to return to Dalishar's caves.

It was when he tried to turn back that the *stahra* suddenly quivered with life for the first time, trembling like an animal and pulling like a strong wind against taut sails. Startled, he'd yelped and dropped it.

It lay absolutely still on the ground, looking very ordinary while he stared at it for so long that his eyes started to ache. When he finally found the courage to pick it up again ... nothing happened.

Until, that is, he once again tried to turn back.

This time, when it trembled and tugged, he realized what it meant. This time he understood.

Stay in the current you have found.

He'd been right, after all! He was indeed meant to follow Tansen when the warrior left Dalishar. The gods were helping him. Just as well, considering how difficult Tansen was being.

Let it carry you.

So he did. He continued his pursuit, confident now. Each time he chose the wrong direction, the *stahra* led him the right way. Zarien had no idea where Tansen was or how long it would take to catch up to him—*shalla-heen* walked a lot faster than he did—but now had no doubt that he would eventually find him.

Are all stahra enchanted? Tansen had asked him.

It had seemed a strange—even ignorant—question at the time. Now he wondered how Tansen knew. Did the sea king have instincts which he hadn't yet recognized as a sign of his destiny, or had Tansen seen the *stahra* do something which Zarien hadn't?

On his own again now, Zarien was very hungry. Despite their taste for cooked flesh, the mountain rebels enjoyed good food. It was plentiful, too; Tansen had explained this was because Josarian had convinced Silerians to stop letting the Valdani take most of it. Now Zarien missed the food at Dalishar. He didn't enjoy returning to a diet of hastily gathered wild things.

Sister Rahilar's treatment had helped his feet, but by sunset of his second full day in pursuit of Tansen, they hurt abominably. He was pleased that some of the blisters had become calluses, but very sorry indeed that some of the sores were worse than ever. He was also pleased that the *stahra* now led him on an ever-descending trail into a lush, wooded valley. This was easier on his abused body than those high mountain trails, which the *shallaheen* scrambled over as if pushed by a good wind in calm waters.

However, at least the other minor pains he'd acquired during his sojourn on the dryland were improving. The blisters on his burned hand, acquired while retrieving the *stahra* from the Guardians' fire, were withering now. The cold burning sensation caused by Najdan's *shir* pressed against his throat was fading.

Drylanders.

It was no wonder, he thought, that the Lascari chose, long ago, to become sea-bound.

He approached a thick grove of olive trees, thinking perhaps it was time to stop for the evening. The tortured twisting of the trees' ancient branches looked eerie in the dim light of the wildly dramatic sunset; but he could tell that there was water in the grove, and he was both thirsty and sticky from the day's exertion. He brushed past a gnarled tree with dull green leaves and considered how pleasant it would be to bathe his stinging feet in the cool—

"Umph!" He grunted in surprise as the *stahra* suddenly leapt out of his hand.

Zarien's eyes flew wide and a gasp caught in his throat as the weapon leaped towards an assassin who appeared out of nowhere, his dark face fierce, his two *yahr* swinging—

"Galian?" Zarien said in confusion.

Impervious to Galian's blows, the *stahra* slapped the black-clad *shallah* so hard he fell down and lay there without moving.

"*Zarien?*"

He heard Tansen's incredulous voice and whirled to face him. Like Galian, Tansen was wearing the black clothes and red *jashar* of an assassin. He looked sleek and deadly. The surprised expression on his face quickly changed to an angry scowl. Zarien suddenly realized he should have prepared in advance for this moment. Smooth explanations would clearly be needed to appease Tansen. Instead, Zarien's mouth just worked silently as he glanced stupidly from Tansen to the now quiescent *stahra* to Galian— whose prone body was alarmingly still—back to Tansen.

"Um . . ."

Tansen looked at the *stahra,* then back at Zarien. "So now you know?"

"Yes. You knew. I didn't understand . . . when you . . . I . . ." His voice sounded thin and breathless in his own ears. "I . . ."

"What in the Fires are you doing here?" Tansen demanded sharply.

Zarien pointed at Galian. "Is he all right?"

Radyan now appeared, as did three other men. All clad in black, two of them wearing the other two red *jashareen* Tansen had taken from the assassins he'd slain on the path to Dalishar. Radyan bent over Galian's body and spoke his name. He was answered by a groan.

Radyan looked up. "Just stunned."

"Why are you all disguised as assassins?" Zarien asked.

"Ohhhh." Galian opened his eyes and put a hand to his face. "What happened?"

"Counterattack," Radyan said. "By an oar."

"An oar?" Galian repeated incredulously, trying to lift his head.

"Never happened before?" Radyan asked. "No oar wars in your clan's past?"

"An oar?" Galian repeated. With Radyan's help he finally succeeded in lifting his head. That's when he said, "*Zarien?*"

"And Zarien's oar," Radyan added.

"It's a *stahra,*" Zarien said wearily, uneasy with the extremely displeased way Tansen was looking at him.

"It protects the boy," Tansen explained.

"Does that mean we can't kill him?" Galian asked with a distinctly disappointed look.

"*I* didn't make it hit you," Zarien insisted.

"I suppose it just did that by itself," Galian snapped.

"It did!"

"Wish *I* had one of those," Radyan murmured.

"He's telling the truth," Tansen said.

"You see?" Zarien said to the others.

"He's also," Tansen continued, "in so much trouble, I don't think even that *stahra* is going to be able to protect him."

"Now wait a moment," Zarien said, alarmed.

Tansen took his arm in a grip of steel and said to the others, "Would you excuse us?"

"I had to follow you!" Zarien protested as Tansen dragged him away with far more haste than dignity.

"What did I tell you?" Tansen snapped. "Didn't I tell you to stay at—"

"Well, Sharifar told me differently. I am to stay close to you," Zarien argued, tripping as Tansen tugged him through the trees and beyond the hearing of the others.

"Oh, for the love of Dar." Tansen released his arm and faced him, his expression radiating exasperation. "I evidently haven't made this clear enough yet: For your own safety, you are to do exactly as I tell you at all times."

The cold fury in Tansen's voice upset him. "It is the will of the goddess that I—"

"No matter what."

"—follow you now!"

"You have no business disobeying my orders!"

"She told me so in that—that—" He made a vague gesture.

"Do you think I give you orders for the pleasure of hearing myself talk?"

"—that strange fire in the cave."

"Do you think I'm being whimsical when I tell you to wait for me in safety?" Tansen demanded.

"The fire that your friends say is sacred."

"Do you think you have the right to risk my men's safety the way you just did?"

"Ask Mirabar if you don't believe me!"

"What do you suppose people at Dalishar are doing right now? What if they have to neglect their duties to go in search of *you*?"

"Ask Cheylan! They saw it, too! They were there! Ask them, if you don't believe me!"

"I believe you." Tansen looked up at the darkening sky. "I believe you," he repeated, evidently trying to master his temper.

"Then why can't I—"

"Because what we're about to do is extremely dangerous—"

"I don't mean to—"

"—and we're in territory ruled by an enemy."

"—fight assassins. I just want to—"

"Do you know what that means?"

"—stay close to . . ." He paused. "Um. I'm not sure. What does that mean?"

"Waterlords are not like other men," Tansen said.

"I know that, but—"

"I couldn't protect Josarian from Kiloran."

"—surely if I—"

"And I doubt I can protect you from Wyldon."

"Who?"

"The waterlord we've come to . . . harass." Tansen nodded in the direction of the colorfully streaked sunset. "He lives a short trek that way." He added significantly, "At our pace, not yours."

"I'm getting faster. I caught up to you, didn't I?"

"We stopped today to ambush some of Wyldon's assassins."

"Oh." Zarien felt slightly deflated by the news, but relieved he hadn't stumbled across more bodies. "I guess you didn't fight them right there on the path this time."

"No, we were obliged to deviate," Tansen said with a touch of sarcasm.

"I'll keep up w—"

"Wyldon is a waterlord. A sorcerer. Much less powerful than Kiloran, true, but still not the sort of opponent I was actually trained to face. Not someone I can protect y—"

"Then maybe you shouldn't be here, either," Zarien said, suddenly worried.

"It's necessary."

"You can come back later," he urged. "Who knows what power Sharifar might grant you in her embrace, what protec—"

"This has to be done *now*, Zarien." Tansen sighed and looked at the ground. "How did you track us, anyhow?"

"The *stahra* led me."

Tansen's head jerked up and a look of surprise washed across his face. "I see."

"Can you understand?" Zarien asked eagerly. "Can you accept your—"

"I can accept," Tansen said slowly, "that I'm evidently obliged to keep you with me for the time being."

Frustration boiled over in Zarien's blood. "Why are you so unwilling to—"

"And I suppose I'll have to count on that *stahra* to protect you when I can't." Tansen frowned as he added, "If Sharifar's weapon is a match for a waterlord."

Zarien considered this, then looked over his shoulder to where the others awaited them. "Perhaps I should not leave it lying on the ground."

"Perhaps not." Tansen's voice was dry.

Zarien eyed him suspiciously. "And you will not try to leave me behind again?"

"No, I won't leave you behind again." Tansen added wryly, "I've learned that it's more trouble than it's worth."

"PLEASE, SIRAN, A gift, a gift, spare me a gift." The beggar didn't look much older than Armian, but he was worn down by life. Dirty and smelly, with red-rimmed rheumy eyes and rotting teeth, he was also more persistent than a Valdani priest of the Three collecting tribute goats. *"A gift, siran, if you please."*

"A gift?" Armian repeated, brushing past the beggar and proceeding through the streets of Shaljir.

"Money," Tansen clarified to Armian as the beggar followed them, encouraged by Armian's having noticed him.

"Money? Then why doesn't he just say so?" Armian said.

Tansen shrugged. "It's good manners to say 'gift' instead." He said to the beggar, "Go away. We have nothing for you."

"A gift, a gift," the beggar demanded. "Give me something!"

Tansen shrugged off the dirty hand that tugged at his arm. Valdani-ruled Sileria was full of beggars. Tansen had always accepted this as normal, but he was learning differently from Torena Elelar. She insisted that Valdani laws were responsible for the homeless, starving beggars crowding the streets of every city and wandering the roads of every district.

He'd asked Armian if he thought Elelar was right when she said that, in the absence of the Valdani, someday things would be different. Armian doubted it. A few men were born to wield power, the rest were born to obey them, and some were born to scramble for scraps. That, Armian said, was the way of the world.

"Give me something!" the beggar demanded again, following Tansen and Armian.

Tansen ignored him.

"You who have so much—you will offer nothing?" the beggar cried, attracting momentary attention with his loud voice. "You are sheep molesters! You are dung-eaters!"

Now Armian turned to stare at him.

"A gift!" the beggar insisted.

"I will only say this once." Armian's voice was calm, even pleasant, but Tansen felt a chill of tension creep through him. "The boy told you that we have nothing for you. Now do as he says, and go away."

"Go," Tansen urged. His heart was starting to pound.

To speak to a beggar, to acknowledge a beggar and engage him in conversation . . . It was encouragement. Tansen should have known better. He should explain this to Armian now. "Father," he began. The beggar put his hand on Armian's sleeve, crumpling the material in his fist. "A gift, and I will go," he promised, breathing into Armian's face.

Armian looked down at the hand on his arm.

No one else noticed. Not a soul in the street paid them any attention. No one but Tansen realized what would happen now.

"No," Tansen said, dread flooding him. He started forward. Too late.

In a flurry of movement so fast Tansen could scarcely follow it, Armian clapped his hand over the man's fist, trapping it, then sharply rolled the edge of his forearm down into the beggar's wrist, driving him to his knees with a cry of pain.

The beggar lashed out, ineffectually flailing at Armian with his free hand.

"Father, don't!" Tansen blurted.

Armian grabbed the beggar by the hair, let go of his hand, and seized his chin. With one sharp, experienced twist, he broke the man's neck.

A woman shrieked as the corpse fell to the ground.

Tansen stared stupidly at the lifeless body. His heart raged as if it was on fire. His breath sounded like wind gusting through a mountain pass.

Dar help me! Dar shield me. Dar . . .

He felt a hand on his arm, dragging him away from the sight. He heard Armian's curses ringing in his ears.

"Come on," Armian urged him through gritted teeth.

"Wh—what?"

Tansen looked up in a daze, stumbling as Armian dragged him through the crowded street. He saw Valdani faces everywhere. That was bad, he knew. Unlike Silerians, Valdani would tell the Outlookers what they had seen.

"They'll be looking for you," he murmured, his mind still locked on the vision of the beggar lying dead in the street.

"Who?" Armian asked absently, still hauling him along.

"The Outlookers. They'll hunt for you."

"Because one Silerian killed another?" Armian gave him an amused look. "I doubt it."

WYLDON THE WATERLORD was notoriously bad-tempered. He'd been known to kill men for merely smiling the wrong way or for interrupting him once too often. Excessively skinny due to bad health, he'd been heard grumbling more than once that Kiloran, though twenty years older, was merely waiting for him to die so he could increase his power by taking over Wyldon's territory.

Tansen figured that if anyone could be driven to disrupt the Society with swift, rabid, unreasoning fury, it was Wyldon.

Now, in the middle of the night, Tansen addressed his men. Their faces, like his, were blackened with soot. The moons overhead, both on the wane now, were eerily red, lending no charm to the occasion. The men were attacking Wyldon's stronghold tonight, and timing was crucial. The ambush must be swift, and they must be well out of Wyldon's reach by dawn.

He went over their objectives one last time. "I must kill an assassin with one of Kiloran's *shir* and leave it behind as evidence," he said. "The rest of you give them a good battle and then get away fast. Even if you can, don't kill them all. We want a few of them left alive to talk about how Kiloran's assassins ambushed them at Wyldon's very door." He paused and added, "Above all, don't let them kill *you*."

He hadn't allowed Lann or Yorin to accompany him here because Lann's immense size and bushy beard, like Yorin's scarred, one-eyed face, were too distinctive. If one of Wyldon's assassins saw them up close and survived to describe them, someone might soon realize that the attack had been a ruse by Josarian's loyalists. The five men who'd come here with Tansen tonight were, like him, fairly average in size and appearance. The brand on Tansen's chest was his only distinguishing feature, and it was well covered now by his black tunic. He was leaving his two swords, as notorious as his Kintish scar, in Zarien's care for the duration of the attack.

There were six assassins Kiloran couldn't account for, since Mirabar had burned their bodies on Mount Dalishar; now six assassins, apparently Kiloran's, would be witnessed harassing another waterlord. Tansen and his men had already ambushed and killed four of Wyldon's assassins, prior to encountering Zarien, and they made sure that some local *shallaheen* saw them in the area, so Wyldon was bound to hear about it. The waterlords enforced *lirtahar,* the law of silence, but they expected the people dependent on them for water and goodwill to tell them everything that happened in their territories.

"And if we see Wyldon himself?" Radyan asked now.

"Retreat immediately," Tansen replied tersely. "We're not here to kill him or be killed by him. We just need to make sure he wants to kill Kiloran."

He ensured that everyone knew the positions they were to take in anticipation of his signal, then sent them off into the darkness. Now he turned to Zarien and said, "And you are going to stay here, exactly as ordered. Right?"

"Yes, Tansen."

"And what will happen if you don't?" he prompted.

Zarien heaved a weary sigh and replied, "You'll kill me yourself." They had gone over this before. More than once.

"Good. I'm glad we've got that clear at last."

Tansen glanced at the metal-tipped oar in Zarien's hand. The *stahra* had led the boy to him after he'd left him behind at Dalishar, and Tansen had learned by now, albeit reluctantly, that some things were better quickly accepted than long resisted. He knew it frustrated Zarien that he didn't agree this meant he was Sharifar's mate, let alone that he should immediately abandon his responsibilities and go to sea. He was, however, convinced that it meant he must protect the boy and keep him close for the time being. Inconvenient, but evidently inescapable. As for the possibility that he might be the sea king . . . He shook off the thought, knowing that tonight he must focus on the task at hand.

When Tansen turned to go, Zarien forestalled him by saying, "I would appreciate it . . ."

He paused. "Yes?"

". . . if you wouldn't get yourself killed."

He smiled at the boy's irritable tone. "I'll do my best."

ARMIAN WAS WRONG. *The Outlookers might not care that one Silerian had killed another, but they minded very much—as did their citizens—that a Silerian had committed a violent murder in the streets of Shaljir, surrounded by hundreds of Valdani.*

"They think you might just as easily have lost your temper with a Valdan," Elelar *explained to the assassin that evening, "so they're determined to arrest and execute you, lest you break one of their own people's necks next time." She arched a delicate brow and added coldly, "They also feel that Silerians killing each other in their mountain villages, which the Outlookers readily overlook, is a different thing altogether from doing it in the streets of Shaljir right in front of Valdani women and children."*

Armian shrugged in the dim light of the tirshah *where they were still staying. "Then let's leave Shaljir. I'm tired of all this waiting."*

Tansen saw the young torena's *jaw work briefly before she said, "They've locked all the city gates and are searching high and low for you. The Outlookers don't know who you are—ironically—so absolutely no Silerian gets out of the city until they've found the one who committed today's murder." She made an exasperated sound. "Do you understand how serious this is?"*

Armian's expression was forbidding. "I suggest you find a solution, torena. *If, that is, you're at all interested in securing Sileria's freedom."*

Tansen never knew what Elelar would have said or done next if a manservant hadn't stuck his head through the window and said, "Torena! Outlookers!"

Elelar went pale. "It's too late."

Tansen jumped to his feet. "How do they know we're here?"

Elelar glared at Armian and said, "It couldn't be because you were a little careless about covering your retreat, could it?"

"Isn't there another way out of here?" Tansen asked.

Armian reached for his shir.

"Don't be a fool," Elelar snapped.

"They will not take me," Armian growled.

Elelar came to a sudden decision. She turned to the chubby keeper of the tir-shah and said, *"We must hide them with our old friends."*

He glanced doubtfully at Armian and Tansen, but said only, *"As you wish, torena. I will stall the Outlookers as long as I can."*

"Come with me," she ordered Armian and Tansen, then turned and hurried down a murky hallway which led to the back of the building.

There was clearly no time to argue, so Tansen grabbed Armian's arm and, on this occasion, did the dragging. *"Let's do as she says, father,"* he insisted.

They followed her down a set of sagging stairs, along a low-ceilinged corridor, and into a dank little room eerily lit by a flickering candle.

She closed the door behind her and studied their faces with a strange, desperate expression, suddenly looking very young.

"They'll search here." Armian sounded annoyed.

"They'll kill you," she said.

"I can fight Out—"

"They'll kill you right here, cornered like a rat in this little room."

"What are you doing?" Tansen demanded, truly afraid now. Did she mean to betray them, after all?

"I can save you," she said. *"I can hide you where they'll never find you, and I can get you out of the city."*

Armian glared at her, understanding before Tansen did. *"But?"*

"But you must swear on your life, on your soul, on your mother's honor . . ."

"Yes?" Armian prodded impatiently.

"You will never tell anyone, not a single soul, what I'm about to reveal to you. You will never betray the place I'll take you or the friends who will protect you."

They heard stomping overhead. The loud voices of the Outlookers.

"Father," Tansen urged.

"Fine," Armian said. *"I swear. Whatever your secret is, no one will ever learn about it from me."*

"Or me," Tansen added quickly. *"Torena . . . "*

"Help me." Elelar crossed the room and crouched on the floor in the corner. *"It's a trap door."* She glanced at Armian. *"Use the blade of your shir to pry it open."*

He frowned. *"I don't see any—"*

"Right here." She pointed to a spot where hard stone met crumbling grout.

"I don't see—"

Tansen snatched the shir from Armian. It hurt worse than any bloodpact cut, worse than all the Fires. It burned his flesh with cold fury, like holding a live coal, but he held onto it long enough to slip the blade against the stone. His eyes widened when the shir found a space which he'd have sworn wasn't there. He pulled, felt the give, and opened the trap door.

Elelar slid her hands under the door and yanked it open. Grinding his teeth *against the pain, Tansen dropped the* shir *on the floor. Armian picked it up and joined him in looking down into the dark hole now yawning beneath them.*

They heard footsteps on the stairs, descending towards this room.

Elelar started down the steep, dark, winding steps now revealed to them. "Hurry!" she whispered. "Hurry!"

Tansen followed her. Armian was next, pausing only long enough to close the trap door behind him.

Dar be praised, we got away, Tansen thought, lightly shaking his throbbing hand as if that might ease the pain.

He hadn't even reached the bottom of the winding, slippery staircase when he heard footsteps directly overhead and realized his prayer of thanksgiving may have been a little premature.

Dar shield us! Don't let them find the trap door.

Moving cautiously in the opaque darkness, he felt Elelar's hand at his elbow, guiding him when he reached the last step. Armian bumped into him, then steadied himself with a hand on Tan's shoulder. They both knew better than to speak, lest even a faint hint of sound carry to the Outlookers overhead.

Elelar took Tansen's hand. It was a gesture he had dreamed of ever since meeting her, but he had always pictured it happening under vastly different circumstances. Now her touch, coming so soon after he'd held the shir, *made him want to howl. He ground his teeth some more instead. She guided him to a wall. It was rough and very uneven, like a cave wall, damp and slightly slimy. His head brushed the ceiling above him, and he realized Armian was undoubtedly obliged to crouch.*

In complete silence and total darkness, they felt their way along the wall, guided by Elelar. They were evidently in some sort of tunnel; it occasionally grew so narrow he could feel the opposite wall brushing his shoulder. Tansen hoped Elelar knew where she was going.

Only after he believed they couldn't possibly be anywhere near the tirshah *anymore, let alone within reach of the Outlookers—who had not pursued them down here—did he risk whispering, "Where are we? Where are we going?"*

"We're nearly there," she whispered back. "Can you see up ahead?"

"I can't see anyth—" No, that was wrong. Now he realized there was a faint glow in the distance. Reassured by this, he held his silence until they finally reached it.

"A candle?" he said incredulously. "Who keeps a candle down here? And why?"

"Our old friends always leave a light here for us, since we find their world confusing and might miss the entrance."

"Their world?" Armian's expression, visible in the faint light, was suspicious. "Entrance?"

"Here." Elelar took the candle and held it up to illuminate a dark crevice. "Through there."

Tansen's eyes adjusted, and he recognized a shadowy entrance to another underground chamber.

"We must go further down, further underground," Elelar said. "But this is the way."

"And what will we find through here?" Armian asked darkly.

Elelar's smile was strange. "The Beyah-Olvari."

19

HE WHO SEEKS ME SEEKS DEATH.

—Wyldon the Waterlord

TANSEN CREPT THROUGH the damp foliage, moving carefully in the dark so as to make no sound. Up ahead, he could see the faint glow of torches lighting the perimeter of Wyldon's stronghold. As he drew closer, he could hear the sounds of running water.

Emperor Jarell of Valdania had sworn to destroy the Society during his lifetime, and the Empire's Outlookers had worked towards this goal for some forty years. Consequently, the waterlords had lived in hiding and on the run since well before Tansen was born, though they had never relinquished their power over Sileria's water or her people. In a wealthier, easier era, the Society might well have felt that joining Josarian's cause was too risky to be worth the effort. Fortunately for Sileria, though, the Valdani had ensured that the waterlords had little to lose and were willing to follow destiny and join the rebellion. Tansen was the Society's enemy now, but he knew—as he told Josarian long ago—the rebels had needed them to defeat the Valdani. Unity had been essential, just as enmity was now inescapable.

Although Valdania had lost its grip on almost all of Sileria except for the city of Shaljir, the waterlords hadn't yet fully adjusted to their new situation, so most of them still lived in the secret, hidden places to which they and their forebears had retreated years ago. Kiloran inhabited an inaccessible palace of water beneath the surface of Lake Kandahar, Baran squatted in Harlon's ancient, abandoned ruins at Belitar, surrounded by an ensorcelled lake, and Wyldon . . . Wyldon's stronghold was a cave, deep in the forest, whose entrance was hidden by a waterfall.

However, in the absence of the Valdani, Wyldon had abandoned caution and now boldly announced his presence here with a stunning display of waterworks. Tansen hid in the lush—and annoyingly wet—plant life growing in thick abundance all around Wyldon's dwelling and looked for assassins patrolling in the torchlight. Most would be asleep now, but there were bound to be sentries posted. He'd have to rely strictly on sight to find them, because Wyldon's residence was so damn noisy.

The waterfall itself filled the night air with a steady rushing sound which might have been soothing under vastly different circumstances. It split into dozens of shimmering strands halfway down the stone wall along which it flowed. The sparkling strands twisted to become coils which formed an elegant barrier of gleaming bars over the entrance to Wyldon's cave before weaving together again and flowing into a pool that lay in the center of the small torchlit clearing.

With his clothes now soaking, Tansen sincerely hoped that Wyldon's cave was so damp it gave him rheumatism and made his worldly possessions rust and rot.

The pool of water, in turn, spewed an enormous fountain which arched high upward to feed the waterfall, completing the enchanted cycle. A billion dancing droplets of water, glittering even at night, flew away from the fountain's sky-reaching curve. Wyldon, not content with this display, also indulged in water sculpture. Men, women, and beasts inspired by Silerian history and myth, as well as by Wyldon's own fancy, populated the clearing around the pool, all of them fashioned from water.

Just a trifle ostentatious, Tansen thought.

Rumor had it that Wyldon was touchy about his artistic talents and had once killed an assassin who'd said the wrong thing about one of his sculptures. People also claimed that several local *toreni* not only praised but actually paid for his art, just to appease him. Looking at some of Wyldon's efforts now, Tansen suspected those *toreni* had probably promptly put the sculptures in the darkest, most forgotten corners of their residences.

Hiding amidst soaking foliage and with nothing to occupy him as he waited, Tansen was chilly and bored by the time an assassin finally wandered into view.

It's about time.

An attack which met with no opposition was normally the ideal situation, but since the goal tonight was to be seen and noticed, he'd had to wait until now.

Uttering a piercing, high-pitched battle cry that he hoped would carry above the noise of the water and alert any assassin within earshot, as well as inform his own men to commence the attack, Tansen leaped out of the foliage with a *shir* in each hand, launched himself at the assassin—and immediately slipped in the mud created by Wyldon's copious waterworks.

Oh, damn it.

The soles of his wet boots slid out from under him, and his arms flailed gracelessly as he went careening wildly into the stunned assassin.

"What th— Ooof!" The assassin went down, winded by the violent collision.

Tansen reached out to stab him—and missed completely as he went sliding past his opponent and straight towards the geysering pool of water.

He scrabbled wildly at the slick mud as he slid downhill.

A slope? This didn't look like a slope!

He crashed into the low—previously unnoticed—barrier surrounding the pool. Winded and smarting in a dozen places, he hauled himself to his feet and turned to face the assassin—who'd already risen and now came at him in a flying tackle.

They went tumbling backwards together into the water pool—which was not, Dar be thanked, ensorcelled against enemies. Wet and cold, yes, but it didn't freeze Tansen's parts off.

He rose to his feet again, glad that the pool wasn't deep—he'd sunk only to his waist—and peered through the heavy shower of water raining down on him from Wyldon's magical fountain. The assassin was on the other side of its dense core.

They both started to circle it at the same time. Unfortunately, in the same direction. Tansen stopped and switched direction—again, at the same moment the assassin did. They stopped again and stared at each other in consternation.

Resisting the urge to roll his eyes, Tansen shouted, "I'll wait here."

He didn't know if the assassin—now looking very annoyed—had heard him, but the man came tromping laboriously through the waist-high water while Tansen awaited him. Meanwhile, a few shrill sounds coming faintly from around them suggested that others were fighting now. Squinting against the water pouring down on him, Tansen glanced quickly over his shoulder and saw frantic movement beyond the edge of the pond. The battle was on.

The pond, he realized suddenly.

Yes, he could leave a *shir* sticking out of the assassin's body, but what if it got dislodged somehow, after his escape, and sank to the bottom of the pool?

That would be just my luck.

Realizing he needed to kill the man on solid ground to ensure that someone would definitely discover the *shir,* Tansen found himself obliged to run away from his approaching opponent. He glimpsed the assassin's incredulous expression as he started retreating, making his way to the edge of the pond.

This is embarrassing.

They were close enough together now that he could hear clearly when the assassin bellowed, "Come here, you coward!"

"Come catch me!" he replied.

I sound like a coy virgin.

Tansen placed his hands on the solid barrier surrounding the pool and, pausing just long enough to ensure he wasn't leaping into another assassin's arms, heaved himself up out of the water. The still-healing *shir* wound on his hand protested bitterly, but he ignored it. He stalled his opponent's oncoming attack with a quick backward kick in the face, then rolled onto the ground. Well, the mud.

The assassin tried to follow, but he slipped and fell back into the water—hitting his head on the solid barrier. He floated face down in the pool, unconscious and drowning in peace.

I don't believe this.

Tansen looked around for another opponent. Someone he could actually kill with the damned *shir* this time. There were a number of men struggling together all around him now, mostly rolling around on the slippery ground. It was pretty dark, the men were all dressed in black, and they were all covered in mud. He couldn't tell Wyldon's assassins from his own men.

Maybe I should just wait around for someone to attack me, he reflected sourly.

However, the combatants were all so occupied with each other that no one seemed to notice him. The steady rumble of the water ensured that he couldn't hear anyone's voices; certainly not well enough to distinguish friend from foe, anyhow. He supposed he could just drop a *shir* on the ground, but that seemed so obvious that even Wyldon might suspect it had been left behind on purpose.

"Wouldn't anyone like to fight *me?*" he invited.

He took a few quick steps backwards as two mud-coated tumbling bodies came hurtling towards him across the ground. When he backed into something solid and icy cold, he stopped abruptly and spun around—or tried to. Two chill arms encircled him from behind with astonishing speed and held him fast.

He saw water enfolding him. Felt water against his body. Sensed the cold evil of water magic engulfing him.

Wyldon's sculptures! They weren't just there for decoration, he now realized, they were sentries. Less effective than Wyldon perhaps supposed, since all Tansen's men had slipped past them and were wreaking havoc now; but the statues were not without their uses, he acknowledged as he struggled futilely against this one.

The *shir,* he thought suddenly. His own Kintish blades had always proved ineffective against water magic, but a *shir* was different; its watery origin was the same as this ensorcelled statue's. And the *shir* was harder than this creature, in the way that a steel blade was harder than flesh. The arms which held him now possessed demonic strength, but they were nonetheless soft, fluid, full of give.

Yes.

He gave up his struggle and, lowering one hand, reached back and plunged the *shir* into what passed for a leg on Wyldon's water-born sculpture, then ripped sideways, destroying the limb.

The thing lost balance and started to wobble. The creature's grip on him loosened, and Tansen twisted in its cold embrace. Aiming at what could best be described as its torso, he plunged the *shir* into it and pulled it downward, gutting the creature like a fish. It released him and collapsed, the *shir* still stuck in its ruined body. Only one *shir* in hand now, he stared as the statue started to disintegrate, melting into mere water again, a puddle growing around the *shir* he had left sticking out of it.

Now killing *that* thing, Tan figured, was a believable reason for an assassin to forget his *shir.*

Time to go.

He stumbled away from the corpse—so to speak—and started yelling, "Retreat! Fall back!" The men didn't seem to hear him, so he entered the fray, still shouting for retreat. Someone barreled towards him, and he nearly killed him in sheer reflex before a familiar voice howled, "No! Don't! It's me!"

"Galian?" The man was a mountain of mud. "Go! Go! Now!"

"But—"

"That's an order!"

Suddenly Wyldon's waterfall roared angrily, a totally different sound from its usual rumbling rush. The coiling bars over his cave's entrance began hissing like angry snakes as they parted like curtains.

He's coming.

"Retreat!" Tansen shouted again, worried now.

"I'm *trying!*" Radyan shouted back.

Tansen whirled in the direction of that familiar voice. He recognized Radyan just in time to see him slip and fall yet again, locked in deadly struggle with an assassin.

The sudden angry roar of the waterfall had attracted another of the men's attention, and he was already making for the forest.

Taking care not to lose his footing, Tansen made his way to where Radyan was struggling in the mud. He meant to deliver a fatal blow to Wyldon's assassin with his *shir,* but the two men were rolling around so much that he only got the shoulder. No matter, it was enough to stop the struggle and let Radyan escape, which was what counted right now.

The violent roaring and hissing of the water all around them was enough to alert his remaining men to make their escape, though one was pinned down by one the water sculptures—which were actively stalking the intruders now.

That does it. I am never coming back here.

The *shallah* struggled violently, grunting in pain beneath the watery claws of some huge, fantastic, catlike creature. Tan leapt upon it and used the *shir* to cut off its head. Then he grabbed the muddy, bleeding, dumb-founded man by the arm and dragged him into the thick foliage, where they made a wet and undignified retreat, with all due haste, from the scene of their battle.

WAITING IN THE dark with the men's supplies—food, water, ordinary clothing, Tansen's swords—Zarien listened intently for any sound of his companions' return. Unfortunately, there were so many strange sounds on the dryland at night that he could have sworn he heard them coming twenty different times, only to be mistaken every time.

His head was drooping sleepily and he could barely keep his eyes open when he heard the sound—unmistakable even to his ears, this time—of someone (or something?) stalking through the dense forest.

Please, please, please, he prayed to all the gods of the wind and the sea, *don't let it be a mountain cat.*

Then he remembered the *stahra*. Theoretically, it wouldn't let a moun-tain cat kill him. Or even hurt him badly.

All the same, he'd rather not test the theory right now, alone and in the dark.

He heard more crashing through the foliage and decided that, whatever was out there, it couldn't be an assassin. Wouldn't they use a little stealth? And he knew by now that Tansen and his men wouldn't make that much noise. Well, not unless speed was suddenly more important than silence, he reflected worriedly.

Life wasn't hard enough, no, now Tansen had to go around attacking waterlords.

As the noise drew closer, Zarien raised his head from his hiding place—a tumble of rocks—and peered out into the darkness. Yes, he could see it now, something moving through the faint, dappled moonlight. A shadowy figure which was tall like a person rather than short like a moun-tain cat.

Only when it was fairly close did he realize that it was a woman. The roundness of certain areas was unmistakable when she paused and turned slightly, silhouetted in the faint moonlight.

A woman lost out here in the dark? He wasn't sure what he should do, but he didn't think that simply ignoring her was right. He rose slowly to his feet and said, in a loud whisper, "Don't be afraid."

She froze in the shadows, then shifted slightly, as if turning to him.

"Are you lost?" he asked. "I'll help you." She started moving towards him. He continued, "My name is Zarien, and there's—" His words ended in an appalled gasp when she was close enough for him to truly see her.

"Yaggghhh!" He backed away as fast as his feet would move, his horrified gaze fixed on her ... *it* ... this inhuman thing coming at him from out of the dark!

He stumbled and tripped, falling down hard on his rump. The thing came closer, moving with strange fluidity, pale as moonlight, translucent and lifeless. It was without color or expression, without eyes or—

"Gah!" He gave a choked cry of protest as it reached down and seized his arm. Its touch was chilling, its grasp painfully strong. It drew him to his feet and pulled him closer. "No!"

He felt something hard force its way into his hand.

The *stahra,* he realized dimly amidst the chaotic whirl of his fear. What was he supposed to do with it?

The creature now seized his throat and started to strangle him. Choking and eyes watering, Zarien punched it in the belly with the handle of his *stahra*.

It responded in total silence, with physical reflexes hideously similar to a person's, flinching backwards and doubling over slightly. Its texture rippled fluidly, like sloshing water in the bottom of an oarboat. Zarien stumbled away from its chilly touch, took a firm grip on his weapon, and hit the creature in the head as hard as he could with the broad side of the paddle.

The translucent monster spun away from him. Terrified into aggressive action, Zarien pursued it, whacking it twice more. When it fell to the ground, he brought the edge of the paddle down on it, hard, again and again. He stopped when he thought it was dead, but then it moved menacingly again, trying to rise and renew its assault upon him.

The winds take me!

He starting beating the thing again, trying not to see how much like a shapely, defenseless woman it looked as it attempted to shield itself from his blows. He thought he was going to be sick, but he knew he couldn't stop attacking it long enough to indulge in his nausea.

When he heard someone—something?—else coming through the forest, nearly upon him, he wanted to cry. He couldn't fight *two* of these grotesque things!

"Zarien!" The familiar voice was urgent.

"Tansen!" he exclaimed with relief, afraid to look away from his never-still opponent for even a moment. He clobbered it again with the *stahra*. "What is it? What do I do?"

"Get away from it!"

"What is it? What do I do?" he repeated, indulging his panic now that help was at hand.

The warrior's strong hands pushed him aside. Then Tansen attacked the thing, tumbling to the ground and rolling over and over as he fought it.

Someone else arrived on the scene. "What *is* that?" Galian demanded, breathing hard as he grabbed Zarien's shoulder.

Zarien's gaze was riveted on the struggle. "I don't know! It came from out of nowhere!"

Tansen raised his *shir,* which glittered with deadly sorcery, and tried to stab the monster. It resisted, seizing his arm in both hands and fighting for control of the wavy blade.

"I'll hit it again," Zarien announced, raising his *stahra.*

"No, you might hit Tansen!" Galian's arm—thick with mud—blocked him.

"It'll stab him!" Zarien protested.

"That's Tansen's *shir,*" Galian argued. "It can't hurt him."

"How is that possible?"

"Could we discuss water magic some other time?" Galian snapped.

In a sudden flurry of movement, Tansen grabbed the *shir* with his free hand and plunged it into the creature's face. He made a violent motion, like he was ripping its head open. The strange monster's whole body convulsed, sagged, then lay quiescent. Tansen tried to rise, but the thing's hands were still clinging to his arm. With a strange noise and an expression of profound disgust, he pried its fingers off his flesh.

Then he looked at Zarien and demanded, "Why didn't the *stahra* protect you, for the love of—"

"It did, sort of. I mean, it jumped into my hand." He shrugged and added, "My father told me you can never count on the gods—"

"Are you all right?" Galian asked Tansen in a dazed voice.

Zarien glanced at him—and finally noticed that he was covered in mud, virtually every bit of him, head to toe. "What in the Fires happened to you?"

Galian grimaced, cracking some of the mud caked on his face. "Don't ask."

"Fires of Dar!" said a voice behind Zarien.

Zarien turned and saw someone—Radyan, he realized an instant later—coming up behind him. Radyan was as filthy as Galian. Zarien asked, "How did you get so—"

"I don't want to talk about it," Radyan answered. "What happened here?"

"We're not entirely sure," Galian said as the rest of the men—all covered in mud—joined them and began asking questions about the bizarre scene here.

Tansen retrieved the *shir* he'd used to kill the monster, then rose to his feet. He was muddy, too—and absolutely, completely soaking wet.

Zarien asked him, "Why are you all—"

"Let's not dwell on it now," Tansen suggested.

Zarien stepped forward and gingerly nudged the dead creature with his *stahra.* The motionless form began diminishing, slowly turning into . . . a puddle of water. "What *is* it?"

"Water magic," Tansen replied briefly.

"Is this a White Dragon?" Zarien asked in awe.

Tansen actually snorted. "Not even close." The warrior retrieved his swords and his satchel from their hiding place and announced, "Those assassins are right behind us, and Wyldon's bound to attempt some more tricks like this if we don't make tracks. Let's go."

"Where are we going?" Zarien asked.

"North, to Zilar."

He'd learned a few things by now, so he asked worriedly, "Isn't Kiloran's territory north of here?"

Tansen took his arm to hurry him along. "Exactly. Wyldon's men will track us as far as Kiloran's territory, and then confirm to him that we are indeed Kiloran's assass—"

"But we aren't, so is it wise to risk—"

"Kiloran's in Cavasar. Can't you move any faster? We *are* still in deadly peril, you know."

Zarien picked up his pace and tried not to resent the way Tansen dragged him through the dark forest while the other men pulled ahead of them. "But won't Kiloran attack us if w—"

"We'll be out of his territory again before he knows—"

"I thought it was a big territory."

"Very big. But we're traveling in secret and will—"

"How long will it take to cross—"

"A lot longer than it needs to if you keep wasting your breath talking."

Zarien scowled at him in the dark and ventured one more question. "How did the attack go?"

"Oh," Tansen replied, "let's not dwell on it."

20

WAR IS THE BUSINESS OF ONE KIND OF MAN, AND
PEACE THE BUSINESS OF ANOTHER.
—*Toren* Varian

ELELAR HAD SPENT many long hours in Santorell Palace before today. As Imperial Advisor Borell's mistress, she had even acted as hostess here on several occasions. Now, a few days after Searlon had come to her bedchamber by night, she hoped and prayed that this afternoon's visit to

Santorell Palace would result in the end of Valdani rule in Sileria. She and Searlon had used the time between that late-night discussion and this moment to prepare the elements needed for their hastily concocted plan.

Other members of the Alliance had hoped to participate in this historic moment. Indeed, it might be better if they were here. Men like *Toren* Varian probably had more influence with Advisor Kaynall than Elelar did. But Varian was at home in Adalian and possibly even still unaware—like the other signatories to the secret treaty—of Josarian's recent death. That, however, was a detail which neither she nor Searlon had any intention of revealing to the Valdani. As for the other leaders of the Alliance who were currently here in Shaljir . . . In truth, Elelar didn't want them to learn today that she had helped destroy the Firebringer.

Now, as she entered the council hall of Santorell Palace, following the formal announcement of her arrival, she found Advisor Kaynall and Commander Cyrill awaiting her. Kaynall, an older man of elegant if unremarkable appearance, was sitting at the massive table which dominated the richly furnished hall. Cyrill was standing by the tall glass doors which led out onto the balcony overlooking Santorell Square. While not revealing himself to the crowd which had massed below, he was watching it intently with a dark scowl.

Elelar had just fought her way through that crowd, when coming here, and she knew how restless and eager the people were. Indeed, she and Searlon had ensured they would be so—by actively spreading the rumor that Advisor Kaynall would announce Valdania's surrender today.

Even here, one story above the crowd and shielded by these thick Valdani walls, she could hear voices from the crowd wafting through the windows along with the spring breeze.

"Free Sileria!"

"*Roshaheen* go home!"

"Native rule in Sileria!"

"Surrender to Josarian!"

"Free Sileria *now*!"

Elelar acknowledged Advisor Kaynall's greeting and replied courteously to his insincere questions about her journey to Shaljir and her health. Evidently even this foreign goat-molester appreciated that a *torena* was due a certain measure of respect.

Cyrill's greeting, however, was abrupt. He inclined his head so slightly that it barely moved, and muttered, "*Torena*."

She smiled and asked after his family.

"I have sent my wife to the mainland." His tone was brusque.

"Very wise," she replied gravely. "To stay with your parents?"

He gave her a look of burning hatred as he answered, "No. My mother is still in mourning. Her brother—my uncle—died this past year. As you know."

He was Borell's nephew and blamed Elelar, Borell's traitorous Silerian lover, for his death. She frowned with feigned sympathy and murmured, "Suicide, I understand."

"Yes," Cyrill snapped.

"Such a pity." She sighed. "Suicide is anathema in Sileria, of course." She arched a brow. "But you're probably no more familiar with our customs and values than your uncle was."

Cyrill lost his precarious hold on his temper. "May the Three curse you, woman!"

"Dar will shield me from your petty Valdani gods," she replied, enjoying the way his face colored with anger. Really, it was a pity they'd never gotten to know each other better; she'd always appreciated men who were this easy to manipulate.

Kaynall raised a hand as Cyrill took a reflexive step towards Elelar. "That's enough," he admonished mildly.

Elelar nodded and changed the subject. "I don't feel I can commence this discussion—"

"What discussion?" Cyrill demanded.

"—without Searlon. Could I prevail upon you, Eminence," she asked Kaynall, "to request his presence?"

Although Kaynall's face could hardly be called an expressive one, Elelar saw his surprise. He studied her with curiosity and veiled suspicion as he said, "Of course." He nodded to Cyrill, who went to the door, opened it, and briefly ordered one of the guards in the corridor to summon the assassin.

After closing the door and giving Elelar a look of hot loathing, Cyrill returned his attention to the crowd below in Santorell Square. "I estimate their numbers have doubled since we dispersed them at midday, Eminence," he said.

"They keep coming back?" Elelar asked innocently.

Cyrill ignored her, but she thought she saw his ears redden. He had Borell's bad temper but wasn't nearly as intelligent. Now he turned and addressed Kaynall as if Elelar wasn't even there.

"I suggest we send mounted Outlookers into the crowd to disperse them again."

Kaynall looked directly at Elelar. "They'll only come back, won't they?"

"It seems likely," she agreed.

"Why?" Cyrill demanded. "Why are they doing this now? Why today?"

"Why, indeed?" Kaynall murmured, studying Elelar.

Cyrill asked, "Shall I order it, Eminence?"

Elelar said, "You don't think it will start a riot?"

"Stay out of this, woman," Cyrill ordered.

"The kind of rioting," Elelar continued, "that tore Cavasar apart before it fell to the rebels."

"And does Josarian mind," Kaynall asked, "that it is Kiloran who holds that city now?"

"Josarian," she said, "is in no position to mind anything. Ever again."

"Then it's true!" Cyrill pounced. "I thought that Outlooker had lost his wits out there in the mountains. But it's true? Josarian's really dead?"

Elelar ignored him and addressed Kaynall. "The Alliance has met the conditions of the treaty."

"It was my understanding that Kiloran killed him," Kaynall said. "If he is indeed dead."

"He's dead."

"Then produce his body."

"We can't. Your men blundered the attack and our people had to improvise."

"You're referring to this water monster that our man described?"

"Before he disappeared," Cyrill muttered darkly.

"Yes," Elelar replied. "We call it the White Dragon."

"Which leaves no corpse?"

"Precisely."

Kaynall sat back. "How convenient."

"Far from it, obviously."

"Then why not just kill Josarian the ordinary way?"

"That was the part your men blundered," she reminded Kaynall.

"But surely—"

"Josarian was surrounded by powerful friends: the *shatai,* a fire sorceress, nearly ten *shallah* rebels, and some fifty *zanareen,* all willing to die to protect him. And on our side . . ." Her stomach churned with shame and hatred as she used the words *our side,* but she shrugged and continued, "There was one sole Outlooker who'd survived the ambush against Josarian and had been taken prisoner." She gave him a cool look as she asked, "Under the circumstances, what would you recommend?"

"I would recommend producing a body."

"Water magic was the only way to kill him," she persisted.

"Kiloran was his enemy," Cyrill said. "If Josarian is indeed dead, how do we know—"

"All you need to know is that Josarian is dead," she interrupted.

"But if the Alliance didn't kill him . . ." Kaynall let the implication dangle.

"You would refuse to honor the treaty?" She made sure that no shadow of pleading, panic, or fear colored her tone.

"We would have to await instructions from the Imperial Council," he said judiciously.

"Yes, I see." She smiled with open malice. "And, of course, you have so much time before Kiloran rolls the Idalar River back on itself to starve Shaljir of water, the Guardians burn down its walls—"

"The walls are stone," Cyrill argued.

"—with their fire magic, and Tansen leads the rebels in a bloodbath against every last Valdan in the city." She paused for effect, then purred, "Yes, I'm sure there's plenty of time."

"You're not r—"

Kaynall's comment was interrupted by shattering glass and the noisy clatter of a candelabra which keeled over as something flew into it. Elelar flinched with surprise, as did both men.

"A rock," she said shakily, spotting it on the floor. Someone had thrown a rock through the window.

"Damn them!" Cyrill started drawing curtains across the windows, moving hastily from one to the next. "Eminence, we must disperse—"

"What brought them here?" Kaynall demanded of Elelar. "What put them in this humor?"

The heavy doors swung open then, and Searlon entered the hall. The Outlookers closed the tall, formal doors behind him, leaving the four enemies in privacy.

"*Torena*." Searlon crossed his fists and bowed his head. "I heard you were back in Shaljir. I've been awaiting your arrival here."

She nodded cordially. "Searlon."

He searched her gaze. "It is done, then?"

"Yes." She glanced at the two Valdani and added, "But they seem skeptical."

"The Outlooker's story was not entirely convincing," Searlon replied politely.

Kaynall studied them with a cynical expression. "You expect me to believe you worked together?"

They looked at him, then at each other, then back at him.

"Believe what you like," Elelar said indifferently.

She had agreed with Searlon that they couldn't produce some *shallah*'s body for him to falsely identify as Josarian's, not after the Outlooker's testimony about the failure of the ambush followed by Josarian's horrifying death by sorcery. Searlon hadn't contradicted the Outlooker's tale at the time, so he'd make Kaynall suspicious if he did so now. Moreover, a substitute corpse would be their downfall if Kaynall had a second witness, one they didn't know about, available to verify or deny that it was Josarian. So they must instead convince the Advisor that Kiloran's destruction of Josarian had been the Alliance's backup plan.

"We expect you," Searlon said, "to honor your treaty with us."

Now Cyrill entered the fray. "You've never before mentioned this close association you have with *Torena* Elelar," he challenged Searlon.

Searlon's expression suggested Cyrill was even stupider than he had supposed. "Apart from the master I serve, have I mentioned *any* of my associates to you, *roshah*?"

"Oh, for the love of Dar." Elelar sighed. "Who do you think escorted me to the meeting where we negotiated the secret treaty?"

Kaynall's gaze flashed to Searlon, who'd been her escort, and she saw that he remembered. Cyrill sneered and said, "Ah. For a moment I had forgotten who we're dealing with: the most experienced whore in Sileria."

"Watch your tongue." Searlon's cold voice cut across Elelar's gasp of outrage.

"Does she warm your bed now that my uncle is dead?" Cyrill asked Searlon nastily. "Is she your wh—"

"She is a Silerian woman," Searlon replied in a chilly tone, "and therefore I cannot permit you to insult her in my presence."

"*Permit?*" Cyrill repeated.

"We're getting off the subject," Kaynall pointed out tersely.

"Indeed," Searlon agreed.

"If Kiloran's murder of Josarian was due to their quarrel," Kaynall began, "then—"

"Then it changes nothing," Searlon pointed out. "Josarian is dead, as p—"

"Not having a corpse changes a great deal."

"That is the fault of the Outlookers," Searlon insisted. "We are not to blame."

It was, of course, much more complicated than that—Najdan's betrayal of Kiloran, Tansen's rescue of Josarian—but that was none of Kaynall's business.

The Advisor shook his head. "Nevertheless—"

"My master," Searlon said, "has been in the Alliance since long before you came to Sileria. Since long before I went to serve him, and even long before the *torena* was born. My master was the first waterlord to join the Alliance."

Kaynall stared at him now, interested, perhaps even swayed. Elelar realized that he hadn't guessed this, had perhaps never even guessed that Kiloran was in the Alliance at all.

"The *torena*'s grandfather, who founded the Alliance," Searlon continued, "broke centuries of tradition by extending his hand in friendship to a waterlord." He arched one brow and added, "This was, of course, after the Emperor swore to destroy the Society, and the Outlookers began to make war on it. If not for that . . ." Searlon's scar elongated into a dimple as he said, "Well, Eminence, none of this might have happened."

Kaynall looked consideringly from one Silerian to the other. After a long moment, he murmured, "So. I almost feel sorry for Josarian."

"That," Searlon said, "is because you never knew him, Eminence."

A cry came through the window: "Free Sileria!"

Kaynall glared at Elelar. "You arranged this, didn't you?"

"Her?" Cyrill asked stupidly. Then his eyes widened as he gazed at Elelar. "Of course!"

Elelar took the plunge. "I strongly suggest, Eminence, that you announce the Valdani surrender to that crowd out there."

"No Silerian whore," Cyrill snarled, "tells us—"

"Be reasonable, *torena,*" Kaynall suggested, giving Cyrill a warning glance. "To relinquish Sileria based on—"

"You've already lost Sileria," she said. "Even as we speak, rebel groups are descending on the last of your scattered outposts in the countryside. You've lost everything but Shaljir, and how long can you really hold on here?"

"A lot longer than you seem to think," Cyrill said.

"Beyond the city walls," she persisted, "lie the power and the determination which fought for and seized all you have lost here, from Liron to Cavasar. And it's all now fully concentrated on taking Shaljir."

"I understood," Kaynall said shrewdly, "there was some division among the rebel forces."

"It has not prevented us from hating you more than we hate each other," she replied, "nor will it prevent us from staying unified long enough to destroy you all, if you make that necessary." She caught Cyrill's eye now. "We sacrificed Josarian. We destroyed the mines of Alizar. We—"

"I thought they were merely flooded," Kaynall said.

"They can never be mined again," Searlon lied smoothly.

"We poisoned our own wells, killed our own traitors, and sent our own loved ones to certain death." Elelar leaned towards Kaynall. "So just imagine, Eminence, what we're willing to do to *you,* the remaining Valdani, in order to free Sileria now."

"A bit of patience," Kaynall warned, "is needed when—"

"We've run out of patience," Searlon said. "Surrender."

"Or what?" Cyrill prompted with open disdain.

"If you do not announce your surrender by sundown," Elelar lied, "our allies will make the secret treaty public in Valda."

Kaynall looked startled, but he argued, "Then they couldn't keep it from becoming public here, too. Do you really want all of Sileria to know that the Alliance betrayed the proclaimed Firebringer?"

The Valdani had, of course, always remained highly skeptical—even openly contemptuous—of Josarian's divine rebirth in the Fires of Dar. But no one in Sileria cared what they thought, least of all Elelar.

"No, we don't," she admitted, "but if you refuse to honor your treaty— now, today, before sundown—then you leave us no choice. There are very few of our names on that treaty, and we are willing to accept the consequences of exposure." Her gaze encompassed both Valdani men as she said, "Neither of you has been in Sileria very long, Eminence, but perhaps it has been long enough for you to observe that we are not afraid to die."

"Long enough to observe that life is cheap here," Cyrill amended contemptuously.

She ignored him as she continued, "The consequences to Sileria, if the treaty becomes public, will be minor. Five of us signed a dishonorable treaty in secret, and five of us will die for it. Tansen had no part of it and, as the dead Firebringer's brother—"

"His what?" Cyrill blurted.

"—he will be elevated to even greater heroic status—"

"They weren't brothers," Cyrill said uncertainly. The Outlookers had learned all they could, which wasn't much, about the rebel leaders.

"—than he already enjoys. Nothing in writing connects Kiloran or the Society with the treaty, either. Whereas," she pointed out, "it will look very bad, indeed, when the citizens of Valdania find out how you, acting on the orders of the Imperial Council, sacrificed Outlookers, cities, rural districts, Valdani-owned lands, and even High Commander Koroll's life, giving up the jewel of the Middle Sea piece by piece because you were too weak—and the Outlookers too corrupt—to hold it while you waged your costly wars on the mainland."

The crowd outside, in Santorell Square, was growing dangerously impatient. *"Free Sileria!"*

"Exposure will be more than a little awkward for you, Eminence," Searlon joined in. "And as for the Imperial Council's fate . . ." He shrugged gracefully. "Well, this is the sort of incident that foments riot, rebellion, and revolution, isn't it?"

"You know little of Valda," Cyrill said with a noticeable lack of conviction.

"Our dispatches tell us," Elelar said, "that there is rioting in Valda over high taxes, food shortages, and enforced conscription into the Emperor's armies."

"How long has the current dynasty been in power?" Searlon asked. "Might not some ambitious Valdan with military and political power convince his supporters, in view of Emperor Jarell's shameful loss of Sileria, that it's time for new blood to seize the throne?"

"As for you . . ." Elelar shook her head. "Well, your fate, like that of the Imperial Councilors, is easy enough to guess should the treaty become public knowledge."

"Free Sileria! Free Sileria! Free Sileria!"

"Eminence," Cyrill said, sounding a little breathless, "surely you're not listening to—"

"Be quiet," Kaynall snapped. "This is a political matter, not a military one."

"Well, Eminence?" Searlon said.

"If you have indeed arranged to expose the treaty . . ." Kaynall said slowly.

"Yes?"

"*If* that is so . . . You must arrange for a postponement."

Elelar felt her heart sink with disappointment. "We cannot."

"I don't believe you."

"It's true," she lied. There were, of course, no arrangements in place to expose the treaty; there hadn't been time. However, Elelar knew that Tansen couldn't afford any delays. He was counting on her to secure Shaljir for him *now*. So she maintained her bluff.

"I cannot surrender Sileria," Kaynall argued, "without communicating with the Imperial Council. That will take time."

"A ship to the mainland?" Elelar let some of her anger show. "Debates in the Council? Another ship back? Too much time, Eminence."

"Nonetheless—"

"And there should be no need. The treaty stipulates—"

"That you would produce a body!"

"And had we produced a body," Searlon said, "would you surrender now? Or would there still be this need for delay, for consultation with the Council, for—"

Cyrill was emboldened to say, "We'll never know, will we?"

"Did you ever intend to honor the treaty?" Elelar demanded.

"I have stated my terms," Kaynall insisted. "Postpone—"

"Enough of this," Searlon said.

He moved so fast that Elelar scarcely understood what was happening until it was over. There was a short, sharp cry of mingled surprise and pain from Cyrill as Searlon jumped forward and hit him in the face. Some drops of blood sprayed Kaynall when Cyrill's head snapped around. Kaynall jumped to his feet as Searlon roughly seized Cyrill's head and made a violent twisting motion. Elelar heard a strange *snap!* and stared in confusion as Cyrill suddenly went limp and unresisting in Searlon's grasp.

Only when the body hit the floor with a dull thud did she realize what the assassin had done.

"*Free Sileria! Free Sileria! Free Sileria!*"

Kaynall was backing away, stumbling clumsily in his haste to escape Searlon. His mouth worked, but only a whispered, "Gu—gua—guar—" came out.

"Stop him," Searlon commanded.

Heart pounding with panic and horror, Elelar obeyed without conscious volition. She stretched out a slippered foot and shoved a chair behind Kaynall, obstructing his retreat. He backed into it, flailed briefly, and fell to the floor. Searlon was upon him before he'd even recovered his breath, let alone tried to get up.

As Searlon hauled him to his feet, Elelar choked out, "What are you *doing?*"

The assassin ignored her. "Time to make that announcement, Eminence."

"I . . . ah . . . ah . . ."

"Dar have mercy," Elelar said hoarsely, staring at Cyrill's corpse, "you've killed him!"

This was not part of the plan.

Searlon shook Kaynall. "Do we need to tell you what to say?"

Gasping for air, Kaynall shook his head.

Searlon hadn't used his *shir*, Elelar thought in a daze. No, of course not, she realized; the Valdani wouldn't let an armed assassin roam the halls of Santorell Palace. He was probably searched every time he entered Kaynall's presence. So he'd had to kill Cyrill with his bare hands.

This was not the plan!

Not the plan they'd made together, anyhow. Searlon was in charge now, moving events along according to his own plan, one he hadn't confided to her. "Then onto the balcony, Eminence." He glanced at Elelar. "Would you mind opening the doors, *torena*?"

"Free Sileria! Free Sileria! Free Sileria!"

She gaped at Searlon in horrified silence for a moment, then numbly moved to do as he asked, opening the glass doors which led onto the balcony overlooking the immense crowd now gathered in Santorell Square. The thousands of people gathered below them abandoned their chant as the doors opened; now they began cheering wildly in expectation of the announcement.

Searlon shoved the trembling Imperial Advisor onto the balcony and warned him, "I'm right here, Eminence."

Kaynall nodded his understanding. He was sweating. Drops of Cyrill's blood stained his imperial robe. Elelar and Searlon stood on either side of him. Kaynall flashed Elelar a desperate, pleading glance.

"He'll do it, Eminence," she said with a coolness she was far from feeling. "The crowd will only cheer him on, and as for your guards..."

Fires of Dar, we've murdered a Valdan right in the heart of Santorell Palace! We'll never leave here alive!

She shrugged indifferently. "Well, they can only arrest us once, after all."

"I suggest," Searlon said, raising his voice to be heard above the cheering crowd, "that you listen to *Torena* Elelar."

Lips trembling, Kaynall raised his arms to ask for the crowd's silence. It took more than a few moments, during which time Elelar kept listening for the sound of palace guards coming to arrest her. In the square below, the immense and gaudy Sign of the Three, erected here two hundred years ago, gleamed under the dazzling Silerian sunshine, making her eyes water slightly as she stared at it with an unfocused gaze. As the noise of the crowd slowly faded, the pounding of Elelar's heart filled her ears. Finally, when he knew he could be heard, the Imperial Advisor addressed the conquered populace of Shaljir.

"People of Sileria," he began, "after long and difficult negotiations with the rebel alliance . . ." He was obliged to pause as another cheer floated up from Santorell Square. "The Empire of Valdania has agreed to surrender Sileria to native rule!"

The crowd went wild. The roar of victory made Elelar's head spin. For a moment, she forgot her horror, Searlon's reckless ploy, the Valdani corpse lying only a few paces behind her . . . For a moment, she forgot everything as she realized with a sensation of utter shock that it had happened.

The Valdani had surrendered.

The long years of sacrifice, the hard work, the bitter intrigues, the subterfuge which had ruled her life . . .

Done. Over. Finished.

Success.

The Valdani were leaving Sileria.

Pillars of fire rose from the crowd, startling her. She looked down and saw four Guardians—now openly revealing their identity, free of Valdani laws for the first time in two hundred years—with golden flames leaping skyward from their bare palms, faces jubilant as they celebrated.

Women threw their hand-painted scarves high into the air, creating a dance of floating color in the golden glow of the late afternoon sun. Men raised their children aloft, holding them high, making sure they could see Kaynall, the last Imperial Advisor in Sileria, at the moment the Valdani surrendered. The moment Sileria become free for the first time in a thousand years.

Free. We're free.

The thousands of deaths, the hundreds of funeral pyres, the lives cut short, the bloody battles, the razed villages, the burned crops . . . It had all been worth it. They had not been wrong. They had not fought, died, or sacrificed in vain.

She heard a new chant commencing in the square, a new creed for Sileria to live by.

"Native rule! Native rule! Native rule!"

From the sacred rainbow chalk cliffs of Liron to the exotic port city of Cavasar, from the snow-capped peak of Darshon to the crumbling Guardian temples of Adalian, from the golden beaches of the coasts to the merciless beauty of the mountains, Sileria belonged only to the Silerians now.

She felt tears streaming down her face and didn't bother to wipe them away. Her heart pounded with what she recognized as the only pure, uncomplicated moment of happiness she'd ever known.

She had been born to a humiliated race, a people whose faces had been forced into the dust centuries ago. And for the first time in a thousand years, they had lifted their heads and proven to a skeptical world that they could, once again, be the strongest, proudest, bravest people in the three corners of the world.

Overcome by emotion, she turned to Searlon, the only other Silerian within reach, and met his gaze. He looked unusually solemn, with no trace of the sardonic light which was normally present in his dark eyes.

"We're free," she choked out. "We're free."

He nodded and smiled, for once, without cynicism or irony. "We're free." She could barely hear his soft voice over the din of the joyous crowd below.

Their gazes held for a long moment of mutual understanding before Searlon's eyes flickered back towards Kaynall. "But it never hurts to be sure." He leaned closer to Kaynall and said, "Tell them when you're leaving."

Kaynall flashed another panicked look at Elelar. "But we've made no plans, no—"

"Make them now," Searlon advised. "Quickly, Eminence."

Kaynall held up his hands again. It took even longer, this time, for the crowd to quiet down. "At sunrise tomorrow, we will commence preparations for evacuation of Sileria and the unconditional surrender of Shaljir!"

When the cheering finally died down enough for him to speak again, Kaynall continued, "I ask you now, as people who have shared this city with us for two hundred years . . ." Kaynall was obliged to raise his voice as his audience started shouting him down. ". . . to let these final days we spend together . . ." He paused in consternation at the derisive sounds coming from below. ". . . be peaceful ones!"

Distinctly uninterested in the wishes of the departing Valdani, the crowd became increasingly noisy. "And for those Valdani . . . who wish to leave Shaljir . . ." Kaynall tried harder to be heard. ". . . with the departing imperial Outlookers . . . report . . . *report to Santorell Palace*—"

Searlon interrupted him. "I think you've made your point, Eminence."

In a sad attempt to regain some dignity, Kaynall said coldly, "Then may I go inside?"

"Yes," Searlon said. "There is still the treaty to sign."

This, at least, was part of the plan the assassin had made with Elelar. While it was unlikely that Kaynall would deny such a public proclamation of surrender, it never hurt, as Searlon would say, to be sure. Elelar had prepared a document for Kaynall's signature which would further bind the Imperial Advisor in Sileria—and thus his government—to the promises he had just made on this balcony. She reached beneath the broad sash tied around the waist of her long silk tunic and produced the document now, a single sheet of parchment.

She unfolded it, handed it to the Advisor, and said, "It requires only your signature and seal."

He looked at the document, then let his gaze travel over the celebrating crowd in Santorell Square. "Well," he said at last. "You thought of everything, didn't you?"

"I certainly hope so," she replied.

"Josarian! Josarian! Josarian!"

As the crowd took up the new chant, Elelar met Searlon's eyes again. Their moment of communion was already long past. He arched one brow as the betrayed Firebringer's name floated through the air. His killer's eyes glinted with mockery. Her own gaze, she knew, was hard and cold.

"*Josarian! Josarian! Josarian!*"

"This way, Eminence," Searlon said, reentering the council hall.

Kaynall followed him inside.

A moment later, Elelar heard Searlon's voice behind her, prodding her to join him in witnessing Kaynall's signature. "*Torena?*"

"I've worked my whole life for this day," she said over her shoulder. "I'll be with you in a moment."

"As you wish, *torena*."

His insincere courtesy might have grated on her nerves if her head wasn't already reeling with a new, desperate plan.

"*Josarian! Josarian! Josarian!*"

She had betrayed nearly everyone who had ever trusted her. And now it was time to betray Searlon.

She slowly raised her arms, praying for the crowd to notice her and fall silent. Praying for Dar's help as she had never prayed before, because so much depended on the next few moments.

She heard voices below shouting as people took notice of the Silerian *torena* on Kaynall's balcony. The din slowly faded again as more and more people silenced those around them to find out what she wanted to say on this extraordinary occasion.

When she thought many of them could hear her, she announced, "I am Elelar mar Odilan shah Hasnari!" She prudently left out the portion of her name—yesh Ronall—which identified her as the wife of a Valdan.

She was famous throughout Shaljir, she knew, not only as the daughter of an old aristocratic family, but as a close ally of Josarian's, as a loyalist spy who had been beaten, imprisoned, and sentenced to death before making a daring escape and joining the rebel forces living in the mountains.

She thrust her palms outward in a gesture meant to silence the crowd's cries of welcome and approbation. She knew she had only moments before Searlon stopped her.

"Kiloran has killed Josarian!" she shouted. "Avenge the Firebringer! Kiloran the waterlord murdered the Firebringer in the mountains only days ago! Josarian is dead! Kiloran killed Josarian! Tansen himself witnessed it and told me! *Avenge the Firebringer!* Kilor—" She lost her words in a breathless cry of pain as Searlon yanked her backwards by her hair, nearly breaking her neck.

"You'll die for that, *torena*!" His voice was so vicious she scarcely recognized it.

"It's too late," she said triumphantly as he dragged her off the balcony.

"They know. They *know*, and nothing you can do will ever change—" The hard blow to her face stunned her.

She didn't want to die. Not in her first moments of freedom. Not at the moment of the victory which she had worked her whole life to achieve.

She saw Searlon's coldly angry face. She felt his hand at her neck.

No, no, no!

"Guards! Guards!" Kaynall's voice. Seizing his opportunity. "Assassin! *Help!*"

Searlon's concentration slipped. Fueled by terror and the overpowering will to live, Elelar found the strength to break his hold, fell to the floor, and rolled away from him with more speed than dignity.

Two Outlookers rushed into the room. Searlon whirled to face them.

"Kill him!" Kaynall screamed. "Kill him!"

Searlon moved to fight—then stopped abruptly when four more Outlookers poured through the door, undoubtedly alerted by all the shouting.

Backing towards the balcony and keeping his eyes on the Outlookers, Searlon said, "This isn't over, *torena*."

Her voice was hoarse as she replied, "I know."

He disappeared through the balcony doors. The Outlookers pursued him, several of them hanging back slightly since they were unable to all invade the tight space at once. Elelar heard a shout, a thud, and some unpleasant noises. An Outlooker staggered backwards into the room and collapsed. A sword was sticking out of his belly.

Elelar gasped and looked away. She heard someone else on the balcony shouting instructions down to the square below, repeatedly urging the Outlookers on the ground outside to "capture the Silerian."

He got away.

"Eminence," another gray-clad Outlooker announced breathlessly upon coming back inside, "he's escaping."

"How in the Three can he possibly escape?" Kaynall snapped.

"He jumped."

"And he hasn't broken a leg?" Kaynall demanded, striding towards the balcony to see for himself.

"He's, uh, very athletic, Eminence."

The council hall surrendered to chaos now, with Outlookers running in and out, exclaiming over the two corpses Searlon had left behind, staring curiously at the battered Silerian woman nursing a bloody lip, and receiving orders about pursuit of the murderer.

Keeping her wits about her, Elelar seized the document she'd prepared for this occasion and, after checking to make sure Kaynall had indeed signed and sealed it, she carefully folded it and tucked it back inside her sash. Then, drawn by the angry screams outside, she returned to the balcony to see what was happening now in Santorell Square.

There was, of course, no sign of Searlon below. If he had needed any help escaping, any shielding from the Outlookers, he would have received it. The crowd had no idea who he was; they'd have seen only a Silerian fleeing from the Valdani.

But Searlon already seemed forgotten, as did Kaynall. The crowd was wailing over Josarian's death, people shrieking with mourning, with fury, with rage. Others were shoving their way through the crowd and streaming into the side streets leading away from the square. Going to tell the rest of Shaljir the news: The Valdani had surrendered; Josarian was dead; Kiloran was his murderer.

Who knew what would happen now? Not Elelar. She knew only one thing for sure: Searlon was right, it wasn't over.

"So," Kaynall said from behind her, "you and Searlon aren't as close as you've just tried to make me believe."

"Well," she said, turning away from the sight of the volatile, wildly emotional crowd and reentering the council hall, "we have our little differences."

Kaynall made his way to a chair and sank shakily into it. "I find it remarkable, *Torena* Elelar," he said, "that no one has yet murdered you."

She rubbed her throat. "Searlon just came very close." She wanted to cry now in reaction, but she would not weep in front of a Valdan.

"Now that it's done . . ." He sighed. "I confess I'm personally rather relieved."

"Oh?"

"I will be glad to leave Sileria. You are a difficult people."

"Yes," she agreed. "We are."

He shook his head. "I only wish you had brought me Josarian's body. All of this . . ." He made a vague gesture, encompassing Cyrill's death and the surrender of Shaljir. "It would be easier to explain in Valda if I could parade Josarian's head before our insulted people."

"Oh, really, Eminence." She didn't bother to conceal her disdain. "How did such unimaginative fools as the Valdani ever manage to conquer so much of the world?"

"Unimaginative?" he repeated wearily, evidently too tired to take offense at her rudeness.

"Sileria is full of dead *shallaheen*." Her voice was bitter. "Who in Valda could tell Josarian's corpse from another?"

His gaze sharpened. "Take someone else's corpse home with me and claim it's Josarian's?"

"Why not?"

"What about the tales here of Kiloran's White Dr—"

"How many people in Valda will believe that, if they even hear of it?"

He gazed at her for a long moment, a faint smile forming on his lips. "Ah, *Torena* Elelar, if you'd been on our side . . ."

"That, Eminence," she replied as she took her leave of him for the last time, "would be when all the Fires of Dar freeze over."

He didn't summon guards to arrest her for collusion in Cyrill's murder. No one tried to prevent her from leaving the palace, which was swarming with panic-stricken Valdani arguing hotly about Kaynall's announcement. Stunned Outlookers were everywhere, trying to organize pursuit of Searlon while simultaneously worrying about the increasingly aggressive crowd just outside Santorell Palace. Built with Valdani confidence and arrogance, the palace had not been designed for defense against the city's populace.

Elelar was so overwhelmed by all that had just happened in Kaynall's council hall that she hadn't considered how the people of Shaljir would respond to her sudden appearance on the palace steps as she made her exit.

"The *torena*!" someone cried.

"*Torena* Elelar!"

"Elelar shah Hasnari!"

Some of them came surging towards her. Sixty, seventy . . . perhaps a hundred of them. Maybe more. People of all classes, all ages, all factions. Men and women, young and old, some dressed in rags, some dressed in garments as rich as her own. All of them Silerians.

"No," she said as they seized her. "No!" she shouted, confused and suddenly afraid.

"*Elelar! Elelar! Elelar!*"

They hoisted her on their shoulders, high above their heads, handling her roughly but with love. Palms were reaching up to her, fingers seeking to touch her. They carried her away from the palace and paraded her through the dense, wild, passionate crowd.

"Dar bless the *torena*!"

"Dar shield Elelar!"

They were jubilant about their freedom. Filled with sorrow over Josarian's death. Caught between fear and rage at Kiloran's betrayal of the Firebringer.

"*Elelar! Elelar! Elelar!*"

They were delirious, she realized, with imagined love for her. She, who had betrayed Josarian. She, whom Mirabar so badly wanted dead.

She wanted to hide, to go home, to weep, to be alone.

She glanced wildly around, convinced she couldn't escape them. The sun gleamed off the golden monument to the Three. Silerians now climbed agilely all over it—a mark of disrespect never before permitted. Now no Outlookers interfered. The gray-clad Valdani forces huddled in fear, their backs to the walls of Santorell Palace, while the people of Shaljir abused the Sign of the Three.

A laborer dressed in humble clothing climbed atop the monument and took a sledgehammer to it. He waved briefly in acknowledgment of the crowd's noisy encouragement, then returned to his task of destroying this famous symbol of Valdani might and power in Sileria.

Elelar felt a hot thrill rush through her, her personal shame and sorrows forgotten as she suddenly remembered something Mirabar had said once said about her visions.

"I have seen Daurion's sword smash the Sign of the Three, a great structure made of marble and gold . . ."

It was happening. It was really happening! Elelar scarcely noticed the way she was roughly passed from shoulder to shoulder, pushed, shoved, tugged, and tossed among the crowd like a trophy. She barely felt the hands grabbing her, clutching at her, reaching out to claim, seize, bless, and bruise the normally sacrosanct person of a *torena*. She hardly heard the way they cheered and chanted her name.

Her gaze was fixed on the gold-and-marble Sign of the Three, which her people had just started tearing down.

She would tell Mirabar when they met. It was true. It was exactly as the Guardian had seen in her visions.

Yes. I must tell her . . . when she comes to kill me.

21

IN VALDA, MEN LOVE POWER.
IN THE MOORLANDS, THEY LOVE HORSES.
AND IN SILERIA, THEY LOVE TO HATE.
—Kintish Proverb

THE NEWS SPREAD across Sileria like wildfire.

By the time Tansen arrived in Zilar, where Mirabar awaited him, the town was already celebrating.

It was a stranger who first told him as he, leading a footsore sea-born boy and five men dressed again as ordinary *shallaheen,* arrived on the outskirts of this, one of Sileria's most beautiful towns.

"A rider arrived from Shaljir this morning to spread the word!" the stranger replied in response to his question about the wildly festive celebration in progress which, considering that Josarian was dead, was the last thing Tansen had expected to find here. "The Valdani have declared unconditional surrender!"

Tansen thought he felt his heart stop. Then it resumed beating, thundering in his chest with joy, relief, and victory.

"They are turning Sileria over to native rule!" the man cried. "They are leaving Shaljir! Leaving Sileria!"

The stranger was so overcome that he impulsively embraced Tansen. Normally reserved, Tansen now returned the embrace.

We've won!

"The Valdani have surrendered?" Radyan demanded in a high voice.

"They've surrendered!"

"We've won!"

Tansen staggered away from the stranger's bear hug and grinned at his companions. Galian whooped wildly and started slapping everyone on the back, even people he'd never seen before.

"No battle for the port of Shaljir?" Zarien asked. "No . . . no sea-born slain?"

"Without a fight!" the stranger confirmed in exultation. "The Imperial Advisor simply gathered the people in Santorell Square and announced surrender!"

Tansen grasped Zarien's shoulder. "Your family is safe," he assured him.

Radyan shouted, "We're free!" He slung his arms around both their necks and hugged them fiercely as he spun in a circle. The other men in their group joined in, jumping on top of them, slapping their backs, shouting, whirling them around.

It's done!

"We've won!"

"Dar be praised!"

"Blessed be Josarian's memory!"

Tansen heard that and wanted to sink to his knees, suddenly swamped with sorrow that his brother hadn't lived to see this moment, the achievement to which he had dedicated his life and consecrated his death.

His head was spinning when his men released him. Zarien looked disheveled and happy. Radyan glowed with triumph. Galian bayed to the tiled rooftops.

There was music, raucous laughter, singing. People shared their wine-skins with each other, as well as with Tansen and his men. They even raised the skins high to pour wine over each other's heads in gleeful abandon. The people of Zilar danced in the streets, in their fountains, even on their roofs. So did the strangers among them, the rebels who had come from all over Sileria to join Josarian in the siege of Shaljir—a battle which now would never be necessary.

"Blessed be Josarian's memory," Tan repeated quietly.

MIRABAR KNEW HE was in Zilar before she saw him. He'd been recognized and, without ever glimpsing him, she heard the people of Zilar chanting his name.

"Tansen! Tansen! Tansen!"

Mirabar and her escorts, including Najdan, had not made good time coming here from Dalishar, since Najdan had deemed it wise not only to avoid Kiloran's territory entirely, but to also avoid the river valley which was the most direct route. They had arrived last night and slept in the Sanctuary just beyond the edge of town, surrounded by countless rebels who were mourning Josarian's death—and who were also, as requested by the runner he had sent ahead of him, awaiting Tansen's arrival.

Mirabar's vague notion of inspiring the mourning masses with visionary hope until Tansen got here had been swept away in a torrent of rejoicing when the news arrived from Shaljir.

Freedom in Sileria.

Her eyes kept misting over. Even Najdan was moved by the extraordinary event. There was no one in Sileria who had not risked or lost or suffered because of the rebellion; but Najdan's life, like Mirabar's, had changed beyond recognition since the day they met. He, like she, had given everything to their cause.

"Sirana!" Pyron, who had come to Zilar with her and Najdan, came bounding up to her, as buoyant as a child. Stinking of the wine someone had poured all over him, he proffered the last thing she would have expected.

"Thank you, I don't need a hammer," she said. "Where is Tansen?"

"Coming, *sirana*. The crowd is slowing him down." He grinned and extended the rejected hammer to her again. "We wanted to offer you the honor of the first blow."

She eyed the hammer. "Blow?"

"The Sign of the Three! We're going to tear it down!"

"Oh!" She took the hammer in her hand, caught Najdan's eye, and said, "Yes. Thank you. It would be my pleasure."

Zilar was known for its relative wealth, its fabulous views, its lush foliage, and for the vast gold-tiled Kintish temple which dominated its main square. Not even the repairs which were obviously needed could detract from the beauty of this exquisite structure, which Kintish craftsmen, now dead for centuries, had made a thing of eternal grace. One hundred years ago, the Valdani had erected a garish Sign of the Three in front of the temple and reconsecrated the building to their trinity.

From this day forward, though, the Three would never again hold sway in Sileria. It would indeed be a pleasure to demolish the symbol of foreign gods which had, for a century, marred the beauty of Zilar's main square. Mirabar followed Pyron as he pushed through the crowd, creating a path for her.

She was famous throughout Sileria now, the fire-eyed flame-haired prophetess whom Josarian had trusted and Kiloran had respected. People cheered her as she passed, chanting her name noisily enough to compete with the praises being heaped upon Tansen. Only a year ago it had been dangerous for her to travel anywhere in Sileria, where she was still sometimes taken for a demon and often regarded with fear and loathing. Now the people of Zilar, and all the rebels who had come to join them, reached out to touch her, sang her praises, applauded her very presence, and pressed forward to help her, with more enthusiasm than deftness, as she clambered up onto the Sign of the Three. Having grown up wild in the mountains, though, she needed no assistance and progressed faster after shaking off the helping hands.

When she reached the top of the gaudy monument to Valdania's dominant religion, she saw hundreds upon hundreds of faces looking at her expectantly. She suddenly realized she was supposed to say something suited to the occasion.

"Today," she began, thinking fast, "as promised in prophecy for centuries, we are finally free! And Dar will no longer tolerate the gods of the *roshaheen* profaning Her land!"

It was good enough. Their approbation was thunderous. Mirabar raised the hammer high and brought it down with all her might on the gold-and-granite monument.

"Ow!"

She felt as if her arm would fall off. Who'd have thought banging into solid granite would be so bone-jarring?

"Having trouble?" a familiar voice asked.

Her gaze flew to where Tansen stood on the ground directly below her. His humble clothes, unkempt from all the pulling and tugging of the crowd, were those of an ordinary *shallah,* but no one would ever, she knew, take him for an ordinary man. Her heart flooded with life as she met his gaze. His dark eyes were alight with rare happiness and laughter. His long black hair absorbed the brilliant sunlight, and his bronzed skin glowed with inner fire.

Mirabar waved the hammer. "It's harder than it looks," she called back, trying to be heard above the shouting and chanting.

"Well, you're only a little thing," he replied.

She arched her brows at him and proffered the hammer. "Care to try it yourself?"

The crowd loved it. A roar of laughter and encouragement followed Tansen as he scrambled up to join her atop the monument. Before Mirabar handed him the hammer, she warned, "Don't ever call me 'a little thing' again. I don't like it."

He grinned, took the hammer, and warned, "Stand back."

With muscles which were, admittedly, a lot bigger than hers, he took a heavy swing, brought the hammer smashing against a corner of the monument, and chipped a piece off.

While hundreds cheered the first piece of rubble to fly off the Sign of the Three, Tansen winced slightly and admitted, "That does hurt a bit."

She laughed. "Perhaps we should leave the rest to people who've had too much wine to care."

He nodded and gazed out across the crowd. "Perhaps we should take advantage of their attention while we have it, and their spirits while they're high."

She looked at the countless people gathered here. Their faces were full of triumph. Even the shadow of Josarian's death couldn't stifle their joy in the wake of the news from Shaljir. She supposed that perhaps even the thought of opposing the Society wouldn't daunt them right now. Not at this particular moment.

"Yes," she agreed. "Better not wait until they're too drunk to listen, or until they're calm enough to think too much and get scared. It's best to speak now, when they feel ready for anything . . . and believe that *you* can achieve anything."

His expression revealed mingled amusement and consternation at this assessment, but he nodded his agreement and raised his hands to ask for quiet. When he had it, he addressed his people in a strong, confident voice.

"Until now, we've thought only of driving the *roshaheen* from our land. Only of freedom!" He paused as the crowd responded, then continued, "Now we must consider what kind of nation we want to be. Josarian might have led us, but he is dead, murdered by Kiloran . . ." He waited again, but when the crowd started chanting his name, he stopped them. "I'm a warrior, not a ruler!"

"Tansen! Tansen! Tansen!"

"But a new ruler is coming! The first Yahrdan in a thousand years will soon take his place at the head of this nation, to rule us in freedom and prosperity." This startling news quieted them again.

Under his breath, he said to Mirabar, "I am telling the truth, aren't I?"

"I hope so."

"I was counting on a more positive answer."

"I only repeat—"

"Forget I asked." Addressing the crowd again in a full voice, he announced, "Mirabar, who foresaw the coming of the Firebringer, has envisioned a new ruler, chosen by Dar, who will soon take his place among us!"

He turned and gave her a piercing look. Recognizing her cue, Mirabar blew flame into her palms then raised her hands, creating an impressive arc of fire overhead. "He is coming!" she proclaimed. Sensing that Tansen wanted a little more, she added, "He is coming in a blaze of glory, in a river of Dar-blessed fire, to rule this land in peace and prosperity!"

"But he's young," Tansen added, "and we must shield him." Mirabar was momentarily surprised that he announced this, but then understood when he continued, "We must shield him from Kiloran, who betrayed and slaughtered the Firebringer!"

Ah.

"Our freedom, our ruler, our nation's future depends on destroying Kiloran, who has sworn to oppose the Yahrdan as he opposed the Firebringer!"

Kiloran didn't even know yet about Mirabar's visions of the Yahrdan, but she supposed a minor lie was excusable. Kiloran undoubtedly *would* oppose him, whoever he was, when he finally appeared among them.

"Who will be brave and stand with me," Tansen demanded, "in defense of the new Yahrdan?" When he got the response he had hoped for, he added, "Who will avenge Josarian?" They were Silerians, so they liked this notion even better, and the sheer volume of their voices proved it. "Who will help me fight Kiloran and the Society for ultimate rule of Sileria?"

In the glow of victory against the Valdani, their response suggested they could do anything.

ZARIEN HAD NEVER been squashed among so many people in his life. Their ebullience was inspiring, but the noise, the jostling, the press of strangers' bodies, and, above all, the *smell* of all these flesh-eating drylanders in one place, under the hot sun ... He felt dizzy and overwhelmed, as enthusiastic rebels and loyalists responded to Tansen and Mirabar's appearance atop the Sign of the Three—a monument which was kind of pretty, actually, though Zarien knew it had to come down.

"Avenge Josarian!"

"Fight for the Yahrdan!"

"Free water for all!"

The people were whipped into a warlike frenzy, emboldened by victory against the Valdani and incited by their fury over Josarian's murder. A year ago, Zarien could well guess, opposing Kiloran would have been unthinkable amongst the landfolk. Now, however, these people—and many thousands of others like them, all across Sileria—were the nation which had fought Valdania and won, and that changed everything. Perhaps the Honored Society looked like a worthy opponent when you had brought the greatest empire in history to its knees.

Sooner or later it would occur to them that the Honored Society had been an important part of Sileria's victory against the Valdani. However, Tansen had chosen his moment well, so no one seemed to be questioning his plans right now. The wind was at his back, the current in his favor, the waves melting before his bow.

And when Sharifar embraced him and the sea-born recognized him as their king ...

Maybe he can really do it, Zarien suddenly realized. *Maybe he can really bring down Kiloran and the Society.*

The sooner he convinced Tansen to go to sea, the better.

"Radyan! Galian!" cried a vaguely familiar voice.

Zarien searched the crowd to see who had recognized them. He spotted Pyron even as the *shallah* blurted, "Darfire! Zarien? Then you're not dead yet."

"Of course I'm not dead," he replied, the *shallah* dialect coming to his tongue with increasing ease.

Pyron shrugged. "We were worried. A sea-born boy disappearing into the night like that, and all the strange activity at Darshon . . ."

"What strange activity?" Radyan demanded.

"Of course!" Pyron said, slapping his forehead. "You left Dalishar before it started. We haven't seen it either since we came down from the summit of—"

"Pyron," Galian interrupted, "seen what?"

He described lightning, whirling clouds, rising and falling plumes of colored smoke and steam . . .

"What did Mirabar say?" Galian asked.

"She was vague—"

"Imagine that," Radyan murmured.

"—and Cheylan was even vaguer."

"So they don't know?"

Pyron shrugged. "Could be Dar is angry about Josarian."

"Could it," Galian asked, "have something to do with the coming of the new Yahrdan?"

"Don't ask me," Pyron said. "But Mirabar says that the vision we saw that same night—"

"What vision?" Galian demanded.

"Oh, I didn't tell you already?"

"Pyron," Radyan prodded impatiently.

"Glowing golden eyes in the sky over Darshon."

"Really?" Zarien asked, fascinated.

"You mean this was another vision that everyone saw, not just the *sirana*?" Galian asked.

"Yes. I tell you, things are getting very strange aroun—"

"Just the glowing golden eyes?" said Radyan.

"And a voice inside my head. Inside everyone's head."

"What did it say?" Galian asked.

" 'He is coming.' "

"He, who?" Zarien asked.

"Mirabar says it's a sign of this Yahrdan she has promised." Pyron glanced uncertainly at Radyan. "Do you think that sounds right?"

"Listen," Radyan said suddenly, directing their attention back to the speakers atop the Sign of the Three. "Tan's calling for a bloodvow."

"A bloodvow?" Zarien knew about this custom and had seen the many scars on his companions' palms, but he had never witnessed anyone actually making a bloodvow before. It was almost exclusively a *shallah* custom.

Now he watched in mingled awe and distaste as Tansen convinced the countless people here today to swear a bloodvow with him against Kiloran and the Society. Guardians—he hadn't realized there were more Guardians here!—blew fires into life all around the thickly peopled main square of the town, and one even did so up on the gold-tiled roof of the Kintish temple.

Tansen set the example by slicing open his own palm with one of his swords and letting the blood flow freely, holding it up for the crowd to see. Then, to Zarien's astonishment, Mirabar held out her hand, and Tansen cut her, too. A woman! The *shatai* didn't even hesitate, just ran his blade across her flesh. They let the blood drip into the magical fire at Mirabar's feet as they recited their pledge, Tansen's voice carrying far, Mirabar's barely audible.

"I swear by Dar, by the memory of the slain Firebringer, and on behalf of the Yahrdan foretold in prophecy," Tansen vowed, "their enemies are my enemies, and I will not rest until the blood of Kiloran, his friends, and the friends of his friends flows as mine flows now!"

There was a moment of solemnity as Mirabar prayed to Dar, asking for Her blessing.

Then someone cried, "Avenge the Firebringer!"

"Avenge Josarian!"

Radyan nudged Pyron. "Give me your knife."

"Where's yours?"

"I lost it at Wyldon's stronghold."

"How did you—"

"I don't want to talk about it," Radyan replied impatiently. "Give me your knife."

"I'll do it, I'll do it." Pyron evaded Radyan's grasp and pushed his way through the passionate crowd to thrust his blade into the nearest Guardian fire.

People around them were already bleeding, vowing, swearing vengeance against Kiloran and the Society in loud, emotional voices while the Guardians prayed for Dar's blessing. When Pyron returned with his fire-blessed blade, he sliced his palm open first, then handed the knife to Radyan. Radyan cut himself, then gave it to another man. None of the *shallaheen* even winced, though Zarien knew it had to hurt. However, this was their way, so he supposed they were used to it.

When the knife had come full circle in their little group, Galian handed the blade to Zarien.

He frowned at it and shook his head.

They all looked stunned.

"Zarien . . . ," Pyron prompted.

"No," he said.

Galian said, "I don't know why you travel with Tansen, but as long as you do—"

"No," Zarien repeated. "I am sea-born."

"Even so . . ."

"We do not need to shed blood for our promises to be binding."

"But—"

"Let him be," Radyan said.

"Radyan, he can't just—"

"He's sea-born, he's . . . a little unusual, and he's, well, young," Radyan reasoned.

That smarted. Zarien protested, "I am a ma—"

"He's also," Radyan continued, "Tansen's responsibility. So let Tan deal with this. It's . . ." He shrugged and concluded. "It's not our place."

The others considered this and finally agreed. But it made a difference. Zarien's refusal to open his palm like a *shallah* had set him apart and created a renewed distance between him and these men.

He realized he might have made a mistake by refusing. Then again, what did it matter what these *shallaheen* thought of him? He was not of their world. He intended to return to sea as soon as possible. He wanted to go home. What did he care about the bloodfeuds of the landfolk?

Ah, but the sea-born had sworn loyalty to Josarian, as Tansen had pointed out to him.

But against the Valdani.

In the end, though, the Society had proven to be every bit as inimical to Josarian as the Valdani had. And now Sharifar wanted to unite the sea-born under the leadership of her consort, who would be chosen by Dar . . . So perhaps the sea-born were meant to take sides in the current struggle. Indeed, he realized, they must be, for it would undoubtedly be the first thing Tansen asked of them after Sharifar embraced him.

Maybe Zarien should accept this primitive *shallah* custom, after all, as a show of good faith with Tansen's people. Maybe he should let them cut his palm and then swear by Dar . . .

But it was too late. The other men had turned away and were gathered around the magical Guardian flames, reciting their vows. He was forgotten. A sea-born stranger. An outsider. A *roshah* who had rejected their demand for a gesture of loyalty.

Zarien sighed and wished, yet again, that he could just go home.

22

IT'S LUCKY TO BE SMART, BUT IT'S SMARTER TO BE
LUCKY.

—Zimran shah Emeldari

TANSEN ESTABLISHED HIS temporary headquarters inside Zilar's
famous Kintish temple. It was a bit noisy, since nearly a dozen Guardians
were busily destroying everything inside the temple which related to the
Three, but otherwise convenient, since it stood in the center of Zilar.

As the sun set over Sileria, people gathered around the enchanted
Guardian fires blazing throughout Zilar. Sharing food and wine and laughter, they exchanged stories of the war—tales which often grew taller in the
telling—and shared their sorrows as well as their victories. Inside the old
temple, glowing lantern-light flickered off the richly elaborate mosaics
depicting Kintish gods, idols, and myths; elegant and mysterious figures
which danced in the shifting light almost as if they had come back to life to
celebrate along with the Silerians.

Tansen had issued instructions that anyone present in Zilar who was a
clan leader or who commanded a rebel group should come speak with him.
As twilight turned into night, he discussed with these men, singly and in
groups, plans for opposing the Society in their villages and cities. These men
had come from all over Sileria, from as far away as Liron and Adalian in
some cases, and were eager to return home and celebrate Sileria's freedom
with their own families and clans.

Some of them, Tansen saw, understood what was coming. They
acknowledged and accepted the hardships they were bound to face as they
challenged the Society in its attempt to fill the power void left by the Valdani. Others, Tansen realized, were simply riding high on victory and wine,
flushed with excitement and triumph. They would sober up soon enough,
in more ways than one, and possibly quiver in their boots when they realized what Tansen had asked of them. It was a good thing he'd made them
swear a bloodvow while their spirits were still bold.

As Josarian had once observed, once men had sworn a bloodvow, they
could be relentless, fearless, even brutal in pursuit of its fulfillment. Now,
with fresh cuts on their palms and fresh vows in their hearts, the honor of

all these men—and more than a few women, too—depended upon them
heeding their commitment, no matter what the cost.

There were ways in which organizing opposition to the Society was easier than starting the rebellion had been. During the time Josarian had
waged war against the Valdani, rebels throughout Sileria had gradually created bases of operation and chains of command. Tansen's task was to redi-
rect these now-established systems, created for the rebellion, towards their
new enemy.

The waterlords not only commanded life's most essential resource, but
also many highly trained killers. The assassins, like their masters, knew the
structure and methods which supported the rebellion, because they had
been part of it. They spoke the common language and various dialects of
Sileria, they were born to its customs, and they knew its terrain as well as
Tansen himself did. They had relatives and bloodpact relations among the
very people now pledged to wage war against them. And no one was harder
to defeat than an enemy who knew you so well—an enemy who was, in fact,
one of you.

Nothing was worse than a civil war. And Tansen knew he must win this
one quickly. The Valdani were surrendering Shaljir and withdrawing their
remaining forces from Sileria, but there was no doubt that they deeply
resented losing the jewel of the Middle Sea. They might try to get it back, if
the mainland wars favored them, their economy recovered, and they
thought they saw their chance. Or if not them, then some other conquering
power might arise from the ashes of the mainland wars, see Sileria's independence as merely a brief anomaly in its long history of foreign domination, and attack.

If Sileria was weakened and depleted by a long and destructive civil war,
then all that Josarian had won might be lost, Tansen feared, despite prophecies claiming that the Firebringer would drive out the foreigners forever.
Tansen never favored leaving anything to fate, and even Mirabar often said
that destiny required effort, commitment, and sacrifice—it didn't just happen by itself.

The very best way to fight an enemy, his *kaj* had taught him, was to
avoid conflict by making it unnecessary. If Tansen could foil Kiloran's plots
and ruin his alliances, there would be less need for battle, bloodshed, and
suffering.

"Take this home with you," Tansen instructed Kiman shah Moynari, a
clan leader from the east. He held up one of the five *shir* of Kiloran's which
he still possessed. It glittered with cold sorcery in the flickering golden light
of the Kintish temple. "No, don't try to touch it," he cautioned Kiman. "I'll
wrap it and put it in your satchel."

"What am I to do with it?" Kiman asked, watching him.

Kiman somehow reminded Tansen of Zimran, though he was a few
years older. He didn't wear the fine clothes Zimran had always favored, but

he was every bit as handsome in his own way. Tansen noticed the marriage
mark on the man's palm and briefly wondered if a wife might have changed
Zimran's philandering ways. Tansen thought not, but perhaps he was
wrong.

In any event, there were at least two important ways in which Kiman
was completely *unlike* Zimran: He was a leader, and he had been totally
committed to the rebellion. Now he seemed equally committed to war
against the Society; the cloth wrapped around his left hand was dark with
blood from the fresh cut on his palm.

"The *shir* was made by Kiloran," Tansen explained to Kiman as he finished wrapping it in his threadbare old tunic, which Zarien had been wearing ever since saving his life in that shallow cave on Mount Dalishar. He had
given Zarien money (stolen from the Valdani) and sent him forth this evening to buy new clothes and, more important, some well-made boots for his
abused feet. Victory celebrations notwithstanding, the shrewd merchants of
Zilar were doing business at all hours while their town was flooded with
people from all over Sileria.

"Kiloran made this *shir*?" Kiman's eyes widened.

"When you get back home, I want you to join up with the Lironi,"
Tansen instructed, "who are already in open conflict with Verlon. Meet
with their clan leader—"

"Yes, I've met him before," Kiman confirmed. "His name is Jagodan."

"That's right." Tansen knew him slightly. An impressive and intelligent
man in his forties, Jagodan had held the Lironi—possibly the largest clan in
Sileria, and certainly the largest in the east—together through years of
hunger, hardship, bloodfeuds, and rebellion; and now he was, according to
Cheylan's news, leading them against the Society. There was no more valuable ally than a man like Jagodan. "And keep the meeting private. The
fewer people who know about this the better."

"Yes?"

"A small party should dress as assassins, ambush some of Verlon's men,
and leave this *shir* behind in the battle."

"So Verlon will believe Kiloran is plotting against him?"

"Or at least suspect it," Tansen confirmed. "And when Verlon makes
inquiries and learns that other waterlords are making similar complaints . . ."

Tansen intended to send two more *shir* out into Sileria with rebels returning home, with similar instructions for their use; the remaining two, he
would keep for himself. Sooner or later—and the sooner the better—one of
the insulted waterlords would respond to this offense by attacking Kiloran.

"As soon as the waterlords start quarreling among themselves," Tansen
told Kiman, "they'll be weakened and we'll have our chance to destroy the
Society. Perhaps our only chance."

"Do you really think they'll start fighting with each other?" Kiman
asked hopefully, his handsome face reflecting worried doubt.

"They always have before. In fact, after Harlon's death, they nearly destroyed themselves with their quarreling."

"But they've always united against a common threat."

"Well, we'll just have to change that," Tansen said.

NAJDAN DIDN'T LEAVE Mirabar's side all evening, nor did he partake in any of the wine which had flowed so freely in the hours since Tansen's speech before the vast crowd. He remained watchful and vigilant, fearing for the *sirana*'s safety in this seething mass of people.

He had watched the passionate, enthusiastic crowd very carefully today, so he knew that not everyone had sworn a bloodvow as Tansen had asked. Some people had left the square with furtive haste. Some had hidden in the shadows, muttering and shaking their heads. Throughout Sileria, there were people who had been loyal to the Society much longer than they'd been loyal to Josarian. Some had abandoned the Firebringer at the start of his quarrel with Kiloran. How many more might abandon Tansen now that Kiloran had succeeded in killing the Firebringer?

A practical man, Najdan was utterly convinced that Kiloran must die. The old waterlord would never accept the new Yahrdan whom Mirabar—and therefore Najdan—was fully convinced was coming to rule Sileria in peace and prosperity. Najdan just wished the man . . . child . . . Yahrdan would arrive soon. Just as it had been easier to attract people to Josarian's cause after he became the Firebringer, so it would be easier for Tansen to gain support and destroy Kiloran if he actually presented Sileria with a Yahrdan for the people to follow.

Details were so important.

Najdan thought it wisest to assume that there were also assassins here now, disguised as ordinary men. They might have been here for many days, previously hoping for a chance to kill Josarian, and now looking for an opportunity to slay Tansen. There might even be those bold enough among them to attack Mirabar, despite her reputation for fierce and terrible fire sorcery. Najdan absently fingered a scar acquired in a cage of shifting lava where she had imprisoned him upon their first meeting.

He glanced at her. She was sitting near a woodless fire, absorbed in conversation with a number of other Guardians, both male and female. A crowd surrounded them, evidently fascinated by their words. Najdan studied each person in turn, as he had numerous times already, but still saw nothing which required action or intervention. Beyond them, he saw only the happy, drunken, triumphant people of Sileria, celebrating victory.

Nonetheless, he felt uneasy. As he kept watch over the *sirana,* his hand rested absently on his *shir,* which was shuddering violently in response to all the Guardian magic around him in Zilar. If anyone was going to attack Mirabar, tonight would be the perfect time. A successful assault on Sileria's famous prophetess could incite terror in those around her and spread doubt throughout the nation. Surely her death, so soon after Josarian's, would convince everyone that Tansen's cause was doomed to failure? Even men who had sworn a bloodvow might think twice about opposing the Society then.

Najdan had not survived twenty years as an assassin through sheer luck. He had learned long ago to listen to his instincts and to act upon them even when others doubted him.

He was therefore both relieved and apprehensive when he saw Mirabar finally rise from her place by the fire and approach him to say, "Let's go now. I'm tired."

"It is late," he agreed. "We should return to Sanctuary."

He looked around for some familiar faces, feeling it wisest to ensure she had an escort of at least five additional men. The familiar face he saw, however, nearly froze his blood.

Acting on reflex, he shoved Mirabar to the ground, following her down with a knee planted in her back.

"Quiet!" he ordered her.

She immediately ceased her muffled sounds of protest. The idiots around them, however, required several warnings. And by then, he realized it was pointless.

The face he knew—Candan, an assassin of Kiloran's—had already moved on. Najdan rose to his feet and watched his retreating back. Candan moved with intent but without haste.

"He didn't see me," Najdan murmured. "Or you."

"Who?" Mirabar demanded, rising to her feet and brushing herself off. She nodded to the Guardians and *shallaheen* now asking after her well-being in view of the assassin's rough treatment. "Yes, yes, I'm fine." But she hissed at Najdan, "That hurt."

Najdan climbed atop a stone water trough and peered across the crowd, thankful that the many fires and torches provided enough light for him to see . . . two other men join Candan. Najdan didn't recognize them, but he recognized the confidence and the intent purpose of his own kind.

Assassins. Headed for the temple.

"Tansen," he said suddenly, realizing it wasn't Mirabar they were after tonight.

"What about him?" Mirabar asked.

"Stay here," he ordered her.

"Why?"

Najdan grabbed two nearby *shallaheen* who were both armed and looked sturdy. "Guard the *sirana*," he ordered.

"What?"

"Guard the *sirana*!" He didn't like this, but there was no time for something better, and he no longer suspected Mirabar was the target. He glared at the two *shallaheen* and added in his most menacing tone, "If anything happens to her, I promise I will hunt you down and, when I find you, take a very long time about killing you."

"Najdan," Mirabar admonished.

"Stay with them," he told her.

As he shoved his way through the crowd, he heard Mirabar saying, "No, no, it's best to just do as he says." He was glad that she, at least, showed sense.

He didn't want to risk shouting "assassins!" That would only serve to create enough general panic for Candan and his companions, all disguised as ordinary men, to escape safely. It was always best to corner and kill your enemies; if you let them get away, they would inevitably return to make you regret your mistakes. Kiloran himself had taught Najdan this, long ago; and now Kiloran's worst enemy, Tansen, was living proof of the lesson.

When Najdan reached the temple, rudely shoving his way through the throng, he found Galian, the one-eyed Yorin, and two other men posted at the main entrance. They were drinking, laughing, and gossiping, relaxed and happy.

"Who's come through here?" Najdan demanded.

"Hmmm?" Galian looked up.

"I said—"

Yorin shrugged. "I've stopped getting all the names. Everyone who—"

"Three men?"

"Recently? Sure. Well, I think it was three. Was it three? I think . . ." Yorin was still pondering this as Najdan shoved past him and opened one of the heavy doors of the temple. "A lot of people have been going in and—"

"And there are some Guardians in there," Galian added. "Been in there forever, it seems, tearing down—"

"Come with me!" Najdan snapped, hoping they were sober enough to fight, and not caring if they got themselves killed in the process.

"Now just a moment," another of the men objected as Yorin and Galian followed Najdan. "Who's he to gi— What's that?"

The steel clang of Tansen's swords rang through the temple, audible above cries for help and screams of pain. Najdan pulled his *shir* from his *jashar* and ran forward into the flickering light of the lanterns.

"Darfire!" Yorin blurted. "Get help!"

One of the *shallaheen* sobered up fast enough to spin around and run out of the temple shouting, "Assassins! Assassins!" before Najdan could warn him not to create a panic.

Typical.

There were more than three assassins here. A lot more. They had evidently been insinuating themselves into the temple all evening, a few at a time, dressed as *shallaheen,* until there were . . . Actually, Najdan wasn't even sure how many there were now. Since none of them were dressed as assassins, the scene was very confusing. He hesitated, reluctant to attack someone who might be an ally, and unwilling to turn his back on anyone who might be an enemy.

One man lay dead near Tansen, who was currently fighting three more. A scream attracted Najdan's attention. He looked to his right and saw a Guardian strangling someone with what appeared to be a rope of glowing orange. . . . *Lava,* he suddenly realized. It burned through the flesh and severed the man's neck. Another Guardian blew flames at someone and set his clothes on fire. The screams were terrible. The sudden bursts of their fire sorcery made Najdan's *shir* shake even more wildly in his hand. Other Guardians, however, already lay dead on the floor, which didn't surprise him; Guardians were primarily spiritual leaders, and many had no combat experience at all. Now some woman, absurdly, started shrieking that they mustn't risk setting the temple on fire.

It was only when Najdan saw one Guardian slit the throat of another with a *shir* that he realized that not all of the Guardians in here were really Guardians.

He raised his *shir* to attack one running towards him, but the Guardian raised his arms and cried, "No! No! Please, don't! No!"

Najdan lowered his *shir* and acknowledged his mistake. . . . Until he noticed, due to long association with Mirabar, that something was wrong. "Where's your insignia?"

"My what?"

There was no broach depicting a single flame inside a circle of fire, the proud symbol of Mirabar's sect.

"Your insignia," Najdan repeated.

The man moved suddenly, a *shir* appearing in his hand as if by magic, but Najdan was faster. He stabbed the stranger through the belly and ripped open his vitals. A hot and messy death, he noted with distaste as blood and innards flowed over him, and then onto the floor, as the dying man sank to his knees. Najdan bent over the corpse and took the *shir,* the very first one of Kiloran's he had ever touched except his own.

He heard another woman scream, but he couldn't see her. His path was blocked by an enormous, blinding fire which suddenly seemed to be raging out of control. If its creator had lost command of it—if its creator was, in fact, dead—it could indeed destroy the temple. Half of Zilar, as well. Guardian fire needed no fuel and could destroy what ordinary flames couldn't, including the town's stone dwellings.

Najdan circled the growing fire, moving in the direction of the woman's continuing screams. He finally saw a female Guardian trying to fight off an attacker. He didn't reach her side in time to save her, but he quickly killed the assassin who had gutted her, surrounded by dancing flames and twirling whips of lava.

They're killing women now.

"Najdan."

He spun around and met the eyes of someone who had once been an ally. "Candan."

"You will pay for your betrayal, *sriliah*," Candan spat.

"Perhaps."

"Perhaps?" Candan repeated disdainfully. "Without a doubt! You can't really imagine they'll win? *Shallaheen* and Guardia—"

Candan jumped as Najdan threw the newly acquired *shir* at him—and didn't regain his balance before Najdan slid the other one between his ribs and sought his heart.

"You always did talk too much," Najdan said as Candan gazed at him with wide, astonished eyes.

"Na...Na..."

"This will hurt," Najdan promised. He twisted the hilt and yanked the wavy-edged blade out of Candan's body.

The assassin gurgled in agony, then slumped to the floor, jerking awkwardly in his death throes.

From behind Najdan came more terrible screams.

He turned, thinking the noise signaled a fresh attack; but all he saw behind him were Pyron—who must have arrived in the last few moments—and Galian, killing another assassin. Well, Galian was doing the killing, using his two *yahr*. Pyron was doing the shouting, as well as the jumping up and down.

When the assassin lay dead, Pyron said feelingly, "I hate assassins! I just hate them!" He saw Najdan standing nearby, armed and blood-soaked, and added, "Nothing personal."

Tansen shouted, "Don't let him get away!"

Najdan saw that the *shatai* had cornered his remaining opponent while another assassin wounded a *shallah* who stood in his path and then ran for the doors at the back of the temple. Najdan followed. The assassin made it out the door and into a shadowy covered walkway. He escaped into the densely crowded street ahead. Najdan pursued him—and ran smack into someone who suddenly appeared out of nowhere, blocking the exit of the covered walkway. Najdan's speed was such that the two of them went flying straight into the crowded street, knocking several people over and creating general chaos.

By the time Najdan had picked himself up, the fleeing assassin was long gone. There'd be no chance of catching him in this densely packed throng. He looked down with displeasure at the young man whose sudden appearance had brought such an abrupt end to his chase. "You are a tiresome boy."

"You know," Zarien said, glaring up at him, "we'd get along much better if you just never came anywhere near me."

"I agree. Watch where you're going in future."

"You can't blame—"

"Get up," Najdan ordered, tucking his *shir* back into his *jashar*. "We've attracted quite enough attention, I think."

Zarien looked around and finally noticed how everyone was chattering and staring at the armed assassin and the sea-born boy who had just brought down half a dozen people in their tumbling drama. He flushed and rose to his feet. Dusting himself off ostentatiously, he added, "These clothes are new."

Najdan absently noted that the boy addressed him in *shallah* now, rather than the common Silerian he had used at Dalishar. He supposed he shouldn't just leave Zarien out here on the street, so he said, "Come inside."

Zarien followed him with a look of long-suffering tolerance. The boy's expression changed once they entered the burning temple, however. Najdan suspected he'd made a mistake and perhaps should have instructed the boy to wait outside for Tansen.

"By the eight winds!" Zarien's face contorted with horror as his gaze encompassed the aftermath of the attack: the wounded, the dead, the blood, the fire. "What in the Fires is going on?"

"An attack by assassins," Najdan replied briefly.

More people had been alerted by now. They came pouring through the doors to help, albeit too late. Amidst the confusion, Najdan saw Tansen. He was covered in blood, but unharmed, and shouting for the crowd to organize water supplies and to fight the fire in case the Guardians couldn't bring it under control. Then he turned and saw Najdan and the boy.

"Zarien!" Tansen's expression, so often unreadable, now revealed tremendous relief. Najdan suddenly realized the *shatai* had grown to care about the boy. "You're safe!"

"What . . . What . . . ." Zarien sounded dazed.

"We'll talk about it later." Tansen's gaze flashed to Najdan as he asked, "Mirabar?"

"Safe. When I saw Candan coming here, I left her in someone else's care." He glanced at Zarien and added, "The other assassin got away."

"I left this one alive just in case." Tansen nodded to where Yorin and Pyron were finishing their task of tying up the man Tansen had been fighting when Najdan had gone in pursuit of the escaped assassin.

"For questioning?" Najdan guessed.

"Yes. Do you recognize him?"

Najdan studied the man. "No. Let me see his *shir*." Tansen showed him where it lay on the floor, useless to anyone else as long as its owner was alive.

Najdan studied it a moment, then nodded with certainty. "It was made by one of the brothers. Abidan or Liadon. Their work is too similar for me to say which one, but it's one of theirs."

Tansen nodded and thought for a moment. "And this other man—Candan?—whom you recognized. One of Kiloran's men?"

"Yes."

"Do you recognize any of the other dead men?"

Accustomed to death, Najdan didn't shrink from examining the corpses. "I recognize those two," he finally told Tansen. "Both Kiloran's men. But I don't know the others." He eyed the daggers of the dead men. "Most of them were Abidan and Liadon's men. Which makes sense. Zilar lies within their territory."

"None of Baran's assassins," Tansen mused, studying the various *shir*. He scoured his face with a dirty hand, suddenly looking weary. Only a few days ago, Najdan recalled, he had been dying of a serious wound. "Perhaps Baran hasn't joined them yet. Perhaps there's still time to win him over to our side."

"I know that he hates Kiloran beyond reason," Najdan offered, "but I don't know why."

"Hatred might not be enough to make him side with us against Kiloran now," Tansen said pensively.

"True. He and Kiloran have declared a truce several times in the past. Whenever they agreed that something mattered more than their private feud."

"And what could matter more," Tansen asked, "than the fate of Sileria?"

"Tansen!" Someone Najdan didn't know, a man wearing the Guardian insignia, rushed up to them and said, "We've got the fire under control. It'll be out shortly."

"Good work." Tansen frowned. "Did you burn yourself?"

"It happens," the Guardian said, dismissing his singed sleeve and reddening skin. He turned away to return to his task.

Najdan had seen some of Mirabar's burns and knew that even Guardians were not always impervious to fire.

"I will show you where I left the *sirana*," Najdan said, coming to a sudden decision. "I think a very large escort would be advisable for both of you on your way to Sanctuary for the night."

Tansen glanced at Zarien, who was slowly edging towards the main exit and looking as if he might vomit at any moment. "Yes, that's a good idea. The boy shouldn't stay . . ." He sighed and looked at Najdan again. "And you?"

"I will question the assassin."

"Are you sure—"

"He is my kind," Najdan said. "If he can be made to talk—which, I admit, is unlikely—then it will take another assassin to force him to speak."

Tansen accepted this without expression. "I'll leave some men here to make sure that you're not surprised the way I was just surprised. Just in case."

Najdan glanced over the devastation all around them in this previously immaculate shrine to various foreign gods. "It's been a very interesting day."

"You have a gift for understatement."

"And you," Najdan observed, "are very lucky."

"In more ways than one," Tansen agreed.

"Indeed. I am beginning to lose count of the ways."

"Yes, well," Tansen said dryly, "my grandfather always told me that it's wise to be lucky . . ."

"Ah."

". . . but foolish to rely on luck."

23

THERE'S ONE SURE WAY OF WINNING AN ARGUMENT
WITH A WOMAN. UNFORTUNATELY, NO ONE KNOWS
WHAT IT IS.

—Moorlander Proverb

RONALL SAT DRINKING in the library of his wife's palatial house in Shaljir. He drank heavily, with a terrible thirst, as if his life depended on it.

Not wine, not ale. Not tonight. Tonight, nothing less than Kintish fire brandy would do. Tonight, the world was coming to an end, and he wanted to be blissfully unconscious by the time it finally happened.

His head was reeling, but he was still alert enough to hear Elelar's slippered feet when she entered the library and, unaware of his presence, closed the doors behind her. She didn't see him. He was sitting in a massive chair, with his back to the door.

And living with my back to the wall.

Only when Elelar came forward to stare into the flames still burning magically in the hearth—would Derlen never douse that damn fire?—did she notice him. She gave a startled gasp and flinched, a much bigger reaction than he'd expected, then relaxed.

"Damn you," she snapped, "don't sneak around this house like some . . . assassin."

"An interesting choice of words." Ronall vaguely wondered about the bruises on her face and throat. He didn't remember putting them there. "Are we expecting your friend Searlon?"

"He's not my friend." She glanced at him briefly and added, "Or yours. He'd kill you just to spite me."

"If he's as clever as you said, he'd leave me alive to continue tormenting you."

"True enough. What are you doing here?" she demanded.

"Waiting for my wife."

She made no attempt to hide her impatience. "What do you want?"

"Waiting for my heroic wife," he elaborated, "who stood by the Imperial Advisor's side while he publicly announced Valdania's surrender to the Silerian rebels." The tale had quickly spread throughout the city. Naturally, Ronall had heard it from someone other than his dear wife. Now he smiled suggestively. "Dare I ask how you convinced Kaynall to do it? Or would a husband find the answer too shocking?"

"Searlon got him to do it," she replied tersely. "By killing Cyrill."

That stunned him into momentary silence.

Elelar added, "Right in front of me and Kaynall."

"Three Into One, you're a ruthless woman," he murmured.

"It wasn't my plan, you fool! I had no idea—"

"But you took advantage of the moment, all the same."

She hesitated, as if remembering. "Yes. I did." She whirled on him, angry now. "And why shouldn't I? Cyrill spilled so much Silerian blood, like all the rest of them. What is his blood to me?"

"And my father's blood?"

"Your father?" she said in confusion. "He wasn't there."

He downed some more of the fire brandy, so named for its glowing orange-gold color, not to mention its effects. He felt the burn going all the way down, and he welcomed it. "He was killed this afternoon."

He was pleased to see how stunned she looked. "*What?*"

"I gather you hadn't heard."

"Your father was killed?"

"By Silerians on a rampage. Looting, burning, and killing every Valdan in their path."

"What about your mother?"

"Dead, too, beside her Valdani husband."

She sank to her knees beside her pet Guardian's perpetual fire and whispered, "Dar have mercy."

"The Silerian servants escaped alive," he continued, "except for the one who tried to protect my mother. Two of the servants came here to tell me what had happened and to ask my help in getting out of Shaljir before things get worse."

"I'll deal with it," she said absently.

"Damn you, woman!" How useless did she think he was? "I already did!"

"Oh." She seemed not to notice his flare of temper. "Good."

"You heard nothing about this?" he demanded.

"I heard there'd been violence, some attacks on Valdani civilians, a few people killed . . ." She shook her head. "That's all. I was busy all day . . ."

"Celebrating?" he snarled.

"Working. With the Alliance. We must consider . . . consider how to govern ourselves . . ." Her voice faltered.

"After you're done killing all the remaining Valdani in Sileria, you mean?"

"No!" She spoke sharply. "I had nothing to do with this!"

"Didn't you?"

"No! The Alliance has never condoned—"

"They massacred my parents!"

"An angry mob, Ronall! Not—"

"My mother, Elelar! Silerians slaughtered my helpless mother like some—"

"And how many of their mothers do you suppose the Valdani killed?" she asked furiously. "Ask Tansen, sometime, how his whole family died! His whole village! Ask Faradar how her parents d—"

"I hope you're happy with the new nation you've brought into this world! Angry mobs and bloodthirsty killers—"

"That is not the nation I helped free! It's just an enraged crowd who knew the Outlookers meant to sacrifice them, perhaps even kill them, if the city was besieged! A furious and resentful people suddenly free of restraint and—"

"Dar help me, you're defending them!"

"No!" She sat back on her heels and made an obvious effort to cool her temper. "I'm not defending them. I'm . . . trying to understand them."

"So you can be understanding about what they did to my parents?" he snarled.

She met his gaze. "So I can understand how to stop them."

That surprised him. "Do you really intend to?"

"Of course. Enough incidents like this, and the Emperor might ignore the treaty and send—"

"I see. Angry mobs could jeopardize Sileria's independence."

She had the decency to look a little shamefaced. "I'm very sorry about your parents, Ronall."

"Why?" He changed tactics. "You never cared about them."

"I'm sorry for anyone who dies the way they did."

"Even Cyrill?"

She was silent.

He prodded, "They're all just . . . Valdani to you, aren't they?"

"They *are* Val . . . were Valdani. What else—"

"My father tried to save your life when you were in prison," he reminded her. "He petitioned the Imperial Council—"

"Only because I was your wife."

"My father cared about Silerians, Elelar," he insisted. "He married one."

Her dark eyes were remarkably cold now. "Yet he opposed independence, and he actively supported a government whose laws didn't even nominally protect Silerians from rape, theft, assault, torture, or murder when the crime was committed by a Valdan."

"So you're glad he's dead."

"I'm not glad a Silerian mob killed him."

"And my mother?"

She looked away.

"Answer me, Elelar."

She finally said, "Your mother was what I pretended, for so long, to be. And I hated what I pretended to be."

The brandy burned his belly and made his head reel. "So you hated them both."

"Why do you want to talk about this now?"

"Call me whimsical."

"You're drunk, as always."

"If you knew for certain that the Emperor wouldn't change his mind, the people of Valda wouldn't clamor for reprisals, some imperial army wouldn't swoop down on us . . . You wouldn't care if the people slaughtered every last Valdan in Sileria, would you?"

"I refuse to argue with you." She rose and started to leave.

Rage burned inside him. It blocked out the sorrow and fed on the liquor. He surged unsteadily to his feet and stopped her departure. "And if they killed me . . . me, most of all . . . that would send you dancing into the streets, wouldn't it?"

Rage. Hot and sweet. So much better than pain.

"Get out of my way," Elelar ordered.

The rage bubbled over like lava erupting from Darshon. He grabbed Elelar, feeling the way her soft flesh gave beneath his cruelly squeezing fingers. "Answer me!"

"Let go of me!" She struggled to escape him.

He shook her. Shook her hard. Whether he meant to shake the truth from her or to punish her for wounding him, he didn't know. He only knew that he, the husband sworn to cherish and protect this delicate female, brutally enjoyed the way she flopped helplessly in his grip as he shouted into her face, "You would love it if they killed everyone with Valdani blood, wouldn't you?"

"Stop it!"

"You'll only be happy when they finally kill me, too!"

Desperate to be free, she aimed a blow at his groin. He twisted just in time to avoid it, then let go of her to take a furious swing at her. His fist connected with her face, and she went reeling backwards to fall on the floor.

Shock and shame flooded his veins. Liquor clouded his mind and made his balance unsteady. Rage and fear made his heart pound so loudly it deafened him. Yet above the roar of his own blood, he could hear her words clearly.

"Yes," she hissed. "I pray to Dar nightly that you'll die, and if the mob kills you, I'll throw open the doors of the house and offer a reward!"

Tears of sorrow, guilt, and fury misted his vision. He saw the blood running down from her nose now. Saw what he had done to the only woman he had ever loved, the woman he had made hate him with such venomous loathing.

"Elelar . . ." He heard the whine in his own voice and hated it. He took an unsteady step forward, alternately hoping for her forgiveness and damning her for not wanting his.

"Get away from me." She sounded like a growling dog. "If you ever touch me again, if you ever come near me again, I swear I'll go out into the street and *beg* the mob to come here and kill you!"

"Don't—"

"Get out of my house!" she screamed, flinching away from the hand he extended without thinking. "*Get out! Get out! Get out!*"

He stumbled out of the room, pursued by her hate-filled voice. When he found himself outside, he didn't even remember how he'd left the house. Her vicious screams still rang in his ears.

The stables, he thought blearily. He could go farther if he had a horse. He could go *very* far away from his wife on a horse.

Get out! Get out! Get out!

He wasn't sure how he found his way to the stables, staggering drunk and blinded by the dark. Habit, he supposed. Good thing no one had moved the stables.

He shook awake a sleeping groom and ordered a horse to be saddled. Elelar's favorite horse, he decided. Yes, that was the one he'd take with him, away from his wife, far away, so far away she'd never see it again.

Luckily, it was a patient gelding, because it took him a few tries before he awkwardly hauled himself into the saddle.

"*Toren,*" the groom ventured hesitantly. "May I ask where you're going? In case the *torena* inquires?"

Get out! Get out! Get out!

He thought it over for a moment, hoping for something crushingly witty to come to him. The best he could manage, though, was, "Tell the *torena* that I am going to embrace the mob."

"But—"

He kicked the horse and clung to its back, out of habit, as it trotted out of the stable yard and into the dark streets of Shaljir, where surely someone would oblige Elelar by killing him.

* * *

TANSEN STOOD IN *the rain, staring down at Armian's corpse. After a moment, he sank to his knees.*

"Forgive me, father," he whispered.

The night rained down upon him in dark condemnation for what he had done. Dar would punish him terribly for this, he knew. How could She not?

He picked up Armian's shir—*which was his own now, by right of victorious combat. . . . It came into his hand as if awaiting his touch, as if it knew it belonged to him now. Its previously unbearable cold fire was now a soothing coolness, and it seemed to extend its strange ensorcelled power to him, making him stronger, faster, deadlier . . .*

He thought he would be sick. Head reeling, stomach churning, whole body shaking in reaction to what he had just done, he stood upright again in the rain with Armian's shir *in his hand.*

He stared down at the body of his slain bloodfather, his mind blank, his heart burning with sorrow and with shame.

Then Elelar's screams pierced the dark, rainy night, carried to him on the winds sweeping across the high cliffs of the southern coast overlooking the cove below.

He felt her hands on his shoulders, pushing him away from Armian. He staggered back, unresisting, and watched her examining the body, shouting Armian's name as if she could raise him from the dead. Then she turned on Tansen.

"What have you done? What have you done? Sweet Dar, WHAT HAVE YOU DONE?*"*

Rain pelted her, soaking her tangled, wind-whipped black hair, running down her smooth cheeks, clinging to her long lashes and making her blink as it crept into her eyes. The delicately painted silk scarf which had covered her hair earlier was now a soaked rag falling carelessly around her shoulders. Her clothes were wet and dirty, and she was panting with exertion and panic.

"What have you done?" she kept screaming.

He pushed her away from Armian's body and, after taking one last look at his father, shoved the corpse off the cliff. Elelar screamed in horror as it bounced off the rocks below and plummeted to the beach. The wind, the rain, and Elelar all ensured that Tansen didn't hear it hit the ground, but he felt the final thud somewhere inside his heart.

Elelar backed away from him, screaming wildly.

"Torena . . ."

"No, no, no!" She staggered backwards, as if afraid of him, and fell down on the uneven ground. When he stepped forward to help her, she crawled away on unsteady limbs, still screaming.

He backed away, hoping she would see he wouldn't hurt her, and waited. She was not a silly woman, and her screaming stopped as soon as she realized he meant her no harm. She lay there on the ground, wet and muddy, gaping at him as her body heaved with panting breaths.

At last she said, "Have you gone mad?"

"The Moorlanders will find the body. They will take it as Kiloran's answer."

"I've grasped that!" she shouted. "What in the Fires can you possibly be think—"

"Now the Moorlanders' plan will fall apart," he said, willing her to understand. "Now the Society will not rule Sileria."

"You idiot!" she screamed. "Now the Valdani will continue to be our masters!"

"We will find another way to fight them, to defeat them. We need not exchange this master for an even crueler—"

"You are out of your mind, aren't you?"

He stared in dismay as she pushed herself to her feet and stalked towards him. He had thought that she, of all people, would understand.

"How do you imagine," she shouted, "we can do this without the Moorlanders?"

"But the Alliance—"

"The Alliance needs Kiloran, and you've just made us his enemies with this ins—"

"He is our enemy! You've told me so yourself!" he shouted back. " 'Who rules the mountains through bloodshed and terror?' " He quoted her own words back at her, things she had taught him during their flight from Shaljir, their journey through Sileria to find Kiloran, and their stay in the waterlord's camp. "Who controls the toreni with abductions, ransom demands, and murder? Who destroyed Sileria's last Yahrdan? Who has already killed more shallaheen than the Valdani ever will?"

"And who," she raged, "just killed our best chance of freedom in centuries?"

"You saw what kind of man Armian was. You know what kind of man Kiloran is. You heard them, just as I did, plan their future, our future, Sileria's future!"

"I heard them plan armed resistance to the Val—"

"There was no place in their new Sileria for you or me. No place for shallaheen, toreni, Guardians, or anyone else!"

"We'd have made our place!"

"How? The Moorlanders' plan only included the Society! Kiloran and Armian were going to take over the whole country with the Moorlanders' help, rule the whole nation with terror, bloodshed, and drought. They'd have all the power in Sileria if the plan succeeded! How were you planning to take it away from them then?"

"Nothing is as important as driving out the Valdani! No other enemy matters!"

He saw that she meant it. She, who had helped him see what the waterlords and the assassins really were; she, who had unknowingly revealed his terrible duty to him; she thought he was wrong. She hated the Valdani with such blind passion that she thought Kiloran and Armian would be better masters of Sileria, and was willing to help them steal the nation from its own people.

"You're wrong," he said desperately, but he knew she wouldn't listen to an illiterate peasant boy from Gamalan. "You're so wrong."

"What's that?" She was suddenly alert, looking past him, down at the cove.

He followed her gaze, turning to peer through the murky night. Now he saw it: a Moorlander vessel, its lanterns blazing in the dark, drifting into the cove.

"They're here," she said, her voice calmer.

"They'll send an oarboat ashore. They'll find the body."

"Not if I can prevent it," she said with sudden determination.

"Torena, no!"

She shook off his restraining hand. "I'm going to salvage this proposed alliance with the Moorlanders." Her voice was hard as she added, "The only way you can stop me is by killing me, too. Now get out of my way."

She tried to move past him. He doubted that she could find her way safely down to the beach, in the dark and without his help, in time to meet the Moorlanders; but he couldn't risk it. He had never handled a woman roughly in his life, but now he came to a sudden decision and grabbed the torena.

She shrieked a protest—perhaps afraid he really would kill her—as he bore her to the ground with a knee planted in her back. He tore the sodden silk scarf away from her shoulders and used it to bind her wrists together behind her back. Then he rose, hoisted her over his shoulder, and carried her away from the site of Armian's death like a sack of grain. He didn't release her until dawn, when he knew there'd be no chance whatsoever of her contacting the Moorlander ship.

While untying her wrists, he explained that he would escort her safely back to Shaljir.

"I'm not going to Shaljir." Her voice was hoarse, but still rich with fury.

"Where shall I take you then?"

"I'm going back to Kiloran. To tell him what you've done. To tell him that I tried to stop you and that the Alliance had no part in this insanity." She glared at him with anger which had only grown hotter with the passage of hours. "I will not let one bloodthirsty peasant destroy what my grandfather has spent his whole life building."

"Elelar . . ." He heard the pleading in his voice and hated it.

"What do the shallaheen call someone like you?" she prodded. "Sriliah?"

Traitor. The very worst thing one Silerian could call another.

He stared at her in dumbfounded silence as she rose to her feet and declared, "Kiloran will swear a bloodvow against you, and I will celebrate on the day I learn of your death."

"But you . . ." He made a helpless gesture. "You showed me the way. It was—"

"Don't you dare try to blame this on me." She gave him one last look as she said, "You've destroyed everything, and I will pray to Dar to punish you as you deserve."

He watched her stalk away from him, knowing she would soon find the coastal road if she kept going in that direction.

She'd probably find Kiloran before long, too.

A bloodvow. From Kiloran himself.

He knew he'd never survive it. No one could survive that. And he had no doubt about how relentless Kiloran would be, given what Tansen had done.

A bloodvow.

What could he do? Even fleeing to the farthest corner of Sileria wouldn't save him, not with Kiloran as determined to kill him as he undoubtedly would be.

The early morning wind shifted. He caught a whiff of sea air.

The sea.

He had never been to sea. If truth be known, he was afraid of the sea and found the notion of entrusting his life to a boat more than a little frightening. He had, of course, never been out of Sileria in his life.

He trembled as he realized what he was considering.

A bloodvow lasted for nine years, and then it must be honorably withdrawn if the enemy had not been killed during all that time. This rule was part of a centuries-old code of conduct established by the waterlords to help keep the Society from tearing itself apart with the same unquenchable lust for vengeance which regularly destroyed clans like Tansen's.

He had no chance of surviving Kiloran's wrath for nine years in Sileria, but if he went away now . . . and only came back when the nine years were over . . .

His family was dead, his clan gone, his village destroyed. He had nowhere to go, no one to turn to. No one would miss him once he was gone, just as no one would care if Kiloran killed him.

He might die on a faulty boat crossing the Middle Sea. He might starve, lost and alone, in some foreign place. He might be imprisoned or killed by whatever manner of men lived on the mainland . . . But he had to try. His only other choice was to cower in hiding until Society assassins finally cornered and killed him, as they inevitably would.

He wasn't ready to die. He was only fifteen, and he wanted to live. So he had to try. He would flee Sileria and try to survive on the mainland. And if he lived . . . then, someday, he would come home.

Tears misted his eyes. He blinked them back. His boyhood was over forever. It had ended in the night, on a rainy, windswept cliff. Now he must be a man.

Nine years. Perhaps it will not seem such a long time.

He wrapped Armian's shir *in the finely painted scarf he had used to bind Elelar's wrists, then rose to his feet and began his journey. By nightfall, he reached the port of Adalian. The next day, offering to work for his passage, he boarded a ship bound for the port city of Kashala in the Kintish Kingdoms, where his new life would begin.*

24

TANSEN CLIMBED SLOWLY out of the dark well of his dreams. Groping for escape from his memories, he struggled vaguely in the land between sleep and waking.

A strange snuffling sound finally fully roused him. Something cold and wet prodded him, startling him. Swimming blindly away from the past, he cautiously opened one eye.

A pair of soulful eyes, glinting faintly as they reflected a stray beam of moonlight, met his gaze in the dark room where he had been sleeping. He blinked, opened both eyes now, and focused on a hairy face wearing a hesitant expression.

"Oh. Hello," he said without enthusiasm.

Pleased that Tansen wasn't wasting the night in sleep like everyone else, the dog licked his face.

"Go away," he ordered.

The dog wagged its tail, then started poking him and snuffling around him again, evidently convinced he didn't mind.

Tansen sighed. Sister Shannibar, whose Sanctuary he was sleeping in on the outskirts of Zilar, loved animals and kept several here. Sister Norimar, who shared the Sanctuary with Shannibar, detested them. Although the two women had renounced violence upon joining the Sisterhood, Tansen—who'd only been here a few hours—had already seen them come close to exchanging blows over this difference of opinion. However, he doubted Norimar would be around long. The way she flirted with his men suggested she'd soon find herself a second husband and abandon the Sisterhood. He supposed she had taken her vows when grief over her first husband's death was still fresh and she hadn't considered how unsuited to the life of a Sister she was.

Fortunately, Norimar was none of his concern. Unfortunately, Shannibar's dog clearly wasn't going to let him go back to sleep. It was running around the room almost frantically now, sniffing and snuffling, occasionally whining . . . and regularly returning to his side to poke him with its cold nose.

Tiring of this, Tansen rolled to his feet. Just as well, he supposed. His dreams were far from restful.

The Sanctuary was a large one, built to accommodate guests seeking shelter or safety, so he and his men were able to sleep inside tonight. Not wanting the dog to wake Zarien, who was still young enough to need a lot of sleep—not to mention a lot of food—Tansen urged the dog to follow him out of the room and into the main common area of the Sanctuary.

Only a few moments later, however, the animal's whining and scratching became so insistent that Tansen began to worry it would wind up waking everyone in the Sanctuary. When it pestered an equally restless cat, the cat responded with a show of bad temper that made the dog bark. Tansen decided to take the dog outside before everyone else's night was ruined, too.

Outside, the waning moons still glowed with a faint orange-red color, but the stars were clearly visible for the first time in recent nights.

"Who let the dog out?" someone demanded, startling him for a moment before he recognized Mirabar's voice coming from near the enormous old fig tree which dominated the Sanctuary's garden.

"I did," he replied, his heart tugging him in her direction. "Is he bothering you?"

"She," Mirabar corrected dryly.

He saw the fiery glow of her eyes now, blazing out of the dark shadows. As she stepped forward, the faint moonlight shimmered along the thick red curls which fell past her shoulders. She had washed and changed into clean clothes, pale homespun which emphasized the golden color of her skin even at night.

"She?" he repeated. "Oh. Well, she's . . . restless."

Tansen heard the distraction in his voice as he stared at Mirabar and wondered if she noticed it. He was glad he had washed and changed, too, after coming here from the temple. He hadn't liked her seeing him covered in blood yet again.

Always more blood, it seemed. The blood of his family, his friends, his enemies. Would there ever be an end to it?

"She woke me," Mirabar said, and he welcomed the intrusion on his thoughts. "She's so noisy and pushy."

"That nose." Tansen smiled.

Mirabar smiled back, pleasing him. "It's startling in the middle of the night, isn't it?"

He grinned. "I think Sister Shannibar spoils her."

"Clearly. Anyhow, she kept pestering me even after I gave her some food. So I came outside. I don't know what she wants, and Shannibar . . ." Mirabar's gesture suggested exasperation. "Shannibar sleeps like a log."

"And you wouldn't want to wake Norimar to tend the dog."

A puff of laughter escaped her. "Definitely not."

Together, they watched the dog running around the yard with the same agitation she had shown inside. Finally, Tansen noted, "Animals are often restless before an earthquake."

Mirabar shivered and rubbed her arms, taking a seat on a stone bench near the well. "That's all we need now."

He joined her on the bench, close enough to smell her warm, clean scent; far enough away to be courteous. Almost as if she were an ordinary woman and he an ordinary man come to court her.

But they weren't. They were what Dar and destiny had made them, and nothing between them would ever be so simple or normal, he knew. Especially not in these strange times.

"Today I heard some stories," he prompted, "about clouds of colored smoke dancing above Mount Darshon, visible even at night."

"You haven't seen it?" She quickly answered her own question by adding, "No, of course you wouldn't, not if you haven't been high up since you left Dalishar."

He asked her to tell him about it, happy to sit in the dark and listen to her soft, earthy voice speaking the mountain dialect of his innocent youth—in her case, with the slight inflection that reflected her upbringing in western rather than eastern Sileria. When she finished her description of the lightning and colored clouds swirling violently around Darshon's peak, he knew she was awaiting his reaction; but he could only think to ask her opinion about it.

"I don't know." She sighed. "I've asked many of the other Guardians in Zilar."

"Have they seen it?"

She nodded. "Some came from high in the mountains, from summits where they saw it as recently as two nights ago."

"So it's continuing," he mused.

"Yes. But no one has any more useful ideas than I do."

"What are your ideas?"

"Only that something is beginning. Something..." She shrugged. "Something we have never seen before."

"Pyron says that, for the second time, everyone at Dalishar saw a vision: golden eyes in the night sky. And they felt as if they heard a phrase—"

" 'He is coming.' "

"Yes."

"I asked the other Guardians," Mirabar said, "and the vision has only appeared at Dalishar. No one elsewhere has seen it."

The dog came up to them, whining for comfort. Tansen absently stroked its head while he considered Mirabar's words. "There were quite a lot of Guardians today," he said at last. "More than I had expected."

"Some of the ones I spoke with told me they saw portents in the circle of fire. Shades of the dead guiding them here."

"Do they know why?"

"They think it was to join your bloodvow, and to hear us promise them a new ruler. They want to support him, to help him." She lowered her head. "So I . . . I haven't told them everything."

"What do you mean?"

"Fire and water, water and fire . . . A child of fire, a child of water, a child of sorrow . . ." She made an abrupt sound of frustration. "Until I know more, unless I can reassure the Guardians . . . I don't think it would be wise to tell all I know."

"They might be afraid you're seeing a waterlord in our future," he guessed.

"And if I can't guarantee that I'm not—"

"Are you?"

"I don't know."

"The, uh, the Beckoner," he began hesitantly.

"Yes?"

"Have you asked him if it's a waterlord? I mean . . . can you ask the Beckoner questions?"

"I ask him questions all the time," she said wearily. "I am very seldom answered."

"And he hasn't answered you—"

"About this?" She shook her head. "No."

"Is he . . ." He wasn't sure he wanted to open this subject, but he went ahead anyhow. "Is he like Armian?"

"Like Armian?" she repeated blankly.

"You've said that Armian wasn't like other shades. Because he spoke directly to us, rather than through you. Because after I gave Armian's *shir* back to Kiloran as a peace offering, you were still able to Call Armian even without it."

"Only for a little while," she reminded him. "Only during the days when we needed Armian to convince some of the waterlords to join the rebellion. It was special and strange, yes, but it was nothing like this."

"How is this different?" he prodded, wanting to understand, to know her secret world better.

"Well, for one thing, I don't Call the Beckoner, he Calls me. Which is something shades don't do. Ever."

"Oh."

"He doesn't just speak to me. He can create . . ." She paused as she searched for the right words. "Not just visions, images which I see. He can create sensations. He can cause me physical pain."

"He causes you pain?" He didn't like that.

"Yes." As if relieved to speak about it to someone, she rushed on, "And he can also make me feel powerful emotions which aren't my own: shame, sorrow, bitterness, love, courage . . ."

"Why does he do it?"

"To make me understand." He was captivated by her vibrancy as she tried to explain her mystical experiences to him. "So I can recognize who I'm sent to seek or what I'm meant to achieve. So I can accept the urgency and the importance of things which seem . . . well, incomprehensible at first, even outrageous." She added reflectively, "Perhaps the Beckoner knows I must be driven to the edge of madness sometimes so that I'll have the will to do what I must." Her posture slumped a bit and her voice, when she spoke again, was weary. "But it's so hard, sometimes, because no one but me has ever seen him. For a long time, many of the Guardians in my circle were even convinced that these visitations were a sign that I was going mad—or possessed by evil."

"So no one knows who . . . what . . ." He trailed off, feeling inadequate. These were matters far outside of a *shatai*'s realm.

"What the Beckoner's nature is?" she supplied.

"Yes."

"No." Her voice sounded hollow. "No one knows. No one can tell me or help me."

He thought how lonely living with these visions must be for her. Finally, he asked, "Could the Beckoner be a manifestation of Dar?"

She shrugged. "Why would Dar manifest Herself as a man?"

"Could he be some sort of god, though?"

"He could be," she agreed. "I don't think he's a sorcerer, and I'm positive he's not a shade, but . . ." She sighed, weary and confused. "I've thought about it and thought about it until my heads reels, and I don't know. I just don't know."

Her voice broke in doubt and frustration. He wanted to comfort her, to reach out and stroke her hair, take her in his arms. But after the things they had said to each other at Dalishar, he wasn't sure she would find that as comforting as he would right now. And a good man, his grandfather had taught him, didn't use a woman for what would please him unless she'd made it clear it would please her, too.

He had always tried to be a good man. He had failed more than once, but he didn't want to keep failing with her. Not anymore.

Wanting to distract her, and unable to resist at least some contact, he reached out and lightly touched her left hand, the one he had cut with his engraved Kintish blade today. "Does it hurt?"

"Hmm?" As he had hoped, the question coaxed her attention away from the thoughts which tormented her. She looked down now at the fresh bandage on her fine-boned hand. "Oh, that." She shrugged with a *shallah* woman's contempt for pain. "Not really."

"You did very well today."

"So did you," she replied. "You were good with the people."

"Josarian was good with people. I'm good with weapons." He had left his swords inside, though. Now that the Valdani had surrendered, he and Mirabar were safe here. Kiloran had circumvented custom once in the past by arranging for Outlookers to ambush Josarian in Sanctuary; but no Silerian would violate centuries of custom by attacking an enemy on Sanctuary grounds, so Tansen could relax his vigilance tonight.

"No, you've improved," Mirabar said. "You were very good with the crowd today. You gave them what they wanted and knew how to get what we wanted."

It pleased him, because he hoped it was true—and because she had bothered to notice and troubled to say so.

After a moment of companionable silence, Mirabar said, "I suppose you have new duties for me t—"

"I do."

"But there's something I need to do first."

"Yes?" he invited.

"I want to go to Mount Niran. To see Tashinar."

He knew that Mirabar was very close to the old woman who had been her teacher ever since finding her wild in the mountains years ago. He also knew that Tashinar was sick and increasingly frail.

"I don't know what's happened on Mount Niran since Josarian's death," Mirabar said. "And I'm worried, too, because of these earthquakes we've been having."

"Of course you can go," he assured her.

"I need to see her. Speak with her," she continued. "I need . . . guidance."

"I can understand that."

"There's so much I can't tell the other Guardians . . ."

Not even Cheylan?

He wanted to say it, but he didn't. He didn't want to bring the other man into this garden with them.

". . . but I can trust Tashinar to keep my confidence and listen to me without panicking or jumping to conclusions."

"When do you want to leave?" He wouldn't keep her here. He could hear how much she wanted to see Tashinar. But he would be sorry to see her go.

Insurrection, he reflected wryly, hadn't left him much time for women since his return to Sileria. And he knew now that he had wasted too much of the time he had spent with *this* woman.

"I want to go right away," she said.

"After sunrise?" He tried to hide his disappointment. He probably succeeded. His life had made him good at that.

"Yes. Unless I'm still needed here?"

It was tempting to tell her she was, but he'd be lying. "No, if you need to go, you can go."

"After Najdan gets back and rests a bit, we'll set out." She drew in a shaky breath. "I guess he's still in the temple. What a . . . a long interrogation that has been."

"He may have saved my life tonight," Tansen told her. "I was alone in the temple with nothing but assassins who took me by surprise, and a few Guardians—some of whom died so fast I never even saw it happen."

"They weren't warriors."

"No." Tansen had fought that many men before and survived, but the odds certainly weren't ideal, and his *kaj* had given him a few object lessons in the dangers of arrogance. "I was lucky Najdan recognized one of the assassins in the crowd and came to help me."

"That attack was a bold move," she said.

"We can count on more." He didn't hesitate as he reached out to touch her again, because it was imperative that she understand. "I want you to be extremely careful at all times—"

"I will."

"You must be vigilant. Najdan will be, but it's instinct to him after all these years. You must concentrate on it."

"I will," she promised again.

"It'll be a dangerous journey." He could feel fear for her rising inside him just thinking about it.

"I know. But I need to do this." Then she asked, "What shall I do after Niran?"

"Go to Sister Velikar's Sanctuary. When she returns from Belitar, find out what Baran's answer is to our offer of friendship. If it's favorable, we need to make immediate plans with him. And if it's unfavorable . . ."

"Yes?"

He frowned. "Then I need you to change his mind." He didn't like this, but he knew it was necessary. If Baran was recalcitrant, then only the strongest Guardian in Sileria was likely to find a way to influence such a powerful waterlord. "You're a great sorceress. Maybe you can—"

"He's a waterlord and I'm a Guardian," she said doubtfully.

"He respects you."

"Perhaps," she conceded, "but not that much." Her gaze searched his face in the dark. "Are you afraid his answer might be unfavorable?"

"I'm not sure." Tansen studied the night sky overhead. "He didn't join the rebellion for freedom. Not even for power. He joined it because the Outlookers were such a distraction. So long as the Valdani ruled Sileria, they interfered with his private war against Kiloran."

"Does anyone know why he hates Kiloran so much?"

"No. I used to think it was just a power struggle."

She shook her head. "It's more than that. Najdan has said it's personal, though even he doesn't know why."

"I suppose I realized that, too, when Baran stayed on our side, in defiance of the other waterlords, after Josarian killed Srijan. Baran went against the Society just because Josarian made Kiloran bleed by killing his son." Tansen had met Baran a few times and had always found him chilling, in a different way from Kiloran. "He's so strange and unpredictable. You'd think he'd join us now because we're Kiloran's enemies, but . . ."

"But, what?"

"Baran's smart, despite his eccentricities," Tansen said, thinking out loud. "He'll realize how much we need him; and he may feel he has no need of us. After all, from his perspective, why shouldn't the Society rule Sileria?"

"So the only thing that will interest him in our friendship . . ."

"Is if he becomes convinced he needs us to destroy Kiloran."

"And you, I hope," she said dryly, "have a long list of suggestions about how I can convince him of this?"

"Just one," he admitted.

"Which is?"

"Do whatever you have to."

"Vague and demanding," she noted. "Rather like the Beckoner."

He smiled faintly. "If something better comes to me, I'll get a message to you at Sister Velikar's Sanctuary."

"Where will you be?"

"I have a lot more to do here, but when I can, I'll leave for Shaljir."

"Ah. Shaljir . . . and its port." She nodded. "Perhaps it's time to do as Zarien wishes."

He was as uneasy with the notion as he had been from the start, but he agreed. "If I don't want that damned *stahra* following me all over Sileria, I suppose I must."

She cleared her throat. "There are better reasons, actually, than just—"

"I know." He sighed. "His goddess wants him by my side, that much is clear." He absently pressed a hand against the magically healed *shir* wound beneath his tunic. "And I still don't know who or what saved my life in that cave. Or why."

"But you don't feel a calling," she guessed.

"I truly don't." He shrugged and added, "I don't even like the sea, to be honest."

He heard her soft puff of amusement. "Still," she said, "the boy is full of riddles, and you must find the answers."

He believed it, too. "Oh, well. Whatever happens, at least it won't be a wasted journey. There's plenty to accomplish in Shaljir. Among other things, I need to speak with the leaders of the Alliance."

"The Alliance?" She sounded appalled, undoubtedly remembering it was the Alliance which betrayed Josarian to the Valdani.

He pointed out, "Only a few of them even knew about that secret treaty, Mira."

"But still—"

"I don't like them much, either," he admitted. "They're probably already plotting and scheming about how to govern the nation and, more to the point, who'll have the power. But we need them as much as we ever did; they're part of us, just as we're part of them. We can only survive if we all remember that. So I mean to tell them that Sileria needs them to stand with us against the Society. And also that we're awaiting a new Yahrdan; one who probably won't," he concluded with pleasure, "be one of them."

Mirabar was quiet for a long moment before saying, "So you'll see her."

He didn't have to ask whom she meant. "Yes."

Elelar was, in fact, the reason he didn't intend to bring Mirabar to Shaljir with him despite the strong impression she could undoubtedly make on the Alliance as she delivered fiery prophecy about their future.

"In Shaljir, at this very moment, the *torena* is probably being hailed as a heroine of the rebellion." Mirabar's voice could have chilled wine.

Tansen wondered if she had learned that tone from Najdan. "She did as I asked, Mira, as she promised. She got Searlon to help her secure Kaynall's compliance with the trea—"

"You don't know that she had anything to do with it!"

"Yes, I do," he said quietly. "And so do you."

"What I know is that as long as she lives, Josarian goes unavenged—"

"She didn't kill—"

"Don't mince words! She betrayed him! And you," Mirabar concluded, "are a man without honor until you fulfill the vow you made to me and punish her for it."

Deep down, it was what he believed, too, what he had been raised to understand and taught to accept. However, he was not an ignorant *shallah* boy anymore, even if that child still lived somewhere inside him. Mirabar could see visions, but he could envision the future. "We can't live like that anymore," he began, "not if we're to—"

"A very convenient excuse," she snapped, "especially coming from the man who today urged thousands to avenge Josarian by destroying Kiloran and the Society!"

"That was different." He forced himself to remain calm and reasonable. That was probably a mistake, since it only seemed to enrage her. "Of course it's different! Kiloran isn't a beautiful woman who knows how to make a fool of every man, especially you!"

He didn't want to have this argument again, he really didn't. He tried to end it by saying flatly, "I'm not going to kill her, Mirabar."

Her eyes glowed with hot fire as she said slowly, "If you won't . . ."

"Don't," he warned. "Don't make vows you'll regret."

"Then I will."

"I know you understand violence," he said. "Who in this damned country doesn't? But killing another person isn't something you should . . . should take . . . take . . ."

He lost track of his words as the dog howled frantically and the rumbling started. The sound was distant at first, then suddenly all around them.

"Earthquake!" Mirabar jumped off the bench.

"Open ground!" Tansen shouted, taking her arm and guiding her away from the looming fig tree.

They tripped over the dog, who cowered at their feet, yowling and begging for comfort. Tansen rose, shoved it out of the way, and dragged Mirabar beyond the reach of the tree's heavily sagging branches.

Then they fell down again as the ground shook wildly beneath their feet. This time Tansen ordered Mirabar, "Stay here!"

"But everyone inside—"

"I'll get them out!"

"I'm coming with—"

He shoved her back down—hard—as she rose, and he repeated, "Stay here!" He grabbed the dog by the neck. "And keep this damned dog out of my way!"

She nodded and took hold of the dog. Tansen ran towards the rambling building where their companions were sleeping. Inside, crockery was tumbling off walls and tables, chairs were sliding across the floor, the cat was having strong hysterics—and so was Sister Norimar.

It all ceased a moment later, stopping as suddenly as it had started. Knowing that it might be just the beginning, rather than the whole event, Tansen got everyone out of the building, a task which included shoving a frightened and sleepy sea-born boy out of his bedchamber window.

Once everyone was outside, Tansen determined that no one was hurt. They were all shaken though; and, not surprisingly, they quickly grew irritable.

"How long is this going to keep happening?" Sister Shannibar demanded, cuddling the panting, whining dog. "How many more times will—"

"I just want to go back to sea," Zarien said. "I'd really, really like to go back to sea."

"They don't have earthquakes at sea?" Pyron asked.

Zarien squinted at him. "How could there be an *earth*quake at sea?"

"I mean—"

"All this activity," Tansen mused. "We've never had three earthquakes so close together. Not in my lifetime."

"And none this bad," Shannibar added. "Not that I can remember."

"We hadn't had one at *all* in years," Pyron pointed out, "until that first one which hit the night we were at Dalishar and Tansen was missing." He looked at Zarien. "So I guess it began soon after you decided to come ashore. I wonder if it's got something to do with you?"

"You can't blame this on me," Zarien protested. "And besides, I didn't *decide* to come ashore, I was—"

"No one's blaming you," Tansen interrupted, thinking it might be wiser if Zarien didn't, in a fit of irritation, blurt out his strange personal history to the assembled group.

Pyron apologized by saying, "It was just an idle thought."

"Extremely idle," Tansen agreed.

The dog suddenly started barking.

"Oh, no!" Sister Norimar cried. "I'm going to be sick if it happens again!"

"No, no," Sister Shannibar assured her. "She just hears someone coming."

"At this time of night?" Norimar demanded.

"Maybe it's Najdan," Pyron suggested.

"He shouldn't be coming here alone in the dark," Mirabar said, rising to her feet.

It was indeed Najdan. As he pointed out, in response to Mirabar's scolding, a soft-footed man in black clothing wasn't all that easy a target when traveling alone in the empty hours before dawn. He accepted Shannibar's offer to draw some water from the well for him so he could wash off "all that disgusting blood and soot" before entering her Sanctuary.

Moving away from the group, Tansen asked him, "Did the assassin tell you anything?"

Najdan looked very tired. "Only that Kiloran is calling for unity and cooperation among the waterlords."

"Which we expected."

"Other than that . . ." Najdan idly studied the assassin's *shir,* which he now held in his hand. "He was not a talker."

"We had to try." Realizing that Najdan had probably done things tonight which even he didn't want to think about, Tansen amended, "You had to try."

Najdan nodded, then set the *shir* aside as he prepared to wash. "I will find a use for this. Your idea is a good one—planting stray *shir* among the waterlords. Even after they realize what we're doing, they'll continue to suspect each other."

"That's what's good about having enemies who don't really trust each other."

"Indeed," Najdan agreed dryly.

Sister Norimar called, "Najdan, would you like some food?"

"No, thank you," he replied.

"Food?" Sitting slumped on the ground, Zarien suddenly perked up. "Did you mention food? Because if you're getting some, anyhow . . ."

Tansen smiled as he heard the Sister assure Zarien it would be no trouble.

25

GOOD JUDGMENT USUALLY COMES FROM EXPERIENCE; AND EXPERIENCE USUALLY COMES FROM BAD JUDGMENT.

—Silerian Proverb

THE BLINDING SUNLIGHT was the first sensation to pierce the black void of Ronall's senses. When it caused him enough discomfort to inspire a voluntary response, he squeezed his eyes more tightly shut.

This action quickly produced an agonizing pounding of blood at his temples, each *thud-thud* more piercing than the last. He clenched his jaw against the pain.

Mistake.

The act of jaw-clenching awoke his throat, which worked convulsively to alert his chest that another glorious day in Sileria had begun. Without thinking, he drew in a deep breath . . . And immediately felt nauseated beyond belief.

Three have mercy.

Ronall rolled over and vomited.

"Ohhh. D . . . Dar help . . ."

It was too much trouble to finish the thought. He scrubbed feebly at his sticky mouth and rolled back away from the mess he had just made.

One of the servants would clean it up. They were used to it by now. He pitied them sometimes; but that's what the poor clods got for being born hungry peasants rather than wealthy *toreni.*

Someone has to do the puking, and someone has to do the cleaning up. That's the way of the world.

He pressed his face into the mattress . . . and spat out dirt. Three Into One, what in the Fires had happened to his bed? It was filled with soil and was as hard as . . .

Rocks?

Yes, he realized, slowly pulling his reluctant senses together. Dirt and rocks. He wasn't in bed. He wasn't at home. He was lying on the ground. Outside. Under the open sky.

With the Dar-cursed sun in my eyes.

Very cautiously, he turned his head to the side and, bit by bit, opened one eye. The world reeled and the sunlight made his eye stream stingingly.

Where am I?

Panic filled him. It made his heart pound. This, in turn, made his temples pound. With a groan of unbearable pain, he closed his eye again and willed the world to stop whirling. Willed himself to remember where he was.

It was no good. Nothing was coming to him. His mind was absolutely blank.

After all the mornings—the countless times—he had awoken with no recognition of where he was and no memories of the night before, you'd think he'd be used to it by now. But no. It still sent his mind reeling in horrified panic every time, throwing him into a desperate confusion which, to his shame, had produced tears on more than one occasion.

By all the gods above and below, he was a puny, pathetic, disgusting excuse of a man. No wonder his wife hated him so. . . .

His wife.

A memory started to stir. He could tell by the way his heart seemed to curl inward that it was a bad one.

Get out! Get out! Get out!

He was pretty sure he didn't want to remember any more right now. In fact, he was pretty sure that slipping back into an unconscious stupor was far and away his best alternative. But he wouldn't be able to now. He was increasingly uncomfortable, lying on the hard ground with the sun in his face.

Damn.

His skin was crawling. . . . Were there insects scurrying across his skin? He brushed at them, but the crawling continued. Nausea rolled over him again. The rhythmic pounding in his skull threatened to break it wide open.

With a great deal of effort, he opened his aching eyes again. They watered in response to the sun. He groaned and pushed himself away from the dirt on shaking arms, clumsily working himself into a sitting position. The effort left him sweating and breathing in short, hard pants.

He looked around. He appeared to be in a lemon grove.

No, this wasn't right. . . . Surely he had been in Shaljir?

The very thought seemed to trigger more nausea. He leaned over, bracing himself on his hands, and retched. Again and again. When he finally stopped and sat back gasping, drool filled his mouth and dribbled down his chin.

"Dar . . . ," he croaked, wiping his face with the back of his sleeve, disgusted with himself.

Where in the Fires am I?

This setting was beyond his comprehension. With monumental effort, he rose to his feet. The accomplishment left him shaking and swaying, but he didn't fall down. With slow, painstaking steps, he turned in a complete circle, looking for something familiar, something to stir his memory.

Nothing.

He didn't even know which way to walk. Here he was, shaking, weak, sweating, dizzy, nauseated, and badly in need of a drink. . . . And he was utterly lost in the middle of nowhere. Why, in the name of the Three, had he left the city? And when?

How much had he had last night? *What* had he had?

I can't keep doing this, he thought, *I'm going to get myself killed if this keeps up.*

"Killed?" he said aloud.

Memory came flooding back. Ronall sank to his knees under its weight. The violent scene which had erupted out of his argument with Elelar blurred in his mind with so many other similar events in their marriage . . . except this one was worse.

I pray to Dar nightly that you'll die. . . .

When Elelar publicly flaunted her affair with Advisor Borell, when she turned Ronall away from her bed, when she regarded him with open contempt . . .

. . . and if the mob kills you . . .

When Ronall learned of Elelar's duplicity on behalf of the rebellion, when she openly admitted to marrying him for the benefit of the Alliance, when she escaped from prison and made no effort to contact him, when he rotted in prison in her stead, begging his guards for liquor, dreamweed, *anything . . .*

. . . I'll throw open the doors of the house and offer a reward!

Somehow, none of those injuries and wounds, bad as they were, hurt as much as Elelar's shrieking prayer that the mob which killed his parents should now kill Ronall. Nothing had ever hurt like hearing her long for his death.

Yes, they had been fighting, tempers high, but he knew she wouldn't later regret her words. She meant it. If he wouldn't leave Sileria and thereby free her from their marriage, then she wanted him dead.

Why *wouldn't* she, considering the kind of husband he was?

Not that she had been an ideal wife.

He had been so wounded, so hurt, so appalled . . .

Or maybe it was fear, he acknowledged. After what had happened to his parents, he knew his own death could come at any moment. He couldn't leave Sileria; but how could he stay, either?

He and the many other Silerian-born Valdani were living with their backs to the wall now. After what had happened in Shaljir, it was only a matter of time before Silerians began gleefully slaughtering every Valdan left in Sileria.

No, Elelar's wish for his violent death was not an idle one. Darfire, she could even arrange it, if she wanted to. Who would even care now if a drunken half—caste Valdan were slaughtered by the mob? In the absence of Outlooker protection, who would shield Ronall or seek justice for his murder? He had cronies and companions, but no real friends, no one who would mourn his death or risk their own safety for him. Only his parents had cared, and perhaps only because it had been their duty. And now that they were gone, dead, murdered by a Silerian mob . . .

Three have mercy, they had killed his mother! His silly, contented, vapid Silerian mother who had never harmed anyone, even if she had habitually neglected everyone. They'd slaughtered her with raging violence in her own home, brutally punishing her for the sin of marrying a Valdan.

And his father . . . implacable, demanding, and usually absent. Ronall's father had always been a stranger to him, a familiar face, a cool gaze, and time-worn gestures concealing a largely unknown character. Perhaps the bravest thing Ronall had ever done in his life was go to his eternally disappointed father and ask him to save Elelar's life after Borell had her imprisoned on charges of treason.

The heavy weight in Ronall's chest now was proof of all the things he had secretly, foolishly hoped for; all the things which had been bludgeoned to death by a bloodthirsty mob in Shaljir. His father would never look upon him with approval, let alone warmth, now. They would never get to know each other, never cease to be strangers. His mother would never look *at* him instead of past him. Never praise him instead of make excuses for him. His parents would never even see a grandchild from him now, one with Elelar's intelligence and beauty, one with . . .

Grandchild. The heir he and Elelar had never gotten.

It was just as well, really.

If his parents' violent deaths left a heavy weight of grief pressing on him, then the death of his marriage . . .

No. He was a fool, of course. His marriage had died the day it had begun, a stillborn thing which he had been too unfit to bring forth; a bitter harvest which left him starving.

The *end* of his marriage last night, which he supposed was a more accurate description than its "death" . . . yes, the end of his marriage was a mortal wound. He was bleeding to death. The pain was excruciating. It left him . . . yes, it left him ready to die.

Get out! Get out! Get out!

Ah, yes, now he remembered. Well, a little, anyhow.

He had ridden through the streets of Shaljir, but he couldn't find anyone to kill him. Then he had decided to flee the city, to get as far away from Elelar as he could. He couldn't bear to look into her eyes, not ever again, not after what he had seen in them that night. He wanted to die. He was ready . . . but he needed someone else to do it for him. Even in this, the final act of his life—and his only worthwhile achievement—he would be a helpless coward.

He'd had some vague notion that if no one in the city would kill him, then surely the mountain rebels would. He had no idea how he'd gotten through the city gates. Either the Outlookers were no longer guarding them, or else they couldn't be bothered to stop a drunken *toren* from riding out to his well-deserved death.

He had no idea how far he had come, nor where he was now. The morning sun was blazing down with offensive cheeriness on a place he'd never seen before. Dar, he needed a drink! He was just starting to wonder what had happened to the damn horse, because he really didn't want to set out on foot, when he heard its nervous whinny somewhere in the grove. It was just close enough to make his head reel painfully from the high-pitched sound; just far enough away to make his search for it a sweat-producing ordeal.

His heart filled briefly with hope when he saw a stone structure; but as he approached it, he realized it was just an empty hut, the sort of place where lowlanders slept during harvest time, when they were in the fields and groves from sunrise to sundown. This hut looked particularly dilapidated. The roof had caved in and there were big cracks in the walls, as if an earthquake . . .

A chill swept over him. Yes, an earthquake. There had been another one, hadn't there? Was that when he had fallen off the gelding? He thought so, but he wasn't sure. He just remembered the animalistic terror he had shared with the horse while the world shook and roared around them. Dar was angry and meant to make Sileria know the cost of offending Her.

Ronall was trembling and panting with fatigue as he came up to Elelar's grazing gelding and took its reins in hand. Patient and well trained—no showy stallion for his practical wife—it evidently recognized his unwashed and liquor-soaked scent and decided to tolerate him until someone better came along. With tremendous effort, Ronall hauled himself into the saddle. He held the gelding still for a moment, concentrating on not retching again. Then, when he thought he could stand it, he slackened his hold on the horse's mouth and let it move forward.

Presumably there was some sort of road or trail around here. They'd stumble across it sooner or later. And they'd follow it deep into the mountains. Ronall had no intention of returning to Shaljir. There was nothing for him there now. Nothing for him anywhere.

Somewhere in those mountains were thousands of angry rebels slavering for more Valdani blood. Somewhere, sooner or later, someone would oblige Elelar by killing him.

Meanwhile, he wanted a drink.

He had, of course, neglected to bring any money with him. It didn't matter. He wore a ring he could sell; it was worth a veritable fortune by the miserable standards of the *shallaheen*. That would keep him in liquor for a while. If need be, he could sell the horse, too. And his boots.

He didn't care. He didn't intend to live long, after all. There was nothing left for him. Not anywhere.

It was a dark place full of light, a bright place shadowed by darkness. A vast cavern, heavy yet airy, immense yet encroaching.

Fire and water were all around Cheylan. The churning lava of the restless volcano extended its reach to this forgotten place, dripping into the water which flowed through strange tunnels lit by eerie glowing shapes. Each time lava touched water, angry hissing filled the air and steam rose to obscure his vision.

Some of the phosphorescent lumps on the walls and ceilings were plants, but not all. Some of them had long, spindly legs, some had no legs at all, and some had what appeared to be a thousand tiny legs.

When Cheylan moved past them, they all scurried away, as frightened as any helpless creature was in the presence of a stronger one. Born to this secret, long-forgotten, underground world of fire and water, they were strangers to the sun. These crawling little glowing creatures had never seen daylight or breathed any air other than the hot, dank, ancient miasma which filled these steamy tunnels beneath the coastal mountain range north of Liron.

Fire and water . . .

He heard lava rumbling somewhere deep in the belly of the world. The walls of this strange sanctuary trembled, but they held. They always would. Cheylan was sure of it. Since the first time he had stumbled across this secret stronghold years ago, while fleeing from his grandfather's deadly wrath, he had known it was a sacred place, eternally protected by Dar. Blessed by the twin powers of fire and water which ruled Sileria. Sanctified for him and him alone.

Water and fire . . .

This was his place, his domain, the cradle of his destiny. He had always believed that Dar had created it for him; and now that Mirabar had seen it in her visions, he was sure of it. He had kept silent, not yet sure he should trust her with this secret; but he had recognized his private kingdom in her confused words, in her breathless description that night at Dalishar.

Something great would happen here. His destiny was indeed unfolding. Josarian had freed Sileria and then died, leaving the way open for his successor. Cheylan had been the Firebringer's willing servant, always believing that his own fate would be revealed to him if he was patient and shrewd. He had realized, of course, that no one else could rule Sileria while Josarian lived.

The Firebringer was so greatly loved, there was no question of whom the people would choose to lead them if they won the war against the Valdani.

Cheylan had minded this far less than he imagined Kiloran did. The waterlord lived for absolute power and demanded total obedience. Cheylan had spent some time with Kiloran during the rebellion, and he had quickly recognized that the old wizard didn't know how to compromise, let alone cooperate. In Kiloran's world, there was his way and no other. He was intelligent, cunning, and immensely powerful, but he was inflexible. That was his weakness. He couldn't share power with the Firebringer, couldn't share Sileria with anyone. Consequently, he could never be anyone's ally; only an enemy. He could never be an asset; only a threat. And threats, like enemies, had to be eliminated.

It was inevitable that Kiloran turned on Josarian, and inescapable that Josarian—and now Tansen—felt it essential to destroy Kiloran. Cheylan, whose life had taught him the value of compromise, not to mention subterfuge, might have found his true destiny under the Firebringer's rule of Sileria; but he had, of course, privately hoped for more. Josarian, although beloved of Dar and survivor of the volcano's sacred embrace, was nonetheless a mere *shallah*. Neither a *toren* nor a sorcerer. Whereas Cheylan was both, though he had been born to a world where his unique qualities had, so far, cost him more than they had earned him.

Cheylan had known that if anyone could kill the Firebringer, it would be Kiloran. Since murdering Josarian would have terrible repercussions, no matter who did it, Cheylan himself had never intended to try; cooperating with the Firebringer was far better than killing him. However, living to see Josarian dead and Kiloran blamed for his murder was best of all.

Whether this was Dar's way of opening the door to Cheylan's destiny or merely luck, he was grateful. Now the future was at hand.

A child of sorrow . . .

Cheylan had spent so much of his life alone, shunned, and unwanted, that he always found the darkly glowing solitude of these rumbling water and fire-filled tunnels soothing rather than frightening.

Some of the walls here bore the mysterious paintings of the Beyah-Olvari, that long-extinct race of water wizards who had inhabited Sileria, according to Verlon, eons ago. The paintings were eerily beautiful, graceful in a disturbingly inhuman way; but Cheylan found it hard to believe they revealed the secrets of water magic. They seemed too abstract, too symbolic. He certainly couldn't interpret them, and he found it rather improbable that Marjan, the very first waterlord, had managed it. Silerians loved their legends, but Cheylan suspected that a more practical explanation, or even dumb luck, accounted for Marjan's resurrection of the ancient magic which he had used to destroy Daurion, scatter the Guardians, and change Sileria forever.

A child of fire . . .

Lava oozed through the walls, coming in slow trickles now rather than in the hesitant droplets which usually festooned these tunnels. It was another sign of Dar's restive passion, Her steadily increasing activity. Eastern Sileria was in turmoil, her people panicking, her air thick with tension. While fighting raged between the Lironi and the Society, with heavy losses punishing the great clan of the east for its disobedience to Verlon, the volcano was never silent or still now. The ground trembled almost daily all around Darshon, quivering in response to Her fiery will, Her hot blood, even when it didn't shake in a genuine earthquake.

Some people were evacuating their homes and villages, already fleeing in fear from the colored columns of shifting smoke and dancing lightning surrounding the caldera day and night now. Meanwhile, others were attracted to Darshon by this same spectacle. Some of the *zanareen* claimed Dar was summoning them again for a mysterious purpose. Other sects and factions were coming to Her, too, risking death to approach the tempestuous volcano. Some brought offerings to soothe the goddess, including bones of the dead which had survived the sacred fires of their funeral pyres.

Cheylan didn't flee when Dar rumbled, and he didn't bring Her puny offerings. He knew She wanted what only he could offer, what he alone had been born for. And he was ready. Honed by hardship, shaped by bitter experience, he knew his time had finally come. Lava trickled over him now, coming from the domed ceiling of the tunnels. It blessed him, consecrating his life to Dar's divine plan.

Born to this magic, born for this power, Cheylan seized a trickle of lava and pulled it through the air like a ribbon of glowing silk. He raised it overhead like a banner and swore, in his heart, to fulfill his destiny. Dar and Verlon had made him what he was, who he was. The goddess had given him gifts, and his bloodthirsty grandfather had taught him others. There was no one in Sileria like Cheylan. No one in the three corners of the world who was his equal.

A child of water . . .

He walked across the surface of the water flowing through these tunnels. His feet sank slightly into its resilient coolness with each step, the water supporting his weight as he commanded it to, responding to his power, his will, his sorcery. Just as Verlon had taught him, long ago, before they had become enemies.

Fire and water, water and fire . . .

Who else in Sileria could command the two? Who, in all the world, besides Cheylan had mastered both elements? Cheylan floated past more of the faded, ancient paintings of the Beyah-Olvari, letting the current carry him as he stood still on the flowing water's surface. Even Marjan, a Guardian who unlocked the mysteries of the dead Beyah-Olvari and learned their magic, hadn't been this great a sorcerer. He had given up fire for water, turning his back on one sorcery in favor of another. Since that time, everyone in Sileria believed that only one power or the other was possible, never both together.

Fire and water, competing for ascendancy in Sileria for a thousand years. Forever apart, forever at odds. Now all of Sileria, even Mirabar, believed that one must finally vanquish the other.

There would always be water magic in Sileria, just as there would always be fire magic. Nothing could change that. Not even the passion of Silerians' hatred for each other.

He is coming.

Only Cheylan could unite fire and water. Only he understood them both. Only he could challenge them both and defend against them both.

Only he could be the one Mirabar awaited, the one she saw in her visions.

Protect what you most long to destroy.

There were still things he didn't understand, though. Factors he couldn't yet control. Was the Society meant to be destroyed by Tansen, or to come under Cheylan's influence? Should he kill Verlon now, or try to win back his grandfather's trust and use him as an ally until he no longer needed him? Could Tansen really eliminate Kiloran for him? And if not, how should he deal with Kiloran?

Or, he wondered, was that particular message even about the Society? The Beckoner spoke to Mirabar, after all. And Cheylan thought he knew whom Mirabar herself most longed to destroy; he just couldn't guess why it mattered one way or the other.

The one thing he remained convinced of, however, was that Mirabar's visions were leading him in the right direction. He needed her. He recognized that. And he didn't like leaving her in the company of Tansen, who had the potential to wield more influence over her than did anyone but Dar Herself.

The *shatai,* fortunately, seemed a little inept at handling women, but Cheylan had nonetheless been concerned by the sharp two-edged blade of Mirabar's anger at Tansen. Love tended to look so much like hatred. She was the sort of woman whose devotion, once fixed, would be steadfast. That was an advantage if Cheylan could win her soon; a serious problem if he couldn't. She was too powerful, too important, for him to let another man have her—least of all Tansen, who learned too quickly, thought too clearly, and might even, it seemed, soon become a demigod himself if the sea-born boy had his way.

No, Cheylan didn't like leaving Mirabar with Tansen. He especially didn't like the high-handed way Tansen had given him orders and sent him east again, barely bothering to conceal his real motivation: getting Cheylan away from Mirabar.

Cheylan might well have decided to refuse, had he not realized he had an important task to perform here. Anyone could deliver Tansen's messages to the Lironi about mutual support against the waterlords. But there was Semeon to consider—the red-haired fire-eyed child that he had once told Mirabar about, the one whom she and Tansen now wanted to protect. Cheylan knew he must deal with that. So he had come east again, as ordered.

And when he had done what he must, he meant to return to Mirabar's side and stay there. If Tansen caused trouble or got in the way . . .

Well, Cheylan could deal with that, too.

ZILAR POSSESSED PERHAPS the largest population in Sileria, outside of the country's four major coastal cities. It had too many people to displace, and it was too important to surrender to the enemy. It lay at the delta of two rivers, and it overlooked the coastal plains between Cavasar and Shaljir. Its citizens had sworn to oppose the Society, and now Tansen must show them how to do it.

The most important thing, of course, was to store water against the inevitable shortage which an offended waterlord would inflict without mercy. Many towns and villages did this every year, anyhow; but now they all faced a bloodfeud with the Society. Moreover, the dry season was approaching. Ideally, Tansen should have started the war against the Society during the long rains; but this wasn't an ideal world. Josarian's loyalists couldn't wait until the long rains to defend the nation against the waterlords' bid for absolute power. Now Zilar—and the rest of Sileria—must begin preparing for a drought like they had never known.

The Guardians could light rings of protective fire around Zilar's wells, troughs, fountains, water barrels, and water towers, thus shielding them from water magic, but they could do nothing to protect the Shaljir River, the town's primary source of water, from its two masters: Abidan and Liadon, the brothers whose assassins had attacked Tansen in the temple here.

Tansen assigned crews to siphon extra water off the Shaljir River as it flowed past Zilar, then he organized other crews to devise additional means to store the water. Every supplementary water source around Zilar— streams, springs, ponds—was examined by the Guardians. They determined whether or not it was ensorcelled and therefore dangerous. If it wasn't, they tried to devise ways to protect it from the waterlords.

It seemed highly unlikely that assassins would launch an all-out assault on such a large town. The waterlords had never used them as an army. They were ambush fighters, primarily accustomed to working alone or in small groups. Their attack on Tansen in the Kintish temple represented precisely the sort of challenges he expected from them: stealth, disguise, surprise. They might, like the Outlookers, raze a few villages or commit a few massacres to set an example, to remind Silerians of the penalty for opposing the

Society; but they would only do so in places where the population was small and weak. And unlike the Outlookers, Dar be thanked, they would only kill men—and any male children old enough to be counted as men.

Male children Zarien's age, perhaps.

The thought kept creeping back to distract Tansen from his work. He regretted leaving Zarien down at the riverside while he instructed people in the town itself on the general principles of defense and security. However, since the sea-bound Lascari were familiar with the problems of water supply and storage, if in a totally different setting, the boy had become interested in the work at the river and chose to stay there.

"Outlookers and Valdani have always been easy to recognize," Tansen said now to the gathering of volunteers in Zilar's main square, "but assassins aren't, not if they choose to wear an ordinary man's clothing." To a trained fighter like Tansen or Najdan, actually, there were clues—habits, posture, body language—which frequently gave away another of their kind. It took time, though, to develop this instinctive recognition.

"In a small village, every stranger is noticeable, easy to identify; but a large and busy market town like Zilar is usually full of strangers. So your work," he explained to the crowd, "is to limit access to the town and determine the business of everyone coming and going. We'll work out a system today. Above all," he concluded, "you must ensure that no assassins enter Zilar. Fortunately, that's easy."

"How can that be easy?" someone asked.

"Once you have control of access to Zilar, search every man who comes here." Tansen shrugged. "If he's carrying a *shir,* he's an assassin."

"What if he doesn't want to be searched?"

"Tell him what you're looking for."

"And if he still doesn't want to be searched?"

"Then he's an assassin."

"And we know," someone else cried, "what to do with an assassin!"

They all shouted their agreement. Which was encouraging, Tansen thought, considering that they were all sober today.

However, simply hoarding water and keeping assassins out was, as Armian would have told him, merely defensive. In order for Zilar to be free, the Shaljir River would have to be free. That meant getting rid of Abidan and Liadon. And killing waterlords was a lot harder than killing Valdani.

Experience had taught him that sorcery was the best weapon against sorcery, so he was counting on the Guardians. A few days after arriving here to celebrate Sileria's freedom from the Valdani, Tansen met with nearly a hundred Guardians in the old Kintish temple. He regretted that Mirabar had left Zilar, since she was held in great respect by her kind, but he could do this without her.

He mostly regretted that she had left with so many things still unresolved between them. It was another thought that kept distracting him.

Focus on the task at hand.

"Some of you," he said to the gathered Guardians, "will tell me that you're not warriors. And I'm afraid there's only one answer to that: then you'll die."

He waited for their outraged protests to die down, then continued, "That's not my decision. That's the waterlords' decision. If you'd like, I'll be happy to send a message to Kiloran suggesting that since so many of you aren't fighters, he refrain from attacking you. What do you suppose his response will be?"

Some of them looked upset, others uneasy. The practical ones nodded their agreement. Those who had learned to fight during the rebellion now urged the others to remember that their forebears, the Guardians who had ruled Sileria for centuries before the Conquest, had been a race of warriors as well as sorcerers.

"That's true," Tansen said, raising his voice to be heard above the others. "Mirabar has told me. And Daurion himself was a Guardian. Daurion, who ruled this island with a fist of iron in a velvet glove, who drove back the Moorlander invasions again and again." His gaze swept the crowd, vaguely wishing for a pair of fire-gold eyes among them; but she was on her way to Mount Niran. "Daurion, who was betrayed by Marjan."

"A thousand years of foreign domination was the curse of the water-lords!" Ealian, an elderly Guardian, proclaimed. "Tansen's right! We must take back our nation!"

"How—by going up against the waterlords in combat?" someone else protested. "We can't defeat them in direct confrontation!"

"If you can't, then who can?" Tansen demanded. "The Guardians possess the only power in Sileria which can challenge the waterlords' sorcery."

"Fire and water have competed for ascendancy since the time of Marjan," Ealian said. "It is time for one to vanquish the other!"

"And if they vanquish us?"

"Then," Tansen said, "that's your answer."

This brought an uneasy hush upon the temple. Tansen let it engulf them for a moment, then said, "You're the only group in Sileria with absolutely nothing left to lose. If the Society rules Sileria, then the waterlords will squeeze the *toreni,* the *shallaheen,* the lowlanders, the city-dwellers, and everyone else for everything they've got, and rule them through terror and bloodshed—but, after the initial massacres to punish everyone who opposed them, they'll let most of Sileria live."

He paused before stating the obvious. "However, they won't let any of you live. If the Society wins this war, they'll hunt down and kill every last one of you, their ancient blood enemies. And forever after, they'll kill anyone born with the potential to become one of you." He let this sink in for a moment. "Does anyone here doubt it?"

No one did.

"Now you can retreat to the highest mountains, abandon your people, hide from the waterlords the way you've been hiding for centuries, and hope for the best," he said. "Or you can take part in your fate, in Sileria's fate, and fight for your lives."

"We swore a bloodvow!" Ealian reminded the others.

"You are the Guardians of the Otherworld," Tansen added, "blessed by Dar and sworn to serve Her will. Who will prepare the way for the new Yahrdan if not you?" He saw his words affect them, saw fire enter eyes which in no way resembled Mirabar's.

But Ealian knew what would motivate them most: "Avenge the Fire-bringer!"

"Avenge Josarian!"

Leadership called for compromise, and war called for expedience. So Tansen urged them, "Avenge the Firebringer!"

A young woman rose to her feet. Typically *shallah* in appearance, with olive skin, brown eyes, and coarse black hair, she was not much older than Mirabar. And like Mirabar, she wore a Guardian broach made of copper. "I will fight," she said. "And I will shame any man who won't do what I am willing to do!"

Tansen decided he liked her. "What's your name?"

"Iyadar."

"Iyadar," he said with a grin, "Josarian might not have stayed a widower had he been lucky enough to meet you."

It wasn't true, of course. Josarian had never gotten over his wife's death, and he had also been the beloved of a very jealous volcano goddess; but the compliment pleased the young woman and influenced the Guardians, as Tansen had hoped.

"What must I do?" Iyadar asked.

Before Tansen could reply, the rest of the Guardians present began jumping to their feet with similar questions. He raised his arms to quiet them, then replied, "The first thing you must do is get rid of Abidan and Liadon."

"How?" Iyadar asked.

"I want all of you to start asking around town today to find out everything you can about them," Tansen instructed. "Where are their strongholds? How powerful is their sorcery? How many assassins do they have? What is the extent of their territory? What are their strengths, their weaknesses, their peculiar habits?" He explained, "The servant always knows the master best. The people of Zilar have paid tribute to these two brothers for years, have lived under their influence for a long time. They know things about them which they don't even realize they know, things which they may have no idea are useful. So find out *everything*."

"And then?" Ealian asked.

"We'll meet again tomorrow and develop a plan. Then you will accompany me, along with any fighting men who volunteer, to implement our plan."

The first major assault on the Society had to be successful or Sileria would lose heart. The nation needed proof that the Society could be fought and beaten. And the Guardians needed to learn—right away—how to fight the waterlords rather than run from them.

"After that, some of you will stay here to help protect Zilar. The rest of you," he concluded, "will go back to your own circles, or to other Guardian circles, and teach them what you've learned here. There are perhaps as many as one hundred waterlords whom we've got to defeat, and we can't waste any time."

He dismissed them all. As he watched them leave the temple, excited and scared, he knew with burning regret that he was leading some of them straight to their deaths.

26

IT IS BETTER TO REMAIN SILENT AND BE THOUGHT A
FOOL THAN TO SPEAK AND REMOVE ALL DOUBT.
                                    —Silerian Proverb

THERE WAS NO way to reach Mount Niran from Zilar without traveling through lands controlled by waterlords, including Kiloran's traditional territory. Indeed, the journey took Mirabar far too close to Lake Kandahar for comfort. Kiloran wasn't there, but that only made the trip marginally safer. His assassins still patrolled the whole district, and his power over the major water sources here had not slackened.

In addition, Mount Niran, Mirabar's destination, was much closer to Cavasar than she had gone ever since Kiloran seized the city. With so many deaths during the war and so much shifting of power in the wake of the Valdani withdrawal from Cavasar, who knew what additional lands Kiloran now controlled, what greater power he now wielded?

The journey itself made Mirabar jumpy with fear, but Najdan's ever-increasing tension practically made her skin tingle. He had served Kiloran for twenty years, often carrying out his duties in this very region. He knew better than anyone just how dangerous this journey was for Mirabar, especially since she was so easily identified. She kept the hood of her cloak pulled over her flaming hair at all times and shielded her burning eyes from view whenever they encountered people; but just one slip—a stray lock of red hair escaping her hood, a shifting ray of sunlight seeking out her fire-rich eyes—would alert people to her presence here. Anyone loyal to Josarian's memory would stay silent; anyone loyal to Kiloran would betray her.

The cloak, she reflected irritably, was an increasingly impractical disguise. The days were growing warmer, the sun hotter. At least Najdan's disguise didn't make him sweat like an overworked horse, she thought enviously. Although he wasn't enthusiastic about it, he had agreed to eschew his own black clothes and red *jashar* in favor of ordinary clothing left in Shannibar's Sanctuary by someone who had never returned for it.

The tale of Josarian's death was spreading like wildfire through the mountains, as was news of the Valdani surrender in Shaljir. Sileria was delirious with volatile emotions. Whole communities were wracked by mourning even in the midst of their victory celebrations. Whole villages were already disintegrating into violence as everyone in Sileria learned of Kiloran's triumph over Josarian and of Tansen's vow to destroy the Society. Fighting the Valdani had united the people. Now the ancient blood hatred which ran so deep in Sileria was tearing them apart again.

Hanging to the rear of her group, and keeping her face and hair hidden with what must look like absurd modesty, Mirabar listened to the vows, the fears, the opinions, and the wild predictions of the people they encountered on the high mountain paths, narrow goat trails, and crumbling roads of rural Sileria. When she and her six-man escort needed food or additional supplies, Pyron or one of the others would enter a village to make the necessary purchases, then come back full of news and gossip.

The normally reticent *shallaheen,* the traditionally timid lowlanders, the cautious *toreni,* and the calculating merchants all knew that destiny was at hand and everyone must choose his fate before it was chosen for him.

The mountains were erupting with precisely the sort of brother-against-brother rage that Mirabar knew Tansen had feared from the moment Kiloran first betrayed Josarian and Josarian responded by killing his son. Now, in the wake of victory against the Empire, Mirabar believed there was only one real question: Did Sileria drive out the Valdani to live under the yoke of the Society, or to pursue a future of peace and prosperity under the leadership of Dar's chosen ruler?

However, she knew that many people would never view things her way. Some were too frightened of the Society to oppose it. Others were too used to its rule to seriously consider challenging it. Even worse, many genuinely loved the Society, loved Kiloran. Filled with a rapt devotion to the waterlords which Mirabar had never understood, they believed Kiloran and his kind had stood between them and the *roshaheen* for centuries, had protected them when there was no one else to do it, had given them justice when there was no law to avenge their injuries.

Would the people choose Kiloran or Tansen? Which power would finally triumph in Sileria, fire or water? Did Silerians fear the waterlords too much to trust in the Guardians?

Mirabar shivered beneath the hot sun by day, chilled by uncertainty and fears. She wanted to reveal herself to the people she and her escort met, wanted to proclaim prophecy in the main square of every village in western Sileria. But she was too vulnerable to attack. Once her whereabouts were known to the waterlords, she'd never live to reach Mount Niran, let alone Sister Velikar's Sanctuary back on the slopes of Dalishar.

Others carried her words, though: people who had been in Zilar on the day freedom was announced and Tansen's bloodfeud against the Society was proclaimed; people who knew, as Mirabar did, that their sacrifices would all be in vain if they surrendered now to the Society; people who believed, as Mirabar desperately wanted to, that Dar Herself would help them triumph.

Mirabar trembled under the waning reddish moons by night, mourning her loss of innocence, the death of her absolute faith in the goddess.

Why did You let him die, Dar?

Had the goddess betrayed Her Chosen One? Sacrificed him? Neglected him? Or had She been too weak to shield him from Kiloran?

If Dar was too weak to shield Josarian, then how could Mirabar possibly shield the coming ruler?

A child of fire, a child of water, a child of sorrow . . .

How will I know him? Where will I find him? Give me a sign. Please give me a sign.

Lying in the dark now, in a particularly poor Sanctuary, Mirabar suddenly heard a strange rumbling sound outside.

Another earthquake?

She rose from her bedroll, grabbed the chubby Sister who was their hostess tonight, and dragged her towards the door, eager to escape the distinctly unstable stone dwelling before any ground-shaking began in earnest.

"What are you doing?" the Sister cried.

"Get outside!" Mirabar instructed, raising her voice to be heard above the rumbling filling the air. "The roof's not sturdy!"

The Sister blinked at her in bewilderment. Mirabar couldn't believe that she could be so stupid. Even a child knew what to do during an earthquake, and they'd endured enough of them recently that the Sister's reflexes ought to be a little more honed.

"Come *on*." Mirabar dragged her away from the dwelling and the overhanging rockface sheltering it—and tripped over Pyron, who was sleeping like the dead. She kicked him. "Get up! Get up!"

"Ow! What are you doing?"

The other men were all sleeping, too. How could anyone sleep through this racket? The roaring filled her head now, flooded the night. And the *heat* . . . It was terrible, suddenly. Covering her skin, burning through her clothes, shimmering through the night until her vision was blurry.

"*Sirana!* What's wrong?"

Mirabar whirled and saw Najdan approaching her through a heat-haze. Steam was rising in thick columns all around him.

The ground wasn't shaking she realized. It wasn't an earthquake. . . . But the heat was burning through her now, scorching her flesh. She started pulling her clothing away from her sweat-drenched body, shaking in reaction to the noise and the steam spewing skyward.

Now she heard chanting. Trilling. Ululating. A bewildering mixture of voices filled with passion and fervor, ghostly praise-singing flooding the hot, roaring night with even more urgency.

She looked around wildly. The men were all awake now. All staring at her. She felt a hand on her arm.

"*Sirana?*" Najdan said uncertainly.

She met his perplexed, concerned gaze. "Don't you feel it?" she demanded, hearing the panic in her voice.

"Why are you shouting?" he asked.

To be heard above the . . . "Can't you hear it?" Her head was reeling with it!

"Hear what?" Pyron asked, plainly bewildered.

Najdan tightened his grip on her arm, staring at her with increasing worry.

She was wrong, the ground *was* shaking, but this still wasn't an earthquake. This was power, tremendous power. . . . Lava moving through the veins of the earth, flowing somewhere beneath their feet, making the ground tremble with Dar's blood, Dar's breath, Dar's life. . . . Mirabar gasped and leaped back, dragging Najdan with her, as lava erupted at her feet.

"What's wrong with her?" Pyron jumped to his feet.

"Quiet!" Najdan ordered. "*Sirana,* what do you see?"

How could they not see it, not feel its heat? She was burning up! The fumes, the sudden flames erupting out of the glowing ooze of the lava spilling forth from the world's womb. . . .

A woman was screaming. Mirabar clapped a hand over her mouth, but the screams continued, so it wasn't her. She peered through the steam and the fire and the smoke . . . but, no, the Sister wasn't screaming, either.

"Where is she?" Mirabar cried.

"Who?"

Screaming! Screaming for help. For mercy. Screaming in pain, in terror!

"We've got to help her!" Mirabar shouted, wading through the lava. Oh, how it burned! The agony was unbearable, but the screams pulled her on.

"Who's she looking for?"

"Don't let her go beyond Sanctuary grounds!"

Strong arms grabbed Mirabar from behind and lifted her off her feet. Najdan, wading waist-deep through the lava, carried her back to safety.

"No!" Mirabar cried. "We've got to help her!"

"Who?" he demanded.

She didn't know. She only knew that something was driving her to help whoever was crying out to her. The screams beckoned to her even over the lava's roar and the intense, almost hysterical trilling of the unseen singers.

"*Sirana* . . ."

"Shh. Quiet!" she ordered, suddenly hearing a new sound, a helpless cry of innocence.

For a moment, she thought a goat was wailing, perhaps being swallowed by the lava. Then she recognized the sound, realized what it really was.

She met Najdan's gaze. "A baby."

"Where?"

"Crying."

He cocked his head. "I don't hear anything."

Lava circled the assassin, whirled around him, flowed over his body. Flames ignited in his long hair. He stood staring at Mirabar, his dark face creased with concentration and concern.

"You don't see . . . anything," Mirabar said at last, pulling her wits together, "do you?"

He slowly shook his head. "No."

She glanced at Pyron. "And you?"

"I see a Guardian losing her mind right in front of—"

"Shut up," Najdan snapped.

Mirabar looked through the misty, glowing night and saw the baby now. He flowed past her on a river of lava. The infant's orange eyes glowed like all the Fires of Dar. His skin was smeared with blood and he wailed like any baby, but he seemed at home in the liquid fire which carried him away into the clouds of steam as the passionate trilling and chanting filled Mirabar's head, as the rumbling roar echoed all around her. . . .

The night fell silent. Blissfully, mercifully silent.

The lava dissolved and faded from view. The thick steam peeled away from the night even as Mirabar peered through it in search of the child. The heat dissipated and died away.

Nothing was left but the dark night and its ordinary, subtle sounds. And her own panting breath.

Mirabar came back to her normal senses. She felt the cool air on her skin, inhaled the heady scents of the mountains at night, heard her heart pounding in response to the terrifying vision, and tasted the aftermath of fear in her mouth.

The Sister was regarding her with wide-eyed horror. Najdan looked bemused. Pyron looked like he wanted to hit her. The other men were shifting restlessly, waiting for some assurance that, despite her wailing panic a few moments ago, there was really nothing to fear.

"There's really nothing to fear." Her voice sounded hoarse.

"Well, that's good to know," Pyron said sourly, "because, you know, for a moment there, I thought there was room for doubt."

"If you must be a fool," Najdan told him, "you could at least be a silent one."

"There's no need to be insulting," Pyron protested.

"Do you need anything, *sirana*?" Najdan asked.

"No. No, it was just a . . ." She looked around and asked plaintively, "No one else saw that?"

"Saw what?" Pyron sounded plaintive, too.

"A . . . There was . . ." Mirabar sighed. "Never mind."

"Fine," Pyron said. "Would anyone besides me like to get some more sleep before dawn?"

"You're sure we're safe?" the Sister asked Mirabar, her eyes still round and distressed.

"Quite safe. Go back to bed."

"And you, *sirana*?"

"Oh, I think I'll stay up." Mirabar brushed her hair away from her face with a shaky hand.

Najdan announced, "Then I will stay w—"

"No," she said. "You need to be alert when we leave here. Go back to sleep."

He hesitated, then nodded his agreement. Mirabar wasn't sure, though, that any of them would be able to sleep after the way she had just frightened them.

Keeping watch alone in the dark safety of Sanctuary grounds for the rest of the night, Mirabar hugged her knees to her chest and tried to understand exactly what the terrifying vision meant.

RONALL RODE SOUTH, following the Idalar River, going deep into the heart of Sileria. He stopped frequently to ease his sorrows with whatever was available in the war-torn villages and valleys through which he passed. Not that much *was* available. The war had depleted Sileria. Kintish dreamweed was hard to find, and Moorlander cloud syrup had become so expensive that Ronall couldn't buy any with what little money he was carrying now.

Mercifully, he had found the town of Illan the same day he'd awakened lost and bewildered in the lemon grove. He'd been able to sell his ring there for a decent price, though certainly for less than it was worth. Although the air was already thick with talk of civil war, many merchants and traders were eager to do business. They viewed the immediate future with mercenary optimism now that the Valdani had surrendered.

"Whatever happens next in Sileria, and even if the Society requires heavy tribute to keep the water flowing during the coming dry season," the trader who bought Ronall's ring had said, "at least we can resume trade with the rest of Sirkara now that the war is over. And from now on," he added, "half our profits won't go to the damned Valdani."

The damned Valdani, Ronall knew, had taxed native Silerians at a much higher rate than the Valdani themselves paid. It was one of Elelar's many grievances against them. Indeed, all the laws in Valdani-occupied Sileria favored the conquerors at the expense of the natives. Luckily for Ronall, the privileges of his Valdani blood had always protected him from the burdens of his Silerian blood; that, too, had been the law here under imperial rule.

Now his Valdani blood was a death sentence.

However, the friendly trader who bought his ring evidently had no idea he was dealing with one of the "damned Valdani." If he even noticed that Ronall's clothes owed more to Valdani than to Silerian fashion, he evidently thought nothing of it. After all, Ronall was a *toren,* and they did as they pleased.

Ronall had tensed with fear when Guardians in Illan, at the urging of the town's citizens, set fire to a Shrine of the Three. Yes, he meant to die . . . but not while he was so appallingly sober. However, no one in Illan paid any attention to him, beyond extending the deferential courtesy most people usually showed a *toren*. It was the same everywhere he had gone since then.

Although Valdan had been the official language of Sileria for two hundred years, Ronall's mother and all his family's servants were Silerian, so he'd grown up speaking common Silerian. His coloring was more Silerian than Valdani. In fact, as long as he didn't reveal his name, there was nothing to identify him to any of the people he now encountered as a . . . What did the *shallaheen* say—a *roshah?* A foreigner. Not nearly as foreign as he would be on the mainland, of course. Elelar had recently made it abundantly clear that he wasn't a real Silerian; but more than a few Valdani visiting Sileria, over the years, had made it abundantly clear that he wasn't really a Valdan, either.

He hadn't bathed since leaving Shaljir, and the days were growing hotter; he supposed he was pretty rank by now. Not that the woman he had paid for last night had complained. Unlike his wife, women who charged money for his pleasure never complained to him about anything. That was their greatest charm. However, their accommodating ways had never eased the ache of loneliness, even while eliminating a more prosaic ache, and last night had been no different.

Get out! Get out! Get out!

His misery curled its claws more sharply into his heart every time he remembered Elelar.

He didn't want to think about her. He wanted a drink.

The Idalar River flowed steadily through the mountains, and he kept following it upriver. It was bigger than the Shaljir River, which lay west of here, and a far more important water source. The waterlords who controlled the Shaljir River cooperated with Kiloran, keeping the capital city under the Society's heel, but this was the river the city relied upon for the majority of its water. This was the chief source of Kiloran's wealth; he demanded heavy tribute from Shaljir for its water. Ronall had only a vague notion of what waterlords used their money for, though he supposed that assassins were expensive. Most assassins were said to live well, eat well, and wear fine clothes, which suggested that the waterlords paid them well. As the most powerful waterlord, Kiloran would presumably have the most men and, therefore, the biggest expenses.

The Idalar River looked placid and innocent as Ronall rode Elelar's calm gelding along its west bank. It looked like . . . just a river. The kind of ordinary sorcery-free water he'd heard they had on the mainland. It was hard to believe this gently flowing river was a fierce battleground between Kiloran and Baran. He wondered if they were fighting for it even now, or if they were resting, gathering their strength to fight Josarian's people for ultimate control of Sileria.

The waterlords hated the Valdani as much as Elelar did. Ronall supposed they had every reason to, considering that the Valdani had tried to destroy them.

So things would be grim for Ronall's kind—the Valdani who couldn't go home because *this* was home—no matter who emerged victorious in the current struggle to rule the island nation.

Several days out from Shaljir, Ronall found a reasonably pleasant village on the banks of the Idalar. He hadn't had a drink since morning and it was past midday now. So he might as well stop here. He was in no hurry, after all. He had no destination. No one awaited him, and no one would miss him.

He tethered his horse outside the village *tirshah* and went inside. There were perhaps twenty men in there, mostly *shallaheen*. They stared at him, the stranger among them. The outsider, the *roshah*. He asked for the strongest drink available.

The keeper, a scarred and elderly *shallah,* briefly studied his dirty but extremely expensive clothing. "I've got some silver wine, *toren*. From Valdania."

Ronall wondered if the man had guessed he was half-Valdan. However, a moment later, the old *shallah* added, "It's expensive. Not much call for it here, as you can imagine."

"Why keep it, then?"

"Used to have some Valdani customers." He shrugged. "Couldn't keep them out. That was the law."

"They're all gone now?"

"Most of them. Abandoned their estates around here."

"I don't like silver wine," Ronall said.

"Don't blame you. Bitter stuff."

"Yes."

"Got some good volcano brew."

"That'll do." A little rough going down, but he suddenly felt like drinking something Silerian. "Plenty of it."

As the old man poured him a mug, Ronall asked, "The Valdani who abandoned their estates . . . Will any of them be back?"

"For what? Everyone around here is already fighting over their lands. The *toreni* families they took the estates from want them back. The *shallaheen* and lowlanders who fought for freedom want to enjoy prosperity and are demanding a share of the lands. In fact, some of them have already simply taken them."

"What about the waterlords?"

The man shook his head. "They don't seem interested. I guess they're not farmers or landowners by nature."

The brew went down like burning lava. Ronall cleared his throat and commented, "Sorcerers."

"Yes. The waterlords have power over whoever winds up owning the land, and that's all they care about."

A young *shallah,* apparently emboldened by the keeper's easy chat with Ronall, approached them. "Who do you favor now, *toren?*" he asked. "Kiloran or Tansen?"

Ronall eyed the *shallah* and considered rebuking him for his impertinence just so he wouldn't have to think up an answer. "I favor . . . As I always favor . . ."

"Yes?"

"A good drink, a soft bed, and a warm woman," Ronall said.

A few men grinned or laughed in response, but the young *shallah* persisted. "People say the *toreni* will favor Tansen because the waterlords have drained them of their wealth for centuries."

"It would be hard," Ronall admitted, "to side with those who make a regular practice of abducting us for ransom." He drained his mug. "More," he said, handing the mug to the keeper.

"Are you just passing through, *toren?*" the keeper asked.

"I'm . . . looking for something," he replied at last, suddenly sad. The brew went down a little easier this time.

The young one now asked, "What?"

Ronall smiled wryly. "A solution to my problems."

"A *toren*'s problems." The young *shallah* looked at the other men and said, his voice now tinged with sarcasm, "Which new boots to wear with your new clothes? Which of your estates to spend the dry season at? Which horse to ride on the hunt?"

"Precisely," Ronall said, feeling better now that he'd quenched his thirst a little. Now he remembered what he had come here for. Now he felt the courage to make it happen. He swallowed more fiery brew and then looked right into the young man's eyes. "Which *shallah* to have punished for waking me too early after I've spent the night drinking. Which serving maid to force my attentions on. Which tenants to squeeze so I can pay my gambling debts. Which—"

"*Toren,*" the keeper interrupted, "please pay no attention to this young fool's comments." A sensible businessman, the elderly *shallah* prodded the younger one, "Apologize to my customer, you clod, if you expect to be welcome here any longer."

The young man's complexion darkened. "I . . . I beg your pardon, *toren.* I . . . We have known such hard times here."

"And you can see by looking at the *toren* that he has known hard times, too," the elderly keeper insisted.

Ronall lifted a brow at this assessment, but the young *shallah* bobbed his head in agreement and repeated his apology. Then he shuffled away, leaving Ronall in solitary conversation with the keeper. There was an awkward silence while the elderly *shallah* refilled Ronall's mug, but then everyone returned to their own conversations.

"Would you believe," Ronall said quietly to the keeper, "I've done all those things?"

The old man looked unsurprised by the admission. "These have been hard years. We've all done things we regret, *toren.*"

Ronall snorted into his brew. "Believe me, I've done nothing I regret as much as just being born."

"And wouldn't many, born to Valdani-ruled Sileria, say the same, *toren?*"

"Would they?"

"With the future of Sileria now so uncertain," the elderly *shallah* added, "who knows how many more of us will yet live to regret ever being born?"

Ronall sighed and drained his mug. Again. Then he decided to get good and stinking drunk. As usual.

"WE'LL ATTACK IN six different groups," Tansen explained to Radyan, outlining the plan for assaulting Abidan and Liadon. "Three groups per brother. Two separate attacks. Simultaneous, so neither brother will be free to help the other. We'll begin when . . . Are you paying attention?"

Radyan was looking past him with a frown. "What? Um, no."

"Radyan, this is im—"

"He's going to hurt someone."

Tansen turned and saw what Radyan was staring at in the fading sunlight. Galian was practicing with the *shir* he'd taken from the assassin he had slain during the fight in the old Kintish temple a few nights ago.

"Hurting someone," Tansen said dryly, "is the basic idea behind a *shir,* you know."

"Ah, but if we could narrow it down to only hurting the *enemy,*" Radyan suggested as Galian, fighting an imaginary opponent, came close to stabbing a Guardian who was innocently passing behind him.

The Guardian spurted flames everywhere in reflexive response, causing Galian to howl in startled alarm. The two started arguing in angry voices which carried easily to where Tansen and Radyan stood making plans.

"And making *new* enemies," Tansen noted, "hardly seems productive at this juncture."

"I wish someone could take that thing away from him."

Tansen grinned. "Actually, you can, but—"

"But I'd have to kill him first," Radyan concluded. While they watched, Galian evidently forgot he was holding the deadly *shir* and nearly poked the Guardian in the eye while they argued. "Which I may soon be willing to do," Radyan added.

"Oh, well. At least it may be useful in our attack." Tansen shrugged. "Najdan says one of the brothers made it."

"I can't stand this any longer." Radyan left Tansen's side, walked up to Galian, and seized him by the shoulder. "Come talk to me and Tansen," he ordered loudly.

"But I—"

"Make your apologies and come."

"But—"

"*Now.*"

They were all on a bluff overlooking the Shaljir River, which flowed smoothly past the town of Zilar. The water's innocent surface revealed nothing of the sorcery which ruled it. The bustle of activity continued throughout the town, and people were especially busy at the water's edge. If the plan Tansen had made with the Guardians failed to destroy Abidan and Liadon, then Zilar would need all the water it could store. If his plan succeeded, then they could safeguard the stored water against a future shortage, in case other waterlords captured the river, or else share the water with others in need.

His gaze swept the riverside and sought Zarien. Although not much of a walker, the boy was certainly a hard worker. Throughout their stay in Zilar, he had invested seemingly tireless effort in harvesting and storing water, evidently enjoying the work. Tansen supposed that after feeling out of his element for so long on the dryland, it was a pleasure for him to find something he was comfortable with, something he was good at. Tansen well remembered how utterly bewildered and inept he himself had felt during his first few months in the Kintish Kingdoms, after fleeing Sileria as a boy; he supposed Zarien was experiencing similar frustrations.

While Tansen watched Zarien working at the water's edge, he heard Radyan's irritable voice clearly as he returned to Tansen's side with Galian. "How anyone who handles not one but two *yahr* so well could possibly be so clumsy—"

"It's a new weapon," Galian protested. "And new weapons take time—"

"Exactly! So why would you practice with it in a busy, crowded—"

"Just ask Tansen. New weapons—"

"*Tansen!*"

Galian and Radyan stopped arguing as Yorin, having spotted Tansen, approached them at a run.

"What is it?" Tansen asked.

Yorin's scarred face was troubled. "It's bad news."

"What?" Radyan prompted.

"Word has come from Cavasar," Yorin said. "The people there have declared their loyalty to Kiloran. They will not join us."

Tansen rubbed his neck and tried to view this admittedly disappointing news in perspective. "I expected this. He holds the city, after all."

"Yes, if any place is completely at Kiloran's mercy . . ." Radyan sighed and looked away.

Galian said, "Let's just hope Shaljir is tired of paying tribute."

"Liron is resisting Verlon," Tansen reminded them.

"No word yet from Adalian," Yorin said.

Tansen's gaze sought out Zarien again. "Maybe if we could get the sea-born to declare themselves on our side . . ."

"Shaljir is what matters most now," Radyan insisted. "If you can—"

"Something's wrong," Tansen said suddenly, his gaze still fixed on Zarien.

The boy waved his tattooed arms and shouted at people to get away from the water. He dragged several men back from the river's edge. Tansen could faintly hear him urging people on the main dock to get back, run, go.

Radyan drew in a sharp breath. "What in the Fires . . ."

Suddenly the whole river started churning, foaming and bubbling as if animated by a thousand different currents.

"It's them," Galian breathed. "The waterlords."

"Get away from the river!" Tansen's voice attracted the attention of many people, but not that of the sea-born boy he was shouting at. Zarien was still near the water, his energy being spent in yelling frantic instructions to a well-dressed fat man—a merchant, by the look of him—who stood on the dock, staring transfixed at the wildly churning water.

"Zarien!" Tan shouted. "Get away!"

Tansen scrambled down the bluff, pushing his way through the people rushing towards him as they escaped the waterside.

A torrent of water crashed into the dock. It collapsed. The horrified screams of Zilar's panicking citizens assaulted Tansen's ears as the fat merchant fell into the heaving, roiling water.

"Zarien!" Tansen saw what the boy meant to do and shouted, "*No!*"

Zarien dived in after the merchant.

Tansen lost his footing and slid into two women climbing up the embankment. He tumbled over them, fell against some rocks, felt something jagged bite into his shoulder and cheek, then scrambled to his feet and continued his frantic descent to the river's edge.

His heart pounded with terror as his eyes scanned the foaming, turbulent water.

"Zarien! *Zarien!*"

He almost jumped in, but reason prevailed. He was a competent swimmer at best. He'd be of no help to the boy in the water.

He glanced around frantically, searching the water for Zarien, searching the ground for the *stahra*. Sharifar wouldn't let the boy die, surely she wouldn't.

He found the enchanted oar, seized it, and searched the churning river again for some sign of Zarien.

There!

Zarien was holding the fat merchant around the neck and trying desperately to keep his own head above water.

"Zarien!"

If you let him die, Sharifar, I will never come to sea. Never.

Tansen threw the oar like a spear. It landed close to Zarien . . . but the unpredictable bubbling water immediately carried it away from him. Tansen didn't think he even saw it.

He looked around for something else. Something he could throw to Zarien. Something the boy could grab . . . He spotted an ordinary oar, one which lay beside a small dugout lying on the embankment.

He seized it, estimated how far he needed to throw it, and . . . and stopped when he realized how much closer to the riverbank Zarien was getting with each strong stroke of his free arm, each powerful kick of his legs.

Darfire. He's not drowning.

Almost numb with surprise, Tansen leaned over and extended the oar as Zarien neared shore. The boy saw it, seized it, and let Tansen pull him up onto the bank. Then he turned and started hauling the fat merchant out of the water.

"Help," Zarien croaked. "He's even heavier than he looks."

When they had pulled the merchant to safety, Zarien leaned over, braced his hands on his knees, and panted, "That was hard." He sounded absurdly surprised.

Tansen resisted the urge to hit him. "What did you think you were doing?" he demanded.

Zarien squinted up at him. "What's wrong now?"

"You could have been killed!"

Zarien looked at Tansen, looked at the roiling water, and looked back at Tansen. "By that?" He sounded almost contemptuous.

"Dar give me patience," Tansen muttered.

"The sea-born," Zarien informed him, "do not drown in a little foamy river water." He glanced down at the merchant and added, "But landfolk do."

The merchant was choking and wheezing. "Thank . . . Thank . . ."

"He's thanking you," Tansen pointed out.

Zarien was staring at Tansen. "You're bleeding."

He glanced down at his arm and saw a gash. "Oh."

"Your face, too."

The words made him realize that his cheek was stinging. He touched it. His fingers came away smeared with blood. "I fell," he said wearily.

"You should be more care—"

"Don't. Even. Say it."

Zarien sighed. "Never mind."

Tansen shook his head. "I don't know whether to praise you for saving his life or beat you for scaring me t—"

"Something's wrong," Zarien said, staring at the water.

"Of *course* something's—"

"No, something else," Zarien said. "The water's doing something—"

"*Yes*, it's doing something—"

"Something else, something new," Zarien persisted.

"Get back," Tansen ordered. "Let's get away from it." He kicked the gurgling, disoriented merchant. "Get up. We're not carrying you—"

"Where's my *stahra*?" Zarien asked. "I'm sure it was here—"

"Uh, sorry about that." Tansen seized his arm and started dragging him forcibly up the embankment, once again aware of the terrified screams of the crowd. "I threw it in the river."

"You threw it in the river?" Zarien repeated incredulously.

"I thought it would save you."

"I didn't need saving!"

"Which is presumably why it didn't save you."

Zarien shook off his grasp and turned back to the river. "I'm not leaving without my *stahra*!"

"No!"

Tansen grabbed for him. Zarien pulled away. And slipped. He went tumbling downhill, dragging Tansen with him. They careened into the merchant . . . who fell backwards into the river.

"Dar curse you and all your . . ." Tansen's voice faded as he realized the merchant wasn't sinking. He lay atop the surface of the water . . . which was now silent, still, smooth, and glowing eerily in the dying sunlight.

"That's really interesting." Zarien stretched out one leg and cautiously tapped the surface with the toe of his new boot. Then he turned a puzzled gaze on Tansen. "It's as hard as rock."

The merchant started praying. Tansen resisted the urge to kick him again.

Zarien stepped onto the river and started walking across it, awkwardly slipping on its glassy surface every few steps.

"What are you doing?" Tansen demanded, gritting his teeth as he followed the boy.

"Looking for my *stahra*." He looked over his shoulder at Tansen. "If it's embedded in this stuff . . ."

"Then we'll let Sharifar worry about how to get it out," Tansen snapped. "Zarien, I'm ordering you, get out of . . ." He slipped. "Off of . . . Away from—"

"There it is!"

Tansen looked to where the boy was pointing. Sure enough, an object which could only be the *stahra* lay downriver, resting atop the crystal-hard water.

"All right," Tansen said, "I'll get the damned *stahra*. You do as you're told, for once, and get away from the river."

"I'll get it."

"*Now*, Zarien."

Zarien sighed. His expression was one of long-suffering tolerance. "Very well." His tone indicated clearly that he was merely humoring Tansen. He turned and started stumbling and skidding his way back to the riverbank.

Tansen sighed and went after the *stahra*, fully realizing what a stupid risk he was taking for the boy's damned oar. The crystallization of the river seemed to be the waterlords' final act here, but Tansen knew better than to take chances with water magic. He should be up on the bluff with the rest of the town, cowering at a marginally safe distance, not sliding around on the surface of Abidan's and Liadon's actively enchanted river, practically inviting them to kill him.

Really, it was amazing that Zarien's parents, in a totally understandable and forgivable fit of exasperation, hadn't ever thrown him overboard and sailed away as fast as they could.

After Tansen retrieved the *stahra* and returned to the riverbank, he wasn't at all surprised, alas, to find the boy right there, rather than up on the bluff where he ought to be. Tansen was now feeling the aftereffects of the sort of emotional panic he never indulged in, and he found he was simply too tired to keep snapping at Zarien.

Maybe a boy's true passage into manhood, Tansen reflected wryly, occurred when his parents simply ran out of the strength to keep trying to govern him.

Zarien was studying the hard, shiny, unmoving surface of the water with amazed fascination. He took the *stahra* from Tansen and used it to poke at the river several times. When Tansen failed to admonish him, he was emboldened to step onto its surface again.

However, once he started drumming on it with the sturdy heels of his new boots, Tansen said, "*Must* you?"

"It's incredible!" Zarien bent over and touched the hard surface. "How do they do that?"

"That's what everyone in Sileria would like to know." Tansen gazed out across what had been a river only minutes ago. "It's the source of all their power over us."

Zarien's head jerked up, his expression shocked as he met Tansen's eyes. "This is it, isn't it?"

"This is the beginning." Tansen nodded. "They know by now what we intend. And they're punishing us." Perhaps the assassin who had escaped Najdan's pursuit told Abidan and Liadon, but not necessarily. Anyone could have alerted them. Tansen's declaration of war had been very public, and word would have spread fast.

Zarien looked down at the river again. "No one can drink this. No one can . . . use this now."

"Exactly."

"That's terrible." He looked up at the bluff, where hundreds of people were gathering to stare in fear and dismay at the river. They had known this could happen, but it horrified them, even so. "All those people . . ."

"This is why we have to fight the Society, Zarien."

Zarien nodded. "Yes."

"No one should be allowed to do this to us. No one should hold this kind of power over us. No one should rule us through the threat of doing this to us whenever we fail to obey, to please, to submit."

The young face was thoughtful. "Yes, now I understand."

"I hope you do." Tansen looked up at the crowd gathered on the bluff. He saw their frightened, appalled faces and murmured, "I hope everyone in Sileria does."

27

EMELDAR WAS AN ordinary *shallah* village. Precariously
perched near the summit of a craggy mountain in western Sileria, it had a
main square of modest size. Its streets were narrow and ancient, its dwellings
mostly made of stone quarried from the mountain itself. The traditional
sacred lava stone and the fire-scarred offering-ground were at the edge of the
village, where there was a cherished, if distant, view of Mount Darshon.

Indeed, the only remarkable thing about this village, so much like hundreds of other villages in Sileria, was that it was the birthplace of the Firebringer.

Here in Emeldar, Josarian was born, grew to manhood, fell in love, and
married. It was here that his wife died in the unfortunate horrors of childbirth. It was here that he mourned her and, in his despondence, allowed
himself to be coaxed into his cousin Zimran's modestly profitable smuggling
trade; and it was not far from here that he was caught by Outlookers one
night.

In the normal course of events, Josarian and Zimran would have been
arrested and sentenced to a year or two in the mines of Alizar. But a single
moment of bad judgment—and to this day, no one could really say
whose—had changed the world. If Josarian had not tried to warn his cousin
before the Outlookers caught Zimran, too; if the Outlookers had not lost
their heads and started beating Josarian for his impetuous warning; if Josarian had not fought back and killed two of them . . .

Well, actually, everything would probably have turned out the same,
anyhow. He wasn't the Firebringer because he'd killed a couple of Outlookers and become an outlaw that night. He was the Firebringer because Dar
chose him.

Even Kiloran, who had turned his back upon Dar long ago, understood
and accepted this.

Now, as Kiloran entered the main square of Emeldar for the first time
ever, he could only marvel that such an extraordinary man had come from

such an ordinary place. They had been mortal enemies, and Kiloran had tried to kill him more than once, true; but Kiloran did not believe in undervaluing a man (or woman) just because of enmity. Josarian had indeed been extraordinary—even before becoming the Firebringer.

Kiloran had reached an age when travel was more of a trial than a pleasure, so he wasn't pleased about having to come to Emeldar, but the journey was necessary. Having secured the loyalty of Cavasar, he now needed to ensure that Baran wouldn't be a problem—as he could be, if he chose.

As Kiloran's even-tempered gelding approached the main fountain, he reined him in. He had never doubted the tale of how Josarian had ruined his village's water supply to destroy the Outlooker forces sent here against him, but now he scented the water for himself.

Poison. It was indeed true. A waterlord could recognize tainted water instantly, though the Outlookers had drunk it like thirsty goats.

Fortunately, this wasn't a problem. Kiloran had five assassins with him, all of them mounted on horses which had, until recently, belonged to the Outlookers in Cavasar. He saw no point in expending the energy needed to cure the entire water supply, especially since the Emeldari were now his blood enemies, but he could certainly cleanse enough of it to keep his men and horses watered for the duration of their stay in Emeldar. Considering what a dreary little village this was, he hoped that their visit would be a short one.

Kiloran sent one of his men in search of a comfortable place for him to stay, if such accommodation was possible in Josarian's deserted birthplace. Another of the men took charge of the horses, and two more began transferring water from the main fountain to a large bone-dry trough. When there was enough of it in there for the horses, Kiloran would extract the poison so they could drink. Meanwhile, Searlon drew enough water to quench the men's thirst.

"If you please, *siran*," Searlon said, presenting the bucket to Kiloran for him to cure the water.

While pondering the ramifications of Dar's dramatic activities in the distant volcano lately, Kiloran held his hand over the broad-rimmed bucket and felt the water inside it respond to his will. He had little understanding of the goddess; the colored pillars of smoke, sky-reaching bolts of flame, and angry lightning dancing all around the summit of Darshon concerned him now. He did not hate the goddess, and he refused to fear Her. He could not, however, afford to ignore Her.

Despite the coming of the Firebringer, Kiloran remained convinced that the *zanareen* were essentially mad and unreliable, so he didn't intend to count solely on their noisy proclamations about the strange new events at Darshon. If anyone could sensibly interpret this unprecedented display of Dar's, he supposed it would be the Guardians. Consequently, he had recently made arrangements to have several of them captured, in the hopes that at least one of them could be made to talk.

After only a few moments, a silvery mist arose from the bucket of water beneath Kiloran's palm. The poison hissed into the air, the water rejecting it as he commanded.

"You and the men may drink now," he advised Searlon.

"Not before you, *siran*," Searlon said. "The journey has been a long one, and the sun is hot."

Though an immensely powerful and influential assassin, Searlon proffered the first cup of water to his master like a common servant. And not, Kiloran knew, because he wanted to test the water before drinking it himself. During more than ten years of loyal service, Searlon had never failed to show his master the greatest courtesy and most attentive respect. It was one of his many virtues.

Kiloran was pleased to have Searlon back. The assassin had stolen a horse in Shaljir, made his escape, and taken the coastal road to Cavasar to join his master. Kiloran had therefore been the first person in Cavasar to learn of the Valdani surrender. He had used the information to his advantage, gaining more of Cavasar's love as he made the announcement. He accepted credit for the victory in the wake of Josarian's death without, of course, discussing the details of how the Firebringer had died.

Unfortunately, though, the circumstances of Searlon's return to Cavasar were a mixed blessing. *Torena* Elelar was a fanatic, which had proved useful, but Kiloran had always known she wasn't a fool. Her proposed alliance with Searlon was sensible, despite how much it must have galled her to suggest it. And, in the end, she had needed Searlon to force Kaynall to honor his own treaty. Sadly, though, Elelar had shown her appreciation by betraying Kiloran. It was a bold and unexpected move, one which took even Searlon by surprise.

Ah, mistakes. They are so easily made.

Kiloran knew that frightened whispers in Cavasar were spreading the story of Josarian's death. That was as it should be. He held the city now. Nothing could threaten that. The rumors that he had proved to be even more powerful than the Firebringer would ultimately be to his advantage there. Fear and love were so closely entwined in Sileria, and knowing how to balance them was one of his great strengths.

However, Kiloran was not loved at all in Shaljir, and the *torena*'s dramatic announcement, made to the masses at such a volatile moment, had roused the people of the city to passionate hatred. That was unfortunate. Shaljir's citizens had responded enthusiastically to their aristocratic heroine's public call for vengeance, effectively eliminating Kiloran's options there.

It was therefore essential that Baran accept a truce and relinquish full control of the Idalar River to Kiloran. Sileria's ancient capital must be brought to its knees. If Shaljir resisted, then the rest of Sileria would see that disobedience was possible. And that was unacceptable.

Nothing happened in Sileria without Kiloran's knowledge, so he was already well informed about Tansen's public proclamation of war. It took little imagination to realize that Tansen had killed the six assassins Kiloran had sent to ambush him at Dalishar after Josarian's death. Tansen was alive, urging the populace to civil war, and Kiloran's men were missing without a trace. Yes, it was disappointing, but Kiloran knew that persistence was an inherent requirement of victory. He would merely keep trying.

Meanwhile, thousands had already joined Tansen in declaring a blood-feud against the Society, news from the east revealed that the Lironi were opposing Verlon, Mirabar had offered public prophecy about the coming of a new Yahrdan, and the waterlords were already struggling for dominance over their people.

In the wake of the Valdani surrender, chaos was sweeping across Sileria. Far from being distressed by it, Kiloran found it exhilarating. He had carved his small empire out of the chaos which followed Harlon's death nearly forty years ago. Blessed with a cold intelligence which resisted panic and impulse, he had risen to preeminence by recognizing his opportunities during those years of terrible turmoil in the Society. Now he would do so again. Only this time, the prize wasn't just leadership of the Honored Society. This time, he would rule all of Sileria.

As for Mirabar's prophesied Yahrdan ... Well, Kiloran had already defeated the Firebringer, and he could destroy whomever the fire-eyed Guardian now foresaw in her visions. He had already proven that prophecy did not make a man invincible or his future assured. He had already demonstrated that he was the king of his kind, and soon he would triumph over all his enemies and lead Sileria into a new age.

It was a fitting climax to an extraordinary life. He had only two regrets. He wished he could be ten years younger when he assumed control of the nation ... and perhaps he might have been, had Tansen not killed Armian and destroyed their chances ten years ago. And he wished he had a suitable heir to carry on his legacy after his death.

Kiloran loved Sileria and didn't want chaos once again sweeping through the land after he died. This was his time, his destiny. He would bring order to the nation, unite the people under his vision, and secure the island against more foreign invasions. He would wipe out the Guardians once and for all, including Mirabar. He would destroy dissenters. He would eliminate Tansen, his friends, and the friends of his friends. . . . And when Sileria was safely his forever, Kiloran would forgive the people for having strayed. They were his children, and they would return to him in love and in fear. It was their history. It was their destiny. There could be no other way. Not in Sileria.

However, he didn't want to do all that, to devote the rest of his life to his beloved nation, only to die knowing he left behind no one to maintain order, inherit and secure his legacy, and carry on in his name.

There had been prospects over the years, potential heirs to his legacy as the preeminent waterlord of the Honored Society, but they had come to nothing. Armian was dead. His own son, Srijan, had been bereft of water magic, as was Searlon. And Baran, the whimsical and frustratingly unambitious young man of enormous natural talent whom Kiloran himself had first apprenticed to water magic . . . Baran had turned on him in vengeful wrath.

Kiloran sighed at the memory. Honesty compelled him to admit, in the privacy of his own heart, that he had erred, both in judgment and in sense. Through uncharacteristically rash acts which he remembered with bemusement, he had driven Baran to this demented hatred. Then he had compounded the error by failing to kill him.

Ah, mistakes. They are so easily made.

He silenced his regrets. What was done was done. He had created Baran, and now he must deal with the consequences. Eventually he would destroy him, but not now. It would take too much sustained effort. He couldn't spare the energy now, and he couldn't afford the potential damages. Later, after Tansen and Mirabar were dead, the Guardians were all ashes, and Sileria was his. Then, yes, then he would finally succeed where he had failed so many times over the years; he would finally destroy Baran.

Each thing must come in its time, however, and this was the time for the Honored Society to unite against a common enemy.

Kiloran chose to rest as the hot sun rose high over Emeldar. One of his men had found a dwelling which, though spare and simple, was moderately comfortable. Kiloran wondered with cool irony if it had been Josarian's house.

As requested, several other waterlords arrived throughout the day, each one accompanied by assassins, to attend this truce meeting. Baran, however, did not arrive that day; nor the following day. Searlon privately suggested to Kiloran that this was a sign of disrespect, perhaps even an open insult. The assassin advised his master that it would be best to leave if Baran didn't arrive the following morning.

"It is not fitting, *siran*," he said, "that you should be seen to wait upon his pleasure. It is beneath you."

What Searlon meant, of course, was that if Kiloran waited another full day, he would be seen as needing Baran's cooperation too desperately. This, in turn, would lead to the suspicion that he was vulnerable.

As another night in Emeldar fell with no sign of Baran, a cold fury boiled slowly inside of Kiloran. Did Baran mean to reject his offer of a truce? Even worse, did Baran mean to make a fool of him by not even acknowledging it?

He was Kiloran, the greatest waterlord in Sileria, the greatest waterlord who had ever lived! This display of disrespect was intolerable!

Kiloran saw the predatory instinct lurking in the dark eyes of the other waterlords who had gathered here in Emeldar at his request, but he didn't let it worry him. He had dominated the rest of them for more than thirty years, and he would continue to do so with or without Baran.

Unfortunately, though, Baran was placing him in an inconvenient position. If that half-mad upstart didn't arrive tomorrow, then Kiloran, for the sake of his dignity, would indeed be obliged to leave Emeldar without securing a truce. He would also be obliged to swiftly and ruthlessly punish Baran for this show of disrespect. And that possibility represented both energy and attention which Kiloran couldn't afford to spare right now.

It was often hard to decide which man he most regretted not having killed long ago, Baran or Tansen.

As if Baran's disrespect weren't annoying enough, Wyldon hadn't shown up yet, either. Searlon raised the subject that night in the privacy of Kiloran's temporary quarters, away from the watchful eyes and eager ears of the other waterlords and assassins quartering in Emeldar.

"I do not believe Wyldon would simply defy you," Searlon said. "Something has happened."

"It's not a serious concern right now," Kiloran replied. "If he's dead, his loss is of little consequence, and his territory will be open for conquest. If he's alive and merely offering me an insult . . . well, he will be much easier than Baran to punish."

Searlon nodded. "When we leave here, I will initiate inquiries." He lifted one dark brow and prodded, "We are leaving tomorrow, are we not, *siran?*"

He knew the assassin was right. It was best to adjust quickly to disappointments and move on. "Yes, before midday." He paused, then added, "While you're making inquiries, I also want to know more about the demon-girl's prophecy."

"Of the coming Yahrdan?"

"Yes. I waited too long to kill Josarian, let him become too influential. The task would have been so much easier had we eliminated him as soon as we knew he was the Firebringer."

"And if the Yahrdan is young, as Tansen and Mirabar said in Zilar, and in need of protection . . ."

"They've been vague, but they may already know who he is."

"And if not, they're certainly trying to learn."

Kiloran nodded, considering this. "If there was some way we could find out before the rest of Sileria . . ."

"I doubt that can be done, *siran*. This information comes only to Mirabar, in her visions. Unless we can capture her alive . . ."

"Perhaps we should find someone easier to take alive. Someone Mirabar trusts."

"Ah. Someone she confides in." Searlon rubbed his chin as he considered the possibilities. "Najdan, for example."

"He won't betray her."

"No," Searlon agreed sadly, "I suppose not. If we captured him, though, perhaps he could be forced to talk."

"We can try, but I must admit that I don't anticipate satisfactory results."

"Still, we must deal with him. One way or another."

"True. I count on you to make him regret betraying me."

"I intend to, *siran*." The assassin added, "After all, Najdan is more than a mere enemy."

"Yes." For twenty years Kiloran had trusted Najdan, favored him, rewarded him, counted on him, and shielded him. Only to be repaid, when it mattered most, with betrayal. "Much more."

Even now, he wondered what hold, what fascination or fear Mirabar exerted over the assassin. Even now, he tried to imagine what had lured Najdan—always so devoted, so faithful, so obedient—away from his own kind after twenty years. Even now, he was as puzzled as he was enraged.

"You will secure great honor for yourself," he told Searlon, his voice rich with promise, "when you slay him for me."

"I could ask for no more, *siran*."

"Ah, but you will," Kiloran replied dryly. Although unfailingly courteous, Searlon was neither modest about his skills nor shy about asking for his due. He would expect to be richly rewarded for shedding Najdan's blood. And Kiloran would not disappoint him. It was a waterlord's duty to cherish, protect, and reward those who were loyal to him.

Searlon grinned. "Yes, *siran*. I will."

Kiloran stared at the wavering lantern-light as he considered the other news they had received from Zilar. "About this sea-born youth seen in Zilar with Tansen . . ."

"By all accounts," Searlon responded, "he's too young to be there as a representative of the sea-born, and he's alone. It still seems most likely, with the Valdani withdrawing now, that the sea-born will ignore our quarrels on land."

"So the lad is just some runaway, then? Chasing after youthful dreams of glory with a famous rebel leader?"

Searlon frowned. "Why does he worry you, *siran*?"

"A sea-born lad, that far inland." Kiloran shook his head. "It may be nothing, but he's out of place. Things that are out of place bother me. Especially where Tansen is concerned."

"You would like to know more," Searlon surmised.

"Yes. If only to put my mind at ease." He supposed that he wouldn't trouble himself over an equally minor anomaly of a different nature. But the sea-born ... well, the sight of them, even the mention of them—it always brought back memories. And the memories always bothered him. He supposed it was the same for Baran. "Just see what you can learn," he instructed, pulling his thoughts away from the past.

"As you wish, *siran.*"

The night passed uncomfortably. Accommodations were far from luxurious in Emeldar, and the presence of other waterlords was a drain on Kiloran's senses. Cooperation wasn't the same thing as trust, after all. He didn't actually believe that any of them would make an attempt on his life here, but he wasn't about to wallow in misplaced confidence and relax his vigilance so that one—or all—of them could ensorcel the poisoned fountain in the main square and ambush him with it. Such an act was strictly forbidden by the centuries-old protocol of a Society truce meeting ... but that didn't mean no one had ever tried it.

And as if all that weren't enough to disturb his rest, Dar gave a loud crack of rage in the middle of the night, setting some of the assassins to gibbering like frightened virgins.

All in all, Kiloran was feeling distinctly bad-tempered by the time he arose, dressed, and left his quarters to announce to the other waterlords that he would endure no further insult from Baran.

"We're leaving." He looked around at the five waterlords and thirty assassins gathered here. He had no intention, of course, of leaving them behind to gossip and plot together in his absence. "We're *all* leaving."

Gulstan, who ruled the springs all around Britar, said, "You're right, *siran.* He has insulted you." He could hardly keep the satisfaction out of his voice.

"He has insulted us all," Meriten said pointedly. He was young and not particularly powerful. He was smart enough, however, to offer unswerving friendship to Kiloran in exchange for occasional protection and help.

"Perhaps we should give him another day." This suggestion came from Dulien, who was still sulking over Kiloran's recent acquisition of the Zilar River. Dulien had tried for years, without success, to bring it under his control.

"I've offered to be his ally," Kiloran said. "He has failed to seize his opportunity. The consequences are his to bear."

"He might be—"

"We have all discussed our plans while we've awaited him," Kiloran pointed out. "We have nothing left to say. We are agreed on our obligations, our promises, and our ... our ...." His voice trailed off as something intruded on his thoughts, whispering across his senses.

Kariman, a waterlord from the Amalidar Mountains, prodded, "You were saying?"

Kiloran ignored him. He stared sightlessly into the distance, waiting until he was sure.

"Is something wrong?" asked Ferolen, whose territory was north of Adalian.

"*Siran?*" Searlon ventured politely.

Kiloran lifted his hand, now sure, as he sensed the awaited approach. "Baran is coming," he told Searlon.

He needed to say no more. Searlon ordered the men to stop harnessing the horses for departure, then took his place beside his master and waited for Baran to appear. The other waterlords took their places, too, aligning themselves formally in the village's main square, with their assassins behind them.

Kiloran glanced briefly over the scene, pleased with the dignity and the imposing menace of his kind—even the ones he detested. What *toren* wouldn't beg for mercy when confronted with this solemn spectacle? What Guardian wouldn't flee for his life? He was pleased that Baran would see the full impact of this assembly when he entered the square. It was time for Baran to remember who he was, what obeisance was due the gift of water magic. He should realize to whom he owed his loyalty; he was one of them, and no one should turn his back on his own kind.

"He's getting closer," Kiloran said.

"No, don't," Searlon snapped at one of the assassins who reached for his *shir*. "Unless I say otherwise, you will act as if made of stone."

Great power recognized great power. That's why Kiloran could always tell when Mirabar was approaching, and he knew that she felt his presence just as strongly. That smirking aristocratic Guardian, Cheylan, had it, too. A presence which filled the air, which vibrated along senses attuned to a life beyond the one ordinary people knew and understood. It was rare, and it took years to develop. A sorcerer's power must be very great to announce his presence in this way, a tremendous natural talent additionally honed and enhanced through practice and dedication. They didn't all have it. They didn't all recognize it.

Kiloran could feel the stinging chill which emanated from Baran as he approached Emeldar. And when Baran's horses entered the main square, followed by only two mounted assassins, Kiloran also felt something far more ordinary emanating from Baran: the obsessive hatred for him which had shaped Baran's life.

Baran was perhaps Najdan's age, though Kiloran was surprised by how much older he looked now. However, it had been years since they'd met face-to-face, and changes were inevitable. Born to a merchant family, Baran was a big, muscular man, though thinner now than Kiloran remembered. His long black hair was thick, unruly, and uncombed—that, at least, had not changed. His skin was rather fair for a Silerian, his lips full like a woman's, and his eyes two dark windows into a tormented soul.

He reined his horse to a halt in the middle of the square and surveyed the scene. A grin split his face. Even Kiloran marveled that a smile could look so malevolent.

"Ah, how I've missed you all!" Baran's deep voice rang with good cheer and patent insincerity.

He dismounted, gave the reins to one of his men, and nodded towards a trough which held cleansed water. No one chose to object as Baran's assassins watered their horses without asking.

Baran, meanwhile, crossed the square on foot and began greeting his compatriots one by one, examining them like a *toren* looking over prospective servants.

"Gulstan! You really are trying to become the fattest waterlord in Sileria, aren't you? Meriten," he exclaimed, moving on while Gulstan's mouth worked in sputtering outrage. "Ah, Meriten, pretty as ever, I see. Kariman! Ferolen . . . No, I really can't think of anything to say to you. And Dulien!" He leaned forward and murmured into Dulien's ear, loudly enough for the others to hear, "Don't sulk, Dulien, it doesn't become you."

"No one likes you," Dulien replied. "No one has ever liked you."

"Ah, but they do envy me," Baran replied easily, "don't they, Dulien?"

Kiloran said coldly, "Did you come all the way from Belitar just to insult your betters and cause ill feeling?"

Baran smiled at him, his eyes dancing with the hot hatred which was the ruling force in his life. "If you were my betters, you wouldn't be so worried about what I'm going to do now that Josarian's dead, would you?"

"You are one of us," Meriten said. "And now that Tan—"

"Yes, yes, yes," Baran interrupted, strolling away and studying the fountain as he babbled, "unity is crucial against a common enemy, this is what makes the Society stronger than any other faction in Sileria, it's why we've survived for a thousand years against so many foes . . . and so on and so forth. I know the doctrine by heart." He suddenly whirled around and confronted Kiloran again, his expression that of a hesitant houseguest. "You know . . . it was such a long journey, and I suddenly find I'm so terribly thirsty."

"Indeed," Kiloran said.

"Could I trouble you?" Baran raised his brows in seemingly innocent inquiry.

"It's no trouble." Kiloran nodded to an assassin, who brought Baran a cup of water.

"How gracious of you," Baran said. "Perhaps sometime I'll honor your home, eat at your table, sleep beneath your roof." The words of the traditional welcome flowed smoothly from his tongue. Then he snapped his fingers in sudden recollection. "No! Come to think of it . . ." He gasped. "Why, yes! I've already done that. And it didn't work out so well, did it?"

Kiloran felt Searlon's puzzled glance. The other waterlords looked confused. For as long as any of them had known Baran, he had been Kiloran's enemy. They had no idea that once, long ago, Baran had been welcome in his home, as his apprentice.

"I believe you said you were thirsty," Kiloran remarked, ignoring Baran's jibes.

"Yes." Baran sniffed the water in the cup. "But this somehow seems stale." He spilled it out onto the ground, then walked over to the fountain, dipped the cup into the tainted water, and drank.

Kiloran heard Searlon draw a sharp breath of surprise through his nostrils. Meriten took a hesitant step forward. Ferolen and Kariman exchanged a glance. There was no doubt that Baran could tell the fountain was poisoned, even if he'd never heard the story of Josarian's devious destruction of the Outlookers here.

Gulstan simply said, "You really are mad, aren't you? And here I thought people were just being unkind."

"I don't like to drink alone," Baran said suddenly. He held the cup out to Kiloran, his eyes full of strange delight. "Won't you join me, *siran?*"

It was an absurd gesture, a childish challenge. However, with so many people here, Kiloran knew he couldn't refuse. Not only would the tale be repeated, it would grow bigger with every telling. He felt a desire to wrap the fountain's waters around Baran's neck and strangle him. However, this was a truce meeting. Besides, Baran would just fight back and turn the whole day into a messy disaster. So Kiloran accepted the cup. He knew there wasn't enough poison in a few sips, or even a whole cup, to actually kill an ordinary man, let alone a waterlord. And he could certainly command the water to protect him from what little poison he swallowed. This was merely one of Baran's bizarre rites.

Kiloran drained the cup, then suggested they sit in the shade to discuss their mutual concerns. Baran agreed with a buoyant enthusiasm that suggested he was looking forward to a day spent among long-lost friends. Gulstan ground his teeth. Meriten looked confused. Even Searlon seemed a bit off balance. Dulien sulked, and the other two waterlords regarded Baran with lively interest.

Once they were all seated in the shade, Baran said, "I must apologize for keeping you waiting, Kiloran. I wouldn't have dreamed of such disrespect, but I had so many visitors at Belitar that it was hard to get away."

Kiloran considered ignoring the comment, but decided the conversation would move more quickly if he simply took the bait. "Visitors?"

"Well, of course, Tansen has sent a messenger," Baran said chattily. "The ugliest and meanest Sister you can possibly imagine, in fact. What was Tansen thinking of? That's no way to influence a red-blooded man in the prime of life!"

"Perhaps he could find no other volunteer," Gulstan suggested dryly. "I'm just guessing, of course."

Kiloran could easily imagine what sort of message Tansen had sent to Baran, and he knew better than to waste time asking what Baran's response was. He would get no straight answer; indeed, he doubted that Tansen would get a straight answer.

"I've asked you here to propose a formal truce," Kiloran said, already tired of Baran's company and eager to complete his task. "You and I—"

"But don't you want to hear about my other visitor?"

"No."

Baran pouted. "It hurts me when you speak to me that way."

Kiloran was starting to regret having called this meeting under a banner of truce. How satisfying it would be to simply abandon sense and caution, and—finally, after all these years—kill Baran right now.

Unfortunately, he mustn't do it. Not here and now. No member of the Society could, with impunity, violate a truce meeting with an act of violence. Not even Kiloran. It was undoubtedly the only reason Baran had abandoned the safety of Belitar to meet him face-to-face today. It was among the inflexible rules which had made the Society strong for centuries. Kiloran himself had ruthlessly punished anyone who had ever violated this tenet, and he knew that killing Baran today was one of the few things he could do to destroy his own supremacy in the Society.

"Shall we proceed?" Kiloran suggested.

Baran leaned forward, grinning again. "You'd love to kill me right now, wouldn't you? Doesn't it just eat at your heart? Doesn't even *your* blood run hot when you think of finally putting an end to me, old man?"

"Baran . . ." Kariman said uneasily.

"But maybe I'm wrong," Baran admitted. "Maybe nothing could warm your blood, you grizzly old reptile."

The horses at the trough suddenly whinnied in panic and danced away from it. Some assassins started shouting. Several drew their *shir*. Others responded, taking their weapons in hand, too. The other waterlords jumped to their feet. Kiloran knew what they saw even before he himself turned to look.

The water he had cleansed was boiling coldly with his rage, droplets spraying everywhere. Steam spewed skyward, the chilly mist of ensorcelled water dancing in a ghostly display of anger. And it took only this small manifestation of sudden fury from one of their masters to push all the assassins to the brink of violence.

Baran folded his arms, leaned back, and laughed.

"Stop it," Gulstan insisted, glaring at Kiloran. "This is a truce meeting!"

Searlon was shouting orders, demanding the assassins disarm. To make his point, he knocked down an assassin of Dulien's who didn't immediately obey.

Kiloran regarded Baran with real displeasure. "Are you satisfied now?"

"Satisfaction is such a thorough word," Baran replied. "Let's just say I'm pleased."

Kiloran willed his fury to subside. The water responded by sinking tranquilly back into the trough. The silvery mist blew away. The assassins all hesitated, then slowly began backing away from each other. Searlon offered a hand to the man he had knocked down and helped him to his feet. The horses danced nervously while the men tried to calm them. The waterlords resumed their seats, one by one.

Kiloran decided he'd had enough. "I have no more time to waste with you," he advised Baran. "Your cooperation with us isn't needed enough to—"

"That's what Wyldon thought."

Kiloran paused. "What?"

"That his cooperation wasn't needed," Baran said casually. He saw Kiloran's puzzled frown. "Oh, didn't I mention? Wyldon was my other visitor."

"Wyldon has been to Belitar?" Kiloran didn't believe it. Nothing could convince Wyldon, or any other sane waterlord, to enter Baran's lair.

"Not exactly to Belitar, I must admit." Baran smiled. "As hard as this may be for you to believe, he doesn't trust me."

"Imagine that," Gulstan murmured.

"We met nearby, in Sanctuary." Baran sighed. "He was so distressed. So angry. I tried to appeal to him on your behalf, truly I did, but nothing could calm him down."

"Go on," Kiloran prodded impatiently.

"He's not going to forgive you for the night you sent six assassins to his stronghold to kill him."

"What?" Meriten blurted.

"Well," Baran added casually, "he thinks it was six, but he admits that things were very confusing, and it might have been four. Or maybe eight."

"*What?*" Dulien said.

"I didn't—" Kiloran suddenly realized. Six of his men missing ever since they'd gone after Tansen . . .

Oh, the *shatai* was clever. He knew that the other waterlords would suspect Kiloran of the attack no matter what he said; and he knew that Kiloran wouldn't explain he'd lost six assassins, *shir* and all, trying to ambush Tansen. It was hardly an admission designed to increase the others' respect for him, after all.

"It seems that one of your assassins left a *shir* behind," Baran said. "Very careless. But I can see how the poor fellow might have forgotten it, given that he'd just used it to gut one of those hideous sculptures that Wyldon's so proud of. Frankly, they even give *me* nightmares." He shook his head sadly. "Someone really needs to be honest with Wyldon about his art, but I fear my heart's just too tender for the task."

The five other waterlords flew into a fury.

Dulien jumped to his feet again. "You sent assassins after Wyldon?"

"Who are you planning to attack next?"

Gulstan said, "So you finally got tired of waiting for him to die?"

"Are your assassins invading my territory even now? Is that why you wanted me to come all this way to watch you declare a truce with this madman?"

"I resent that," Baran protested.

"You tried to kill Wyldon, Kiloran?"

Meriten argued, "If he did, it's not our concern."

"Watch out, you spineless sycophant," Gulstan warned, "you'll be next."

Kiloran heard Searlon's voice raised again, warning the assassins against using their *shir*. The agitated shouts of their masters were urging their blood to violence again. They circled and stalked each other as the waterlords continued arguing.

"This meeting is just a pretense, isn't it?"

"We mustn't turn on each other now. This is exactly what—"

"Wyldon is a fool who deserves whatever happ—"

"And will we say that about *you* next?"

Through the chaos, Baran smiled at Kiloran. His now-thin and surprisingly lined face was rich with laughter and satisfaction as he said, "We really don't get together often enough, do we?"

28

ALLIES NEED NOT BE FRIENDS.

—Kiloran

BARAN'S INSIDES BURNED with the dull, ever-present physical pain which was becoming increasingly difficult to ignore, but he was nonetheless thoroughly enjoying the spectacle of half a dozen waterlords and more than thirty assassins all at each other's throats. The rage which lived inside Baran was the only thing stronger than his endless sorrow, and it fed off their hatred and suspicion, their mistrust and enmity, their short-tempered intolerance and cold-blooded greed.

While Gulstan demanded an explanation of Kiloran's attack on Wyldon, his fat face growing red with fury, Baran blessed the impulse that had led Wyldon to seek his support. Baran was the only waterlord alive who had ever challenged Kiloran. Oh, there had been others, to be sure; but Baran was the only one still *alive*. So Kiloran's enemies always sought Baran's support. Josarian, Wyldon, Tansen . . . they were just the most recent petitioners for his friendship. Every enemy of Kiloran's—and there had been more than a few during the dozen years Baran had openly opposed the old water-lord—came to him sooner or later.

Baran ignored most of them. He neither needed nor wanted their friendship. He didn't care whose territories Kiloran threatened or stole, whose relatives Kiloran killed or abducted, whose honor Kiloran impugned or offended. He didn't want Kiloran's territory for his own, he had no interest in winning the loyalty of Kiloran's men, and he was indifferent to Kiloran's wealth.

Baran cared for one thing and one thing alone: vengeance. Personal, private, and profound vengeance. Apart from that, nothing and no one mattered. He needed no friend, no ally who could not actively further his quest for revenge.

While the waterlords shouted all around him, Baran idly fingered the necklace—Kintish silver with jade inlays—which he had worn ever since Kiloran destroyed his world, years ago.

Ah, well, at least a little amusement, now and then, made this bitter thing called life so much more bearable. Wyldon's seething, self-righteous anger, when he met with Baran in Sanctuary, had been wonderful. And the pleasure of delivering Wyldon's scathing denouncement to Kiloran, in front of five other waterlords at a truce meeting—well! Baran hadn't enjoyed anything this much in years.

Above all, it delighted him to make Kiloran angry, to drive him to an indiscreet display of rage, to unsettle his icy demeanor with a verbal ambush. Baran was pleased to see proof today that he had improved significantly at this over the years. There was a time, long ago, when Baran would rage with helpless frustration and blind fury while Kiloran remained cool and indifferent. Even now, the memory of those days was like a merciless fist around Baran's heart. How wonderfully satisfying it was now to make Kiloran angry, appalled, and alarmed, all in one day. Why, this was such a delicious feeling, it almost inspired Baran to let Kiloran live a few more years, just to enjoy the sheer pleasure of tormenting him now and then.

The sudden grip of fire on Baran's vitals, however, reminded him that he didn't have a few years. When Tansen's emissary, Sister Velikar, discovered him vomiting blood in the damp ruins of Belitar, she had examined him. He hadn't permitted it, but she had done it anyhow. It would take more than a waterlord to menace Velikar, Baran discovered; and since she was a Sister, he couldn't harm or kill her when she ignored his commands and threats. There were certain rules governing life in Sileria which even Baran obeyed, and the inviolability of the Sisters and their Sanctuaries was among them.

Anyhow, Velikar's pronouncements about his illness, like her prescriptions for its treatment, would have terrified a man who had something to live for. If there was anything human left in Baran's soul, though, it had been yearning for death for years and would embrace it when it finally came—as, indeed, Velikar believed it soon would.

The rest of him, though . . . the rest of him craved fulfillment of a monumental goal and raged against the possibility of dying before it was achieved.

Baran had denied his own affable nature, forsaken his clan and his family, consecrated his life to vengeance, and helped reshape the destiny of Sileria, all so that he could destroy Kiloran. The risks he had taken in pursuit of this dream defied all reason. The dedication Baran had brought to the art and craft of Kiloran's own sorcery eventually made him one of the most powerful waterlords who had ever lived. The ruthlessness he had employed in carving out his place in the Society would make the man he used to be sick with horror, wild with shame, demented with guilt. But that genial man had died years ago; Kiloran had ensured that. All that remained now was the merciless and half-mad waterlord who lived only to destroy Kiloran and who would do anything, hurt anyone, and risk everything to accomplish this.

If Velikar was right, though—and he supposed she was, because surely no one could feel this way who wasn't mortally ill—then he had little time left to achieve the goal to which he had dedicated his life, the ultimate ambition which had already led him to do so many extraordinary things.

He must discover the best way to have his vengeance before he died. No matter what it took. No matter who he had to betray or how many of Sileria's laws and customs he would ultimately violate, he meant to see Kiloran die before he did.

The immediate question was, of course, should he side with Tansen's seemingly hopeless war against the Society, or accept Kiloran's offer of a truce? He looked at the quarreling waterlords surrounding him and searched for some inspiration about what path he should take.

Not surprisingly, Dulien decided to go home and sulk. He turned his back on the other waterlords and ordered his assassins to prepare to ride out. Gulstan—who was probably just bluffing—announced he was leaving, too. Then Kariman, who never bluffed and who had a lot to lose if Kiloran moved against him, rose to leave, too. Meriten, who knew where his cup was filled, stayed by Kiloran. Ferolen, possibly the most tedious man in Sileria, just kept shouting that Kiloran owed him an explanation. Kiloran looked as if his head ached.

This is going so well. I must remember to send Wyldon a gift.

"Aren't you going to stop them, *siran?*" Meriten demanded as three waterlords and nearly twenty assassins began mounting their horses.

"Is anyone hungry?" Baran asked. "I find all this excitement has stimulated my appetite. I don't suppose there's anything to eat in this Darforsaken place?"

This use of the goddess's name made Ferolen stumble briefly over his words, but he quickly recovered. "What is between you and Wyldon is your own affair, Kiloran, but I—"

"Yes," Kiloran interrupted, speaking at last. "It is."

"But not exclusively," Baran pointed out cheerfully. "After all, he does want me to help him kill you."

That finally shut Ferolen up. He stared at Baran with mingled curiosity and exasperation. Meriten's eyes narrowed.

"When you do that," Baran informed Meriten, "it makes you look a little like a wild boar. Strange that I hadn't noticed the resemblance until—"

"This is a truce meeting," Meriten snapped. "If you came here to kill—"

"You wound me!" Baran spread his hands in supplication. "Would I do anything so crude as disgrace a truce meeting with violence?"

"No, of course not," Ferolen said. "Just bad manners, veiled threats, boorish behavior, de—"

"And unfounded accusations," Kiloran said coolly. When Meriten and Ferolen glanced at him in surprise, he added, "Do you really believe Wyldon would confide in him?"

"Oh, that's good," Baran said. "Very good."

"You want us to believe he's lying?" Ferolen asked.

Kiloran didn't bother to answer. Instead, he told Baran, "You weary me."

"That happens easily," Baran replied, "when you get to be old, fat, and forgetful."

"I forget nothing," Kiloran said, his voice chilling the very air. "No promise. No dream. No friend or enemy. No favor or insult." He leaned slightly towards Baran as he added, "No mistake."

Mistake.

The word cut through Baran like a *shir*. As it was no doubt intended to. To hear Kiloran speak so casually of what he had done, to use such a barren word as *mistake* . . . A red haze of rage clouded Baran's mind for a moment. For an instant, he was young and blind with white-hot anger, agonizing loss, violent sorrow . . .

"*No.*" He willed the feeling away, rejected the loss of control. He strangled the surge of devouring emotion which would have driven him mad long ago, had he given in to it.

But Kiloran knew. Kiloran had seen that brief moment of wild animal pain. He smiled, enjoying victory once again.

Now, Baran thought, *I could do it now. Who cares if it's forbidden? Who cares if they all descend on me and kill me right here, as long as he dies first?*

He called to the water in the fountain, that tainted, sad water which Josarian had used so ruthlessly to defeat his enemies. Baran touched it now with his senses and coaxed it to his will . . . Only to find it was already in someone else's grasp.

"Damn you," he whispered, feeling the sting of Kiloran's sorcery in conflict with his own. He knew the sensation of Kiloran's magic well, having felt it daily throughout their years-long war for control of the Idalar River.

Kiloran was still stronger, still the best. Baran could challenge him and survive. Baran could seize hold of Kiloran's water and cling to it with ferocious tenacity, violating Kiloran's command of it, mitigating his power. But Baran couldn't take the Idalar away from him, no matter how hard he tried. Now Kiloran had grasped Emeldar's central fountain before Baran reached for it, and Baran couldn't take this away either.

Baran might have fought for it, might have let this be the day he killed Kiloran or died trying . . . but fiery pain suddenly seized his innards. The world disappeared as he squeezed his eyes shut, clenched his jaw, and tried not to cry out in agony.

"Thank you." The voice was Kiloran's, satisfied and snide. He had felt Baran lose his grasp of the fountain's waters. Perhaps he even thought Baran had let go willingly.

He must master the pain. Mustn't let them see he was ill. He should have chewed some of those disgusting leaves of Velikar's before entering the village. Oh, well, too late to worry about it now. All he could do now was invoke the iron will which had made him who and what he was.

"You're welcome," he murmured, hoping his voice sounded dry rather than pain-fogged. He opened his eyes but kept his gaze lowered. "I wouldn't want to be rude."

A moment later, he heard Ferolen gasp. The gush of water filled Baran's ears as the sudden flare of sorcery filled his senses. If he didn't hate Kiloran so much, he would admire him; there was a time, actually, when he had. Now he heard Meriten rise to his feet, heard assassins shouting. As the pain faded, slowly receding into a dull ache, he finally looked up, though he could already guess what was happening.

A tower of water rose straight up from the fountain to loom over the square. At its peak, it divided into hundreds of strands which shot through the air, curving gracefully as they descended to touch the ground all around the square. An impressive spectacle, Baran acknowledged in silence, and one which effectively made a watery cage of Emeldar. Although most of the riders reined in their mounts, one frightened horse lost its wits and careened straight into the silvery glowing bars which stood between it and the rest of Sileria. Baran winced as he heard the solid *thud* of horse and rider hitting crystallized water.

"Ouch." He told Kiloran, "I don't like to criticize, but you could cause ill feeling with tricks like that."

"Oh, do shut up," Ferolen snapped.

"Are you always this edgy," Baran asked, "or do I bring it out in you?"

"You bring it out in everyone," Meriten muttered.

Gulstan bellowed in outrage. His voice carried clearly across the square as he ordered, "Stop this at once or we will respond in kind!"

"Oh, this should be good," Baran crooned. "I can't tell you how glad I am that I came here tod—"

"It'll be a bloodbath," Meriten snapped.

"Exactly," Baran said. "You're keeping up better than I expected."

Meriten's eyes iced over with fury. "If you—"

"That's enough," Kiloran said. "From all of you." The old waterlord caught Searlon's eye and nodded.

"*Sirani,*" Searlon said, raising his voice to be heard above the threats of the trapped waterlords and their assassins. "My master means you no harm. Let us all remember that this is a truce meeting." He glanced briefly over his shoulder at Baran, his handsome, scarred face disdainful. "And let us also remember that only one waterlord present is actually my master's enemy."

"I wish I had one like him," Baran remarked pleasantly. "But then, of course, so does everyone in Sileria." It was common knowledge that even some of the lesser waterlords feared Searlon—and all of the Society's assassins did.

"Unfortunately for you," Meriten advised him, "a waterlord must be wise and, oh, *sane* to command an assassin of Searlon's abilities."

"Why, Meriten," Baran said, "that was almost amusing. If you keep working at it, you may soon stop being the dreariest cuckold I've ever met. And speaking of your wife, tell her I—"

Meriten made an inarticulate sound of rage and leaped for Baran. Baran tried to block the first blow, but he was too slow. Meriten drove him to the ground. Baran fought back, but he could tell how his illness was weakening him. His defense was ineffectual, and Meriten's hands around his neck were making his vision go dark. Fortunately, someone plucked Meriten off him.

Choking and trying to conceal how shaken he was, Baran gasped for air. When his vision started to clear, he saw one of his own assassins, Vinn, holding a *shir* to Meriten's throat. As his gaze focused, he realized he was surrounded by seven or eight assassins now, all loyal to different masters, all with their *shir* drawn as they tried to decide what to do.

"Well." Baran suddenly felt very weary. "That was interesting."

"Get up," Ferolen snapped.

When Baran spoke this time, still lying on the ground, it was to conceal that he needed time to gather strength before he could rise to his feet. "Do you know, Ferolen, from this angle, you don't look nearly so bald."

Ferolen's face contorted in a truly splendid surge of sputtering vexation. Baran eyed him doubtfully, but the waterlord stepped back rather than giving in to the impulse to kick him while he was down.

"Shall I kill him, *siran?*" Vinn asked Baran, still holding his *shir* to Meriten's throat. The jade-and-silver inlays, which always made Baran's *shir* among the most easily identified in Sileria, gleamed beautifully on the hilt of Vinn's wavy-edged dagger.

Meriten stood very still, as vulnerable as anyone was to a *shir*. But, red-faced with rage, he ordered his men, "If I die here, kill them all! Kill them all!"

"You're going to upset people with talk like that." Feeling a little stronger, Baran now rose to his feet. "This *is* a truce meeting," he admonished.

"And you have no idea," Kiloran murmured, gazing at Baran with interest, "how much I regret that at this moment."

Baran wondered if Kiloran knew, if he had guessed. Concealing his worry, like his weakness, he grinned. "When did you decide to start practicing honesty?"

The old man ignored the question and turned away to walk into the center of the square, stout, white-haired, dignified, and imbued with immense power. Yes, even Baran had to admit that Kiloran looked impressive as he stood at the center of his own high-domed water-born prison and addressed the other waterlords.

"I sent no one against Wyldon," he said, "and I vow to punish any of my men who took any action against him."

"Rogue assassins?" Baran guessed loudly. "Growing wild and bold as their master grows old and feeble?"

Kiloran ignored him. "However, without Wyldon here, instead of Baran, to speak for himself . . . Without the *shir* which Baran claims is proof that my men were involved . . . Without a Sister present to tell us that Wyldon and Baran did indeed meet at her Sanctuary, as Baran claims . . ." He shrugged. "Who can say what really happened?"

The others were great water wizards, powerful sorcerers who ruled whole territories, commanded hundreds of assassins, and made thousands submit to their will and their whims. But Kiloran was still the greatest, blessed with a fierce, deep, and finely honed power which awed even them. Individually, none of them could escape this prison, while Kiloran lived, unless he willed it. Even working together, they might not be able to break his power and melt the watery bars of this vast cage without Baran's help. With Baran's help, however, they could probably even kill Kiloran if they all united against him; but that kind of unity among them was no more likely than a Sister massacring a whole village. Besides, although none of them personally remembered the chaos which followed Harlon's death forty years ago, all of them knew about it. If Kiloran died violently today at his own truce meeting, the Society would erupt with such ruinous internal violence that Tansen wouldn't have to bother destroying them; they'd do it themselves.

These men knew all of this. Baran could see them consider their options and, one by one, decide that accepting Kiloran's word, rather than Baran's, might be the best choice. For the time being, anyhow.

Kariman, the most sensible of the three departing waterlords, was the first to dismount. He crossed the square, stood directly before Kiloran, and announced, "Perhaps we were too hasty."

"Possibly something distressed you enough to affect your judgment," Kiloran suggested dryly.

Gulstan spoke loudly from his horse. "Forgive me for pointing out the obvious," he said to Kiloran, "but it's your fault that we can't kill him today."

Baran laughed. "Well, you *could* . . . But only think how happy that would make Tansen. All the chaos. All the mistrust and fighting amongst yourselves after my disgraceful murder at a truce meeting. All the condemnation and retribution from the rest of the Society." He nodded. "Yes, if I were going to accept Tansen's offer of friendship and wholeheartedly devote myself to his cause, I think I'd try to get you all to kill me today. He'd be very happy with the results."

Dulien remarked, "Still, it might be worth the risk."

Searlon, seeing sudden movement among the men, said, "There will be no killing here today." His was a voice which commanded more attention than half the waterlords Baran had met.

Gulstan dismounted now, too, and said, "Perhaps Baran's tale about Wyldon's accusations is indeed best ignored for now."

Everyone present seemed to agree, and, as they all dismounted, the tension slowly dissolved. When Kiloran saw that the meeting would go forward according to his desires, he closed his eyes, inhaled deeply, and released the water. The crystal-hard bars melted, curled upward, and soared towards the sky, glaring blindingly under the brilliant sun. One by one, with a speed and grace that made Baran recall his earliest attraction to water magic, they coiled inward and dissolved into the towering pillar of water which rose from the fountain, then it sank slowly in upon itself, giving off a faint glittering mist as it came to rest at last.

Baran shrugged, uninterested in pressing Wyldon's argument on his behalf. If Kiloran meant to kill Wyldon, that was Wyldon's problem, not Baran's. Besides, Baran realized with sudden amusement, there was always the faint possibility that Kiloran was actually telling the truth and knew nothing about the assault on Wyldon's stronghold.

Baran hoped so. It would make this entire volatile scene today all the richer and more delightful in his memory.

Now Kiloran turned to him, impatience revealed in those dark, flat, snakelike eyes. "Will you accept my offer of a truce? Will you become my ally until our enemies are destroyed?"

Baran shook his head. "No, that's not what you really came here to ask me, old man."

Kiloran's lips thinned. "Will you release the Idalar River to my control so that I may ensure that the city belongs to the Society and not to Josarian's people?"

"You really should have thought of these problems before you killed him," Baran chided.

Kiloran's eyes narrowed. "What's done is done. What is your answer? Are you with us or against us? Will you come home to your own kind?"

"The Guardians are with Tansen," Meriten reminded him, as if anyone in Sileria might have forgotten, "and there can only be one victor."

"Fire sorcery and water magic cannot exist together in Sileria," Kariman said. "Not anymore."

"Certainly not since the leader of the Society murdered the Firebringer," Baran agreed reasonably.

"You have no future with them," Kiloran said, ignoring the jibe. "They are not your friends. They cannot be, and they know it. They will use you, abandon you, and finally destroy you."

"All right, I'm confused," Baran said to Kiloran. "*How* would that be different from your friendship?"

"This isn't about you and me. It can't be. And I know you understand that, no matter what kind of games you play," Kiloran said. "Everything is at stake now, Baran. The destiny of Sileria. The future of the Society. The continued existence of the waterlords." Baran felt some of the old man's undeniable charisma as he came closer and insisted, "Water magic itself will now perish or survive in Sileria, based on whether we let Tansen and his followers destroy us, or we destroy them."

Baran almost flinched when Kiloran reached for him, took him by the shoulders, and held him at arm's length like a father imploring a recalcitrant son to listen and understand. It had been a long time since they had stood this close together; even longer since Kiloran had laid a hand upon him in friendship.

But this wasn't friendship. Kiloran had no friends; not now, not then, not ever. This was coercion. And Baran had forgotten how good Kiloran was at it.

"This thing between us," Kiloran said, his voice as warm as it had been in the days when Baran had trusted him, "will be finished someday; but you and I should finish it." His fingers tightened and his voice grew stronger as he demanded, "Do you really want Tansen to finish it for you?"

"No," Baran said honestly. "I don't want Tansen or anyone else to finish it for me."

"Then come home," Kiloran urged. "Join us, join me, in securing the future." He nodded. "After we have put our house in order, then we can afford to fight within the Society. But for now, we must stand un—"

"United against our enemies," Baran said, "for this is what makes us stronger than they, what makes us endure while they perish."

"Do you accept the truce?" Kiloran asked.

Baran nodded. "I accept the truce."

"Will you relinquish control of the Idalar to me?"

"Ah." Baran smiled slowly. "Perhaps if we cooperated . . ."

"Release it," Kiloran demanded.

"He has accepted the truce and offered to cooperate," Kariman pointed out. "That's enough."

"It's not enough," Kiloran insisted. "Shaljir must—"

"Working together," Gulstan said with obvious relish, "you can starve the city of water. Baran has said he will cooperate."

"If his friendship is secure," Dulien said to Kiloran, "why should you demand that he give up his power?"

Baran smiled innocently at Kiloran, thoroughly enjoying the moment. "Shall we confirm our alliance, *siran*?"

He saw the old man struggle with his disappointment and anger. "If you betray me—"

"You'll kill me the way you killed Josarian?" Baran shrugged. "You can certainly try."

Kiloran prodded, "And you vow to help us destroy Tansen?"

"I'll even help you destroy Mirabar," he offered. "Although the rumor out of Zilar is that she's currently well protected by . . . Now who was it again?" Baran snapped his fingers. "Oh, yes! Najdan the assassin. Now isn't that interesting?"

The other waterlords were clearly surprised by this news. So much for the quality of their informants. Kiloran's pasty face seemed to go even paler as his jaw worked, but he held his silence.

"So really," Baran mused, "I suppose there are actually several possible explanations for how one of your *shir* wound up buried in the, er, body of one of Wyldon's hideous sentries. Hmmm?"

"I will deal with Wyldon," Kiloran said coldly. "And also with Najdan."

"And what shall I do?"

"Go home to Belitar. Await my signal. Prepare to pull the Idalar out of Shaljir." Kiloran paused and said with a touch of malice, "I imagine you'll need to rest and save your strength."

So the old man had indeed noticed something. Baran wondered just how much he had guessed. No doubt he would soon attempt to find out more. Fortunately, no one but Velikar knew, and she had promised not to talk. She might be a dreadful woman, but Baran felt certain she kept her promises.

"What about Tansen and Mirabar?" Baran asked.

"Yes," Kiloran said. "We must consider precisely how to eliminate them. But first . . ." The bucket of drinking water which rested in the shade roiled noisily in response to Kiloran's magic. A slender tendril of water arose from it and snaked through the air. "First, shall we confirm our alliance before these witnesses?"

"By all means."

Kiloran extended his arm to Baran, who took it in an elbow clasp. The old man's physical strength had ebbed and weakened over the years, but his sorcery had only grown stronger; Baran was aware of both things now as the snaking tendril of water started coiling around their clasped forearms.

It flowed continuously, never resting, twining and re-twining coldly around their warm flesh as they recited their vows.

"I swear . . ." Kiloran began.

"I swear . . ." Baran echoed, caught in the web of the old man's power, drawn into the seductive beauty of the sorcery they both commanded with a skill unknown to anyone else alive.

". . . by the power born in me, by the cold purity of the . . .

". . . of the element with which I rule men, women, children, even the land itself . . .

". . . by the ancient secrets of water magic entrusted to me and by the inviolable laws of the Honored Society . . .

". . . that I will honor this truce now declared between us, until we vanquish our enemies. I will not harm you . . .

". . . or your friends, or the friends of your friends . . .

". . . until the blood of our enemies flows . . .

". . . even as this water flows now."

Baran felt the water which twined around their joined arms grow even colder with Kiloran's sorcery, so cold that an ordinary man's arm would be damaged by it.

"If you betray me," Kiloran warned, "noth—"

"As you once betrayed me?" Baran suggested, flooded anew with hatred.

The frigid watery coil tightened, squeezing hard. A man would be in agony. Even a waterlord should be uncomfortable now. But Baran was not just anyone, and the hot flood of hatred brought a return of his strength. Smiling coldly into Kiloran's dark eyes, Baran started melting the water which bound them.

"I taught you well," Kiloran observed, struggling for supremacy, holding onto the water with his will, freezing it even as Baran melted it. The water glowed and writhed in torment as they wrestled for control of it.

"You were his teacher?" Meriten blurted, reminding them of the others' presence.

"Now we know who to blame," Dulien grumbled.

Ferolen sputtered, "You— You— You made him a waterlord? *You're* the one who—"

"Made him what he is," Kiloran agreed with a flash of bitterness.

Baran laughed, enjoying the moment, feeling revived. "You don't really believe *you* taught me everything I know, old man?"

The comment startled Kiloran enough to distract him from the liquid shackles binding them together. Baran felt the old wizard's will fall away from the icy coil around their arms. Pleased, Baran melted the water. It dissolved into a silvery mist, freeing him from Kiloran's grasp.

"So you had another teacher," Kiloran murmured thoughtfully. "Of course. That explains a great deal that used to puzzle me."

"How I became so powerful based only on what I learned from you?" Baran suggested.

"Yes."

"At least," Ferolen said to Kiloran, "you evidently had the sense to stop teaching him when you realized what a madma—"

"No, that's not what happened," Baran said, the steel in his voice making Ferolen look at him with surprise.

"Who else taught you?" Kiloran asked, curious enough to betray his interest.

"Good question," Ferolen said. "Who in all of Sileria would be fool enough—"

"Perhaps it was someone," Baran interrupted, "tired of teaching mediocre half-wits, Ferolen." He smiled sweetly and added, "For example."

"Keep in mind," Ferolen warned, "that *I* have not sworn a truce with you."

"If you had the guts to attack me, you'd have done it years ago," Baran said dismissively.

"I've never known who taught you, Baran," Gulstan remarked, raising his voice a little to be heard above Ferolen's sputtering. "And I've always wondered."

"Come to think of it," Kariman added, "I've never known either."

"I always assumed he killed whoever taught him," Dulien muttered.

"And now we know he's tried," Meriten said with a pointed glance at Kiloran. "So maybe he did kill his next teacher."

"I do so enjoy being a man of mystery," Baran said, delighting in Kiloran's scrutiny.

The old wizard shrugged and feigned indifference well. "It doesn't matter now," he said to the others, "does it?"

"And there are so many things in a man's past," Baran murmured, "are there not, *siran?*"

"So many things best left in the past where they always belonged," Kiloran said with deceptive gentleness.

Baran felt it again, as Kiloran meant him to—the hot sorrow of his loss, the futile rage of his helplessness, the murderous frustration inspired by Kiloran's casual indifference to all he had destroyed.

"And so many things yet to avenge," Baran whispered, his voice choked with wild fury.

The threat hovered in the air between them. Kiloran did not deign to reply. His flat eyes merely gazed back at Baran, cold and hard. Snake eyes. Dragonfish eyes. The eyes of a man born without a heart, without a soul. A man who could hurt without regret, betray without shame, destroy without compassion.

The man I've become, too.

The man Baran had made of himself, because it was the only way he could ever become strong enough to destroy the man he now faced.

The other waterlords stared at the two of them in fascinated silence. A breeze swept through the village of Emeldar, stirring Baran's hair, carrying the scents of the mountains to him: The scents of his youth; of everyone's youth.

He lowered his gaze, wracked with sorrow.

"Dare I point out," Meriten said, his voice unusually nasty, "that you've just declared a truce and made your vows before witnesses?"

The tension in the air exhausted Baran. The illness riddling his body consumed his strength. The taste of his life was like ashes in his dry mouth.

"Then our business here is concluded, isn't it?" Baran said. "Much as I regret it, I find I must tear myself away from the pleasures of your company and return to Belitar." He smiled whimsically and added, "Tansen's delightful messenger is still waiting around for my answer to his offer of friendship."

"Ah," Kiloran said, showing some interest. "Then you have sent no answer yet?"

"Didn't I just say so, old man? Do try to keep up."

Ferolen snapped, "Must you be such a—"

"Leave it," Kiloran advised Ferolen. He glanced briefly at Baran and added, "He knows what to do now."

Baran arched one brow. "I know what *you* would do."

"Exactly."

"Ah." Baran considered this. "I am to be the poisoned goat?"

"The what?" Kariman said.

"The poisoned goat?" Meriten repeated.

Baran glanced their way. "In the jungles south of Kinto, when villages are troubled by a man-eating tiger, they leave a poisoned goat tethered to a tree at sunset."

"And what the tiger takes for an easy meal," Kariman surmised, "is really his death in disguise?"

"Yes."

"You've been to the Kintish Kingdoms?" Gulstan asked.

"One of or two of them," he replied vaguely.

"Then you did come from a merchant family, as some say?" Gulstan persisted. "Traveled and traded a bit?"

Baran ignored the waterlord's interest in his past and said to Kiloran, "So I am to make Tansen lower his guard, and then what? Kill him?"

"When the time comes, I'll deal with Tansen myself."

"Ah. Then it's true." Baran smiled and pretended a malicious pleasure he was too weary to feel now. "It's personal. What did he do to you, I wonder?"

Kiloran, of course, ignored this. "You will deal with Mirabar."

"A great sorceress like that? You flatter me, *siran*."

"No, I don't think I do," Kiloran said dryly.

"And regardless of who survives, Mirabar or me, you'll have solved at least one problem when it's done."

Kiloran shrugged. "Of course, if you really feel you're not up to it . . ."

"Oh, that's good," Baran said. "Very good."

"Well?"

Baran caught Vinn's eye and nodded. "Well, the sooner I return home, the sooner we can kill Mirabar, starve Shaljir of water, and bring down Tansen." As his assassin came to his side, he said to the six waterlords before him, "I can't tell you all what a pleasure this has been."

"I know that I shan't soon forget it," Kariman replied.

"Nor do I hope to repeat it," Gulstan added.

"Until we meet again," Baran said to Kiloran. "Which, I sincerely hope, will be when I kill you, old man."

"May the wind be at your back," Kiloran murmured.

A blessing of the sea-born.

Baran's breath stopped. He thought his heart must have stopped. Rage misted his vision. His stomach churned and his throat knotted.

He stared at the grizzled old waterlord in speechless fury for a long, hot moment. Then a *shallah* blessing he hadn't heard—let alone used—in many years came to his lips. "May your son bring you honor and . . . Oops!" he said cheerfully. "Too late for that, isn't it?"

Baran heard someone—he didn't see who—gasp in shock over this callous reference to Srijan's death. He smiled in bitter triumph as Kiloran's dead eyes revealed more emotion than he had ever before seen in them. "Oh, dear, how thoughtless of me," Baran murmured. "Do forgive me, *siran*."

"Get out." Kiloran's voice was flat.

"I fear I've touched a sore spot," Baran confessed to Vinn.

"Then perhaps we should indeed leave, *siran*," the assassin replied, keeping a watchful eye on Kiloran.

"You don't think I should stay and try to cheer him up?"

"With respect, *siran*," Vinn said, "I don't advise it."

Baran shrugged. "Of course, he should have anticipated what happened. If you betray someone like Josarian, you've got to expect retaliation. Don't you agree, Vinn?"

"Get out," Kiloran repeated.

"Oh, very well. If you're going to take that attitude." Baran sighed and turned away, pleased with the taut silence among the waterlords as he walked away from them. All the way across the main square of Emeldar, he could feel Kiloran's gaze burning into his back. He suspected that never had the old man wanted to kill him quite as much as he did at that very moment.

Baran and his two assassins mounted their horses, then headed east out of Josarian's abandoned village, still aware of the tension in their wake.

"Now that was a very entertaining day," Baran said. "Wouldn't you agree, Vinn?"

"It's always an entertaining day when I am with you, *siran,*" the assassin replied. "But today . . . Yes, today was especially good."

29

I AM PREPARED TO DIE TODAY. ARE YOU?

—Tansen

THE NIGHT FELL hard on Mirabar, frustrating her plans at the end of another long day of travel.

Ejara, the second moon, had finally abandoned the night sky. She was not even a sliver-thin crescent overhead anymore. Her absence heralded the end of yet another cycle in the wheel of time which spun as smoothly and relentlessly in this world as it did in the Other one. It was dark of the moons now, nights of syrupy blackness when no ordinary person ventured far from his hearth. In these extraordinary times, however, being ordinary was a luxury which hardly anyone in Sileria could afford.

Tonight Mirabar, Najdan, Pyron, and their companions were camped high up on the steep and treacherous slopes of Mount Niran. They had hoped to reach the Guardian encampment today, but the consuming black of a dark-moon sky made Pyron suggest forcefully that they stop for the night before someone broke an ankle or fell off a cliff. Although longing to speak with Tashinar as soon as possible, Mirabar agreed to stop and make camp for the night.

Far from Sanctuary, exposed and vulnerable, they lit no fire tonight, lest unseen enemies be lurking somewhere in the dark. Najdan lay down to rest almost immediately after eating a cold meal of bread, cheese, smoked meat, olives, and figs. He would rise in a few hours to assume sentry duty during the empty hours when other men were most apt to be sleepy and dull-witted.

Too restless to sleep yet, Mirabar joined Pyron where he perched on a rocky outcrop and kept watch with ears rather than eyes in the impenetrable dark. She heard him shift slightly as she approached him, undoubtedly alerted by her soft footstep. He drew a sharp breath through his nostrils, then sighed in evident relief. "It's you."

"It's me," she agreed.

"Darfire."

"What?" she asked in a whisper.

After a slight hesitation, Pyron admitted, "Your eyes. I used to think they were reflecting firelight or moonlight at night. But I was wrong. They glow on their own."

Since she heard him dusting off a spot on the boulder for her even as he spoke in low tones, she didn't take offense. "Don't bother, I'm dusty already," she whispered, sinking to a sitting position without waiting for him to finish clearing a spot.

"Is something wrong?" he asked, his voice barely audible. It wasn't like her to seek his company.

"No, I'm just . . ."

"Eager to get to the Guardian encampment," he guessed.

She nodded. Then, realizing he probably couldn't see the gesture, she whispered, "Yes."

"Is it far?" Pyron asked.

"The encampment? No. If there were any light tonight, it would have been worth it to press on until we reached it."

Mirabar could have lit the way for them, of course, but Najdan was firmly against so boldly exposing her presence here before reaching the safety of the Guardian encampment. On a night like this, there was no telling who crept stealthily through the darkness on the other side of the fire, and Najdan saw no point in courting trouble.

"Your . . ." Pyron paused. "Your teacher is there?"

"Yes. Tashinar."

"What is she like?"

Mirabar smiled briefly as she considered the question. "Very unlike me," she replied at last. "Calm. Wise. Gentle."

"Old?"

"Yes. A respected elder of our sect. And very brave. She resisted Valdani torture once, long ago. Didn't talk even when they—" Pyron shushed her, and she stopped abruptly.

Together they listened in tense silence for a few long moments. Then he sighed and murmured, "Nothing." She continued listening to the thick darkness until he prodded, "Didn't talk even when they . . . ?"

"They took three of her fingers," Mirabar whispered, her attention still focused on the many subtle sounds of night in the mountains. "They left her for dead, lying in the dust somewhere between Cavasar and the Orban Pass. But she survived."

"Dar curse them and all th—"

"Shh!"

She felt Pyron's tension in the silence that followed, but when they still heard nothing, he finally whispered, "What?"

"I don't know," she said slowly.

She shivered suddenly, sure something was wrong. But what?

Then there was murmuring nearby, from their own companions. It frustrated her attempts to hear and distinguish every faint sound, and it exposed them to whatever she suddenly, blindly feared was out there in the dark.

"*Sirana?*" Najdan's voice.

"Quiet," she snapped loudly, knowing that he'd already revealed their location to anyone within earshot.

There was silence for a moment, and then she heard his approach. His voice, though soft, carried through the darkness to her. "What are you doing?"

"Nothing. Be quiet." Then the realization chilled her. "What woke you?"

"Someone is doing *some*thing," he said grimly.

"Your *shir*." Mirabar rose.

"Yes."

Pyron scrambled to his feet. "What *about* his *shir*?"

"It's not responding to me—I'm not doing anything." Mirabar turned and began picking her way through the dark, adding to Pyron, "You'd better come. We can't stay here."

"But—"

"We're still at some distance from them—"

"The Guardians?" Pyron asked, following her.

"Yes." She spoke at a normal volume now. The time for stealth had passed. "We're not *that* close. If his *shir* is responding to their magic, then—"

"Then," Najdan said, finding Mirabar's arm in the dark and helping her down from her stony perch, "they're invoking a great deal of it."

"That must be this . . . this . . ." Mirabar shook her head. "Whatever I'm feeling. It must be coming from them."

"They're under attack?" Pyron guessed.

"Yes." Najdan's reply was terse, his attention already fixed on the problem. "They must be. My *shir* is shaking so hard it will barely stay in my *jashar*."

"We've got to help them," Mirabar said, aware of the other men gathering around her as they realized what was happening.

"By fighting waterlords? How?" Pyron prodded. "By attacking assassins? How many? And *where*?"

"We've got to help them," Mirabar repeated.

"We cannot risk your safety, *sirana*," said one of the other men. "If there are assassins or waterlords attacking—"

"Then I will fight them, too," she insisted.

"Tansen said—"

"I'm in charge here," she snapped.

"No, you're not. Right now," Pyron pointed out, "Najdan's in charge."

He was right, she realized. Najdan knew more than any of them about what they were facing. They must accept his judgment and follow his orders.

"Najdan?" Mirabar prodded. When the assassin didn't respond, she gripped his thickly muscled arm and said in desperation, "Najdan, *please*. Tashinar is there!"

He hesitated, then briefly covered her hand with his. Coming to a sudden decision, he said, "We must act quickly, then."

RONALL AWOKE IN the dark, alerted by some sound. He lay there listening for a moment, wondering what had disturbed him, but he heard nothing else.

Whatever it was, though, he was wide awake now; moderately alert, albeit still pleasantly drunk. He had rested just enough to feel no interest in going right back to sleep.

With consciousness, however, came the increasingly predictable return of his endless longing. Longing for something. Longing for everything. Longing for *more*.

More Kintish fire brandy. More of the exceptionally good dreamweed he'd been lucky enough to acquire yesterday.... Two days ago? Last night? He wasn't sure. But it was good.

And more of the woman who'd ministered so skillfully to his needs after sundown.

He turned his head and smelled the clean linen of the bedclothes, now perfumed with the heavy scents of sex and sweat. He vaguely remembered bespeaking the sole spare bedchamber in this small, simple, respectable *tirshah* in ... Actually, no, he didn't remember what village he was in. It didn't matter, anyhow. Just another Darforsaken town of stone and dust somewhere in the Threeforsaken mountains of this godsforsaken country.

He did clearly remember, however, the shocked look on the face of the respectable old couple who ran the place when he boldly brought the woman of his choice (for the night) through the front door and commenced enjoying her right there in the public room.

The disdain and disgust on their faces was nothing compared to the way his own wife looked at him every day—

Get out! Get out! Get out!

—so it didn't bother Ronall in the least. His pretty companion, however, had suggested they continue their play in more private surroundings. He had agreed, laughing off the scandalized mutterings he heard behind him as he led the young woman up the stairs to his bedchamber.

Now he rolled over and reached for her.

The bed was empty.

Surprised, Ronall lifted his head and looked around. The room was amazingly dark tonight—dark-moon, he recalled—and the candles had guttered out. He started to speak the girl's name, thinking she might be there, but then realized he didn't know it.

"Are you still here?" he mumbled. "Hello?"

No answer.

He sat up and foggily wondered what had happened to her. She wasn't a professional on the prowl for more customers before the night was over. Outside of the major cities, there were hardly any prostitutes in Sileria; the rigid mores of the lowlanders and the *shallaheen* made life too uncomfortable for such women in rural areas. She was just some adventurous and poorly guarded peasant girl who had understood what was expected of her in exchange for the money Ronall had offered her.

A surprisingly *experienced* peasant girl, he recalled with a satisfied smile. One who gave damn good value for the money.

Oh, well. He now vaguely recalled her saying something about being a local *torena*'s maid, and he supposed she had felt obliged to return to her post before morning. Too bad. The night was no longer precisely young, but there was still plenty of it left.

With the mindless pleasures of the girl no longer available to him, Ronall's thirst suddenly got much stronger. He rose from the bed, carelessly pulled on his dirty and rumpled clothes, and stumbled around searching for his purse. The sour-faced old keepers of this *tirshah* were probably fast asleep by now, in the cold comfort of their joyless marriage bed, but Ronall would leave money for whatever he scavenged from their liquor supply downstairs. Although most of his moral standards were wallowing in the dust, he was nonetheless a *toren* and would not stoop to stealing from the *shallaheen* who owned this dreary little place.

After several fruitless attempts to lay his hands upon his dwindling supply of money, he found a candle and the flint box. Even the light didn't solve his problem, though, and that was when he finally realized.

That little slut stole all my money!

He had ceased caring about almost anything and wouldn't have minded if she'd taken a little more than what he'd already given her—but *all* of it?

"She wasn't *that* good," he muttered.

Women.

You could always count on them to make you feel like sheep dung.

His befuddled vexation turned to hot anger, however, when he discovered she had also taken all his remaining dreamweed.

That does it!

She wasn't going to get away with this. There were limits, after all!

The sound which had awoken him must have been that thieving whore making her escape. His liquor-soaked brain finally recalled the fact that he had a horse stabled in the tidy little lean-to out back; Elelar's long-suffering gelding was probably even getting used to the strange and unpredictable hours at which Ronall suddenly required its services. So all Ronall had to do was find out where the girl was going, and he had every chance of catching up with her and getting his belongings back. In fact, he decided with relish, after what she'd just done, he would positively *enjoy* humiliating her in front of her aristocratic employers, if she made it necessary.

Having determined his course of action, he picked up the candle and staggered out of the bedchamber, shouting for the keeper. The first door he came upon had voices coming from the other side of it, which was promising. Ronall kicked it down (which took several clumsy tries, actually), wishing the woman in the bedchamber he now entered wouldn't scream *quite* so shrilly.

The elderly keeper stood in the middle of his small, spare, tidy bedchamber staring wide-eyed at Ronall's abrupt entrance. The old woman in the bed—his wife—kept screaming.

"Where is she?" Ronall demanded.

"What?" the man cried. "Who? What?"

"*Yaggghhh!*" the woman shrieked.

"Make her stop that," Ronall said.

"Shhh, shhh," the man said to his wife. "*Kadriah,* please, please, stop, please stop, stop, shhh."

Kadriah. Ronall wasn't quite sure what it meant, though he knew it was a *shallah* endearment. One which signified devotion.

Get out! Get out! Get out!

He stood staring while the man tried to quiet his screaming wife. Envy suddenly filled Ronall at the sight of these two old, homely, poor *shallaheen* who had found what had always eluded him. He could see it so clearly now in the way the man tried to shield the woman from him. In the way the woman's plucking hands tried to prevent the man from shielding her at risk to himself. In the simple bed which they had undoubtedly shared for as long as Ronall had been alive. In the two pairs of worn shoes placed side by side on the floor.

"We have done nothing, *toren,* please, we have done nothing!" the old man insisted.

"Where is she?" Ronall demanded again, pulling his thoughts back to his purpose.

"Who?"

"The girl!"

"The one who, um . . . Who, um . . ."

"The one I took upstairs and bedded," Ronall supplied with growing impatience. "Where is she?"

The woman suddenly stopped screaming. The man stared at him blankly. Then the woman said to Ronall, in a voice rich with outrage, "You're looking for her? *That's* why you come bursting in here like some assassin—"

"She's a local girl, you must have recognized her," Ronall insisted.

"—come to murder us in our bed?"

The old man glanced at his wife, who was now shaking with anger rather than terror, and he said, "Actually, no, *toren,* she didn't look familiar."

"This is a respectable place!" the woman shrieked. "We don't see the likes of her in a place like this!"

Ronall's head was starting to ache. "Nonetheless—"

"How dare you!" the old woman screamed, jumping out of bed now and advancing on him with finger-wagging fury. "How dare you profane my house with lewd behavior and then have the gall to terrify me in my own b—"

"She stole my purse," Ronall advised her.

"I don't care if she . . ." The woman paused. "Your purse?"

"My money."

"Your money?"

"*All* my money," he elaborated helpfully.

The old woman scowled at him in exasperation. He had not paid for his bedchamber in advance.

She licked her lips and said with obvious distaste, "Perhaps if you told us her name . . ."

"I don't know it," he admitted.

"Dar have mercy," she muttered in disgust.

"But she mentioned that she's personal servant to a local *torena.*"

The old couple exchanged a long look. A couple so close they spoke without words. Ronall was starting to hate them.

"Porsall?" the old man suggested to his wife.

"Probably," she agreed.

"Valdani," Ronall surmised.

The old man nodded in response. "The *toren* is a Valdan. The family has been here for . . ." He waved a hand and vaguely concluded, "Forever. I suppose that's why he hasn't fled. Perhaps he has nowhere to go."

Then the woman said, "His wife is *Torena* Chasimar."

"Silerian?" Ronall asked, still thinking about Porsall.

"Half."

"Half," he repeated faintly.

The old woman added with emphasis, "Given the *torena*'s own behavior, I can well believe she'd have such a disgraceful girl as her maid."

Ronall remembered the girl, his money, and his dreamweed, all of which he'd forgotten for a moment. "Then I suggest you direct me to Porsall's estate if you cherish any hope of my paying you what I owe you."

They did so willingly. They were considerably more reluctant to provide him with the brandy he demanded, but he was better at insisting than they were at resisting, and so he got his fill before leaving in pursuit of the girl.

It was a thoroughly foolhardy quest, as Elelar would certainly have pointed out, since he didn't know the country and he couldn't see a damn thing. He carried a lantern, but its light was feeble enough in the consuming darkness to ensure a very slow pace even if his wife's gelding *hadn't* suddenly decided to develop a stubborn streak. By the time Ronall reached his destination, he was exhausted from kicking, slapping, urging, and coaxing the balking horse.

By Dar and the Three he'd make that girl sorry for this farce! When he got his hands on . . . on . . .

All thoughts fled from his mind as he became simultaneously aware of the shouts, the screams, and the glow in the sky above the trees. All of it coming from roughly where he expected to find Porsall's estate and the wayward girl.

"What in the Fires . . . ?"

A lone figure came barreling out of the dark, then shied and screamed upon encountering him. His horse responded in kind, demonstrating a heretofore unknown streak of nervousness—which Ronall decided was understandable, under the circumstances.

He was still trying not to fall off the damn horse when he heard a surprised gasp. Then a familiar voice murmured breathlessly, "It's you."

"It's me," he agreed.

The girl recovered her breath and cried, "Dar be praised, it's you, it's you!"

It was the first time he could recall anyone ever being so glad to see him, but he didn't allow that to distract him as he slid off the gelding's back, seized the girl by the arm, and demanded, "Where's my money and my dreamweed, damn you?"

"Help us! Help us!" she screamed right into his face. "They are killing the *toreni*! Help us!"

ABIDAN THE WATERLORD awoke the moment his deepest senses, the senses which only his own kind possessed, alerted him to a change in the Shaljir River.

It was softening, trying to dissolve. Pushing against his will now. Trying to flow again. Trying to escape his grasp, a grasp too weak to hold it alone. A grasp which needed his brother Liadon's strength, too, to command such a river.

Abidan knew instantly that his brother's control had slipped. Something had shifted his focus. Distracted him.

Damn Liadon!

Abidan arose and started scrambling for his clothes in the oppressive darkness of his bedchamber. He hated dark-moon nights. It was unnatural, this opaque blackness which enveloped everything once the sun went down.

As a child he'd been taught that fire-eyed demons prowled on a night like this. As an adult, he had often used the obsidian black of dark-moon nights to attack and slay his enemies, and he'd always known they might do the same.

It's that woman, I just know it's that damned woman! I told Liadon not to let her come back again!

For the past three years, his brother had been in love with possibly the most volatile woman in the three corners of the world. Abidan had already lost count of how many times she had left Liadon after a violent quarrel. Liadon sulked and moped in her absence, which was irritating enough, but things were even worse when she returned to him.

As she always does, damn her!

Abidan yanked on his clothes and shouted for one of the assassins on sentry duty.

The return of Liadon's mistress invariably made him useless. He always expended all his energy in bed with her and left Abidan to worry about such mundane matters as dominating the Shaljir River, collecting tribute, controlling their territory, and dealing with their enemies.

Then Liadon's quarrels with his true love would soon begin, and he'd drive Abidan to distraction complaining and whining about her. When she left, as she inevitably did—usually after wreaking havoc on Liadon's household, and often on Liadon's person, too—Liadon would swear that this was the last time, it was over, he was finished with her. Abidan had actually believed him the first two or three times.

An assassin came to the door of Abidan's bedchamber.

"*Siran?*" He carried a lantern, and Abidan could see his puzzled expression. "Is something wrong?"

"Yes, something's wrong!" Abidan snapped. "Go get my brother!"

"But, *siran* . . . It's the middle of the n—"

"*Now!*" Abidan roared. "You pull him out from between that bitch's legs if you have to, do you hear? And bring him to me!"

"Yes, *siran.*" The assassin departed hastily.

Abidan finished pulling on his boots and strode out of the bedchamber. His own woman was in Sanctuary awaiting the birth of their second child. The first had been stillborn. Recalling how horrible that whole ordeal was, Abidan had sent her to the Sisters several months ago. A smart decision. Between war with the Valdani and now war with Tansen, he didn't have time for such things.

Neither did Liadon. Abidan had thought—had foolishly, naively believed—that his brother truly understood that and wouldn't let that emasculating whore who ruled his wits move back in, yet again, and destroy all their work.

I'll kill him for this! I'll kill her for this!

Abidan marched down the hall of his modest stone house, which squatted deep in the mountains east of Zilar, so high up that Outlookers had never found it.

I'll kill them both and feed their carcasses to the dogs!

He didn't have dogs, but he could get some. It was a small point.

He and Liadon hadn't had a good enough teacher. That's why they weren't as powerful as Kiloran, Verlon, Gulstan, Kariman, or some of the others. But Kiloran had made promises. Oh, yes. If they could help him against Josarian, help him kill Mirabar, help him defeat Tansen, help him dominate the city of Shaljir . . .

Kiloran was old and had no heir. Kiloran knew things about water that no one else did, not even Baran—who, although even crazier than Liadon's mistress, was damned good, Abidan admitted grudgingly. All the brothers had to do was effectively support Kiloran against the Guardians and Josarian's loyalists, and the old waterlord would teach them everything he knew and make them heirs to his immense power and vast territory. Who knew? If his plans succeeded, Abidan and Liadon might even rule Sileria when this was all over!

But not if we can't even maintain control over our own damn river!

They must bring Zilar to its knees. Zilar, where Tansen had publicly declared war against the Society, where he had commenced his bloodfeud against Kiloran and attracted thousands to his cause. Zilar, the jewel of their own territory!

If the brothers failed now, Kiloran would find them unworthy. Actually . . . he might even decide they were expendable.

So when Abidan felt Liadon's grasp on the Shaljir River slacken even a bit, he saw their future crumbling before his very eyes. Liadon understood how much was at stake. Abidan was sure that only one thing could distract him now.

That woman.

Abidan decided he had never hated anyone so much in his life. He stepped out into the clear night air, determined to make Liadon focus all his attention on the Shaljir River, as he damn well knew he should, even if it meant killing that woman right before his very eyes!

"Get a torch!" he snapped at an assassin guarding the door to his house.

"*Siran?*"

"We're going to my brother," he growled. He was too restless to wait here for Liadon. He'd go there. And he'd murder that woman when he got there!

The brothers lived in similar stone houses on opposite sides of a narrow river, the first significant water source they had ever learned to harness and command. Now that the long rains were only a memory and the dry season was fast approaching, the river was shallow and growing sluggish. Abidan couldn't see it from here, not on a night like this, but he could smell it, hear it, feel its presence. He owned it in every way that mattered, as he owned the Shaljir River—as he dreamed of one day owning the Idalar itself, the greatest river in Sileria, the one which determined leadership of the Honored Society and domination of the capital city.

Dreams which would never come to fruition if his idiot brother didn't keep his mind on their work.

Filled with yet another surge of rage, Abidan took the torch which his assassin brought to him and set out for Liadon's house.

I will kill him for this! I will make him watch while I kill her! I will—

These satisfying thoughts were interrupted by shouts and screams coming from across the river.

"Fire! Fire!"

"*Siran!*"

"They are burning the house!"

"Where's it coming from?"

"Watch out!"

"Sound the alarm!"

"*Arrrrgh!*"

Flames erupted in the night. Screams filled the air. There were strange explosions of fire in the trees. A flickering glow painted the sky above where Abidan knew his brother's house lay.

"Wake everyone!" he ordered an assassin.

Many were already awake, alerted by the noise. Half dressed and confused, they emerged from the darkness, from their tents and their quarters, armed with their *shir*. Many weren't even here, though. Assassins weren't Outlookers or soldiers. Many of them had homes of their own. Assassins served him, they lived under his protection, but they didn't live right *here*. Many would hear the alarm, sounding at this very moment, but it would take time for them to get here. Others lived so far away they wouldn't even hear it. Wouldn't even know they were needed. A waterlord's home was always well guarded, but it wasn't a military encampment

It didn't need to be, Abidan reminded himself with growing fury at this outrage. A waterlord could defend himself and his land. A waterlord could destroy anyone who dared to violate his home or attack his person.

Now more men came plunging through the night. *Shallaheen*. Lowlanders. Tansen's people. They flung themselves into combat with his assassins. And the fire . . . Guardians, he realized.

Guardians attacking his home. Attacking him and Liadon. Attacking waterlords.

They'll die for this.

"Liadon!" Abidan shouted.

Liadon's house was burning.

No wonder he was distracted. No wonder his grip on the Shaljir River had slipped.

Abidan started forward at a run, dropping the torch in his hand. He must get to his brother. Together, they would destroy everyone who had the gall to attack them in their homes tonight. He must get to his brother, and they would—

He came to a halt as a strange power tore at him, almost knocking him over in its sudden sweep across his senses.

"Argh!" He fell back a step.

"*Siran?*"

Heat.

Sudden, terrible, intense, fiery heat.

Attacking him. Attacking his water. The river. *His* river!

Not the Shaljir, he realized. It was too big, too powerful, too much for them. This little river. This stream rushing past his house.

They think they can take it from me!

Shaking with rage, he swept the river into the arms of his will and commanded it to turn and attack. He struggled against the hot, alien power playing across the surface of his river. What did the Guardians think they were doing? They couldn't control water, they couldn't take this river from him! A hundred tentacles rose out of the water now, answering his will, responding to his sorcery. And the river reached for his enemies.

A *shallah* screamed in terror as icy tentacles enfolded him and pulled him into the river to drown him. A lowlander struggled against a watery mask which covered his face, smothering him.

Now Abidan felt his brother reaching for the water, too, felt the familiar texture of Liadon's power. But Liadon was pulling the river the wrong way, trying to use it to defend his burning house, his burning land.

"Let it burn!" Abidan screamed, knowing it was futile, knowing his brother couldn't hear him at this distance. "Fight them! Fight the men!"

No fire on my side, Abidan suddenly realized. *Only men.*

Did that mean there was only fire on Liadon's side, and no men? The two brothers would be using the river for different purposes, at odds with each other, if they were fighting different enemies without realizing it.

No, the same enemy, he realized. *But a clever one.*

Kiloran had warned them against underestimating Tansen. "He lets you see what you want to see," Kiloran had once said, "what you expect to see. Then he does what has never occurred to you."

This attack certainly proved that. Who but Tansen would strike a waterlord in his very home, the last place any sane Silerian would choose for a battleground? Even Outlookers had rarely tried such a thing, not since Harlon's day some forty years ago; and they had lost many men before they finally destroyed Harlon.

There was another explosion, and the bridge which spanned the river went up in flames. Hot, violent magic poured forth from it, singeing

Abidan's senses. The Guardians were trying to cut him off from his brother.

Did Liadon even know Abidan was also under attack? Or were he and his men so consumed with fighting the sudden fire, the ensorcelled flames of Guardians, that he didn't even realize—just wondered why Abidan hadn't yet come to his aid?

Didn't Liadon feel Abidan's will exerted on the river, too?

Let go, Liadon, let go. Give it to me now.

But Liadon didn't let go, evidently had no idea that he should. He was trying to pull the water off course and drag it across his land in a vast wave to put out the fire.

A thousand hissing snakes of liquid were writhing across its tormented surface, reaching for Abidan's enemies but weakened by Liadon's call.

I'll let go of it, Abidan decided.

His men were outnumbered, but he was sure they could hold off their attackers until more assassins arrived in response to the alarm. And the people who lived around here, the *shallaheen* who relied on him and Liadon for every sip they drank, they would come, too. Josarian was dead and Tansen's cause was hopeless. The people who lived under the brothers' protection knew who filled their cups, and they would fight loyally.

He would let Liadon have the river, and when he was done, when the fire was out, then Liadon would realize what was happening and they would join forces. It didn't matter what the Guardians thought they were attempting with this strange force they were exerting on the river. They weren't waterlords, and they couldn't command it.

Take it, Liadon, take it.

Abidan released the river completely to his brother's needs.

A moment later, he realized what a huge mistake he had just made.

"Then he does what has never occurred to you."

The surface of the water exploded in flames.

Abidan had never seen anything like it. Had never imagined anything like it. Fire magic battering away at water. Wave after wave of flames sliding across the surface of his river. Spears of glowing lava plunging into it, hurting him as it did so, infecting his ensorcelled domain with something wholly foreign, wholly alien to its magic.

He shouldn't have let go. That was what Tansen had wanted. That was the plan, Abidan realized with horrified fury.

He reached for the river again—and found nothing there but a hot wall of violent resistance. Guardian magic now stood between him and the water which had been his.

"My river! Mine!" he screamed, running forward, determined to seize it physically if he couldn't touch it any other way.

Tansen couldn't have it! Tansen couldn't take away his whole future, his whole life!

"Liadon! Stop them! Stop them!"

He couldn't even tell if his brother was now battling the Guardians for their river, or if he had already lost it, too.

"*Liadon!*" he screamed.

Those spineless fire mages, those scraping servants of the volcano goddess, those mewling, prayer-mouthing, ghost-talking cowards now stood between him and his water, his river, his power! He would kill them all for this!

But as he turned away from the appalling sight of his river obliterated by a roaring display of enchanted fire which lit up the whole night, he realized that he'd have to kill them the old-fashioned way. His water-well certainly wasn't enough of a weapon to fight off the second wave of peasant warriors now emerging from the flickering shadows, now pouring out of the darkness and into this fiery nightmare.

And the water-well was on fire, anyhow.

The Guardians had attacked it, too, while his attention was diverted. Now they were attacking the house, even the land. A wave of men and women—*women,* he realized with shock—were melting out of the dark, flinging glowing spears of flame and hurling balls of fire. Guardian fire needed no fuel to burn, and his stone house would give way if he couldn't stop them. He must fight—

No, he suddenly realized. That was also what Tansen wanted.

The Shaljir River.

It was all he had left. He reached out to it, barely able to feel it through the chaos erupting all around him.

His brother had let go of the Shaljir, he was sure of it.

He closed his eyes and tried to concentrate. Without the Shaljir River now, he was no one and nothing. Without the river that Zilar relied upon, his life was over.

"*Siran!*"

His eyes snapped open just in time to see one of his assassins jump between him and an attacking *shallah* who used two *yahr,* swinging them with deadly skill. Both men were covered in blood, dust, and sweat. Both looked savage and deadly in the glowing light of the enslaved river, in the flickering shadows created by the burning house and the flaming trees.

The *shallah* felled the assassin with four heavy blows of his *yahr,* then turned on Abidan, crouched for attack.

"Abidan?" he asked, his gaze sharp.

Abidan was a waterlord, not a warrior; but if his hour had come, he would die like a man. He circled slowly, keeping at a safe distance from the stalking *shallah.* When he saw his chance, Abidan stooped and seized the *shir* of the fallen assassin whose body lay between them. He himself had made this *shir,* and so he was the only man alive who could touch it besides the assassin . . . or now this *shallah,* if the assassin was indeed dead. Stimulated by the intrusion of Guardian magic on such an immense scale, the wavy-edged dagger quivered so violently it was hard to maintain his grip on it.

The *shallah* hesitated, then dropped one of his *yahr* and, to Abidan's surprise, pulled a wildly shaking *shir* out of his boot.

"That's one of mine," Abidan blurted, furious that this *shallah* upstart had it now.

"You're losing a lot of them," the *shallah* replied.

"Where's Tansen?" Abidan demanded. They'd never met, but he knew this wasn't Tansen; everyone knew that Tansen fought with two Kintish swords.

"He's busy killing your brother."

Abidan struck, but the *shallah* was expecting it. The *yahr* swept through the air and slammed hard across Abidan's face, then the *shir* sought his vitals, creeping cleverly between his ribs to inflict a mortal wound. *Shir* knew how to kill, relished killing. *Shir* could almost think . . . It was a . . . It . . .

Hot and cold life force gushed out of him as he sank heavily to the ground. The fire made everything look like sunset. Sunrise? No, it was growing darker all around. Sunset.

The blood-streaked face of the *shallah* loomed in the distance, floating in his vision.

Making sure I'm dead?

Abidan heard the thought, but no words came out of his mouth.

He did hear a distant voice, though: "Galian!"

It was filled with the panic of the still-living.

The *shallah* whirled, his long black hair catching the firelight. There was a harsh grunt. Falling, falling down . . .

Abidan groaned when the *shallah* fell on top of him.

"*No!*" someone cried. "Galian!"

Scuffling. Fighting. Hard blows. Grunts. A harsh scream of pain. Everything moving in the flickering golden light.

Someone pulled the *shallah*'s heavy body off him.

"*Siran!*"

Abidan tried, but he couldn't answer.

"*Siran,* more are coming. A third wave."

He couldn't see anything now. He was leaving the world.

Where do waterlords go?

"*Siran,* I think we must fall back, abandon . . . *Siran?*"

Please, my only request . . . I just don't want to be with Guardians.

Distant voices.

"Abidan is dying."

"We can't stop them. Not with the *sirani* both dead . . ."

"Liadon may still be alive."

"Not for much longer. Look at that. You can't really believe he'll live through *that?*"

"Yes . . . you're right."

Abidan felt something on his shoulder.

"Good-bye, *siran*. It was an honor to serve you."

"He can't hear you."

"Do it now. Call for retreat."

"I never thought it would end this way."

"It's not over. Tansen will pay for this."

"Yes, you're right. Tansen must pay."

It was the last thing Abidan heard before he died.

30

ONLY TWO THINGS MATTER: LIFE AND DEATH.
—Kintish Proverb

A FULL-SCALE BATTLE raged in the dark forest around the Guardian encampment high up on Mount Niran. Assassins were killing the Guardians, who fought back with bursts of flame and clouds of fire which briefly illuminated the night, then died as quickly as the Guardians did.

"Dar have mercy!" Mirabar cried.

Najdan clapped a hand over her mouth, even though it was unlikely she'd be heard above the noise of the battle and the screams of the dying.

A wave of water had swept across the Guardian encampment, rising out of a stream which lay at some distance from the camp and which had always been free of sorcery. Until now.

The encampment was in a clearing bordered by several caves, all of which were eerily decorated with paintings left by the Beyah-Olvari. Now the clearing was empty—except for the corpses which lay everywhere. Someone—some waterlord—had made the stream water so cold that all he had to do was wash it over them to kill them, pulling death across these Guardians like a watery veil. The water was gone now, only the damp ground and discolored bodies revealing evidence of how these men and women had died. The fatal wave had receded before Mirabar's stealthy arrival, subsiding back into the stream whence it came.

Crouched beside Najdan in the thick forest of gossamer trees just beyond the edge of the clearing, Mirabar stared in horror while faceless voices pierced the night all around them with wordless cries of triumph and of terror.

This had been her circle of companions, her only community in the days before the rebellion. These Guardians were her family. Sorrow and rage flooded her soul with equal fierceness as she stared at the slain. The deadly water had doused all but one torch, so she couldn't make out their faces, their exact identities, in the dim and flickering light. She only knew that each of the eleven corpses she now counted might well be someone she'd known most of her life.

Tashinar.

She made a sudden, clumsy movement in their direction. Najdan's firm grip dragged her back into their dark hiding place. She gasped when her hand touched a stray trickle of ensorcelled water. The cold was unbearable. Instinctively, she filled her breath with fire and blew warming flames onto her dying flesh.

A small burn was left behind, but she had succeeded in eliminating the effects of the water magic on her skin. Just a few drops of water, she reflected in scared amazement, and the pain was so consuming. Her eyes filled with tears as she turned her gaze back to the dead.

Where is Tashinar?

"There were perhaps fifty people camped here?" Najdan whispered into her ear.

She nodded. Half that number had camped here before the rebellion, but now it was always more—a combined group of Guardians and Josarian's men.

"Why aren't they all dead?" Najdan murmured.

"We must help them!"

"Where were most of them when the attack began?" When she didn't respond, he prodded, "Out roaming the forest on a dark-moon night?"

"No, of course not. They'd have been r—" A nearby scream, one which was surely someone dying in agony, made her flinch and try to scramble to her feet. Najdan held her steady.

"Think," he whispered fiercely. "If they were all in camp except for the sentries ..."

"Then ..." She nodded, understanding. "Then why didn't the waterlord, whoever he is, kill them all with his ambush?"

"Why drive them out into the forest? If he couldn't move the water fast enough to kill them all, why not at least trap them in camp, where they'd be easier to kill?" He paused in thought. "Is there something important I don't know about Guardians or about this place?"

"No." Mirabar flinched again, unable to hold still amidst the unseen violence occurring all around them. "How can you just sit here and ask questions? We've got to stop them!"

"Stop them doing what?" he whispered fiercely. "What are the assassins trying to do? This isn't the best way to kill all the Guardians. If I were—" He stopped and drew in a sharp breath. "They're not trying to kill them all. Just most of them."

He finally had her full attention. "Why?"

"Driving them into the forest on a dark-moon night. Separating and confusing them." He nodded. "It's the safest way to capture some of them."

"Capture?" She didn't even want to think about what the Society intended to do with captured Guardians. "How do we stop them?"

"Come."

Keeping his head low and his steps silent, he dragged her back through the thick of the battle, sometimes only a few paces from grunting, struggling combatants. Cloaked in darkness, he retraced their steps until they found their companions where they had left them, hiding on the outskirts of the horrifying battle.

"For the love of Dar," one of the men blurted, "I hear women screaming!"

"We can't just sit here and do nothing!" another insisted.

"Do we have a plan?" Pyron asked.

"Yes," Najdan said crisply. "The *sirana* will encircle this entire battle with a ring of fire and then tighten it on them like a noose."

"What?" she exclaimed.

"You did it at the battle for the mines of Alizar, and that's a much bigger place."

"I had help," she pointed out in panic. "There were nearly a hundred Guardians there."

"There are others here, too," he replied calmly, "and as we rescue them, perhaps they will have enough sense and strength left to assist you."

"What do we do?" Pyron asked.

"You will guard the *sirana* with your lives," Najdan said. "All five of you."

"But—"

"They're killing and capturing Guardians," Najdan explained tersely. "Once the *sirana* reveals her location with fire magic, she will be in terrible danger. And once they realize that she's trying to trap them—"

"*Am* I trying to trap them?"

"—they'll shift their attention to killing her."

"Where will you be?" Mirabar asked, trying to smother the terror that filled her upon hearing his words.

"I'll be trying to capture one of *them*."

"Why?"

"It's our only chance of finding out why they're trying to capture Guardians instead of just killing them."

"That's it?" Pyron demanded. "That's your plan?"

"As long as you don't let them kill the *sirana*, we can disrupt *their* plan and end the battle before they've killed or captured everyone. Under the circumstances, we can hope for little more." Najdan paused and then added in a voice gone cold with menace, "I am leaving the *sirana* in your care. If you want to live past dawn, I strongly suggest that you don't let them kill her."

After the assassin left them to carry out his own plans, Pyron asked no one in particular, "Are you *sure* he's on our side?"

TANSEN WAITED UNTIL he was sure the plan had worked, until he was sure both brothers had lost control of the narrow river which ran between their homes. Then he gave the signal for the next wave of men to attack, and finally joined the battle himself.

Hanging back until now was hard. Fighting was what he did best, but he had to stay alive to implement the second, or even the third, alternate plan in case the first didn't work.

Fortunately, however, Abidan and Liadon had fallen into his trap like bridegrooms falling into their marriage beds. The brothers needed each other, yet they had never learned to think and act as one. This was the weakness Tansen had discerned from the information gathered by the tireless Guardians in Zilar; if Abidan and Liadon could be separated by the attack, unable to communicate in any way, they could be taken. Tansen had further played upon this weakness by giving them different problems, counting on each of them to fail to consider what the other might be dealing with until it was too late. Counting on them to struggle, lose focus, and make uncoordinated decisions, until one or both of them weakened enough for the Guardians to come between them and their water.

Without mastery over water, a waterlord was just a man. His assassins were still formidable fighters with unusually dangerous weapons; but other good fighters—not to mention fire sorcerers—could challenge them, and perhaps even win.

Tansen swept through the inferno which had once been Liadon's garden, slaughtering assassins who stood between him and his target. The roaring Guardian fire consumed Liadon's stone house, blasting Tansen with its fiery heat. The dark-moon night glowed golden with sorcery, making Liadon easy to spot; he was the unarmed man ignoring the battle raging all around him as he desperately tried to regain the power he had just lost.

"*Siran!* Watch out!"

An assassin leaped between Tansen and Liadon, defending his master with his life. Tansen knocked aside his *yahr,* parried the thrust of his *shir,* whirled once, and cut off his head. Blood shot up like a geyser for an ugly moment before the body keeled over.

Liadon, as spattered with blood as Tansen was, stared at him in openmouthed shock. "It's you."

"It's me," he agreed.

"Kiloran warned us. He said—"

Tansen killed him. "I don't care what he said."

*　　*　　*

RONALL, WHOSE BRANDY-FUELED blood was now pounding loudly in his ears, let the girl drag him through the trees until they reached a spot where he could see for himself.

He thought his heart would stop. Instead, it started thundering painfully in his tight chest. Elelar's gelding was dancing uneasily, tugging at the reins by which Ronall led it. He didn't blame the beast a bit.

Toren Porsall's elegant house was ablaze beneath the dark-moon sky. It was slightly smaller than Elelar's country villa, and modest compared to Ronall's father's rural residence. . . . The one which Ronall suddenly realized was now his, since his parents were dead. Porsall didn't appear to be filthy rich by the standards of Valdani *toreni,* but this was a substantial family estate.

It would be ashes by morning.

Dozens of *shallaheen* surrounded the place. The blazing torches in their hands made it quite unnecessary for the girl to scream right in Ronall's ear, "They're burning it down! They're burning the house!"

"Dar have mercy." She was right, he realized. They were killing the *toreni.* The local *shallaheen* were after the lifeblood of the Valdani in their midst.

"Please help us," the girl cried. "Help us, *toren*! Those people are your kind!"

He glanced sharply at her, but he couldn't make out her expression in the dark.

She insisted, "The *shallaheen* will listen to you!"

So she took him for a full-blooded Silerian? Maybe the murderous crowd would, too, in that case.

Or maybe not. Fear flooded his thoughts. These were exactly the kind of bloodthirsty Silerian peasants who had brutally murdered his own parents not long ago.

"I know they are Valdani," the girl said, weeping copiously, "but the *toren* has never been unkind to me, and the *torena* is very good! She took me in when I was driven out of my village in disgrace! When she saw that I worked well, she made me her personal maid and . . . gave me . . . many things . . . And was always . . . Please! Please, help!"

Watching the frenzied mob circling the burning villa, Ronall's throat was tight with fear. His stomach churned sickeningly. He was pretty sure he was shaking. "What makes you think the *toreni* are even still alive?"

"Can't you see?" She pointed. "The fire has driven them to the roof!"

He lifted his gaze and studied the red-tiled roof. Sure enough, a man and a woman were cowering up there, visible in the bright light of the raging fire.

"Where's a waterlord when you need one?" Ronall muttered.

"A waterlord will not help them, they are *toreni*!" she snapped.

"A waterlord won't help them because it's too late to save whatever they owned of value," he corrected absently, concentrating on his terror.

"*You* must help them!"

He suddenly didn't want to die quite as much as he'd thought he did. His palms were sweating so badly that the reins were becoming slippery.

"Stop crying!" he snapped at the girl, afraid he'd start weeping, too.

"Please, *toren,*" she cried. "Even a Valdan is a human being!"

He stared at her, grief sweeping through him.

They're killing them because they're Valdani. They're killing them because they're not real Silerians.

"Dar curse them all," he said on a half-sob.

The girl flinched, then wailed, "If you won't help him, then please, *please,* at least help her! She is half-Silerian! *Toren!* She is half-Silerian! Help her! Help her! *Help her!*"

He wasn't sure if it was the victims' Valdani blood or the girl's shrill hysteria which drove him into the fray, but suddenly he was mounted on Elelar's unhappy horse and galloping straight towards the reeling, raging, murderous crowd of *shallaheen.*

What in the Fires am I doing?

"Stop!" he screamed in common Silerian, his command of *shallah* being almost nonexistent. "Stop! Stop this *now!*"

The wiry bodies of mountain-born peasants careened into his horse as he reined it to a prancing halt in their midst.

Guttural cries assailed his ears.

"Kill the Valdani! Kill the Valdani!"

"Take back what is ours!"

"Kill the *roshaheen!*"

Three have mercy, Ronall knew his time had come. He would die like his parents. He would die like every last Dar-cursed Valdan in Sileria.

"Stop this!" he shouted.

"What's it to you, *toren?*" demanded an old, scarred *shallah* who had finally deigned to notice him. "Who are you?"

He ignored the question and took a wild stab at reason. "The war is over! The Valdani have surrendered!"

"Then why are they still here?" someone screamed.

"This is their home!" he insisted, remembering what the old keeper had said earlier. "This family has been here for generations!"

"They stole it! They took it from Silerian *toreni* like you! Where is your manhood? Where is your pride, *toren?*"

"Then let's talk to the family they took it from!" he suggested. "Let's ask them what—"

"They are long since dead and gone!"

"So now *you're* stealing!" he challenged, waiting for someone to haul him off his horse and beat him to death.

"This is Sileria! It is ours! They have no place here! The Valdani must leave!"

"Kill the *roshaheen*! Kill the *roshaheen*!"

"They were born here!" Ronall's heart thudded so hard it hurt. "Please, let's all talk. Let's act like men, not animals."

"They have made us animals!" the old *shallah* snarled. "And now we will make them pay!"

Someone cried, "They're coming down! They're coming down!"

Ronall looked up. Sure enough, even the roof was flaming now, and the terrified couple up there had no choice but to descend into the violent crowd and meet their end.

I'm going to die here. I'm going to die here.

Elelar would probably never know what had happened to her wayward husband, how or when or where he had died. Nor would she care, since she could declare abandonment after three years and finally be free of him.

She would miss the horse, though.

Tell them who you are. Tell them you're half-Valdan. Finish it. Let it be done at last. Let them finish it.

Or . . . he could just turn around and run away. He looked longingly over his shoulder, knowing no one would follow him, knowing that with one quick jerk of the reins, he could be free of this disaster. Safe. Gone.

Get out! Get out! Get out!

He would never know why he did it, or how he found the guts to do it, but he reached down to grab the old *shallah* by the shoulder and said insistently, "Please. They are unarmed. You've destroyed their home. You're . . . taking over the estate." Until someone more powerful put these *shallaheen* in their place, anyhow. "There is no government left to support any future attempt of theirs to reclaim this place. No Outlookers to protect them." When the old man tried to pull away, he tightened his grip. "*Please.* Let them come with me. You don't need to kill them. Not now."

The old man shook off his grip and turned away, pushing through the crowd to confront the sweating, dirty, frightened aristocrats who had finally made a messy and hazardous descent from their blazing rooftop.

Ronall kicked his reluctant gelding forward. "You don't need to kill them!"

The *toren*—Porsall—was having trouble standing. It looked like he had broken his leg coming off the high roof. The *torena* was clinging to him, shaking with silent sobs.

"Let them come with me!" Ronall shouted again. "You don't need to kill them! Not now!"

The *toren* looked up, noticing him now. "Who are you?"

In a stroke of genius, Ronall announced, "I am the husband of *Torena* Elelar shah Hasnari!"

The bloodthirsty crowd paused in surprise.

"The *torena*?"

"*Torena* Elelar?"

"Dar praise Elelar shah Hasnari!"

"The *torena* has a husband? But didn't she live with . . . Um . . ." The *shallah* who had spoken up now hesitated, then coughed.

Someone interjected, "They did say she was married."

"Yes, I heard she was married," someone else said. "To a Valdan."

"A Valdan?" The scarred old *shallah* eyed Ronall.

Ronall thought he would piss on himself as a perceptible wave of hostility swept across the crowd. A blessed instinct of self-preservation inspired him to say with amazing dryness, "I'm sure I would know if that were the case."

"Why would *Torena* Elelar's husband be trying to save Valdani?" the old *shallah* demanded.

Another lie sprang to his lips. "*Torena* Chasimar is my wife's cousin." His head spinning, he added, "You *do* know you're about to murder a half-Silerian woman, don't you?"

The rabble all around him began murmuring restlessly now. Killing a woman didn't sit well with Silerians, now that they paused to think about it. Killing a *Silerian* woman was even worse.

Ronall pressed his advantage, "When the massacres began in Shaljir, my wife was afraid something like this would happen. Elelar couldn't leave the city herself, so she sent me to protect her cousin." He met *Torena* Chasimar's bewildered, watery gaze and added, "I'm glad I arrived in time. Elelar would be very distressed if I couldn't bring you back with me."

"*Torena* Elelar's cousin . . ." The old *shallah* looked thoughtfully back and forth between Ronall and the woman. Ronall's clothing was more Valdani than Silerian (not to mention dirty and rumpled), but it was, above all, the rich clothing of a *toren*. Besides, Ronall doubted that a mountain peasant knew all that much about fashion. "I suppose," the old *shallah* concluded at last, "it's possible."

Ronall called on long-forgotten lessons in comportment as he looked down his nose at the old man and said with all the pomposity he could muster, "Are you questioning my word, *shallah*?"

"A woman," someone else murmured. "A Silerian wo—"

"*Half* Silerian," the old *shallah* snapped.

"And which half will you kill?" Ronall asked, wondering if any of them noticed how he was trembling. "Which half can you cut out to leave her as pure-blooded as you?"

"I don't want to kill a woman," another *shallah* announced.

"Nor do I," someone else decided.

"But you *do* want to kill an unarmed *toren*?" Ronall persisted. "Just to clarify."

"No one is threatening you, *toren*!" The peasant who addressed him seemed aghast at the idea.

"I was referring to him." Ronall indicated Porsall, who listened in sweat-drenched, wide-eyed silence.

"He must pay," the peasant replied. "Vengeance is our right."

"Vengeance for what?" Ronall demanded.

"He's a Valdan!"

"If you can't be more specific than that . . ." Ronall began.

The scarred old *shallah* came to a decision. "You can take the woman with you, *toren*. We will not harm *Torena* Elelar's cousin."

Another *shallah* argued, "What if he's lying?"

The old man replied, "What if he's not?"

"And Porsall?" Ronall asked, already knowing the answer.

"Take the woman and go," the old man instructed.

"Let me take her husband, too," Ronall urged. "He is Elelar's kin by marr—"

"Take the woman now, *toren,* or she will see us kill him."

Frightened and out of ideas, Ronall met Porsall's eyes.

Porsall looked at his wife. "Go," he said. "You must go."

The *torena* didn't touch or embrace him. Just stared blindly at him while sobs wracked her body.

"Go," he repeated more urgently.

She turned and started stumbling towards Ronall. Her light brown hair was a dusty tangle, her pale sleeping linens streaked with soot and dirt, her face contorted by fear and grief. She hunched her shoulders as she passed through the crowd, flinching at any contact with her would-be killers.

When she reached Ronall, he leaned over and tried to pull her up onto the horse with him. She wasn't heavy, but he wasn't that strong. A life spent lifting mugs and throwing dice didn't build muscle. After two fumbled attempts, someone else assisted the *torena*. She gasped and sobbed at the contact, but Ronall was just glad he was finally able to pull her up behind him.

He looked at Porsall again. He wanted to cry. "I'm sorry."

"Go," was all Porsall again. "Take her where no one knows. Take her . . . Find someplace for her. For people like us."

Ronall nodded, turned his horse's head, and gave it a gentle kick. *For people like us*. Did Porsall know, somehow recognize that Ronall was Valdani, too? Or did he just mean himself and his wife when he said "us"? Ronall supposed he would never know.

Torena Chasimar's sobs became louder as they slowly rode away. Ronall's spine stiffened when he heard a howl of pain behind him, followed by raucous cries of triumph. The *torena* gave a muffled scream against his back and clutched him tighter.

"Oh, Dar," she wept. "Dar have mercy. Where will I go? I am Silerian! Where can I go? Dar help me. Where can my child go?"

Ronall flinched, making the gelding prance nervously again. "Your child?"

"I'm pregnant," she wept. "Where can this child live? Where can we go? Oh, Dar have mercy on us!"

Ronall slumped, feeling the tension leave him on a wave of despair. "Dar won't have mercy," he said bleakly. "She is the destroyer goddess."

MIRABAR WAS SHAKING so hard, it was difficult to maintain control of her fire. Some of her attackers came within moments of killing her before being slaughtered by her defenders. They died so close to her that their blood splattered her. And the power needed to build and maintain this enormous ring of fire was so great that she couldn't defend herself if her companions failed her; she had no strength to spare.

"Did you hear that? They've called for retreat!" Pyron cried, his face streaked with blood. He was breathing hard, his eyes glowing with exultation in the golden light of Mirabar's fire. "Dar be praised, the assassins are retreating!"

"So Najdan's plan worked," someone said.

"He knows how they think," Pyron said, evidently forgetting that he had questioned the plan.

Mirabar didn't comment. If she faltered now, the assassins might realize it and turn back to finish their grim job. She kept plodding through the dark forest, arms spread, coaxing the wall of fire which she dragged with her at enormous cost to her strength.

It became harder with every step. The mountaintop battleground was already three-quarters encircled by fire. If any Guardians were still alive out there in the dark, they were too disoriented or too badly hurt to realize what she was doing and help her. The farther Mirabar got from the spot where she had first blown this fire into life, the harder it became to control it without letting it sizzle out, and to feed it without letting it become an inferno which would destroy the entire forest.

Her breath came harder and thinner as she continued chanting, singing her magic in archaic High Silerian, a tongue which hadn't been used in common speech for centuries but which gave voice to most Guardian rituals.

She faltered weakly in the dark, stumbled, and fell.

"*Sirana!*"

Pyron hauled her to her feet, his blood-slick hands slipping on her bare forearms.

"Look out!"

A black-clad assassin melted out of the dark night and came for her, his *shir* glittering with the cold sorcery of his master. Mirabar watched in an exhausted daze as the shining, wavy-edged dagger descended towards her in a deadly arc.

He ducked as something struck at his face.

Pyron's *yahr,* Mirabar vaguely realized. Missed.

The assassin knocked Pyron aside and lunged for Mirabar. She fell back, scrambling to get away. She tried to ward him off with fire; but nothing came to her palms, and her breath was soft and empty. He was a big, strong man and his grip on her was firm.

"Get him!" Pyron shouted.

"Watch out! Another one behind—"

"No!"

The *shir* flashed at Mirabar again. Terrified and weak, she did the only thing she could think of, and dived straight into the raging wall of fire she had made, taking the assassin with her.

He screamed wildly, and his *shir* cut her in passing as his arms waved. He let go of her, but now she grabbed him. He struggled to get away. Burning. His long hair blazing. His clothes on fire. His flesh burning, melting, *cooking.*

Heat flooded Mirabar. Surrounded her, engulfed her, filled her. The raging inferno of Dar-blessed fire. The gift of the Guardians, the gift of the destroyer goddess.

It would kill her, too, if she lost focus, if she stopped concentrating, if she became too weak. She was flesh and blood just like the horribly screaming assassin dying even now, dying so hideously at her hands. Dying because she was killing him, trapping him here in the fire with her.

"Dar have mercy, what's happening?" someone cried.

"Mirabar! Mirabar!"

She ignored them, ignored everything but the grip she must maintain on the burning, writhing arm, and the fire she must shield herself from.

Lava poured through her veins. The rich blood of the volcano flowed along her senses. Flames toyed with her hair before melting into her shoulders and her back. Her skin glowed like live coals beneath her clothing.

The assassin stopped struggling and became a dead weight.

Dead.

She let go. She didn't know what happened to the body now in the consuming fire, she knew only that it was no longer alive.

Darfire. I've killed a man.

The fire scorched her, hurting her. She tumbled out of the flames, rolling across the ground, escaping the fire before her distraction led to her own death.

Darfire, I've killed a man.

"By all the Fires . . ." Pyron's shocked voice pierced her whirling senses. "*Mirabar?*"

Heat poured off her. She felt it. She opened her eyes and saw steam rising in a thick mist from her flesh. The *shir* wound on her arm—just a scratch really—throbbed with startling coldness against the heat consuming her. Blood flowed freely from it.

"*Sirana!*" Pyron knelt down beside her, his eyes wide with shock. "Are you . . . um . . . ?"

"I thought . . ." She licked her cracked lips.

"Someone get water!" Pyron instructed.

Mirabar tried again. "No." They should stay together as Najdan ordered. "I thought . . ."

"What?"

The cool night air washed over her. The heat exhaustion eased slightly, the consuming fire fading from her skin. "I thought . . ."

"Yes? What, *sirana*?"

The *shir* wound ached with bitter cold. "I thought you said they were retreating."

Pyron sighed. "Oh, for the love of Dar."

THE GIRL WAS waiting where Ronall had left her. She helped *Torena* Chasimar off the horse and embraced her. The two women wept fitfully while Ronall staggered into the bushes and vomited until there was nothing left inside of him.

They were both staring at him when he emerged. He stared back, his mind a complete blank, his limbs shaking in reaction to everything he'd seen and done tonight.

"What do we do now?" the girl asked.

"How in the Fires should I know?" Ronall said irritably. "*You* urged me to save her."

"What about the *toren*?" the girl asked.

When he didn't respond, the girl looked at the *torena*. Chasimar shook her head. The girl started weeping again.

"Oh, stop that!" Ronall snapped. The girl wept harder. Ronall sighed and apologized. "I'm a little on edge," he explained. He could still hear Porsall's scream in his mind, and he had a feeling he'd be hearing it for a long time to come. If he *had* a long time to come, which didn't seem likely.

"Where will we go?" the *torena* asked, weeping.

"What will we do?" the maid wailed.

"Three pity me," Ronall mumbled.

Elelar had her faults, but at least she didn't cry pathetically or fling herself helplessly on someone else's mercy when she was in trouble. Indeed, Ronall desperately wished she were here now, because despite the open insults and contempt she would subject him to, she would undoubtedly know what to do. If she didn't, then she'd figure it out, and get it done.

"No one and nothing defeats Elelar," Ronall muttered, "least of all a pack of rabble, two weeping women, a nervous horse, a dead man, and nowhere to go on a dark-moon night."

Elelar, Ronall knew with bleak certainty, wouldn't have let them kill Porsall. She'd have thought of something.

No, he was wrong, he realized. Porsall and Chasimar were Valdani. Elelar would have watched with pleasure—then urged the crowd to kill Ronall, too.

"What shall we do?" The *torena* turned to Ronall.

He sighed. "You're going to instruct your maid to give back the things she stole from me." He ignored Chasimar's gasp and continued, "Then we're going back to the inn where I paid for the privilege of bedding her earlier this evening. You two can sleep in my bedchamber. I won't be needing it, as I plan to be downstairs, where I will be busy, for the rest of the night, depleting the liquor supply." Hearing no objection to these plans, he added, "In the morning, we'll . . ." He stopped, sighed, and concluded, "We'll confront the morning only when we absolutely have to. Agreed?"

THE MEN HELPED Mirabar to her feet, and she slowly regained control of her wildly blazing wall of fire as it crept over the dark mountainside. But she couldn't drag it any farther, not by herself. Especially not after what she'd just been through.

Darfire, I've killed a man.

She was shaking. His screams, his struggles, the smell of his burning flesh . . .

Tansen was right. Killing someone was not a thing to take lightly. Not a vow to make in haste and in anger.

No more assassins came out of the dark to murder her, so it seemed that Pyron was right, after all; they were retreating.

Eventually two *shallaheen* appeared out of the night; rebel inhabitants of the Guardian camp. They were bloodstained and battered, but still alive. Najdan had instructed them to bring Mirabar back to the encampment, which was now secure. The rest of the men were to round up survivors.

Najdan was already in camp when Mirabar, moving slowly, arrived. He noticed her disheveled condition and scorched clothing, but he made no comment; it had been a battle, after all.

He had succeeded in his attempt to capture an assassin. There was no time to shield Mirabar and the other Guardians from the brutal facts of war with the Society. Najdan staked out the prisoner in one of the caves and began interrogating him.

It was a long, ugly night. Survivors trickled back into camp, wounded, dazed, shocked. All night long, Mirabar identified the dead when she could, and prepared the bodies for the mass funeral pyre she would burn once everyone was accounted for.

All night long, the screams and howls of Najdan's captive echoed around her and the other survivors.

Tears poured hotly down Mirabar's face. More than once, she escaped to the bushes to be sick. More than once, she gazed down at the recovered corpse of someone she'd known since childhood.

The morning sun was bright when Najdan finally emerged from the cave. He looked gray, grim, and exhausted. Mirabar thought she knew what the sudden silence meant.

"The assassin is dead?" she asked hoarsely.

Najdan nodded and accepted the hot tisane she offered him. No one else would even look in his direction. She ignored them and sat beside him.

"Najdan . . . ," she began, trying not to weep. More tears would not help now.

"He admitted they'd been sent to capture some Guardians," Najdan said wearily. "At least two, no more than four."

"Why?" she asked, cold with fear.

"He insisted he didn't know." Najdan closed his eyes. They looked sunken. "I think he was telling the truth."

"Who was the waterlord?"

"Geriden."

"I don't know that name."

"He's very minor." Najdan opened his eyes again. "His allegiance is to Kiloran."

She started trembling. "Kiloran wanted them captured?"

"The assassin didn't know, but it's what I believe. Now that the sun is up, we can start tracking them. If, as I suspect, the trail leads to Lake Kandahar—"

"Najdan." More tears flowed down her face. She couldn't stop them.

He saw her tears, her trembling, her horror. "*Sirana?*"

"Tashinar is gone."

He knew what was worse than death. "The searchers have missed the body, that's all," he said quickly. "You and I will look—"

"I've searched. I've made the men search again. She's gone." Mirabar shuddered. "They've taken Tashinar to Kiloran."

TANSEN KNELT ON the banks of the stream which ran between the smoldering ruins of Abidan and Liadon's houses. He'd just ordered his people to prepare to retreat and scatter, in case unexpected Society reinforcements arrived later. Abidan and Liadon were dead, and the Shaljir River was free; Tansen didn't intend to lose any more people today now that these goals were accomplished. The blazing funeral pyres here were already big enough. The chanting of the Guardians shivered through him, darkening his mood even as the sun brightened the sky.

However, this water was free now, and he was filthy and thirsty. So he pulled his tunic over his head and sluiced water over his torso, letting it wash away the blood, though the soot was more stubborn. Then, battle-weary and heartsick over lives lost, he drank . . .

. . . Josarian had helped Tansen down to the river when the fighting was over; but he had not yet spoken a word to him. Not since Tansen had slaughtered Zimran even as Josarian begged him not to.

Feeling light-headed and weak, Tansen let the icy waters of the Zilar wash the blood off his skin, knowing that Josarian would continue to see it there long after it was gone. The zanareen, *who had sent Tansen's rescue party in the right direction in time to save Josarian's life, now stood guard around Josarian, chanting, praying, giving thanks that the Firebringer was safe. He ignored them. They elevated Tansen in their praises, for he had come to save their leader. He ignored them, too.*

Weak, exhausted, and in pain, Tansen barely had the strength to sluice the bitterly cold water over his body.

"Here," Josarian said at last, his voice subdued, "let me. You're going to fall in headfirst in another minute."

"No, I—"

"Sit back," Josarian snapped.

He sat back.

Josarian soaked a cloth in the water and then wiped gingerly at the edges of Tan's seeping shir *wound. "It looks worse again."*

"Oh."

"You should rest."

"We must leave here."

"Did you know about . . ." Josarian's voice broke. He looked away for a moment. "Did you know Zimran would be the one to lead me into the trap?"

"I . . ." He took a shallow breath, trying not to strain the wound. "Yes, Josarian."

"We . . . We were born only three months apart." Josarian dunked the cloth into the river again. "We shared everything as boys. As men, we . . ."

"I'm sorry."

I'm sorry he betrayed you. I'm sorry I had to kill him. I'm sorry.

A tear streamed slowly down Josarian's face, glistening beneath the brilliant light of the full twin moons. "I know."

Tansen would not ask for forgiveness. He said only, "It had to be done."

"If only . . ." Josarian bowed his head and gulped for air. He scrubbed at his face and finally said, "We will meet again in the Otherworld. Mirabar says that our earthly concerns and quarrels will not matter there."

"Mirabar . . ."

"Mirabar," Tansen murmured, trying to tear himself away from memories of the night Josarian had died. That sad, subdued conversation beside the Zilar River was the last time he'd ever spoken with his brother.

After that, Josarian waded across the shallow, icily cold river, and Kiloran ambushed him with the White Dragon. Tansen was with Mirabar, insisting it was time to leave before more Outlookers came along.

A blood-chilling scream split the night wide open. It came from the river-bank. Tansen was already running towards the sound when he heard more voices—screaming, shouting, crying out. Above it all, there was a terrible roaring unlike anything he'd ever heard in his life, a sound which was so terrifying it made his hair stand on end and a clammy sweat break out on his skin.

His side was burning and his head was spinning by the time he reached the riverbank. What he saw there made him forget his pain, his exhaustion, his weakness. Made him forget everything but the horror confronting him.

"Tan?"

Tansen whirled around, ready for battle, nearly startled into attacking the intruder without conscious thought.

"Radyan." Tansen froze.

Radyan eyed the sword in his hand. "Something I said?" The joke sounded flat and tired.

Tansen glanced down at the engraved blade. He didn't even remember seizing it. "Years of training," he muttered absently.

"We're done here," Radyan said. "The last pyre is burning. Everyone is moving out now."

Tansen nodded and donned his filthy tunic again. He didn't know why he bothered, since it was completely ruined. "Let's go."

A hand on his arm stopped him. "Tan."

He glanced at Radyan's strained face. He knew that look. "Who?" he asked, dreading the answer.

"Galian."

"Galian," he repeated, sadness washing over him.

"May Dar have mercy on his soul."

Tansen wanted to curse Dar, but he didn't. "We will miss him," was all he said.

They turned away from the river and began following their retreating companions, disappearing back into the mountains.

"What now?" Radyan asked.

"We'll announce the names of the dead in Zilar so their families can be notified. I'll send a runner to Lann at Dalishar to give him new instructions. You'll work with the Guardians. Now that we've freed the Shaljir River, they've got to try to prevent another waterlord from taking control of it."

"Where will you be?"

"Shaljir. But I'll be back as soon as I can. We've won Zilar. We must keep our presence there strong."

"And the boy?"

"Zarien? I'm taking him with me."

"Ah. The *stahra*. He goes where you go."

"He goes where I go," Tansen agreed.

"I must admit, I've been wondering: Why?"

Despite everything, Tansen smiled. "You wouldn't believe me if I told you."

"And would I believe how that fresh wound became an old scar?" Radyan asked with a pointed glance at where Tansen's silvery *shir* scar lay beneath his shirt.

"Are people talking about it?" he asked quietly.

"What do *you* think?"

Tansen sighed. "It's a long story, and one without an ending. The truth is, I don't know how it healed."

Radyan frowned for a moment, then smiled and looked away. "Have it your way." Then something caught his attention. "Look!"

Someone had used heavy hemp rope to make a simple *jashar* which now hung like a banner from a free-standing, fire-blackened arch that had once been the entrance to Liadon's house.

Tansen studied the knotted, woven cords. " 'Free water for all.' "

Radyan's gaze remained fixed on it for a long moment. "I like it," he announced with a grin. "Free water for all." He glanced at Tansen and urged, "Let's make it come true."

"You might say," Tansen replied, "that it's been my life's work."

31

HE WHO HAS NOT CARRIED YOUR BURDEN DOES NOT
KNOW WHAT IT WEIGHS.

—Silerian Proverb

THE BOY WAS dawdling near the enormous old fig tree in the Sanctuary garden, staring moodily at his motionless *stahra* when Tansen first saw him.

Safe. Alive. Unharmed. Moderately obedient, it seemed, since he was, for once, right where he was supposed to be.

And taller? Tansen thought incredulously. It had only been a few days, for the love of Dar!

"I trust that Sisters Shannibar and Norimar are feeding you well?" Tan said dryly.

Startled, Zarien whirled around, letting the oar fall to the ground. "You're alive!"

"I'm alive," Tansen agreed, smiling at the mingled relief and astonishment in the boy's expression.

"You're— I thought . . . I mean . . . *waterlords*."

Tansen gathered from this garbled pronouncement that Zarien hadn't expected him to survive his admittedly audacious plan.

"Without water," he advised the boy, "they are only men."

"But they *had* water. They had . . . They were . . ." Zarien started taking air in big gulps. "Even when the Shaljir River melted and flowed again yesterday, I . . . I thought you might not be . . . um . . ."

Tansen surprised himself by putting his arms around Zarien and hugging him, much the way Josarian used to hug *him*. Then, lest the boy's sense of manly fortitude be compromised, he slapped him on the back and said, "Is there any food left for me, or have you eaten it all?"

"SANCTUARY? BUT I don't want to go to Sanctuary!" *Torena* Chasimar protested.

Ronall's head was pounding. His tongue tasted so vile he half-wished someone would cut it out. Sitting in the public room of the *tirshah*, he squinted against the sunlight which poured through a window—along with the fresh air that flooded his nostrils and made him want to vomit again. He had drunk himself unconscious, as planned, and was now feeling the effects of too little sleep gotten in too awkward a position at the very table where he still sat—now facing the two women he had reluctantly rescued in the night.

With any luck at all, things will look better after a generous quantity of ale, he decided.

He ignored the scandalized scowls of the elderly keeper and his wife, to whom he hadn't bothered to explain why he now kept *two* women in his bedchamber. He had never explained his actions to servants or peasants, and he certainly didn't intend to start now.

With enormous effort, Ronall focused his gaze on the two women who were now, for better or worse, his responsibility. He deeply regretted ever bedding the maid—Yenibar, as she'd informed him—and getting into this whole mess. Why hadn't he just let the wench steal his money and dreamweed? Or, having impetuously pursued her, why didn't he turn around and run away when he saw *shallaheen* killing Valdani? It seemed incredible that he, of all people, had come to Chasimar's rescue—and outrageously unfair that, refreshed by sleep and invigorated by the light of day, she didn't seem very appreciative of what was surely the sole heroic act of his life.

"We can't stay here," he explained through gritted teeth. "I don't know exactly who your husband's murderers were, but they were obviously local people. You can't seriously believe that *she,*" he indicated the keeper's wife, "won't spread gossip about me to every ear in this area by sundown tomorrow, which means that everyone will also know that *you're* here. And it's just possible they'll reconsider letting you live."

"So we have to leave here," *Torena* Chasimar conceded, "but I don't see why I have to go into Sanctuary."

Ronall sighed. "Where do you want to go?"

She gazed helplessly at him.

"Do you have a family?" he prodded. "Someone who'll take you in?"

"In Cavasar."

"Now that's just lovely," he replied.

"You won't take me there?"

"Certainly not. Haven't you heard? Kiloran is in charge of the whole city now. If anyone hates Valdani even more than the *shallaheen* do, it's the Society."

"My mother's people are there, too," Chasimar explained. "Full-blooded Silerians."

"Just how safe do you think Silerian *toreni* will be in a district now completely controlled by Kiloran?" he demanded.

"You think they're dead?" she gasped.

"No, he won't kill them. He'll just make them pay whatever he asks." He paused, then added, "And if they refuse, *then* he'll kill them. I don't even want to enter a district where—"

"Are you saying I can never see them again?" Tears welled up in her eyes.

"No. I'm saying that if you want to stay in Sileria—"

"I do! Where else can I go? I've never been to the mainland! I know no one there! And I have nothing—no money, no clothes, no relati—"

"Then you'd better pray for Tansen," he advised.

"Josarian's brother," she murmured with a distressed frown.

That startled him. "They were brothers?"

"Bloodbrothers," she elaborated.

Which, he knew, meant as much to a *shallah* as a birth relationship. "Are you sure?" he asked curiously.

"Of course I'm sure," she replied impatiently. "I knew Zim . . ." She stopped herself, shrugged, and said faintly, "Everyone knows." Her suddenly heightened color and shifting eyes stirred some vague unease in him.

"*I* didn't know," he pointed out a little irritably.

"*Torena* Elelar knows. She knows them both." She paused and, evidently remembering Josarian was now dead, amended, "Knew."

"Yes," he agreed morosely. "She knew them both."

Chasimar frowned. "Why wouldn't her own husband know they were bloodbrothers?"

"My wife and I are, um, not close. We don't talk much." Ronall poured some more ale and mused, "Bloodbrothers."

What a country, he thought blearily, feeling only slightly better as he drained his mug yet again. Guardians setting things on fire and talking to the dead, waterlords ensorcelling whole lakes and rivers, assassins capturing *toreni* and holding them for ransom, *shallaheen* cutting their own flesh in bloodpact commitments which ruled their lives, *zanareen* flinging themselves into the volcano, sea-born folk covering themselves in indigo tattoos and ignoring the whole rest of the country with open disdain.... And in the end, Sileria had murdered its own savior, the Firebringer. Why had the Valdani even bothered fighting Josarian, Ronall wondered, when some Silerian or other was bound to turn on him sooner or later? What a nation.

Really, he decided, any sensible person would be positively gleeful about fleeing to the mainland.

"But you and I are still half-Silerian," he muttered, "and therefore incapable of sense."

Yenibar gasped. "You, too?"

He shrugged, the strong ale helping him recover his sense of fatalism. "My name is Ronall. My father was a pure-blooded Valdan. Fourth generation to be born in Sileria. My mother . . ."

"Silerian," Chasimar breathed, "like mine."

"From Adalian."

"Can you . . ." Yenibar glanced at the *torena,* then continued, "Can you take us to them?"

"They're dead. Murdered by a mob in Shaljir."

Chasimar lowered her head and started weeping again. Ronall felt like hitting her, but he restrained himself.

"And *Torena* Elelar," Yenibar persisted. "She really is your wife?"

"She really is my wife," he replied glumly.

"Where is she now?"

"Shaljir, I assume."

"Has she a country home?" Yenibar asked.

He nodded. "She inherited the family estate from her grandfather."

"Would she give us shelter there?"

"I don't think she'd give any Val—"

"Elelar shah Hasnari?" Chasimar lifted her head and stared at Ronall. "That's right. You . . . told them I was her cousin."

"Yes," he agreed absently.

"Perhaps you could tell the same to her servants at her estate."

He shrugged. "I suppose I could."

"Elelar shah Hasnari's home, of all places, will be safe under native rule. Her relatives will be respected, as you proved last night. If she's in Shaljir," Chasimar added, "perhaps I wouldn't inconvenience her by staying at her country estate for the time being."

"Inconvenience her?" Ronall repeated pensively, starting to appreciate the ironic beauty of the suggestion.

"And if you tell her . . ." Chasimar licked her lips and continued, "Tell her I'm Porsall's wife. I'm the one who—"

"I don't have to tell her anything. I'm her husband. She'll do as she's told," he lied, beginning to genuinely like this new development.

Even Elelar wouldn't banish a homeless, pregnant, half-Valdani *torena* from her house to starve in the streets or be murdered by a mob. Even Elelar, whose morals were as depleted as Ronall's, would have compassion for an unborn child. She had her faults, but Elelar was a creature of duty who maintained certain rigorous standards (while wholly disregarding others).

Elelar would almost certainly leave Shaljir before long. She was a conscientious manager of her property. Since Elelar was a fugitive after escaping the Valdani prison in Shaljir, Ronall thought it unlikely she had been able to visit her grandfather's estate in months, and he knew that meant she'd be eager to go now.

When she got there, Ronall relished the image of her finding Chasimar and, against all personal preference, feeling obliged to shelter the woman. Elelar would have applauded while the mob in Shaljir killed her own loathed husband, but even Chasimar's Valdani blood wouldn't compel Elelar to abandon the widow's unborn child to hunger, violence, and death.

"That's an excellent plan," Ronall said at last, aware of Chasimar's and Yenibar's hopeful gazes. "I'll take you to my wife's estate." He grinned and added, "I need a change of clothing, anyhow."

MIRABAR PROTESTED VIOLENTLY, but Najdan won the argument. So she fled to Sanctuary while he attempted to track the assassins who had successfully abducted two Guardians: Tashinar and an initiate named Suligar, whom Mirabar knew only slightly.

Mirabar hated meekly allowing Pyron to escort her to safety while Tashinar was carried off to Kiloran. She hated waiting while Najdan and a dozen other men tried to follow and rescue the two captive Guardians. But Najdan was right when he said that if she accompanied them, they would waste most of their energy trying to ensure that she wasn't killed or captured, too.

She knew—and hated knowing—that Najdan was right when he said she was too valuable to risk losing in an attempt to save Tashinar. She was born to shield the new Yahrdan, whose destiny was to rule Sileria in freedom and prosperity; not even Tashinar's life could take precedence over that.

So now she huddled in the safety of Sister Basimar's mountain Sanctuary, where Pyron and an escort of five men had brought her, hooded and cloaked, with all due haste after the battle on Mount Niran. The other survivors of the massacre on Niran had fled, too, going to join another Guardian circle.

Upon arriving here in Sanctuary, Mirabar had the unpleasant task of confirming Zimran's death to Sister Basimar, who had loved him. Heartbroken, the Sister wept for him.

Basimar couldn't do much about the *shir* wound on Mirabar's arm. Just a scratch, it wouldn't have bothered her if it had been made by an ordinary blade. But everything she'd ever been taught about *shir* was true; nothing hurt the way an assassin's water-born dagger did. The scratch burned with an ever-present cold fire, and it kept reopening, bleeding afresh. It would leave a scar, ensuring that she always remembered the assassin who'd cut her. As if she could ever forget.

Darfire, I've killed a man.

She had seen people die before, had even felt responsible for people's deaths before; but she had never held a struggling man in her hands and killed him before. She had never before heard a man scream in agony while she burned him to death. She had never felt a living person squirm in desperate, smoldering agony while she murdered him.

I've killed someone.

Tansen was right. It was not a thing to be done lightly.

I had no choice. He'd have killed me. I was defending myself.

She knew that was true. Yet the knowledge of death in her hands, the memory of murder in her nostrils, the song of her victim's screams in her ears . . . it changed her.

Elelar deserved to die. Mirabar still believed that with all her heart; but now she wasn't sure what to do about it.

If only Tansen had killed her as he promised to do. If only it were already over and done with.

If only . . .

What was she to do about Elelar now? Tansen had made it clear he would do nothing, and now Mirabar felt nauseated every time she considered doing to Elelar what she had recently done to that assassin.

If only . . .

He should have killed Elelar. It was his duty. It was his right.

He can't. Part of him belongs to her. Part of him will always belong to her.

Mirabar wanted to weep. There was no safe direction for her thoughts to turn anymore.

Why did the strange display of whirling smoke, colored clouds, and flashing lightning continue at the peak of distant Mount Darshon? What did Dar want? What was She preparing for? The coming of the prophesied Yahrdan? Or something else?

And how would Mirabar know him? In the wake of her recent vision, she wondered if he was an infant. But what about Semeon, the flame-haired fire-eyed child whom Cheylan had promised to protect? No infant, but a child nonetheless, and one whose coloring matched that of the infant in her vision.

How will I know him?

Above all, how would she protect him when she'd been unable to protect Josarian himself, the Firebringer, a strong warrior in the prime of manhood?

Why did You let him die, Dar? Why?

What would happen to Tashinar? Why did Kiloran want Guardians captured? What would he do to the woman who had tamed, taught, and loved Mirabar? Did he know what Tashinar meant to her, or was it merely chance that she was one of the Guardians he had captured? Since he'd wanted more than one, and the assassin whom Najdan had tortured knew of no instructions to take someone in particular, Mirabar prayed that Kiloran at least didn't know that Tashinar was dear to her.

If only I had gotten to Mount Niran sooner. If only we had pressed on and arrived that night, before the attack. If only there had been moonlight.

If only . . .

Her mind was whirling, her thoughts as tumultuous as her emotions. Basimar's frequent weeping over Zimran's disgraceful death didn't help. Nor did the sulky fear of Haydar, Najdan's mostly silent mistress, improve Mirabar's state of mind.

"Stop looking at me like that," Mirabar snapped at Haydar as the three women sat down to supper the day after Mirabar's arrival here. Pyron and the other men had already prudently decided to take all their meals outside, safely distant from the three overwrought women. "I'm not a demon."

"Forgive me, *sirana*," Haydar murmured, casting her dark gaze down to her untouched food.

"Why should I forgive you?" Mirabar demanded, all out of patience.

"Mira," Basimar admonished in watery tones.

"No, let's settle this now," Mirabar insisted, eager to unleash a little temper on someone.

Basimar's plump, rosy face was distressed. Her steadfast devotion to Zimran, who'd once been her occasional lover, had always baffled Mirabar, since it was certainly no secret that he slept with many other women. However, though unable to understand, Mirabar nonetheless sympathized with Basimar's broken heart when Zimran developed an unprecedented, faithful, and intense devotion to *Torena* Elelar after helping her escape from prison.

Now Zimran was dead, and Sister Basimar's mourning was tinged with bitterness over his passion for another woman and with shame over his betrayal of Josarian.

Mirabar felt guilty about upsetting Basimar even more, but the demon inside her must be fed. So she now turned angrily on Haydar and demanded, "Why do you flinch when I move, shift your gaze when our eyes meet, cringe when I talk, sulk when I—"

"Because he will die for you!" Haydar suddenly cried, her dark eyes flashing with startling fury.

Taken aback by the first sign of spirit she had ever seen in Najdan's woman, Mirabar gaped at Haydar in stunned silence.

"I do not fear you. He says you are no demon," Haydar continued, her voice filled with hot emotion, "and I believe him, because he always knows best."

Now Mirabar had something to say. "So *you're* the one who convinced Najdan that he always knows b—"

"Mira," Basimar snapped.

"Well, I knew it wasn't me," she protested.

"He left me to follow you," Haydar said in growing anger, "and I endured it, because that is a woman's duty."

"Oh, for the love of—"

"He spoke of your visions, your power, your courage, your honor—"

"He did?" Mirabar asked, startled.

"I agreed that a man must serve such a great destiny." Consumed by emotion, Haydar suddenly swept her arm across the table, knocking her plate, food, and cup onto the floor. Basimar gasped and jumped, but Mirabar remained riveted on Haydar's tormented expression and passionate words. "But then you made him betray Kiloran."

"No, Haydar," Mirabar said softly. "I didn't make him—"

"He did it for you!"

"He did it because it was right," Mirabar insisted quietly.

"No. It was because Kiloran ordered him to kill you, and he could not do it."

And they all knew it wasn't because Najdan was afraid.

"Then surely," Mirabar said, "it was Kiloran who caused his betrayal."

"Najdan served Kiloran loyally for twenty years." Haydar grasped Mirabar's wrist with a strong, work-roughened hand and demanded, "Do you think he'd have betrayed his master for anyone but you?"

"It is Dar who—"

"He doesn't care about Dar! He serves you, not the goddess!"

Wondering if there'd perhaps been a huge misunderstanding, Mirabar cautiously said, "But he loves you, Haydar. There's no question of . . . um . . ."

"I don't fear you as a woman," Haydar snapped. "You're young enough to be his daughter."

"That," said Basimar, her tone laced with uncharacteristic cynicism, "has never mattered to any man of my acquaintance."

"Be quiet," Mirabar suggested.

Haydar glanced at Basimar. "He's the most honorable man I've ever known."

"He's an assassin," Basimar protested.

Mirabar kicked her and suggested, more forcefully this time, "Be quiet."

"He loves me." Calmer now, Haydar let go of Mirabar's wrist. "I have never doubted his love."

Basimar's eyes clouded and she looked down at her plate. Even Mirabar felt a sharp stab of envy. Haydar spoke with simple, warm confidence. She sounded like a woman who'd always been given every reason to know that she was loved—permanently, faithfully, exclusively.

Haydar sighed. "But he has betrayed Kiloran, and he will die for it. For you. Very soon. Kiloran will not let such a deep insult go unpunished for long."

"Tansen will destroy Kiloran," Mirabar said.

"How can he?" Haydar asked quietly. "How can anyone destroy Kiloran?"

"He will," Mirabar insisted, feeling her stomach churning again. She pushed away her plate, leaving the food untouched.

"Since the day Najdan paid my father a bride-price and took me to live with him near Lake Kandahar, I have learned many times over that no one can challenge Kiloran and live."

There seemed little to say in response to this. The Firebringer himself had died for challenging Kiloran, just like everyone else who had ever done so.

Almost everyone else.

"What about Baran?" Mirabar asked suddenly.

Haydar shrugged. "Yes, it's true, he has lasted a long time."

Mirabar nodded slowly. "We *must* make him our ally."

Sister Basimar looked at her thoughtfully. "He did side with Josarian against Kiloran."

"But the Firebringer is dead," Haydar said, "and Baran has always been as shrewd as he is crazy."

"Yes, I've met him," Mirabar said. "It's a very unsettling combination."

"He knows too much to become your ally now," Haydar said with certainty. "He will never believe that Tansen can win, not with Josarian dead and Kiloran already in complete control of Cavasar."

"If I could make him believe in the coming of the Yahrdan, in the visions of—"

"He's a waterlord," Haydar pointed out. "This vision will not attract him."

Mirabar remembered Tansen's words with regard to Baran: *Do whatever you have to.*

What could she do? If Baran didn't want to join them, what would convince him to change his mind?

And how, she wondered wearily, could she ever be sure Baran was sincere, that whatever he might say or promise was at all reliable?

She sat slumped in her chair, worrying until her head ached. Baran. Tashinar. Kiloran. Elelar. Tansen. Zarien, his watery goddess, and his search for the sea king. The Beckoner. Cheylan. Dar. The Firebringer. The Yahrdan. The visions . . .

Together, they were all a burden which was driving her to her knees.

Please, Dar, as I have been faithful and true, as I have served You with an open heart and fire in my soul . . . Please help me. Please lead the way. Please show me what to do.

Weary beyond bearing, yet knowing she wouldn't sleep tonight, she finally searched for the only comforting words she could find: "Whatever happens next, Haydar, I won't let Najdan die for me."

Haydar replied with a Silerian woman's resignation, "If he means to die for you, there's nothing you can do to stop him."

I ROSE OUT *of the water, looming over the shallow Zilar River like some monster from a madman's worst nightmares. Tansen knew what it was even before he heard Najdan's hoarse, shocked voice utter the words: the White Dragon. A voracious, evil creature born of a magical union between water and a wizard.*

It was huge, far bigger than a Widowbeast or a dragonfish, and its fierce roar made the very ground tremble with awe. It shifted and glittered beneath the brilliant light of the moons, gleaming like the blade of a shir, *shining like the diamonds of Alizar. Its long, serpentlike neck swayed and twisted, the sharp icicles inside its great mouth snapping at its enemies. If it had eyes and ears, Tansen could not see them, so he didn't know how it had found its intended prey—the Firebringer—with such unerring accuracy.*

Tansen ran forward through the shallow water, feeling its deadly chill. This was Kiloran's river now. He had given birth to this monstrous creature here in the heart of Josarian's territory.

"No!" Tansen screamed, running straight at the enormous, dripping beast, his swords drawn.

He swung at its haunches. His blade cut through pure water. He swung again, cutting, stabbing, slicing, thrusting. He circled the roaring beast, plunging through thigh-deep water, his flesh burning in a thousand places from the bitterly cold, ensorcelled droplets flying off the White Dragon. Each splash was like the touch of a shir. *Tears streamed down his face from the pain.*

"Josarian!" he howled, attacking the creature again.

An enormous claw came down and struck him. It was like being hit by a galloping horse. He flew backwards. The waters of the Zilar closed over his head as he fell. He lunged to the surface, still hanging onto his swords. The great dragonlike head lowered, following him, the hungry jaws snapping and seeking him. He swung a sword with an arm that felt heavy and numb. His blade scraped along the shir-*like fangs. The cold breath of the beast froze his wet flesh.*

"Tansen!" *Josarian screamed.*

"Josarian!" Tansen sat bolt upright, shouting his brother's name.

"What? What! *What?*" Zarien howled, flinging himself around in the dark, his voice high with panic.

Heart pounding, breath coming hard, Tansen quickly said, "Nothing. It's nothing. I'm sorry."

"What!" Zarien repeated, his voice loud enough to wake shades of the dead. "What's happening?"

Tansen heard the clatter of wood and guessed the boy was fumbling for his *stahra* in the dark chamber they shared here in Sister Shannibar's Sanctuary.

"Nothing," Tan repeated. "Nothing. It's all right."

"It's not all right!" Zarien cried. "I . . . I'm . . ." There was a long, dark silence, punctuated only by the sound of their racing breath. "It was m . . ." Zarien gulped air. Tansen heard him sink to the floor. "It was more of those dreams of yours, wasn't it?"

"Yes."

"Don't you ever just . . . *sleep?* Like other people?"

"Not lately," he muttered. "Not often."

"Did you ever?" Zarien asked plaintively.

"A long time ago. When I was . . ." He sighed gustily. "When I was your age."

"A *long* time ago," Zarien agreed.

"Sorry I woke you."

"What do you dream about?"

Mostly about the night I murdered my bloodfather.

No, perhaps he wouldn't share that with the child. "Things."

"That's it?" He heard outrage in the youthful voice. "That's all you're going to tell me, after scaring me half to d—"

"Josarian," he snapped.

"What?"

He sighed again. "I was dreaming about Josarian. About the night he died."

He heard Zarien draw a sharp breath. "The night Kiloran killed him."

"Yes."

"Tell me."

"What?"

"About the night he died. About the White Dragon."

"No," Tan said firmly. "That's not a good story for the dark." No point in *both* of them having nightmares.

"Then tell me about Josarian," Zarien persisted. "What was the Fire-bringer like?"

Oh, this boy could pierce the heart with such accuracy.

Tansen drew up his knees and rested his chin on them, grateful that the dark hid his expression. He made a fist with his hand, then opened it again. The *shir* wound there, gotten during the ambush he'd survived on the way to Dalishar, had started troubling him again after the attack on Abidan and Liadon. Sister Norimar had tended it for him this evening—weeping copiously the whole time over Galian's death. Tansen hadn't realized there'd been a spark between those two. Now they'd never know if there could have been flames.

So much is lost with every death. So much.

"Tell me about Josarian," Zarien repeated insistently. "You knew the Firebringer better than anyone, they say."

Josarian.

Think about something besides the night he died. Think about something good.

"He . . ." Tansen breathed away the tension, the horror of the nightmare, the pain of the memory. He closed his eyes and remembered the man whom he had taken as his brother. "He had the biggest, most generous heart of anyone I've ever known. He was . . . all that's good about Sileria, about the *shallaheen*. He was very brave and loyal, strong and practical, shrewd and honorable. But he was also compassionate and fair, which are not virtues taught to everyone in the mountains," Tansen admitted wryly. "Josarian treated everyone with respect, and anyone who met him responded with respect, from the poorest *shallah* to the loftiest *toren*. He . . ." Tansen hesitated, but then told the boy with honesty, "Perhaps he loved too much, when he loved. He couldn't get over his wife's death, and he probably never would have, had he lived. He couldn't see the flaws in his cousin, Zimran, who betrayed him. He was very wise in some ways, but terribly innocent in others."

"How did you become bloodbrothers?"

"It's late," Tansen pointed out.

"My heart has jumped out of my chest and is even now halfway to sea," Zarien replied. "I'm not going back to sleep soon."

Tansen smiled. "I'll light a candle."

"And perhaps there's some food left?"

Tansen laughed softly. "Yes, we can look."

"Good!"

So they brought light into the dark night, found something to keep Zarien from starving to death before morning, and talked. Tansen answered the boy's questions about how, after being arrested by Outlookers in Cavasar, he had first met Josarian by tracking down the mountain bandit on the pretense of killing him for the Valdani—but really, in fact, to join Josarian in harassing them.

"We became bloodbrothers the night before we attacked the Outlooker fortress at Britar, where we freed Josarian's imprisoned friends and relatives."

"I've heard that story!"

"Good, then I don't have to tell it now."

"Yes, you must!" the boy insisted. "You were *there*."

Tansen acquiesced and, in truth, didn't try very hard to shrug off the admiration shining in Zarien's eyes. The battle at Britar remained, to this very day, one of his and Josarian's most famous feats; they had been two men against perhaps one hundred Outlookers. Knowing full well that one or both of them was likely to die, they swore a bloodpact together the night before they attacked, thus becoming brothers. Tansen also joined Josarian that night in swearing a bloodfeud against the Valdani.

"That was the start of the rebellion," he told Zarien, watching Sanctuary shadows flicker in the candlelight. Sister Shannibar's clumsy dog stared soulfully at Zarien, using everything but words to suggest that she, too, might expire of hunger before morning if no one fed her some scraps. "Of course, we didn't know then, never dreamed that day, where it would eventually lead us. Lead all of Sileria."

"Go away," Zarien told the dog. "That's the last piece you're getting."

Since he had already said this three or four times—prior to giving in and feeding it some more—the dog quite sensibly ignored the command and continued to gaze at him with an expression of mingled hope and deprivation.

After Britar, the Outlookers had failed to count on Josarian's charisma, let alone his determination, and so his bloodfeud against the Valdani grew faster than they could suppress it—though they certainly tried, and their measures in the mountains were usually brutal beyond what Tansen was willing to describe to the sea-born boy.

"When did Josarian come to Kiloran's attention?"

Now they were into the awkward part of the story, Tansen realized. Josarian hadn't come to Kiloran's attention; Tansen had. However, Tan had no intention of telling this child that Kiloran sought him in vengeance, even after all those years, for murdering Armian.

So he simply replied, "Well, Josarian became very famous, you know. Among the drylanders. It was inevitable that Kiloran would take an interest."

"And Mirabar? When did she join you?"

"When Kiloran did."

"Who is the woman she wants you to kill?"

The question came at him like an arrow out of the dark. It had been a long time since anyone had actually made him flinch in surprise.

"It's a long story," he replied.

"The sun is still far away." Zarien's dark eyes were watchful in his tattooed face.

Tansen tried another tactic. "It's not my place to talk about it," he lied.

"If not yours, then whose?"

He regarded the boy uneasily. "Mirabar's, perhaps." And he thought she was unlikely to share the tale with Zarien.

"Why did you not do it? Kill the woman, I mean."

"Have you ever killed a woman?"

Zarien recoiled. "No!"

Tansen lifted his brows. "Neither have I. And I don't intend to start."

"But Mirabar said—"

"Never mind what Mirabar said." Time to take charge, he decided. "Tell me more about what Sharifar said."

"What Sharifar said?" Zarien seemed startled by the question.

"I am," Tansen said dryly, "more interested than I have, perhaps, led you to believe."

"Then you won't change your mind? We're leaving for Shaljir?"

"The day after tomorrow," Tansen confirmed. "What are your plans?"

"*My* plans?" the boy asked cautiously.

Tansen studied his expression for a moment, wondering what he saw there. "Yes," he said at last. "What do you expect me to do?"

"Oh!" Tansen was sure this time; he saw relief. "I will arrange for a boat to take us to sea."

"And?"

Zarien shrugged, seemingly unconcerned. "That's all I know. I must bring you to sea."

"How will . . ." Darfire, he didn't even know how to phrase it. He tried, "How will I meet Sharifar, if I am indeed—"

"She will decide," Zarien said simply.

"I see. That's all?"

Zarien blinked. "Yes. Should there be more?"

"Damned if I know." Whatever he had to do, he hoped it would be easier than jumping into a volcano.

Zarien shrugged and ate some more.

Watching him, Tansen tried again. "Have you told me everything Sharifar said to you?"

Zarien paused, keeping his eyes on his food. "I've told you everything you need to know."

Far from it, Tansen reflected with some exasperation; but something in the boy's choice of words distracted him. "Everything *I* need to know?"

"Yes."

"But not," he guessed slowly, "everything that was said?"

Zarien became preoccupied with the dog. "Everything that was said about you."

"What else was said?"

"Sea-born matters," Zarien said evasively. "It doesn't concern you."

Tansen tried not to smile. "Ah, but if I'm the sea king—"

"Private matters," Zarien amended, his tone distinctly defensive now. "Nothing that you need to know about."

"Whatever she said," Tansen noted, "it bothered you."

A sulky shrug was his only reply.

A chilly foreboding crept across Tansen. Those scars of Zarien's evinced a terrible dragonfish attack, one which should have killed him; one which *had* killed him, in fact, if his tale was accurate. A sea-born boy who'd never be searched for, because he was believed to be dead . . . Just how long a life had the goddess offered him in exchange for hunting down her consort?

"Zarien."

The boy heard the sudden, dark seriousness in his tone and looked up from his food.

"Did she tell you . . ." Tansen hesitated. "What happens to you when Sharifar finds her consort?"

Zarien looked puzzled. "To me?"

"Did Sharifar say that would be the end of your life?" He couldn't go to sea, not ever, if it might mean this boy's death.

Zarien's eyes flew wide. "You mean, will she give me back to the dragonfish then?" Tansen nodded. A look of outrage washed across the tattooed young face. "She had better not!"

Tansen sat back. Whatever was on Zarien's mind, this was clearly a brand-new idea to him. Fortunately, however, it seemed to inspire far more indignation than fear.

"She had no right to send me ashore in disgrace if she meant me to die anyhow. There was no reason for her to tell me that I . . ." His complexion darkened as he stumbled to an awkward halt.

"Tell you what?" Tansen prodded.

"Um . . ."

"Let's try another question," Tansen said suddenly, a new suspicion dawning on him. "Will *I* die when I meet Sharifar?"

Zarien's looked surprised. "How could you die? The sea king is supposed to unite the sea-born folk. How could a dead man do that?" He regarded Tansen with an expression suggesting the *shatai* was considerably less intelligent than he had previously thought. "Landfolk," he muttered, rising to his feet.

"Where are you going?" Tansen asked.

"Back to sleep. I'm full now."

"Full," Tansen murmured, regarding the Sisters' decimated supply of bread and cheese. "And you've only consumed the weight of six adult sheep. Imagine."

"I do not eat sheep," Zarien reminded him.

"Just their excretions."

"Ugh!" Zarien stomped away. "Landfolk."

"Goodnight, son."

"Goodnight, Tansen."

Tansen sat up for a while longer, absently petting the dog—who noisily mourned Zarien's absence—and thinking about the conversation.

He wished he knew more about boys, but he had stopped being one so long ago—and so abruptly. He was convinced there was something Zarien wasn't telling him. He thought he'd covered the most significant possibilities, and now he was reasonably certain that if embracing Sharifar was going to kill either him or Zarien, the boy didn't know about it.

Whatever Zarien was keeping from him, Tansen just hoped it wasn't important.

32

No one wins wars; some merely lose less than others do.

—Kintish Proverb

THE SCREAMS COMING from the depths of Kiloran's watery palace were giving him a headache. This shifting mansion of water and air, of flickering light and silvery dark, now reverberated loudly with the anguish of the young Guardian being interrogated at some distance from the hall where Kiloran was trying to concentrate on other business.

It had taken tremendous will and skill to shape this palace out of the deep waters of Lake Kandahar long ago. Maintaining it was a drain on Kiloran's strength, but one he was accustomed to, having done it for so long. Besides, his power had grown so much greater over the years that holding up these fluidly quivering walls of water was, by now, merely a minor demand, not the noticeable effort it had been once upon a time.

He controlled the walls, floors, and ceilings of his unique home as easily as a man controlled the fingers of his hand. This was what made Kandahar impregnable, the most envied stronghold in the entire Society—and one which would die with him, if he couldn't find a suitable heir. The ensorcelled palace could not survive on its own, so closely entwined was it with its owner's will. At a whim, Kiloran could create or destroy whole rooms, trap and drown prisoners, admit guests from the lake's surface high overhead, and change the very size and shape of the palace.

Not that he did it often. It was a luxurious, well-furnished home, and he didn't like destroying his cherished possessions. His water-born stronghold was filled with treasures from all over Sileria, and from all over the nations of Sirkara. Kiloran loved beautiful things, fine craftsmanship, rare and exotic possessions of exquisite loveliness. The palace was also filled with symbols of who he was and reminders of all he had achieved and endured in his long life: enemies destroyed, territory conquered, loved ones lost, mistakes made, lessons learned . . . Yes, much of his life was represented in the keepsakes housed here.

Enemies destroyed . . . Kiloran kept two glittering diamonds from Alizar here, a symbol of the mines he had helped take from the vanquished Valdani and which he now possessed, though he had yet to free them of his sorcery and access their endless wealth. There was also a bronze broach, a single flame in a circle of fire, taken from the first Guardian he had ever killed.

Territory conquered . . . Kiloran liked to receive visitors in the main hall, where he sat on a throne of enormous gold-encrusted shells. A gaudy but impressive reminder of the waterlord from whom he had taken Lake Kandahar itself, many years ago.

One entire vast wall in the main hall was covered with *shir*; some taken from formidable enemies slain over the years, some treasured remembrances of dead comrades.

Loved ones lost . . . Srijan's *shir* was among the daggers on that wall now. Josarian had not taken it upon killing him, and so Kiloran had ordered its retrieval.

Mistakes made, lessons learned . . . Armian's *shir* was among them, too, its magnificent workmanship standing out even in this unparalleled collection. Though young at the time, Kiloran had done fine work on the weapon he made for Harlon's son so long ago.

Mistakes made . . .

Kiloran's gaze strayed, for the first time in longer than he could remember, to the bracelet which lay alone on a shimmering protrusion of crystallized water emerging from another wall.

Kintish silver with jade inlays.

He hadn't been surprised to see Baran wearing the matching necklace. Baran always wore it.

Lessons learned . . .

The bracelet lived here as a reminder to Kiloran of something he had once forgotten and never intended to forget again: Impetuous acts and ungoverned passions always cost too much and should never be indulged.

No, he never intended to forget again.

Indeed, Kiloran thought his own recent conduct at Emeldar proved just how thoroughly he had banished impetuosity and now governed his passions. He was convinced the greatest self-control he'd ever exerted in his life was that day in Josarian's abandoned village when Baran tried everything but physical violence to goad him into an attack.

The temptation to finally kill that mad, embittered agitator became even greater when Kiloran realized that Baran's surprisingly changed appearance was the result of illness. A serious one, Kiloran suspected. Baran, a big and previously agile man, was already physically weakened. After all, Meriten, rather small and certainly no warrior, had managed to choke him half to death before Baran's assassin came to his rescue. How soon before ꞁ Baran's sorcery weakened, too? Perhaps it already had. What a temptation it had been to try to find out right then and there!

Baran ill . . . Perhaps even dying? It was such a pleasing prospect, it almost made Kiloran feel young again.

Baran weak, vulnerable, and finally vanquishable . . .

To ambush Baran. To take back the Idalar River at last. To destroy and humiliate him. To pull the moat at Belitar right up over the ancient ruins there and drown Baran in his own bed one night . . . Oh, yes, these were immensely pleasing thoughts.

However, when the rage Kiloran had felt in Emeldar cooled into clear-headed reason, he realized that, after all these years, the problem of Baran might soon simply solve itself. Kiloran was a practical man, and he much preferred the possibility of Baran dying quietly of a wasting disease to the cumbersome reality of expending even more of his own energy trying to destroy Baran after their new truce ended—as it unquestionably would once their enemies were defeated and dead.

Yes, Kiloran had learned his lesson well. His fury over Baran's behavior at Emeldar that day must not cloud his judgment or incite him to impetuous acts. Even now, Searlon was attempting to learn just how ill Baran really was. If Baran was going to die soon on his own, if patience was all that was now needed to finally defeat him, Kiloran could wait. After all these years, to win with no effort would be the sweetest victory of all.

Meanwhile, he would let Baran make himself useful. After all, bringing Shaljir to its knees would indeed be easier if he had Baran's help in holding back the Idalar River. And if Baran killed Mirabar, then that was one less task Kiloran must accomplish.

Another long, piercing scream of pain and anguish floated through the watery halls and echoed around the palace.

It had been going on since last night, and Kiloran, whose head was starting to throb, had had enough of it.

When Kiloran tried hard enough, he could hear the Firebringer's perpetual agony through the barrier of death. The extraordinary means of Josarian's demise, the powerful sorcery needed to defeat him, ensured that the two of them were linked for the rest of Kiloran's life. That was the way of the White Dragon. Fortunately, this mystical bond very rarely intruded on Kiloran's thoughts. Whereas it was becoming impossible to ignore the Guardian's howls of pain. Feeling his temper fray, Kiloran sent for Dyshon the assassin, who was interrogating the young woman.

"If she hasn't talked by now," Kiloran advised Dyshon, when he appeared, "then she knows nothing."

Dyshon looked tired and a little gray-faced. Well, interrogation was, admittedly, an unpleasant business.

Dyshon asked, "You want me to kill her, *siran?*"

"Yes. There's no point in persisting."

"So we're going to question the older one?"

Kiloran nodded. "Yes, it's time to revive her."

"I regret, *siran,*" Dyshon said, "that I have been unable to make the younger prisoner useful to you."

Kiloran shook his head. "If the woman knows nothing, then she cannot be made to tell anything." He sighed. "It's a pity. Only two Guardians captured, and one clearly useless."

"With respect, *siran,* perhaps it was a mistake to entrust the capture to another waterlord's assassins."

"Ah, mistakes, they are so easily made," Kiloran replied philosophically. "Geriden assured me he and his men could handle it. And despite coming under attack unexpectedly while engaged in their ambush, his men did manage to bring back two Guardians, which was the minimum number I requested."

"Has there been any word about the hunt for Mirabar?"

"Not yet. But I remain hopeful."

The battle at Niran had, unfortunately, turned into a general bloodbath. Just when Geriden and his assassins felt confident of killing all but four Guardians and then hauling away their captives without interference, Mirabar and an unspecified number of men—*Najdan among them, no doubt,* Kiloran thought with a twinge of fury—had attacked the ambushers. Consequently, Geriden had lost half the men he'd taken to Niran, and only two Guardians had been brought to Kandahar. One of Geriden's assassins had seen Mirabar, illuminated in the dark night by her own deadly fire; her demonic appearance was unmistakable. It was lucky the assassin had been prudent enough to retreat and remain alive, rather than attacking and dying as others had done, or Kiloran might never have known exactly what happened that night.

Or that Mirabar had, quite unexpectedly, been in the region. Far from Tansen, whose last known location was Zilar. Far from Dalishar, which was virtually impregnable.

Geriden hadn't thought to track Mirabar at the time, a mistake which ensured he received a blistering verbal attack from Kiloran upon arriving at Kandahar. The mediocrity of Geriden's sorcery was only one reason he remained such a minor waterlord.

Kiloran knew with regret that it was almost certainly too late to track Mirabar now. Najdan would have known the risks of her being seen, and he'd have ensured her quick disappearance after the battle. However, one must try. So Kiloran had assigned every assassin he could spare to go search for her.

Mirabar's surprise appearance on Mount Niran led to a number of questions, all of them still unanswered. Was she there that night by chance or intent? Had someone betrayed Kiloran and warned Mirabar of his plans? Although this was a disturbing possibility, which must be investigated, Kiloran was at least convinced that the Guardians themselves had not been warned; they were completely unprepared for such an assault, according to Geriden, and the ambush would have succeeded perfectly if not for Mirabar's arrival. And if Mirabar was there that night by chance, then what had brought her to Mount Niran *now*? What could have been worth such a risk to her safety?

Kiloran sincerely hoped the older Guardian, the one they hadn't yet begun to interrogate, had some answers. In any event, she promised to be more rewarding than the young one. Whereas the young one was relatively helpless, the old one's fire sorcery was so powerful that the assassins had only been able to capture and transport her by keeping her unconscious.

Such a powerful elder was likely to know the things Kiloran wanted to know, though extracting the information would be a challenge, one which would require his personal attention. Here at Kandahar, Kiloran used potions acquired from the Sisterhood to keep her weak and befuddled until such time as it was obvious—as it now was—that they'd have to risk reviving her.

"Yes," Kiloran concluded, nodding to Dyshon. "Let's begin questioning her."

"THEY'VE TAKEN THE two Guardians to Kandahar," Najdan advised Mirabar. "We followed them as far as we could." He took a breath and concluded slowly, "I regret, *sirana,* that I cannot retrieve Tashinar from Kiloran's lair. She is lost."

Mirabar was vaguely aware of the way Basimar gasped at Najdan's statement. She herself felt the words—*she is lost*—like blows, but at least they were real. At least she knew.

Tashinar is lost.

Each word was a blow which drove Mirabar to her knees.

"Tashinar," she murmured brokenly, too shocked at first to feel the full weight of her grief.

"You cannot go after her," Najdan said. "You must accept that."

Once upon a time, Mirabar had invaded Kiloran's underwater palace and saved Tansen's life; probably Josarian's, too, that fateful night. She couldn't do so again, though. Even now, as she started weeping for Tashinar, Najdan was telling her that Kiloran, aware that she'd been at Mount Niran, already had assassins prowling the mountains in search of her. It was very unlikely she could reach Kandahar alive, and quite certain that Kiloran would kill her there if she did.

She heard the words, understood the danger, and recognized her duty. But she could only collapse facedown onto the ground and wail, "*Tashinar!*"

Now she felt it. Now it assaulted her in hot waves of anguish.

"We must leave immediately, *sirana,*" Najdan advised her, "or we'll become trapped here."

"No," she cried. "No! No! No!"

"When they learn you're here," Najdan said urgently, trying to pull her up, "they'll make it impossible for you to leave."

She shoved him away. Her fingers clutched fistfuls of dirt as she lay on the ground. "*Tashinar . . . No!*" In Kiloran's keeping; in Kiloran's lair. In the grip of Kiloran's cruelty.

"You will be cut off from everyone else," Najdan warned, raising his voice. "A prisoner of this Sanctuary."

He tugged on her, forcing her to rise to her knees.

"Go back for her!" she wailed. "Get her!"

"No."

"You can get her!" She hit him. "You know Kandahar. You know Kiloran's secrets! Go back! Get her!" She hit him harder.

His face was lined and gray. His eyes glittered darkly. "I can't. No one can."

"*Nooooo . . .*"

"We must go now," he insisted.

He tried to drag her to her feet. She lashed out in blind, animal pain, fire shimmering over her skin, burning him so he'd release her. She heard him draw a sharp breath as he dropped her.

Then Haydar's frightened voice: "Najdan!"

"It's all right," he said. "She won't hurt me."

"She just did!"

"Go get ready," he ordered. "All of you. We're leaving *now*."

"Tashinar . . ." Mirabar sobbed.

Najdan knelt beside her again. "We will avenge her," he promised.

"I don't want vengeance," she wept. "I want Tashinar!"

His hands were gentler now. He pulled her upright, pushed her hair off her face, and then embraced her. "I know," he said quietly. "I'm sorry."

TANSEN, FOLLOWED BY Zarien, entered the old Kintish temple in Zilar early in the morning, meaning to attend to a few final details before he departed for Shaljir. He looked questioningly at Radyan, who awaited him there, wondering what could have put such a big grin on his face.

"You'll never guess," Radyan said, "who's brought the latest messages from Dalishar."

Tansen glanced in the direction Radyan indicated and saw a friend emerge from the shadows. "Emelen!"

Josarian's brother-in-law crossed the vast temple to embrace him in greeting. "Praise Dar that you, at least, are safe," Emelen said.

"When did you get to Dalishar?" Tansen asked.

"A few days ago," Emelen replied. "Did you know Lann slept through that first big earthquake we had? Let's remember never to leave him on sentry duty."

Tansen grinned, briefly introduced Emelen to Zarien, then advised the boy they'd be here a little longer than expected. Seeing Zarien's impatient expression, Tan distracted him by suggesting, "Go get something to eat. Here's some money." As expected, the ploy worked, and Zarien promised to leave him in peace long enough to talk with Emelen.

"I've got Guardians to deal with," Radyan said, excusing himself.

"Where's Jalilar?" Tansen asked, sitting down with Emelen.

"In Sanctuary, and not happy about it."

That didn't surprise Tansen. Josarian's sister had never liked confinement *or* being separated from her husband. "How is she?"

"Taking Josarian's death hard," Emelen admitted, his own face sad. "She knew it could come. We all did. But they were close."

"I know," Tansen murmured, remembering.

"Their parents are dead. Now he's gone." Emelen sighed. "To be honest, we fought badly before I left her in Sanctuary. She says . . ." Emelen shrugged and looked sadder. "Well, we still have no child, and with her family dead, there is only me. She said I could either stay there with her or take her with me, but I couldn't leave her alone in Sanctuary and go running off to die without her."

"So what did you do? You just said that she's in Sanc—"

"I left in the middle of the night. While she slept. And I, uh . . ." He cleared his throat awkwardly. "I made the Sister give her something to keep her asleep for a full day, so she couldn't possibly follow me."

"Fires of Dar."

"Uh-huh."

"I wouldn't be you for all the diamonds in Alizar," Tan said with feeling.

"No," Emelen agreed.

"She'll make you very sorry for that."

"I know." Emelen made a frustrated gesture. "I just didn't know what else to do. There was no time to keep fighting about it. I knew you'd need me to get back as soon as possible."

"I did," Tansen admitted.

"She simply wouldn't stay there. Not unless I made it, well, impossible for her to come with me. And she couldn't come, she mustn't. Who knows what Kiloran will do to the Firebringer's sister if she leaves Sanctuary now?"

Jalilar was a strong and sensible woman, and Tansen was positive she understood what was at stake. "But the war has taken everything from her," Tansen said, thinking aloud. "Her family, her village, her friends, her way of life . . ."

According to the customs of the *shallaheen,* Tansen would, as her dead brother's bloodbrother, be responsible for her if anything happened to her husband now. He would protect her, but it wasn't enough, he knew, not after all that Jalilar had lost. Yes, she could certainly be forgiven for quarreling with Emelen, whom she loved so passionately, about leaving her behind in safety while he went off to probable death at Tansen's side.

Whether or not Emelen, however, would be forgiven for employing such drastic measures to both protect and desert her . . . Tansen almost shuddered. He had enough problems of his own with women without contemplating Emelen's too closely.

Emelen said, "They told me at Dalishar. Zimran betrayed Josarian."

"Yes." He waited to see how much Emelen knew.

No more than anyone else, apparently, since Emelen only said, "To be honest, I never really liked Zimran, never understood why Josarian loved him so much. But I never, ever thought he would do something like that."

"No."

"Why?" Emelen asked. "*Why?*"

Tansen shrugged, concealing his discomfort with the subject. "Maybe because he could. You know the old saying: He who betrays you is never one from afar."

"Do you think it was because of you?"

That surprised him. "Me?"

"He was always jealous of you, you know. Josarian made you his brother. Loved you best. Trusted you the most. Relied on you more than anyone. Even when you weren't around, Josarian was always saying, 'Tansen says,' or 'Tansen told me,' or even, 'What would Tansen do now?' And Zimran hated that. Hated you for it. Maybe started hating Josarian for it, too."

Tansen shook his head. "Zimran was a complicated man." One whom Elelar had played like a harp.

"Do you think Zim was in collusion with Kiloran?" When Tansen frowned, Emelen elaborated, "How else would Kiloran have known when and where to attack Josarian?"

How indeed?

Maybe I really should kill Elelar.

But he knew he wouldn't.

"Kiloran had tried before to kill Josarian, and he would have tried again if he'd failed that night. It was just another attempt," Tansen suggested. "The one that worked."

"And which one will work on you?"

"That's a cheerful thought."

Emelen smiled. "Sorry. Perhaps thoughts of imminent castration by my own wife are making me glum."

"Perhaps missing her is making you glum," Tan suggested morosely. "Women can do that to a man."

"There is good news, though."

"What?"

"Well . . . *strange* news, rather."

"Yes?"

"The visions at Dalishar are continuing."

Tansen stared at him. "What?"

Emelen nodded. "I've seen it myself. It doesn't happen every night, and it's not always the same thing. But once in while . . . I've never seen a vision before, but this could be nothing else."

Tansen listened while Emelen described the same sort of thing he'd heard before. Sometimes people saw glowing golden eyes in the night sky over Dalishar. Sometimes they saw an image like a fist—a symbol reminiscent of Daurion, the last great Yahrdan, who ruled Sileria, as songs and stories said, with a fist of iron in a velvet glove.

"And a voice?" Tansen prodded.

"Yes. Well, not a voice exactly, but something you hear in your head."

" 'He is coming.' "

"Yes. You've seen . . . heard it?"

"No, but I've heard *about* it." A few times, by now. "So it's not connected to Mirabar," he mused. "It's something all on its own."

"Something amazing."

"How are people responding?"

"Everyone from Chandar and other nearby villages is crowding the camp at Dalishar now, eager to see it."

"They're not afraid?"

"Depends on who you ask. I mean . . . who is 'he,' and what's he going to do when he comes? People are either excited or afraid depending on what they think the vision means."

"Mirabar said—"

"That it's a promise of this new ruler she has foreseen," Emelen concluded. "I know, and so does everyone else. It helps. It definitely helps."

"But some people disagree?"

"Of course. This is Sileria. Some people insist it means terrible things."

"Of course," Tansen said dryly. This was Sileria. "What does Lann say?"

"Lann says visions make him queasy, and he wants you to put someone else in charge at Dalishar so he can go kill assassins and be happy again."

Tansen grinned. "Fair enough."

"Dalishar's not the only place where strange things are happening."

"The colored smoke and lights at Mount Darshon," Tansen murmured.

"When Jalilar and I left the east, after Jalan brought us news of Josarian's death and word started spreading, the *zanareen* went mad."

"The *zanareen* have always been mad," Tan pointed out.

"I mean, they got even stranger. Haven't you seen any of them lately?"

"I've been busy," he said dryly.

"They're raving about how Dar is angry, Dar wants vengeance, Dar will have blood—"

"But that's good," Tansen interrupted. "The Society killed the Firebringer, so surely Dar's fury will help us convince people they've got to oppose the waterlords now."

"They're also saying Dar wants sacrifices."

"Such as?"

"So far it's just the usual: flowers, fruit, grain, wine, livestock, gold, jewels, bones of the dead . . ."

"But?"

"The *zanareen* say if it's not enough, She'll take more."

"That's Her way," Tansen said with resignation. "It always has been."

"People are already afraid. Traveling west, Jalilar and I met people going east, men and women. They were 'Called' to Darshon, they said. Called to worship and praise Dar. They didn't seem to know what in the Fires they would actually do once they got there, but they were going."

"Where's Jalan?" Tansen asked suddenly. Jalan the *zanar* was a raving religious fanatic and possibly Tansen's least favorite person; but he'd been right all along about Josarian's true identity, and maybe he'd now have something useful to say about all of this.

"He came with us as far as the Sanctuary where I left Jalilar. When he was sure the Firebringer's sister was in a safe place, he left us to return to Darshon." Emelen added, "And I would rather face a White Dragon myself than travel with Jalan again. So, I can assure you, would my wife."

"Even Josarian didn't like him."

"I doubt that Dar Herself likes him," Emelen said with feeling.

Tansen smiled wryly, then asked, "What about the fighting in the east?"

"Jagodan shah Lironi won't back down," Emelen said, "and his entire clan, as well as several others, are with him. He lost a brother and a son in the rebellion, and he says they didn't give their lives just so the Lironi could spend the next thousand years being ruled by the Society instead of by the *roshaheen*."

"That's good," Tansen said, feeling encouraged. He remembered meeting here with Kiman shah Moynari. "Other clans are joining them, or soon will. I sent Cheylan east again, to pledge our support to Jagodan and encourage the Lironi."

"What would encourage *everyone*," Emelen pointed out, "is presenting this new ruler you and Mirabar have promised Sileria."

"I know." He spread his hands helplessly. "I don't think anyone but Mirabar can find him, and she's . . . frustrated by the vagueness of her visions."

"Where is she now?"

"Mount Niran."

"Niran?" Emelen exclaimed. "Have you lost her mind? Kiloran could get to her—"

"She needed to go."

"What could be so important—"

"She's hoping her teacher can help her understand these visions, unravel their meaning. She's seen . . . things that disturb her."

"Like what?"

"I don't know," he lied. No need to spread the worry around, he thought.

"Why not have her teacher brought here, or somewhere safe?"

"Tashinar is very old. I doubt she can travel this far anymore. And Mirabar was . . . restless. She needed to go." More worried than he wanted to admit, he added, "I've learned it's usually best to let her follow her instincts."

"What about you? Radyan says you're leaving for Shaljir."

Tansen nodded. "There are things I need to do there."

"And who," Emelen asked with emphasis, "is that sea-born boy?"

"A runaway."

"With an enchanted oar." Emelen's tone was pointed.

"Ah, so you've heard about that?"

"What's going on, Tansen?"

"It's a long story." He was getting tired of saying that.

"You used to trust me," Emelen snapped.

Tansen met his friend's dark gaze. "I still do." He rubbed a hand across his face, coming to a sudden decision. "All right. I'll tell you about the boy. Someone besides Mira and Cheylan ought to know—"

"If *Cheylan* knows, then *I* certainly deserve to—"

"—in case I don't come back."

"Don't come back?" Emelen pounced. "From where?"

"Or in case . . . Zarien's right and it comes to pass." He still didn't believe it though. Not at all.

"Right about what?"

Tansen frowned and wondered where to begin. "How much do you know about the sea-born?"

"Nothing, of course. I'm a *shallah*."

"Then this will sound very strange."

"Oh, I don't know," Emelen said. "After all that's happened, I've become pretty hard to surprise."

BARAN RESTED AND tried to regain some strength here in the damp and cavernous ruins of Belitar, the eerie home he had claimed more than a dozen years ago. Sweating profusely in the aftermath of a particularly painful episode in his increasingly dire illness, he eyed the absolutely disgusting tisane that Sister Velikar offered him. He sniffed it cautiously and said to her, "Perhaps not."

"Fine," the ugly old woman replied. "Don't drink it. What's it to me if your guts fester and rot a day sooner?"

"I think it's your charm that draws people to you," Baran opined.

"As a Sister," she retorted, "I am obliged to tend the sick and ease their suffering as best I can. But I am not obliged to force them to accept my help, or to like them personally."

"If I drink it, will you kiss me?"

Her lips curled. A strange grating sound emerged from her barrel-like chest. When she recovered from her amusement, she countered, "I'll kiss you if you don't."

"A wise man knows when he's defeated." He took a sip, grimaced, and then downed the entire thing as fast as he could. "Be honest," he said, gasping and trying not to vomit. "Tansen really sent you here to poison me."

"Who told you?"

He shot a sharp glance at her. Then he rolled his eyes when she started laughing again. "We're going to have to take turns at being crazy," he advised her. "It's too confusing when we're both doing it at once."

"Someone's coming," she said suddenly, turning towards the door.

He only heard the footsteps after she did, after being warned. It worried him. His senses were starting to diminish, he realized, overwhelmed by the struggle against this disease. He wasn't concerned about his safety yet. Belitar was virtually impregnable. No one could cross its encircling moat without his blessing, and his men would certainly alert him to any attempts which he himself failed to perceive. But the clouding of his ordinary senses was another sign that his time was running out.

The moment an assassin entered the room, however, Baran threw off his weakness by force of will and rose to greet him. "Vinn."

The assassin crossed his fists over his chest and bowed his head respectfully. "*Siran*." Then he glanced resignedly at Velikar. "Sister."

"We've missed you," Baran said, "haven't we, Velikar?"

"No," she said.

"I'm glad to be back," Vinn replied, ignoring Velikar. "And the news was as you expected, *siran*."

"Someone has started asking about me," Baran surmised. He'd instructed Vinn to have inquiries made at the three Sanctuaries within a day's journey of Belitar.

"Yes," Vinn replied. "Someone wants to know if you have been ill. Have you required medicine or treatment? What is your condition?"

"Who has been asking?" Baran prodded.

Vinn shook his head. "Not Searlon himself. He'd be too easy to recognize when described to us—that scar of his."

"An assassin, though?"

"The man asking wasn't dressed as an assassin, but the Sisters at one Sanctuary nonetheless suspected he was one, and the Sisters at another weren't sure."

"And at the third?"

"No inquiries there yet."

"Ah."

"So we did as you ordered, *siran*."

He smiled. "Good. The Sisters cooperated?"

"Yes. For a generous donation, they agreed to tell Kiloran's spy, should he appear, that you were ill during the rains but are now almost completely recovered, getting stronger every day and steadily regaining the weight you lost."

Vinn, as well as a few other trusted assassins, knew by now that he wasn't well. There was no way to hide it from them any longer. Only Velikar, however, knew just how sick he was. And he intended to make sure that Kiloran didn't find out the truth.

"Well done, Vinn."

"What now, *siran*?"

"I haven't made up my mind yet, but it's possible we may take a little trip."

"Absolutely not," Velikar said. "Out of the question."

Vinn frowned at her. "No one tells the *siran* what to do."

Velikar frowned back. "Well, if he wants to be a fool—"

"And no one," Vinn added with menace, "calls my master a fool, woman."

Velikar stepped forward. "And no assassin speaks to m—"

"Now, now," Baran admonished. "That's enough. Both of you."

Vinn turned to him. "Why is this pestilent woman still here, *siran*? Surely it's past time to send her back to Tansen?"

"If my presence offends you," Velikar said, "I will be happy to remove myself." She met Baran's eyes and added, "I need to gather more herbs today."

He nodded and watched her leave the room.

"If you need a Sister to tend you until you're better, *siran,*" Vinn said as soon as she was gone, "at least let me find one who isn't so—"

"Try to be a little patient with her, Vinn," Baran insisted. "She may be with us for a while. I've become quite fond of her, you know."

After a stunned pause, the assassin laughed and relaxed. "Only you, *siran*. Only you."

"I strive," Baran assured him, "to keep you amused."

"And you succeed, *siran*. You always succeed."

"How heartening."

Returning to business, Vinn said, "Kiloran's spy asked about Wyldon at the Sanctuaries, too."

"And?"

"They confirmed everything at the Sanctuary where you met with him."

"Then Kiloran will know it's true," Baran murmured, feeling the effects of Velikar's disgusting tisane start to soothe him. "Wyldon really did seek my support against him."

"Will we give it?"

"Probably not," Baran admitted.

"Because of the truce," Vinn guessed.

"Because Wyldon is a weak and hot-headed fool who can't be useful to us, and who could even conceivably become a burden." He smiled and added, "Besides, I can't stand his sculptures."

"Yes, you are right, *siran*."

"I love those words."

"Do you think Kiloran really did attack him?"

"Ah, I hope not."

"But if not Kiloran, then who?"

Baran smiled, thinking of Tansen, and suggested, "Perhaps someone who wanted to see Wyldon sowing dissent among the waterlords."

"Then Kiloran might be innocent?"

"My dear Vinn, Kiloran was not even innocent at birth. But, after seeing his reaction to the news while we were in Emeldar, I do think it possible he's not actually responsible for the attack on Wyldon." Baran sighed with pleasure. "Wouldn't it be wonderful if Kiloran will now pay for something he didn't do?"

"Will he pay, *siran*?"

"Of course. It has never occurred to *Wyldon* that Kiloran didn't order the attack. So he's beside himself with vengeful rage. I doubt I'm the only waterlord he's trying to get to side with him against Kiloran, and there will surely be others."

"Until Kiloran eliminates him."

"Yes, as Kiloran will unquestionably have to do in the end."

"Can we benefit from their struggle?"

"That," Baran said, "is what I'm pondering even as we speak, Vinn."

"Somehow, *siran,* I thought so."

"But these are very complicated times."

"We will prevail, *siran.* You are a complicated man. So surely these are your times."

And my time is running out.

"Hmmm." Baran turned his back on the assassin and said, "That will be all for now, Vinn."

"Shall I go home, *siran?*"

Baran thought it over for a moment. "No. Stay close."

"The trip you mentioned?"

"I'm thinking it over," Baran admitted.

"Then I shall be prepared to leave at a moment's notice."

"I know you will." Baran's assassins were used to their master's habits after all these years.

"*Siran.*" Vinn bowed and took his leave.

Alone now, Baran took a long, deep breath, then let it out slowly, searching for pain. He found none. That was good. He was feeling stronger now. That was good, too. But he had already learned through bitter experience that it was temporary. He would only grow weaker. He was spiraling towards death. No one could change that. The time would come when he couldn't hide it.

Yes, according to Velikar, the time would come soon.

He didn't pray. Dar had not listened when it mattered most, and he had never spoken to Her since. Dar could burn in that volcano, bereft of the Firebringer, through all eternity for all Baran cared. Indeed, he hoped She did. Baran hoped She knew the heartache and loneliness he did.

He doubted it, though. She was the destroyer goddess, after all, and a female who used Her lovers ill. Once, long ago, in a time lost to most memory, Mount Shaljir had raged with the fires of Dar's consort. He had burned out eventually, consumed by Dar's needs, leaving only the hollow, looming mountain behind; it dominated the capital city to this day, a harmless shell of what it had once been, honeycombed with caves and tunnels where once lava had flowed. And before that, in an age distant beyond imagining, Dar's previous consort—perhaps Her very first—had blown up and crumbled into the sea, leaving behind only the rainbow chalk cliffs of Liron to show that he had ever ruled with the goddess who dwelled in Darshon.

Long ago, in another life, as another man, Baran had sailed past those cliffs more than once on trading expeditions to the Kintish Kingdoms. They were extraordinary, the cliffs of Liron—so extraordinary that people still called them sacred, thousands of years after the death of the god who had once dwelled there, the consort whom Dar had consumed in Her destructive hunger.

Poor Josarian. He never had a chance.

And what will I do now?

Baran didn't want to die without killing Kiloran. It was all he had lived for. All that mattered to him.

Every thought, every word, every deed must be consecrated to that goal now, lest he die with it unfulfilled.

But if he did die before Kiloran, if Dar could really be that cruel . . . Yes, of course She could. Baran knew that better than anyone. If he did die before destroying Kiloran, then he could think of only one possible way to exact revenge after his death, one sole chance to reach past mortality and vanquish his enemy. It wasn't a perfect plan, but he scented the acrid odor of destiny whenever he thought of it. He suspected it might even be his just fate. His and Kiloran's. And, frankly, he rather enjoyed the irony.

It was a huge step, though, as well as an audacious one. He wanted to be sure. As sure as he could be, anyhow.

So, now that he was alone, he descended into the moldy depths of Belitar's ruins, to the ancient foundations, to the stones placed here a thousand years ago during Sileria's last great era in the sun, before the clouds of betrayal, terror, and humiliation had swept across the land. He passed through deep cellars built before the Conquest, and then he sought the ancient, hidden passageways—crumbling, damp, ruined beyond repair— which led even further down. Down to the mysterious origins of Belitar's oft-rebuilt ruins, thousands of years old at this depth.

Down, down, down to the murky netherworld of another time, another race, another domain entirely. Down to the secrets which had died with Harlon. The secrets which, indeed, had died many times over the centuries, only to be rediscovered again and again. Always by someone desperate, as Baran had been. Always by someone who made the discovery through senses belonging only to those with water in their veins and ice in their souls, to those who possessed a great talent, a terrible thirst, and a heart of stone.

Down here, in the belly of the world, hidden from the fiery sunshine where the New Race thrived, lived Baran's teacher. And Baran hoped she would have the wisdom to help him prevail even now, when time was against him and Kiloran had never been more powerful.

33

A POWERFUL FRIEND BECOMES A POWERFUL ENEMY.
—Silerian Proverb

THE OLD FEMALE Guardian was tough. Kiloran respected a strong opponent and could acknowledge his admiration for this one. He always gave his enemies their due. After all, the weak, the foolish, and the embittered might be briefly annoying from time to time, but they had no real chance of becoming genuine *enemies* of a strong man, let alone of a powerful waterlord. If a man's greatness could indeed be judged by his foes, then he lost nothing by acknowledging, even admiring, their strength.

As Kiloran expected, the old woman had tried to immolate herself as soon as she realized she was his prisoner. Dyshon couldn't have stopped her, but Kiloran could. However, the interrogation had not proved very fruitful thereafter, since the struggle left the Guardian so exhausted. After learning too little from her to hold his attention yesterday, Kiloran had instructed Dyshon to sedate her again.

Now she was awake again, and the interrogation would begin anew. It was a tedious business, but it must never be forgotten that persistence was an inherit quality of victory.

The woman was small, white-haired, and frail. A severe cough indicated to Kiloran that death might have come soon for her, anyhow, even if he had not intervened and altered her destiny. This wasn't the first time she had endured interrogation, either. Three fingers were missing from one of her hands.

Valdani torture. Long ago, he guessed, studying the old scars of the small hand he now took in his.

The prisoner was shackled, held immobile by coils of water which should be making her distinctly uncomfortable. She was soaking wet and shivering, her skin so bloodless now that she looked almost as pale as a Valdan.

"They left me for dead," the old woman said suddenly, her voice weary and cracked. She met Kiloran's gaze, then looked down at the mutilated hand he held so gently. He heard liquid in her breath when she paused before speaking again. Yes, she was very sick. "I told them nothing, as I will tell you nothing. Kill me or release me. You're wasting your time."

"At the risk of repeating myself," Kiloran replied, dropping her hand, "I can end your suffering quickly if you cooperate. And if you don't, you'll be here for a very long time."

She shrugged and closed her sunken eyes again. "Perhaps I'll learn to like it here."

Yes, she was tough. And her power was undeniable—every *shir* in Kandahar was shaking now that she was awake again. But she was nonetheless terrified. Kiloran had seen the horror in her eyes yesterday when she'd first realized whose prisoner she was. As a Guardian, she'd have lived her whole life in fear of the Society, of the waterlords—of him. And with good reason.

If she knew anything worth knowing, soon Kiloran would know it, too. If she could explain the unprecedented activity at Mount Darshon or reveal whatever the Guardians might know about Mirabar's visions, then Kiloran would make sure she did so before she died.

He watched her shiver and listened to her cough. He willed the watery shackles to tighten around her limbs, to grow even colder; and he heard her gasp in response.

"I am not a Valdan," Kiloran whispered softly.

Her dark eyes watered with mingled pain and fear. "I know. You are something much worse."

"And you know that what they did to you is nothing compared to what I will do."

Her mouth trembled briefly, but she said only, "Let's get on with it."

He paused for a moment in appreciation. No Valdan would ever show such courage, least of all a Valdani woman. It was so fitting that the Valdani had surrendered Sileria at last, finally leaving Silerians to settle their differences without interference. No outsider could understand the feelings which now bound Kiloran and this woman together. No *roshah* could share the intimate history which united the waterlord and the Guardian in their mutually satisfying enmity. No Valdan could truly appreciate the depth of hatred between them as the woman screamed in pain and Kiloran focused on the demanding task of breaking her.

"FATHER . . ."

Armian froze, like a statue, when he saw Tansen standing above him on that windswept cliff, swinging his yahr with deadly intent.

If Tan lived for all eternity, he would never forget the sound of Armian's voice as he said, "Tansen?"

His trusted child, his beloved son, his murderer . . .

"Tansen?" His voice torn by shock and disbelief.

"Father."

"Tansen?" Wounded by betrayal and treachery.

"Father!"

"Tansen? Wake up."

He reached for his sword harness even before he was fully awake. Breathing hard, he looked around him in confusion.

"We're in Sanctuary," Zarien said, backing away cautiously. "You don't need that."

Sanctuary? Yes. They had stopped here for the night on their journey to Shaljir. Just the two of them. Traveling quietly and being discreet.

"What?" Tansen demanded. "What's wrong?"

"I don't know."

Zarien turned and gestured to the door of the bedchamber. Now Tansen saw a Sister standing there, holding a sputtering candle.

"Assassins," she said simply. "Four of them."

Zarien gasped.

"Where?" Tansen unsheathed his swords.

The Sister gurgled in alarm. Zarien quickly stepped between Tansen and the Sister, who took a few steps back while she hurriedly explained, "They're waiting outside. They've requested shelter for the night."

"It's very late," Tansen said suspiciously.

The Sister shrugged and, evidently realizing he didn't mean to gut her, said more calmly, "I think they're in danger."

"From what?" he asked.

"Who knows?"

"Do they know we're here?"

"They know I have other guests," she replied. "They don't know who." When Tansen didn't respond, she prodded, "This is Sanctuary. I really can't turn them away."

"They're assassins!" Zarien objected.

"Sanctuary is for everyone," the Sister pointed out. "And no one can harm anyone else here."

Tansen thought it over. "Damn." He sighed, then said, "Let them in, but don't tell them anything."

"Let them in?" Zarien exclaimed as the Sister nodded and scurried away. "Have you lost your—"

"If she turns them away, they'll wonder why. They might even wait for us just beyond Sanctuary grounds," Tansen explained, "and ambush us as soon as we leave tomorrow."

"You think they'd guess who's here?"

Tansen shrugged. "I doubt it. It's more likely they'd suspect we're *toreni* ripe for a profitable abduction."

"But if they find out who you are, then surely—"

"Keep your friends close, but keep your enemies closer," Tansen quoted. "At least this way we'll know where they are, and we can avoid nasty surprises when we leave."

Tansen pulled his humble homespun tunic over his head and laced up the neck to ensure that no one could see even a hint of the notorious brand on his chest.

"What are you doing?" Zarien kept his voice to a whisper now that they could hear the assassins entering the main room of the Sanctuary.

"I'm going to find out whatever I can."

"Maybe we should just stay in here," the boy suggested.

"*You* should stay in here," Tansen said pointedly, keeping his voice low, too.

"But . . . Oh." Zarien sighed. "They'll wonder, like everyone else, what I'm doing so far inland."

"They may even have heard of the lone sea-born boy who's been seen with me, and if so—"

"Seeing me, they might guess who you are." Zarien sat down suddenly. "Maybe we should just sneak out through the window now?"

"Don't worry," Tansen murmured. "There are only four. I can handle them."

"Only four," Zarien repeated faintly.

Tansen grinned wryly at the distinct lack of confidence he heard in the boy's voice, then stuck his head out the door and peered into the main room. Despite the late hour, the four assassins were talking noisily and accepting food and drink from the Sister. None of them noticed Tansen, which gave him time to get a good look at them in the dim light without being studied in return. He didn't recognize any of them. It was, of course, nonetheless possible that they might recognize him, since he was by now more famous than any assassin, but he decided to risk it. They wouldn't attack him here, and he could certainly deal with them in the morning as long as he knew where they were. Meanwhile, if they didn't recognize him, perhaps he could learn something from them.

Two of them rose abruptly to their feet the moment they noticed Tansen enter the main room. He shuffled forward slowly, in a submissive posture.

"Who are you?" one of them demanded rudely.

Tansen crossed his fists over his chest, lowered his head respectfully, and murmured, "*Sirani.*" Without raising his eyes, he said, "Forgive me for intruding."

They saw what they wanted to see, a humble *shallah,* an ordinary mountain peasant, a common man who held the Honored Society in awe. He submissively answered their terse questions about his presence here, telling them he was returning from Shaljir, after working there for some years, taking his city-born wife home to meet his family now that the Valdani had surrendered the city and Silerians could finally come and go in freedom.

No one asked why his wife remained hidden in her bedchamber; apart from a Sister, any respectable woman would avoid such men in the middle of the night, and city-dwellers were particularly afraid of assassins.

Tansen fawned enough to please them, and he pretended to be honored when one of them suggested he take a seat and join them at the simple wooden table where they were eating and drinking. As Tansen sat, he finally got a good look at one of their *shir*. He recognized the workmanship, having seen it before. He kept his face impassive, wondering what Wyldon's men were doing here, so far from their own territory.

As soon as the assassins drained their cups, Tansen refilled them. When the wineskin was finally empty, he fetched another—the Sister had gone to bed by now—and kept their cups full thereafter. He encouraged the assassins to tell bloody tales of the men they'd killed and the *toreni* they'd abducted. He admired their *shir* and made them laugh by gasping in pain when he accepted their mocking invitation to touch one of the wavy-bladed daggers.

When he judged the moment ripe, Tansen decided to get them gossiping. "Is it true," he asked, "what they say about how Josarian died?" A tense silence followed his question. He leaned forward and whispered, "Kiloran. The White Dragon. Is it true?"

"Kiloran," the youngest one said, practically spitting the name.

"He thinks he can do anything now," muttered the one sitting next to Tansen.

"He's wrong," said the young one. "He'll pay for what he did to us."

So ...

Evidently Wyldon did blame Kiloran for the attack on his stronghold. Tansen wondered if any of these four assassins had been among those whom his own men fought that night. In retrospect, perhaps it was fortunate that the ambush had been such a messy affair, he reflected wryly. If any of these men had indeed been there that night—had seen Tansen there—they'd never recognize their water-drenched mud-covered enemy in the tidy person now sitting with them.

"So you ..." Tansen hesitated shyly for a moment, then rushed on, "You are not Kiloran's men?"

"Kiloran's men? Hah!" This from the young one again, who was wonderfully talkative. "We've just left Kiloran's men lying dead in—"

"Quiet!" The one sitting next to Tansen was more sensible.

"Why? Even if the rest of them tracked us this far, th—"

"You talk too much," the sensible one snapped.

The young one glowered and shrugged.

"Kiloran and Tansen are feuding now, they say," Tansen ventured, hoping to get the youngest assassin to blurt out more indiscreet and interesting news.

"He can't get along with *anyone,* can he?" said the assassin sitting directly across from Tansen. "Baran's feuded with him for years, the Firebringer quarreled with him, now Tansen's sworn a bloodvow against him ..." The man scratched his belly, then scratched his ear. "And now he's feuding with our master."

"That truce meeting was probably just a trick," the young one said. Tansen noticed he was starting to slur his words. "Wyldon was right not to go. He would be dead now if he had gone."

Tansen wanted to ask about the truce meeting, but he was afraid that another question from him might make the sensible one silence the others again.

"Tansen and Kiloran will tear each other apart," said the scratching one—now he was scratching his groin. Tansen worried briefly about lice as the man continued, "It's a lot more than a feud. It's another damn war, only worse than Josarian's war, because—"

"So what? Wyldon will rule Sileria when they're both dead!" vowed the young one.

"You think Wyldon can trust Baran?" Now the itchy assassin was trying to scratch his own back.

The fourth assassin, who'd been silent so far, now murmured, "No one can trust Baran."

"True enough," agreed the scratcher.

The young one opined, "But Baran and Wyldon want the same thing now."

The quiet one spoke again. "No one really knows what Baran wants."

"He wants Kiloran dead," asserted the sensible one, momentarily forgetting that they shouldn't discuss their business in front of the *shallah* in their midst.

The scratching one, who was twisting and contorting while he spoke, said, "Baran wants Kiloran to suffer more than he wants him dead."

The young one said with fuzzy conviction, "He wants both things."

"Do you think Baran went to the truce meeting?"

"No."

"Baran? Hah!"

"If he did, he's probably dead now. Surely it was a trap?"

"No, I'll bet even Kiloran wouldn't violate a truce meeting that way. He's smart, he must know the whole Society would turn on him if he did that."

The scratching one grunted, and then they all fell silent. Unable to resist, Tansen finally asked, "Truce meeting?"

"Kiloran called a truce meeting," the young one began. "To put aside his—"

But the sensible one interrupted him by saying to Tansen, "You ask a lot of questions."

"I'm sorry," Tansen said quickly. He let admiration warm his voice as he added, "I have never talked to assassins before."

"Oh?" The man leaned closer. "Or maybe you have and you've just forgotten."

Tansen caught the hint. "Perhaps. It's true that I have a terrible memory."

"Is that so?" The man suggestively fingered his *shir*.

Tansen kept his eyes on it as he assured him, "Definitely."

After a tense moment, the man grinned and leaned back in his chair. "I thought so."

"If you'll excuse me, *sirani* . . ." Tansen rose to his feet. "My wife needs me."

They nodded and returned to drinking and talking, forgetting the timid peasant before he was even out of the room.

The bedchamber was dark, but Zarien was wide awake.

"Well?" the boy prodded in a whisper.

"Their conversation is limited, but nonetheless very interesting," Tansen replied quietly.

"Are we leaving now?"

"No."

"But—"

"After they fall asleep—which should be soon, at the rate they're guzzling wine."

"You're sure they don't suspect who you are?"

"They saw what they wanted to see," Tansen assured him. "Someone admiring and afraid. Someone they could talk in front of with impunity."

"No," Zarien said after a moment, "I think they saw what *you* wanted them to see."

CHEYLAN FINALLY LOCATED Semeon, the fire-haired, flame-eyed boy whom he sought—and located him, of all places, in Tansen's long-deserted native village of Gamalan. Now that Outlookers no longer menaced the Guardians, the child's circle of companions had grown bold, despite the danger from waterlords and assassins, and were permanently inhabiting the abandoned ruins of this forgotten village rather than living on the run in one temporary encampment after another.

Cheylan considered the possibilities and, after some thought, decided that this could work to his advantage.

Semeon was still very young. His exact age was unknown, since he'd been abandoned by his parents. That was a typical fate for such a child, and better than the usual alternative—to be murdered by one's parents. As far as Cheylan knew, he himself was the only "demon" child in centuries whose parents hadn't killed him or abandoned him in fear and despair. Not that his own childhood had been enviable. Cheylan hadn't starved or lived like an animal, as had Mirabar and Semeon in their early years, but he had seen his mother shrink from him every time he'd ever sought her affection. He had consistently seen distaste and suspicion in his father's eyes. He'd known, as far back as he could remember, that his parents considered him a burden rather than a blessing, and that they dreaded rather than loved him.

Cheylan sometimes thought that abandonment might have been preferable.

However, had he been abandoned, he never would have known Verlon, his grandfather; and thus the gift of water magic which lay hidden in Cheylan's fiery sorcery might have been forever unknown to him. Had his own grandfather not been a waterlord who soon spotted his talent, Cheylan might never have recognized the subtle signs of the cold power born in his veins. Unlike fire magic, the gift of water magic felt like a normal part of your senses until someone else showed you what it truly was and taught you how to harness it.

Of all Cheylan's family, only Verlon had sought his company as a boy. Only Verlon had wanted him, cared for him, seemed to cherish him. Verlon was the only person in the world to whom Cheylan had ever been close. The cold old wizard had been the sole warmth of Cheylan's childhood, as well as his mentor in the fluid mysteries of water magic.

However, Verlon was a waterlord, and they were all the same in the end. By the time Cheylan was a young man, he'd realized that Verlon only wanted to use him. The old waterlord merely saw his grandson as a means of expanding his own power and influence. Through Cheylan, Verlon thought he could have access to fire magic, to communion with the Otherworld, and to the Guardians themselves.

Resentful and ambitious, Cheylan resisted the old man's attempts to use him to achieve his own ends. And when Cheylan thought he was powerful enough, when he felt ready to become a waterlord in his own right, he turned on the grandfather who had abused his trust.

Unfortunately, Cheylan had underestimated the old man. Or perhaps, he acknowledged now with the wisdom of additional years, he had overestimated himself at the time. In any event, his bold and bitter attempt to take Verlon's place had failed disastrously, earning him a bloodvow from his grandfather. So Cheylan had prudently joined a Guardian circle and disappeared into the mountains.

Even so, Verlon's persistent wrath made Cheylan's life inconveniently dangerous while he remained in eastern Sileria. Since Guardians stuck together, especially when menaced by the Society, Cheylan's circle of companions eventually elected to migrate west as a group, rather than let him go alone. Soon after entering the western region, Cheylan met Josarian and was drawn into the rebellion.

Cheylan hadn't seen his former circle of companions in many months now, nor could he honestly say he missed them. He didn't even know where they were anymore, nor did he care. His destiny was far greater, after all, than that of the impoverished fire mystics whom he had joined in desperation years ago.

However, as Mirabar herself had said more than once, destiny didn't just happen by itself; it required effort, courage, commitment, sacrifice. Destiny also required, Cheylan knew, bold acts and shrewd intervention. So he had traced young Semeon to the forgotten ruins of Gamalan, the sad little place which he knew—due to their reluctantly close association for a while during the rebellion—still came vividly to life in Tansen's nightmares.

Maybe Semeon was no threat to Cheylan's destiny. But if life in the shadow of Darshon had taught Cheylan anything, it was that only the ruthless prevailed. This was the land of the destroyer goddess and Her fire-raining volcano; of the Firebringer, who'd slaughtered thousands of Valdani in his bloody quest for freedom; of the White Dragon, which had slain the Firebringer in vengeance and agony; of the Honored Society, with its waterlords and assassins; of bloodfeuds and bloodvows and clan warfare which lasted for generations. This was a nation which betrayed its own leaders and sacrificed its own heroes.

There was no place for mercy in Sileria, Cheylan knew, and there was no room in his heart, nursed on the bitter milk of his demonic birth, for compassion. In a land which granted no second chances, Cheylan would willingly go further than this to eliminate any potential risk to the powerful future he envisioned for himself. And so he felt no guilt or regret as he plotted the murder of Semeon, a boy barely old enough to leave his own mentor's side.

MIRABAR SAT MUTELY on the horse Najdan had acquired for her as they traveled towards Mount Dalishar. She was disguised as a *torena* now, albeit a relatively humble one. At Sister Basimar's suggestion, Haydar had purchased a wig in Islanar for Mirabar, effectively hiding her flame-bright hair. The elaborate woven headdress Mirabar now also wore, the *jashar* of a *torena,* modestly shielded her face, making it fairly easy to hide her golden eyes from strangers as long as she kept her gaze lowered behind the beaded and knotted strands which hung down past her neck.

Mirabar had never even seen a wig before. She would have laughed had her mood not been so dire with grief. Did elderly aristocratic women with thinning hair really wear such absurd things? Mirabar thought it felt, at best, as if a small animal were sleeping on her head.

Haydar, whose most notable feature was not a colorful imagination, said no, it was merely like wearing someone else's old hair. A charming thought indeed.

Still, at least the hungry *shallah* who had sold this hair to a wigmaker had evidently had clean habits, as there was nothing offensive in the shiny black hair. And the clothes Haydar had purchased to complete Mirabar's disguise as a *torena* traveling with her small entourage . . . well, they were much finer than anything Mirabar had ever worn before.

If Tashinar could see me now . . .

Mirabar felt tears welling up again. She held them back and, instead of crying yet again in vain, prayed to Dar for Tashinar's quick and merciful death; there was nothing better to hope for once someone became a prisoner in Kiloran's impregnable lair.

Haydar, posing as Mirabar's maid, disliked horses—like most *shalla-heen*—and walked at some distance from Mirabar. The men, including Najdan, looked rather bedraggled for a *torena*'s escort; but these were hard times for everyone, after all, even *toreni*. Mirabar didn't know where Najdan intended to install Haydar once they reached their destination, and she was too numb with sorrow to feel any interest in the subject anyhow. She was growing used to Najdan's mistress, however, and supposed she could accept the woman's regular company from now on if Najdan expected her to do so.

The sun was hot overhead, riding high in the flawlessly blue sky, when Mirabar, swaying slightly on her mount, heard the Beckoning.

"Why?" she demanded instantly.

"Why what?" Pyron asked, walking beside the horse.

"Why," Mirabar continued, "did you let Kiloran take Tashinar?"

"*Sirana,*" Pyron replied uneasily, "you know that we—"

"Not you," she snapped.

Mirabar looked around for the Beckoner, hearing his silent song, and finally spotted him floating amidst the trees on the north side of the narrow road.

She drew her horse to a halt and repeated, "Why?"

"*Sirana* . . ." Najdan's voice. "Is it . . ." She heard him draw in a sharp breath, as if he'd suddenly touched something fiery-hot or watery-cold. "It's a vision, isn't it?"

"He is here," she replied absently.

"Kiloran?" Pyron bleated.

"No," Mirabar said, her gaze moving distantly into the mysterious world of the Beckoner.

"Najdan?" Haydar's nervous voice.

Najdan said quietly, "She sees him. The one who brings her visions. Stay back. Don't interfere."

Pyron assured him, "I wasn't going to."

"Why didn't you prevent Kiloran from capturing Tashinar?" Mirabar demanded of the Beckoner, whose glowing gold gaze now held hers so fiercely that it seemed to dominate even the brassy sunshine. "Why did you permit Geriden's assassins take her?"

I prevent nothing. I permit nothing.

"An answer." She started crying. "You finally answer a question . . . and your answer is so useless."

Pyron muttered, "Should she be talking to him that way?"

"Quiet," Najdan snapped.

"Why," Mirabar pleaded, "didn't you warn me so I could go to her? Stop the assassins. Save her."

You went to her, the silent voice replied. *You tried to stop them. You tried to save her.*

"I was too late," she wept. "I failed."

Then you were destined to fail, and she is destined to die in Kandahar.

"Did you decide this destiny?" Mirabar asked hotly, her heart full of hatred.

I decide nothing.

"Nothing?" She sighed and repeated, "Nothing."

It was true, Mirabar supposed. The Beckoner was her guide and her tormentor, pushing her hard towards destiny, but he had never claimed to create or craft the fate he revealed to her.

Hot tears rolled down her cheeks. "Can't I save Tashinar?"

You're not strong enough for Kandahar now.

"Will I ever be?"

Perhaps when the child is with you . . .

"The child," she repeated wearily.

To shield you.

"But you've always told me to shield the child . . ."

She will be part of you . . .

"She?" Mirabar blurted.

And you will shield each other . . .

"Shield each . . ." A wave of mingled hot and cold shock washed across her. "Part of me?" she whispered. "Will I . . . Am I going to bear the—"

Belitar.

"What?"

The truth is in Belitar.

"I can't go there," she protested. "Not n—"

A child of fire . . .

"In Belitar?"

A child of water . . .

"Belitar?" Najdan repeated uneasily. "*Sirana?*"

A child of sorrow. . . .

"A girl?" Mirabar asked desperately. "Am I looking for a girl?"

You are looking for me.

"What?"

The girl is looking for you.

"My girl?" she whispered.

Welcome her, the Beckoner urged, drifting into the Otherworld. *Welcome him. Welcome your fate.*

34

THE CITY OF Shaljir was in chaos. When Tansen arrived at the Lion's Gate with Zarien, he scarcely recognized it, even though he had passed through it several times in the past.

"May the winds have mercy . . . ," Zarien murmured, his tattooed face stricken with horror as he stared at the severed heads grotesquely decorating the gate. "Those . . . Those are . . ."

"Valdani heads," Tansen confirmed, his mind blank with shock as he stared. "There were . . . There were Silerian heads . . ." But that was before the Valdani surrendered. Now Silerians in Shaljir were slaughtering Valdani men . . . and women and children, just as the conquerors had slaughtered unarmed Silerians—and displaying their severed heads at the city gates.

Tansen felt strange. He had personally killed more Valdani than he could count. He couldn't even guess at the figure, though he supposed it was several hundred. He was aware of the weight of his slaughtering swords, discreetly wrapped and bundled today with the satchel he carried, so that he wouldn't attract attention.

And now he, who had slain so many Valdani, was sickened by what he saw as he reached the city of Shaljir. Maybe he felt this way because there were women and children among the Valdani dead, and he knew, without being told, that these people had died as the victims of mindless mobs rather than in battle.

Or, he thought darkly, maybe he felt sick because if Silerians could do this, then they were no better than Valdani.

"The landfolk . . . The landfolk . . ."

Tansen's attention was diverted to the boy. Zarien looked as if he was going to vomit. Tansen put a steadying hand on the back of his neck. Zarien drew in a deep breath. Unfortunately, he did it just as a breeze stirred the air. And since they were standing downwind of the grisly display on the gate . . . Zarien let out a horrible moan and threw up all over his new boots.

Tansen dragged him away from the chaotic crowd bustling through the gate, then held his head as vigorous heaves consumed the boy's body. It hurt, Darfire, it hurt to see him losing his innocence day by day.

When Zarien was finally done, he carelessly wiped his mouth with his sleeve, then leaned against Tansen, who supported him with one arm while wiping hesitantly at his face with his free hand.

Zarien drew a few cautious breaths and blinked away tears, looking dizzy and ill. "The landfolk . . . love killing, don't they?"

"I don't know," Tansen murmured, at a loss.

"Is this Dar's will?" Zarien whispered, searching his face.

"I don't know Dar's will."

"Couldn't we just . . . let them go? Let them return to Valdania?"

"I don't kn—"

"If you don't know, who does?" Zarien pleaded. "You *have* to know!"

"I'm sorry," Tansen said, feeling the weight of being less than this boy expected of him. "I'm sorry."

"All the killing . . ." Zarien's legs seemed to sag under him. "Must it always be this way here?"

"I've wondered that . . . since I was your age." He met the boy's dazed, sorrowful gaze. "Come, let's get away from this."

Zarien pulled away from him. "You mean . . . go through the gate?"

"Don't look," he advised.

Zarien sighed, squared his shoulders, and rubbed a hand through his short hair. "And don't breathe," the boy said wearily.

"Somewhere on the other side of this," Tansen promised him, "is the port."

"The port." The idea revived Zarien slightly. "We're going straight there?"

"No."

"But—"

"We have to see the *torena* first."

"What *torena*?" Zarien asked suspiciously.

"*Torena* Elelar shah Hasnari." He made sure he kept the irony out of his voice as he said, "A great heroine of the rebellion."

"Oh." Zarien studied him with a frown for a moment. "Is she the one the *sirana* wants you to kill?"

He'd have flinched if he hadn't been expecting it. "Why do you ask?"

Zarien shrugged. "You don't seem to know all that many women. I just wondered."

"I know plenty of women," he countered, trying to shift the focus of the conversation.

"And this one—"

"Will feed you well," Tansen promised.

But Zarien would not be distracted this time. "You're not going to kill her, are you?"

"No."

Zarien squinted up at the gate, where a woman's head was swarming with flies and being consumed by maggots. "Good," was all he said.

KILORAN CURLED ICY, razor-sharp tentacles of water into the old Guardian woman's guts, toying with her innards. Only the ensorcelled chill of water magic kept her from bleeding to death. The dreaded Valdani methods of slow torture were nothing compared to this; their victims usually died within hours, and never lasted more than two days. Only a waterlord could torture his victims this brutally for this long without killing them. And only Kiloran could break a sorceress of this woman's strength.

She was truly a worthy foe.

He felt the heat she conjured, even in her exhausted, pain-ridden, fear-weakened condition. He felt the fire she drew from the mysterious spiritual source understood only by Guardians, the hot wave of opposition she brought against him even now. She Called fire into her body, into the dark hidden crevices and cavities, into her organs and veins. She Called silently, trying to warm herself, perhaps even to defeat the frozen agony Kiloran created and to free herself with a very bloody death—because enough warmth now might well make her lacerated, coldly tormented insides bleed until she was dead.

Yes, she tried—but he was stronger. So much stronger. Whatever heat she Called, Kiloran met with the cold waves of his will and the bitter ice of his power. The struggle exhilarated him and further drained her.

There were no external flames, though. Not anymore. She had given up such attempts more than a full day ago. However, Kiloran didn't underestimate her; she would seize the first opportunity he gave her, so he gave her none. He kept her drenched. Drenched, cold, exhausted, and in pain.

"Tell me about the one Mirabar awaits," he said.

She didn't answer, but he saw the flicker in her eyes, just as he had upon broaching this subject several other times, and now he was sure of his earlier suspicion: She was relieved.

Whenever Kiloran asked about the size, strength, and location of various Guardian circles, her tension was palpable; she was afraid she'd break and tell him. When he asked about the colored lights and shifting clouds around Darshon, she was worried, though perhaps less so. But she seemed, yes, *relieved*—he was sure of it now—whenever he broached the subject of Mirabar's visions.

Which meant she knew nothing about the visions. Nothing significant, anyhow.

He dropped the subject again—permanently, this time. He also released his grip on her vitals and withdrew the snake of torment from her belly. The twisting, seeking water was stained with her blood as it emerged from her body. The old woman's eyes remained squeezed shut. Then, just as she took a steadying breath, Kiloran molded a mask of water over her face. He heard the coughing and choking, saw it wrack her whole body, watched impassively as she struggled. She was growing physically weaker again, he noticed. He'd have to stop soon, since he couldn't risk actually killing her. Not yet.

Yes, several more questions, and then he'd let her rest for a few hours, he decided. Let her regain just enough strength to stay alive for more questioning. He was close to breaking her. He could tell. He had been doing this for nearly forty years, and he knew the signs. Tonight perhaps, or maybe tomorrow morning. Yes, very soon now, he would know what she knew, and then she could die.

She wheezed and sputtered violently when he finally willed the liquid mask to peel away from her face and free her to breathe again. Kiloran watched her closely, pleased he had timed it well; another moment or two, and she'd have passed out. Now, however, she was merely terrified and filled with the natural panic of imminent suffocation.

"What is Dar doing?" he asked her.

He saw the glow of flame begin to ripple across her skin. Yes, as he suspected—another attempt to immolate herself. With less effort than it took him to smile, Kiloran opened the ceiling over her head and brought a bitterly cold shower of water crashing down upon her with vicious ferocity. She was too weak by now to scream, so her agony came out as a choked whimper.

"Is She preparing for something?" he asked.

The old woman rolled her head sideways against the crystal-smooth wall to which he kept her shackled with coils of water. She seemed to be listening to something.

He prodded, "If you answer me—"

"Shhh," she replied.

It amused him. After a moment of silence, during which her glassy gaze became a bit more focused, she murmured, "He's here."

Surprised, Kiloran listened to the waters of Kandahar, felt the lake's mysteries flow through him, and smelled its peaceful translucence.

No new arrivals. No disturbances. Nothing unusual.

Yet the old woman said with convincing certainty, "Yes . . . He is here."

A delusion? A Guardian vision? Or just a trick?

He was curious enough to ask, "Who?"

Tears rolled down her cheeks. "The Firebringer."

"Oh." Nothing very interesting, after all.

"He's here," she repeated.

"In a way." Guardians talked to the dead, after all, so perhaps it wasn't surprising that the old woman could hear the Firebringer's silent screams.

"Ohhhh . . ." More tears. A sob. "His agony is terrible."

"And never ending," Kiloran said, bored. "Whereas yours can end as soon as you—"

"No," the old woman said, showing an unexpected return of energy. "My pain is like Hers."

"Whose?"

"Dar's," she whispered. "We weep fire for Sileria."

"How sad."

"And it can never end. Not while lava runs through the veins of the land."

"Tell me about Mount Darshon," he prodded.

"You'll find out soon enough," she promised.

Kiloran sighed. "I only do this because you force me."

Calling on his will, he drew dagger-sharp needles from the lake and used them to pierce the old woman's already-maimed limbs again. She didn't scream, but her face contorted so horribly that, for a moment, she almost didn't look human.

Kiloran ordered, "Tell me about the lights flickering around Darshon. The colored, dancing clouds."

The old woman's gaze focused in the distance. "She awaits him. She wants him."

"Who? The one Mirabar awaits?"

"She's not done with him."

"She—Dar or Mirabar?"

The old woman laughed suddenly, and Kiloran, though interested in her statements, began to suspect that she was either delirious or pretending to be.

"He is here," she whispered, her eyes closing, her face taking on a strange expression—almost like ecstasy.

"Yes, we've established that."

"And he is waiting."

His interest sharpened. "Josarian?"

"The Firebringer is waiting . . ."

"The Firebringer is dead," he advised her.

"No, I can hear him." Her voice was getting stronger.

"So can I, but the White Dragon has destroyed—"

"The flesh. I know. The flesh is forever dead."

For the first time in many years, Kiloran felt a sudden chill. "Will Josarian's spirit take a new form?"

She smiled. "You're afraid."

Which was probably the old woman's intention. "What form?"

"If he succeeds, it will be because you fail."

He plunged an icy spear of writhing water back into her tormented body and wrapped it around her damaged organs. "*What form?*" he repeated, feeling the unwelcome heat of emotion creep into his soul as he squeezed her ruined innards. The pain made her gasp and writhe, yet it didn't weaken her as it had before.

Her face almost seemed to glow. He suddenly thought she must have been a lovely young woman, long ago. An incongruous thought, under the circumstances. But as soon as he banished it, he already knew it was too late. His momentary distraction, her desperate heat, perhaps even the intrusive spirit of the Firebringer—he couldn't know for sure how it happened; but something was burgeoning inside her now.

"What form?" he demanded, knowing it was already too late.

"*Fire*," she whispered, her voice hot and husky like a woman in the throes of passion.

"*Siran!*" The stunned voices of the forgotten assassins behind him. "What's happening?"

"She's burning, *siran!*"

Heat. Burning heat. The fierce power of a Guardian. *Fire*. The intense flame of the Otherworld. He had fought it all his life. The anarchic force of his enemies, the wild danger and destructive glory of their sorcery. They weren't immune to their own fire magic, and neither was he.

Kiloran grunted in pain as the old woman's power, reinforced by something Kiloran could barely even sense beyond his pain, overcame him. His grip on her vitals melted like wax. Flames licked the part of his senses trapped inside of her. Fire singed the icy will which kept shackles around her hands and feet.

"*No*." But he had lost. He knew he had lost.

A glow like lava covered her skin. Heat like a volcanic vent emanated from her.

Kiloran backed away, deliberately collapsing the walls and the ceiling as he stumbled across the floor. As water hit her, steam rose from the old woman's fiery flesh, filling the room with thick mist.

"*Siran!*"

He heard a *shir* clatter to the floor, then keep clattering as it shook wildly against the hard surface. One of his men leaped forward to attack the Guardian, then fell back as more heat assaulted him.

"Stay back," Kiloran said. "It's too late." He doubted his men heard his voice above the hissing of the steam and the chaos of their own shouts.

She didn't go up in flames, as Kiloran had feared from the start. No, she glowed hotter and hotter, her fire coming from her core and radiating outward, until she crumbled into ashes.

Her death left behind a deafening silence. The *shir* stopped shaking. The men stopped shouting. Kiloran absentmindedly made the water drift back into walls and ceilings while he stared at the pile of ashes—now soggy and spreading slowly across the water-drenched and blood-smeared floor.

"What was *that?*" one of the assassins demanded at last, his voice stunned.

"That," Kiloran said, "was an example of why we need to kill them all."

"How did she—"

Kiloran turned to face Dyshon, who had witnessed the interrogation in hopes of learning more effective sorcery. The assassin was diligent, if only modestly talented. Kiloran now met his green-eyed gaze. "Have someone clean up this mess."

"Yes, *siran.*"

"Scatter the ashes. Far from Kandahar."

"Right away, *siran.*"

"But first . . ." Kiloran looked back at the ashes again.

"*Siran?*"

"Leave me alone for a moment."

"Of course."

He heard someone retrieve the *shir* which had fallen to the floor. He heard footsteps behind him, men obeying his every command, because he was their master. Because he was the greatest waterlord in Sileria.

What form will he take?

Fire.

Now that he found himself without much hope of getting answers to the additional questions this puzzling statement raised, he almost regretted capturing and questioning the old woman in the first place.

However, the old Kintish proverb was wrong. Knowledge was *not,* in fact, hollow. It was just sometimes very hard to apply to a given situation.

Kiloran let the silence of the empty room fill him, and then he closed his eyes and listened. The screams of the Firebringer now filled his senses. So wracked with pain, so steeped in agony that it almost hurt just to listen. Yes, Josarian was as humbled as ever. As thoroughly defeated as Kiloran had believed ever since consuming him with the White Dragon. There was nothing new in those cries of torment. Neither the grief nor the pain had diminished; not even a little.

The Firebringer was still Kiloran's victim. His conquered enemy. His dead and humiliated challenger.

That had not changed.

The old woman had been in terrible pain. She had been crazed with it. She was also strong and shrewd. Her final words could have been a deliberate ploy to disquiet Kiloran before she disintegrated into a useless pile of ashes.

Nonetheless, her dying whisper hung in the air as he turned to leave the room and attend to other business. Was it a promise? A plea? A threat? Or a prayer?

Fire.

* * *

TANSEN HAD NOT seen her since the night he had nearly killed her—the night he crept into her bedchamber in Chandar to confront her with her betrayal of Josarian.

Since then, Elelar had accomplished precisely what he had sent her to Shaljir to accomplish: Kaynall had surrendered Sileria to native rule. Another man might think Tansen could execute Elelar with impunity now; certainly another woman thought so.

Mira . . .

No, he knew better than to think about one woman while preparing to face the other. He banished all thoughts of red hair and golden eyes, of fire and heat, of an earthy *shallah* girl blossoming into womanhood amidst war and bloodshed, amidst prophetic visions and flawed men.

Well, at least he *tried* to banish all such thoughts.

Zarien unwittingly helped by asking, as he gazed at the entrance to Elelar's palatial city dwelling, "*You* know a woman who lives *here?*"

"I have a broad acquaintance," Tansen told him.

The boy had not gawked, stumbled, or stammered in amazement and awe as Tansen had upon first entering Shaljir at a similar age. Of course, Zarien's thoughts were still partially fixed on the grisly heads decorating the Lion's Gate. Tansen also discovered, upon asking the boy a few questions, that Zarien had seen many more races and classes of people than Tansen had as a boy. The sea-bound never ventured ashore, but they mixed and mingled in the floating markets, transported passengers to and from the mainland, and anchored their boats in every bustling port of the nations of Sirkara.

"But I've never spoken to a *toren*," Zarien said, casting a doubtful expression at Tansen. "Well, except for Cheylan, and he doesn't really count, being a Guardian and all."

"Actually, I've never met this *toren*," Tansen said, regarding the grand entrance to the house and thinking briefly of Elelar's despised half-Valdani husband. "He may not even be here." Had Ronall abandoned Elelar, the rebel wife who had betrayed him, and gone to the mainland?

"I've never spoken to a *torena*, either," Zarien elaborated.

Tansen shrugged. "Just be polite."

The boy who perched outside Elelar's house as sentry asked their names and, upon hearing Tansen's, didn't even bother going inside to ask for instructions. The young city-dweller's eyes grew wide with astonishment, then glowed with admiration. He took them inside to another servant who, showing similar deference, immediately escorted them into a large, elegant reception room.

Zarien looked at the departing servant, then studied their surroundings. "I guess," he concluded, "this woman likes you better than most others do."

Tansen smiled. "Perhaps this one just doesn't know me well."

"Oh, better than most, I think," came a familiar voice. It rippled through him like the aftershock of an earthquake as he whirled to face her.

"Where did you come from?" Zarien blurted, staring at Elelar.

Tansen was aware of his heart beating faster. "The *torena*'s house has secret passages."

"And hidden doorways," Elelar added, studying Tansen's young companion with curiosity.

After a tense, awkward pause, Tansen set an example for the boy by crossing his fists over his chest and bowing his head. "*Torena*," he murmured respectfully. "I hope I find you well."

"Oh!" Zarien glanced at Tansen, caught his eye, then crossed his fists and bowed his head. "Um . . ."

"Zarien, this is *Torena* Elelar shah Hasnari." When Zarien just stared mutely at the first *torena* of his acquaintance, Tansen looked at Elelar and said dryly, "He's honored."

Smiling politely, Elelar said, "The honor is mine . . ."

"Zarien," Tansen supplied.

"Of the sea-bound Lascari," Zarien added, blinking a little.

Elelar glanced back and forth between them. "Sea-bound?"

Zarien suddenly flushed. Tansen sighed. "It's a long story."

She lifted one dark brow. "Do you intend to tell it to me?"

Zarien looked at him inquisitively.

"Yes," Tansen admitted. "I think I'd better."

She looked faintly surprised, as well she should. He'd always been stingy with his trust, and she had nonetheless found a way to betray his bloodbrother. However, if Tansen, of all people, was about to disappear into the sea, Elelar needed to know.

Elelar's gaze dropped to where Tansen's torso was concealed by his threadbare tunic. "Your wound is healing?" she asked. The last time she had seen him, the *shir* wound in his side had been bleeding, and it soon thereafter came close to killing him.

Tansen exchanged a glance with Zarien. "Yes, *torena*."

"I'm pleased you are well," she said simply.

The door through which he had entered the room now opened again. Two servants came in, bearing trays of food and drink.

"I'm sure you've had a long journey," Elelar said to Tansen, her polished manners failing to ease the palpable tension between them. "I hope you will honor my home, eat at my table, sleep beneath my roof."

Zarien was already perking up at the sight of food, his nausea at the Lion's Gate forgotten for the moment. Tansen was grateful for the boy's presence here today, realizing that having a third party present—someone innocent of everything that had ever happened between him and Elelar—made this first meeting since Chandar easier than it would otherwise have been. It was still far from easy, though.

The last time he had seen her, he had held a sword to that delicate throat. He had craved the death of his own shame nearly as much as he lusted for vengeance. Now her long-lashed, sloe-eyed stare told him that she remembered those moments perfectly; remembered everything they had said to each other in the shadowy light of that rage-filled night in her bed-chamber at Chandar.

"We thank you for your generosity," Tansen said, nodding briefly to Zarien—who immediately began a bold attack on the food tray. "But we'll stay elsewhere."

She nodded. "Santorell Palace, perhaps?"

Zarien laughed in surprise. Tansen blinked.

Elelar glided gracefully over to a chair and sat down, her elegant silk tunic molding itself to her body. "Things have changed a great deal since you were last in Shaljir," she pointed out.

He accepted a glass of water, flavored with a touch of lemon and honey, from a servant and then took a chair opposite Elelar. The servant left the room as Elelar told Tansen about changes in the city since the Valdani surrender.

"The Alliance is establishing a temporary government in Santorell Palace. *Toren* Varian of Adalian is now in residence there. So are a number of other important members of the Alliance from other districts." She smiled slightly. "You're no longer an outlaw or rebel who must hide his identity in the capital city. You're a great hero, and people will want to know you've come to Shaljir."

He sighed, wishing—would he ever stop wishing?—that Josarian were here. "I don't want to put myself on display—"

"It doesn't matter what you want," she said gently. "And you know that." As if the silence which followed this statement wasn't already awk-ward enough, she added, "You've always known that."

Tansen glanced at Zarien, who was busy shoving all the shining baby onions to one remote corner of the food platter, and said, "I haven't got much time."

She looked at the boy, too. Zarien, chewing enthusiastically, stared back at both of them, his eyes wide and ingenuous in his dark, tattooed face.

Elelar ignored Tansen's assertion about time in favor of saying, "There are additional matters you must attend to."

"Such as?"

"The Alliance is . . . in dispute about the eventual distribution of power—"

"You mean they're squabbling like dogs over the scraps the Valdani have left behind."

He heard Zarien choke on surprised laughter at his rudeness, but he didn't take his gaze from Elelar's. Her expression, of course, gave nothing away. "There are disagreements," she said tactfully. "Peculiar tales are float-ing freely into the city now."

"If those peculiar tales come from the mountains, then they're probably true," he replied.

"Stories about you, Mirabar, Josarian's followers, and a bloodfeud against the Society proclaimed at Zilar."

"All true." He sipped his drink.

"Fighting in the mountains. Guardians against waterlords."

"Keep going."

"Visions at Dalishar. Pilgrims at Darshon."

"You're very well informed," he observed. Unable to resist, he added, "As always."

"Some things never change," she said. "Others can never be mended."

"That," he agreed, awash in his shame, in his neglected vengeance, with every breath that Elelar took, "is also true."

"And you and I both know," she said, her voice dropping to a murmur, "what it is to live with regret. With deeds we can never erase."

"*I* know what it is to live with regret," he said. "You know what it is to get away with murder."

Elelar snapped, "I didn't murder—"

"His blood is—"

Zarien gasped. "She *is* the one!"

Tansen ground his teeth together, furious at himself for not thinking before he spoke. For forgetting the boy's presence for even a moment. He glanced briefly at Elelar, whose sudden pallor belied her rigidly controlled expression, then said to Zarien, "Are you done eating?"

The answer was plainly *no,* but the boy took the hint. Staring at them both with open curiosity, he nonetheless rose to his feet and said, "Yes. Uh, maybe I should go down to the port now?"

"No, not alone," Tansen said absently.

Elelar added, "The port is really a mess right now. These earthquakes we've been having . . ."

"Please," Zarien said to Tansen. "I can smell the sea from here."

"Later."

Zarien sounded exasperated as he insisted, "I won't get lost."

"Not alone," Tansen repeated.

Elelar rose to her feet, catching Tansen off guard. He rose politely, but she was already halfway across the room. "A servant can take him," she said, her voice distantly gracious. She opened the door, called for a servant, and instructed Teyaban, the young man who entered the room, to take Zarien to the port and later escort him back here.

"Satisfied?" Zarien asked Tansen.

"Don't leave Teyaban's side," Tansen instructed Zarien.

"Don't worry. Even if I get separated from him, I'll find you again." Zarien picked his oar up off the floor. "I've got *this,* after all."

As Elelar gave the boy a puzzled look, Tansen said, "Be back before dark. The streets are—"

"Unsafe at night," Zarien said on a sigh. "Yes, yes, you've mentioned that. A few times." He glanced doubtfully at the *torena,* then back at Tansen. "So . . . I'll make arrangements, yes?"

"Yes," Tansen agreed.

Zarien came very close to Tansen, hesitated, and then stood on his toes to whisper into Tan's ear, "And you won't . . . *do* anything, will you?"

"Do anything?" Tansen repeated, not bothering to whisper.

"You know," Zarien whispered again.

"No," Tan replied irritably, "I don't know."

Exasperated, Zarien gave up whispering. "What the *sirana* wants."

"What the *sir*—" Tansen was surprised into a rude snort. "No. Now will you just go? Quietly. Immediately. Without another word."

Zarien shrugged, as if disclaiming all responsibility for Tansen, and headed towards the door. It was nearly shut behind him when he suddenly opened it again, nearly hitting Elelar with it in the process, to say, "It was, um, a great honor to meet you, *torena.*"

"Yes, I can tell," she said dryly. "I'm sure we'll have the pleasure again."

Zarien gazed doubtfully at her for a moment, as if contemplating a reply to this remark, then gave up and left.

Now that they were finally alone, Elelar turned to face Tansen. "So," she said, getting right to the point, "Mirabar wants you to kill me?"

Dar curse that boy.

"That can hardly come as a surprise to you, *torena.*"

"No," she admitted, "it doesn't." She came closer. Close enough for him to smell her scented skin. "Where are your swords?"

"I'm not going to do it, Elelar," he said tersely, "and you know I'm not, so let's just—"

"That's good," she murmured, turning away from him. She walked to the empty fireplace and stared pensively at its charred stones. "I didn't think you would, but that's good, all the same."

He didn't understand her preoccupied manner. "Good?"

"Yes." She seemed to come to a sudden decision. "I need a favor."

He almost laughed. "You of all people shouldn't—"

"No, you'll like this one."

He folded his arms across his chest. "What?"

"About Mirabar . . ."

"Yes?"

He saw the fire in her eyes now. It wasn't what he was used to from her, wasn't what he expected. Her face was alight with it as she said, "It's something the Olvar told me."

"The Olvar?" He recalled the gentle, wizened leader of the Beyah-

Olvari living in the secret maze of tunnels and caves beneath Shaljir. "What did he tell you?"

It wasn't the cold light of shrewd calculation, nor even the hot light of her fanaticism, both of which had been so dangerous and deadly on many occasions in the past. This was different, the glow in those dark, kohl-rimmed eyes, the fervent warmth in that lovely face . . . Different but somehow familiar, as if he'd seen this look elsewhere . . .

"He told me," Elelar said, her voice rich with tension, "that Mirabar's going to kill me."

"She wants to, it's true," he said, years of practice helping him keep his voice steady and reassuring, "but I won't—"

"Yes!" she said, her face brilliant with intensity. "That's the favor I want!"

"Of course," he promised, realizing how Mirabar's fiery power could frighten a woman of merely human gifts. "I'll stop her if sh—"

"No!" she said. "Don't stop her! *Promise* me you won't try to stop her."

His first thought was that Elelar was planning a trap for Mirabar. His second thought was that the one thing that could make him kill Elelar would be if she hurt Mirabar.

"Elelar . . . ," he began slowly. But he didn't even need to ask. Now he understood what he saw in her face. No cunning plan, no double meaning, no concealed motive. He knew this expression, so strange and unfamiliar on Elelar's face, because he'd seen it elsewhere, on other loved faces: Josarian, Mirabar, Zarien. And on the scarcely tolerated face of Jalan the *zanar,* too.

It was the look of believers. The look of people who could not be dissuaded or intimidated or stopped, because they had been touched by something so much greater than themselves that they were beyond the fears and reasoning of an ordinary man like him.

"What's happened to you?" he asked suspiciously, taking her by the shoulders.

"The Olvar told me . . ."

He was astonished to see tears well up in her eyes. Her smile told him these were tears of joy. Of relief.

"What?" Tansen demanded, shaking her slightly. "What did he tell you?"

"I must surrender."

He let her go. "Surrender?"

"When the one with eyes of fire comes for me, I must not resist."

Tansen was completely taken aback. He didn't want to kill her. He knew she should die, but he didn't want to let someone else kill her, either. And he didn't want Mirabar to have the blood of vengeance on her hands. Mirabar had no idea what that was like, and he never wanted her to find out.

"Tansen . . ."

He shook his head. He couldn't think of anything to say except, "No."

"The fate of Sileria depends on this."

"On Mirabar killing you? No." He shook his head. "I want to speak to the Olvar."

She came closer again. Pressed her palm to his arm. Then raised her hand to touch his cheek. A soft palm. Silken fingers. The skin so fair by Silerian standards. So different from the work-hardened, burn-scarred, sun-kissed hand of the woman who wanted her dead. The woman whom Elelar now claimed was destined to kill her.

"Don't you see?" Elelar whispered. "Surely you, of all people, can understand?"

"No," he repeated, knowing what she would say next.

"It's my redemption."

He didn't want to lose her. That was the ugly truth.

Forgive me, Josarian. I can't let go. Not even now. Forgive me.

He was ashamed and humiliated. And afraid.

"My death, for Sileria," Elelar said. "I'm ready."

"*I'm* not."

"My guilt expunged. My shame healed. My soul purified for the Otherworld." She leaned closer, so close their breath mingled. "Let her do it. Let her kill me. *Promise* me."

"No."

"Let me be redeemed," she urged, seducing him with her desire to be sacrificed.

He took her face between his hands. Her lovely, treacherous, yearning face. "Not like this." He tried to make her understand. "Not Mirabar."

She placed her hands over his, stroking his fingers, his wrists. "Don't you see? It must be her destiny, as it is mine."

"I don't care. I won't let it happen."

"Sileria's destiny—"

"No."

"Let her cleanse me with her vengeance," she whispered, kissing his neck, pressing her lush breasts against his chest.

He shivered, then pushed her roughly away.

"And who will cleanse Mirabar for murdering you in vengeance?" he snarled.

"She's a *shallah*. She won't need—"

"Oh, yes, she will," he interrupted. "And I will not let your death become her burden. I'm a *shallah,* too, and I can tell you the weight never grows lighter. Not ever."

Angry now that she was failing to win him over, she said, "*She* will not be killing her own father."

He'd been expecting that, but it made him hotly angry even so. "Darfire, maybe I *should* just kill you and get it over with!"

"After you just promised the boy you wouldn't?" she taunted.

"*Zarien*." It was like a bucket of cold water. He realized that he had let her distract him. Well, nothing new in that. "Zarien," he repeated. "By all the gods above and below." He ran a hand through his long, tangled hair and said wearily, "Actually, I may not be around to keep you from flinging yourself into the fires of redemption at Mira's expense."

She frowned at him. "Something to do with that boy?" When he nodded, she added, "What is a sea-bound boy doing ashore? And with *you*?"

"You and I have a lot to talk about," he said, "and there's not much time. The boy is impatient, and with good reason."

"A lot to talk about," she agreed. "The fighting in the mountains. The Society. These visions that people are talking about. The new government. The massacres of Valdani. And there are people at Santorell Palace whom you should—"

"Yes," he agreed. "I'll see them, speak to them before I go."

"But where are you going?"

He sighed. "To sea."

35

A FIRE IN THE SOUL IS LIKE A TIGER IN THE CAGE;
BOTH ARE RECKLESS IN THEIR FEROCITY.
—Kintish Proverb

ZARIEN MADE A conscious effort to shake off the unbearable tension between Tansen and the *torena* as he left Elelar's house with her servant. Sometimes Tansen could be a little too damn quick to reach for those swords of his, and there was a tumultuous anger in him as he faced the *torena,* a darkness which Zarien had never before sensed in him. For a moment, Zarien worried about leaving the two of them alone. No, he didn't believe Tansen would consciously choose to kill a woman, not even a woman who upset him as much as this one evidently did. Besides, Zarien wasn't blind; he could clearly see that there was also a man-woman current flowing between them which Tansen couldn't entirely resist.

However, although Tansen might be against killing the *torena,* Zarien had seen many times by now just how fast those swords could come out of their sheaths. No wonder people thought they leapt out by themselves! And Tansen didn't always think before drawing his weapons, intent on violence. Tansen was so fast that, when startled or surprised—or awakening from one of his nightmares—he sometimes didn't even seem to know he had already unsheathed his swords and was holding them poised for combat. So whatever made Mirabar hate Elelar, and whatever made Tansen seem like a wounded dragonfish in the *torena*'s presence, Zarien had decided it might be prudent to make sure, before leaving them alone together, that nothing deadly would happen.

Of course, Tansen's irritable response made it clear that nothing would, despite all the air-snapping tension.

Landfolk.

No matter. Soon—very soon now—he and Tansen would be at sea. Sharifar would welcome them, and they could leave behind forever the volatile ways of the drylanders. Of course, Tansen would still care about what happened on land; and, after all this time ashore, Zarien could understand and accept that—at least a little. Waterlords and assassins shouldn't be allowed to rule and ruin Sileria in the wake of the Valdani surrender. There were some good people in the mountains. There were also plenty whom Zarien didn't like, but that could be said about life at sea, too.

Nonetheless, he was glad to be going home at last. Glad to be taking the sea king to Sharifar, as vowed. If he was right, if Tansen was the one the goddess sought and Zarien was the one who brought the sea-born their king . . . well, who knew? Perhaps the Lascari would even break centuries of tradition and overlook his little sojourn on land.

It could happen.

His parents would be so glad to see him alive. They would—

My parents . . .

His newly full stomach churned a little. Glad to see him alive? Yes. They had loved him, he believed that. But to welcome him back into the clan, after his sojourn on land, when he now knew that he wasn't even a Lascari?

Perhaps not, he admitted privately.

Everything about the night he had died now came back to him, including Sharifar's humiliating claim that his father was a drylander and his mother . . . well, not Palomar, in any event.

One thing at a time, he decided.

He had to get to port and find someone to take him and Tansen to sea. Tomorrow, he hoped. The day after, at the latest. Get to sea. Find out Tansen's true destiny.

Then find out who my parents really were.

With his course of action clarified in his mind, he lifted his face to the breeze wafting through Shaljir's narrow streets and took a deep breath.

He immediately choked on the city's overripe smells: sewage, many unwashed bodies, the unmistakable odor of a funeral pyre, some livestock and their associated mess, the perfume of a passing Kintish courtesan, and a few barrels of volcano ale that had fallen from a cart and splattered the street in front of him.

Somewhere in the midst of all that, though, he smelled water. Not just the sweetwater these city-dwellers had been hoarding in barrels in preparation for Kiloran's assault on the Idalar River. Not just the water gushing from their fountains, singing to him almost as sweetly as Palomar used to. Not just the water he felt swelling in their wells and their basins. No. In addition to all that, he smelled the *sea*.

He inhaled and sighed like a lover. "Ohhhh, can you smell that?" he said to Teyaban, the servant whom *Torena* Elelar had sent with him.

"Hmmm." Teyaban sniffed the air and sighed, too. "That perfume. They say it induces visions."

"Huh?"

"Not the war-and-glory kind that Mirabar the Guardian gets, mind you," Teyaban continued cheerfully. "I mean the kind that make a man's body stand up and say hello."

Zarien blinked at him. "What are you talking about?"

Teyaban nodded to where the courtesan was entering a house as palatial as *Torena* Elelar's. "The perfume of Kintish courtesans. They've got all sorts of womanly arts, you know."

Zarien watched her disappear into the house. Her servant—a huge, hairy, scarred Moorlander—waited outside. "Oh. Uh-huh."

"Ever been with a Kint?"

"Yes, of course." Zarien answered absently, thinking of Kintish ports and seafarers and passengers. Then he realized what Teyaban meant by "been with." His truthful answer to *that* would be quite different, but he decided to let it go.

Teyaban, however, had a few tales he wanted to share; Zarien mostly ignored his conversation and followed his nose to the port of Shaljir, leading the servant assigned to lead him. Soon he could hear the seabirds, taste the salt on his tongue, see the salt-air stains on tattered *jashareen* hanging in doorways and grimy shutters bordering windows left open to benefit from whatever stray breeze might be bold enough to waft through the narrow streets. Soon he could recognize sea-brought goods from the mainland being carted up from port and see the tallest ships' masts rising proudly above the city's Kintish red-tiled roofs.

"Ugh!" Teyaban grimaced as they turned into a narrow street with slippery cobblestones. "Fish market."

The thick, briny scent pervading the air here smelled wonderful to Zarien, despite being different from the sweetly plump smell of freshly caught fish which he was used to in sea-bound life. He smelled seaweed now, too, and could hardly wait for the longed-for feel of a boat deck rocking beneath his feet.

The fishmongers of Sileria were tattooed, like their sea-born kindred. Zarien laughed with relief, with a sense of homecoming. Now, for the first time since he had died in the jaws of the dragonfish, he was among his own kind and no one would stare at his tattoos with avid curiosity.

A moment later, he realized he was wrong about that. Already, tattooed fishmongers were indeed staring at him. Staring hard.

"What are *you* looking at?" Teyaban challenged one. Typical of the landfolk, he had deliberately provoked the biggest, meanest-looking person in sight.

"It doesn't matter," Zarien said quietly, dragging Teyaban with him as they passed the big man and left him behind. He knew what everyone was staring at. Unlike the drylanders, these people recognized his tattoos, identified the primary pattern and knew what it meant: *sea-bound*. A sea-bound lad walking the dryland. An unheard of anomaly. Something they were unlikely to see twice in their lifetime. Of course they stared.

"What's going on?" Teyaban asked.

They reached the end of the street and came upon the port. Zarien ignored the question as he stared in astonishment.

What had *Torena* Elelar said? "The port is . . ."

"A mess. I know," Teyaban replied.

"Earthquakes did this?" Zarien stared in shock at the wreckage of smashed boats, collapsed docks, and damaged warehouses.

"Yes." Seeing Zarien's bewildered expression, Teyaban elaborated, "You know. Surely a sea-born fellow knows."

"I've never . . . There haven't been any earthquakes in my lifetime. None that I remember, anyhow."

Teyaban made a clucking sound. "Oh, I hadn't thought of that. Before all the recent ones, I guess it *had* been a quite a few years since the last one. And now they're coming close together, and they're pretty bad—"

"But that's land," Zarien protested. "How did *this* happen?"

Teyaban looked surprised. "Well, after all, there's land under the water, Zarien." He pointed out to sea. "When Dar moves the mountains, She moves a lot of *that*, too." Teyaban nodded. "The water responds."

"By the eight winds," Zarien murmured. "Waves big enough to do this . . ." He had been caught in some terrible storms. Waves so big they blotted out the sky, and you soon forgot which way was up. His clan had lost a boat and four family members in such a storm two years ago. When Zarien was younger, he had seen two boats of the Kurvari clan smashed against the sacred chalk cliffs of Liron; no one survived. He had thought he knew what waves could do. "But I've never seen anything like this . . ."

"That's the destroyer goddess for you," Teyaban said philosophically. "If the Valdani had any sense, they'd never have tried to conquer Her in the first place, eh?" He pointed west. "Just the other side of Mount Shaljir, as you leave the bay, a Valdani ship was hurled against the rocks during the most recent earthquake. A bunch of the passengers actually lived, but the salvageable cargo was all plundered." Teyaban grinned. "So I guess the survivors from that wreck will be empty-handed when they reach Valda." He shrugged and added, "If they ever do. They might have been slaughtered by the mob when they came ashore."

Zarien now deeply regretted eating the *torena*'s food, since it was threatening to come right back up. He didn't want to think about the killings, nor about the heads displayed on the city gates. However, even that wasn't as bad as the fear rushing through him. He had never realized—had never had reason to know—that the earthquakes which so terrified him on land were equally devastating at sea.

"I need to find out about my family," he said.

Teyaban slapped his forehead. "Darfire, I'm sorry Zarien. I didn't realize . . ."

Zarien ignored the apology and started forward, barely aware of Teyaban close at his heels, still babbling.

Now they were mostly surrounded by sea-born folk. The short hair, the tattoos, the simple clothing—tighter and more colorful than that of the *shallaheen*. Many of the grown males carried *stahra*, so no one stared at Zarien's. They stared at him, though. Oh, yes, they stared at *him*.

He ventured far out onto the docks, hoping to find someone he knew, someone he could trust. Adalian was his clan's home port, not Shaljir, but they were related to other clans and were friendly with a few more.

He heard the lap of waves against wood, felt the salt on his tongue, and rejoiced at being home again, even as he worried about his family's well-being. Even as he wondered how to explain everything now that he was here.

"Are you a Kurvari?" someone called in sea-born dialect.

Zarien turned into the wind to find who had asked the question. He saw an old sea-born woman and a boy, together in an oarboat.

"No," he replied. "Lascari."

"Oh. Saw the tattoos. Sea-bound." Zarien nodded, seeing from her tattoos that she was not sea-bound. She shrugged and added, "Thought you might be Kurvari."

"Why?" he asked.

"There are three Kurvari boats at the floating market today."

His heart started pounding. "We're related. Could you take me to them? I can pay you." It felt wonderful to speak his own language again, and to listen to someone without having to concentrate.

She looked at him and the drylander standing beside him. "Both of you?"

"No," Zarien said, "just me." He turned to Teyaban and added in common Silerian, "Wait here."

"No, we're supposed to stay togeth—"

"I'll be back," Zarien said, nimbly scrambling into the old woman's oarboat and pushing off before Teyaban had time to cause trouble. "Just wait for me here."

"Zarien!"

Zarien waved, then turned his back on land. Darfire, it felt good to be in a boat again! He tentatively reached for the old woman's oar. "Shall I row?"

She smiled. "What nice manners you have."

He dipped the oar into the water, felt the sea ease to his stroke, and began paddling. He grinned, despite his worries, so happy to be here at last.

"Is your boat anchored at the floating market, too?" he asked the old woman.

She shook her head. "Our boat was destroyed in the second earthquake. My grandson and I happened to be ashore for trading, or we'd have died with everyone else."

"I'm sorry. What happened?"

"We don't know." She looked at the distant horizon, where the azure waters of the Middle Sea met the brilliant blue of Sileria's sky, now drenched in the gold of the sun. "They never came back from sea. No one ever saw them again." She brushed a weathered hand across her face. "Maybe a big wave capsized them and sent them under straight away. Otherwise . . . well, my son was a fine sailor. He could have survived anything that was . . . survivable."

"I'm sorry," Zarien repeated.

After a long pause, she said, "May I ask what you were doing ashore?"

"It's a really long story."

"I believe that."

"And I don't know yet how it ends."

She considered this. "Do the Lascari still accept you?"

"I don't know that, either."

"The sea-bound shun anyone who—"

"Yes," he agreed.

Still curious, she prodded, "It must have been something very big, to make you abandon the sea and go ashore."

He thought of the scars, now concealed beneath his tunic, which the dragonfish had left on him. "Oh, it was big, all right."

"This is unbelievable," Cheylan murmured to himself, looking around at the hundreds of people on the road to Mount Darshon.

One might have thought that the advent of the Firebringer, followed by his death, would have forever destroyed the cult of the *zanareen*, those fanatics who worshipped at the snow-capped peak of Darshon and occasionally flung themselves into the volcano in doomed attempts to become the Firebringer.

"But this is Sileria," he muttered wryly, pushing against the flow of traffic on the decaying Kintish road which ran all the way through the war-torn lands of the Lironi, the most powerful clan in the east. Whereas the *zanareen* would probably never have even existed in a more sensible country, they continued to thrive here even after the ignominious death of their Awaited One.

Poor Josarian—he was surrounded by those dreary fanatics day and night after surviving the leap into Darshon's volcano to embrace the destroyer goddess. Being the Firebringer had so many disadvantages—an early death being the most obvious one—that Cheylan would always be thankful that it had been that mountain peasant and not him.

Now the *zanareen* were preaching about Dar's fury over the Firebringer's death. The dancing clouds and flashing lights around Darshon frightened the masses, as did the earthquakes, and every foaming-at-the-mouth *zanar* in Sileria seemed to have a different explanation for it all. Cheylan wondered if Kiloran, the chief villain in many of these theories, believed a single one of them.

The offerings and the prayers were old news around Darshon, nothing Cheylan hadn't seen before. However, all the fevered chanting, mournful singing, and euphoric warbling was a new habit, and it was getting on his nerves: pilgrims everywhere were trilling, ululating, wailing. . . . It was a nonstop cacophony which Cheylan had a feeling would still be ringing in his ears when he was halfway back to the western districts and far from Darshon—which he hoped would be fairly soon.

He had left Mirabar alone, under the influence of other men, for too long already. His business for Tansen was nearly concluded here, and he had only a little more personal business to attend to. He expected to head west on the Adalian coastal road, riding a fast mount, in a few more days if all went well.

Meanwhile, he made his way past the pilgrims streaming towards Mount Darshon to worship, praise, and pacify Dar. They brought generous offerings; some of them were so heavily burdened with worldly goods, it looked as if they were offering Her everything they owned. Others came barefooted and empty-handed, having already lost everything—to the Valdani, to the Society, or to the recent earthquakes. Strangely, these were often the most ecstatic of the travelers, and some of them were feverishly determined to ascend Darshon, despite the heat vents now opening on the mountainside, the terrifying colored smoke spewing from the caldera, and the strange light dancing around the summit.

Cheylan had seen pilgrims all his life, of course, but most of these were different from those he was used to. These weren't just people paying homage to Dar; many of these people seemed as crazy as the *zanareen*. The feverish light in their glassy eyes reminded him of Jalan, one of the maddest *zanareen* he'd ever met. Their babbling talk, their apparent indifference to hunger and exhaustion, their noisy passion for the destroyer goddess, their mingled terror and exultation . . . no, these pilgrims, however normal they may have been before, were now no saner than Jalan.

However, Jalan had been right about Josarian; so Cheylan wondered what these people might be right about. Unfortunately, even they didn't seem to know.

Most of them claimed Dar had Called them here, had summoned them from all over Sileria, from all walks of life, from every part of the nation. But although they were positive She wanted them here, they were all nonetheless rather vague—and incoherent—about *why*. Some said it was to witness a birth, others said it was to consecrate a death. But whose birth and whose death, no one knew. Some even claimed that Sileria was destined for destruction and only Darshon would be left standing after the Middle Sea swept the rest of the island away.

Even the sea-born folk were becoming infected by the mystical hysteria sweeping across Sileria. They didn't come inland, of course, but some of their clans were gathering in the waters off the eastern coast, abandoning their traditional fishing territories to float in the shadows cast on the sea by the looming Lironi mountains and wait . . . without, it seemed, having any idea what they awaited.

The rains had been generous this year, and the dry season had yet to seize the island nation in its thirsty grip. The brilliant verdure of the landscape displayed Sileria at her loveliest, and the almond trees held their blossoms late into the season. On a day like this, Cheylan's homeland was a beautiful country to live in, to love, and to dream of ruling through one means or another. And Mount Darshon, looming over eastern Sileria, rising above the surrounding mountains to pierce the clouds in fire and fury . . . Darshon, snow-capped dwelling place of the destroyer goddess, inspired awe in everyone, including Cheylan.

Some pilgrims crossed their fists and bowed respectfully as Cheylan passed them on the road, his flame-bright eyes revealing his special status in Dar's domain, his insignia identifying him as a member of Her favored sect, and his rich clothing marking him as a *toren*. Here in the east, he was almost as famous now as Mirabar was throughout Sileria; but many of these pilgrims had come from afar and so didn't know his name. Nonetheless, he heard a few people whisper it here and there. Some even called out their blessings to him, praised him for serving Dar, or even asked him for answers to the questions which had brought them here: What was truly happening at the summit of Darshon? What did Dar want of them now? What would be the fate of Sileria?

He wanted to know the answers, too, of course. He had Called shades of the dead, made his own offerings to Dar, and sought answers in the sacred flames of enchanted Guardian fire. However, he still found no answers, and he was eager to return to the side of the one person in Sileria who he knew saw and understood what no one else did. Soon he would see Mirabar again, and his destiny would unfold in all its glory.

The sun was high and hot when Cheylan finally reached his destination: Marendar, the village from which Jagodan shah Lironi was leading his clan in a bloodfeud against Verlon. Cheylan knew that Tansen liked Jagodan, but he didn't see the attraction. True, Jagodan had the strength and charisma needed to lead the Lironi, who were notorious for their violent bloodlust, but Cheylan thought he was nonetheless ignorant, hot-headed, and vulgar. Of course, Cheylan reflected, there was no reason to suppose these qualities would bother Tansen, an illiterate *shallah* from an obscure clan which had destroyed itself with bloodfeuds. Tansen had accomplished so much that one sometimes forgot where he came from and perhaps overestimated him.

The sentries recognized Cheylan instantly, welcomed him to Marendar, and told him Jagodan was probably in his house. Having been there before, Cheylan knew the way and so needed no escort to find the humble stone dwelling perched on a hill overlooking the rest of the village. When he got there, though, some children playing outside assured him he had been misinformed; Jagodan wasn't home. Since *shallaheen* always lied to strangers, and since they started young, he didn't believe them and went inside anyhow.

He found a man and a woman in the main room of Jagodan's simple home, standing close together by the stone hearth on the north wall. They heard Cheylan's footstep and jumped guiltily apart at the same moment that he realized the man wasn't Jagodan, although the woman was most certainly Jagodan's wife.

"Kiman," Cheylan said, recognizing the young leader of the Moynari clan who had recently returned from Zilar, where he had joined in Tansen's bloodvow against the Society.

"Cheylan." Kiman attempted a blank-faced stare, but his eyes were restless—nervous.

Not surprising. The *shallaheen* were very touchy about their women, and just being alone with the wife of a man from another clan was sometimes enough to start a bloodfeud. However, Cheylan was not a *shallah* and didn't care whose wife Kiman talked to.

Cheylan greeted Viramar, the young woman Jagodan had married several years ago after mourning (for years, it was said) the death of his first wife when she was bearing their fourth child. Viramar murmured a reply, looking even more nervous than Kiman did.

"Where's Jagodan?" Cheylan asked.

He delivered the question abruptly, eager to get on with his business and leave Marendar without delay. However, he immediately perceived it was taken as an accusation. Kiman suddenly looked defensive and hostile. Viramar stammered guiltily.

Cheylan watched them with amusement as he realized the truth: It wasn't the *appearance* of impropriety which made them so nervous.

Now that's very interesting.

He wondered if Jagodan suspected. Probably not. Not yet. If he did, he'd surely have killed Kiman already.

Cheylan smiled, recalling that Tansen was the one who had instructed Kiman to ally himself with Jagodan. So the Lironi, who probably didn't have a cool-headed thinker in the entire clan, would probably blame Tansen for this. At least, Cheylan certainly hoped they did. In any event, he had no doubt the Lironi would find out about Kiman and Viramar. *He* had already found out, after all, and he hardly knew these people.

Dishonoring Jagodan shah Lironi's wife was a very dangerous mistake. Had Kiman been emboldened by love, or just overcome by lust? Cheylan smiled, enjoying Kiman's growing unease as they stared at each other.

I wonder—are you braver than I gave you credit for, or even dumber than I thought?

ZARIEN WAS ALMOST shaking with nerves by the time they reached the floating market. The oarboat bumped into an unusually large piece of flotsam, and Zarien noticed there was rather a lot of it bobbing on the surface. More damage from the earthquakes, he realized; more boats which the sea had chewed up and swallowed screaming.

Nonetheless, the floating market was crowded and busy today. Boats from all over the Middle Sea clustered together here, though most belonged to the sea-born folk of Sileria. The bobbing boats formed an area the size of a typical *shallah* village, and they were anchored so closely together that planks were rarely even needed to traverse from one boat to the next.

A *toren*'s yacht nearly sailed straight into the oarboat. Zarien and the old woman's grandson paddled hard to get out of its way, then watched as the crew lowered a plank and three *toreni,* one of them a woman even more beautiful than Elelar, made their way across it and into the bustling, bobbing marketplace to examine and purchase goods which came from all over Sirkara.

"Let's go around," Zarien said, pulling his oars again.

The old woman nodded. "The Kurvari have anchored—"

"On the windward flank of the market," Zarien concluded, rejoicing in his homecoming. "They always do."

Once they were in the right vicinity, it didn't take Zarien long to spot a familiar hull. The boat belonged to Gillien, who was distantly related to his mo— to Palomar.

Too excited now for decorum, Zarien secured his oars, stood up, and shouted, "Gillien! *Gillien!*"

He heard voices from the deck above his head. Gillien, Gillien's wife, one of their children, a dog . . . then Gillien's dark face peered over the rail.

"Gillien!" Zarien grinned up at him.

Gillien drew a sharp breath. "Forgive me. You look just like . . ." His jaw dropped and he stared in disbelief. "*Zarien?*"

"It's me!" The expression on Gillien's face made him laugh. "It's me, Gillien! I'm alive!"

"You're alive!"

"I'm alive!"

The old woman asked, "They thought you were dead?"

Gillien shouted to the rest of his family. They all rushed to the rail and peered down at Zarien. One of the girls squealed with delight. The baby started crying and the dog barked. Zarien laughed again, unable to make out anyone's words through the noise.

He shouted, "Aren't you going to invite me aboard?"

Laughing now, Gillien reached down to clasp his extended hands and hoisted him aboard. Then Zarien was being embraced by his distant kin, his own kind. Their salt-pure scent, their wind-burned flesh, their joyful tattoos, the roll and sway of the deck beneath his feet . . .

"Oh, the gods are merciful," Gillien murmured, "the gods be praised."

"It's good to be here," Zarien replied fervently. "It's so good to be here."

Gillien pushed him away and took a good look at him, holding him by the shoulders. "We thought you were dead! Everyone thought you were dead! Killed during the *bharata*. Your family was certain. There was no doubt, no—"

"I know, I know," Zarien said. "I'll explain everything later. But right now—"

"What *is* that?"

"What's what?"

Gillien sniffed. "That smell." He leaned closer and sniffed again. "That's you!" He laughed and said, "Are you *sure* you're not dead? What is that awful smell? It smells like . . . like . . ." His voice trailed off as a strange expression washed across his face. Now his gaze traveled slowly over Zarien, as he stared in astonishment at the *shallah* clothing he wore. When he looked at Zarien's feet, he fell back a step, his mouth hanging open.

Zarien looked down and suddenly saw what Gillien's whole family, now grown silent, saw, too: the dusty boots he wore, with some dried mud caked on one of the toes.

"Smells like . . ." Gillien looked into his eyes, his gaze asking Zarien to deny it. "Like landfolk."

"They . . ." Zarien nodded, suddenly remembering what he had never expected to forget. "They stink when they come aboard."

"Yes," Gillien whispered.

"Stink of cheese and milk and . . ." And other things he'd been eating daily while on the dryland.

"Oh, Zarien," Gillien said in a low, sad voice.

"I had to," Zarien said. "There was a reason."

"It doesn't matter," Gillien said.

"But I—"

"Zarien." Gillien shook his head.

Zarien closed his mouth. He knew. He had known from the very first what going ashore would mean.

Still, maybe it would be different with his own family. His own clan. Maybe when he explained everything to them.

Or not. He wasn't Lascari. Not in any way. Not really. Not anymore.

Even so, he had to see them. There was so much he wanted to tell them. Such important things he wanted to ask them now.

Gillien sighed and said, "Look, I don't pretend to understand. And I'm sorry, because you could have stayed with us, but . . ." He shrugged. "I don't know. Maybe it's just as well."

Zarien frowned. "Why would it be just as well?"

Gillien's face changed again. Sadness and pity washed across his dark features. "You've been . . . with them, haven't you? With the drylanders, I mean. So you don't know, do you? No, I suppose you couldn't."

"Know what?" he asked suspiciously. But he knew. He already knew. He could see it written all over Gillien's sad face.

"Your clan was sailing to Shaljir, after the *bharata*. After mourning you. They were along the eastern coast—"

"No," Zarien said, shaking his head.

"—when the first earthquake, the really big one, hit."

"No." Zarien took a step backward, still shaking his head.

"Maybe if they hadn't made such good time, if they'd been further south . . . We were further south, you see, and we lost no boats."

"*No.*" Zarien felt tears stinging his eyes.

"Your grandparents survived. And four other boats, too. But most didn't." He paused. "Your parents didn't, Zarien."

He mouthed the word *no,* but no sound came out of his constricted throat.

"You can't imagine what it was like on the water that night," Gillien said. "Like the sea was trying to swallow the whole world, or maybe fling it against the sky. And it was worse farther north, they say, where the Lascari were. Much worse."

Zarien's legs gave way. He hit the deck hard, then sat there rocking slowly, still listening.

His parents. His brothers. All dead. Most of the rest of the clan dead, too.

"They say your father's boat was thrown out of the water like a toy, then fell onto the shoals, where it broke apart. It was swept out to open sea then. No remains, no survivors."

Sorin, Palomar, Orman, Morven . . .

Zarien's shoulders were shaking. Tears streamed down his face. He couldn't speak, couldn't think.

"They're gone," Gillien said. "I'm sorry."

"The sea took them," Zarien murmured, as one was meant to upon receiving such news . . . but he couldn't finish the blessing.

"As she will take us all in the end," Gillien continued for him. "And then we will be together again, sailing to that shore which has no other shore."

Zarien hauled himself to his feet, needing to move, to do something to relieve the terrible pain in his heart. He saw the knife sheathed in Gillien's belt and seized it. Gillien didn't move. Zarien drew the blade down his forearm, cutting himself in mourning. It hurt, but not enough; not enough to ease the howling sorrow of his heart. He cut his shoulder, too, pressing the blade through the fabric of his tunic. He felt the sharp bite of the blade. Saw the cloth turn red with his blood and felt it cling wetly to his flesh. He made another cut, his body numb and unresponsive compared to his raging grief.

Gillien put a hand over the one which held the blade and said quietly, "That's enough."

"No." He felt the terrible scars on his torso burning as if they had just been branded there. "No, it's not enough." He drew the knife across his belly, making a long slash of scarlet vengeance against his fate.

"Zarien!" Gillien seized the knife from his stiff hand, then lifted his tunic to examine the wound. He gasped loudly at what he saw there. "May the winds have mercy . . ." His gaze flew up to meet Zarien's. "How did you live through *that*?"

"I didn't," Zarien said stonily.

He looked down at his scarred belly. Blood dribbled down in a strange pattern. The scars didn't bleed; only the unmarred flesh showed any sign of his slash with the knife.

"What's happened to you?" Gillien whispered.

"It doesn't matter." Zarien felt more tears pour out of his eyes, but now fury and betrayal mingled with his sorrow. Now he hated as ferociously as he grieved. "It doesn't matter anymore."

"Zarien . . ."

"I don't belong here," he said suddenly. He saw the dazed confusion in Gillien's eyes. Saw the expressions on the faces of the rest of the family—fear, shock, even suspicion. "I can never belong here again."

"You're still sea-born," Gillien said kindly. "Just not—"

"No, I'm not." The steel in Zarien's voice matched the hardness in his heart. "I don't want to be here. I don't want to be here ever again."

"Don't say that. The sea will always—"

"Sharifar had no right," Zarien said bitterly.

"All the nine goddesses—"

"*Sharifar had no right!*" he shouted, his hatred consuming him, the bitter gall of her cruelty turning his heart to fire inside his chest.

Gillien's wife murmured something which Zarien scarcely heard. Gillien took Zarien by the shoulders. "Calm yourself. Your voice is carrying."

Zarien looked around him in a daze and realized that people from other boats were staring avidly at him, listening to him curse one of the goddesses.

He trembled with emotions too wild to be contained within his body. He wanted to mourn. He wanted to die with his family. He wanted to spit in Sharifar's face and let the dragonfish kill him. He wanted to . . . He wanted to leave. To end the most bitter homecoming he could have imagined.

"Good-bye, Gillien," he said. Gillien didn't try to stop him as he climbed over the rail, moving as slowly as an old man. "May the wind be at your back."

"May the wind be forever at yours, too, Zarien," Gillien murmured, his voice full of regret.

But Zarien was already caught in the whirlwind, and he would never sail calm waters again.

He lowered himself into the oarboat and said, "Let's go."

The old woman eyed him curiously. He didn't know how much she had heard, nor did he care. "Back to port?" she asked.

"Yes." He didn't offer to row this time. He sat staring at nothing, scarcely aware of their movement through the water.

He had realized, upon seeing the port so badly damaged, that his family might be hurt, even dead. He had known that—but he hadn't believed it. Not really. Not for a moment.

Sharifar had no right.

She had asked everything of him. And now she had taken all that was left. She and Dar, together.

He would hate them forever. He would never serve them. Not now. Not ever.

His gaze finally focused on something: the *stahra* lying at his feet. Sharifar's gift, which had led him around the dryland like a dog following its master, like a dragonfish following the scent of blood. He picked it up. He had never touched the *stahra* his father had gotten for him and never had a chance to give him. That *stahra*, like the boat in which it was hidden, was now somewhere at the bottom of the Middle Sea, as lost to him as his family.

And he would never again touch the *stahra* which Sharifar had given him. He rose to his feet and, holding the *stahra* like a harpoon, threw it into the sea. The old woman gasped and bleated questions. The boy tried to retrieve it.

"No," Zarien said. "Take me back to port."

He watched the *stahra* float away for a moment, then sat down again.

Take it back, he told Sharifar in the grieving silence of his heart. *Our bargain is broken. If you want the sea king, go find him yourself.*

He waited, wondering if she would bring fury to the sea to sink the boat and kill him before he reached shore. He hoped so, because he was more than willing to die if it meant he could try to gut the goddess like a fish before he drowned.

Take me before we reach the shore, Sharifar, he urged. *Because you'll never have another chance.*

He would turn his back on the sea forever after this. He would never return.

And you will never have Tansen, he swore to Sharifar. *Never.*

36

NEVER FOLLOW A BEAST TO ITS LAIR.
                                        —Moorlander Proverb

CHEYLAN HIT THE ground with a thud, his face scraping the rocky soil while icy tentacles, which had grabbed his ankles with lightning speed, dragged him on his belly towards a boiling torrent of hissing water which, only moments ago, had been a peaceful stream.

He didn't waste time or energy in physical struggle. Instead, he reached for the stream with the force of his will and tried to seize it from Verlon's control. The frigid tentacles twining around his legs quivered briefly, then jerked him fiercely and continued pulling him inexorably towards the churning water. He didn't panic, didn't lose focus, just struggled for mastery of the stream . . .

Rocks scraped across his skin and thorns snatched at his clothing as he was dragged closer to the water, which was boiling so violently that dead fish, killed instantly, were bobbing wildly on its surface.

Feel the water. Smell it. Hear it. Know it better than you know your own blood, your own heartbeat, your own skin . . . Taste it in your mind, see it with your heart. Let it be you, so that it will let you be it.

All Verlon had ever taught him, all he had ever taught himself, everything he knew about the liquid mystery of water magic swelled into one tidal wave of effort as he fought to keep Verlon from killing him.

Let the water be in you, that you may be in the water. Answer when it whispers, so it will answer when you whisper.

Cheylan whispered with all his might, praying that he had listened long and hard enough, through all the years of study and practice, to survive this confrontation with the great waterlord who had trained him—and who hated him enough to kill him.

Let it seduce you, that it will be seduced by you, too.

Guardians were the servants of fire, but a waterlord was the master of his element. If a waterlord's talent was great enough and his concentration good enough, all the listening eventually led to being heard. All the seduction led to love.

Love the water, so that it can love you in return.

This was where a waterlord gave his heart of stone. To *this*. To the crystal-clear element which sought his love even more jealously than the destroyer goddess did. To the pure chill of power which rewarded his talent beyond anything Dar could ever offer. This great gift drank a man's heart like wine, and he never missed what lesser men thought of as love.

Now, fighting for his life—for the life which held such promise of greatness yet to come—Cheylan reached for the water, coaxed it, whispered to it, seduced it. And felt it yield to his love.

And when the water loves you, then you will own it and do with it as you will.

He felt Verlon now, too, felt him the way a suitor felt his rival in his midst. They struggled against each other, their fierce wills clashing in watery silence, in chilly rage, in a desperate struggle which was, as it had always been, about so much more than the water itself.

Then suddenly Cheylan felt the stream yield to his will. The tentacles around his feet collapsed into a puddle. The stream stopped bubbling and hissing, subsiding into a weary stalemate as steam rose from its now-calm surface.

Cheylan didn't let go, and neither did Verlon.

"It's the Idalar River all over again," Cheylan murmured dryly. This was why the most important waterway in Sileria usually looked uncannily peaceful; Baran and Kiloran were in a constant battle with each other for complete mastery of it, and water without a decisive master tended to look just like unensorcelled water—to everyone but another waterlord, that was.

Cheylan knew what would happen next, so he simply waited. Sure enough, before long, a small party of men appeared on the crest of the hill which rose above the far side of the stream. Cheylan watched impassively as the old man, dressed in richly elegant clothes and using a cane, which looked (ostentatiously, Cheylan thought) like a giant *shir,* began making his way down the hill, flanked by two assassins, their red *jashareen* brilliant against their black tunics.

When the old man finally stood on the other side of the stream, Cheylan crossed his fists over his chest and bowed his head. "Grandfather," he asked innocently, "what have I done to deserve such a violent welcome?"

Verlon glared coldly at him. "You mean apart from plotting against me with the Lironi?"

"Is that what you believe?"

"Hmmm, let me think," Verlon snarled, his voice dripping with sarcasm. "*Yes.*"

"And you think I came alone to your stronghold—"

"You're still a few strides outside of my stronghold," Verlon pointed out testily. The stream warded his home.

"—because I have a death wish. That would be your theory?"

Verlon studied him suspiciously. "Are you here as an envoy? To speak on their behalf?"

"No."

The water on Verlon's side of the stream bubbled briefly. "Then what *are* you doing here?"

"Were you really going to kill me?"

"The rebellion's over. The war is between the Society and Josarian's loyalists now, and you've sided with them." Verlon nodded. "Of course I was going to kill you."

"You can't," Cheylan replied.

"You've continued practicing," Verlon noted sourly.

"And you're old."

"True," Verlon said, his face darkening, "but if you make me mad enough, I might even exert myself, *sriliah*."

Cheylan had heard the *shallah* word for "traitor" from his grandfather too often to be angered by it, so he only replied, "We're not peasants, so why do you insist on talking like one?"

"Because there isn't a word in common Silerian bad enough to describe you!"

"It's so good to be home," Cheylan said dryly.

"This isn't your home. This hasn't been your home for years."

"As much as I enjoy these reunions, grandfather, I don't have much time, so perhaps we could stop exchanging barbs and—"

"Come to the point? Please do," Verlon invited nastily.

Cheylan made it simple: "I am with you, not them."

Verlon was so startled that Cheylan felt the old man's grip on the stream give way. Just a little. Then Verlon snorted with open disdain. "Why? Has something happened that I don't know about?"

"Plenty," Cheylan assured him. "And don't you *want* to know? Doesn't it make sense that *someone* among us should know?"

"Us?" Verlon repeated.

"The waterlords."

"You're not a—"

"Aren't I?" Cheylan challenged. "No, I'm not in the Honored Society, and I have no territory or assassins; but how many waterlords in Sileria could battle you for control of your own moat," he said, gesturing to the stream between them, "and win?"

"You haven't won!" Verlon hurled, infuriated. "It isn't yours yet, you—"

"But it's not entirely yours anymore, either, is it?" Cheylan didn't like raising his voice, but he usually had to when trying to make the old man listen to him. That hadn't changed.

Verlon's face darkened. "Give it back!" he ordered.

"After you've calmed down," Cheylan promised. Seeing his grandfather on the verge of a tantrum, he added, "I don't want it. Not yet, anyhow. You can have it back as soon as I'm sure you're not going to attack me again."

"*I won't attack you again!*" Verlon screamed.

"That," Cheylan opined, "wasn't entirely convincing, grandfather."

Verlon exploded in an inarticulate vent of rage, making noises not unlike the cries of a mountain cat in rut. He threw his cane on the ground, then immediately shouted at one of his assassins to pick it up.

Tired of wasting time, Cheylan continued, "You ambushed me—"

"You should have been expecting it!"

"I admit, I wasn't anticipating a warm welcome. Not in *our* family—"

"*You* have some nerve talking to me about—"

"And I can't claim to be entirely surprised that you—"

"I have every right!" Verlon shouted. "I should have killed you years ago!"

"Have you completely forgotten," Cheylan asked with a touch of irritation, "that you rescinded the bloodvow you swore against me?"

"I've changed my mind!"

Cheylan sighed.

Verlon stomped around, waving his cane, hurling insults and abuse—and trying, without any success, to pull his stream away from Cheylan's will. When he had finally worn himself out a little, Cheylan tried to reason with him again.

"They think I am with them because that's what I want them to think," he told the old man.

"Yes, you're good at that," Verlon said bitterly.

"But the Guardians are doomed, as are Josarian's followers. Tansen is locked in a quarrel with Kiloran which he can never win, and how long can Mirabar survive with every waterlord and assassin in Sileria looking for her?"

He was pleased to see that Verlon was listening to him now, albeit with a suspicious expression on his weathered face.

"I want to come home, grandfather," he said.

"I don't want you to come home," Verlon replied baldly.

"Can you stand alone against the Lironi *and* Kiloran?"

Verlon's head jerked with surprise. "How do you know about—" Then he stopped himself.

"About Kiloran?"

Verlon nodded.

"He's making a move on your territory."

Verlon stepped forward. "How do *you* know?"

"I know because Tansen knows."

Actually, Cheylan knew that Verlon had been duped. Kiman shah Moynari had described the whole plan to him, as explained to him by Tansen in Zilar's gold-tiled temple. The Moynari had recently helped the Lironi slaughter eleven of Verlon's assassins, leaving no survivors to tell who had done it—and leaving behind one of Kiloran's *shir* to cast blame on the waterlord and promote feuding within the Society.

It was a good plan, and it served Cheylan's purposes, too. He didn't want any of the waterlords too strong, and he certainly didn't want them united.

Verlon fumed, "Kiloran already has Cavasar, the mines of Alizar, the Idalar River—"

"Well, not the Idalar—not entirely, that is."

"Oh. True. There are moments in which I could almost love that madman Baran." Verlon was briefly amused, but then he scowled again. "Kiloran won't be satisfied until he rules all of Sileria," he continued angrily, "and he knows I'm powerful enough to oppose him. That fat, snake-eyed old lizard wants it all, and—"

"And we must deny it to him."

"*We?*" Verlon said scathingly.

"This is the east, and the east has always been ours, grandfather."

"Ours?"

"You have been the supreme waterlord here for thirty years. Your territory is a birthright passed down to you from your teacher. Now that the Valdani are finally gone, now that the Firebringer is safely dead, now that the Society's destiny is at hand and the waterlords will finally rule Sileria . . . now is your time, at last, grandfather. Who in all of Sileria deserves to rule the east as much as you do?"

"And why are *you* being so generous?"

"I'm being practical," Cheylan corrected.

"So you've already decided what's in it for you," Verlon translated.

Cheylan nodded. "Who deserves more than I to inherit your legacy? To take your place after you're gone?"

"I know you," Verlon growled, "and you won't wait until I'm gone."

"So you'd rather see Kiloran take it?"

Verlon glared at him, his face contorting unattractively as he considered and dismissed various possible responses to this.

"Even if you chose someone else," Cheylan continued gently, "would they have a chance of standing against him, as I would?" Upon receiving no reply, he added ruthlessly, "Would they have a chance of standing against me when I decided to take back what should have been mine in the first place?"

"You flatter yourself," Verlon snapped.

"Do I, grandfather?" He didn't even glance at the stream. He didn't need to. He knew Verlon could feel his firm grasp on all its fluid potential.

"How many waterlords in all of Sileria could do this to you? Two? Three? Five? No more than that, surely."

Verlon shrugged.

Cheylan waved his hand and suddenly set the surface of the stream on fire. Verlon didn't move, but Cheylan was pleased at the way the assassins edged away from the flaming water, their *shir* twitching so wildly he could see it from here.

"And I," Cheylan added, "am so much more than a waterlord."

"Show some respect, boy," Verlon growled.

Cheylan glanced over his shoulder, looking up at the clouds, up to where Darshon's sacred snow-capped peak, still violent with mysterious tumult, dominated the sky. "What other water wizard in all of Sileria enjoys Her favor? Of all of us, who but me can make peace with Her?"

"Peace . . ." Verlon frowned in puzzlement.

"You know there must be peace, at last, between fire and water in Sileria."

"No," Verlon said. "It must be us or them. We can never exist together."

Cheylan shrugged. "I didn't say we wouldn't have to kill a lot of them. But *eliminate* the Guardians of the Otherworld?" He shook his head. "There will be no need, with me at your side."

"And with your dagger in my back."

"You're very old, grandfather," Cheylan pointed out, "and I have learned patience."

"A great deal more than patience," Verlon replied cynically—but Cheylan could see him giving in.

"If you reject me now, grandfather," he said, looking across the burning water, "you will be alone, against Kiloran and the Lironi. Alone, and with no one strong enough to honor your legacy after you die. But if you welcome me home, we can defeat them all, make peace with the destroyer goddess, protect what is ours . . . and someday claim what is also theirs. Then, grandfather, even after you're gone, your blood will run through the veins of the most powerful ruler Sileria has ever known."

"You've become very ambitious," Verlon noted.

"I've always been ambitious," he replied. "I just never knew what to do about it before."

"Apart from trying to kill me, you mean."

"As Kiloran says," Cheylan replied philosophically, "mistakes are so easily made."

Verlon snorted, then began pacing back and forth slowly, leaning on his cane, his face intent and serious as he considered his grandson's words. "These are extraordinary times," he said at last. "Josarian changed everything. This is no longer the world to which either you or I were born." He nodded and kept pacing. "New answers must be sought, because all of the questions are new." He lifted his face and looked up to where Darshon loomed above them, swimming in the churning colors of Dar's choosing. "The waterlord who rules the east must heed Dar's warnings and learn to exist with Her," he admitted. "Not like those fools in the west who can dismiss Her so easily in their dank ruins and underwater lairs, so far from Her wrath, so far from the smoke and fire of Her fury."

Cheylan waited.

Verlon turned to face him across the enchanted flames and ensorcelled water. "You can protect my legacy. I believe that." Cheylan knew this was a huge admission from the old man. "And you can build from it to create a great one of your own." He nodded. "There has never been another man like you. Not in Sileria. At least not that I know of. No one with the range of your talents." He paused for a moment. "I have no intention of losing everything I have achieved, everything I hold through power and will. Not to Kiloran. Not to the Lironi." His eyes were hard as he added, "Not to you."

Cheylan said nothing.

"Your strength combined with mine would ensure my place until I die," Verlon continued. "And I would indeed like my heir to rule all of Sileria." He looked down, staring moodily at the fiery stream for a moment, then met Cheylan's eyes again. "But how can I trust you? How can I possibly trust you?"

Now Cheylan spoke. "Tell me what it will take to win your trust again."

"I don't know."

"I do."

Verlon looked both interested and suspicious. "What?"

"Do you know the greatest threat to you? To all of us?" He didn't wait for an answer. "It's not the Lironi, or Tansen, or Kiloran, or even Mirabar. It's Dar's chosen one."

"Mirabar's vision of a new Yahrdan."

"You've heard, then?"

"The same rumors everyone else has heard."

Cheylan sprang the trap: "I know who it is."

"*What?*"

Oh, he had the old man, yes, he had him now. And he would get what he wanted. "There's still time to stop him, to get rid of him. Only it must be done soon. He'll be more powerful than the Firebringer, harder to kill, impossible to control, if he's allowed to reach manhood."

"A child?" Verlon murmured. When Cheylan nodded, Verlon asked, "How can you be sure it's him?"

"Because I'm in Mirabar's confidence."

"But isn't she protecting him?"

"She doesn't know where he is. Only I do."

"Then why haven't you killed him already, if he's such a threat?"

"Think! How can I remain in Mirabar's confidence if I do that?

Besides, what would better establish *your* preeminence than killing him?" He added gently, "Especially since it was Kiloran, not you, who destroyed the Firebringer."

Verlon glowered briefly. "Then this boy *can* be killed?"

"Oh, yes. He can be killed. It won't be easy, but the longer you wait, the harder it'll get." Cheylan paused. "This is my gift to you, grandfather, whether or not you decide to let me come home. If you don't get rid of him, this boy will fulfill Mirabar's prophecies and destroy you, along with everyone else who opposes him or the Guardians."

"If he's your gift to me," Verlon said coldly, "then *give* him to me. Where is he?"

"Gamalan. His name is Semeon." Cheylan smiled. "I know the weaknesses in his Guardian circle's defenses. I'll help you plan the attack. Only . . ."

"Only what?" Verlon prodded.

"Only you mustn't do it until I'm elsewhere and surrounded by witnesses. If I'm to keep you informed about Mirabar and Tansen's plans, then they need to believe I had nothing to do with Semeon's death."

Verlon started to smile. "Agreed," he said. "So . . ." He cast an annoyed glance at the fire-locked stream before inviting, with no more warmth than Cheylan expected, "Why don't you come honor my home, eat at my table, sleep beneath my roof . . . and tell me how to kill this boy?"

Knowing he had won, Cheylan blew gently upon the stream, and released his grip on its waters as his fire started to fade. "Gladly, grandfather."

RONALL WAS AMUSED by how astonished Elelar's servants were to see him when he reached her country estate with Yenibar and *Torena* Chasimar in tow. They didn't even recognize him at first, which wasn't surprising; he seldom came here, since he'd always hated rusticating, and Elelar didn't like him visiting her estate, anyhow. In addition, he supposed he was scarcely recognizable after so long without a bath or anything resembling personal grooming. Some earnest young lowlander in the household immediately decided to take him into hand, and Ronall let himself be taken: bathing, shaving, hair trimming, nail trimming, a massage . . .

Oh, it's good to be a toren, he thought, sinking into the pleasures of his class. *It's good to be rich and pampered.*

But, as always, his pleasures were fleeting and their price was soon made clear. Half of Elelar's servants treated him with open disdain. They knew he was half-Valdani, and they knew how his wife loathed him. They had always shown him courtesy in the past, but that was because the Valdani ruled Sileria and the penalties were appalling for any Silerian who crossed a Valdan. Now, in a free and chaotic Sileria, despite his status as a *toren,*

Ronall's Valdani birthright held him hostage to the rudeness, contempt, and resentment of Silerians. Even, as he well knew, to their violence and deadly hatred.

Meanwhile, the other half of the servants were so glad to see someone, *anyone,* with authority over the estate (however nominal and seldom-exercised it was in Ronall's case) that they fell all over themselves in an effort to force their bewildering concerns upon him. Three have mercy, didn't they understand he knew nothing about running an estate? He couldn't answer their questions about planting, harvesting, property disputes, repairs on old buildings, construction on new buildings, a new Guardian encampment on Elelar's land, how much to put aside for taxes this year, whether there would even *be* any taxation this year, what to do about the Valdani buried in one of the fields (Silerians considered burial a repulsive custom, and the servants wanted permission to dig up and burn the bodies), what to do about all the pilgrims begging for food at the *torena*'s gates, and how to respond to Ferolen's demands for tribute.

"Ferolen the waterlord?" Ronall asked. "I thought Elelar paid tribute to . . . oh, what's-his-name? You know who I mean."

"Yes, *toren*. She did," a servant replied. "But he died during the rebellion, and now Ferolen controls our water. What shall we do, *toren*?"

It was an easy decision. An obvious one. The only decision possible in Sileria. "Pay Ferolen," Ronall instructed.

"Are you sure, *toren*? Tansen has declared—"

"Yes, but Tansen isn't here to deal with Ferolen when he decides to make us suffer for not paying, is he?"

"No . . ." was the uncertain reply.

"So pay the tribute."

"Yes, *toren*. Now about the Guar—"

"Everything else will have to wait until the *torena* arrives," Ronall said. "Get me some fire brandy."

"I'm afraid it's all gone, *toren*. The Valdani took it."

He sighed. "Well, bring me whatever you have. And bring me lots of it."

"Of course." The servant hesitated and then asked, "Is the *torena* coming soon?"

"You don't know?"

"She sent money and a few instructions right after the Valdani surrendered Shaljir. She said she would come as soon as she could, to deal with everything; but we haven't heard from her since then, and we don't know quite when to exp—"

"Well, you know the *torena*," Ronall said. "Always so busy."

"Yes, *toren*."

"However, if she said she'll come soon, then you can count on it."

"I know, *toren*." The servant's dark face brightened when he added, "Only imagine how pleased the *torena* will be to find her cousin here!"

"Yes," Ronall agreed dryly. "Only imagine."

"Dar be praised for sparing *Torena* Chasimar's life."

"Yes. Now, I believe you were going to bring me something to drink?"

"Dar curse those Valdani dung-eaters for killing *Torena* Chasimar's husband!"

"As you say." Ronall had altered the truth a little to ensure Elelar's servants would accept Chasimar.

"The war took so much from so many," the servant continued, warming to his theme. "And now there will be more bloodshed. More loss."

"All this talking is making me terribly thirsty," Ronall prodded.

"Oh! Yes. Of course, *toren*. And shall we send something soothing to *Torena* Chasimar's room? I understand she's crying."

"Crying?" he repeated without much interest.

"The death of her husband must be a terrible sorrow to her."

"Yes, well, whatever you think best," Ronall murmured, not wanting to know more about it. He could still hear Porsall's dying scream in his head, and he wished it would go away.

Ronall finally got something to drink—some particularly good strawberry wine, in fact—but the servants simply would *not* stop pestering him for answers, advice, and decisions. He staggered up to his scarcely familiar bedroom that night, pleasantly drunk and annoyingly burdened with Elelar's worries. He'd sleep in a clean bed for a few nights, he decided, and then leave with some money in his purse. He didn't want to see his wife again, and he particularly didn't want her people nagging him until she got here.

His bed, when he found it, wasn't empty.

"Yenibar," he said without much enthusiasm. He lifted the bedclothes, saw she was naked, and felt some moderate interest begin to stir. He didn't encourage it, though. He was tired. "There's plenty to steal in this house," he explained. "You don't need to come to me for that."

She didn't rise to the bait. "I wanted company. I thought maybe you did, too, *toren*."

He sighed. "Considering our history together, however brief, I think you can call me Ronall when we're alone."

"Everything is so strange now," she murmured, using one shapely leg to push the bedclothes off the bed. Her flesh was golden, young, and smooth in the glowing candlelight. "Strange places, strange people—"

"Strange bedfellows," he added dryly. "But then, these are strange times."

"The *torena* is inconsolable."

He nodded and sat down on the bed, depressed. "Porsall."

Yenibar made a dismissive puffing sound. "No. Although that has certainly upset her, too. He was the father of her child, after all."

"Well, of course he was . . ." Ronall stopped, studied her expression, and figured it out. "There was someone else."

She rolled towards him and started unfastening his clothes. He watched her impassively as she said, "Yes."

"Is he still—"

"No. He's dead."

"During the war?"

She placed her hand boldly between his legs and massaged him. He sighed and relaxed a little more. "In a way," she whispered.

"In what way?"

"It was not an honorable death," she explained.

"What happened?" he asked, sliding down onto the mattress to lie bedside her, pressing his hand over hers, showing her what he liked.

"It's a sad story," she warned him.

"I'm in the mood for a sad story," he replied, his head swimming with good wine and a woman's clever touch.

"Tansen killed him."

"That's it?"

"Yes."

"You're not much of a storyteller," he noted. "Why did Tansen kill Chasimar's lover?"

"For betraying Josarian."

He pressed his face against her neck, pleased that she had bathed, too. "This man, this, uh, *sriliah*—"

"Zimran," she murmured, arching her back into him.

"Mmmm. Faster," he instructed. Then he realized what she had said. "I thought Zimran was Josarian's cousin?"

"He was. And he betrayed him."

Sileria. "So Tansen killed him."

"Yes," she whispered.

"And Chasimar weeps for Zimran," he mused, getting distracted. "More than for her dead Valdani husband."

"She loved Zimran. She even helped the rebellion for him."

That surprised him. "A half-Valdani woman helped the rebellion?"

"That crowd trying to kill her that night," Yenibar murmured. "If only they knew. *Torena* Chasimar did more for Josarian than any of them."

"Such as?"

"She was one of Josarian's first abduction victims—"

"When he was trying to raise money." Ronall remembered; he had been terrified, at one point, by a rumor that he was among Josarian's intended victims. Elelar must have found that particularly amusing.

"*Torena* Chasimar was a voluntary victim, because she loved Zimran," Yenibar explained. "Even after *Toren* Porsall paid the ransom, the *torena* didn't want to come home. She was so happy living with Zimran in the mountains."

"That must have annoyed the *toren*," Ronall guessed.

"He didn't know. He just thought Josarian was cheating him. Thwarting him." She giggled a little. "But Josarian was trying to convince *Torena* Chasimar to go home, and she was refusing."

"War is terrible," Ronall said solemnly.

"And Zimran was a good lover."

"The *torena* told you that?"

"No. I knew him, too."

"I see. He was a busy man."

Yenibar shrugged. "It's not as if he had ever promised to be faithful to *Torena* Chasimar."

"No, I suppose not." Ronall and Elelar had, in their marriage vows, promised to be faithful to each other, and neither of them had ever done so, so who was he to judge anyone? "So now Chasimar misses Zimran."

"Well, I think being here makes it harder for her," Yenibar said, "even though we really had no other choice."

Ronall pressed himself into her stroking hand and asked, with diminishing interest, "Why does being here make it harder for her?"

"Because of *Torena* Elelar," she replied absently, shifting her hips closer to his. "It reminds Chasimar of . . . Mmmm . . ." She sighed.

"Reminds her of what?" he whispered.

"Of how she lost him."

"To Tansen."

"No. To . . ." She suddenly stopped speaking and went stiff.

He noticed. "To—?" he prodded.

She kissed him with as much enthusiasm as if he'd suddenly promised her a sack of gold. He wasn't fooled. He pushed her away and said, "Tell me."

She shook her head. "Ronall, let's just—"

He took her wrists in a punishing grip and rolled on top of her. The liquor fired his sudden shift to restless anger. "*What?*"

She looked wide-eyed and nervous in the flickering light. "She lost Zimran to *Torena* Elelar, and it wounded her. Now we are here, in Elelar's home, and *Torena* Chasimar keeps thinking about it." When he stared down at her in blank astonishment, she quickly added, "I mean no disrespect, *toren*."

"You're saying that Elelar and Zimran . . ."

"They loved each other. It was well known."

"Elelar let it be known that she was sleeping with a *shallah*?" he said doubtfully. He didn't bother asking about the assertion that Elelar had *loved* Zimran, which he doubted even more.

"They lived openly together near the village of Chandar."

Ronall rolled away, losing all interest in the girl. "Why?" he wondered.

Yenibar reached for him tentatively. "Because Zimran was a special man."

"Zimran was close to Josarian," Ronall mused, staring into the darkness. "He was someone Josarian trusted." Someone in a position to betray Josarian. "Fires of Dar," he murmured, starting to remember Elelar's homecoming that night in Shaljir. The errand she had sent him on—getting a Society assassin to meet her in secret right after Josarian's death.

"Sweet merciful bloodstained gods," he whispered.

"*Toren?*"

He didn't know how it all fit together. He'd probably never know. But Elelar was somehow involved in Josarian's death. He knew her well enough to know that. There was no such thing as coincidence where his scheming wife was concerned. Zimran had loved Elelar and betrayed Josarian. Elelar had needed so much power over Zimran that she, a *torena,* had lived openly with a *shallah,* letting him think she loved him that much. What else would she have needed so much influence for except convincing him to betray the Firebringer?

And who in all of Sileria was powerful and cunning enough to have convinced Elelar, with her vehement hatred of the Valdani, to sacrifice Josarian? Who except . . .

"*Kiloran,*" Ronall concluded, feeling sick.

"Yes, he's the one who killed Josarian, but Zim—"

"Tell me," Ronall said quickly, pushing her hands away from him. "Think hard. Have you ever heard of an assassin named . . ." He tried to focus, tried to remember. "Searlon?"

"Yes," she said, surprised. "Everyone has heard of Sear—"

Ronall sat up. "Who's his master?"

"You know, *toren.*" She looked confused. "You just said it: Kiloran."

He slumped over on the bed. "Don't touch me," he snapped a moment later. "I think I'm going to throw up."

"What's wrong?" Yenibar asked.

"Dar have mercy," he groaned, feeling the room spin. "I hate my wife." What a fool he had been to marry her! To hope for her love—to long for it even now. How had he ever expected to master Elelar when the Firebringer himself couldn't do it?

"I hate my life," Ronall said with feeling. Less than a full day in Elelar's house, and he was already back to fervently wishing someone would just kill him and get it over with.

"I'm leaving this place," he announced blearily. "I'm leaving as soon as I wake up. You and Chasimar will have to manage for yourselves here until Elelar shows up. I can't stay here."

"I . . . I'm sorry, Ronall."

"Oh, don't even bother," he said morosely. "It's hardly the worst news I've had this year."

"Can I get you something?" Yenibar asked, sliding cautiously off the bed.

"Go see if there's another bottle of that strawberry wine somewhere."

Ronall lay upon the bed and closed his eyes as she left the room. "I wish," he said to the four walls and empty silence, "that my ancestors had never left Valda."

37

AT THE POINT OF A SWORD, LOVE AND FRIENDSHIP
BECOME JUST ANOTHER POINT OF VIEW.
—Valdani Proverb

IT WAS LATE. Elelar waited in a shadowed hallway of her home, pacing slowly outside of the bedchamber to which Teyaban had brought Zarien before coming to Santorell Palace to inform her and Tansen that something had evidently gone terribly wrong in the Bay of Shaljir today. After rowing out to the floating market, Zarien had eventually returned to shore in a fiercely destructive mood, according to Teyaban. Angry, bitter, hostile, raging without making much sense, fighting tears, and altogether looking as if the world was about to end.

Well, maybe it is.

Elelar banished the fatalistic thought as soon as it came to her. The Guardians flowing into Shaljir believed profoundly in Mirabar's visions. A new leader was coming, they said, a ruler of great potential, the first Yahrdan in a thousand years . . . If Mirabar could just find him—and, oh, yes, keep the Society from slaughtering him.

If he's such a great leader, why doesn't he step forward? Why don't we already know who he is? And just how young is he?

Elelar sighed and continued pacing, casting a doubtful glance at the door to Zarien's bedchamber. Tansen had been in there with him for a long time. Elelar went to the door and pressed her ear against it, listening. She heard nothing. Which was all she had heard the other times she had done this while waiting for Tansen to come out and tell her what was wrong.

The sea king.

Imagine that. Tansen, embracing some goddess—much as his own bloodbrother had done at Darshon—and becoming the prophesied leader of the scattered sea-born folk of Sileria.

In truth, it made no sense to Elelar. Tansen's place was in the mountains.

All his strength and influence were needed to lead the *shallaheen* and to destroy the Society. Though he himself scarcely knew it, he was loved, feared, and respected in the mountains; not with the same religious fervor as the Firebringer, but in a deep and enduring way. During the rebellion, Elelar had spent enough time among the *shallaheen* to know that.

The sea-born folk knew his name, knew his deeds, and no doubt regarded him with the same kind of legendary awe that the city-dwellers and the lowlanders did. But it was hard to believe that his true destiny was at sea—or even inside the walls of Shaljir. With Josarian dead, the *shallaheen* needed Tansen too much to part with him. Surely Dar could see that? Surely Sharifar, this sea spirit in search of a consort, could understand that?

Elelar walked away from the bedchamber door and continued pacing the hallway, thinking idly while she waited.

So Tansen didn't want Mirabar to kill her? Elelar almost sneered. So Tansen worried about blood on that razor-tongued girl's hands?

So Tansen, Elelar thought with an unfamiliar twinge of jealousy, *is in love?*

He wasn't just protecting Mirabar. Elelar could tell; she knew too much about men to mistake the signs: He was protecting *himself* when he protected Mirabar—she had become that important to him.

Elelar wondered if Mirabar felt the same way. Tansen wasn't giving any hints, either way, which didn't surprise Elelar. Regardless of all he had seen and done in his life, Tansen was still a *shallah,* and they had very strict views about a woman's honor. Short of announcing his intention to marry Mirabar (or at least to offer a good bride-price for her), there was relatively little Tansen could say about his interest in an unmarried young woman without dishonoring her, according to the rigid customs of the *shallaheen.*

And marriage is probably out of the question, since he's about to go seduce a sea goddess—or let one seduce him.

Elelar turned when she heard light footsteps behind her.

"Faradar," she said, addressing her personal maid, a young woman who knew many of her secrets—though certainly not all—and who had endured countless challenges with her during the past few years.

"They're asking in the kitchen, *torena,*" Faradar said, glancing at the door at she spoke softly. "Do you want an evening meal, and how many guests will there be?"

Elelar shook her head. "I don't know. Tell them to put out some cold food and just leave it there."

"Do you know yet why the boy—"

"No. I've been waiting here since we returned to the house."

"They've been in there for a long time," Faradar mused, staring at the door. "The *siran* seemed very worried about him when you returned to the house together."

"Yes," Elelar agreed. Tansen's concern for Zarien was something he couldn't hide, not even from the servants.

"The *siran* loves that boy," Faradar stated plainly.

"Yes," Elelar said slowly, only just now realizing what had been obvious from the moment Zarien had first arrived here with Tansen. "He does."

"Do you think—"

They turned when the door clicked open. Tansen came out, his lean face drawn and sad, and closed the door behind him.

"Well?" Elelar asked.

"His family is dead," Tansen's voice was soft. "Most of his clan. He . . . It's come as a terrible shock to him."

Wanting to get rid of Faradar, Elelar said to her, "Go have some food brought up to Z—"

"No," Tansen interrupted. "I asked. He won't eat. Not tonight."

Faradar, however, understood Elelar's hint and politely took her leave, offering to have some cold food set out for Elelar and Tansen downstairs.

"No," he said. "I want to stay close to him, in case he calls for me."

"I'll have something brought to you here, *siran*," Faradar promised.

"Thank you. Just some wine. I'm not hungry."

"*Torena?*" Faradar asked.

"I'll be down later," Elelar replied, guessing that Tansen wouldn't want her company for long. She'd rarely seen him so tired. His concern for this boy drained him in a way that physical demands rarely did.

Tansen stared at Zarien's door for a long moment, then said absently to Elelar, "He needs some time by himself. I'll go back in and sit with him a little later, after he's asleep." He sank into a chair, for once neglecting his manners, and looked up at Elelar, who stood before him. "I don't want him to wake up alone."

Elelar glanced over her shoulder to make sure Faradar was gone, then asked, "What does this mean for his plans? Your plans?"

"He says we're not going to sea. He says . . . uh, vulgar things about Sharifar which I really can't repeat to a woman."

"But—"

"He blames the goddess, Elelar. He blames Dar, too. He's . . . very, very angry."

"Yes, but—"

"He won't go. And I can't go without him."

She thought this over. "No, I suppose not."

"I have no idea what to do."

"Except float around in a boat and hope for the best."

"Which seems like a waste of time, given the circumstances on land. Besides . . . surely someone would need to speak to the sea-born. Someone credible."

"Like a fourteen-year-old boy?" she murmured doubtfully.

He shrugged. "More credible than me. He's got those dragonfish scars. Besides, he's one of them. You know what the sea-born are like. Josarian's the only 'drylander' any of them have ever cared about."

The Firebringer's named dropped between them like a volcanic rock, still glowing hot and red with Dar's fury.

But Elelar knew now how she would pay for that betrayal, even if Tansen didn't accept the destiny the Olvar foresaw for her and Mirabar, so she didn't let the sudden anger and sorrow in Tansen's face distract her.

"So what are you going to do?" she asked.

"Take care of business in Shaljir." Looking a little more focused now, he continued, "All those vultures in the Alliance will have to abide by Dar's will and accept the Yahrdan whom Mirabar and the Guardians recognize."

"*If* they ev—"

"We're only going to use the word *when* with regard to that, Elelar," he instructed, "particularly whenever *toreni* and members of the Alliance can hear us."

She sighed. "Nonetheless—"

"Meanwhile, Shaljir has got to prepare for Kiloran's assault. Especially with the dry season upon us."

"We've stored water—"

"I noticed. But you'll need to do more than that."

"We're trying to find out Kiloran's plans. Trying to learn what Baran will do."

"So are we."

"Kiloran can't withhold the Idalar River from Shaljir unless Baran helps him."

"Or just fails to hinder him," Tansen pointed out.

"Oh. Yes. True enough." She made a helpless gesture and asked, "What else must the city do?"

"I'll work with the Guardians. Only they have any chance of protecting Shaljir from the Society. And the city-dwellers need to see the Guardians fighting for them, the way the lowlanders and *shallaheen* are seeing it now."

"Derlen the Guardian is here," she advised him, "in my household. He can help you organize the Guardians coming into the city, as well as the ones already here."

"I need to leave soon. But tomorrow I'll send for Radyan to come work with Derlen and the Alliance after I'm gone."

"Radyan? I don't know him."

"He's very shrewd. And he comes from Illan—"

"On the banks of the Idalar."

"Yes, so he's quite familiar with what Kiloran can do."

She nodded and raised a new problem with regard to Kiloran. "We need to access the mines of Alizar. The country needs money, Tansen."

He sighed. "I know. I just don't know how to loosen Kiloran's grip on Alizar."

"We've tried to consider—"

"I'm not sure anyone but another waterlord can do it."

"Is there any possibility that another waterlord might?"

Tansen shrugged. "We're working on it."

She saw he didn't mean to tell her more than that, but she knew something of how his mind worked, so she guessed his plan. "You're trying to sow dissension within the Society."

He looked a little annoyed, but she saw that he hadn't really expected to keep it a secret from her. "Fortunately, it's not very difficult."

"How can the Alliance hel—"

"The Alliance," he interrupted, "should be concentrating on stopping the massacres. Here and throughout Sileria."

She made an exasperated gesture. "Do you think we don't know that? Do you think we don't know the danger of offending the Emperor in Valda at this point?"

"The killing of women and children offends *me,* Elelar," he said tersely. "The rebellion is over, and even the Valdani *men* remaining in Sileria are mostly unarmed now. No one hates the Valdani more than I do, but this has to stop."

"How?"

He rubbed his forehead. "I don't know. We have to find a way, though." He frowned a moment later and asked, "Where's your husband? Has he been killed, or did he leave Sil—"

"I don't know where he is." She shook her head. "He took my favorite horse and disappeared. I've had no word of him since. He may well be dead now, for all I know."

Tansen accepted a goblet of wine from a servant who came up the stairs. When the two of them were alone again, he said, "You married a Valdan. You can convince the people—"

She gasped. "Half-Valdan, and I only married him because—"

"It doesn't matter," he insisted. "You're a heroine of the rebellion, loved by the people. You have influence with the Alliance, you're probably the most powerful woman in Shaljir now, and your name is legend even in the mountains. So tell the whole nation that you love Ronall."

"*What?*"

"Pray he's still alive, find him, and make an example of him: the half-Valdani husband who supported your secret work—"

"He never knew!" she protested.

"Who begged the Imperial Council to spare your life, and who went to prison for you after—"

"He didn't go to prison voluntarily!"

"Who endured torture and suffering in prison to protect—"

"He knew nothing! There was nothing he could tell Commander Koroll! And if he had known anything, he'd have told it all for just one drink, the filthy—"

"Find him and make him a hero, Elelar," Tansen ordered. "Make the people love him the way they love you."

She was aghast. "I can't—"

"You have to," he said inflexibly. "If you don't, everyone in Sileria with Valdani blood will be slaughtered within the year. That's not what Josarian wanted, despite how many he killed."

She felt ill. "Tansen . . ."

He leaned forward. "Don't let Sileria exist as a place where we murder women and children." Their eyes held. "Don't let that be our future, *torena*."

Elelar sighed and nodded. She would do her duty. She always had. She supposed that she could bear this, too. Besides, it wasn't as if she expected to live long enough to endure Ronall's company into old age. "But I don't know how to find my husband," she said honestly.

"I'll help. He should be easier to find than a *shallah* or a lowlander. Everyone notices a *toren*. When we go back into the mountains—"

"We? You're taking the boy, then?"

He blinked. "Of course. He goes where I go."

She heard pride in his weary voice and supposed it shouldn't startle her. "Even now?"

"Where else would he go?" Tansen replied. "His family is dead. His clan is mostly dead. The sea-bound shun him now. I'm all he has. There is no one else."

It wasn't her affair, but she was fond enough of Tansen to be concerned. "That boy . . . any boy . . . any child is a big responsibility, Tansen, and this one is diff—"

"Is that why you've never had one?" he asked coldly.

She almost flinched. She was surprised at how much his bald question and chilly tone hurt on this subject. She replied with dignity, "I've never had a child because it has never been Dar's will that I do."

He sighed. "I apologize, *torena*. I was rude." Their gazes held for a moment, and he added, "I'm sorry, Elelar. It was unkind of me."

She acknowledged the apology, but nonetheless persisted, asking softly, "Do you know what you're doing?"

"Yes." Seeing that this didn't satisfy her, he added, "Whether chance or destiny brought this boy into my life, Elelar, he has been a gift to me." He looked down and clearly tried not to make the words cut as he concluded, "It's as if he was sent to fill the place left empty in my heart when Josarian died."

She wanted to weep for the things she had done. "Or was that place in your heart so empty that it seized upon this boy and now will not let him go?"

"Go where?" he challenged.

She thought about it and admitted, "Nowhere, I suppose. If he has no home left and he has abandoned his quest for the sea king . . ." She smiled sadly. "I suppose he's yours now whether you want him or not."

There was a dark, thoughtful expression on his face as he stared at the closed door to Zarien's chamber. "He's a very strong boy," Tansen murmured. "We'll be fine."

"Good," was all she said, though she didn't feel as certain as Tansen did. "I'll leave you alone now. There'll be a servant at the bottom of the stairs all night, in case you want anything."

"Thank you."

She turned to go.

His voice stopped her. "Elelar?"

She didn't turn around. "Yes?"

"I haven't forgotten," he warned her. "I want to see the Olvar."

"Very well." She spoke over her shoulder. "I'll arrange it."

What Tansen thought didn't matter. What he did wouldn't change her plans or her destiny. She could let him talk to the Olvar. It wouldn't do him any good.

"YOU WERE RIGHT, *siran,*" Searlon informed Kiloran in the watery splendor of Kandahar. "Baran is very ill."

"What is it?" Kiloran asked, pleased.

Searlon shook his head. "No one knows for sure. He's been very secretive. But it's been going on for a while, and he's sick enough to have bribed the Sisterhood to tell my informants that he's getting well."

"Ah." Kiloran nodded. Searlon was not like other men, and Baran was a fool to think he could trick the assassin with such a ploy. "Dying?"

"It seems likely, *siran.* But we should consider that it could take a long time."

"Or not," Kiloran said, trying to be optimistic. He considered another problem. "Do you think he's strong enough to kill Mirabar?"

Searlon shrugged. "Possibly. If he catches her off guard."

"Then that will be his plan."

"And what is *our* plan regarding the territory left vacant by Abidan and Liadon?"

Kiloran made a sound of weary anger. "I warned them about Tansen. I warned them, yet those fools still let—"

"We should look forward, not backward, *siran,*" Searlon suggested politely.

He mastered his rage and agreed, "Yes, of course."

"Is Meriten having any success reclaiming the brothers' territory from the Guardians?"

"Not yet, but I'm willing to give him time."

"We don't intend to . . . step in?"

Kiloran shook his head. "Meriten is loyal to me, and it would be foolish for me to expend energy right now on that particular territory."

Searlon considered this and then indicated his agreement with a nod. "Perhaps if I assisted him, though?"

Kiloran nodded, understanding that Searlon meant he would advise Meriten on making the most effective use of his assassins in his struggle with the Guardians over the Shaljir River. "If you can spare the time."

Searlon mused, "It would, however, mean further delays in my dealing with Najdan."

"Since we don't even know where Najdan is at the moment—"

"Finding Mirabar is the key, of course. And that's proving harder than I anticipated," Searlon admitted.

"Ah. We return again to the question of befriending someone who will betray her, if Baran can't manage to kill her soon."

"Sooner or later—"

"No doubt. In the meantime, however, if you feel you can help Meriten without neglecting more important matters . . ."

Searlon nodded, then continued, "You wanted to know more about that sea-born boy."

"The one traveling with Tansen."

Searlon shrugged. "Little is known. He appeared out of nowhere one day, shortly after Josarian's death, and hasn't left Tansen's side since then."

"But why? And where does he come from?"

"*Why* is anyone's guess, although there is strange talk of an enchanted *stahra*—that's an oar which the sea-born use as—"

"I know what it is," Kiloran interrupted. "Enchanted? Is that just *shallah* talk, or is there something to it?"

"I don't know yet. But the most interesting thing is that this boy is—*was*—sea-bound."

Kiloran leaned forward. "Sea-bound?" he repeated, scarcely able to hear his own voice above the sudden pounding of his heart.

"I've never heard of one coming ashore before." Searlon stroked his scarred cheek and admitted, "I find it interesting. Your instincts were right, *siran*. The boy is more out of place than we realized. I intend to find out more, but Tansen has disapp—"

"What clan?" Kiloran demanded.

"The boy? Lascari, they say."

After all these years, it was like being slapped suddenly, unexpectedly, and without provocation. "Lascari," he whispered.

"Yes." Searlon gave him a puzzled look. "What does that mean to you, *siran*?"

He stared at the fluidly solid walls of his underwater palace and pondered the possibilities. Perhaps it was merely coincidence. "But I don't like coincidences."

"And I don't believe in them," Searlon said. "However, I don't understand. What—"

"Is anyone else asking about this boy?"

"I don't know. Is that important?"

"Is *Baran* asking about this boy?"

Searlon frowned. "Not that I know of, but—"

"See if you can find out."

"Yes, *siran*."

"But without calling Baran's attention to the boy, if he's not already interested in him."

"Of course." Searlon waited. When Kiloran didn't speak, the assassin did. "May I ask what this is all about?"

Kiloran sighed, feeling his heart slowly return to a normal pace. "It may be nothing." He nodded. "In fact, it's *probably* nothing. But the Lascari . . ."

"Do you know them, *siran*?"

He shook his head. "I knew one of them once. She's been dead for years, though." He had tried to make sure. He had been obsessed with being certain. A soft shadow of doubt had remained for a while, only fading gradually as he watched from a distance while Baran grew more bitter and insane with each passing season. It was Baran's spiral into madness which had fully convinced Kiloran many years ago that the woman was truly dead.

Impetuous acts and ungoverned passions always cost too much and should never be indulged.

And now . . . Now another Lascari had come ashore, after all these years.

Searlon asked the obvious question: "Do you think this boy has come ashore seeking vengeance for her death?"

"Possibly. Or not. The sea-born aren't like *shallaheen*, you know. Vengeance is not a way of life for them, and I'm not at all convinced it would be reason enough for one of the sea-bound to set foot upon land. Besides . . ." He thought it through. "Would the Lascari have waited so long to avenge her? Even if they somehow learned her fate, would they have wanted to avenge her?" They had shunned her once she came ashore. "And even if they did, would they have sent a mere boy to do a man's work?"

"I will learn whatever else there is to learn about this boy," Searlon promised. "I will do whatever I must."

"What's his name?"

"Zarien."

It meant nothing to Kiloran. "I'll look forward to hearing what you learn." He had no intention of telling Searlon more unless it was actually necessary. So many things in the past were best left undisturbed.

"Meanwhile," Searlon said, changing the subject and Kiloran's pensive mood, "there is troubling news from the east. Verlon claims you're trying to move in on his territory."

Kiloran frowned. "Why would he claim that?"

"One of your *shir* was found alongside more than ten of his assassins, all dead."

Kiloran felt an icy fury sweep through him. "Damn that insolent *shal-lah*!"

Searlon didn't have to ask whom he meant. Tansen had made very good use of the *shir* he'd collected from the bodies of Kiloran's assassins who had tried to ambush him after Josarian's death.

"And with Wyldon loudly claiming the same thing as Verlon," Searlon added, "they each give credibility to the other's story."

"You mean others are starting to listen," Kiloran surmised. "Meanwhile, Wyldon's assassins are attacking mine."

"I suggest a truce meeting with Wyldon."

Kiloran shook his head. "I've already tried that. While you were away. His refusal came yesterday—we found the body of my envoy, headless, with one of my *shir* sticking out of his belly. The *shir,* I assume, which Tansen left behind when he attacked Wyldon."

"That's discouraging," Searlon admitted.

"And annoying," Kiloran added. "It means we'll have to deal with Wyldon immediately."

"And Verlon?"

Kiloran thought it over. "He's a hot-headed fool who rarely listens to anything, let alone reason. However, he's powerful. It would be too much of a strain to fight him right now."

"So we must make sure that Wyldon's fate gives him pause."

Kiloran nodded. "So that he'll pause long enough for us to deal with the rest of our business, untroubled by him."

"How shall we draw Wyldon out?" Searlon asked.

"I've been considering that," Kiloran replied. He reached for the bracelet he had not, until forming this plan, touched in longer than he could remember. Kintish silver with jade inlays. A solid, elegant thing. Brought onto Silerian soil, years ago, by a Lascari. The bracelet was too small for a man's wrist, of course, but Kiloran believed Wyldon would recognize that it matched the necklace Baran always wore. "Wyldon wants Baran's friendship," Kiloran said. "Let's convince him he has it."

"Ah." Searlon took the bracelet and smiled, the scar on his cheek flowing down into the dimple which so unexpectedly suited him. "And then, *siran*?"

"Then we'll teach Wyldon the price of turning his back on *my* friendship."

Baran felt adrenaline flow through him, energizing his ever-weakening body, when Vinn entered the simple stone dwelling to tell him that Mirabar and her party had been sighted approaching Sister Velikar's Sanctuary and would be here momentarily.

"Get out of sight," Baran advised Vinn. "Najdan will be with her, and you know how jumpy he's always been." Kiloran's former assassin, who had slain so many of Baran's men over the years, was likely to kill Vinn before remembering that they were on Sanctuary grounds.

"I will be just behind that door," Vinn said, indicating his proposed hiding place. Then he paused awkwardly and made a few stumbling attempts to address Baran.

"Yes?" Baran prodded dryly. "Something on your mind?"

"*Siran* . . . Are you sure about this?"

"I admit," Baran replied blithely, "it's not really the done thing—"

"It's insane!" Vinn blurted.

"Then I'm living up to my reputation."

"Begging your pardon, *siran*."

"No, no," he insisted, "I'm not sensitive about it."

"What we're about to do— Can this really be right, *siran*?"

"These are very difficult times, and we must be innovative about solving our problems, Vinn." Baran smiled cynically. "You surely don't imagine Kiloran is sitting around just doing the same old thing these days, do you?"

"No . . ." Vinn shrugged and looked around the Sanctuary. "But *this* is nothing I ever thought we would do."

"Me, neither," Baran admitted. "Yet if the world persists in giving me unpleasant surprises, then I must keep returning the favor."

"This is more than an unpleasant surprise." Vinn's voice dropped to a whisper. "This has never been done."

"Yes," Baran agreed. "That's what I like best about it."

"Do you think—" Vinn stopped speaking, listened, and then met Baran's eyes. "I hear them," he said, before disappearing out the back door of the Sanctuary to eavesdrop and make sure his master's plan went smoothly.

Baran stood up and waited, briefly worrying about not having heard the new arrivals when Vinn did. The world, once so full of vivid sensation, was fading with every passing day, almost as if he now lived at a distance from it.

However, he felt Mirabar's power now, felt that pleasingly disturbing presence which so few had, that intangible signature of extraordinary sorcery which identified only the best—the most skilled, the most innately powerful—to each other. *He* had once had it, but he suspected it was now fading, too, like everything else about him.

Their voices came to him a moment later. Mirabar's voice, warm and feminine, so different from that of Sister Velikar, the only woman Baran had spoken to lately. Najdan's voice, deep, dark, a little rough, revealing all the sharp violence of the man. Another man's voice, too—energetic, facetious, saying something about Josarian's almond wine at Dalishar.

It was this second man, the one Baran didn't know, who pushed open the door to the Sanctuary and called, "Sister Velikar? Oh, Velikarrrrr?"

"She's not here," Baran informed him.

The man's head turned in startled surprise and he saw Baran. "Oh! Hello. We didn't reali . . . Uh . . . Ah! Hah!" His face contorted into a comical expression of fear as he recognized Baran. The man staggered backwards, speaking over his shoulder to someone else, "It's— It's—"

Mirabar's voice came faintly from outside, irritated now. "What? Oh, Pyron, just get out of the way, will you?"

"*Sirana* . . . wait!" Najdan's voice.

Baran saw the bright cloud of Mirabar's volcanic hair as she reached the open door, then she grunted as Najdan elbowed her aside and entered the Sanctuary.

Najdan saw Baran, made some kind of wordlessly vicious noise, drew his *shir,* and leaped forward.

"We're in Sanctuary," Baran protested mildly.

Najdan stopped as if he'd been frozen on the spot. He stared at Baran with a fierce, glowering expression. "What are you doing here?"

Mirabar saw Baran and gasped. He looked from Najdan to her. Those eerie Dar-blessed eyes were wide open in her sun-kissed face. She was, as he recalled, rather pretty in her Otherworldly way. A little small, perhaps, but then many *shallaheen* were; they usually didn't get much to eat as children, and she had probably gotten less than most.

"What a pleasure to see you again," Baran said politely. "Was your journey successful?"

"No," she answered absently, staring at him. Then she realized what she had said and blinked. "I mean—"

"Too late," he chided.

"What are you doing here?" Najdan repeated, still poised for attack.

"Tansen sent Velikar to me as an emissary; but I thought to myself, really, why should we all speak through intermediaries?"

"Because we don't trust each other?" Mirabar suggested.

"And how can we foster trust if we don't speak face-to-face?" Baran countered.

"Where's Velikar?" Najdan growled. "What have you done with her?"

"I don't think I like your tone," Baran pouted. "Surely you're not suggesting that I would harm a Sister?"

"Where's Velikar?" Mirabar snapped.

"Out gathering . . . something or other," Baran replied. "We only arrived yesterday, so there's a great deal for her to catch up on."

"Velikar only got back . . . *We?*" Mirabar frowned. "She's been with you at Belitar all this time?"

"I'm every bit as capable of hospitality as the next murderous sorcerer, you know."

The one they called Pyron hesitantly approached the door again, armed with a Valdani sword now. From the far side of the threshold, he asked his companions, "Has he killed you? Has he killed Velikar? Is he alone? What should we do?"

Najdan snapped over his shoulder, "You could start by calming down."

"Good advice," Baran agreed.

"Shut up," Najdan said.

"I thought you wanted my friendship," Baran admonished.

Najdan's jaw worked, but he took a steadying breath and said, "*Sirana?*"

Mirabar took a deep breath, too. It delighted Baran to see how afraid of him they were. Ah, there were still some good things left in life.

"Yes," Mirabar said, composing herself, "we want to talk to you face-to-face, and we want your friendship. We're just a little . . . surprised to come upon you so suddenly, without warning."

"I'd have written," Baran said, "but you're all illiterate."

"And we'd be more polite," Pyron said, "but you're crazy."

"Wait outside," Mirabar ordered Pyron.

"I *am* outside."

Baran shook his head in wonder. "These are the forces that hope to defeat Kiloran?"

Najdan's expression got darker. "*Sirana,* if we kill him n—"

"This is Sanctuary!" she reminded the assassin.

Najdan looked ashamed, but Baran said, "There's a first time for everything."

"Not for this," Mirabar said.

She approached the assassin and placed a hand on his arm. Baran noticed how Najdan's *shir,* already trembling from Mirabar's presence, shook even harder when she got that close to it. Najdan, however, seemed quite accustomed to the phenomenon.

"Najdan," she murmured, "I'd like to speak alone with him."

Baran said apologetically to Mirabar, "I'm making him agitated, aren't I? I seem to have that effect on some people."

"You have that effect on everyone," Najdan said, his tone very unflattering.

Baran shrugged. "I can't understand it, myself."

Mirabar ignored him and repeated, "Najdan, please."

"No," the assassin replied.

"It's Sanctuary," she reminded him again. "What can he do?"

"I don't know," Najdan said, "but I know *him.*"

Baran objected, "I hardly think that killing nearly twenty of my men over the years qualifies as a social acquaintance."

Mirabar said to Najdan, "I'm not helpless, and he knows it."

Baran added, "In fact, I find it your most enchanting quality, *sirana*."

Najdan stepped forward, raised his shaking *shir*, and touched the fine fabric of Baran's clothing with it. Baran clenched his teeth but gave no outward sign of how powerfully, bitterly cold he found the *shir* which Kiloran had made so long ago for the assassin whom he would one day lose to Mirabar.

Najdan's voice was low and deadly as he ordered, "You will show the *sirana* respect."

"Always," Baran assured him innocently.

"If you even insult her, never mind hurt her—"

"Yes, yes," Baran said, steeling himself to show no pain when he placed a hand on Najdan's wavy-edged blade and pushed it casually aside. *Damn,* that would hurt for days; but it was worth it. Najdan looked surprised and Mirabar looked impressed. "I understand the terms. Now, can I be left alone with the *sirana*? I have a matter of some delicacy to discuss with her."

He watched Najdan and Mirabar exchange a glance, and he recognized what he suspected Kiloran would never realize because Kiloran could never accept it: There was great devotion between those two. An assassin and a Guardian.

Baran pondered the ramifications of the relationship as he watched the assassin head for the door to wait outside. Thinking of Vinn, he realized that this could make things even stickier; the prospect amused him.

When the door closed behind Najdan, Mirabar turned to face Baran, her glowing eyes wary and watchful. He didn't know her well, but he had met with her often enough to know she was a direct woman, impatient with implication and inference, so he got right to the point.

"To oppose Kiloran is unhealthy," he said.

"Yet you've survived this long."

"Longer than Josarian, certainly, who was even betrayed by his own."

She flinched. "You mean Zimran?"

His interest sharpened. "Who else might I mean, *sirana*?"

She recovered. "I can never tell, with you."

He smiled, *very* interested now. "Ah. So Zimran wasn't the only one of Josarian's people plotting against him."

"Did you come here just to discuss Josarian's death?" But her face darkened, and he knew he was right.

"Let me guess: the Alliance?" He watched her sink slowly onto a bench, staring at him as if *he* were the demonic one. Seeing that he was right, but also that she wouldn't supply the specifics, he shook his head. "Well, what did you expect? *Toreni*, wealthy merchants—people with something to lose. People who had dealt with Kiloran for years before Josarian came along to steal everyone's thunder." He considered this and mused aloud, "And who in the Alliance had the most influence over Zimran? Could it be the *torena* who was sharing his bed?" He grinned when Mirabar's expression revealed he'd guessed the truth. "Ahhhh . . . she is a very interesting woman, isn't she, *sirana*?"

"What do you want?" she asked suspiciously.

"What everyone wants, of course," he admitted cheerfully, letting her change the subject. "To resurrect my loved ones, to correct the mistakes which blighted my youth, to—"

"To drink Kiloran's blood from his own skull."

He made a face. "Do you take me for some Moorlander savage? I'd be quite content just to see him dead."

"No," she said. "I think you want to see him suffer first."

Baran shook his head. "I've seen him suffer. The satisfaction is modest and fleeting. He doesn't suffer like other people. You might say he's just not good at it."

"And do you suffer well?" she asked, watching him closely with those glowing eyes.

"*Sirana,* I suffer so well, they say it drove me insane."

"He's the one who made you suffer," she guessed. When Baran didn't deny it, she asked, "So you will join us now? Because you want him dead and believe this is the way to accomplish it?"

"Yes, but only if I get what I want, in return."

"Kiloran's death is not enough?"

"It would be, but you can't guarantee it."

"What *can* I guarantee that will satisfy you?" Something about the way she said it gave him hope, made him believe that she was willing to do almost anything to win him to her cause.

He sat down next to her and felt her go tense. When he took her hand, she tried to pull it away. He held onto it, and her eyes glowed almost yellow with astonishment as she realized what he wanted even before he said it.

"You could guarantee me the future, in case we fail now," he said. "Give me a child."

She looked ready to jump out of her own skin. "A child?" she repeated, her voice scarcely audible.

"Think of it, Mirabar—may I call you Mirabar?" he asked solicitously.

"Oh, stop it." Her reply was too breathless to carry the snap she had presumably intended.

"Think how strong, how powerful a child of ours would be. If we don't survive, then this child would be Sileria's future, Sileria's hope—"

"Your hope. For vengeance." But her protest sounded weak.

"Which, as it happens, coincides with your hope of freeing Sileria from Kiloran."

"But you are of the Honored Society, and I'm—"

"Times change," he said philosophically.

"How do I know times won't changes *back* as soon as Kiloran is dead?"

"Marriage means something even to me, Mirabar. I wouldn't kill my own—"

"Marriage?" she blurted.

"Surely you don't imagine I was proposing to dishonor you? Or that I want our child to be a bastard?"

She looked dizzy. "You want me to marry you and give you—"

"A child of fire," he whispered. "A child of water."

Tears welled up in her eyes, surprising him.

He asked gently, "Is the thought that repellent to you?"

"Fire and water ..." She kept staring at him, those golden eyes dazed and glistening.

"Yes. You and I can do what no one in Sileria has ever done, what no one has even thought of doing."

"Belitar ..."

He nodded. "There are things there that you should know about. That perhaps only you can fully appreciate." He paused and added, enjoying the tumult he envisioned, "Najdan can come with you."

"A child of water. A child of fire." She looked at him, waiting, as if expecting him to say more.

"I can shield you from Kiloran."

"Shield me ..." She placed her hand over her belly and held it there, her face lost in thought.

"Yes. We can shield each other."

"Shield him," she murmured. "Welcome him. Welcome your fate."

"I beg your pardon?"

She came to a decision. Banished the dazed look from her face. Met his gaze. And vowed, "I'll do it."

38

ALL JOY IS BORN IN SORROW AND SUFFERING.
—Silerian Proverb

As TANSEN MADE his way down to the dark underground world of the Beyah-Olvari, far beneath the streets of Shaljir, he remembered the first time he had ever come here: Ten years ago, with Armian.

His bloodfather had been as stunned as he to see the small, fragile, blue-skinned beings living so deep in the bowels of the earth. Like almost everyone in Sileria, Tansen had believed they were extinct—or perhaps that they had never really existed at all. Perhaps they were just another Silerian legend.

However, as Tansen learned, the Beyah-Olvari were real, and so was their story, their sad tale of being driven to near-extinction by the New Race—Tansen's kind—the tall, strong, dark people from the little-known lands south of the Middle Sea, their origins so far from Sirkara that no one knew who they had once been, eons ago, or where their original home was. The New Race were an aggressive, land-hungry people who brought war, disease, violence, and fire magic to Sileria, and nothing had ever been the same since their arrival.

Strong emotion distressed the Beyah-Olvari, and violence terrified them. Armian, a violent man of strong emotions, stirred them to chattering fear and endless chanting in these dank, underground tunnels. So, at Elelar's insistence, the assassin had retreated to an isolated chamber far from the Beyah-Olvari until the young *torena* could arrange for his escape from Shaljir after his impetuous murder of a beggar in the city's streets. Armian was bored and restless, and he counted on Tansen to keep him company. Tansen, however, was intrigued by these strange, gentle creatures living in secret below the densely populated capital city, so he had frequently abandoned Armian, during their brief exile down here, to befriend the Beyah-Olvari.

The original practitioners of water magic in Sileria, the Beyah-Olvari used their power very differently than the waterlords did; indeed, the very mention of waterlords distressed them, causing them to wail banishing prayers to dispel the evil that they believed threatened them just by hearing the name of a sorcerer like Kiloran, Harlon, or Verlon.

Using their gentle magic all those years ago, they had healed the coldly burning pain in Tansen's hand where he had grabbed Armian's *shir* to pry open the secret trapdoor to the underground tunnels. Then they had taught him about Sileria's past, including the dark, conquering history of his own oft-vanquished people.

Tansen had fled Sileria only a few months after meeting the Beyah-Olvari, but they remembered him—and still treated him as a friend—when he returned from exile years later. Now he sought them again, venturing down into the earth's ancient passageways, down to the secret world of another people, down to the dark, dank, hidden existence of Sileria's oldest race.

And he brought a boy with him, just as Armian had. A lad grieving, just as Tansen had been grieving all those years ago. They weren't hiding or seeking escape this time, though. Tansen needed answers, and he thought Zarien needed a distraction. The boy's somber, heartbroken mourning was relieved only by sudden outbursts of fury against Dar and Sharifar. Tansen, who was distressed by the minor wounds Zarien had inflicted upon himself in mourning, didn't know how to comfort him—not when his own bitterly burning question remained unanswered: *Why did You let Josarian die, Dar? Why did You let Kiloran kill the Firebringer?*

"What made these tunnels?" Zarien now asked Tansen, who was pleased to hear the boy's voice energized by curiosity.

"Lava flows," Tan replied. "From Mount Shaljir."

Zarien paused. "Um, there's *lava* in Mount Shaljir?"

"Not anymore. Very long ago."

"Oh." A moment later, Zarien asked, "What's all this glowing stuff?"

Tansen studied the phosphorescent life-forms which dimly illuminated the tunnels. "Plants. Molds. Insects. Slugs." He shrugged. "Everything that lives down here with the Beyah-Olvari." He made sure he could see Zarien's face when he added, "It's what they eat."

He wasn't disappointed. Zarien's surprised disgust was comical. "They *eat* these things?"

"Yes," Tansen replied innocently.

"You're lying," Zarien said with certainty.

Tansen grinned. "No, and they'll offer you a bite, too."

"Not really!"

"Yes. It's good manners to accept."

"Will *you*?" Zarien asked pointedly.

"I've done it before, so I'm excused. But Josarian had to, when I brought him here."

"I'm not going to—"

"Try the mushrooms," Tansen advised. "They're not nearly as revolting as the worms."

"Ugh."

"To be honest, I suspect the Olvar invites visitors to eat just because he finds it amusing."

"What's that noise?" Zarien asked now.

"That's them. They chant and pray and sing and wail almost all of the . . ." He paused, listening.

"What's wrong?" Zarien asked, bumping into him.

"I'm not sure. They sound . . ." Not upset. Not even scared.

"Excited?" Zarien ventured.

"Yes," Tan agreed slowly, "excited."

"They're awfully loud, aren't they? Or is it just the way the sound bounces off the walls down here?"

"We should have met with an escort by now," Tansen realized. Formality, courtesy, blessings, rituals . . . you could never enter the domain of the Beyah-Olvari without enduring all of these things, no matter how tiresome or inconvenient it was. Yet no one was greeting them or proclaiming Tansen's name and deeds as he approached the Chamber of the Sacred Pool, where the Olvar could always be found.

"Something's wrong," Tansen murmured. He didn't draw his swords.

He didn't hear anything indicative of violence or mayhem. Besides, the Beyah-Olvari would probably keel over in a collective faint if he came upon them with his blades unsheathed.

"Wrong? Maybe not," Zarien opined. "It sounds like a celebration to me."

He was right, Tansen realized. Now doubly eager to reach their destination, he picked up his pace, ignoring how the boy stumbled behind him in the poorly lighted passages. When they arrived at the Chamber of the Sacred Pool, which was mercifully easy to find for a change, due to all the noise the Beyah-Olvari were making, they stopped and stared.

"I've never seen so many of them all in one place," Tansen said to Zarien, raising his voice to be heard above the echoing cacophony of the wild singing and chanting.

Zarien stood gaping, his mouth hanging open, his dark eyes wide with wonder. "I've never seen . . ." He watched the small, delicate, blue-skinned creatures dancing, prancing, running about, embracing each other, singing, weeping, and laughing all at once. "I've never seen anything like this."

"Let's find the Olvar."

"What's that language? It's not any Silerian dialect, is it?"

"No." Tansen took Zarien's arm and led him through the jubilant throng. Some individuals noticed them and tried to greet them, but the Followers of the Olvar seemed so overwhelmed with emotion that their usual abundant courtesy deserted them, and they could do little more than chatter at Tansen in their own language and steer him towards the Olvar.

"So you can't understand them?" Zarien asked, starting to look a little edgy as the crowd pressed in on them.

"The Olvar speaks archaic High Silerian."

"So?"

"It's close to *shallah*," Tansen explained. "We'll be able to understand him." A moment later he added, "There he is."

"That's the Olvar?" Zarien asked.

"Yes." Tansen glanced at the boy. "What's wrong?"

Zarien shrugged, looking at the small, slim, wizened old being bent over the Sacred Pool, the glowing waters of which he continually stirred with his small hands. "Nothing's wrong," the boy said. "I guess, after what you told me about him, I just thought he would be . . . grander."

Tansen smiled. "You'll see." He approached the Olvar, crossed his fists and bowed his head respectfully. "*Siran.*" He searched the heavily lined blue face and was astonished to see tears in those ancient eyes. "What's happened here, *siran*?"

"Welcome, my friend," the Olvar said. His voice was thick with emotion, and it was hard for Tansen to hear him above the din of the wildly excited Beyah-Olvari all around them. "All our blessings be upon you. We humbly beg your pardon for not having—"

"There's no need," Tansen assured him. "I can see that something . . . um . . ."

"Something tremendous," the Olvar assured him. "Something I never thought . . ." He blinked, his heavy lids moving slowly over his watery eyes, and then he looked at Zarien. "Who is this one?" His tone was strange, like his expression. Tansen couldn't tell if it indicated curiosity or fear—or both.

"This is Zarien of the sea-bound Lascari." Tansen glanced at the boy, who immediately greeted the Olvar with respectful courtesy. Seeing that the Olvar was still staring strangely at Zarien, instead of enthusiastically blessing him, Tansen added, "He can be trusted, *siran*."

The Olvar looked directly at Zarien. "Can you?"

Zarien blinked. "Be trusted? Yes."

The Olvar stared at Zarien for such a long time that the boy started shifting restlessly under that intense gaze.

Tansen decided to intervene. "*Siran,* this boy—"

"Is very special," the Olvar said slowly.

"Yes," Tansen agreed. "And he—"

"He will be," said the Olvar, looking at Tansen now, "more than you imagine. Perhaps more than you can accept."

The sea king?

As soon as the thought occurred to Tansen, he glanced sharply at Zarien. Had Sharifar sent Zarien ashore not to find the sea king, but rather to become him—to mature into the man she sought?

"I will accept whatever he becomes," Tansen said with certainty. "And y—"

"Will you?" the Olvar asked. "Or will you see the mirror of your sorrows when you gaze upon him?"

Aware of Zarien's barely suppressed irritation at these cryptically dark comments, Tansen replied, "I will always see a strong boy with a good heart."

"May his heart always be worthy of your esteem," the Olvar murmured. "Because he is indeed very strong."

Tansen wondered how Elelar had gotten anything as intelligible as a specific prophecy about her destiny from the Olvar, who was being just as vague and bewildering as Tansen had always found him. He wanted to ask about Elelar and Mirabar, but first he felt compelled to ensure smooth relations between Zarien, who looked ready to leave, and the Olvar—who still studied the boy with an unfathomable expression.

So Tansen said emphatically, "Zarien is trustworthy and won't tell anyone about the Beyah-Olvari, *siran*. I've explained to him how your safety depends on your existence remaining secret."

The Olvar shook his head. "No. That will change now."

"I'm not going to tell." Zarien sounded offended.

"We no longer wish to remain secret."

"Fine. Then *you* tell people," Zarien snapped at the Olvar.

"Zarien," Tansen chided.

Zarien pressed his lips together and looked away.

"Why," Tansen asked the Olvar, "don't you want to remain secret anymore?"

The Olvar stirred the Sacred Pool with his hands, staring into its shimmering water. The glow lit his face with the cool fire of his water magic. "Because I have found another secret. Here in the water. Where it must have been for centuries. And now I know. Now we know what we never imagined."

Tansen studied the exultant glow on the Olvar's face, then looked around at the joyful Beyah-Olvari, making such a racket he could hardly hear his own voice as he asked, "What do you know?"

Tears streamed down the Olvar's face. "We are not alone."

"What?" Tansen asked sharply.

"Others have survived the long years. The eons of darkness and secrecy. Others have lived through the centuries of waiting to enter the sunlight again."

"Others?" Zarien said, looking from the Olvar to Tansen.

Now Tansen understood. "There are other Beyah-Olvari," he said slowly.

The Olvar nodded, still crying. "Others like us. Alive. Somewhere in Sileria."

And like the rest of his kind, he started singing with joy.

TIME WAS HARD *to measure in the tunnels beneath the city, but Tansen guessed that they only spent a few days with the Beyah-Olvari before Elelar devised a way for them to escape Shaljir—and escape the Outlookers searching everywhere for them. Although Tansen had found this sojourn into another world—the secret world of another race—fascinating, he wasn't sorry to leave. In fact, he was starving and could hardly wait to get some decent food into his stomach!*

"The glowing worms didn't appeal to you?" Armian asked dryly as they rode away from the coast on mounts provided by Elelar.

"Not even the glowing mushrooms," Tansen replied without looking at his father. Then, wishing the doubt didn't even occur to him, he asked Armian, "You will keep your word, won't you?"

"Hmmm?"

"Your promise to the torena. *Not to tell anyone about . . ."*

"About our little friends living underground?" Armian didn't seem offended by the question. "Yes, I'll keep my word."

Tansen knew it was rude to persist, a slight to Armian's honor, but he had to be sure. The Beyah-Olvari seemed so helpless, despite their own special power. "Not even Kiloran?"

Armian smiled slyly. "You surely don't imagine that Kiloran's going to tell me everything he knows, do you?"

"I, uh . . ." Tansen hadn't thought about it.

"The most powerful secret," Armian advised him, "is always the one that the fewest people know."

"Oh." It wasn't quite the answer Tansen had hoped for.

"This secret," Armian explained, "can add to our power someday."

"Our power?" Tansen asked, puzzled.

Armian looked faintly surprised. "Yours and mine. Our influence."

"Oh. Yes." After a moment, he asked doubtfully, "How?"

"I don't know yet, son," Armian admitted. "But until I do, I'd be a fool to share it with Kiloran, wouldn't I?"

Tansen sat uncomfortably on his plodding horse, staring blankly at the spot between its ears.

After enduring his silence for a while, Armian asked, "Is something wrong?"

"Huh?" Startled, Tansen nearly slid off the horse. He grabbed at a handful of its mane, then stared at Armian, unsure of what he wanted to say—unsure, even, of what he was thinking. "I . . . No. I'm just hungry, father."

Armian smiled wryly. "I'll ask the torena *how soon we can stop." He rode ahead to join Elelar, leaving Tansen alone with feelings too chaotic to shape into thoughts or pursue to conclusions.*

They headed deep into western Sileria and searched for Kiloran as the dry season began to squeeze the land fiercely in its cruel grip. For a while, much of Tansen's concentration was devoted to staying atop his horse. He had never been on one before, and he found the experience awkward and smelly when it wasn't downright frightening. The humiliation was worst of all, though. He was slow and ungainly about mounting—and, on several occasions, he had been fast and noisy about dismounting without having planned to do so.

While they traveled, Armian helped him improve his horsemanship; the years in the Moorlands, where men practically lived on horseback, had made Armian a fine rider, wise in the ways of these skittish, snorting beasts. When they stopped for the torena's *rest, Armian taught him to fight. Born to a violent clan in dangerous times, Tansen had already learned as much as most shalla-heen knew about combat, but now he realized how little an ordinary peasant knew in comparison to an assassin—to an expert like his bloodfather, who had been taught by assassins.*

Armian was the first person to teach Tansen that violence was a skill, and that practice and discipline were more important than passion and rage. It was Armian who first taught him about surprise attacks, ambush tactics, misdirection, feinting, and conserving his strength. Training with his father in the mornings, in the evenings, and sometimes in the sleepy shade of the afternoons,

Tansen became increasingly fast and effective with his hands and feet, and he learned to swing his yahr with deadly skill and precision.

"But you should have a nicer one than this," Armian said, idly fingering Tansen's yahr one day. "I'll find you a better one."

Tansen nodded, pleased.

"And after you kill someone with it," Armian added, "perhaps Kiloran will make you a shir."

Tansen froze. Armian noticed.

"Isn't that what you want?" Armian asked him. "Didn't you tell me—"

"Yes, father." It must be what he wanted. It was what he had always wanted. Now it was so easily within his reach.

All he had to do was kill a man. He didn't know whom yet, though he had no doubt Armian would choose someone for him to murder, when the time came. Or perhaps Armian would let Kiloran choose the victim.

All he had to do was kill.

"Tansen?"

"Yes, father?"

"You look strange."

Tansen blinked. "Um. The horse. It smells." He dismounted, sliding down as Armian had taught him. "I think I'll walk for a while."

RONALL WAS USED to Elelar's favorite horse by now, and it even seemed to have resigned itself to his company, so he saw no reason to abandon it when he deserted his dear wife's estate and set off again in pursuit of . . . Dar and the Three only knew what.

Death? Maybe. Maybe not. He still had moments—even whole days—when he was so despairing that death seemed to beckon to him like a lover. He was so lonely, lost, and afraid.

And, as always, so hungry for . . . something. Evermore longing for a fulfillment he couldn't even define. His wife's love, perhaps? Hah! The next person that Elelar loved would be the first—and Ronall had no illusions that it would be him.

Poor Zimran. He never had a chance. Not against Elelar.

He could sympathize with, rather than hate or resent, the *shallah* who had lived with his wife. Somewhere along the twisted path of his life, Ronall had lost any desire to take vengeance on his wife's lovers—probably because he knew better than anyone that loving Elelar was its own punishment.

And what, he now wondered, would Dar's vengeance against Elelar be for plotting against the Firebringer? What would the volcano goddess do to her? What would be the penalty for such a sacrilege, such a dark and terrible betrayal?

Ronall's religious training as a boy had been mixed, contradictory, and somewhat indifferent. As a man, he prayed impartially to Dar and to the Three, but usually only in moments of fevered desperation. The rest of the time, he just hoped the gods would leave him alone if he left them alone. Which was more or less how he treated the waterlords and their assassins, too.

Now he wondered with a chill if Elelar expected the Society to protect her from the wrath of Dar. Were the strange events at Darshon related to his wife's transgression? Were the earthquakes evidence of the destroyer goddess reaching out in search of Elelar, all the way from Mount Darshon? Would he beat Elelar to the Otherworld, or would Dar send her there first in a fury of fiery rage?

He pondered these and other depressing questions as he wandered south, idly taking whatever detours appealed to him, and stopping often. By night—and often by day—he drank whatever was available, usually to such excess that he blacked out and awoke in uncomfortable (even embarrassing) situations with little or no memory of what had passed. He mostly kept away from women, not so much because of his recent disastrous experiences with Yenibar, but mostly because sex started to seem like too much effort for too little ease of his desperate longing, his gnawing loneliness—especially here, deep in the mountains, where the bloodthirsty *shallaheen* were so quick to punish any insult to their women.

He had taken enough money from Elelar's house to supply his taste for Kintish dreamweed and Moorlander cloud syrup, but there was very little of these luxuries to be had in Sileria these days. There were plenty of beggars, though, and sometimes he even tossed them a coin or two, just because it was easy.

There were also an extraordinary number of pilgrims on the crumbling roads and narrow mountain paths lately. More every day, it seemed. It was almost as if everyone who wasn't busy plotting, scheming, and fighting in Sileria's civil war (better known, in select *shallah* circles, as Tansen's bloodfeud against Kiloran) was rushing headlong to Mount Darshon to . . .

To do what? Commune with Dar? Become a *zanar*? Die in the massive eruption which any sensible person could plainly see was a very real possibility? Suffocate in the clouds of gas—or whatever it was—swirling around Darshon's summit? Get swallowed by the lava which was starting to force its way out of cracks in the mountain's rocky skin, just as deadly vapors were doing?

"Dar has Called me to dance on the blood of her heart, *toren*!" a proud young *shallah* proclaimed to him one day on the road.

"And that would mean *what*, in ordinary language?" he asked.

He was astonished to learn it meant lava-walking, or some such insanity. People who weren't even Guardians were racing headlong to Darshon to dance on the fresh lava flows and thereby prove themselves beloved of Dar.

"And the singing?" Ronall asked someone else one day. "All that singing and chanting and wailing . . ." Which was making his aching head want to split open under the blazing sunshine. "It couldn't wait until you get to Darshon and actually start dancing?"

No one answered. They were too busy ululating.

"Dar is Calling us to inhale the scents of Her womb!" two wild-eyed Sisters told him early one evening as he entered their crowded Sanctuary and requested a place to sleep for the night.

"That doesn't sound pleasant," he replied, desperate for some wine or ale in the absence of anything stronger.

"To breathe in the fire-blessed perfume of Her secret places!"

"Are you sure you want to do that?" he asked skeptically.

"All who survive will be beloved of Dar!" promised a painfully skinny *zanar* who was helping the Sisters pack up their meager belongings.

"And all who don't will be smelly corpses on the mountain slope," Ronall pointed out. "I don't think inhaling those vapors is going to be a nice way to die."

The *zanar* seized him by the shoulders, looked deep into his face with eyes which appeared less than perfectly sane, and cried, "Not all deaths can be the pleasure which Dar has proclaimed yours to be, *toren*!"

Ronall wiped the *zanar*'s flecks of spittle off his cheek. "Isn't that a shame?"

"Each will serve Her in his own way! Each will rise or fall according to his merit in Dar's heart!" the *zanar* shouted.

"Yes, yes, I know." It was the sort of thing the *zanareen* were always saying, and one of the reasons he had sympathized with the Imperial Advisor for having them banned from Shaljir for many years. They could be incredibly tedious. "Is there anything to drink around here?"

"If Dar has forsaken you, then that is your destiny!"

"Indeed. You know, even just some volcano ale would be f—"

"But Dar knows where you belong!"

Ronall sighed. "Then I do wish She would tell *me*." He turned to one of the Sisters and tried hard to get her attention. "Look, I can pay for—"

"Sanctuary and its blessings are free to all, *toren*," she replied, not even looking at him. "But we've run out of food and drink."

"I'm not surprised," he muttered. There was already barely enough room to breathe in here, and he had little doubt that even more travelers would arrive before night descended completely. "Perhaps I'll press on."

"May we go with you, *toren*?" the Sister asked, bothering to look at him now that she wanted something from him.

"With me?" he repeated doubtfully.

"Just until our paths separate." She paused and added, "You're not going to Darshon, are you?"

"Of course not. The way the volcano's been acting lately? Believe me, I'd be as far away as Cavasar right now, if I weren't even more afraid of Kiloran than I am of Dar."

"But you can protect us until our ways must part," the Sister said decisively. She returned to her frantic packing.

Less than thrilled with this prospect, he suggested, "Don't you want to wait until morning to leave? It'll be dark in just another—"

"The moons are full, and we know the paths around here very well."

"But surely you can wait—"

"No, *toren*. Dar has Called us, and we must go."

"Fine," he said. "Whatever."

They followed him until after dark, babbling with holy fervor the whole while. It was a relief to bid them and their mad *zanar* farewell under the glowing faces of Abayara and Ejara.

"Things just keep getting stranger and stranger," he muttered, cautiously wandering the countryside until he found an abandoned Kintish shrine in which to spend the night.

It stank of sheep.

THEY FINALLY FOUND Kiloran's tented camp deep in the mountains. He was on the move, maintaining his power over his vast territory, administering punishments and rewards according to who angered him and who pleased him; who paid tribute and who did not; who rebelled and who obeyed.

He was all that Tansen had ever heard he was, a man whom any sane person would fear. His power was immense, his strength unparalleled, and his soul as cold as the bitter chill of his sorcery.

Although the location of his permanent home was a secret which he did not share even with Armian, he couldn't keep his movements a complete secret from the Outlookers. Yet instead of attacking him, they accepted bribes to leave him alone. Many even, Tansen soon realized, simply left Kiloran alone out of sheer fear.

A master of subterfuge, Kiloran advised Armian to use a false name, even among his most trusted assassins. Apart from Tansen, Elelar, and her grandfather, Kiloran was the only person in Sileria who knew Armian's true identity, and the waterlord wanted it to remain that way for the time being. So Armian took the name of Tansen's original father, Dustan, and pretended to be a relative of Kiloran's who now spent most of his time on the mainland.

Kiloran treated Armian with affectionate courtesy and, in private, recalled many tales of Armian's father, Harlon. He admonished Tansen to listen and learn, to take pride in these tales of great power and terrible destruction.

"As Armian's bloodson," Kiloran told Tansen, "this is your history, too."

Tansen wanted to protest. His history lay among the ashes of the dead Gamalani. He said nothing, though, because it would be rude to argue. Also, he quickly recognized that it was safer to let Kiloran see what he wanted to see.

Kiloran treated Torena *Elelar with the good manners due a young woman of her rank. Tansen could tell from their conversations, not all of which he understood, that Kiloran was an educated man, and that the rumors about his elevated birth were probably true.*

The old waterlord was not prone to reckless haste, and so he carefully considered Armian's proposal—the Moorlanders' proposal for the overthrow of Valdani rule in Sileria—posing many questions, pondering numerous possibilities. He was concerned that the plan might fail, and that the Honored Society would bear the full weight of the Emperor's fury—a destructive force which had already weakened the waterlords badly in these hard times—while the Moorlanders abandoned them to face the consequences alone. He also agreed with Elelar, who spoke for her grandfather, Toren *Gaborian, when she said that Sileria must, above all, be sure that the Moorlanders would indeed leave when the Valdani were driven out.*

Armian had the answers to most of their questions. He was empowered to speak for the chieftains of the Moorlands, for the hairy, demon-fearing blood-drinkers who offered the hope of freedom to Sileria. He seemed to trust the promises of the savage barbarians who had sheltered him during the long years his people believed him dead, lost, or hidden somewhere in the Kintish Kingdoms.

"A ship will come to a hidden cove on the Adalian coast," Armian explained to Kiloran. "I am to give them the Society's answer then."

"When?" Elelar asked.

"After the dry season," Armian replied. "When the rains come."

"Oh, we'll have an answer for them by then," Kiloran said. A slight smile nearly warmed his cold, stern face as he assured Armian, "By then, I'm sure, you and I will be as close as father and son."

Tansen felt cold as he watched his father offer a son's embrace to the old wizard with the heart of stone.

TANSEN WORRIED ABOUT Zarien's lack of complaint as he led the boy up a steep and rocky footpath on the ancient slopes of Mount Shaljir. He knew it was a hard climb for the sea-born boy. He had grown to expect—yes, perhaps even enjoy—the boy's breathless and caustic comments about treks which few *shallaheen* even considered demanding. Zarien's sarcastic but basically good-natured commentary usually made Tansen smile.

The boy was still grieving hard. Too hard to object, as he otherwise would have, to being coaxed, urged, prodded, and dragged up Mount Shaljir on a hot, dry day like this. Tansen felt helpless to ease his pain. The loss of his family was a terrible wound in Zarien's heart. The betrayal of a goddess was, perhaps, even worse. Tansen had experienced both things, too, and knew that the pain of each was so great that it was impossible to measure.

To sacrifice so much, to believe so profoundly, and then to lose everything, even his faith . . .

Tansen knew he couldn't make the pain go away. Like all pain, it would fade in its own time; and like all wounds, it would leave a scar. Healing was a slow thing, and Tansen knew he must be patient. He and Zarien talked often. They also often kept each other company in silence. It felt like too little to do for the boy, yet he knew that there was no more to be done.

No more . . . except perhaps what he meant to do today.

He kept climbing, following his instincts, looking for the right place to stop. The pace was too slow for him, too fast for Zarien—precisely the way they had become used to traveling together.

Going higher, they came across ancient Guardian altars, long-forgotten sites consecrated to Dar. Though forbidden to Guardians by the Valdani for two hundred years, Mount Shaljir was a holy place. Once, so long ago that Dar had stopped mourning centuries before the Conquest, Her consort had dwelled here, a fiery lover spewing lava in response to Her longings and rages. Whether he had been a mortal blessed with godhood, or a god cursed with mortal flaws, no one really knew; but one day he had burned himself out and faded away, leaving only the mountain behind him, honeycombed with tunnels and caves created by ancient lava flows and forgotten eruptions. And some of these places bore the paintings left thousands of years ago by the Beyah-Olvari.

Tansen suppressed a surge of frustration as he thought of the Olvar again. He had learned nothing useful from the wizened old wizard. The Olvar didn't even acknowledge his questions about Elelar—or anything else. Oh, well. It was understandable.

"Others like us. Alive. Somewhere in Sileria."

It was an extraordinary announcement, even in these extraordinary times. Unfortunately, the Olvar apparently knew no more than that, at least not yet, and the euphoria produced by this discovery . . . vision . . . prophecy . . . whatever it was—well, it made the Olvar virtually incoherent with joy, effectively eliminating all further discussion.

Zarien didn't mind. Zarien said the Sacred Pool smelled funny and made him feel strange. Tansen suspected it was more likely the dankness of the tunnels which the sea-born boy smelled, and the feeling of being enclosed in those narrow, low-ceilinged caverns that he didn't like. Tansen didn't particularly like it, either. Anyhow, Zarien was more than ready to leave, and Tansen saw no reason not to humor him.

The rest of their stay in Shaljir had been extremely busy for Tansen, and hard on Zarien—who could smell the sea every waking and sleeping moment that they remained in the city. They shared a vast bedchamber in Santorell Palace where once, Tansen soon learned, Imperial Advisor Borell had regularly entertained his mistress—*Torena* Elelar. So Tansen didn't like their quarters any better than the restless sea-born boy did. Tansen spent long days, starting early and stretching well into the night, meeting with high-ranking members of the Alliance to discuss governing the newly independent nation, addressing vast crowds of city-dwellers about the past and the future (and the massacres), and working closely with people from all walks of life—particularly Guardians—to prepare for Kiloran's assault on the city's water supply.

It was all important work. It was also exhausting and frequently frustrating. He loathed cooperating with the same people who had sacrificed Josarian's life in the secret peace treaty with the Valdani. He distrusted them all—including Elelar, whose public manner towards him revealed none of the private tumult they had always known. He missed Josarian most of all when he had to appear before vast, cheering crowds whose adulation embarrassed him as much as it impressed Zarien. He found the threatening dispatches from Valda as alarming as they were insulting, and he was furious when someone left a Valdani corpse where Zarien, of all people, was the first to come upon it.

Tansen was eager to return to the mountains, where the fighting was getting fiercer every day according to the latest news Elelar had received. The dry season, which was settling into the land now, would be a huge challenge to his bloodfeud against the Society. It was also making Shaljir an increasingly unpleasant environment. Even Tansen, an eastern-born *shallah,* knew that most of the wealthy citizens of Shaljir usually abandoned it at this time of year for their country homes, only returning to the city after the long rains began. Yes, he would be glad to leave the city soon—and rather pleased to leave behind Elelar, *Toren* Varian, and their kind roasting in the hot, airless, stench-filled city. They had little chance of enjoying their usual rural leisure this year, with so much work demanding their attention in Shaljir while civil war raged across the mountains and the lowlands.

However, although he and Zarien wouldn't be in Shaljir for much longer, Tansen had every intention of visiting the Olvar again, in the hopes of finding him calmer and getting some answers.

Maybe I'll leave Zarien behind next time, though.

The Olvar's vague comments bothered Zarien, who hadn't particularly liked him. Tansen decided not to share his private musings about the possibility that Zarien himself was the sea king. It could perhaps explain how the boy had healed his *shir* wound, if that was indeed what had happened, but it was a discussion which could wait until Zarien was done mourning and his anger at Sharifar had finally dimmed a bit. Meanwhile, Tansen was at least pleased that a visit to the mythical (or so Zarien had thought) Beyah-Olvari, however disappointing, had lifted the boy's sorrow-laden spirits for a few hours. That alone had made the trip worthwhile.

Hearing no tortured scrambling behind him now on Mount Shaljir's steep slope, Tansen realized he had absentmindedly increased his speed and left Zarien far behind. He paused and waited for the boy to catch up.

Overall, Zarien seemed deeply grateful that Tansen didn't insist on going to sea. Zarien was still convinced Tansen was the sea king, but now he was fiercely determined to deny him to Sharifar. For his part, Tansen was almost guiltily relieved. He didn't want to be beloved of a goddess, as Josarian had been. There was a woman in the mountains whom Tansen wanted to claim, and he couldn't have her if he was Sharifar's consort. Mirabar had made it very clear that sharing was not in her nature, and he rather doubted that Sharifar would like such an arrangement, either. Dar, after all, had been very jealous of Josarian's love for his dead wife, forbidding him to mourn Calidar any longer; so Tansen didn't believe a sea goddess would be more inclined to tolerate his love for another woman—one who was not only alive, but fiercely powerful in her own right.

Now that he was going back to her soon, he hoped the decision about their future together would be as clear to Mirabar as it had become to him ever since Zarien announced that Tansen would not, after all, embrace Sharifar.

Of course, Mirabar—like Elelar—was a creature of duty. She might insist Tansen try approaching Sharifar anyhow, with or without Zarien's help. However, being close to the sea left Tansen as indifferent to Sharifar's desire as he had been in the mountains. He still believed that whomever she sought, it wasn't him; and the more he thought about it, the more he believed Zarien was the most likely possibility. Now, if only Tansen could convince Mirabar that he wasn't the sea king, perhaps he could convince her, too, of his sincerity about forsaking all others—*all* others—for her, if she would accept him.

He didn't want to think about Elelar's conviction that Mirabar was destined to kill her; that the fate of Sileria rested upon it. He tried not to remember how much Mirabar wanted the *torena* dead. He . . .

He sighed and admitted that he still had a lot of problems with women to worry about, even if Sharifar was no longer his concern—or at least not his concern until Zarien had traveled far enough from his grief to think about the goddess without such harsh feelings.

And who knew when that would be? Not Tansen, who doubted he would ever forgive Dar for letting Josarian die.

He heard weary footsteps and panting breath behind him. He glanced over his shoulder and saw Zarien, drenched in sweat and—he was glad to see—glowering at him with uncomplicated bad temper. "Where," Zarien demanded, "are we going?"

"I'm not entirely sure," Tansen admitted.

Zarien's face froze in an expression of comical outrage. After a moment in which he seemed too offended to summon coherent words, he threw down the heavy stick he was using as a staff and announced, "Then *I* will decide."

"Oh?" Tansen lifted a brow.

"Yes," Zarien snapped. He staggered over to a rock and sank down upon it, breathing hard as he dragged a forearm across his tattooed forehead. "*This* is a good place. *This* is our destination." He added with a portentous glare, "And there had better be a very good reason that I had to come here."

Tansen suppressed a grin. "There is." He looked around. The boy had chosen the place, and it was his right to do so. A break in the rocks, from some long ago avalanche perhaps, gave them a breathtaking view of Shaljir, in all her weary glory, and of the sea beyond. In the other direction, they could see the mountains from which they had come together, and to which they would soon return together. The dry heat of the season eliminated any mist or cloud which might normally soften those jagged, merciless peaks in the distance.

"Yes," he said. "This is the right place."

"For what?" Zarien asked breathlessly, shaking his empty waterskin. "I'm thirsty. Aren't you thirsty?"

Tansen walked over to him and handed him his own waterskin.

Zarien felt its weight and seemed reassured. "Oh, good. There's no water around here, is there?"

"I don't know," Tansen admitted. He wasn't familiar with Mount Shaljir.

Zarien sniffed the air, then shook his head. "No," he said absently, then drank gratefully.

Zarien's sensitive nose was presumably a sea-bound trait, Tan supposed, acquired among generations who spent their lives carefully hoarding drinking water amidst the undrinkable expanse of the sea. Zarien could easily distinguish between the smell of seawater and what he called "sweetwater," and he was usually the first to find a place to replenish their water supply when they were traveling.

When Zarien was done drinking, he asked, "So why are we here?"

Tansen prepared himself. Zarien wasn't a *shallah*. He might not understand. He might even dislike the idea. "A mountain is the only fitting place for this," he explained to the boy, "and this is the only one close enough to Shaljir for us to do this now."

Zarien shrugged. "Do what?"

Tansen held out his scarred palms and waited for the boy to look at them. "You know about bloodvows and bloodpact relations among the *shallaheen,* don't you?"

Zarien shifted uncomfortably. "If this is about my not swearing the bloodvow against Kiloran at Zilar—"

"No," Tan said quickly. "This is . . . the only way I can give you something of value in place of what the sea has taken from you."

Zarien's wide-eyed gaze flew up to meet his, and Tansen saw that he knew and understood.

"No one can take your father's place, Zarien. But a boy needs a father. Even a very brave, strong boy who is nearly a m—"

"He wasn't— He—" Zarien made an anguished sound and jumped to his feet, pushing past Tansen to stare out at the sea beyond Mount Shaljir.

"I will honor his memory in your heart," Tansen began.

"I didn't want to tell you. I didn't want to tell anyone," Zarien babbled. "I didn't want anyone to know. Not when I can't even . . . can't even . . ."

Frowning in puzzlement, Tansen came closer and put a hand on the boy's shoulder. "What? What is it?"

"He wasn't . . . *Oh, damn Sharifar.*"

The grief in the boy's voice hurt him. Tansen said nothing, waiting.

Zarien was shaking now. Trembling with emotions Tansen couldn't interpret. Keeping his back to Tansen, the boy finally choked out, "He wasn't my father."

"What?" Tansen didn't understand.

"Sharifar . . ." Zarien took a deep breath. Then another. He hugged himself with his arms. "The night I died. The night she told me I had a choice between staying dead or coming ashore . . ."

Damn Sharifar.

"She told me . . . Sorin and Palomar weren't my real parents."

"Ah." Tansen thought he understood. "I see."

"No," Zarien insisted. "You don't."

"It's no disg—"

"No, there's more."

"Tell me." Seeing Zarien's reluctance, Tansen promised, "You can tell me anything. Always."

"My father wasn't sea-bound. Not even sea-born. My father was a dry-lander." The words were choppy and harsh.

"Who was he?" Tansen asked.

"I don't know."

"I see. And your mother?"

Zarien shook his head. "I don't know."

Now he understood. "That's your secret, then? That's what you didn't want me—or anyone—to know?"

"Yes."

Tansen proceeded cautiously. It meant less than nothing to him who Zarien's true parents were. The dead sea-bound couple who had raised and loved the boy had obviously done it well. However, Tansen was *shallah* enough to understand what pride was involved in clan identity and blood-lines, and what disoriented shame came from not knowing one's true origins. He didn't remember his own real father, but at least he had always known who he was.

"And now," Tansen said, "you can never even ask Sorin who your real father was."

"No." Zarien was trying not to cry.

"Or thank Sorin for becoming your father."

Zarien nodded and swallowed a sob.

Tansen looked out to sea. "Would any of the survivors in your clan know the truth?"

Zarien shrugged.

"Now that Sorin and Palomar, who were your parents in the ways that matter most, are dead . . . do you care who the real ones were?"

Zarien turned to stare at him in surprise.

Tansen shrugged. "We can try to find out—look for the remaining Lascari and see what they know. If it matters to you." When Zarien didn't reply, he added, "But it doesn't matter to me."

Zarien lowered his head again. "I am sea-bound, but shunned. Sea-born, but fathered by some drylander whose name I don't even know. Dead, but still walking around. Enemies with a goddess." His tone broke Tansen's heart when he said, "I am nothing and no one now. I have no place. No beginning, and no destiny left."

Tansen had forgotten just how utterly hopeless things could seem when you were *that* young and inexperienced. When you didn't yet know that the terrible thing you couldn't live through was, in fact, not nearly as bad as the next ten terrible things you'd have to live through. He had forgotten how hard life seemed before you learned to accept how few of your desperate questions would ever be answered and how little justice you would ever see in the world.

"You are," Tansen told him, "the best young man in Sileria, and I would like you to be my son."

A tear dropped from one dark eye and rolled down a tattooed cheek as Zarien met his gaze. "I would be . . . a *shallah*?"

"I, uh . . . I don't know," Tansen admitted. "I've never heard of anyone but a *shallah* becoming a bloodpact relation, so I don't know—"

"No," Zarien suddenly said decisively. Tansen's heart stopped until the boy added, "I will still be sea-born. Gillien was right. Unless someone can tell me for certain that I was not born in the sea to a sea-born woman, no one can take that away from me, even if I am not Lascari and can never be sea-bound again."

"That seems fair," Tansen said, using a word he knew the young liked. "Then, Zarien, will you honor me and—"

"Sharifar said—" Zarien blurted suddenly, then stopped and stared at him, as if seeing him for the first time.

"Sharifar said?" Tansen prodded.

"She said it was time for me to seek my true father on land. I thought she meant . . ." Zarien's tormented face smoothed out into an expression that, at last, almost looked happy. "Maybe she meant you." He frowned a moment later and asked, "Um, fifteen years ago, did you perh—"

"I was younger than you are now," Tansen assured him, "and had never yet, uh, done what one must do to father a child."

"Oh."

"But," he added, "a *shallah* bloodpact relationship is as binding as a birth relationship. If you become my son today, it makes me your true father from now on."

"Then perhaps," Zarien said slowly, "Sharifar did mean you."

Tansen spoke the truth when he said, "I don't care what Sharifar meant. This is a vow between people, a kind of new birth in the eyes of Dar, and a sea goddess has nothing to do with it."

"Unless she sent me to you," Zarien said. "But I will not take you to her, even so."

"You may never need to," Tansen offered.

Zarien looked around. "What do I have to do?"

Tansen smiled, feeling relieved, pleased—even excited. He was about to become a father. It gave his life—so eventful, even so legendary—a meaning, a fulfillment which it had lacked until now. It gave him a stature which, as a *shallah,* was even more important than his achievements as a warrior. It gave him, who had spent so many years alone, someone to love and protect; and that, he knew suddenly, was what he had been born to do.

For the first time ever, he wondered how Armian had felt at this moment so many years ago. Had Armian felt this mingled humility and exultation? This quiet joy and glowing pride? Had Armian, too, been eager to meet the challenge yet afraid of not being worthy of it? Had Armian, upon gaining a son, been happy?

That conversation had gone more smoothly, of course, since Tansen's response had not been complicated by Zarien's concerns, and since Tansen and Armian were of a kind, despite having grown up in separate worlds. When Armian asked, Tansen knew how to respond, and knew what to do.

Now Tansen shook off his memories of that night. He didn't want to think about the bloodfather he had slain. Not now. He only wanted to promise Dar, in his heart, that he would be a much better father than he was a son. He only wanted to promise Zarien that he, as a son, would never face the decisions or have the regrets which Tansen had.

"We have to build a fire," Tansen told him, "pray to Dar . . ." *And hearing from me, of all people, ought to shock Her right into an eruption.* "Then cut our palms—"

"I knew that was coming," Zarien said resignedly.

"And mix our blood to become . . . family."

Zarien glanced down at his calloused sea-born palm. "It's not the pain," he insisted. "I don't mind that. It's just the drylander strangeness of the whole thing."

Tansen smiled again. "I know," he assured him. "I know."

Interregnum

I DANCE IN DAR'S SACRED FIRE,
HER ASHES ARE MY RAGS OF GLORY.

—Song of the Faithful

THE FAITHFUL OF Sileria heard Dar Call them, and so they came to offer Her their prayers, their devotion, and their dying cries of ecstatic agony as She engulfed them in Her fiery tantrums.

The tormented slopes of Mount Darshon were streaked with rivers of fire. Pilgrims to the sacred mountain sought proof of Dar's love by dancing on the lava flows; some of them were so beloved as to survive, while others died screaming.

From all over Sileria, they came to worship, praise, and pacify the volcano goddess, but She would not be pacified.

Explosions of burning rock opened new wounds in the mountainside every night, and Dar's worshippers inhaled the deadly fumes pouring forth; some of the faithful died in agony, while others won Dar's favor and survived.

They came from the war-torn mountains, from the thirsty lowlands, from the sea-scented coasts, from the teeming cities. They brought Her generous offerings of flowers, fruit, grain, wine, livestock, gold, jewels, and bones of the dead. When that was not enough, they willingly offered their lives to Dar. She took all that was offered, and still She would not be appeased.

Deep in the heart of Darshon's fiery caldera, the destroyer goddess prepared to make Sileria bleed.

End of Part One
This story concludes with Part Two,
The Destroyer Goddess

Author's Note

No, I'M NOT trying to be coy or force readers to buy an additional book. *In Fire Forged* just turned out to be such a big novel that it wasn't feasible for Tor Books to publish it in one volume. I know this can be frustrating for readers, but the only other option was to hack away so much of the story that it wouldn't have made any sense. So I am grateful to my editor and the other folks at Tor Books who've given this problematically huge novel their support.

If you want to know what happens to Tansen, Mirabar, Zarien, Baran, Elelar, Ronall, Kiloran, Cheylan, and everyone else, their story concludes in *The Destroyer Goddess: In Fire Forged, Part Two*—which is already written and edited even as this first volume goes to press, so readers won't have to wait long for it (in fact, depending on when you're reading these words, it may already be available).

Meanwhile, I want to thank all the readers who wrote enthusiastic, patient, and also impatient letters asking when *In Fire Forged* would finally be finished and published. Knowing there was actually someone waiting for it (besides my editor, I mean) was what inspired me to keep going.

I also offer profound thanks to Mary Jo Putney, Valerie Taylor, and Cindy Person, who all read and commented on the original manuscript for me; none of these noble people even tried to back out of this task when I presented them each with a stack of paper big enough to make whole forests fear my name. Nor is this the only way in which these dear friends helped me out.

Many thanks to my agent, Russell Galen, who acted above and beyond the call of duty on numerous occasions, and also to my patient foreign agent, Danny Baror.

If Tansen, his friends, and his enemies know how to kill people convincingly, it's primarily due to all that I've learned from my friend and teacher Jerry Spradlin. (Additional thanks to some of my classmates, who let me practice on them.)

I hope Martin H. Greenberg, Denise Little, John Helfers, and Larry Segriff all know how much I value their friendship—never more so than during the endurance feat of writing this book. Other cherished people who helped me survive this marathon include Elizabeth Haydon, Julie Pahutski, Lee Ann Thomas, Karen Luken, Toni Herzog, Kathy Chwedyk, my parents, my webmaster, Scott Street, the Sisters Foundation, and so many supportive friends that I won't name you all because I know I'll forget someone—so just consider me indebted to you.

Finally, I deeply regret that I didn't complete this book in time for my grandfather to read it. Bill Resnick, who kept asking me when *In Fire Forged* would be done, died shortly after I finished writing it. I miss the old man, and I'm so sorry that, in the end, I missed placing this book in his hands.

—Laura Resnick
November 2002

About the Author

LAURA RESNICK HAS lived and worked in several countries and has crossed Africa from Morocco to the Cape. The Campbell Award–winning author of numerous science fiction and fantasy short stories and several fantasy novels, she is also an award-winning romance writer under the pseudonym Laura Leone. Instead of enjoying a well-deserved rest after writing *In Fire Forged, Parts One and Two,* she is currently hard at work on her next fantasy novel, *Arena.* You can find her on the Web at www.sff.net/people/laresnick.